He knelt on th
before the alta
the discomfor
spine. But no longer did he try to alleviate
them.

He knew, with deep, motionless excitement, that something came towards him, out
of the forest.

It was the foreground which moved aside.
And there, against the tapestry of the
unending trees, was a tree greater than the
rest, a trunk like a basalt pillar that soared
into eternity or nothingness.

Below the tree stood a young man. He was
quite nude, but his unblemished and
proportioned body was itself a garment, and
embellished at the head and neck by a hood of
glowing hair.

When he raised his hand, Beljunion had
seen that, from the wrist like ivory, ran a
ribbon of crimson blood, while by the other
hand a cup was held to catch it. Everything
was defined, even the cup was glassy black,
like jet.

The blood, the priest thought, in an ecstacy,
the blood of the Redeemer –

Also in Legend by Tanith Lee

DEATH'S MASTER
DELIRIUMS'S MISTRESS
DELUSION'S MASTER
KILL THE DEAD
LYCANTHIA
NIGHT'S SORCERIES
VOLKHAVAAR
COMPANIONS ON THE ROAD
EAST OF MIDNIGHT

THE BLOOD OF ROSES

ROSES

Tanith Lee

A Legend Book

Published by Arrow Books Limited
20 Vauxhall Bridge Road, London SW1V 2SA

An imprint of Random Century Group

London Melbourne Sydney Auckland Johannesburg
and agencies throughout the world

First published in Great Britain in 1990 by Legend
Legend paperback edition 1991

Printed and bound in Great Britain by
Courier International Ltd, Tiptree, Essex

ISBN 0 09 967860 8

Pater omnipotens, mittere digneris sanctum
Angelum tuum de Paradis

Contents

Book One   –   MECHAIL 1

Book Two   –   ANILLIA 211

Book Three –   JUN 361

Book Four   –   EUJASIA 577

Book Five   –   MECHAILUS 653

Book One

MECHAIL

Chapter One

In the beginning there was silence, winter night, and the great moon burning on the snow. The earth was frozen like a glass ball. Timeless. Not a pleat of the ground, not a branch of the forests stirred.

Then came the sound. A dull, faint drumming. A little snow shook and shifted. The drum pushed and swelled and grew into a noise of thunder. Out of the trees and along the white rim of the world, against the black of the sky, there bolted a stream of riders, mailed and armed, their horses stretched to headlong speed, and the red torches ripping down the night.

The hunt was up. A wild hunt.

The faces of the men were maddened and colourless. Some shouted as they rode, and then were voiceless again. The horses snorted. The soldiers kicked with their spurs, and fire bubbled, and here and there a sword flashed, held naked up between the brands to cleave the moon.

But the quarry – what was that?

The foremost rider, a captain of twenty-nine years, was Carg Vrost. He did not seem himself for sure, but then he had been at the inn drinking deep, not an hour earlier, and with a girl waiting upstairs . . . Forgotten now, certainly. He looked as the others did, crazy, murderous, and afraid. And suddenly, like them, he gave a cry, and pointed, and his eyes were terrible, as if he beheld something from a nightmare. *What?*

The torches flared, and the shadows of soldiers and horses patterned the snow, and the moon was before them, westering, as they plunged again towards the trees. And there – *there* – silhouetted for a few moments on the moon's disc—

The torchlight touched it, adding to the blackness of the flying wings two hems of flame, and giving the pin of the body the aspect of a spindle. Above this, clearly, the horned head showed. And, impossibly, for though of its kind the creature was large, yet it was very slight against the dark, the moon, the massed pursuit. But the horns of its head ended each in a glinting spark, redder than a fire. Of all things, what the soldiers hunted was a moth.

The trees opened. The riders tore among them, down obscure precarious avenues, as if to collide with the sinking moon. Blackness swallowed them. They were gone.

The old slave woman had been sleeping. That was her crime, for which, before morning, she would die. The infant had been sleeping too, but to sleep was his night-time function. He lay in the small wooden bed with its hangings of green, purple and russet, on the posts of which was carved, in miniature, the Raven of the Korhlen. Landholder Vre Korhlen's son, three years of age, the last child got on an ailing wife, and therefore maybe the last child of all, if the Church Fathers did not permit the Landholder another marriage.

He was no trouble, the boy. he did not fret. He lay and slumbered. And the hearth roasted itself quietly, and past the window the winter, with its nocturnal snow and wolves, kept out. The window was shuttered, but the shutters had warped a trifle. There was a gap which let in the cold, so that the woman had plugged the place, as usual, with a piece of woollen cloth.

When she woke the first thing she saw was the cloth lying under the window, at the foot of the bed. Perhaps the draught had roused her. She stood up sleepily, and taking the iron, poked at the hearth fire. Then she went to pick up her cloth and replace it between the shutters.

As she came to the bed the old woman glanced past the hangings at Vre Korhlen's child.

4

She saw something so awful, she could not take it in. Her initial thought was that the boy had been decapitated. His head was turned on the pillow, and across his throat ran a vehement line of purest bright red blood. Yet even while she stared in horror, she observed that into the blood had dropped a winter flower with two black petals. Which abruptly quivered.

It was only fright which released her shrieks. Nevertheless they came, a torrent of them, irresistible as retching.

As she shrieked, she backed away, and her thin sere hands made over and over the sign of the cross of the Christus, and, too, some other defensive mark. But neither worked. Even the shrieking did not seem to. And so with her outcry wrung from her she had retreated almost to the door when the stampede of feet, the scrape and clank of metal, started up the stair. After all rescue was coming. Male strength and the power of the sword. And yet.

And yet, against this thing, what use?

The black flower of the moth trembled again upon the neck of the unconscious child.

The woman supposed it would fly up, perhaps dart at her, and a final wail erupted from her mouth.

But something less credible was happening. The moth indeed was lifting from the bed, and as it rose it brought the body of the child – somehow – upward with it.

The image was beyond truth, and reason. The woman, if she had lived, would have borne it scorched into her brain all her life.

The moth had the child. He hung like a heavy doll from its fragile breathing petalled nail. Even as it gripped him it ascended, away from the bed, into the raftered ceiling. And there, as the door crashed wide, it cast him off.

The boy plummeted to the flagged floor. His body made a harsh response when it struck, breaking a little at the impact. This did not wake him. He sprawled motionless before the Landholder's two soldiers and the old woman with a piece of wool in her hands.

Through the gap in the shutters where the wool had been, the moth eased itself. And the soldiers, transfixed, cursing, watched, and the woman gibbered.

There was no amazement. Terror and revulsion, and rage, but no disbelief. Such things might happen, had done so in the past. They returned like seasons, or the night.

One soldier fell to his knees, praying, a sort of spasm. The other ran out bellowing.

The old woman bent over the child, of whom she had been fond, and did not dare set a finger on him. She knew in her heart already, with a fresh and personal fear, what waited for her now.

The moon had leapt before them down into the valleys of darkness. The forest was everywhere, rushing as it went by, the pillars of trees, the pines in their hides of snow, rocks, defiles, the summer riverbeds altered to Hell's pits. Three men had fallen, one with a scream, a horse toppled, rolling off the edge of vision into a well of night.

Branches whipped. Someone had lost the sight of an eye, but still rode pelting with the rest, half his face a mask of ink.

Carg Vrost kept his head low to the withers of his horse.

He could taste bile; not pausing in the hunt's career, he had leaned from the saddle half an hour before, to cough out his ale.

He did not therefore know if he were drunk still or only crazed. He chased the Devil, and the fiend drew him on.

A concussion behind him, cries, and another horse shrilly neighing and going down.

God knew, the men they sloughed, maimed and lamed, and horseless, would be handy meat for roaming wolves.

Carg Vrost swore as he ducked beneath a bough snapping at him like the neck of a serpent, whirled off over his skull.

Ahead, a fluttering mirage, black ash and two horned

eyes of fire. He could see it, constantly. It was *there*. But this hunt was an insanity.

Vrost glanced over his shoulder. Startled, he noted two men only. They appeared tangled in the wood, netted and pulled away, and he gestured at them violently to come on, and goaded them with foul names. And turned again to see, between his horse's ears, the trees had ended ten paces in front of him, a brink of space.

'*Christus!*'

Carg Vrost hauled on the reins of the charging horse, so it reared upward, floundering and skidding, the replica of a lunatic chesspiece. And in this barbaric shape, mount and rider cavorted to the brink and slid over towards the moon.

She was standing at the window when he entered, Vre Korhlen's wife, the Lady Nilya. She had stood there since they told her: two hours. If she had moved at all, a hand, or her eyes, he could not make out. She looked just the same as when he left her, a figure of the snow night in her white mantle, and her black hair thickly streaked with thirty years of frost. He had seen the first grey on his wedding eve, though her woman had hidden it under the ribboned veil. They must have used some dye before that.

'Sit in the chair,' he said brutally and loudly, 'or take yourself to bed. What can you do, just stand rigid as if you were in church? Did you even go to look at him? Well, Nilya, you'll answer me.'

'No,' she said, 'I can do nothing.'

Vre Korhlen glared at her sightless spine, and turned to the jug of liquor on the table. She was his bane, this woman. Since he had got her, only bad luck. Though fortune had hardly beamed on him with the first one. *She* had been a moron and able besides to cook up only daughters in her oven. Her wits had turned to slush soon enough and she died from a choking fit. For his second wife, this Nilya, he had used agents in the town of Khish. She came from a house having links both to the town governorship and to the Church. Not of the savage forest nobility, but something finer, or so they would have him believe. When he saw her, he wanted her. He had ridden out of the woods to look. They had sent her to be schooled, she could read and write. He had thought this might be of use to him too. He felt a fire building down in his loins, and that boded well for the making of sons. But she disappointed him in bed. She was scarcely present. And then she fruited years after, and it did not suit her, she turned into a skeleton with a great bag where her flat little belly had been. And bearing the child had almost killed her. Had killed her in fact, for she died ever since, a fraction more with every day. Her hands were the way he had seen his own mother's in her last months, transparent and fleshless, and some mornings her face was like a sallow crystal; to look too closely would be to see her bones.

He was not now about to inform her of the surgeon's words, which had disgusted him, angered him beyond endurance. Their gist being that, if the boy were carefully tended, he would not be crippled. *Lies*, blatant as the fawning cowardice of the liar.

For the bloody slave crone, she would be beaten to death in the yard.

As for the supernatural thing, at first he had refused to give it credence, ranting and striking out at his men, sending for more soldiers from his barracks, roaring them away to hunt down some animal or feral malcontent. He would not entertain the story of a demon insect, bathing and drinking at the neck-vein of his son—

He had grown with such legends all around him, Vre Korhlen. He had heard all the tales, and believed them too. But not here, within the boundaries of his private life.

The stone of the house, its winter smells of smoke and wrapped bodies, old food, cold and damp and secrets, pressed upon the Landholder.

He drank his wine and watched without pity his dying wife standing like marble at the window, against the wall of night.

★

Carg Vrost saw, as it seemed to him without opening his eyes, a sky which had nothing in it. This sky was very high and far off, and it would be simple to drift up to it and float there. But he was aware of pain; he lay in a coffin of flesh and muscle that ached and stabbed and anchored him to the earth.

He put himself together slowly, as if fashioning himself out of the pain, and the heaped snow (cold suddenly, like biting fangs, when he moved), and the smashed body of the horse which had broken his own fall into the valley.

The evaporating heat of the horse had also kept him from freezing. He had a lot to thank it for, poor brute. He had had good service out of it, and rewarded it with this.

Vrost found it would be possible to stand. He did so. He had use of all his torso and his limbs, everything but for the four fingers of his left hand, which were unkindly fractured, he could see, although the snow had granted him the mercy of non-feeling. Vrost stared at his hand a moment after he had lurched upright. He already knew he would lose it, back at the Landholder's Tower, if he ever got there. The disaster seemed remote. How had he come to this?

Then he remembered, and put his sound hand on the sword and pulled it from its sheath. Stepping over the dead horse, Vrost glanced around him. There was no hint that any other man had survived or got down here with him. The forest wall craned on the brink above and at various heights round about, and here the valley pitched away, the snowy trees scattered more thinly. The sky was no longer black, but widening with the long leaden twilight before dawn.

When the sun rose, no demon creature could stay abroad.

It came to Carg Vrost, standing one-handed, sword drawn, in the waste of winter, that the madness of the night had also been invited. For the moth which was the demon, having such a form, could surely have escaped a hundred ways. Instead it led them on, like a marsh light,

9

to danger and death. And now it had vanished. Quite properly.

For himself there was no choice but to continue. He could not climb the steep cliff up into the wood. The sloping downward path, (as they told you in Scripture), was much easier. Vrost almost smiled. Then he thought of his hand, and a pang went through him, not of pain, but of hopeless, helpless fury. And then too he put that off, and only trudged forward between the trees.

When the woodland separated, giving all at once a view of the whole valley, it came as no surprise to him to behold the low bleak building, like a casket of stone, left there by the slope, as it were at his feet. Some part of him had expected it. Maybe, even, he had hunted legitimate game in this district of the forest last summer, noticing, some morning, the architecture in the valley, and knowing it as he did now for one of the wild lorn chapels dotted on the landscape like thrown pebbles. Often they were ruinous, although it was hard to tell here, from the higher ground. In summer the walls would have been banked among the green, mossy and painted perhaps with flowers. But the snow had piled upon them, settled to them, next picking out their features, white on umber. The arched door looked closed, but more likely only shadow had shut it, the timbers years ago carried off by outlaws or peasants in the wood, who made nothing if they could steal it first.

The sky was a blank grey. The morning star had appeared, and glittered like an icicle above the chapel roof. The sun would rise there.

And what he sought, what he had hunted, that was there too. He understood this, as if it had been whispered to him when he lay stunned on the valley floor.

The task was only his to do.

Carg Vrost marked himself slowly with the cross of the Christus. As he did it, the numbed, wrecked hand gave off a spurt of vivid agony. The Landholder's captain kneeled, and levered the hand into a snow mound, and stayed it there a little while, to let the winter put it to sleep again. Not more than a minute. He must reach the

10

chapel before the sun. There would be time, if he did not
dawdle.

'No pain. He mustn't suffer. Pain is fruitless and terrible.'
The nervous surgeon, a sawbones kept to tend the Vre's
garrison of thirty soldiers, glimpsed Korhlen's lady wife,
who had evolved like a ghost in the chamber, unseen,
unheard. She too, he had long known from his limited
sights of her, required a physician. But in this wretched
spot, trees and wolves and endless nights, they had not
bothered to find her one. Himself, he was accustomed to
patching and stitching, and cutting and dismembering
when needful. He had set the child's broken arm and
cranked the shoulder back into position, and bound the
ribs. Something was amiss with the spine. He had enough
wit to tell that, but not the learning – or, God knew, the
means – to be effective. The moment he had been brought
to see the boy, the surgeon had begun to plan his exit
from the Landholder's Tower. He hated the situation in
any case, and feared the Landholder like the plague.
They had beaten the old slave woman, he gathered. She
was finished. Slaves were expendable, and barren wives,
and incompetent surgeons.
'Madam?' he queried politely, having picked up courtesy if not skill in a small city to the south.
'I mean,' she said, 'to alleviate my son's pain – you
must have drugs.'
'I've done my best, madam. The injury was distressing.'
He had not believed the hysterical tale current in the
Tower. Was it not more likely the brutish father had
hammered the child to bits in a fit of wrath? 'He'll need
great attention, but he's a healthy boy.'
'Not so,' she said, damning his platitude. 'As a baby
he was often sick. My fault. And this—' Her death-mask
face, never beautiful surely, gaped from its hollow eyes
and parted lips. 'Please. Do everything you can. Don't let
my son suffer.'
Does she perhaps mean I'm to smother him before he rouses?
Astonished at the unconscionable idea, the surgeon

11

breathed quickly, frightened. Controlling himself, he said, 'All care will be taken, madam. He's peaceful now. Did you wish . . . ?'

She only stared at him and shook her head.

She said, nearly idly, 'I've done him enough hurt. I won't go near him.'

Then she turned and drifted out of the chamber again, with the mantle sweeping after her along the floor.

She was insane, like the rest here. (It would be prudent to get away.) She had seemed to say she was to blame for the boy's condition. A mother's guilt at neglect? (Once the ice thawed and the tide of snow receded – he could prevaricate until then.)

In the adjacent room the child suddenly groaned noisily in his stupor. The surgeon was thankful that she had not heard. *Pain!* When the boy did wake, they might have to strap him down. In fact it would be wise to see to it now. There was not sufficient of the Black Poppy. It could come to the use of a swift blow. More compassionate than to leave him to shriek. So much damage was already done the three-year-old body, one would hardly scruple. If he had been an animal, Vre Korhlen's son and heir, they would have cut his throat.

The door was a shadow door.

The soldier approached it over the snow, through a light also of shadow. The valley seemed to ring like a glass goblet; maybe the note was in his head.

Carg Vrost's sword hung heavy in his grasp and it seemed to him his body moved with a dragging ponderousness, while he himself was unhampered, weightless, alert, seated somewhere high up in his brain behind the eyes.

When he reached the shadow door, automatically, and clumsy with the sword, he crossed himself again, and walked over the threshold.

The stone box of the chapel was not, after all, and despite its pilfered entrance, ruined. It had only an awesome biting cold, and a cache of darkness. Four broad pillars upheld the roof, and ahead a tall screen of fretted obsidian framed and interrupted the one window rising beyond the altar. The altar itself was hidden by the screen, on which several masks of saints glimmered, old gilding intact, but not the nacre optics, which had become skull-holes. The robbers would have had the screen, he mused vaguely, but it was too heavy to move. The religion of the wood was older, and picking out the portable eyes of saints did not trouble it. Was the altar desecrated?

'Who's there?'

The whispered cry rose like thin smoke from a source behind the screen. Carg Vrost stood speechless, repeating it over in his mind, wondering if he had heard it. A girl's tremulous voice, or mist, speaking.

Transfixed, he waited.

'Whoever you are,' whispered the mist voice, 'help me.'

And around the screen she came.

There were sisterhoods in the forest, he had heard of them. The girl wore a bleached ascetic's robe, but her head was uncovered. Her face was like the saint-faces on the screen, pale and luminous, and the eyes like craters, until some straying of the half-light found them. They lit, awful with frantic, held-in terror. And with them, two rubies in her hair.

'So *horrible*,' she breathed. '*Help* me.'

Carg Vrost listened intently to his own voice answering her.

'Has it harmed you?'

'No, but I – can't—'

'If God is here,' said Vrost, as he listened, 'He'll watch over us. Stay very still, lady. Still as the dead.'

As he went towards her, she cringed, and then she forced herself to the stillness he had imposed. She shut her eyes and took her lip hard between her teeth. *Don't*, he thought, in confused vehemence, *don't break the skin*. He saw in his mind a fleck of blood on her lip, and the black moth churning in the skein of her black hair, hair and moth stuck to her mouth—

He went without speed, his stony footfalls on the stone

floor, granite sword dragging, eyes not moving from the lock of hair where the moth had webbed itself. Had it flown into this place for sanctuary, or through some obscure element of an evil game played out through the forest? Was it mischance, the snare it had been taken in, so like a weird song of the winter night, a fable, or a dream?

He must not dwell on these things. The task was before him, unforeseen in its conclusion. In spite of his words to her, he knew the girl might become the sacrifice.

A hand's breadth from her, near enough to smell her woman's scent, ferny, rare, and the acid tang of fear across it . . . near enough to kiss, he halted again. Tears were running like silk down her face, no blood.

The moth too was motionless. He could observe its strange and sheer reality. The wings were folded together. They had no device, their blackness was like charred paper. The scrolled body, the horns with their ruby points, were dainty as jeweller's work. But to study this too great a time was unclever.

He seized the girl's hair in his left fist – in that unearthly moment *forgetting*—

Carg Vrost screamed in anguish, an ecstasy of crimson pain. The broken fingers, the deadened palm, woken, unusable – somehow, caught on a fence of mail and warped and splintered bone, the tresses of hair reeled out. Blind, mindless, Vrost raised the granite sword that had the weight of all the world, and *struck*.

The girl cried shrilly. She fell away like a light down his eyeball. And on his wrecked fingers was the weave of hair, and the moth fluttering.

He flung it down and his hand seemed to go with it. He was screaming again and again in agony, but he stamped upon the nest of hair, and lifted his boot – and saw a black flower beat up and away over the screen.

He lunged forward. The edge of the screen took him by the shoulder. Detained, he hung there, and looked into the altar place.

The window was a gape of white air held in a lattice of

iron that had the construction of roses and thorns. The bare altar upheld an iron Christus, crucified against the light. And above, a mysterious yellow flame seemed suspended in nothingness. It was the watch fire of the chapel. Perhaps the girl, lying so silent behind him, had come to tend the lamp. He could make out the slender chain now, and the shallow bowl where the fire gleamed.

The moth flew into it. The moth flew into the fire and was consumed.

Vrost stood and saw, with some other part of him that was unimpaired and distant, and still pure, the blazing up of the demon, black flame in yellow. And then something poured out of the watch lamp, like a breath of unconquerable night.

On the writhing static icon, its naked arms outflung among the gnawing nails, a man's image was superimposing. It engorged, enveloping the cross, the Christus. But the position and the gesture were the same. The legs and torso stretched, the head thrown back, the arms outflung. And in its breast one single nail of scarlet thunder that burst into a thousand shards.

Carg Vrost stared, his body racked and far off from him, as the shower of fiery lights came down, and the fragments of the shattered lamp. And the dawn pierced the window with its talons. And it was day.

Chapter Two

An enormous cathedral, winter had been constructed in the forest, its masonry of ice, the organ peal of wind. The tiny artisans of the tribes of the fox and the ermine had excavated and ornamented its aisles, printed its paving. Its windows were paned with cold mauve and blue and yellowish skies and the deadly reds of frozen sunsets. The cathedral endured. Then spring, the destroying angel, stalked the wilderness sword in hand. Spring smote the cathedral. Its roofs of snow collapsed. After the thaw, green trickled into the arteries of the wood, and spears of sunlight divided the trees one from another.

A wolf trotted through the green church of the wood, a shadow that hardened abruptly to life in shafts of sun. Its eyes, like those of a fierce young man, searched the undergrowth and the canopy above. Birds sang and flickered in the weft of leaves. Other small meals foraged through the grasses.

Where a stream sprang over a knot of tree roots, the wolf paused to drink, then leapt the water, padded on.

Down a slope, among the boulders, something was lying. It had lain there since midwinter eighteen years ago. The wolf, reaching it, hesitated again to nose the thing, and assemblage of bones and metal links, tarnished and dropped apart. A human skull in a cap of brown iron rust laughed up at the wolf: *Too late for you!* The meat was nearly two decades lost. The Raven badge lying in the fern the wolf trod beneath its long foot.

16

The trees opened half a mile above this spot where a Korhlen soldier had slept his sleep, undiscovered or ignored, since the night of the vampire hunting. The wolf passed up this way and on to the brow of the hill, stopped and seemed to look off to where a great swart chimney pushed from the earth. The Tower, with its hive of necessary buildings clutched to the walls, the Tower village, the ill-made road, and the slovenly inn, everything eased by the springing green, the blossom trees and black fields pricked with grain.

The wolf oversaw the image. Then trotted away along the palisade of pines, shadow once more.

His death began on a day in spring, when he was twenty-one years of age. He did not know. He woke prepared for another sort of terror.

The slave, Boroi, was thumping at the door. When he entered he carried the usual things, the water and razor, the wine and bread.

Mechail said, 'Do you think I've got time for all that, you oaf?'

And as he spoke, Mechail heard his father's tones and choice of words. He wondered, for a split second, *How is it that I imitate him, when I hate him?*

The slave in any case had taken no special notice. He set down the accessories of breakfast and shaving, and then stood there, ready to assist, or have himself berated again. Boroi had been a house slave all his forty years, his neck clamped in the bronze slave-torque featuring the Korhlen Raven, his face an old brown juiceless vegetable.

'Well, do it, then. Shave me.'

As the razor diligently slicked across his jaw, Mechail sat in the carved wooden chair which had once been a possession of his dead mother. He held his body and his mind still. When Boroi wiped his face, Mechail reached out and took the wine and gulped it. Wine had helped him last night. He had ceased caring after the fifth cup. Something had made him stop, too, before he was quite drunk. This morning there was only a slight queasiness

17

that would have been there anyway, seeing what he would have to accomplish.

Boroi dressed him. Mechail needed the slave particularly for that. There was still a slight difficulty over the tunic with its ugly inset panel, unskilfully stitched to accommodate the bulging lumpen shoulder, and in manoeuvring the stiff arm with its well-shaped hand that had no strength. Boroi thrust on Mechail's boots and found the belt, which had been flung somewhere by the fireplace. In the shield over the hearth, Mechail caught a sudden vision of himself, a mask of bones covered with skin, two pale eyes with black arches of brow, a black rage of hair.

Who am I? A Landholder's get. For his sins. For mine.

He was full of misery. He had become so used to it. No one must see. They were all his enemies, the father who wanted these things, and the half-brother who aped such wanting, all their friends and hangers-on. The very servants and slaves, before whom nothing must be shown.

This slave was watching him. Mechail caught the stare in the shield, and turned on him. *'What?'*

'My lord's knife.'

'Oh, that. Yes. I'll be wanting it, won't I?'

The slave came over and put the knife, honed bright, into Mechail's good hand.

Something, and he did not know what, made Mechail remember his mother, the last legal wife. He had lost her face long ago, but not the black rain of hair with its weave of silver, her scent, that of a sweet flower which died – he had been just four years old. Someone had said to him that God had taken her, and he had screamed and railed against God. And then the priest beat him. Yes, the day of his mother's death, the priest took the rod to his back, being careful always to aim at the sound right side. He recalled the strange dichotomy: the shoulder which did not hurt hurting worse then the shoulder which always did.

'My lord,' said Boroi.

Mechail glared at him, not seeing, this brown turnip with flint eyes.

'For the Christus – you're *hurrying* me? I know. I've an appointment with an enemy from the house of my father's foes. An Esnias.' Mechail struck the slave abruptly across the head. It was what his father, his brother Krau – and all their line – would have done. What a man did when a slave strayed unbelievably above his station, in only a little way.

Boroi accepted the blow as his due.

There was no sense yet of spring inside the Tower, but in the yard, as he came down the stair from the Cup Hall, between the two ravens of stone, the spring had found entrance.

He had smelled the spring last night, sparkling yet soft. It had done something to Mechail, like the wine, but less coherently and without aftertaste.

Day's sunlight splashed about. Green things were growing where they should not and the slaves raking them away from between the stones. A gloss slipped on the ivy that overhung the wall of the Women's Garden. Above was a wan blue sky with glinting bubbles of cloud.

Below, ten men of his father's garrison stood in the courtyard, with the tough captain and the elderly priest of watery eyes and wiry hands.

No one spoke to Mechail. They knew their business and expected him to know his.

He did. He had known for five years. Before that, he had never quite believed it.

The slaves in the yard went on raking, but watched with their slavish eyes that, though so often dead and cold, seemed to miss nothing. The groom led Mechail's horse up him, the docile mare they had given him because he could not manage much, cripple that he was. He was wary of the mare even so, and she knew it. She rolled her chestnut eye at him. He used the bottom step and swung into her saddle, arriving awkwardly as the power of his legs gave way to the half-power of his upper body. His back hurt as it always did in the morning, or late at night. In the summer, sometimes, he was free of pain, but not for long. Exertion brought it home to him again, a demanding guest who knew the way to his door. But he was so used to the pain, it would seldom discompose him.

He kicked at the mare lightly and she started off, solid with contempt. The gates had been dragged wide, and outside lay the bad road, muddy from dawn rain.

Mechail rode through. The captain fell in behind, and the soldiers. The priest walked along, telling his beads, which were a gift from Vre Korhlen's whore-wife. Painted ceramic globules, or little spheres of coloured glass, and one opal for chastity, and one dull, exquisite emerald for piousness.

The fields spread out under the sky, and at their edges the forest, rising like the humps of a sleeping dragon.

The slaves in the fields paused, most of them, for a few seconds, to peer and stare. They did not risk longer, the overseers would not allow it.

All's well, Mechail thought, *you fetid vermin. All is as it should be. The Landholder's legal heir is going out to make of himself a man.*

First blood.

Krau, the bastard son, he had already done it. Last year. Krau, then aged fifteen, had gone to the grove and used his knife. The feud had still been with Esnias then. This Esnias feud had gone on for a decade. Mechail could recall the horse-stealing and the carrying off of female field slaves which began it.

Out here, recompense from the law was finite and rarely invoked. Even religion was flown in the face of. The Church Fathers had refused Vre Korhlen a third marriage after the death of the Lady Nilya, but even so he took the woman Veksa, sowed and wed her. The priest had joined them. Mechail had not seen the wedding, as they had not let him see the burial of his mother a few months earlier, only the closed vault afterwards. He went there sometimes as a child. But talking to a grave-wall had not helped him. The peasant stories of the voice of the dead one hovering on the wind, though he had credited them, were not able to bring him speech with Nilya.

They turned on to the mill track, past the mill, which was grinding dolorously, and went up towards the forest's edge.

A woman by a well crossed herself, then returned to drawing water, her strong arms and neck curved to the work.

Mechail would have had to perform her task one-handed.

They had taught him to fight, and forced him to exercise the natural arm, so it was pliant and steely with muscle. (They had taught him to read, too, somewhat, and beaten him for everything when he was lax or stupid.)

He thought early on his right arm paid dearly for the left. He had hated his left side, waist to throat. Perhaps he still did hate it, poor useless thing, a passenger tied on his body.

Krau, the son of the third wife, unrecognized in law, he should have been the heir. Then they might have left the cripple in peace.

Only very occasionally did Mechail, as a child, recollect that, but for the dog which had savaged him in infancy, he would have been like other men.

The track thinned and vanished as they came in under the trees. Ahead was visible the clearing, and there the grove of white birches, nearly naked in their new green.

Of course it was a pagan place. In previous times the Raven Lords had taken clutches of slaves and enemies each year to immolate on the black stone. If there was no war or feud, men were chosen by lot. It had been the fertility ritual for the fields.

Mechail caught himself listening for sounds from the grove. Maybe he had expected the Esnias soldier to be cursing, or screaming. But there was nothing. Only the tinkling notes of birds deeper in the trees.

The mare trod her way forward, the ferns brushing her breast, and the black corrupt pine cones snapping under her hooves.

Then the old priest, Godbrother Beljunion, started his quavering chanting. Mechail tensed, his mouth tight, his eyes fixed burning as if blind, in the 'look of the Devil' Beljunion had warned him of as a boy, and thrashed him because of, along with other punishments. Beljunion had come into Mechail's life in the year of Nilya's death, a perfect counterpoise, untiring salt in a measureless wound.

Mechail saw the priest with the rod in his hand, old even then. 'We are, all of us, God's things. He may do with us as He pleases.' The child had shrieked that God had taken his mother and had no right. 'Erase this blasphemy from your thoughts. Know now and for ever, God is God. Accept his will, little fiend.'

Never. I never did. Eyes of the Christus. The will of Vre Korhlen is enough to bear. Hear me, God, I struggle against Your injustice and Your bloody will.

The slim stems of the birches parted and the young man rode into the ancient grove, his head full of invisible flames.

The grass had been high, but recently lopped by the scythe. The black stone leaned at the centre. It was elder as the wood, perhaps. The song of the birds waned, and the light altered, pale and harsh. The sky looked bottomless.

The victim had been tied to the stone. He was from the garrison of the Esnias Tower. In the last days of winter Vre Korhlen's men had caught him at their hem of the forest. He admitted to being after a girl in the Korhlen village, and to stealing a chicken. At another date, probably he would have been ransomed off, and might thereby have provided a truce between Esnias and Korhlen, perhaps leading to the resolvement of a feud which was not yet open and ceaseless warfare. But it was the wrong time. He should have realized and kept off, for many of the Towers of the northern forest held to old customs.

He was a man in middle life, soon derelict by captivity. He had a seven-day beard, and a couple of his front teeth were smashed, quite discernibly since his mouth hung open. His eyes contrastingly were almost shut, yet they moved, looking for Mechail. The soldier was like a man nearly asleep, gazing after a faintly abnormal sight or noise, not really bothered by it.

He wore only his drawers. The stench of his body was ripe. At some point he had dirtied himself, in fright, but he seemed beyond that now.

Mechail sat on the horse. He thought, *I have to kill him*.

Two others of Vre Korhlen's soldiers stood by the stone, and, under a tree, the Landholder's second steward, the needful witness aside from the captain and priest. Nearby waited the final assistant to the morning's work, the Tower butcher, detailed, if essential, to complete the act.

The soldiers were forming up around the grove. The priest went straight across to the dazed, filthy Esnias, offering him, with disgusting and shocking arrogance, the silver cross on its chain of pretty beads.

And with an equally appalling acceptance, the Esnias turned his head and put his lolling mouth against the cross.

Beljunion stepped away and lowered his devout eyes, slinking the emerald through and through his fingers.

'Can I help you, sir?'

Startled, Mechail glanced down, and found a soldier holding the mare, awkwardly , insolently, asking if he should aid the cripple's descent.

A scalding lash went through Mechail's belly, his sex and bowels. It had arrived. The moment. It was no longer rumour or threat, dread or nightmare. It was the present, and there was no escaping it.

He hoisted himself and dropped down from the horse.

The Esnias had put his head over on one shoulder, in the posture of the dying Christus. That was revoltingly funny. He looked fully gone now, and breathed like an exhausted sleeper.

Get it right. Don't botch.

The Esnias was nothing to Mechail, not even meaningful as an enemy. But he would cry out, and the uproar and the spasms of death must be abbreviated.

23

At least Krau was not here. With a girl, doubtless, maybe one of his half-sisters, the daughters of the first wife that Mechail had never known. The first wife had been addled, and her progeny were fey. They did as they wanted, like cats.

Stop dawdling. Attend to it.

The knife was out, in his right hand. He was walking forward. He wanted to pray that the Esnias soldier was unconscious and would not open his eyes again or look to see who came. But Mechail would not pray. It would do no good.

And yes, at the approaching footfall, the Esnias had rolled up his lids and gazed.

Their eyes met.

Mechail had understood this would happen.

The Esnias grinned. Loose-lipped, he murmured, 'First blood, eh?'

Mechail must not answer.

He stood now close to the trussed man, between him and the others, and the spring sun, the trees, the pale sacrificial illuminance, and all things.

Mechail heard himself say, 'It will be quick.'

'It'll still rotting hurt me. And then Hell, with all my transgressions.'

'You fool there is no Hell,' said Mechail, and drove the knife into the man's body, horrified and surprised at the resistance of his flesh and muscle, numbed to the blaze of jetting blood hitting his face, stinging in his eyes, and the man's long wail and the terrible breath. The knife forced up and up so the stomach was carved. Indecently, the white ribs showed, the broken belly-sack, and the flicker of the ending heart.

His sound right shoulder ached from effort. The knife had lodged, and he could not get it free for a minute. The man died. His body relaxed. The pathos of his carcass, defensive and sealed when living, now undressed to its organs.

Mechail had believed he would have to prevent himself

at once from vomiting, but he felt only weak and listless as at the onset of fever.

He turned slowly, and his father's butcher came over the grass, to be certain of the death. Before the man reached the corpse, however, Vre Korhlen's captain raised his hand and the soldiers of the Korhlen garrison gave a hoarse loud shout. It was a formality.

Blinking the blood from his eyes, Mechail wondered what the blood was.

He found Beljunion in his path.

'Go home and bathe yourself,' said the priest. 'Then get yourself smartly into the chapel.'

'I know,' said Mechail. 'You told me.'

After the pagan rite – the feud-murder – a penance to God. Supposedly a light one.

The slaves would behold him riding home, with the blood – it was the blood that was so wet, and which stung and which stank – the blood upon him as the symbol of his courage and his masculinity.

Out of the mask of bones and skin and blood, his eyes like clear winter water froze upon the priest who had thrashed his child's back.

'My knife's stuck in the Esnias. Someone must get it for me.'

The priest flinched delicately. 'Tell one of the soldiers.'

'You tell them, godbrother.'

The priest's face wriggled, set.

'Very well, Lord Mechail. You must hurry and wash off the blood, or it will smear your soul.'

I have no soul. Say that to him, say it.

But the ultimate impertinence would not come, not after all the years under his hand.

Mechail turned to his horse. She sidled at the reek of offal. He caught her hair and the bridle to steady himself, pretending the difficulty was with his arm.

He could feel the nausea now, coming rhythmically towards him. He had had much practice in physical control, in holding in tears and questions, dreams and wants and despair.

The core of him was always crying like a bell beneath a lake. He knew its clamour like the beat of his own pulse. But no remedy.

When Mechail went to the chapel, it was past noon, and he had left Beljunion waiting. The slight to God and his priest was not properly intentional. Having got to his chamber, sloughed his clothes and washed his body, he had forced sickness away with the wine that stood ready on the chest. Then he flung himself on the rocking bed and slept. He woke with a pain behind his eyes, a sense of misplacement, and thought for a second it was still to do. But he had done it. It was finished.

The chapel lay behind the Women's Garden, along a brief avenue that smelled of the peach trees over the wall.

In the cool shadow of an archway some women had grouped, to look at the new-made man. He heard a silly weightless laughter as he approached. He had no friends either among the female tribe. Three of his stepmother's girls were loitering, and Veksa herself was sitting on a stool, making no pretence; she had come to see.

She had been got pregnant at fourteen by the Vre, and never since, having proved her worth with Krau. They said her quaint ways between the sheets meanwhile kept the Landholder happy. She had brought a rich dowry too. She was no Tower Lady, but a miller's daughter. The eager dad had put her forward one evening when his lord was hunting the edges of Korhlen land. She was herself a forward wench, large-breasted and sleek, with a vixen's face, and yellow hair uncommon in the north. She had waxed taller and sleeker in the Tower, used to her own way. Where a peasant woman could be a hag at twenty, at more than thirty Veksa stayed young. Her hair was abundant still and coloured like saffron, some flowing free and some bound up in a plait stabbed with amber pins. For Mechail, who had seen her since his fifth year, she never exactly grew mature, only more apparent. Today the white linen dress was thickly bordered with embroideries of birds and cornflowers, and her wrists were composed of bangles. The sly, slanted smoke-blue eyes were what made her face so dangerous. He did not like to meet them, or any piece of her.

As he came level with the women, he wondered if Veksa would speak. He went by, she did not.

He had reached the chapel door before she called out.

'No courtesy? Not for the godbrother, not for his lord's wife?'

Mechail stopped. Without looking back, he said, 'Good day to you, Lady.'

'And good day to *you*, sir.'

And the girls chorused: 'Good day, Lord Mechail.'

He put his hand on the chapel door.

'Mechail,' called Veksa, 'Felicities on your first blood.'

The women were not recommended to mention this deed.

He knew also that Krau had had bets laid the Landholder's heir would fail. At sixteen Mechail had been confronted by an eleven-year-old Krau strutting before him, his knife sticky with the gore of a pig-killing. Krau had said: 'Do you know about the first blood? You have to kill a man. Not in a fight, but cold, on the stone. And you'll mess yourself. You'll faint.'

Mechail pushed the door. It gave. The hollow of the chapel offered itself, the bright window, and Beljunion's form at the altar.

Veksa exclaimed suddenly: 'My father's dogs had better manners.' She was always boastful of her lowly inception.

Mechail walked into the chapel, where the next adversary was readying to meet him.

Godbrother Beljunion had spent some time preparing for this interview. He had anticipated Mechail's delay. The godbrother was a little frightened, as now and then he had been before when dealing with Mechail Korhlen, the Devil-cursed.

The godbrother knew the superstitions of these forest peoples very well, for he had been born in the northern forest. His schooling and religious training at Khish instilled in him the principles of rigid faith, and a mathematical attitude towards happenings occult or profane. He did not believe in the events as they had been portrayed to him – the winged creature at the neck of the child, the fall, the flight, the hunting from which only stragglers had returned without news, even the captain vanishing in the snow-locked winter waste. It was all an anecdote, dramatized into credence. Vampires, those servants of Hell, were unreal in themselves, yet nevertheless abroad on the earth as ciphers, and warnings. What had truly occurred that night in the child's infancy Beljunion did not choose to fathom, but he was sure of its interpretation. The child was under the thrall of the demoniac. It might break out at any hour, even as the ignorant fears of the Landholder had inclined to predict. But it was not that the boy would become a demon. It was that already – and perhaps immutably – evil had him in its grasp.

Evil was the element then which Godbrother Beljunion had tried so hard to keep at bay, to beat out of him by the rod, and starve out with fasting.

Now the priest waited beside the altar, under the small burning lamp that symbolized God's attention, and the afternoon window poured brilliance upon the young man who walked slowly towards him.

Mechail did not know. They had never told *him* the mythic story, afraid it would bring him on the sooner to some crisis of malevolence.

Nor did he know, evidently, in other ways, what he was.

An innocent, a burnished apple aware only of the maggot eating its heart.

Aside from the ruined left side, the body was tall and leanly muscled, while a shifting promise of rarity in the child had by now fulfilled itself. An animal face, between cat and wolf, chiselled to the features of a human beauty, with savage eyes, half mad, irresistible. Not only handsomeness but some sort of potent power, male and lawless.

Beljunion had had to set himself against this also. A

need to touch or to caress found its outlet in the striking rod.

He had, of course, his interpretation for that, too. He was not at a loss, not ashamed. It was the Devil alone he had to fear.

'Have you cleansed yourself?'

'Oh, yes, godbrother.'

'Have you prayed?'

'No. I got drunk, and needed to sleep it off.'

Beljunion classified this as the defiance the unsure child had formerly shown him.

'Then we will pray now.'

Mechail looked at him. For a moment the priest sensed an urge to opposition far stronger than any Mechail had ever displayed. But it faded.

'Kneel,' said the priest sternly. He was relieved when Mechail obeyed.

Beljunion looked down upon the bowed head in its luxuriance of hair, the straight shoulder and the distorted rock which made up the other. The couth body seemed turned to stone at that juncture, the arm was like some petrified substance – it had barely the shape of an arm.

The priest commenced his prayer for the forgiveness of sin, and Mechail spoke the responses at each proper place.

'You have killed a man, Mechail Korhlen. It's the tradition here, but blood was spilled. Do you confess this error?'

'As you say.'

'*Do you confess this error?*'

'I do confess it.'

'You will not take meat for three days. You will abstain from hard drink for three days. Each morning for five days, on rising, you will repeat the prayer of contrition beginning *Father, in my fault.* This is for the protection of your soul.'

'And did you protect the soul of Krau in this way?'

The priest was faintly shocked. He disliked and feared the Landholder's illegal son, the part-bastard Krau, in an ordinary fashion. Krau was a ruffian. Had Beljunion

29

awarded *him* a penance for first blood? If so, it would not have been observed – or maybe Krau would have had the hideous dwarf (his pet for three years) carry it out in his stead.

'We are concerned with your sins and needs, Mechail, not those of your brother.'

Beljunion moved away from the altar, and crossing to the screen, he passed behind it. On the wall, flanked by the gilded faces of two saints, was the carved and painted cupboard containing sanctified wine.

The priest blessed himself, and opening the cupboard, drew out the cup. It was of iron, cold and heavy. The dregs of wine looked black, and from them rose a sour sharp taint. He regretted the poverty of the wine. But there, even the best that went to the high table was not much daintier.

As he turned to take the reconciling sip to Mechail, an old memory came upon the old priest. It stayed him, the cup in his hands.

Why think of this? This peculiar, this haunting and troubling and unsuitable thing? It was not the Korhlen sacrifice – he had long ago reasoned that out of his mind as something else he must put up with, in order to save them in other ways. Not that. It was the kneeling man, the weight of the cup . . .

His ordainment into the lower ranks of the priesthood had been at Khish. The town had seemed important to him then. Oddly, distanced from it by years, and the uncivilization to which he was sent back, these woods, he saw by now that Khish had not been much.

The church was grey, holed and chipped like a mildewed cheese. He had knelt for the Watching, three hours with the others on the icy floor, before the dim steep altar. Here they must remain until ordination should sweep down on them like a golden wind, with candles and singing. Then, the uplifting, the magic of the wine which became the blood of the Christus, the transforming of men into priests.

There had been fasts and prayers, weeks of them. There

had been the endless inquisition of faith, the testing, the tricks, to be sure.

Dizzy and chilled, Beljunion knelt on the church floor, sometimes feeling he would swoon and sprawl, at other times merely impatient, and sweating. His legs were burning wires and knobs of cramp. Surreptitiously he tried, over and again infinitesimally to ease them.

And throughout, he yearned, *lusted* for a revelation, some special hint of God, to whom he was offering up his life.

He had supposed it was a vision. But maybe it was a fantasy. Afterwards he was by turns proud of it – and unnerved. It did not fit the scheme of his holiness. He took time to learn to see it in his terms of cipher, to explain it away as something other than it was.

Now, as then, almost with the same intensity (yet surely not), the image rose unbidden, like a bud in water.

He had seemed to be, aptly, in a vast forest. But it was not the forest of his physical beginnings. The trees were of gigantic size and ascended apparently for miles into a canopy of perfect blackness. The lower boughs, the foliage, the undergrowth, were dense and curiously wound together. There appeared no way through this wood, and in the darkness everything was visible and yet impassable.

He knelt on the earth as he had knelt so long before the altar of Khish church. He still felt the discomforts of his knees and thighs and spine. But no longer did he try to alleviate them.

He knew, with deep, motionless excitement, that something came towards him, out of the forest.

It was the foreground which moved aside. And there, against the tapestry of the unending trees, was a tree greater than the rest, a trunk like a basalt pillar that soared into eternity or nothingness.

Below the tree stood a young man. He was quite nude, but his unblemished and proportioned body was itself a garment, and embellished at the head and neck by a hood of glowing hair.

When he raised his hand, Beljunion had seen that, from

31

the wrist like ivory, ran a ribbon of crimson blood, while by the other hand a cup was held to catch it. Everything was defined, even the cup was glassy black, like jet.

The blood, the priest thought, in an ecstacy, *the blood of the Redeemer—*

And in the second that the picture winked away he reached out to take and drink the blood of the young god out of the wood, pagan and intrinsic, the altar-icon of the Christus, and not God at all, some wondrous, awful, inexplicable essence – long since explained and exorcized.

The old priest stood gripping the iron cup of the Korhlen chapel.

He shuddered, and muttered a phrase of protection.

And beyond the screen, heard Mechail's restlessness as he too kneeled there, waiting.

Withhold the cup. He deserves nothing. The soul is spoiled.

But it was only a few dregs of sour wine, what did it matter? No, no, the invoked presence of the Christus lingered in them.

The priest broke out around the screen, almost trotting, hurrying to Mechail.

In a hoarse ramble, he spoke the final prayer, and Mechail's pale eyes glanced at him, searchingly.

'Drink,' said the priest, 'for here is the wine of the Immolation. Did he not say to them, *This is my blood.*'

He put the iron cup against Mechail's mouth.

Mechail sipped the dregs of the wine. His brain was suddenly full of a beating of red wings, and the word *blood* flew there in its many forms. But the wine was only vinegar, and he got it down.

The spring dusk spangled with rain. The sinking sun went into the forest. In the Korhlen village, as in the cots and huts of the wood, they would like as not be casting a handful of meal on to the cook fire, a sacrifice to the sun that he should return. In the Tower kitchen it went on too, if the overseer was absent.

Mechail could recall the slave woman, his nurse faint as a wraith in his memory, casting meal or breadcrumbs in the hearth. But elsewhere she had been lax. The biting dog had reached Mechail because of her carelessness. They had whipped her, and she died. This he could remember nothing of. There was a sort of empty subsidence in his mind at this point. The first events of childhood existed, then after the emptiness began whorled tunnels of pain and fever. But illness had visited him often as a child, such recollections were not unusual. And somehow also his brain had reworked time. For it seemed to him, looking back, he had never had a sound left arm; even before the dog he was a cripple, although that was not the case.

He slept again, following the attrition of the chapel. The day passed as, approaching it in dread, he would have thought impossible.

But tonight, in the Cup Hall, surely there must come an acknowledgement. When Krau killed his victim, there was boasting, all his crew of admirers and henchlings vaunting him, shouting and howling. The dwarf turning somersaults. And the Landholder that permitted it. He had even allowed the open naming of the act, before the women and after the table grace was said.

Chapter Three

A scene carved in yellow amber, the Korhlen Cup Hall. The candles were an hour lit, swollen with drippings thicker than a man's wrist. The brands burned and smoked. Over the stonework a skeleton of pine rafters, and from these wooden bones, the swords and lances hanging down, and the rust and green banner with its purple Raven, above the high table.

The Korhlen Hall had overlooked the first ferocious triumphs as the land was wrested and the oaths were made. Feasts and betrothals, some dozen murders, a score of fights that left dead men for meat in the trenchers. The forest was a wild place still, and even now on certain nights formality broke down once the women took their leave. It became then a cave of firelight and male noise, drink, dice and brawling.

At the high table the Landholder had positioned himself for dining, with his garrison captain to his right. They appeared to be discussing the virtues of a new pair of mailed gloves that lay between the salt cellar and the wine. The priest was habitually seated nearby, sorting his beads, preparing to say the grace. On the women's side, to the lord's left hand, the Lady Veksa was herself engaged in a conniving giggling converse with two familiars. But the Korhlen daughters, missing in one way, were, as normal, missing too in person.

Right of the table, the places of the Korhlen sons stood, both of them vacant.

The remainder of the high, wide room was perched

with Korhlen's human creatures, making their preparatory feeding din. The servants moved about with a first service of wine and bread. And at the massive hearth halfway up the Hall, six or seven black and brown dogs, pack leaders and favourites, poised quivering to the rising scent of food. Two of these gleam-eyed dogs were Krau's, unmistakable, for he kept them muzzled, having trained them to viciousness.

Mechail, who had some cause to dislike any dog, paid them no attention as he came in at the south door, crossed by the hearth, and proceeded up the Hall.

The servants made avenues for him, and his father's men and women offered customary nods and dipping eyelids. Mechail gazed before him, as if seeing none of them. It was his only method of dealing with this nightly walk.

Underfoot, the flagstones, painted with stale raw ochre and red, drew the eye senselessly, their patterns observed so often they were meaningless. His father's stare was on him; that he could tell, without a glance. Unmet, Mechail knew also the instant it was withdrawn.

Krau's chair was empty; the dwarf was absent from the Hall.

Mechail reached the high table.

'Lord father.'

He spoke the expected address quickly and loudly. (In childhood, he had been wont to slur and mumble it, acutely embarrassed that he must draw down notice on himself. But the courtesy omitted could earn a blow. Several times Vre Korhlen had cuffed his boys at the board. It was what fathers did. Krau made not much of it. Mechail had received correction differently, inwardly.)

Now again his father's eyes veered at him, moved away.

'Yes. Take your seat, Mechail.'

Take your seat. Was this to be all?

Startled despite himself, Mechail found he had looked into his father's face, to meet the enduring things he met there always.

Korhlen's was a countenance of light northern skin, black bearded, black haired, with no decline to grey, carved deep on brow and jaws. A plate of stone, but for the mouth, which was loose, a pink beast in the undergrowth. Wise writings in books told you you might judge a man's character by his features, yet for this mouth there was no supporting evidence, save maybe in the presence of Veksa, the whore-wife.

'Sit, then. Sit, I said.'

The stone turned itself back to the captain and the metal gloves.

The captain had been there, at the grove. He must have spoken.

Mechail reached for a ewer of unmixed wine. His arm and hand were shaking tautly, as if after too fierce exercise. He saw Beljunion flicker his priest eyes – strong drink had been forbidden – but there was no penance if there was no recognition of the deed. Mechail filled his cup, and as he did so, heard the servers' door opening at his back.

'Good evening, lord father!' sang out the voice.

Krau, the second son, had come in at the door behind the table. It was his most frequent route.

He jaunted around the board, and from the Hall welled up at once the choral greetings, the raised goblets, which Krau admitted with a flaunting wave. He went to Veksa, and kissed her hand. And she reached up to rub the smooth plane of his cheek.

Krau had always been a good-looking boy. He had his mother's blond hair, tilting smoky eyes. His body was athletic and strong, without discrepancy. Tonight he had come wearing his best, as if for a festival: the scarlet tunic Veksa's girls had been half a year embroidering with yellow fruit and silver bears, with the shirt of darker red visible through eyelets of soft gold. Gold wristlets, and a gold cross for a buckle on the calf-hide belt. His breeches were doeskin, he had hunted them himself. His boots he had taken from a well-dressed Esnias captain last summer, after a fight in enemy woods.

Krau straightened from his mother. He smiled directly at Mechail.

The smile was all complicity. It said: *Well*, we *know*, *don't we?*

Several times as a small boy Krau, or Krau's small boy's smile, or his casually trusting hand seeking Mechail's, the sudden unlooked-for sharing of something – such as these had misled Mechail. For a day or a moment they had made him believe Krau might be vulnerable. Until little Krau drew him where little Krau wished him to go, at which the curtain lifted and truth came out, articulate as a sharpened stick.

Now, Mechail knew that the smile was a promise.

He met the sixteen-year-old eyes of Krau, and his flesh stung under the skin. Krau intended to recognize the deed at the black stone.

'Where's the dwarf?' asked Veksa, as if on a cue. Krau's eyes in her face slid now to Mechail, and her own special smile slipped across her mouth like a worm.

'Oh, Dwarfy will be coming in.'

'So funny,' she said, 'what he can do.'

'Yes, I hope it will tickle us.'

'Krau,' said the Landholder, 'sit.'

There was only a terse idleness in the tone. No reprimand, or inquiry.

Krau bowed to his father. He moved to his seat, one chair's breadth from Mechail.

'How's the wine tonight?' said Krau to his elder brother. 'It's been filthy stuff. Old Beljunion cranks up better.'

The priest nervously caught the words, told his beads.

Vre Korhlen said clearly, not looking at Krau again, 'If you bring your pet to table, keep him in check.'

The pet (the dwarf), in the opinion of the Tower, was not human, but a magical devil-thing, part beast, part sprite. Krau had stolen or purchased it from travellers at some forest drinking hut. The facts were vague. At the time the Landholder had beaten Krau, but then the dwarf proved an entertainment. He could perform acrobatics, and mimic the articulation of animals and men. Those that fell from favour in the Tower were fair game. Although sometimes the forms of the mockery were subtle, barely discernible by any but their object, they were feared. Krau had not employed the dwarf in forms of subtle mockery against Mechail for more than a twelvemonth. Perhaps Veksa had persuaded her son it was not currently clever.

How often Mechail had longed to leave the Hall. Sensing the pressure of Krau's will, his instinct was to bolt. But one learned to suppress instinct.

The priest got up and said the grace. Now the dishes of food were coming. A roasted pig for the high table, crackling in its fat, with sauces of green apples and rosy berries, and side dishes of dumplings and sausage. An elaborate dinner; as though to mark something.

It was possible to smell death in the hot pork, but somehow the meal was to be swallowed.

Krau nudged Mechail. 'That's it. You fill your hungry belly, brother. Didn't I say you had a strong stomach?'

Krau's hand lay out by the plate, in its wristlet and its gold ring. Mechail had the urge to drive into that hand the two-pronged table fork.

There was a fresh burst of noise from the Hall below. It came in a wave and hit against the Vre's table.

'What's this?' Mechail heard his father say, in a deep, easy voice. 'Something of yours, Krau?'

'I, my lord? Mine?'

Mechail looked up.

The noise had sunk to a mingled murmur of wondering and cautious disapproval. Faces were turning to see how the lord took it, Krau's new joke.

Into the Hall had come two of Krau's closest attendants, sons of the armourer. They wore hunting leathers and looked sheepish, grinning up at Krau's place hopefully. Between them they propelled a monstrous thing on wooden wheels. There was a black mound to it, from which protruded the pealed boughs of young birches. But the mound also moved a touch, and it seemed likely a further pair of men might be contained under its drape. Nevertheless, it was plain what it represented, for to the mound of cloth and men and boughs was strapped a bloated effigy, a straw-man such as they made for the malicious surrogate burnings of escaped felons. The doll had crude features, a mop of black wool hair, and its enormous gut was clad in a ruddy tunic of the Esnias Tower.

Krau stood.

'What do you mean by it?' he shouted down at his servant-cronies.

'Ah, well, sir,' said the burlier of the armourer's boys, bolder now Krau took the lead, 'it's a foe of the Korhlens we caught in the wood.'

'Death is the only answer, for an Esnias wretch,' said Krau. 'But who is to supply it?'

Mechail was dazedly sure that he betrayed nothing. His body had shut into a rictus. He could not move even his head to see what his father did, whether or not Vre Korhlen would sanction this. The Hall was utterly silent. Some of the women's faces were slightly shocked, but none antagonistic. They waited to learn which way the cat would jump.

And Vre Korhlen said not a word.

'Well, then,' said Krau. 'Who shall it be? Our champion?' Mechail perceived at his eye's corner Krau's inquiring gaze, which fluttered over him, and was gone. 'Look there. *There* he comes.'

And in at the south door shunted forward by another of Krau's playful band, careered a terrible entity of abuse and dream.

The Hall broke into laughter, could not help it. They found this type of show so droll.

The dwarf rode upon one of Krau's malignant dogs, a brown bitch, bridled and saddled like a chestnut mare. The dwarf was clad in dark clothes, with a long dagger at his hip – it was tin, for nothing beyond a carving knife came to the Hall tables. Tin notwithstanding, the effect of garb and weapon was to recreate the morning apparel of the heir. (They must have asked questions.) The dwarf's small humped back, always a paraphrase of Mechail's shoulder, had been accommodatingly padded more on the left side. The dwarf wore his black hair in elf-locks. His face was painted greenish. No sooner were rider and dog-horse in the Hall, and the laughter fading for a second tumult, than the dwarf began to evince extreme paroxysms of fright.

And leaning up on to a table, he made a fearful gagging, and from his mouth a brown frog leapt, and darted away into a chaos of starts, sleeves and curses.

One of Krau's men piped: 'Eeh, poor him. How he trembles and must puke!'

And now, on another table, it was a granary mouse, sprinting under the breads and blood puddings. In a whirl of skirts, women rose squeaking. Men guffawed and aimed blows at the dwarf.

Evasive, the dwarf rode on. He had reached the straw man strapped to the black stone of cloth and boughs and Krau's friends. The dwarf could not dismount. He contorted and floundered. The Hall bellowed.

'Assist a poor cripple!' bleated Krau's spokesman.

Mechail, his body a wound chain of iron, sat expressionless and still, with Krau a blond-bright shadow at his side.

Krau's companions lifted the dwarf tenderly from the dog, which skewed and tried to bite them through the muzzle. There was tremendous mirth. They were banging their goblets on the table now. The women's faces were red with joy.

The dwarf approached the strapped effigy.

The dwarf wept. Handfuls of lead coins clanked on to the paving from his eyes.

Drawing his dagger-sword of tin, the dwarf lunged abruptly at the great belly of straw, which split, exploded. The dwarf sprang into the midst of it in a cloud of chaff, and from the interior began to pitch things out. They fell riotous upon the table-tops, the bodices of dresses – sweets, feathers, bells.

The Cup Hall of the Korhlens rang with merriment and outcry. It was hard enough to catch any individual note. Yet Mechail did so. Beyond Krau's attentive smiling silence, it came, the parody of a sound. Their father's loud, true laughter.

As he pulled himself to his feet, Mechail relinquished vision, hearing and reason. Through a roiling gale of colours and obstacles, of clattering and grunting, he pushed a way. He used the convenient servers' door, as had his brother. No one stayed him. The butt of their joke, even so maybe they had forgotten he was there.

'What's the matter with you? What have I reared? I'd say a girl, but a girl would have better spirit. By God. Your daft sisters have more spunk. He'd never try his tricks on *them*.'

Vre Korhlen spoke the words as an incantation, harsh and blunt, the shield of his body between himself and this man, his son. As he glared into the face of Mechail (named for a saint, *her* fancy, damn her over, even dead), the Landholder did not see in fact Mechail. Only the shell of him. The disappointment. And some other furtive thing Vre Korhlen had never named at all.

'He made a jest of me.'

Mechail was stammering slightly. It happened in his childhood often.

'Yes. A laughing stock. And how do you answer? You run away.'

'What should I do in the Hall—'

'Why something, anything, before God.'

In a white face, Mechail's eyes looked nearly black.

'I heard,' said Mechail. 'I heard you laugh.'

Vre Korhlen now turned physically aside. He was embarrassed and would not display or admit to it. Beneath his external rock, a host of contradictory surges struggled sluggishly in the compost of years. Some piece of the Vre understood that to be amused by this unlucky son was a protection and solace. That, by casting him off in the mind, there was a practice for something crueller and more definite. And too, farther, deeper in the sludge, lay the memory he had put others to guard against. The

41

demon scar upon Mechail. To laugh at it thrust it off, made of it a lie.

Vre Korhlen filled his cup with wine and took a striding step across the chamber, exercising the thick powerful body that disliked ever to be quiet.

'You are your mother,' he said. 'Nilya. That whey face, whining, martyred. Milk for blood. She died bringing me you. It was you killed her off. Nothing but trouble from you. Stir yourself. Fight your fights as you please, don't come whimpering to me. Find something to make me laugh at *Krau*.'

'Krau is straight-backed.'

'Krau is a man.' Vre Korhlen smashed down his cup and spilled the wine. 'Do you think no other ever came out warped? Your grandfather had a twisted leg. He could outride the best. Nor it never stopped him at work in a woman. If any man jibed at him, the lout never did it twice.'

'Are you telling me, sir, to kill Krau?'

Vre Korhlen crossed to his son and slapped him, glancingly, across the cheek.

'Don't gob such talk at me.'

Mechail stood before him. He was the taller, and, to any who had looked, the better made. The ruined shoulder was like a badge upon him, some farce beauty had flung up to mock the remainder of a cloddish world. But he did not know, and would not have believed or cared.

'Then I'm to settle it myself,' he said, choking on the enigma, for he was not to harm Krau and he was not to endure Krau. He must accept but also divorce ridicule. Miracles. It would be miracle enough to live here among enemies, and one day, when this stinking bear died in some fit of his lust or drink, to become himself the Landholder. *He*, Mechail. If it came it would be the labour of a day for Krau to be rid of him. He must always have seen, Mechail, but never so clear, like broken mirror in the mud of this.

Mechail gave his father the clipped bow without which

42

one could not leave the presence. They demanded their courtesies in the stye.

You killed her off. Nilya, his mother. He remembered her lying in the hard bed of a side chamber, put away from her husband not to disturb him. And to Mechail she whispered, 'Don't touch me—' saying he would be hurt by touching her, as if a dreadful heat or poison lingered on her surfaces.

So that was love – what he had felt for her. Back across a void of time. *That* was love. Her fear for him. Grief and loss and terror . . . were *love*.

The women's apartments of the Korhlen hold spread through a stone and wood warren behind the gardens, where in elder times they would have been strictly segregate. Painted wooden balconies overhung from the windows of the apartments, many of which were tenantless, their lower floors allotted to the use of female servants.

A lengthening dusk had merged into a dark. From the patches of grass beneath the balconies might be heard the scurry of rodents. Birds slept in the thatch of roofs. Such human traffic as passed this way trod carefully, particularly by night.

It was Boroi who travelled here now. He had been allowed a visit to a woman, for the getting of children among the slaves was organized and diligent. If he had enjoyed the short, designated convulsion, was not to be judged.

Above, there came a soft rustle along a balcony. It might be ivy moving to the tempo of the night wind, Boroi did not check his pace. Nor did he, when an unseen missile thumped down into the grass, jib or swerve to find its origin.

A ribbon of wordless sound unwove from darkness.

About a pair of wooden posts, two pale women-girls were coiled like two pale cats. They also had names, but now went by suitable cat-titles: *Puss*, and *Chi*.

One day either or both might be given in wedlock (though they were past the normal marriageable age), to consolidate some union of Towers. The bridegrooms would reap thereby a wry harvest. Until that season, Korhlen's daughters did as they wished.

Boroi had disappeared, but they did not care. They were looking for Krau. He had said he would come to call on them, and they had heeded, for he sometimes gave them sexual pleasure. Their antics caused him to laugh, and this too they obscurely liked, that they could amuse. At other persons they regularly threw things from the balcony. Once they had put out the eye of a slave. Puss had been distressed, but Chi did not mind it.

'Is he coming along the walk?' asked Puss now, seemingly of her sister, as both leaned from the rail.

'Is he?' asked Chi in return.

Perhaps they asked, in reality, the night.

But Krau was not on the walk, as yet.

'I shall sit in his lap; he'll fondle me,' said Puss.

Neither looked her age. Strangeness had preserved them. Their hair was blonder than the hair of Krau or Veksa. They were albinos, and had left the womb Puss within minutes of Chi.

There was no light to see their eyes, which were pink.

Vre Korhlen had not deemed himself cursed firstly with Mechail.

The orchard garden was a cloud of peach and mulberry trees, through which a thin moon slowly slit with its silver razor. A night bird sometimes sang there, but not this evening.

Dull lights hung on the Tower and in one or two of the places about, but humankind was packing itself down in its byres or beds. Deadened and blinded after dark, men slept. While in the forest, things with eyes of steel awoke and went about their errands.

Mechail waited among the orchard trees. He was attending on his brother. Krau would most probably come by this path, towards the women's buildings, after sufficient carouse in the Cup Hall. It was the usual formula with him, following a success, to seek the female servants, or his sisters.

Mechail had never had a woman. Even in dreams, he had not partaken. Awake, he burned, as Scripture called it, for hatred of his own body precluded he make love to it.

What Krau did, astride the flesh of women, Mechail knew only from the farmyard.

He did not think of that, or of the wine he had drunk as he waited. He had no idea what he would do. His mind was an empty, scorching wound. He itched with his anger. Again and again he felt the forcing pressure of the knife as it gutted the Esnias soldier. But he had come unarmed.

On three occasions there were huge shouts from the Cup Hall. He listened, as if to alien beings over the border of another country.

And it was under the cover of the third shout that Krau came walking through the trees.

He carried no lamp. He moved limber and stealthy, careful in case, despite everything, his father should gainsay these exploits, of which otherwise he made small secret. He himself, bold handsome Krau, appeared very little as he stole between the trunks in the weird and fractured moonlight.

The bounding of blood in his ears had perhaps deafened Mechail, or his concentration was too much on one point.

Suddenly the foliage above him rushed and broke, took weight and fell down. The impact tumbled Mechail. He dropped, and the parasite arm was crushed. He did not cry out. Something clawed and clung to him – it was the beast which had shot from the tree. Mechail struck at it. It was gone.

Krau poised above him, grinning grey under the moon. The dwarf frolicked at Krau's side, with leaves in his hair. The dwarf still had on the jape-clothes, was still 'Mechail'.

'Good *night*, brother,' said Krau. 'Dwarfy sussed you good and well. Some assignation? Or did you loiter for me?'

Able to use only his right arm, Mechail levered himself

from the earth to which the falling dwarf had thrown him. Krau leaned over, helped.

'There,' said Krau, and dragging Mechail's head forward, kissed him on the lips.

Mechail lashed out. The blow did not reach its target. Krau had danced aside.

'Don't bash me,' said Krau, gently. 'It's not my fault he didn't rate you. The dad's a pig-sot.'

Mechail had heard Krau's insults of their father before. They were worthless.

The razor of the moon crested the trees. It shone into the eyes of the dwarf-man by Krau's waist. The eyes of the dwarf were old and cold, cored of life, though he grimaced and made voiceless gestures of jollity.

'Well, what do you want?' said Krau.

'Fight me,' said Mechail.

'Fool. I could kill you. Only then there'd be a to-do.'

The world seemed to spin. Mechail flinched from them, those torturers; they were changed in the darkness.

'Come on, come see your sisters,' Krau said. 'I'm drunk. You be, too. Come and play with Chi and Puss. And then, we'll hunt Esnias. Give the piss-hog dad something to witness. Not a tied-up slave. Real killing.'

'Esnias,' repeated Mechail. He needed all at once to tell Krau how it had been, to murder the soldier at the stone. But he knew better. And anyway, Krau had done this thing. He knew.

'The woods are full of the bastards, Gaj told me. We're going hunting after midnight. The woods are full of women, too. . . . Did you know? Devilish girls bathing in pools. Girls shut in bothies, scared, won't unbar the door, then following you away through the trees, with thin hot faces. Let's sweat off this dirty wine, eh, brother?'

The dwarf had approached Mechail, staring up with eldritch eyes. It was as if Mechail had seen neither of them ever in his life, the dwarf or his half-brother.

If I go with him, it's another game, some means to dupe me. What does it matter? What's left? Let him. Maybe I can slice him in the wood. Maybe I can kill all Esnias men now.

Veksa, the miller's daughter, entered the bedchamber softly. Her lush hair was loose upon her shoulders, from one of which her mantle had somewhat slipped. Meanwhile she was decorous, her hands clasped before her bosom. She was not afraid in the least, though the summons had been peremptory, tonight.

Her husband, the Landholder, she found drinking and fully clothed, his face swarthy with wine. He scowled at her.

'Now I'll hear *you*,' he said.

Veksa felt the customary contemptuous liking she had always known so perfectly to disguise. She had never feared him, not even the first time in her father's bed. Men could be dealt with. And the lord was only a man. He had lifted her up; she did what she wanted.

'Husband,' she said, using as ever the address common among peasants, 'if Krau's done wrong, you'll chastise him and he won't make any fuss. You know that. He reveres you. I'm just the woman, the mother. I was surprised by his antics. But then, I confess – I laughed.'

As her Landholder had laughed. She had watched for that, and seen it, eaten it up. Her son was canny. He had taken after his mother, there. Only his riskiness was male, silly. But then, it had not failed, the trick. She needed only to get it out of him now, her black-beard, his admission, and not even aloud.

'Mechail is my heir. He was made a clown of.'

'Oh, Krau's jealous. If he thinks Mechail gets more of your regard, Krau tries to make you look at him instead. Boys.'

'The rite at the stone isn't to be mocked.'

'I see it was Mechail he mocked, not the rite. But then again,' she said swiftly, with liquid mildness, 'perhaps it seemed to Krau you and your trusted men were at a loss, how to recognize publicly the significance of the rite . . . in the case of Mechail.'

Vre Korhlen turned to her, glowering. Stupid. How should she quake at that, she who knew him better than his own dam? But she lowered her eyes, kept quiet.

'My legal heir, Veksa. You understand that, so does our bloody boy—' (She noted the familial cast, *Our boy, Krau.* It was the other who was the bastard in everything but fact.) 'There'll be a punishment.'

Veksa did not smile, outwardly. She digested the sweetness, the brevity of his annoyance with her son, ending in this token smack.

'Of course, husband. It was a game, but he'll see reason. Perhaps he wanted to spare you, make a light thing of it, but he'll be ready to take what you give. Strike him. Whatever you like. Krau loves his father. He's staunch.'

Vre Korhlen's face was all she had predicted, now. He was so workable. But it was easy to guide a man to what he wanted. When the time came, it would be easy too for Krau to assay the last step. Besides, he was popular and feared in the Tower, looked up to, things the other one had never tried to be, the cripple. For a moment, unwary, Veksa considered the cripple, there in the bedroom, as her husband imbibed his wine. (*He'll have a heavy head in the morning. I'll need to brew my potion.*) Mechail, wrapped in a mystery, some curious tale she had never properly unearthed, ferret after it as she had. Like a shadow he was, some half-creature of the wood – she had been told enough stories of that kind, in her infancy. Mechail was not exactly as malleable as the others. Beneath his misleading garments of shame and arrogance, a depthless water had beckoned. If he had been some underling, and she differently placed, it could have been pleasing to try of what he was made.

'Where is he?' (*He means Krau.*) 'Still swilling in my Hall? He'll stop that.'

'I think he gathers up his friends there for a – hunt,' said Veksa. 'He never speaks of those things to me, but there's a look he gets.'

Vre Korhlen put down his cup. 'Esnias?'

'They've been a worry to the village on your land. It's early to take your soldiers raiding. I think he wants to clear your woods a little for you, husband, before you engage the feud again. I've heard, those Esnias are nearly

48

as scared of your son as of you.' She stole closer, as if at
some irresistible persuasion. 'Will I pour another cup for
you?'

'Yes. And bring it to bed.'

He rubbed her breast suddenly with his hand. Veksa
pressed herself to him, and licked his lip. He pulled her
nearer and kissed her, filling her mouth with his tongue.
The difficulty was over.

Presently, they would be abed, and she would tell him
she was parched for one very wicked sinful drink that the
priests would refuse her. And she would fill her mouth
again, another way, with the stub of his organ. She would
lip and suck and he would writhe there helpless, uttering
obscenities and moaning to God, this authoritative and
dangerous man. Long, long ago, the old aunt who taught
her had assured Veksa no man would protest a lack of
children if she gave him this. And making believe her
own frenzy, she would swallow down the semen on which,
at the start, she often might have gagged. She would
swallow it now in a happiness of scorn and power.

Adept at her task, able to allow her thoughts to stray,
she did wonder if her bawdy son had found any woman
in the Tower to award him such a thrill.

As for the other, for priestly, chill Mechail, she doubted
he would let any female so practise on him. He would be
wary of the mouths of women, the apple lips, the serpent's
tongue, the biting teeth.

They reached the apartment by a crumbling stair. Puss
heard them as they trod down the vine. She manifested
between the balcony posts.

'Meow,' said Puss. The sisters themselves knew they
were cats.

'Is it Puss? Come here, let me see,' said Krau. Puss
came to him and he made sure of her the way he always
did, opening the buttons of her bodice, finding her right
breast, with its nipple, pale as some candy, encircled by
tiny freckles. Puss purred and reached in turn to caress

Krau in the manner he had shown her. 'Tonight,' said Krau, 'I've brought my hungry brother.'

Over Krau's shoulder lifted the moon of Puss' face in a cirrus of hair. Her eyes were like drops of venom. Mechail stared back at her.

'Who is he?' said Puss.

'I said. Don't you know him? Bad Puss. Kith and kin.'

Puss drew back her lips and hissed at Mechail like a snake.

Krau shook her, enjoying everything. '*Bad* Puss.'

Mechail waited until the two of them, dogged by the dwarf, passed on into the room behind the balcony, then he pushed after, through the shutters. A faint lamplight, mostly invisible from outside, revealed a wide, low chamber of incredible squalor and untidiness. Not only cats, they hoarded like magpies, and in the same way, generally useless glittering things. Cracked vessels and shards of glass, and skeins of cheap beads wrenched from the kitchen sluts, lay piled about, even the skulls of lizards and small mammals were there, and sprays of long-dead flowers and fruits. A mummified civet, moulting and smelling, hung from the rafters; it was their toy. A clump-ish bed suggested where the sisters might sleep amid the mess and trophies.

To Mechail they were strangers, glimpsed now and then at a distance. If he had actually seen them inside three years, he could not recall. But in any event, like all the attributes of this night, they were to him foreign and meaningless.

The dwarf opened a splintery wooden cupboard stand-ing on the floor, producing a flagon of wine. He carried this to Krau. Despite his earlier sentence on drink, Krau hefted it, and negligently offered it to Mechail.

Mechail took the wine, and drank.

Krau laughed.

Chi was sitting on a heap of cushions, ancient worn mounds sewn with tawdry spangles. Across her lap, like a diseased brown bone, stretched a cithra. She plucked and strummed it, conceivably thinking she produced melody. Her eyes were on Mechail, still and unblinking. Chi did not question who Mechail might be.

'Try her,' said Krau, nodding at Chi. 'I've taught her a thing or two. Puss wants *me*, don't you, Puss?' He rolled down on the bed and Puss swam with him, emerging from her dress, never properly put on it seemed, with the ease of a fish in water. Beneath she was unclad.

As in the Hall, Mechail watched.

Krau evidently felt no threat, to lie there on his back with his breeches undone, and the white thing dabbling at him, before Mechail. Already Krau towered, erect. Yet to the towering phallus of hatred and rage, black as night and burning as sex, he was apparently oblivious.

Chi had stopped strumming. She sat on her cushions gazing at Mechail. He could experience her eyes.

The dwarf pawed the civet, made an odd mewing.

'Shut your noise, Dwarfy,' muttered Krau. He hauled naked Puss along his body. There was thin white fur at her groin and in the pits of her raised arms. Krau began to push his weapon into her. She moaned and wriggled. Krau's face was scarlet. Lodged, he gripped her buttocks, moved her.

Unaroused, Mechail looked down at them.

The dwarf had sat against a post in the wall. He rested his head on his stunted knees. His empty eyes appeared fixed on some inner event that almost interested him. Save physically, he was no longer in the room.

Chi rocked the cithara. She had never blinked. Mechail could tell her eyes never left him. He continued to watch Krau. Krau made sounds now, loud enough to fill the chamber. A scent came from the bed, animal and acute. The air itself seemed flickering with odd bright little motes that sheared off from the working bodies.

Puss squealed. Suddenly, unnervingly, she called out *'Mamma! Mamma!'* A wave went through her. She fell down on Krau, and then began to try to pull away. But Krau held her firmly, and thrust himself on, his sounds now glottal and bestial. Puss was pitched and bobbed about on his loins. She was crying. As he subsided, she got herself free of him, and ran away, crouching in a corner under her spiderweb of tresses, weeping for half a minute, before some item by her hand distracted her. She scooped up the object, the leftover of a buckle or earring, and started to pick at it, forgetting.

Krau swung his head lazily, to take in Mechail.

'Well you've had your stare. Now let me see what you can do.'

As if he had told her she must, Chi got up and glided towards Mechail.

She came very close, and he did not prevent her. But she did not touch. She looked up into his face, and now Mechail, not wanting any more to watch the red-hot laxness of his brother, brought his eyes to meet with hers. Their colour had grown visible, like watered rose quartz, pinker than her mouth, or her sister's nipples.

'In the wood, in the wood,' murmured Chi, in a singsong. Her hands made a motion as if bringing harmony up from the discarded cithra, 'be he a man or be he a lord? Give me him skin or give me him blood? In the wood, in the—'

'What nonsense are you tweeting now?' demanded Krau from the bed.

'Wood,' said Chi. 'In the wood.'

The chamber rushed at Mechail. It was strung yet with flying motes of lust, but in the midst the black stone heaved and out spilled the entrails of the dead, shining and uncoiled.

Mechail slammed through the shutters, and leaning on the treacherous balcony, vomited into the dark.

Each tearing spasm seemed to dredge up his own intestines. He felt himself rent, disembowelled, given to the night in a will-less torrent of pain and horror. And in the cave-back of consciousness, he heard Krau laugh on at him.

But when he finished, and leaned on the wall, Krau was at his elbow, and Krau said, 'Come and kill Esnias, brother.'

52

'Yes,' said Mechail. He coughed and spat upon the night.

'In the wood for sure,' said Krau.

God's in the wood. Maybe the Esnias men will do for me. Can You hear me pray to You? End it. Oh God, let me die before morning.

In the wood . . .

The wolf stood above the streamlet with the diamonds of the water falling from his muzzle. Under the stripes of the moon, his eyes, within their leaf-shaped darks, were like the grey-greenish-yellow wines of fine flinty vineyards. His coming had silenced the frogs in the pools. But his ears were lifted. He listened.

He had killed an hour before, the young wolf, a furry citizen of the underbrush, and dined. He came now to drink, and might later roam. He had no pack, and it was spring, a whisper upon the night, the moon in heaven.

But beyond the stream-bed, down through the running aisles of the pines, human beasts had gathered. They too had their kill or catch, which they cooked at a fire. They made a great noise in their cautious quietness.

The wolf walked over the low water, and loped down a parting in the forest. From this high ground, among the stems, the needled boughs that arced to the earth, he might regard the camp of men.

The wolf looked on some while. Their reddish tunics, their haphazard mail, their muted talk, bravado and ignorance, their unkempt ways about the joints of hare, did not engage the wolf's attention much, though once or twice his brows twitched, he raised one elongate foot or the other, silently. He snuffed them, and their burnt feast. His white-wine eyes flamed.

And then, from further off, the wolf – but not the group about the fire – heard with harp-strung ears the quiet, *raucous* advance of other men, tapping and crunching though the forest.

Demon-like, the wolf had changed places with himself, was gone.

To a flash of pallor, one of the Esnias feasters seemed half alerted. He raised an inquiring snout – saw nothing, and sank his teeth again into his meat.

'There they are,' said Gaj, the steward's son. 'The devils. Chomping our Korhlen hares.'

It was Gaj who made comments, but Gralice, his tight-lipped cousin, who had apparently located the trail of Esnias bivouacs. He had known where the Korhlen warriors must come, and led them. The other two men – boys of fifteen – were lesser fry, stable apprentices who hung about with Krau's contingent, messengers and toadies, but handy with knives, so brought.

The Esnias band was eight in number. To destroy it would be prestigious.

The Esnias seemed cosy, in the Korhlen forest. As if they had never heard of a feud. Though they were not loud, they were vigorous for their circumstances, and the fire in the clearing had scant concealment. There were no horses, this riff-raff did not aspire to them. Krau's party had also set out on foot, for the speed of leaving and furtiveness in the trees. The walk had taken an hour. Water courses sprang in the stabbing moon and tiny creatures burst into flight. To go back into the wood, unholy, deep, in the last dense chapter of night, seemed a commonplace to Krau and his men. To Mechail, its supernatural quality was dreamlike. Everywhere might be portents, glowing fungus, starry streams, the shake of bird wings clandestine in a pine-top. His body seemed for the first time incidental and light. He was not impeded. He did not want to acknowledge God; yet, by lying down in the hand of God, he had released himself from bondage. Only death could follow this submission, as in his prayer.

Krau was at his side, hot even now in the coolness, smelling still of his lust.

'What do you think, brother?' wheedled Krau. 'Will we take them?'

Mechail said nothing.

Gaj mouthed: 'Yes, sir. Look, they've eaten and they're

drinking too. Stolen liquor, I'll bet. All they expect is a good sleep.'

'Gaj,' said Krau, 'go to that tree up there. Take Squint. And Gralice, where the split boulder is. You, Pekl, that stump. I'll make the charge with Mechail. We'll run straight at them. On my start.'

His fellows sidled obediently off. They were very relaxed, as indolent as the eight foes lolling by the fire.

Mechail gazed down; the flames drew his eyes. A sort of sleepiness was stealing through him. Then Krau gave him a loving hug. 'You're ready?'

'Yes,' said Mechail. He stood up and went out through the undergrowth even as Krau leapt past him, yelling down the slope.

Mechail's final and pedantic thought was that the Esnias seemed startled.

In their red tunics and dented mail, jumping up from their hearth circle, they were like explosions of the fire.

'*Korhlen!*' Krau screamed. He rammed a man head-on and cut into him under the uplifted arm. As the Esnias reeled away, two others ran at Krau. Gralice, cascading from the opposite side of the clearing, collided with them, as Squint and Pekl poured into the whirlpool. The fire lit the knives. A man squealed and cursed.

Mechail, plunging forth, had no feeling beyond a slight bewilderment. He came against the barrier of a man who reached to clasp him. And the knife in Mechail's grip sheered across the eight fingers of the soldier's hands into his throat.

The Esnias dropped backward and crashed into the fire, banking it. Most of the light was extinguished.

A dislocated immobility clenched upon the clearing with the dark. All at once no one stirred.

Then a leaden blow thundered against Mechail's spine. He knew he fell since the earth smote his face. He felt nothing.

'What do you mean by it, Korhlen? Is this a bargain?'

'Spare me your groans, Esnias turd. Do you think I'd

get by if I hadn't a couple of your rubbish to show, with his priceless body?'

'Our mates.'

'I'll fashion orisons for them in the chapel. Did I hurt you or your friend there? And you brought more men than you said.'

Another young one spoke gruffly. 'It's true. Give him his due, uncle.'

'And I'll be first in the Tower, after my dad, the Vre. Remember that. I won't forget *you*, dear enemies.'

Krau had paid the Esnias. It was arranged. No Korhlen blood on Korhlen hands. Another victory for the bold son, and a sad, appropriate death for the cripple – even an *honourable* death, if it came to it. He would die fighting with his brother in the Korhlen feud.

Two of them were lifting him. His legs had lost sensation from the blow to his back. He hung there, and his head went up without volition, for he surely did not want or need or care to see.

'How shall we do it, Krau Korhlen?' said one of the Esnias standing now by the periphery ripples of the put-out fire.

Krau turned and eyed Mechail. He was smiling, all gaiety. Behind him, Pekl picked his nostrils and Squint squinted at his knife. Gaj and Gralice looked grim. They had condemned Mechail; no Tower could prosper with such an heir. They were *righteous*.

'Not in the back,' said Krau. 'My father would dislike that. No. Let us give him a parting gift, the courage he's never had. In the gut. Let him have a little space over dying. He's taken long enough about his bloody life.'

The two Esnias who held him dragged Mechail against a tree. They held him there then, pinned on the trunk of it.

Mechail knew a momentary terror of the pain to come, but let it go. It was all pain, and this the end of pain. He looked up into the tree. The moon was there, riding over now to the west. Quickly, make it come quickly and put out the moon.

Krau said, 'We'll go off that way, my friends. We shouldn't watch. It isn't on our heads if we don't see.'

One of the six men by the dead fire was coming towards Mechail. Mechail did not look at him, remembering the soldier that morning at the stone, the jarring together of eyes.

Krau had not even bidden him good night.

The Esnias soldier paused a moment, perhaps nerving himself, or wanting some response. Then he muttered, 'Pardon me, God. For my *Tower*—' A rush of his arm, a light—

The second blow, colossal, dashed Mechail through into the black centre of the tree. The Esnias had after all aimed exactly for his heart. There was an instant of shattering and flowing, an inner descent like the plummet of a bird from the sky. And then in truth, nothing.

Nothing.

When the coins had been paid over, and the bodies taken up, the groups of men separated, and went away.

Only then, down from the height, returned the night-shadow of the wolf. Beneath the tree he licked the blood.

And the moon sank under the world.

Chapter Four

The slave, having finished the washing of the icon (his master's corpse), straightened and stepped back.

Boroi knew no existence but his slavery. If he had ever opposed, or dreamed of freedom, that time must be long gone from him. He felt neither unease or triumph at the sight of his death. Mechail Korhlen, that he had seen grow up out of childhood, had surely remained remote to Boroi. Yet, the body was familiar. White as wax now, with the floods of black hair at head and loins, and the vast bruised cavity over the heart that went from red to violet into darkness, a sunset of life.

The deformed shoulder Boroi barely saw any more, he was so used to it. But oddly, he had treated the shoulder with a biased gentleness, even now, when it did not matter.

After the washing came the anointing, and then the dressing. The other slave was already at work with the vials, an elderly woman who could hardly see, rubbing her palms across the dead young flesh. Neither did Boroi apparently feel anything at this, although once, when she made a small noise, perhaps in illicit pleasure or mockery, Boroi lightly cuffed her.

They dressed Mechail in a bleached shirt, dark breeches and tunic, clothes he himself might have put on. (It was supposed unlucky to garb the dead in Tower colours.) The dead hips and waist were curious to handle, as Boroi buckled on the belt with its Raven device. And the feet too were cold in the sunny afternoon, as he pushed home their boots. The Vre must come and choose which jewels his son should take with him.

Despite the warmth of the day, the body gave off no odour, though it had been meat some hours. Nor was there yet any stiffness, even at the penis, which sometimes showed the symptom first.

Mechail's face had only the secretive look the dead have.

Ashamed that his act of the rite was not praised, Mechail had challenged Krau to take him hunting Esnias in the forest – and the Esnias had been too many and had killed him. Krau come back with a pair of bodies in recompense. Someone said the lord sat weeping. Boroi would not believe this, if he thought about it. The lord Vre did not weep. This was what he had wanted.

Expendable, the slave guessed he would be sent now to more menial and harshly labouring duties. Krau would not want or need him, and there were no other recognized sons. But Boroi did not even regret demotion.

Under the gilded sky, the Raven Tower constucted its normal daytime sights and noises. A clank of metal from its forge, the rummage and whicker of horses. A party of soldiers drilled in the garrison yard: there would be open fighting soon, after what had happened. Doves circled about their cot. And over the walls, the slaves worked in the fields, the mill turned her sails. Business went on at the inn.

Had a shadow come? It would soon pass over. There might be some superstitious observance. Then, a memory.

Two men had carried the heir's cadaver down the stairs of the Tower. The corpse was draped over by a pall of green, russet and purple, but beneath was plainly clad, and wore no jewels, never having garnered any beyond a ring of twisted silver, the property once of its mother, the Lady Nilya. The ring lay forgotten in a box.

A trestle stood in the chapel, before the altar. Here they set him, the dead, an offering. The drape was folded under his young man's chin, and his arms, the strong and

59

the warped, drawn out and the hands laid upon an iron sword. That was his right, the mark of esteem, since he had died in a battle, his wound not a coward's. But they would take back the sword, an antique of the Tower, before his burial.

At the head and foot of the bier, a tall pewter candle-stand, each with a candle impaled upon its spike, and lighted. Pale now these candleflames against the burning-glass of the wide window. The fire would deepen as the day went down. Until the dawn, the candles must keep watch. And in the dusk, after such respects as were reckoned necessary had been paid, the priest would come to pray, and four mailed soldiers, to guard the head and foot, the altar-place, and the door. Such were the death-ceremonies of an heir.

His face was not the expected colour, but had a patchy greyish flush. The sunlight of late day came in the western window, and lit like glowing insects on his masculine treasures, the cups of thick glass banded with gold, the ancient swords and knives, the pieces of male adornment, collars and rings in an open chest, the gold cross set with two garnets. The big bed, which he shared so often with Veksa, hid behind its heavy curtains where the purple Raven folded into pleats. An accustomed jug held its eternal fount of wine, now of which today had been offered. Krau stood meekly and gazed on his father.

Krau was not afraid. Even at sun-up, returning, mussed as if from the fight, Gralice, Gaj and the apprentice grooms dragging bodies, even then, Kray had not felt a tremor. There had been uproar, of course, in the house. Krau noted its rising passage until it reached his father's chamber. Veksa had screamed – that would be like her, the witch. The Vre bellowed. But he did not come to see. Not until Mechail was made nice for him, washed and done up like a bride. Watches at the door told how Vre Korhlen entered, stared upon his first-born son for all of twenty heart-beats. Then he had marched out again, pushing his people aside. And since that morning hour, though countless times Krau had had to recount his version of events, the lord had not required it of him. Until now.

And now, there he sat, the old man, mured in his fastness like a bloody bear. Krau could not read anything from his expression, but Krau was of the opinion that there was not anything much to read. Veksa had had the teaching of her son. He had learnt in a myriad ways that this one might be manipulated.

'Krau,' said Vre Korhlen.

(At last.)

'Father, my lord.'

'I'll spare you another recital. You spoke to my stewards.'

'Yes, sir. But—' Krau advanced with seeming caution, as if not to hurt or appear too brazen. As he expected, Vre Korhlen cut him short. Not in the expected form.

'Well, Krau, you killed him.'

Krau, partly stunned at this frankness, kept quiet.

'I say you killed him. Or you had him killed. You'll answer.'

'Father, I don't know – what you want me to say.'

'No damned lie.'

'Father – if I believed—'

'Must I get up and strike you?'

Krau kneeled down. He was unsure of the road, yet less uncertain of where it led.

'Sir, he was whining on and on that you hadn't recognized the sacrifice. He said I must take him after Esnias, warrior killing, to demonstrate his worth. And he was not good at the work.'

'This is what you told my Tower, my stewards. Even your mother, maybe. Now tell me the facts.'

'Father . . . there came a moment when I might have saved him, and I was too slow – I'll blame myself always. I never realized he was this dear to you.'

'Dear to me?' Vre Korhlen's voice expanded into a terrible roar. His face had ignited bull-red. He rose up

61

and the sunlight quivered. 'He was my curse. The curse on my house. *You know it, boy*. Now, give me the truth.'

Krau gazed up into the inflamed and ugly countenance. He made his own soft, receptive. 'My lord, I do know . . . And I hated Mechail. You were just to him, but I never could be. Everything is as I've said. He wanted to go with me and my men to kill Esnias. Then in the forest, in the forest – I let them murder him. If he'd been half a swordsman – but he flailed around. I killed the ones did it. But I let them. And it was in my mind, the moment he asked to go with me. It will damn me to Hell. But I don't mind that. He's off your hands, sir. You're rid of him. And there's no blood-guilt on you. *My* fault. If you want to send me away . . .' Krau paused, lowered his eyes. It was a touch chancy, this gambit. The dad was in a wild mood. After there had been a silence, Krau ventured penitently, 'You see, sir, I've heard them, your enemies, scorn the Korhlen Tower – because of Mechail. Once, I had one of them down, he spat in my face and said: *Where's your half-man brother? One day when he rules we'll take you all.*'

Krau listened to his father sigh. He thought the heavy hand might settle on his shoulder, but there he was wrong.

Vre Korhlen had resorted to his chair.

'There's your suit of mail,' he said, 'ready for the summer. You'll have it fetched and put it on.'

Krau looked up, surprised again. 'Yes, my lord?'

'At the hour, you'll go down and make one of the four, the death guard in the chapel.'

Krau blinked. Something, it had no name, skimmed through him like a lizard through the long grass.

'If that's what you want me to do, my lord.'

'He was your brother. If you'd cared for him, you'd ask to do it. It's necessary. As for penance, you must have one. I don't trust Beljunion to set it. I'll consider that. For now, this will do. Get out, make ready. One day, you'll need to stand a death guard for *me*.'

Krau caught, unmistakably, a crackle of suspicion and malevolence in his father's eyes. To stem it, too quickly, awkwardly, he blurted, 'May the day be far off. Father – will you only say – you've forgiven me?'

'It's what I should have seen to myself.'

Krau found he could breathe more easily.

Yet, as Krau went to the door, Vre Korhlen added: 'But no more will I forgive you, boy, than I'd forgive myself. He was my son. My first. He was better than you, or could have been. Some witchcraft – *I would to God—*' The voice stifled itself and stopped.

A race of rage and disbelief and freshly budding fright swept up Krau. He said levelly, in a supplicant's tone, 'I can't endure it, that I've hurt you, father. Please find some way I can make it right.' And then, like a whipped child, he fled.

Only on the stair did he straighten. And there the fury claimed him and he grinned and gnawed his mouth, sweating with dreadful emotions. *Better than I—*

He wanted to go to his mother and upbraid her. It was her silliness that had led him on, given him unspoken to understand that now the moment was ripe for deeds.

But there was no margin for visits, if he must stand death-guard over the stinking corpse.

Krau arrived at his room, located in a cranny of the Tower but furnished prettily through his mother's auspices. He possessed a few better things than the Vre, maybe.

The dwarf, previously called to the room, curled asleep on the curved chest under the window.

Like any lower animal, Krau observed, the dwarf slept a vast amount, if left to itself.

Krau wanted a woman, but had no time, if he must hasten to mourn Mechail. A drink, however, would be permitted. His body slave must come up, too, to see after the God-rotted mail – all night! To stand watch till morning, over *that*. Well, here was the last time Mechail would get it his way.

Krau bent above his pet dwarf. One of the stubby paws lay out upon the wood of the chest. It had a snagged nail. Krau took up the paw and stroked it, and the dwarf, not waking yet, tensed in his sleep. Krau gripped the broken nail and tore it suddenly downward and away, exposing the tender quick. The dwarf screamed, a suitably beast-like sound, and tumbled from the chest lid.

'Run an errand for me,' said Krau coaxingly.

Like a black gargoyle the dwarf squatted in his agony, clutching at the damaged hand, but already primed. His look, glazed by pain and astonishment, was superficial. Beneath this lens, his eyes were yet composed of nullity. A void which *knew*, and which nothing could amaze.

'Christus. How foul you are, you imp. Fouler than the old dad's motley face. Worse then my smelling brother. Fetch the slave, Dwarfy. Tell him I want wine. And hurry. *Oh*, did I *hurt* you, darling?'

The dwarf gave its slight mewing note. It never spoke, would not use its tongue for some reason.

'Rush along,' said Krau.

He turned to his mirror of dull glass. It was the best in the Tower; it had been the woman Nilya's, until Veksa took it. His mother preferred her copper mirror now, which was kinder.

Krau would make a goodly figure in the mail; he would wear his cloak in the Korhlen colours, those rings . . . He would take some wine along, too. The other three of the deathwatch would hardly object, and Beljunion might go hang.

Gold-leaf sunset, and then the dark inked in, slowly creeping up like water out of the wood.

One night before, how many had lived, that now were laid on biers?

The sails of the Korhlen mill still revolved, and hacked the stars out, but the stars remained when the sails had passed.

The three soldiers emerged at the front of the Tower and went towards the chapel, unspeaking. Beljunion bustled along under the mallow sky, telling his beads. Krau strode last down the garden walk, plucking a spray of peach blossom to perfume the vigil. Under his cloak, a flagon.

The lights of the hold burned low. The dinner in the Hall would be cursory and uncooked, cold meats and loaves and raisins. The women would eat privately.

In her chamber, Veksa before her copper mirror, searching for flaws and eager not to find them, uncomfortable of mind. Aloft, her lord, drinking and pacing, longing to burst out and ride his horse across the land; a little hampered by his perceptions of protocol.

In the women's quarters, Puss and Chi at their aimless play.

The dwarf sucking his torn thumb like a terrible baby in an annex of Krau's room.

Boroi putting out the abandoned gear of his master.

An owl blew across the stars.

In the forest, a fox screeched in desire with the cry of a tortured girl. All the pine needles whispered together.

It was a high place, where he lay, and above was a dome of air, of a translucent darkness, and through it strands of thin cloud floated by, nacreous as if moon-lit, but there was no moon, not a single star. There was a faint murmur of a wind blowing, miles up, in space. There was a fragrant smell, like the wide openness over a hill.

He did not move, perhaps could not. This did not seem of any importance.

Without having looked at it, as if he had memorized it long ago, he was aware of how it was, its aspect, the place of his couching.

A platform had risen from a distant plain. The character of the plain he had forgotten, save that things moved freely there, might come and go, entering and departing constantly. A flight of steps ascended to the platform. He believed that they were made of stone, and narrow, and conceivably incurling, twining some central pillar.

On the platform stood the great altar. A mighty crucifix grew out of it, flung up into the air-dome, where sometimes the threads of clouds seemed to unravel on its apex, a huge wooden tine.

He was lying under the crucifix. It cast a shadow upon him. The shadow had a weight, a bar of merciful lead, that anchored him to calm, unthinking quietude.

Because of it his consciousness began so subtly it infused him like mild light. No jolt of awakening, no onslaught of questioning or fear. He remembered nothing, and sought no change.

The priest closed his fingers upon the opal of chastity, praying for Mechail's soul. The opal, soft and easily scratched, had lost its contained lunar fire behind a film of abrasion. He fingered its scars. Had Mechail been chaste? It would seem so. But then, could any virtue count? He had died in blood. Beljunion shuffled his brain swiftly from the submerged notion of Krau and Krau's designs. It was not any business of a priest, unless someone should come to him to confess.

And for this soul, what help?

O God, hear the entreaty of man, that he be not consumed by Your anger. The deep sins and misdeeds of him are set before You. Forgive, Lord, these transgressions. And of Your boundless compassion take home this spirit, and deliver it not into the bitter wasteland of eternal death.

There was a muted clink behind him, against the wall. It might have been the hilt of a sword knocked inadvertently on the stonework. Assume that this is so. But now it comes again, and, loud in stillness, some noisy gulps, a satisfied jet of breath.

Krau had put himself there, towards the closed chapel door. The three soldiers had taken their stations without fuss, the pair a few paces from head and foot, where the candles were smouldering up on the pewter, and one towards the screen, where he might rest his shoulders as the night wore on. They were a slovenly crew; the death guard would be inadequate. Perhaps one or all would eventually slip down to sit upon the ground, sleep, and snore. Beljunion was prepared for that, and to make no comment. But he had not been prepared for Krau.

Krau was drinking liquor, here in the chapel, swilling so the rest could not miss it.

Their eyes had gone over that way, under the metal helms, glinting in the candleshine.

And now Krau came swaggering up the aisle.

'We're for a heavy night,' he said, pleasantly. 'Who'd like a swig of this?' The man at the head of the bier, after a glance at his opposite, moved towards Krau. 'Tsk. I'm forgetting my manners. The priest first.'

Beljunion began to tremble. Should he only ignore the teasing of this devil? Continue praying as if steeped and impervious in his task?

But Krau pressed against him, leaning down to proffer the flagon. Krau pressed it close enough that the priest might scent strong wine. 'Godbrother? Will you *have* some?' Solicitous, well-meaning. Grin like a dagger sheathed in face.

It was ridiculous and ineffectual to pretend to prayer.

'No. Take that away from me.'

His voice, which should have been adamant, sounded only peevish.

Krau straightened. 'He won't.' He looked at the soldier by Mechail's head. The soldier reached out and took the flagon and drank. Then, stretching right across the corpse, he handed the jug to his fellow.

Beljunion was seared by self-hatred. He must prevent them, their casual sacrilege and blasphemy. He would fail.

His knees creaked as he rose. He turned his dim eyes, watering and afraid, upon them.

'This is not to be done here.'

'But godbrother, it's *been* done. Now, you wouldn't begrudge us a comfort or two. This is a long vigil. No dinner, no merriment. No . . . female companionship.' Krau hesitated, and one of the soldiers laughed. 'But a small drink. To keep us warm.'

'No. You must stop. This is God's place.'

'But you drink wine here,' said Krau. 'Go along, I've done it myself. That stuff from the cupboard.'

Beljunion grappled with the muscles of his body, shaking now, impotent, losing control.

'As you know, Krau, that isn't wine—'

'No? *Not*? It tasted like wine.'

'By the power of God it is made the blood of the Christus, the perfect sacrifice, who died for us upon the tree.'

'But it didn't taste of blood,' said Krau simply.

One of the soldiers, the man by the screen, abruptly marked himself with the cross. Krau looked at him, and shook his head, smiling. 'Don't be taken in,' said Krau. 'It *is* only wine, dear. Beljunion knows that. He tipples sometimes when alone. Don't you, godbrother? Does it taste of blood then?'

The priest felt something give way within him. It was like a column that upheld the floors of his physical being.

'You tell lies, Krau,' he shouted, quavering, hearing his fool's voice, yearning that he and all things might be otherwise.

'Krau?' said Krau. 'No, I think you should call me *sir*, now. I'm a man. And I'm the Vre's son. Mechail let you treat him like a ninny, but Mechail wasn't a man. His mother was a witch, wasn't she, and that got him cursed.' Krau stared at the corpse a moment. Then he took an edge of the drape of colours, and pulled it down an inch more. He prodded at the dead hulk of the crippled shoulder.

The priest snatched after him. Krau moved off, still smiling.

'Are you sick, godbrother?' asked Krau. 'Your spit's thick and your eyes are running.'

'You're the Devil's!' cried the priest. 'Go out! Go out of here!'

'But I can't. My father, the lord, put me here. I must watch all night.'

As if he had lost his reason, the priest fell back to his knees. He crowded into himself, head down and arms clutched, a human tortoise. He prayed insanely, in a gabble, foam darting from his lips.

Krau shrugged. He gestured to have the flagon returned him, and nursed it along the aisle again. He sensed the comradeship of the soldiers. Opening the chapel door a crack, Krau peered forth. 'A lovely evening,' he remarked. He shut the door and went over to the wall. He sat, and taking out a candle, lit it and stuck it down. He next produced dice, began to play them on the flagstones.

It took five minutes for the soldier from the head of the bier to dare to join him. The half of an hour for the other two.

Soon after midnight, the albino girl, Chi, woke from her strange mad dreams. She wanted something. Was she thirsty or hungry? Beside her in the bed, her sister had rolled on to her stomach, rubbing herself and murmuring. Was this what Chi desired? She touched her body experimentally. The response was vague, only consequent. Not that, then.

Getting up, she padded about the big room. Stars shone in at the gaping shutters. The night was cool. Chi took up her shift and dress and pulled them on as she wandered. She came to the civet and petted it. She did not mind its stink, was fond of it, though she never called it by childish names, as did Puss.

Something had happened in the Tower. The servants had muttered things under the windows of the upper storey. The slaves even had had an odd look. One of them Chi had seen down on the grass patches, under the shade of a willow. She was doing something furtively, with her cold face set. When she had gone away, Chi went to look, and found dark liquid had been spilled around the trunk of the tree. But what had caused all this, what had happened, although the atmosphere conducted it, Chi did not know or care.

Going out on to the balcony, Chi gazed about, at the bulk of the Tower, the adjoining buildings, the tops of orchard trees, the stars. Indigo paint flaked along the rail under her hands, and the posts cracked in their sockets ominously.

'Wood,' said Chi. 'In the wood. Who is this coming? He has a white horse. On his shield is a skull. His cloak is red as a rose. Do roses weep? Yes, at the thorns.'

She leaned on the swaying railing, and sang weightlessly to the night, 'Whrrr-waah, whrrr-waah.'

They made a sort of music, the clouds, as they passed. He had begun to hear it. Like silk rustling. And further still, another sound, untranslatable; of no import, yet.

But it was not a cross which leapt up from the altar where he lay. It was a tree. The mighty stem of it was drawn out into space, and somewhere there the branches spread.

A skeleton hung on the tree. The white skull lay over on the right shoulder, a wonder it had not fallen. The ivory was of such purity and cleanness. There was a crown upon the skull. It seemed made of black iron, cruel curled shapes.

There were no leaves on the tree.

Countless miles below, there seemed an alteration in the darkness. A ring of brilliance, like the sheen on alabaster, replacing shadow with only the slightest blending.

And the sound came again, like a footstep a thousand miles below.

'He's nodded away,' said Krau, pointing out Godbrother Beljunion, folded on the edge of the bier. Two of the soldiers laughed. They had all removed their helms. And Krau had learned their names now; he had not been sure, previously. The other soldier too had dropped asleep. 'Your throw,' said Krau.

In the cubby where his master shut him by night, the dwarf sat and slowly licked his torn thumb. It was a method of the Travellers who had trained him, vagabonds of the forest and its measly villages. Saliva held a potent panacea. It could cure most things if properly applied. An animal licked its wounds to cleanse and heal them. The dwarf licked. His blood had ceased to run some while before. The pain had sunk to an umber throb.

The dwarf had no recollections of any better time. All eras were alike to him. In childhood, in a ramshackle woods village further north, mostly unremembered, they had eventually thrust him out. He was a changeling: his mother's wholesome baby having been stolen and replaced by a demon's slough. The Travelling People found him near winter, mostly dead. They accepted him into their reckless lawless tribe. They too were, a few of them, misshaped or lack-witted, although each had some oblique skill, and all were canny.

The dwarf discovered how to perform bodily feats. They came naturally. The Travellers applauded him and gave him rewards, wild honey, and the rot-gut ale they brewed themselves. They had known he would be good for something. Fifteen years he was with them. He earned them pennies. They sold him to Krau (a Landholder's son, drunk on their brew with them in a dry inn of logs), without a second thought.

The dwarf was all in all twenty-one years of age. His wrinkled, nut-knobbed face was that of a man of two hundred. His eyes were waters of a sunless sea. He could not speak, never having learned, as he learned the somersaults and cartwheels. Men would watch, but who would listen?

Krau always told the dwarf exactly what he wished of him; the lessons were succinct. The dwarf got them quickly by heart and performed them without demur or fault. When, at first, he had sometimes been less adept, Krau had punished him. The ripping of the thumbnail had not been a punishment, it was almost an endearment. The real punishments the dwarf did not dwell on. He had small truck with memory. He did not need memory of much duration, it did not help. Past and future were of no account. He existed in the moment. And for now the moment was the cubby in the annex of his master's chamber, lightless and airless, with a bowl of water left for him, and a pan in which he might relieve himself, if he must. Although, if he did, Krau would strike him, the knuckles of his hands and toes, with a thin terrible stick, which once, after some especially heinous mistake, was thrust into his anus.

There had been one incident on the journey to the Tower, after Krau had bought him, which the dwarf's generalized amnesia had somehow left alone. Krau's party had dawdled, and they spent another night in a ruined stone building in a valley. (There were faces on a screen, at which Krau had thrown pebbles.) Next morning they came by a hut in the trees. No one answered the encouraging, sinister shouts of Krau's men. So they drank at a jet of water in the rocks, kicked over a woodpile near the door, smashed a clay jar or two, and urinated on the vegetable patch. An hour later, someone had seemed to follow them up through the wood. There were eyes in the thickets, unseen but seeing. Krau's band did not really notice them. It was not a beast. It kept up too long, then vanished too immediately. The dwarf, who had no words, did not seek to make anything of this detail. Yet it clung on to him like a burr, reasonless. And unreasoningly, as now, licking his wound, he regained the view of it, like the last random sight of his mother's bitter face, some tableau of the Travelling People; equally meaningless.

Having finished with the torn nail, the dwarf went to his bowl of water and lapped sparingly, not wanting to fill his bladder. He had, now, no name. He stretched across the cubby floor, and laid his cheek on his arm, to sleep.

Upon the barren skull, the black irons of the thorns were unpeeling. They moved in a slow dance, stretching and lengthening. Black tongues of leaves flickered undone.

He watched, knowing then, as if by this anomalous token, that he was dead.

And the buds began to come, like crimson beads.

He heard the steps sounding on the stair, a mile below. Yet how swiftly they ascended.

His vision held only the red buds beading the thorns about the skull. But somehow, also, he saw the woman as she climbed, without any apparent speed, with no fatigue, up the enormous flight towards the platform. She wore a mantle of some insignificant bland colour. Her hair was dark, skeined with bright grey. He could not see her face, which was turned from him, but she led by the hand a female child, whose pallid hair rippled as she took each tread.

The buds on the coronet of thorns were opening into burning roses. Drops of moisture stood on their hewn petals.

He felt a famishment. Perhaps it was only for life, that he had lost.

The woman walked up over the final stair, and letting go the child, came to him alone. She leaned above him, into the shadow of the tree. And by the shadow, as if by a fierce light, he beheld the forgotten face framed by the remembered, varied hair. The woman was Nilya. But then, this was the country of the dead.

They did not speak to each other. No sign of recognition was exchanged between them. Suddenly she lifted her left hand, and laid it on his body, above the wrecked heart. He received no sensation in his flesh, only a faint warmth. And some of the petals fell from the rose-crown. Wet with their dew, they had the look of blood.

When Nilya beckoned, the child approached, without hesitation or special interest. Once she was near, Nilya drew aside. The child now reached out. Her arm and hand, with their bird-bones, glimmered before him, and another petal fell across the smoky vein of her wrist. After a moment he saw that it was no longer a petal of the rose, but blood itself, welling up from her skin, trickling over like a tear of fire. In the air, it became a red-hot spark. It smote like a cinder on his lip. And entered his mouth, flaming.

He was conscious of all the passage of it, this curious liquor. There was no taste, only heat. It went, molten, along his tongue, slid into his throat, descended root-like, without assistance, the vessel of his neck and chest. And so it grew into his body, and from it spread the branches. At last he felt, yet only this, flowers opening from the boughs, while the rose began, swelled, erupted, *blazed* in his heart.

Everything was fading. The tree where the skeleton hung became a shadow which cast none. Two ghostly female figures, the woman and the child, were blown away like the clouds that ceased to make a noise. He sank down through the altar and the platform. He knew, unemphatically, a soft despair. He sank down through the ascent of steps. Towards the plain below.

> *Who walks through the wood, from tree to tree?*
> *His cloak of red and his eyes—*
> *His eyes—*

Beljunion, kneeling up against the bier, asleep, dreamed of the round black poles of the forest and the canopy of night. In every bush there scorched the eyes of animals. But something else was walking towards him. In spring the girls hung the male dolls of straw or cloth upon the trees. They were kept hidden from the menfolk, these dolls, for they were wicked, and shameless, having genitalia sewn on them. All summer they hung there, in secret coverts of the wood. To see one was unlucky. You must avert the eyes – the eyes—

Beljunion, wandering unhappily in his own peasant origin, struggled to recall the rest of the rhyme.

But all the while, something walked towards him, through the trees, on one of which maybe it had been hung. A young man, naked.

I must take the cup, and drink.

Beljunion nodded, in the forest, in his sleep, and the action roused him. He became murkily aware of cramp and stiffness, of a dereliction of duty, ordinary distress, and a bleak cold fear.

The chapel. Dark yet. The dicers and drinkers; Krau.

Had they noted his slumber? Why were they here? Ah. One had died. That was why.

Beljunion rode upon the billows of sleep, longing to go under. Yet, within that sea, the being waited, walking ever nearer.

> *His cloak of red and his eyes –*
> *Of swords.*

The priest started back, trying to rise and to cry out. A numbness in his legs instantly prostrated him. He tumbled onto the floor. He lay face down, scrabbling, terrified, hearing one of the mailed man chuckling, not knowing still why that did not matter.

Then it came to him. The reason he was afraid.

'What's up, priest? Wearied by your prayers? Want a little nap, eh?'

One of the soldiers jibing. Irrelevant.

Beljunion managed to get upright. He tottered there, glaring down. The massive candles had burned low into their mounds of yellowish wax. The light was thicker, and more rank. It described the bier, the long lines of the dead man, the white mask above and the white hands on the iron blade.

The priest was afraid because, in half sleep, in waking, he had felt those lines of the dead body *shift* against him.

Only very slowly could Beljunion bring his gaze up over the white hands and the blade, on to the white mask of the dead face.

During a hundred seconds, the priest waited. And it *was* a waiting, an expectancy: for the being finally must walk out between the trees of the night. And then, with a timeless and infinitesimal motion, the face of the dead turned over towards him, and in it the two windows of the eyes were opened wide.

The priest could not move. Could not summon a sound. It was not real and he believed it utterly. *I am dreaming.* No.

The dead eyes were icy and brilliant, and they saw him.

Never in his life had Beljunion met two eyes which saw him so completely.

In a formless way, he knew that he was between this event and the other men, that they could not, because of his interposing shape, behold what had taken place. And he tried to direct himself aside, to show them, and tried to separate his lips to speak or shout. But before he could do either, and conceivably he never would have done, the dead hands clasped hard and live on the sword, and the whole body raised itself.

The drape of colours sloughed off, and the cadaver of Mechail Korhlen rose, stood in an outline of rays – the candles – then surged like some darkness that spilled over.

By the right arm of the dark, and the sword's hilt, the priest was hurled into flight. He flew, unable to save himself, was battered against stone. The light fled. He heard a man call shrilly, and thought, *Now they do see it* – and was spun out after the light.

The two soldiers who had diced were easing back, tardily, carefully, as if not to bruise the air. They looked only at one thing. The man who had shrilly called was the man who had dozed. He was attempting to gain his feet and the door in a single articulation of muscle, but could not achieve it. And death reached him first. On the floor, on his knees, the soldier flailed with his arms against the vast iron bolt. But it heaved through him, sliding over the left arm and breaking the other so it too snapped away. The bolt of iron clove him at the cheek and throat, severing the vital vein and cracking his jaw like eggshell. A gout of fire-slime fountained out. His shriek dashed homeless and bat-like between the walls.

'Draw your swords, fools!'

Krau had reached the doorway, was fumbling at the door. It had struck. A spray of peach blossom was under his boot, crushed, its scent fuming to mingle with the stink of blood and faeces.

'It's alive – it's a dead thing—'

'You fools cut it down. *Make it die twice!*'

The two men fumbled, drew. They swung there, gaping, their blades lopsided.

The dead man came towards them without haste, the black sword dripping and glowing in his hand.

How could they kill him?

'The Devil – the Devil's here—'

'Chop him, Hell blast you.' Krau at the chapel door, pushing and clawing, trampling blossom.

The soldier who had won the dice game shambled forward, aiming at the body of death. But the iron sword clanged down. Taking the steel weapon on the flat, it flung it off by sheer momentum. The soldier saw a pair of eyes like cold white heat. Some part of the corpse swung like a stave and hammered into the soldier's belly. He doubled, choking, and iron carved across his neck above the mail, severing flesh and spine. As he went down, the dead trod over him, and the last soldier broke away. Death wheeled and tapped him across the head. Hair and skull parted. Screeching, the man reeled and drove on into the bier, the altar, sprawling over, kicking, and suddenly still.

The chapel door grated, and undid itself.

A slot of deep blue sky evolved, and under it Krau edged himself. He was grinning again, his eyes bulging.

He watched Mechail, with no idea of incredulity. Krau no longer had a thought inside him but to be gone.

Mechail turned, as Krau slid out through the door, thrusting it closed behind him.

As he ran below the garden walls, beneath the heightening arch of ebbing night, Krau heard a noise begin to bubble in his throat. But not until the crash of the chapel door, a thunder on the taut skin of silence, not until then did the screaming burst out of Krau's mouth.

The world before morning was empty. It was a dream geography of blank shuttered windows and barricades. Running into the courtyard before the Hall, he thought he glimpsed a movement, some slave early about his work, but in another instant the illusion vanished. Krau screamed after it, and up at the featureless rock of the Tower. 'Help me! Help me for the love of the Christus!' And bounded on and reached the stair, tearing between the ravens that would not assist him, into the embrasure of the great Hall door. And there, glancing back, he saw darkness come out of darkness. And darkness took on the figure of Mechail with bleeding iron in its hand.

No one existed in the Korhlen Tower, not any more. It had altered to a phantom architecture, where only Krau and death remained.

Krau rammed himself against the door of the Cup Hall, which gave.

In the nights of former centuries, men had bedded there, and even now sometimes the lower ranks, if drunk, made do about the hearth. But not that night, the night of Mechail's mourning. A solitary dog had slept by the ashes, now she was lifting her lean head. Krau screamed at her: 'Here, girl, to me! Help me, girl—' But the bitch-dog, fearing him and afraid too of the quintessence that came in with him, got up and flashed away into the shadows.

The Hall was black, and the rafters were a web of pitch. Krau staggered towards the south door but, as was usual after dinner, it had been secured; it took two men to manage the bar. The door above the high table was also bolted. Krau lay on it, and lugged his sword out of the scabbard. His throat was raw from screaming, and he had stopped. He breathed in jerks. He could, at any hour, have bested Mechail when Mechail lived. And Mechail, though some demon possessed him now, had stayed in his human body. The death sword was iron. A powerful blow with steel might shatter it, or at least render it unwieldy.

Krau did not deduce these things, only knew them, as he slumped on the door, sweating, urine dribbling on his thigh.

The other truth, the truth of the Devil, of vengeance and the living dead, he knew those too. And his blood was thin and his heart shook him half to bits.

And Mechail stepped into the Hall out of the blue before morning.

Could the undead see him? Maybe not.

Krau kept immobile, but for the huge jumps his heart made. His breathing was noisy; however, he could not much curb it. And he stank too, of terror and its results. He readied the sword of steel. His viscera churned – the Mechail thing was moving up the Hall.

Mechail did not look as Krau had ever seen him. The Devil was plainly there in him. The sky went on lightening, penetrating weirdly, and the pallor of the face and hands seemed to drift, disembodied.

He was at the high table. He did not search.

He came and stood before the bare board. And then, the demon in him ejected a name.

'*Krau.*'

A kind of whirlwind of horror ignited in Krau. Before he could reorganize his limbs, they had thrown him out and most of the way across the table, the steel blade slashing.

And in that moment Mechail's useless left hand, never before employed in anything, clubbed against Krau's forehead. He was flung backward. He hit the floor beyond the table, his sword a body-length from him, and something black sprang down, and Mechail was kneeling on his legs.

Howling, Krau fought, and iron bit into his arms and they flopped to the earth like cut stalks. He tried to scream again, and Mechail sank the hilt of the iron sword between Krau's teeth. Krau heard his molars breaking and the stupid pain dazzled him, but he did not care, only tried to fight still, but the hilt thrust on into the vulnerable avenue of his throat, and gagging, convulsed, he forgot all of it, there was only the mindless urge to struggle and the body's urge to vomit up the intrusion and the impossibility of his own death.

Mechail worked at the sword hilt until it had pierced through the intervening tissue, into the brain. The crosspieces of the hilt had gouged Krau's cheeks into a different structure. He had an idiot's face now, grinning its ruined teeth, and the eyes bulging from their sockets.

Mechail got up from the killed thing, and left it where

it lay, the sword like an iron tongue pointing from its mouth.

He returned down the Cup Hall, a journey his body had often taken, though never in the pre-dawn night.

Outside, the dawn star was above the yard. From the Tower village there stole the narrow notes of shutters, buckets, a readied plough, a cat late-hunting. In the orchard garden a couple of birds trilled.

As he came by the garden way, Boroi was standing there. Boroi observed him. The slave gave evidence of nothing, no fear, no recognition. He stepped aside, and perhaps this alone caused Mechail to go back through the entry. There, he halted.

The shadows clung between the walls, along the walk below the garden and towards the chapel. Boroi did not turn to see the chapel door lying over, nearly unhinged. He looked away to the women's quarters, and a pale needle of a girl was on the path.

The child Nilya might have led by the hand had grown up ahead of Mechail. But her pallid hair fluttered as she moved, as it fluttered in the other dimension.

(Somewhere in the Tower fastness, unheeded, an old woman began to sing with a drizzling voice.)

Chi slipped down the path. Her eyes were opaline, her blonde lips prudish. She approached Mechail as she had done before, not hesitating. If she guessed he had died, she did not seem to consider it.

Boroi merged into the shadows. Chi slit through them. Somewhere she had found a knife or thorn, and unseamed her wrist above the artery. The flow was a trickle merely. It shone, its redness apparent if unseen.

Chi lifted her wrist up to Mechail out of the lake of darkness.

'Give me him blood,' recited Chi, satisfied.

She pressed her wrist to his mouth, and only then did he taste of it. He stared at her with his grey cat-wolf's eyes, and licked the blood from her wrist, and licked it, licked it, without hurry, without a sound.

When he finished he raised his head and she withdrew

her arm, and turned and pattered away. Boroi, who was still watching, saw Mechail turn also and go back across the courtyard. He was a shadow with a man's face that was the face of a beast-god of the wood.

The doors of the yard were closed. The shadow man somehow got up on to the beam, and up to the door-top, and went over, and was gone. Boroi noticed that he had utilized the left arm.

The sky was now very high, and flecked with clouds. Birds sang and the old woman drizzled on in the house.

Boroi went about his business.

He was some way from the Tower when he heard God-brother Beljunion start to shriek. The cries were not like the screams of Krau, which only the slaves had heard, and ignored.

Chapter Five

By night, the hunter would go down to the stream, and stretching to the water, drink. This would be after the kill, if he had made one. Tonight he missed. The forest hare burst away. He had been lucky before, but now the hare had the luck. The hunter lapped at the stream. Then, running back up the slope, dropped suddenly on his right side. His eyes were open, and presently the moon, coming up through a break in the pines, gleamed in them coldly. He might have been dead, the manner in which he lay there, the beast. Then his eyes flickered. A thought ran across them, went out like an ember. What the thought had been, he forgot at once. Like any creature, he was finding what he was by instinct and usage. There was no emendation. No worrying or gnawing at the form of the self. Men did that, but not a beast. Soon, the moonlit eyes shadowed and shut. Accustomed now to hunting in the dark, yet there had been a long season when it was the other way, under the sun the hours of action and being, and night the ultimate stage for sleep. Some slight vacillation then, some blending.

The beast had the frame of a man, and a man's face, newly bearded. The hind legs ended in a man's boots, but the garments on the body were torn and filthy. The left forelimb was oddly quiescent, as it curled over to the ground. The left shoulder hid in the dark. Through the belt of the beast was a narrow knife with blood on it, uncleaned. Sometimes it had been used in a kill, although not always. There was blood too in the short beard, and blood black under the long jagged fingernails.

The beast was sleeping, breath rasping faintly through his parted lips.

He dreamed, also. Not as a beast dreams, this beast.

A blond animal in a red tunic and shirt rushed before him through the meshes of the night wood. It screamed as it went, and the undergrowth coiled and caught it, holding it fast, until the hunter could come up and make the kill. Pressing his mouth to the neck, which had been ripped wide, the hunter drank. The drink was like fire. He guzzled at it, and incandescence scalded his throat and abdomen. But there was no nourishment. So he rent the meat with his fangs, and the meat was salt and strange and he ate it with difficulty.

When at last he raised his head, a luminous shape stood inside the black wings of the forest, watching him. The eyes were visible across distance, yet not to be examined, or defined. The right hand was uplifted, the palm and fingers forming a sort of chalice, from which gleaming fluid suddenly trickled.

But in the dream, the beast did not gaze more than a few moments, before returning to the tearing of his prey. The un-beast brain remembered it had often experienced this mirage, and nothing had come of it. He did not look twice, to see if the watcher vanished, or remained.

Late spring, in cords of jewellery green, wove the lower tiers of the wood. By daylight, he hunted too, slept too. The shades and sombre places, the waterways, and stands of alder, larch and birch, through these he came and went. Fox and wild pig went by him warily. To the human evidence in the forest he was impervious, nearly blind. For several days he slept in a wilderness of rocks, where one vast hemlock grew that was hung with the brown skulls of sheep and horses, and horse-tails, and old bronze rings like mud. Their rattling in the breeze had made him glance at them once, that was all. Five times he came on a village of hovels, perhaps a byre, a dug well, never a church of any kind. From among the trees, he observed such areas. He saw men and women going passively about their lives, a crone unstitching and stitching up her crinkled face over a pot of roots, children shouting after their flock of greasy grey sheep, two men fighting with wooden sticks while the rest of the community gawped. He never went near. Only once, when he came on a woodcutter half a mile off in the pines, did the hunter circle him. But this peasant sensed something. He made a quick sign on his forehead. Then he gave over striking at the tree trunk and glared about. Seeing nothing, he spat at the earth and called out a string of words, unintelligible, next making off with his axe at a fast trot.

At sunset, a burning rose died and fell to ashes through the forest.

In the night, nocturnal presences skittered and whispered. Frogs sang about the pools. Owls sank across the forest's valley canopies. Young foxes fiendishly chuckled.

A wolf howled on certain nights, a crystal of loneliness.

The darkness turned on the wheel and sunset brought light up again from the soil and the leaves which had stored it.

There was a wild snowfall which scattered down in the hour before dawn, out of sequence, and the things of the wood fled before it. But the sun returned and glass dripped from the needles of the pines.

The stone wolf had slept all day in a hollow where a black beech grew. The sun did not much come there, through the pavilion of the tree, but the blowing snow had penetrated. Dropping upon the sleeping wolf, the snow changed it. Stippled and powdered, the mantle of stone had not melted upon the wolf, save a little at the mouth and nose. It was like a stained statue, perhaps of a fountain in some city.

The rose burnt and the ash-light steeped the spaces and the trees faded into sable. The beech was a dark cloud whose leaves whistled faintly as they rubbed together. The eyes of the wolf opened, chill, heatless as its blood – or why had the snow not dissolved? The wolf got to its feet, and sloughed the snow like a skin.

Beyond the hollow, above the forest valleys where the owls drifted and dived, the wolf took his way, under a sky thick with stars.

The upland folded down. There was a gap the length of a wolf's body leaping, deeper than fifty wolves piled one on another. The wolf sprang over the gap, his hirsute structure mystically elongating, pliant. Touching earth, he compacted together again. Magic had happened, if it had been seen.

But the man in the clearing below had not noticed. He was crouched to feed on something he had borne over, snapping a neck, slicing with nails and knife. Occupied.

The wolf stepped daintily down the incline. Coming against a severed branch, the wolf pranced over it, playfully.

At this signal of motion, the man raised his head. His face was bloody, daubed in black blots, tangled in black beard and hair, but the eyes shone, and on the slope the eyes of the wolf met them, also shining.

For a minute, neither animal moved. It was the wolf that firstly did so. Daintily stepping as before, he brought himself into the clearing. He approached the stooped man in a slow, coordinated address, and inches from him abruptly lowered his muzzle to sniff the meat. The carcass was of a polecat, odorous and now mangled. With a polite flicker of his lip, the wolf put his jaw against the kill, tore off a chunk of flesh, and started to devour it. After a moment, the man joined the wolf. They ripped and tore together, filling their mouths, their eyes now and then meeting, without inquiry.

Her gown was dyed black for mourning, and she had had the borders unpicked, the scarlet and the blue taken away. Only the sequins of silver and copper remained. She wore her hair pulled tightly from her face, and a black kerchief over it, like a peasant wife bereaved. Her skin was unpainted, even in the subtle way she had employed by night, when the Vre summoned her. She was no longer clever. She no longer cared.

He might do as he pleased, the husband. He had allowed it. She would never forgive him; already she planned some herb-wise mixture to addle his stomach.

Her only son. Her lovely, precious boy.

Life was worth nothing.

With an edge of her sleeve, the village way, she stemmed the water from her eyes. And the women in her chamber, sitting helplessly subdued and frightened, made a little murmuring moan.

'Hold your noise,' said Veksa. 'What does it matter to you? It's the mother feels it. *My* grief.'

But she thought, flooding again into the sleeve, *They fancied him. They had dreams of him. So fair he was.* And for a moment the incredulous disbelief stormed through her. That he should die – why bother how – some gabble of sorcery, fearsome, false, some error; and the old priest was mad. That he should be *gone, finished with* – no longer in the world.

And after the disbelief, the recognition that this was only so.

Veksa wailed and rocked herself. Her anguish filled the chamber and pressed like huge hands against the walls.

Godbrother Beljunion had heard the Lady of Korhlen's screaming, but there was a continuous uproar of it now always in his skull. Her cries, the cries of the men in the chapel, booming in and out of his consciousness. And then the cry of Krau as he dashed into the lambent dark, and death, risen, silently followed him.

The priest stood before Lord Korhlen, and divided his attention between the voice of the Vre and the scream-notes in his head.

'Do you hear me, priest? You had better. I'll need your witness.'

Godbrother Beljunion faltered. He said, 'But what I saw – how can I bear witness to that?'

'Unless you lied, you will.'

Vre Korhlen was granite. He had ceased drinking even. Sixteen days had waned since that night – *that* night.

The priest could scarcely remember what had gone on. Time seemed interminable yet stuck. It might have been a year, but imprisoned in some endless hour.

No one but Vre Korhlen had questioned him. The people of the Tower shrank away from him. He went by, trembling and abject. It had been difficult to express the truth.

And now, 'You'd better repeat your account,' the Vre said.

The priest found he fumbled. It was a nightmare, and each reiteration made it seem less real, more inescapable. He was exhausted and wished only to sleep. Anything to distance himself from this.

In the Tower, many of them declared it had not been a corpse at all, not dead Mechail but Mechail sorely wounded, tranced. They had heard of such things. And coming to unhinged, Mechail had cut about him, thinking the soldiers were Esnias still. Blundering away, he vanished, probably to die in earnest. Or maybe he had realized at the last that he had slain his own brother. A slave might have assisted his flight. They had been questioned, the slaves, some with whips. But none uttered anything of value.

The other story avowed Esnias had got in and done it all, taking off the cadaver of the heir afterwards, to mutilate.

Beneath all that, Beljunion sensed a perfect knowledge.

One quarter of a mile below the Tower, provision against out-washing winter rains, the Korhlen graveyard cluttered. It was dense with inferior graves, yet dominated, as the village and out crops were dominated by the central Tower, by the Korhlen vault. The slab of stonework was unornamented, effective only in its lurking persistence. Here the generations of Raven Lords were shelved in death, their ladies with them. (Nilya lay here, a heap of bones under her shroud, and for that matter the other woman, the tainted one, older bones.) Krau, covered in a purple pall, his face hooded over, was carried there in lieu of the other, who should have been. The day was hot and crimped with thunder. Beljunion, and this he did recall, was standing by the vault door among the ugly and mostly untended graves, to say the words and issue the prayers. The screaming lady mother of Krau had not come. The court of the Vre stood like posts. Those servants who attended were white and fearful; all the while their eyes flick-flickered to the rim of the forest. And adjacent, in the Korhlen fields, a kind of haze lay on the slaves, toiling and uninvited, as if their breath made smoke. For every sentence Beljunion urged from his throat, another sentence seemed spoken across the sky. And in the fields, a susurration, like frogs or crickets, or some gas that rose from the earth. And when Krau had gone into the dead-house of stench and dark, where spiders spun and maggots waited, it was as if he had been left instead on the bare ground, for ravens and wolves to tear.

A leprous willow grew over behind the chapel. On the morning of the fourteenth day (after the night), Beljunion had seen something hanging pale in the tree. Later it was gone. He had not inspected it. He did not want to acquaint himself with the undercurrents of veracity.

'You must speak.'

Vre Korhlen was insisting. It was like the funeral again. Time still stuck for ever.

Sunk in the meaningless lethargy and horror of his own fear, the priest now dredged up the resistance to reply, 'Why must I, sir? I've said all I can. It's more – more than I can—'

'That won't satisfy me. When the Magister arrives, you'll speak to him.'

The single word plunged Beljunion upward from his abyss.

'A Magister? From Khish?'

'I wrote to the Church Fathers there. They've been useless to me in the past, the Christus knows it. But for this, what else?' Beljunion only stared. The granite man said to him, 'You know Mechail's history. It's that, come back on us. That – thing – from his childhood. I wrote.' Beljunion, in the centre of the whirlpool, thought clearly, *They'll have had some pains to decipher it, then.* 'And here's the answer.' Vre Korhlen held out a sheet of roughest parchment. A great roundel of wax bled at its corner. 'A Magister will be sent to the Tower. In a week or two he'll be here.'

'What can be done,' said Beljunion limply.

'He'll know that, I'd trust. *Christus.* You've seen how my hold is fastened up now, soldiers at every crevice. Do you feel safe when the sun goes down? Yes, maybe you do. You were the only one he left alive.' Vre Korhlen swung about the chamber, his joints of rock propelling him. 'A demon,' he said. 'You and I were to keep it at bay. But we failed, and the demon had all of him. Do you think I've no eyes, godbrother? Every slave and peasant that can get away with the trick is dangling some bloody god-doll from the bushes, calling up some filthy magic. I'd crucify the lot of them, flay them alive, if I had the days to do it. Take this, read it.' He thrust the parchment into the priest's face.

Beljunion took the letter, and read, not seeing many of the words for a rippling and blurring of his vision.

'. . . *this matter of witchcraft . . . that you are worked against . . . you have been no proper son to the Church . . . yet we will do as we are able . . . the Magister Anjelen, who is here with us at this time . . .*'

In the swarthy wax, the imprint of a key, the seal of Khish that Beljunion once knew, now alien to him.

But a Magister. There had been no such exalted one in Khish during his term there.

'Well, then, get out,' said Vre Korhlen. 'You needn't go over it again with me. Go and say your prayers instead. But be ready for this man. He'll want to question you. Perhaps, like you, he can't do anything.' Vre Korhlen paused before the wall. He put out his hand and touched the stonework, as if to judge its thickness and stability.

'Does she still carry on?'

Beljunion said, 'The Lady Veksa, do you mean?'

'That bitch.'

'She has lost her son.'

'Better she'd lost him in the childbed,' Vre Korhlen replied. 'Better they'd all been barren, all the silly bitches.'

The two wolves hunted the forest, moving back and forth on a territorial map constructed in their brains. The killing was more efficient, one driving the prey, the other springing upon it. Usually they acted and fed by night, but sometimes in the daytime they played together. They slept back to back in the hollows beneath trees.

There were other wolves in the woods, and sometimes the wolfish wolf extended vocal signals to them. The man-wolf did not attempt such cries. If they were answered a meeting might ensue, a challenge be issued. (These were also the business of the wolfish wolf, who sidled placatingly or fought, as he saw fit. The man-wolf crouched by, not a participant, but consenting.)

The man-wolf did not know but that he was a wolf, of some sort. He had been born in the normal way; that is, having very slight memory of anything that had gone before, and this retention, what there was of it, soon left him. Only his dreams harried him but, an animal, he let them go on waking. Of the new life he grasped this: that, as he fed upon something he was joined by another. This other, who slaughtered and fed as he did, must therefore demonstrate the kind from which he himself came.

He did not speak any more. Sometimes he made sounds in his sleep. But they were material sighs and growls, such as the wolf-wolf made.

The spring had heightened to summer. The pines held up their malachite fringes, and the sun burst upon streams whose waters were combed over the rocks like glistening hair. An enormous moon haunted the country by night, at white-heat. Where the trees opened, hot valleys broke on bones of stone and lost villages.

Under the tent of an ancient ash tree some girls were bathing in a green pool at twilight. From some Travellers' camp, these women, bold and careless.

The wolfish wolf did not approach the place. But the wolf who was a man went close. He imagined taking hold of one of the women as she scrubbed herself with leaves, the red flowers blooming from her skin, drinking them. But in fact he never tasted her blood or flesh. The women finished their washing, and slid home their bodies into shells of dirty clothing. They went away as the stars began, singing a nonsense song in the dusk, while the night wind rose.

Chapter Six

Two months after the ill-penned demanding words had been sent to the town of Khish, their answer emerged on to the Korhlen road.

The entourage was brief but telling. Three outriders, mailed, with the yellow Key badges of Khish Town garrison. Two pack-mules and a man all liveried dark, and cut by a silver cross of three short upper arms on an elongate and knotted stem: the emblem of the Church Paternal. Central to the column was an ebony horse of some breeding, with mulberry eyes, silver about the harness, and the knot-cross slashed over the saddlecloth. The ebony's rider was clad too in plain black, but the long-skirted tunic was of silk, and had a strand of gold at the throat. His black hair was cut short at the nape and grew straight off a wide forehead that gave way to black brows and blacker eyes; these seemed the only features in the face. The sun's tawny tint was on the skin of the face, the neck and hands. And while a blackish ruby sweated fire in a pendant crucifix of black lacquer, the fingers had no rings. They were severe, like the face which had no features but forehead, eyes and eyebrows, and no meaning or message but of Mind and Thought.

Anjelen.

The man who entered the Raven Cup Hall was a captain from Khish, with the Key on his shoulder. He used little ceremony. He nodded to the Landholder as if to some inn host. Then, swinging up his head announced, 'His grace, the Magister.'

Vre Korhlen, with a stale, stubborn reluctance, turned to confront the figure that came in at his door and along his Hall. With his captain and his first steward, his priest, and five or six of his near kin, the Vre stood waiting for the might of the Church Paternal to reach him. And when it did so, in this forbidding image – tall, and slim as a pen, a man having the light musculature of a boy, but steel in his soul, couth as cities amid his long tunic and ink hair and pale clerk's sunburn – when it did so, the Landholder, with his men, kneeled. And presently a hand like an ivory marker hovered for one half-second above his head, and was withdrawn.

'Get up, Vre.'

'Your grace.'

Even the lord's words grated after the smooth-poured voice of the princely Magister. The accent of the woods was rough. All that, Vre Korhlen knew without knowing, sensible only that he resented this, that even in fear he had wanted some small priests from Khish, not an instrument of the Universal Church.

The Magister Anjelen moved his eyes along the fence of men. He saw them all, and bade them all get up. The decrepit Beljunion, who had suffered an injury, he gave his supporting palm under the elbow, his slender adamantine body bending, retracting. This support startled the godbrother so he nearly fell down again.

Anjelen's waist was belted by a strip of scarlet no wider than a child's thumb, and from this dropped the beads of prayer. They were of unpainted wood, darkened and polished only by use. At Anjelen's back, huge invisible wings stirred ceaselessly. It was power. The power of an angel of God.

'Will you take some wine, Magister?' Vre Korhlen gestured impatiently, vulgarly. A servant jolted forward.

'Water, if your well is clean,' said Anjelen.

'Clean – yes. It'll be strained too. Get water for his grace.'

It was the steward went to see to it. The servant passed among the outriders from Khish, who did not disdain the best wine of the Tower.

'Perhaps your grace would like to sleep after the journey?'

'No,' said the Magister. 'I shall need a chamber in which to interview your household. If you prefer, I'll examine you and your woman in your own rooms. The man there will attend me and put down in writing what transpires.'

The man, who had ridden with the pack-mules, stood dumb and obedient, his writing case ready under one arm.

Vre Korhlen frowned. He said, 'The room given is to be your bedchamber. But if that doesn't suit—'

'Yes. Let me be taken there, then.'

The Khishans drank the best wine, and the Magister waited, his lips unwetted by any refreshment – the water was being drawn, strained, strewn with mint.

A slave in the Raven torque came to conduct the Magister to his apartment, high in the Tower, on the sun-lit southern side, where doves had once nested in the eaves.

Entering, Anjelen looked about the room, the hooded fireplace, screened by a shield, the bed with its antique curtain of purple.

On a low table someone had laid a dish of early peaches, which laved the warm enclosure with their voluptuous scent.

The baggage of the Magister was brought in, a box, perhaps of apparel, another which the scribe opened to reveal books, a chest, which Anjelen unlocked, containing parchments, tinctures in bottles, mysterious essences, waxes, knives, implements of enamel and metal, a globe of vitreous, devices for measurement, and other paraphernalia.

The captain from Khish appeared at the door.

'Is everything as you want it, your grace?'

'It will suffice.'

'One of mine's seeing to your horse, Magister. We don't trust anyone here to do it.'

'Accept a peach, Captain Livdis.'

The captain went greedily to the dish, not touching until Anjelen had pointed out a particular fruit, then seizing it eagerly. The pointing finger had imparted some special resonance. In their ride of fourteen days, the soldiers had come to revere the Magister, who barely spoke to them, who infrequently did anything save exist before their eyes.

The Angel of God did not dine, either in the Hall or in the Vre's sanctuary, both options being offered and refused. He took bread and meat in the upper room, and half a cup of drink, the other half left standing. He called for more candles. He would continue his labours through the night, and those he invited, they must also disregard the hours of sleep.

A procession of people went up and down to the south chamber. He called servants and soldiers, the barbarian nobles of the Korhlen Tower who swaggered there in anxiety and came out pasty-faced and cursing. He did not question any of the slaves, not even Boroi, who had attended the heir, or the piggish man who had waited most often on Krau. To Vre Korhlen he had sent a piece of paper. It read (in the scribe's hand): *I have before me your letter, delivered to the authority at Khish. Is there anything here you would amend or retract? Let me have word. There is no need, as yet, to present yourself in person.* This incredible arrogance went cold to the bottom of the Landholder's belly. He returned indeed only one word: *Nothing.*

At midnight there was rapping on the door of Veksa, the illegal married wife of the lord.

She was not in bed, but had been put into her nightgown by her women, who now wound her into a robe. The pert one brought a belt of gold links with crimson tassels to fasten the garment. But Veksa, moving before her copper speculum, tied back her hair into the mourning kerchief. Her eyes were pouchy in the mirror, her face bloated from the ale she had been drinking for two months, full of liquid years. There was a dreadful complacence there. What can anyone do to me? inquired the baggy and leering face. Everything has been done.

She went up to the south chamber with one woman following. The Tower was leadenly quiet, and from the Hall below there came no noises. Veksa's shadow sprang about her, a fat black beast, from the candles flowering tonight all up the stairs.

The girl knocked upon the door. It was his scribe who opened it. The chamber, despite its two or three lights, was a cave of shadows that reached out and sucked in the women's shades from the lobby.

'My lady is here.'

'The woman Veksa,' said the Angel of God, who would it seemed refer to the lord's wife as nothing of the sort. 'Come into the room, if you please, madam.'

She walked in. She had had reported to her indirectly (her girls' partisan indignation), how the Magister titled her. What she expected, if she had considered him or heeded those who talked of him, was unsure. But his aspect nevertheless checked her. There was still some cunning in Veksa, and still a woman there. The woman felt a bizarre sour little tug that formerly she would, inaccurately, have interpreted, *Well, he's a pretty one*. But the cunning nipped her in the heel. And for the first time in all the days and nights – since they rushed to her and led her down, and she saw her boy under the high table as they tried to pull the long black iron tongue from his mouth – Veksa recollected caution, and that the world was in the charge of them, these men.

'Your grace,' said Veksa. And wished, as he lifted his eyes from the table before him, that she had not come in this manner, in her robe, with only the gold belt to proclaim her value, her face uncoloured, her hair's vanity hidden.

'You may seat yourself, madam.'

She did so.

On the table's two ends a pair of candles burned steadily, giving a fire-life to his black eyes. He was not much of an age. Thirty, maybe. A priest, but not like elderly Beljunion. The name of an angel, was it?

Dared she remove the kerchief on the pretext of the hot night? But her hair was tousled, unwashed, not fit to be shown.

The cunning nipped at her again. She must not dally in her thoughts. And Krau – had she forgotten?

Sudden tears filled her eyes and Veksa let them flow over. She had not really seen in the copper what she had allowed herself to become. She had found tears helpful in the past, if employed sparingly.

'Excuse me, your grace,' she said. She put her fingers up to remove the water, not using her sleeve now in the peasant way. 'You'll know. It was my son was murdered.'

But the Angel of God did not offer her anything for that. He sat, and having looked at her, looked down again into the book before him.

Veksa beheld that it was turned to confront her, legible to herself rather than to him. Not that she could read. Yet she had some notion, from the vast capital and the latticed margin, illumined in blue and emerald and gold leaf. A churchly tome of religion. By law, no common volume, however revered, might be embellished to such an extent.

'I'll ask you, madam,' he said, the interrogator, 'to set your hand on the appellation of God. This is the Book.'

The Scriptures, then. Not from Khish – too costly, and seemingly intact.

'Where is it?' said Veksa. 'You must show me, your grace. I haven't been schooled.'

'Here.'

She put her hand, no longer wet from tears, on to the spot, the gemstone capital, *God*.

'You will tell me what I ask you, without concealment.'

'Yes, your grace. Of course.'

He looked at her again, and she removed her hand from the Book of the Word.

She expected he would begin by inquiring after her birth, her unrecognisable marriage, her son. She wondered if she might permit herself a flash of anger if he referred to Krau as a bastard.

But Anjelen the Magister said, 'I want you to inform me, madam, what you know of the heir, Mechail.'

She was surprised. But then she supposed he was obliged to make this paramount, the hysterical story that it was Mechail, risen from death, who killed the men in the chapel. The old priest had started that. And her husband had given it validity. She knew, oh, yes. Someone had had vengeance on Krau for Mechail's removal. And that the shaggy bear, her husband, had done it, would not shift from Veksa's brain. If so, he was mad. She had never balanced it out, her assessment of him built through long association, her instinctive aversion to him in the wake of Krau's death. She would be certain one day, then she would act. For now, she must say what she knew of Mechail.

'Not much, your grace. He was no kin to me. A cold and solitary boy. His deformity warped his heart. Not generous or loving, like my own lad.'

'You're under a misapprehension, madam. I want you to tell me what you know of Mechail's childhood.'

She thought: *How odd he is, like some grandfather wanting to hear about the baby, and until now he only heard from letters.*

'Nothing,' she said promptly. It was almost exact, exact enough God could not judge her for it. She herself had only heard tales, weird things. Grandda, surely, would not want those.

'The Landholder's wife,' said Anjelen. His voice was low and dark, musical, beautiful – she was abruptly again aware of him, how much the voice was a part of him, how dangerous. That even her thoughts must be wary.

But, 'Yes?' she said, insolently, raising her brows.

'Yes,' he answered.

And she was all at once frightened of his eyes, their remorseless blackness, the way the candles jewelled them, like four lamps in two black waters.

Nilya . . . Veksa had constantly thought of her with

scorn. A ninny, unable to work the man as she needed to. Without knowledge of the herbal medicine of the woods, Nilya's womb had turned to flame and consumed her.

'She was a weakling. Her sickness infected the boy and he grew stunted.'

'Is that all you know?' Anjelen's eyes hung before her. She longed to thrust at them with her nails. 'What of the rumours, the elements of the unnatural?'

'Nilya was a witch and her commerce with demons brought something off on her son,' Veksa blurted.

'What thing?'

'Something which – made a pact with her, and in exchange took the child's blood, marked him for itself.'

'An old worn allegory of the forest. Like the miller's daughter who, with the aid of an imp, bakes loaves into gold to snare the Tower lord. But the imp comes when she is a mother and carries off her child.'

'There are strange things happen.' Veksa heard herself say this, ignoring his obvious sally, and recalled the lessons of her aunt. It might be a fact. These idiots, thinking they could control their masculine world. But the trees were full of supernatural humours.

Veksa had grown hot. She looked away from the Magister.

He said, 'Your godbrother here, Beljunion, swore to the Landholder that Mechail Korhlen rose from his deathbier, after all alive, slaying the death watch, of which your Krau made one. It seems the priest gave no motive for the action. Perhaps there was some slight ill-feeling between your son and the Lady Nilya's.'

'But Mechail's dead. How could he rise to do anything – and in the chapel of God?'

'Madam,' said the Magister, 'don't attempt sophistry upon me.'

A boiling obstruction seemed to swell between Veksa's breasts. Confused, she pushed her hands over her face and took refuge.

'My son was killed, my lovely boy! What do I know? I'm the mother – childless now.'

'Or,' he said, 'emotion. I require only truth from you. Do you see this?'

She put her hands down and perceived he had picked up something from the scatter of objects behind the candles. It was a ring, of twisted silver, not rich, but elegantly shaped.

'Nilya's,' said the Magister. 'Put it on for me.'

Veksa, before she could prevent herself, formed in the air between them a protective sign of the woods villages. She could have bitten off her hand.

'I note you're superstitious of her ghost.'

'Why not? She was my rival, even dead.'

'Still, you've marked yourself now. Perhaps the forest god you invoked, in place of the Christus, will protect you. I can overlook your lapse. Put on the ring.'

She reached out and took it. It felt ordinary. She thrust it halfway on her little finger, but could get it no further, and was glad.

'How does it seem to you?' he said.

'I've finer adornments in my chamber,' she snapped.

'Tell me,' said the priest Magister, 'how it went between your son and hers.'

An intolerable wash of heat flew up through Veksa's throat and head. She was aware her forehead broke into a visible sweat. A deep hatred mounted in her, where the fear had been, and her heart shook with its drum. *He's playing with me: this isn't to learn, but for sport—*

'Mechail was envious of my Krau. How not, when one was fair and whole and the other a mewling cripple. The lord hated his legal son and loved mine.'

'Who dispatched your son?'

'Some *enemy*,' she rasped in a raw hoarse cry. 'I curse him for it. May he writhe in Hell for ever.'

'Take off the ring, madam. Replace it, there. Now you may go back to your apartment.'

Veksa did as he instructed. A hundred phrases jostled at her tongue. She could say none of them, and once she gained her room, she chewed upon those she had said, trying to digest them, his questions, her replies, while her heart continued its uneven throbbing.

There were no bells, no mechanics of time in the forest. Midnight was the moon in a foretold position, reflecting on the earth.

Westerly, the apron of the valley, with its new encroachment of trees, its dry stream bed, and its ruin. Among the boulders the wolves slaughtered and fed. The wish for water led them over, following the tilt of the moon in the first station of black morning. They were obsessed with water, as with blood. They knew streams, pools, urine, spit, but not tears. They knew the wound of another from the wound of the inhabited body, but not, presently, the wine of sacrifice.

West, above the valley, in the pines, a jet of liquid shot from a rock.

A cracked jar stood beneath, bearded with moss. To the wolves, the lupine and the human, no more than another stone.

They drank.

The man-wolf lay down on his belly, favouring his left side. It was the wolfish wolf that ran up the slope, going to sniff the mound with the botched cross compiled from a broken sword, rusted fast and long-haired in ivy. Along the ridge, wrapped into the pines, a bothy stood, made over countlessly against its own decay. How many occasions the walls had buckled, the roof caved in, the door crashed loose after the ice and winter snow. It had no windows, only a smoke-hole, from which, so late, a milky streamer issued to the lit sky.

The wolfish wolf sniffed after the smoke, smelling perhaps a scorched kill. He trotted across the ridge to the door, where an axe leaned on a stair of logs. Feral garlic and some mushrooms hung above the lintel, black cabbage swarted from the soil, and a sorry berry bush. On a frame of sticks one thin shift was stretched after washing.

As the wolf explored the perimeter of the hut, two eyes stared out from a slit in the door.

'Da,' said the slight voice. 'Da, there's a wolf there, and another wolf like a man down at the fountain.'

'Go to sleep,' he mumbled, from his bed of ferns, the pillow of the ancient cloak young eighteen summers before.

The eyes at the door-slit were green by summer firelight, nothing under the westering of the moon. But the wolf eyes blinked peridot as it ran away.

'At mamma's grave. A wolf and a wolf-man.'

The sleeper, wakened, eased up on his elbows, and looked at his daughter.

'You know, Jasha, the wolves won't hurt you, if you're hale.'

'No, Da. But the wolf-man had a poorly arm, the left arm. Like you.'

The man might have shaken his head. He was a decade past such gestures. Sometimes he unremembered everything. They had come and gone from the first, the image of his former self, the fact that he was alive. 'Poorly' though the left arm was. Where he had had to hack off his hand. Had it really happened? And the girl, the other girl, this one's mother. Sometimes singing and sometimes crying. Sometimes sweet, and sometimes screaming in agony. Why had that been? He could recall the birth, the tiny red squealing thing, like a rodent, issued from the womb. That had grown into this, a slim woman with a lizard's face and lizard-coloured eyes. He had trudged her away into some village, but later she came back. She could cook by then and mend. She offered her body to him, for she intimated she had been severally raped in the village; her father's lust was all one with the rest. But he had not wanted her. There had only been lust that once, with the mother, there on the chapel floor. Just once, when he believed the dark mystery had gone from them and they were safe.

But his hand died. And the cleaving sword of her rescue had cut her, touched, he came to think, her brain. She could never say who she had been. Possibly, no one. Some stray, sheltering in the holy vault, hoping to be protected there.

What was his name? He had called *her* Jasha, Jasha's mother, for a girl in another life. And then the daughter, too. And he was Carg. Carg was his name. A Landholder's captain.

It had not been feasible, that he go back, to whatever it was he had come from, chasing whatever it was he had chased. A wolf, then, was it? Some bad dream.

Sometimes he dreamed of a dead horse lying under him. He fornicated with it, and out came the lizard daughter Jasha.

Sometimes, too, he dreamed of destroying her, gently, as she slept. He should have done this with her mother. Not left her to swell, bear, and die, only then shoving her in the ground, breaking his sword for her monument.

'There are things in the woods,' he muttered. Because the lizard girl had bothered him with her vision of wolves who were men.

He killed butterflies always. They terrified him. Once the second Jasha had danced across the cabbage patch after these flying insects, a horde of them with petal wings, and he roared forth and slew them. She wept. She was three then, and then too he carried her to the village. But she came back.

How long had it gone on? Only a year or so. No, he had cut notches in the tree nearest the door. He stopped at fifteen. There were more, more than fifteen . . . each a year.

Where he had taken off his hand the bone had knit into a club. A blight spread from it. His whole arm hurt him all the winters, much of the summers, and now his neck began to stiffen. In the night he could feel his left hand, every sinew and finger, hurting him like the rest.

But he had erected the hut, or found and repaired the hut. And he had cared for the first Jasha until she died. And then for the lizard-rat of a baby.

He could not recollect getting her, only that he had, there on the stone floor, when the sun rose, with a girl

103

weeping and laughing, and a ribbon of blood spreading out with her hair.

'They're gone now,' said the lizard Jasha, 'those wolves.'

It was actually as if they had slept under a long snow, and now something unfathomable, irresistible, woke them. Like stars they moved into a different course, and flakes of life sloughed off from them, Carg Vrost and his daughter.

When Beljunion entered the chamber high in the south of the Tower, he had developed a sensation like a lance stabbing into his left side below the heart. It had enabled him to take some while over the ascent and, on going into the room, to linger. But then the Magister had directed him to a chair, and he must sit before the table.

Sunlight blazed in at a window. It changed the table into gold, and all the things upon the table shone and sparkled. There was a copy of the Book – he would be asked to make a vow on it. Elsewhere were patterns of objects. They distracted the eye. They had some significance. There was a globe of quartz, from the itinerary of a magician rather than a priest.

'Good afternoon, godbrother. Please rest. We're in no hurry, are we? The truth is absolute and always to be come up with.'

Beljunion faltered. He said, inconsequently, 'Your grace is understanding. Is your grace – not from Khish?'

'From one of the southern chapters. I won't tax you with the names of those cities. It isn't what we have to discuss.'

Beljunion held his side, where the pain stabbed. He thought of beating the child Mechail, of lecturing him upon the utterness of God.

Anjelen said quietly, 'Did you yourself believe the story?'

'I – which story, your grace?'

'That a black moth drank the blood of Mechail when he was three years of age. That the moth lifted the boy

104

and flung him down bodily, from which assault he was made a cripple. That Mechail lived as the heir of the Korhlens until Esnias soldiers killed him. That thereafter he rose from the dead, murdered those he took for foes, and went into the forest. Where he continues now, a threat and terror to you all.'

'I myself,' said Beljunion. He collected himself. 'At first in my fear I said irrational things. But Mechail was never dead. This was how he could get up from the bier. I saw him. Do you want me to make an oath on the Book?'

'It isn't necessary in your case, godbrother. You say he was alive, then, not dead?'

'No one rises from the dead, your grace.' The old priest spoke as if encumbered.

'You're wrong, of course, godbrother. The Christus himself was hung to die, impaled through the heart, buried, and rose again on the third day. It's an article of our faith. Do you now deny it?'

'The Christus wasn't a man.'

'Yes, godbrother. God in man.'

'Mechail – was a man only.'

'Perhaps not.' The Magister moved a tiny piece in one of the patterns on the table. It was a miniature crucifix carved in an acorn of marble. On his breast, as he did this, the larger crucifix swung heavily, and the umbrous ruby let out one of its red lightnings. 'Tell me now, godbrother, what you credit to be true. Not what your unease prompts you to say. Nor any guilt, nor any dictates of self-preservation.'

The pain in Beljunion's side was intolerable. The details on the table swirled together. He saw between the fiery cage of their lines Mechail's corpse staring at him, lifting up, and felt the hands of death as they cast him away. Something seemed to split in Beljunion's heart, and the pain gushed out. It was gone. He said, 'The story's as you detected. The vampire moth, if such spirits can be. But I know he was dead. I prayed by him while they drank and diced; yes, dicing and drinking as they did under the cross of the Redeemer. But Mechail's gods were the gods of the wood. And they brought him up again to life. There's a god on the tree, I've seen him, in the forest, and Mechail was like the god. I desired his body, and I mortified my flesh because of it. And I beat the boy, to spare him my caresses. This terrible sin I confess.' Beljunion began to cry like a young man. He looked at the god in the wood who was Mechail, and the cup of night, and the wine-blood he could never drink. Maybe he spoke of this also. The Magister had become a ghost of thunder which listened attentively across a plain of lights, a scarlet nail burning in his breast.

Silence came, and after that, Anjelen began to talk softly to the old priest.

'You have lost your way, godbrother. You must come back to Khish, where they can tend and help you. This has been a grievous task, and you were unable to bear it. Salvation is probable. By telling me, as you have done, you've saved your soul. There are things to be seen to in this place. You will be my minister here, and the minister of the Church. God hasn't forsaken you, Beljunion. Be at peace now.'

And the hand of tawny ivory lay before Beljunion, and he took the hand and pressed his lips to it. The hand had neither much warmth nor any scent. Yet it soothed him. He had been so afraid, but fear was ended.

It seemed the Magister did not need to interview the Vre. *What you know and would say was divulged in your letter.* Anjelen, God's Angel, now had only that remark for the Lord Korhlen.

He stood before the hearth in the Cup Hall, under the banners and weapons, the smoke-stains and blood marks his race had left there. Tonight there should be some relaxation, they would dine as they had, and this Magister might do as he wanted. They were a law in the towns and cities, these priests, but not here. Here the only priests allowed were tame ones like Beljunion.

Anjelen had just made of the Vre a peremptory request, which was to see inside the Korhlen vault. Krau was there, new-stinking. 'I shall look at him,' Anjelen had said. 'I wish you joy of it, your grace,' Vre Korhlen had retorted. And tonight they would eat and drink heartily, and after, there would be the male games, the tussles, wrestling – and then à woman. Not Veksa if she would not (she had grown fat and muddy with grief); some buxom slave, the blonde, or the brown one he had had his eye on for half a year now. A better farewell upon their graves, his sons, to get another. Thus he thought, behind a great door of banked unthinking. But the Magister, who had consented to talk to him here, had begun to speak again.

'Yes, Vre, you can do as you wish. After the vault, there only remains the final dealing. I most locate the creature who was your legal son. I must hunt him in the forest.'

That was to be expected – a witch-finding. Was it conceivable they would come on him – on *Mechail*? There had been no Mechail. To Vre Korhlen by now the exorcism was already complete; the dead were banished. He had eased the guarding of his hold, and he slept at night, nothing came near. The Magister would have performed rites to this end. And for the being itself . . . the woods could swallow anything. Had they not devoured half his soldiers once, along with the phantom they pursued?

Having begun it, he was only eager now to have it done with, to pack off the awkward priest, and to settle back into what he could make of living. It was little enough God had left him; it was damnable. There had been no word of a penance, and that was right, he had penance enough, but doubtless there would be a tithe of money, a *fine* imposed by the Church Fathers. He would pay, and then good riddance.

'I will take with me three of your men, Vre. And my riders from Khish. I'll require dogs, and slaves to handle them. One of these slaves should be the man who waited on your heir.'

'If you need him.'

'I have said I do. Also your other son's familiar, the dwarf.'

Vre Korhlen was momentarily unnerved. 'It's simple, that thing.' Anjelen stood looking at him. 'Whatever you say, your grace. We're at your disposal.'

'Your daughters,' said the Magister.

Vre Korhlen said, determined now, brusquely, 'They're daft, the pair of them, like the dam.'

'I've been told both women are sick.'

'One has a fever. The servant says the girl was bitten by something. A rat. Their apartment's infested. And if one ails, the other starts ailing too. If they died, no loss, God excuse me.'

'Yes, you should ask His pardon. What He creates is for His purpose, Vre, not to be unwished so lightly by you.'

Vre Korhlen begged the pardon of God a second time, and signed himself with the cross. He knew anger at having to do it. He had been kneeling too long, heart and mind, before this churchling.

'If his grace wants to see these girls—'

'No. As with so much here, events speak for themselves.'

Enigma, the seed of doubt. Vre Korhlen refused to let the voice and eyes of the Magister sow it.

'Your hunting,' he said, 'will it want my presence?'

'I should prefer you nowhere near, Vre.'

I am happy to hear it.

Krau's dwarf, who had no name, and now was to be a dog of the hunt, had dwelled like a dog for some while. A kennel in the yards of trodden earth about the kitchen, this had housed him. He had lost his status as a pet in the Tower. He had become a sort of utensil, discarded.

Slaves discovered him five days after the death of Krau, when they went to Krau's chamber. A foulness of odour and scratchings at the cubby alerted them that something was immured there. The steward came and the dwarf's prison was breached.

He emerged, covered in filth and ordure, half-blind from darkness, his tongue and lips ploughed with thirst.

At first they restored him, for it might be likely he was worth something in himself, to the mother of Krau perhaps, who would want to maintain the pet in memory of her son. But no one wanted Krau's beast, and it was tossed into the yards by the kennels. Once they had been the shelter of hunting hounds, in the infancy of the Tower. Now the seven or eight wooden heaps accommodated the strays and runts kept solely to see to vermin. Accordingly, a starved dog or two next duelled with the dwarf for his refuge. The dwarf had not meant to fight. He was scored by teeth and claws, but ended in haphazard possession. Every so often, various canines would return to challenge him. Then the dwarf battled, or shared with them the scraps an elderly slave woman sometimes threw him. One of the dogs became attached to the dwarf, or to the scraps. It was the leanest and most feeble of the scavengers, but, partnered with the dwarf, proved an obstacle to the others.

The dwarf and the dog slept spine to spine in the kennel, on the stinking mildewed straw.

The dwarf, who had no words, few thoughts, fewer memories, did not believe himself a dog. He was only himself and all eras were alike to him.

That Krau was done with he had grasped – even in the cubby he had heard Veksa howling.

A noon came that the dog and the dwarf sat tearing at a bone inside the kennel.

Darkness fell across the sunlight. Men were outside.

They thrust the dog off when it ran out (it cowered, belly flat), and dragged the dwarf into the yard. The dwarf's whimpering they took for fright, and it entertained them. But the noises were reflexive, and soon stopped. The monolithic eyes of the dwarf never changed, gazing up through sun and shadow.

And it was the dog which whined as they bore the dwarf away.

Everything was seen to for the Magister's departure into

the forest. Many hunts had been arranged to a similar formula. That this was quite different was left unsaid. All things to do with the hunting were in the hands of Anjelen, the Angel of God.

The Vre took up former pursuits about his Tower. On the morning of a flamed summer day, they told him the Magister, his three soldiers, the dogs with their handlers, the dwarf, and the three Korhlen men, had ridden off into the trees.

The second steward arrived at the door of the Lady Veksa. 'The Vre requests your company, madam, at table tonight.'

She smiled. She had thoroughly misread her husband for the first time.

Veksa went to the Cup Hall in a black mourning gown embroidered with cream and golden thread. Her hair, washed and perfumed and elaborately dressed, some plaited and some hanging free, had in it two combs of sky-blue lacquer. On her fingers were ten rings, the gifts of her lord. The necklace her father had bought her, from itinerants. It was of thirty gold discs, and hammered in each by now had been the Korhlen Raven. Her face was powdered, and lightly rouged at cheeks, brow and lips, and her eyes sootily masked. She looked her best as her best now was. Her plumpness she thought he would like. She came expressly to captivate him, since the hour she had spent in the south chamber had reminded her: this Vre was her security. Attended by three of her women she swept into the Hall and up to the high table, and there sat down with a mellifluous amenity.

At the empty place, Krau's, she did not glance. She had been thinking. She might yet bear another child. Perhaps she could bring him back, her boy, house him again. The prospect alternately enchanted and dismayed her. There were many items on which she must make up her mind.

But Vre Korhlen, having summoned her to the Hall, was busy talking with his captain. He did not even answer her respectful greeting, let alone take in her fresh magnificence, So, sulking, was he? She would see to that.

The food came, and the Hall ate and drank and made its din.

There were those who had greeted Veksa, wary of her influence. Some had not gone out of their way to do so. She noted that, gradually. Then, she looked across at Krau's empty place, and let a sudden anguish strike her. But at the groan she gave, though her women commiserated, and even the captain frowned and averted his eyes, her husband did nothing.

There was a girl waiting at the board under the steward's patronage. A mousy blonde, a slattern.

Beneath the table, Veksa felt her thighs begin to tremble. After all, she might need to be quick. Or to play a delaying game—

A servant brought a big pie to the table, and it was cut. Veksa fixed her mind upon it, visualizing frogs and mice jumping out. The fool. Did he think she was to be toyed with? She had given him her juiciest years, was in her prime. Through him she had lost her darling. Let the bloody bear be careful—

There was a noise at the south door.

It reminded her of Krau that evening, the straw man and the mockery of the blood rite.

Apprehensively she turned to see. But it was only Beljunion, the lackwit priest, long ago bribed to her faction with presents and flattery. A useful ally there, maybe. He had been absent; the steward had spoken tonight's grace. Now the old priest stamped up the Hall. He did not seem as usually he did. She had heard he had been ill, but he had no appearance of inertia. His face was white and haggard, but with an awful wildness and hardness to it, so that abruptly she felt again the blockage of anxiety between her breasts, and her palms sweated.

'Give me more wine,' she said, and the blonde girl bent to fill her cup.

And then Beljunion started to shout, and the uproar of the Hall sputtered and sank.

'Sir, I come before you from God. I am God's mouthpiece. I claim the protection of my calling. I must say what has to be said.'

Vre Korhlen looked astonished. He offered nothing.

There was not a sound in the Hall, beyond the spatting of the low summer hearth, the clink of a knife here and there.

Then Beljunion shouted again.

'Like a prophet in the Book, I come before you. You have invited a curse, my lord. You have gone against the laws of the Church. These fearful things therefore befell you.'

Veksa stared at the godbrother. He was insane. That was what happened here, their wits turned. And there was something the cold priest from Khish, the Magister, something he must have done, some order given . . .

Vre Korhlen said loudly, 'What are you saying, Beljunion? Eh? Spit it out.'

'Your marriage is a sham and a sin. I abetted you in it, and will go soon to expiate what I did. Put her aside. You must do it. Nilya was your wife. And this one is no wife. Put Veksa aside. You've lost both the heir and your bastard through this fault, and rule a desert.'

'Madness,' said Veksa. Her hand knocked over her cup, and the wine splashed into her lap. She thought: *The Vre has dreamed this up with them.*

Vre Korhlen rose. 'Priest,' he said, 'your calling protects you, as you claim. But get out of my Hall.'

'I'll go,' said Beljunion, 'but you must heed.'

All the strength seemed suddenly drained from him. He withered before them, like a leaf in fire. But it was accomplished.

What will he say now? Will he uphold me? Veksa waited in vain as her husband sat down again. He too wanted wine, and bawled for it.

As the godbrother crept from the Hall, the voices started up like scared birds in a thicket.

Veksa sat where she was for the quarter of one hour. Then, rising smiling, she took herself away.

In her own room she ordered her women from her (their dumbness screeched), and gave way also in silence, afraid to be heard, to a paroxysm of the most appalling horror.

He would send her from him, had wanted only this excuse. After all she had been to him, he reckoned her dross. Of course, he could replace her in a night. There would always be women for a Vre. And she – packed off home to her village, to her father's mill, in disgrace. A dependent, her dowry gone, a laughing stock. Worse than a whore, who at least might keep some profit to shore up her later years.

She writhed against a chair, clutching it, seeing everything before her. It would take him a day or two perhaps to finish the godbrother's work. He might even demand contrition of her, praying in the chapel, a public dissolvement of their marriage bond.

Time enough.

She had always had the means put by, plucked at the proper moments, at the correct phases of the moon and stars. She had cherished her herbs, God help her, to assist him. Now they should be his undoing.

She was sure. It was the lord who had seen to it. Krau's death. *Her husband.*

What she would give him, a few grains of this, and of that. Two sips of wine in her vicinity. This was all it would ask.

Nothing at first. Then a mild colic. But as other natural substances went down into the bowel, the metamorphosis would come. A month from now, long after she was exiled.

She had watched her aunt manage it once, on a neighbour who feuded with them. That house feared Veksa's, and the woman had been extremely unthinking to steal milk from the crock one morning. Later, Veksa had helped her aunt cleanse the crock. This was in the spring. Before summer, Veksa heard the neighbour woman shrieking month-long from her bed that weasels were in her belly, eating her alive. She passed blood and pus for

113

days before death put an end to her punishment. The feud was concluded after that.

They may say he got sick, lacking my tender care.

Veksa smiled as she had in the Hall. She bit her knuckles above and below the rings.

When he came to tell her he had considered and agreed the warning of the priest, then she would be ready with her goblet. Her last loving cup.

Chapter Seven

Summer's heat, the core of a huge brazen bell, had upturned over the forest. Pines burned to coal, the ferns were tinder. Mists scarfed the water-courses, where mosquitoes danced. Cool dawns presaging torrid mornings. The moon by night whiter than clay in a furnace.

They hunted the dead-live wolf from the Tower without a sentence spoken of his nature, whether he was or was not, or could be or never could be. When they camped by the streams they talked of home comforts, women, or their sons. Or of the Magister sometimes, in low murmurs. But not of what they did. Not of Mechail Korhlen.

It was not like the other hunt, the first, eighteen years before. That had been a lawless thing, the Devil's. But God presided now.

God was there in the slender belted form of Anjelen, whose shadow horse picked its way between the glittering knives of sunlight and the pillars of the trees. Anjelen who said for them the grace each sunrise and each evening, as they had, none of them, heard a grace said, the beauty of it, the sorcery of it, brought in to them by the voice, the motionless dominance of eyes and hands.

There is a man you could follow, Christus, to Hell if need be. Evra Livdis, thinking, as he walked his mount through the forest, day after day, behind the Magister, and the other two men of Khish, the three disreputables from the ruffian Tower, in tow. *A commander. The Church gets the sweetest fruit. With an army, what he could do.*

Evra Livdis, at twenty-nine, had served all his fifteen

military years at Khish, son of a soldier in the town garrison, going into soldiering as a vine grows up a cane. A handful of petty wars had called the town to muster for the overlord of the closest city, Chirkess, a name only to such as Livdis, who never saw it. But after the skirmishes, in a dull peace, there was not much to do save keep civil order and kick your boots.

Sent as escort for a Magister, Livdis had been intrigued, and nervous. The authority of the Church Fathers did not extend to Magisters at such towns as Khish. If the priest was from Chirkess, he could not tell and did not learn.

Someone said, Anjelen had worked miracles. He had cured an unhealing wound, had found water in a rock by striking on it. Livdis took these notices with a pinch of salt. Yet, could you not believe it, seeing him, hearing him speak?

When they hunted the woods, bivouacking by night among the oceans of the trees, Livdis grew more fanciful. Taking his watches in the darkness, he was primed for the unusual, which disappointed him, not coming. Probably all they would find, if they did find *him*, was a lunatic, some cretin whose warped strength had outweighed a deathblow. He would be taken, exorcized, burned for the redemption of his soul. That was the calculus, as Livdis knew it.

The dwarf trotted ahead of them, on a long leash controlled by the slave Boroi. The dwarf quested, if it had any notion of what it was supposed to do. The five other dog-hounds were held in check.

It seemed to Livdis they might be meandering in circles, but then he did not understand the forest. His world had been of cut wood and stone.

Despite the heat, and the biting insects, the monotony of the trek, the curious occult burden of it, Livdis was content to follow the Magister. Let it go on.

On the tenth day, the dwarf-dog found. They rode after him, under a tunnel of masonry rock, and came out on the inner rim of a flat valley. The forest wall craned on a brink above and about. Over the valley the sky was wide, enamelled, the crosses of a pair of hawks depending there.

Away along the downward slope lay a ruined building, some chapel or hermitage.

The dwarf set off across the valley. They rode behind. They were a quaint enough picture, the turnip-brown slave man, faceless with slavishness, the uncurling leather lead and the skipping monstrosity at its end, like a toad. Evra Livdis imagined describing this to a girl in the town. The girl allowed Livdis enjoyment of her body, he liked her quite well, though not enough to marry. Slowly jogging in the saddle after the dwarf, Livdis began to recall bed-games in the smothering heat. There was a pressure at his groin. Sometimes they would stop at noon, and if they did he would be able to go absent and toss himself off, but a stop seemed dubious, judging by the dwarf's enthusiasm. Suffer then. Livdis wondered how the Magister Anjelen saw to such urges. Did this priest have them? It was a sin, to waste the seed. How long since Evra Livdis had bothered to confess it? It was a sin too, what his girl did with water, to wash herself free of conception after their unions. He must think of other things.

Livdis saw the dwarf had reached the prolapsed chapel, and was skirting it. They went over the valley floor, and presently to the incline of the further side.

In the trees above, after a scramble, the dwarf lost impetus. Assuredly it had been after something of no relevance, in any case.

They halted. The men began to eat their journey food. Captain Livdis took himself through the wood.

He came on a private space, where there was a rock with a spangled fountain shooting out of it. The sound of the water somehow increased his lust. Livdis seated himself against the stand of a tree, and took himself out, fingering the pole of his flesh to seek the most sensitive pressures. He should not be too vast a time, going by the sensations his hand at once aroused.

Above, through half-closed eyes, the pine needles smoked against the sky, in his ears birds tapped and tined and the water dazzled its ceaseless ejaculation. He thought of the Khishan girl lifting her skirt, and how her legs were and her belly with its root of thick dark fur.

And then something altered. Some coolness or shade, or a sound that did not fit.

Livdis halted the coaxing movement of his hand, opened his eyes, looked. A girl was there, between him and the rock fountain.

He saw nothing about her, save she had breasts and hips. At the same instant he was trying to pack himself away. But she said, 'Will I do it for you?'

And a flame of blood stiffened him so hard he could do nothing then but protect himself with the shield of his fingers.

'What will you do for me?' he said.

'That, or something.'

'Do whatever you like,' he said, and relaxed and let her come to him.

She smelled clean, of the wood and the heat, bark and leaves and human hair.

'What will you give me?' she said.

Obviously. And coins would be no use. He indicated the rolled bacon and the bread. 'This?'

She nodded, and then she raised her skirt, like the girl at Khish. This one was not so dark, yet also darker, brown hair and tan skin, every inch. Her eyes were green. She sat on him carefully, taking him in luscious as a plum, and put her hands on his shoulders. Her breasts were small, but full, like apples. He did not have to do anything. She expected nothing but the food. He gripped her waist and let himself go, pumping upward into her in a ringing blind stampede. Falling back, he thought of the tales he had heard of woods girls, all true it seemed. A sprite in every bush.

She eased herself from him, then sat back on the grass. She took the bacon and tore off a piece, which she ate absently. He had reckoned she would have it all, and next pelt away. Perhaps she had cared for the look of him. She, though, was an oddity. A wide low forehead and a long, slight, straight reptilian nose. Her long eyes were the yellow-green of wine grapes or baby leaves. She looked primal, soulless even. Less like a woman than a snake.

'You're honey,' he said, to be courteous.

'I'll go with you,' she said.

'Ah, no. I'm sorry. I'm on a mission, with a lordly priest. It would never be allowed.'

'I saw the men. I can keep behind them,' she said, unperturbed. 'They won't know I'm there. At night, I'll come to you.'

Livdis licked his lips. There was something to her, sexually, that this quickly tried to harden him again. He could fantasize lying with her under the trees in the blackness, taking longer over it. But he had better get rid of her swiftly. A clinging type, frantic to be ridden off with to a town.

'Don't you have anyone here?' he said.

'My da. He died. I buried him by Mamma.'

She was expressionless. He glanced where she nodded, and glimpsed what might be a grave-mound through the trunks. Further up there looked to be a hut. What had he been doing to plant himself here for his self-abuse, within throwing distance of some peasant cot? But he would swear it had not been there before. *Magic*.

'Well, girlie,' said Evra Livdis, restoring his maleness into the mail. He got up, and she sat there, not stirring. 'Keep the bread. I'll just have a mouthful of the bacon. I'd give you more if I had it.' (There was more packed on his horse; no need to confess that.) 'You're a good sort.'

A cloud went over the sun. It was like a closing of the shutters of heaven.

He had known such things before. Unheralded, a summer storm.

'Rain,' he said. 'Better get to your house.'

Then came the breath of ice, down from the sky, out along the ground.

He saw the girl through a pulsing dimness. The sky darkened yet again, another door shutting. He looked up, and on the pine-tops rested a canopy of unlight. The forest was completely still. The birds did not sing. Only the spring sounded irritatingly from the rock.

Then there was shouting, off where he had left the Magister, the soldiers and horses.

'Farewell,' said Livdis to the woods girl, and he turned, already shivering at the cold, and strode down the ridge.

The girl Jasha waited until he was a way on into the purpling gloom, then she too rose, and went noiselessly after him.

Before he reached the bivouac, the sky had become dusk. The juxtaposition unnerved him, and he reasoned that it was the forest which played up the darkness. The cold was piercing now. Livdis held himself ready for a gale of wind, a groaning and bowing of the trees, but the utter stillness prevailed, in which all little sounds were lost.

When he came up with the men, they were standing like statues, the soldiers, the three slaves. The horses too were immobile, not eating the grass; the dogs huddled together. Only the Magister Anjelen was walking towards him over the earth.

'Threatening weather, captain.'

'Yes, your grace, a storm—'

'Get your men mounted up.'

Livdis shouted an order. They obeyed him. The movement was like sand motivated in a bowl, enclosed and spurious.

At the end of his leash the dwarf picked forward, stumbling now and then. His small curved back seemed loaded by a stone. Presumably he had given signs of finding again.

Anjelen rode after, and Livdis behind him.

They were going down through a dense corridor of pines. The darklight and the shade became night. At any moment torrential rain would smite them. Livdis was conscious of having sinned, as if this were retribution.

Flowers had spiralled from the forest floor and twined the trees here. Primordial roses bloated from the boughs.

The teeth of Livdis began to chatter from the cold. He clenched them. And a drop of moisture wet his hand. It did not have the consistency of rain. He looked, then flung up his head to see. Ropes of snow were sliding down through the pines. The men behind him swore. One called on the Christus.

Anjelen spoke, not turning, his voice carrying effortlessly back to them: 'Don't mind it.' He himself did not hesitate. And the dwarf went on before.

For a mile, two miles they rode between the walls of the wood, and the snow fell. It settled on the ground. Winter was there. Above, the narrow cord of sky was winter night. There was no sound but the wind-chime clinking of harness, and weapons. The trees were heavy with snow and their trunks armoured in flutes of ice. The summer ferns lifted from the snow in fronds of white lace, and in the boughs the roses had changed to crystal. One brushed the face of Livdis. He reached to put it away, and it shattered like a glass. It cut his hands, and the blood burned down his skin. He thought: *A mystery, a vision. Not real.*

He sensed, but could not explain to himself, that by means of this freak or hallucination, they had passed into a realm of infinite possibility. It was here the living dead were to be taken.

Then the pines opened out, and there was a clearing under the metal sky. A wide pool, meady and liquid an hour before, now frozen, a smooth curd of ice.

Evra Livdis gazed down, as if from some enormous height, and saw under the curd of the pool some sombre shapes which loped towards him, running uphill.

'Do you see?' said Anjelen. 'I believe you do. Choose now, Evra Livdis, to exist or die.'

He was so cold he could barely articulate his lips. He said, slurred like a drunkard, 'Life, in your service, Magister.'

Then the frozen pool broke up in shards, and out of it came bursting black wolves, a hundred of them, or maybe only one seen a hundred times over in the exploding prism

121

of the ice. They raced into the forest, and the men on the slope above also broke into screaming shards, flying and trampling away.

Livdis did not turn round to see.

Instead he saw a man crawling out of the ice in the wake of the wolves. In the curtaining snow, he was too a black wolf, black hair about his cheeks and brow and jaw, his mouth blue, his skin like clear aquamarine from the depths of the water. His eyes were only as pale as the ice.

Anjelen the Magister went down to where he lay on his face, and leaning to him somewhat, the priest said, 'Mechail Korhlen, whose silver ring is this?'

And a voice came out of the thing from the pool.

'Hers. My mother's.'

'You are alive,' said Anjelen. 'Come back to yourself.'

And he bent and twisted up the wolf-haired head by its mane, and showed it the world, until the white eyes encountered the face of the Angel of God, the face of Anjelen himself.

'Yes,' said the Angel of God then, 'look at me. Know me. Since you're mine.'

Chapter Eight

The children of the district thought of her as a reptile, and were afraid of her. But when she emerged from the narrow wooden house in one of her green dresses, to walk to the market, there was always the servant man at her back, so they never risked a stone. She had a maid as well, to look after the house, and doubtless the girl could have seen to its provisioning, but the lizard woman was apparently inclined to do this herself. In the same way she started a garden patch in the yard behind the house. A vine had been trained up the flint partitions, which promised grapes in the fall. The lizard woman did not seem likely to promise anything, her belly did not grow round. But then, she was a courtesan not a wife, probably she took precautions. She wore her hair in three plaits, two of which began exactly just behind her temples and ran down to her shoulder blades; the third and central plait, which was the thickest of the three, fell to below her knees. In colour her hair was like a brown walnut, and it shone. The hair might be said to be her beauty. Not her snake-green eyes.

The narrow house was located in the suburb of a conurbation which belonged neither to provincial Khish nor southerly Chirkess. It was summer anyway, and nearby reeked the meaner streets of any city or town. There, were open sewers, butchers' pens, flies. Here, it was a little better: at dusk, in the courtyard behind the house, shielded by walls of its own and other houses, and by a fortuitous neighbouring tree, you could watch the stars appear in the heat-grey amber of twilight. But it was not a forest, even the tree could not make believe it was.

'Why did you come after me, eh?' he would ask her. 'Loved me, did you? Don't you miss your woods?'

'No,' said Jasha. This was true. To miss anything, even something she had not liked, was pointless.

Of course, partly he said these things because he wished to be free of her. He was always in two minds about it, as with much of his new life.

Sometimes, when they lay together in the house bed, after coition, he would say: 'You weren't meant to be there. What did you see? Tell me what it was.' 'Nothing.' 'Not the ice, the flowers breaking? Did you see the black things tear out of the water?' 'What flowers?' she would say.

He had kept her too, maybe, to question her. The verification of what *he* had seen. Which she had seen as well, although with him she feigned ignorance, stupidity.

When she followed him back through the avenues of trees to the soldiers' camp, she had known weirdness filled the forest. But strange atmospheres came and went there often, like currents in the flow of a great river. From her childhood, Jasha was inclined to follow (literally, physically) oddnesses, and those creatures which attracted her attention. She had been born into a peculiar state, the life of the half-man, her father, the ghost-presence of the mad girl who perished at her birth. An earth mound was Jasha's mother, her father a crippled hermit, silently brooding or shouting aloud in fits of intemperate rage, murmuring of a past incomprehensible, tossing in sleep. Her first memory, the bladder of goat's milk held by a man's hand, balanced on the stump of another.

The morning she found him dead, Jasha was not surprised or moved. He had once or twice complained of stiffness in his neck, it had been there for weeks. In the night he sweated and called aloud. He hunted the moon in a dream. It was never to be caught. Then he whispered of a black moth impaled by a nail of blood. He slept; died. She dragged him from the hut in the sunrise, and dug a grave as deep as she was able, by the mound with the rusted sword. She covered him with earth, and laid rocks over the place, but it was learned habit. She had been shown some burials in the village, where she had also been taught to cook and clean, and the task of sex with five disparate and loutish and senseless males, one of them ten years old.

Days after the burying she saw the soldier by the spring. She did what she was always prepared to do. It was not that she was accommodating, merely expedient. (He had explained to her on the ride to Khish that now she was his, and must keep her favours exclusively for him.)

When Evra Livdis went through the woods, Jasha went after him, pursuing – rather than a captain – the high-pitched note of the supernatural.

In the artery of summer, under the winter sky, she tracked the riders, and she experienced the snow winnowing down, and the roses of scarlet glass, smashing, and finally the white pool of ice. When the ice shattered, she saw the black wolves brimming like a flood.

The men about her screamed, the horses neighed and kicked, and the forward static tide turned into a headlong retreat. The slave men ran too, although their flight was different – they had a dwarf on a leash and pulled him with them. The forest rushed as if with mighty waters, the bodies of men and horses, the heat of them in the freezing cold. And the leaping wolves washed after. And they had no heat, no texture, and yet she felt them as they tore by, brushing and snapping the tendrils of the thicket where she had concealed herself, and the cloud of their breath, odourless and unwarm, yet faintly substantial as whey. And when all this was gone, the crashing and tumult drained off into the eternity of the trees, then she saw. By the water, from which the ice had melted now, her soldier, the captain, he alone had stayed, although he knelt there as if before a shrine.

And the other one, the priest in his ruby blackness, he seemed to shine and pulse, as he leaned to something which had crawled out of the water. A drowned wolf which was really a man.

The priest spoke to him and let him go. The priest spoke to the captain. And so the captain bent and picked up the man from the water, and carrying him, got him on to his horse – which, like the horse of the priest, had remained. Then, the priest turned his head towards the thicket. His eyes were like black awls. She knew he beheld her clearly, but he said, 'Who is it, there?'

And then the captain came and rifled the thicket and getting hold of her – she did not assist or resist – pulled her out and thrust her down on to her knees, his own previous posture, which he seemed to think applicable. 'Some slut I met in the wood. Excuse me, your grace . . . She thinks she's got some claim on me.'

'And hasn't she, captain, if you've lain with her?'

'No, your grace, not by my lights. But, if you say she has—'

'Come here,' said the priest to Jasha. And so she rose and went nearer to him, meeting his eyes without evasion, for he was like the earth, the weather, not to be argued with or even feared, since fear and argument were useless. The priest did not say to Jasha: *What did you see?* Probably he understood she had seen everything. He held his open hand before her and in the lean long palm lay a ring of twisted silver. He said, 'What is this?'

Jasha answered, 'Some dead woman's.'

'How do you know?'

Jasha replied, 'It is.'

The priest said, 'A young woman, or old?'

Jasha said, 'Both.' And then she glanced over at the unconscious man's body lying across the captain's horse.

'Look at this cross,' said the priest. He touched the crucifix on his breast. 'What do you make of that?'

Jasha noticed that the cross was also the shape of a black moth, its slender wings outspread, the extended, tapering stem pierced by the jewel like a nail of blood. And she recalled her father's moanings in his death sleep.

'No,' said the priest sharply, 'you will say.'

The captain kept off, over by the horses.

Jasha said, 'A moth, crucified.'

'You're clever,' said the priest. 'He's to go with me, the captain, there. You can come with him. I give you charge over him, for now.'

Jasha inclined her head. Life had no need to be complicated.

Still, it was Evra Livdis who believed he had made the decision, in deference to the morality of the priest, to retain this burden of Jasha. He found her very exciting, sexually, and this gave added credence to his keeping of her. It was not that she was exceptionally adroit, only that she was odd – a woods girl.

Everything else comprised changes. The Magister had taken him on; he had to leave Khish.

When he returned there it was only for two days, and the town already appeared unknown to him, as if he had never been there before, because it was settled now he would be going away.

The journey, all of it, had been bewildering. He was still dazed, after what had happened in the forest. The daze never lifted, he merely got used to it. It was as if he had had an illness, which left a scar. He was not able to say: *I dreamed that*, or to explain it away, or to accept it. He must amalgamate the image, and the alterations which came next.

He remembered raising the dead weight of the unconscious man, bearded and filthy, covered in surface wounds and rags, soaking wet from the water, smelling of wolf . . . When Livdis hauled him over the horse, the gelding did not veer in fright at the stink. Then the girl was got out of her bush and apparently it was his part to take her on, as the priest had taken on him. Livdis had wanted to be in the priest's service. Thereafter, a vague sequence of leading the gelding through the woods with the man slung over it, and the girl walking, and the Magister on his black horse a short space behind her. And it was summer again, the trees congealed with needles and foliage and heat and birds. The heat dried the cold out of him, and dried the soaked man on the horse.

Presently another man emerged from somewhere, either before them or bringing up the rear. This was the Magister's scribe, and though he had seemed to dash away in panic like the others, he came back with the pack animals, and besides he had acquired the leashed dwarf. The slaves, the men from Korhlen and from Khish, were gone.

The Magister made no mention of going to the Raven Tower to say or do anything. The elderly godbrother was there who, Livdis had the impression, had been left the task of finishing the Magister's plan. If any of Korhlen's demented warriors ever went home, they would heighten the confusion and aura of miracles by what they had to tell. And so that act was concluded.

Instead of the Tower, they went straight to Khish along the bad forest road. They were not accosted, although they should have been, a priest, a servant, a shambling dwarf, a girl, a man over a horse who only slept and might have been dead, save he breathed and did not decay, and a single captain on a pack-beast to guard them.

At Khish, while Anjelen did whatever he had a mind to, Livdis was detailed to acquire horses, and to hire four more men. He got these out of the garrison (lying about the ones who were lost). They were decent mulish rank and file, with no prospects. The Magister offered gold, and the prestige of Chirkess, which is where Livdis said they would be going. He did not know, and indeed he was wrong. Yet the picked men, caught up at once by the flimsy web that held them all, did not jib, or grumble.

They followed the reasonable road until it gave out. By then they were in hill country, pale staircases of grassland, from the tallest of which one was yet able to see the interminable forest, like an incorrigible black moss, growing on and on to the north and east. But in the end the forest turned to distant smoke. The hills were grazed by sheep and goats, and skeletal chapels stood on them, mostly deserted, where it was often feasible to sleep. The intermittent priests were of the hill variety. They were obsequious to a Magister.

It must be Anjelen had come this way alone, with only his scribe. And yet, might it not be Anjelen had invented the scribe out of air, or clay, might it not be Anjelen, God's Angel, had flown over the land on wide dark wings, alighting at Khish?

Livdis, in a reverie, considered stories of saints, pilgrims and others under the spell of God, bound surely in just such a dreamlike journeying. Presumably, they did not have access to the carnal pleasure he had been allowed. (He coupled with her each night, once in a chapel, under the screen, before the others came in.) Sacred and profane mingled.

Every few days the girl made a sort of gruel, and fed this to the man who slept. He was able to swallow some of it, and sometimes, on these occasions, his eyes partially opened, but it was the species of blind glare the eyes of human things have before they faint, or sneeze, meaning nothing, awareness otherwise occupied.

Anjelen, in a week, spoke to Evra Livdis perhaps seven times. Ethically once for every day.

After the hills they went down into plains, and there were a pair of rivers, and some slight towns, roughly walled and towered. Livdis knew the names of none of them. He was in an unknown world. One evening, they came among a host of Travelling People going along the track to a town. They were a gaudy, rowdy throng, men in baggy breeches and high boots, jackets and tunics of hide cut open without sleeves, kerchiefs dyed yellow and orange, beards shaped into forks or plaited with laces. The women had earrings and collars and anklets of brass and copper, silver studs sometimes in nostril or lip. They hid their hair under black wigs, and some covered their lower faces. There were luck medallions of corrupt metal all over the hairy ponies they rode, and on their carts, which were painted with trees and thick black crosses. They carried icons of saints in their midst, on poles twined with briar, but there was also a plethora of horse and sheep skulls. They hedged their bets with the gods.

Seeing the small company coming up on them, the Travellers were inclined to jeer and grin. Then, noting the priest, they altered their song. Several men dismounted and came to him like children, craving a blessing. Anjelen sat his horse, *removed*, lifting his hand now and then to mark them for the Christus, among that orchard of skulls and amulets. They pointedly showed him their legitimate holy objects, and then the women came forward displaying tattoos of the cross, and one a tiny silver crucifix set into a front tooth. She could 'smile' God, but she had had to be careful. Twice enemies had tried to knock out her protection.

After the priest, the Travellers gradually noticed the dwarf. As if recognizing a creature of their own kind, they cawed to him, and made kissing noises.

Why the dwarf had been wanted on the journey, Livdis did not guess, but then he did not understand any of it. The dwarf was no longer leashed, and rode on a pony obtained at Khish. He did nothing at all, only stayed with them, got down when necessary to make water, like the other men, got down again at night when they halted, performed those labours he was told to by the soldiers, evidently slept when they slept, was there in the dawn when they rose up again.

Now, he huddled on the pony, the shortened girths and tangle of reins seeming to secure him as the leash had done, his nut-face old and expressionless as damnation.

One of the Traveller men came over to the dwarf. The Magister said nothing. Only the four Khishan soldiers sat bolt upright, demonstrating wariness, and everyone ignored them, even Livdis.

. The Traveller touched the dwarf gently on the thigh. 'What ye do?' The dialect was almost incomprehensible to Livdis, but the dwarf twitched, like an animal that hears its name. 'Come, ye. Do it, ye.' And the dwarf disengaged himself from the pony and slid down, and on the turf, in the clear area between the Magister's horse and the nearest Travelling carts, he became an arc, a hoop, and bowled along the ground.

The Travellers laughed, and cried out shrilly, pleased. They had known he would be good for something.

When the dwarf came near the ebony horse, he stopped wheeling his body, and uncoiled again into his ordinary form of an imp with a hill on its back. The dwarf gazed up at the Magister, right at him, the first time Livdis had seen him do that, too. And Anjelen looked back at him, and nodded, the most infinitesimal of recognitions. What it could mean, Livdis had no idea, of course.

But by then, something else had happened.

A girl had slipped out of the press of people, a maiden – for her dark hair was her own, uncovered by anything but a thin red cloth. She had gone between the horses and arrived where the sleeper lay in his daytime position, tied over his mount, his head hanging. At Khish he had been washed and clad, his hair and beard trimmed. But some twenty days of their excursion had undone most of the improvement. Like a baby's, his bodily functions were random in sleep, and though the woods girl had been detailed to take care of this (she had tended a sick and wandering father, it seemed, and was impervious), there was to him all the pariah quality of illness, absenteeism. Nevertheless the Traveller girl was leaning under him to peer into his face as it hung to the earth in its nest of hair.

'Here, come away,' said Livdis, in a firm sensible tone. He did not want to antagonize the huge band, and checked with half an eye to see what the Magister did, but that was nothing, he was not even looking over. Livdis glanced at a large uncouth man who bore tokens of being one of the leaders. Livdis said, 'Call her off. This fellow's not healthy.' And the man responded immediately, summoning the girl. She went, docile, as if brought from an activity of no moment.

After this, they were able to split aside from the Travellers, who pranced on, with a metallic jangle, cartwheels and calls, towards the selected town.

A ruined inn was perched in the bend of the broader

river, and here the priest's party made its night-time arrangements. Two of the soldiers produced their improvised lines and sat down at the river's edge to snare the fish that rose for midges in the sunset. The third made a fire in the flagged courtyard, uprooting handy immature trees that had seeded between the stones. The fourth man and Livdis between them carried the sleeper into the inn hall, where Jasha, with the dwarf, fashioned for him the usual bed of grass and cloak.

Anjelen walked away from the camp, as was his routine at the nightly halt. Livdis had spied on him sometimes, at prayer or meditation alone, turning the polished plain beads in his long fingers. Otherwise, Livdis had never beheld the priest go off for any other reason. If he even urinated might be the subject for a debate. But the priests were accustomed to be mysterious, obscuring their humanness. As for an angel, naturally an angel did not need to relieve himself. Although he did consume, fastidiously, at his separate place, ascetic portions of food and drink.

The sun scalded down on the river's western bend, making a carnelian bar across the water. The rest of the lower sky was a dense terracotta pink, but the upper vault had already faded, revealing its enormous, hollow height. The depth of the sky was not comfortable to Livdis, he preferred the fixative of clouds or daytime colour, a ceiling rather than a tunnel from which anything might fall. Yet, as a child, he had gone up on to a roof to count the stars. The bigness had not bothered him then.

The horses and mules were feeding peacefully at their stations. Jasha was preparing a stew in the kettle at the fire, while the two soldiers sat and talked, and eyed her with an easy, incurious watchfulness. The dwarf sat too, in a corner of the yard, as if he would sit for ever. It was likely some of the Travellers might stay on the track outside the town, and the men might wish to go over that way, to see if they could get a woman – chastity was quite often rigorous among the People, but it depended. They would have to draw lots for the trip. Livdis did not intend there to be no guard tonight.

The sky swam up higher and higher, and stars emerged in pale white dots without any brilliancy. A fisher bird soared into the air further along the river. Perhaps it had been cheated, like the other two soldiers, who were now returning swearing mildly and empty-handed.

Then something else moved on the landscape, coming down from the track. The last spillage of sun burned red on a red scarf.

'That lass from the carts,' said the second fishing soldier, pointing.

Livdis was not glad. Doubtless she had stolen over to tell fortunes, or maybe sell herself, which might save some of them an extra ride, providing they all fancied her and did not mind taking turns. Yet there was something about her, her body and the way it held itself. Besides, would she not have brought a brace of sisters to share the work and the reward?

'She's up to something,' said the other soldier, vocalizing this idea.

'Yes,' Livdis said.

They stood outside the inn, waiting for her to reach them, and the twilight greyly blued, shading over both sky and land now. And the girl darkened in the twilight, thus strangely becoming less distinct the nearer she got to them. Until she was thirty strides away, a shadow with a pale lightless star of face, not even any more blood in her scarf.

'Stop her,' Livdis said to the soldiers.

One of them went to meet her, blocked her path.

'Where do you think you're going?'

The Traveller girl simply stepped around him, and came on. The soldier obviously had not expected that; he turned and looked at her, surprised. Livdis took it on himself to intercept her.

When he confronted her, he saw into her face. Her eyes were misty, as if she were drunk. She would not halt, so he caught her arm.

'He asked you where you were going.'

She swung in his grip as if part of her was still moving on. At first he believed she would not say anything. Then she said indistinctly, 'To that place.'

'Which place?'

'There.'

She meant the inn ruin. The conversation was inane, and yet oddly fraught with some obtuse inner meaning.

Livdis had a sudden impulse to free her. He did this, and instantly she walked forward again.

He pursued her at the same dogged pace, saying to the soldiers, 'We'll see what she's after,' and tapping his forehead to display an opinion on her wits.

All three fell in behind her. In the inn yard the other two looked over with interest from their dice. Jasha glanced, and went back to stirring her kettle. It was the dwarf that got up, the ancient eyes *seeing*. But this was all the dwarf did.

At the doorless doorway of the inn, the Traveller girl paused. She was staring into the darkness there.

'It's him she wants again,' said one of the soldiers. 'Eh, love at first sight, captain.'

Then she went through the door, and as she merged with the dark, Livdis saw a bluish glint of something.

'The bitch – that's her knife!' The soldier charged through the door, merged also into the dark. There was an upheaval of shadows and noise, something dropped with a clatter, the Traveller girl squealed and the soldier swore. He was trying to drag her, but she fought him. Livdis too walked into the dark of the inn, could see in it, and found the soldier struggling with the girl, preposterously. The soldier waved the stem of the girl's wrist before Livdis as she squeaked and writhed, strong, giving him problems. 'Look, she's opened her own vein. Crazy bitch, what's she at—' And then the girl's wail rising up over the struggle and the dark, 'Let me let me let me—'

Livdis lurched forward and struck her across the face.

Behind him, in the door, Anjelen's beautiful voice spoke a curious litany.

'Let her go.'

Livdis and the soldier stood away from the girl, who flopped there on the uprights of her legs, panting, her arms and neck boneless, a little patter of blood dripping down her hand.

'Come here to me,' said Anjelen.

The hairs stiffened along Livdis' spine. It was the voice from a cathedral. It hung above him, having fallen from the sky.

The girl ambled on her stiff iron legs towards the priest, her body melted wax from the waist.

Livdis saw the hiltless sword of the priest's silhouette in the doormouth, on the lambent omission of twilight. The world might have ended beyond him. Only nothing was there, formless and void.

'What is it?' said the Angel, taking the girl's wrist, seeming to inspect the blood. 'You scratched yourself on a bramble, did you? Tear your skirt and bind it up tightly. Not for you, this.' He lifted his hand from her and at once she began to rip at her skirt. As she made the inadequate bandage, Anjelen said, 'Give her the knife.' Livdis picked up the blade and approached her and held it out. Anjelen said to her, 'Take your knife, now.' Then she took it and put it in her belt. Nearer to Anjelen, Livdis did not like to look at him. There was a sort of wall of solid air, and after this the nothingness. Livdis bowed his head, and Anjelen said to the girl, 'Go back to our people.' And he moved aside, and the air softened, and out there were the country and the river, and the stars growing bright. Into that the girl propelled herself, and walked away again, towards the track.

Livdis heard himself say, sluggishly, 'A mad girl, Magister. Your grace did right.'

But Anjelen was gone from the doorway, and now Livdis could hear frogs sounding by the river, and smell the stew in the kettle Jasha tended.

He thought: *What does she put in the gruel for him? Is it her blood?*

This evil thought blackened like a dead coal almost as

he had it. It went out, and he shook it off, and going to the fire, laughed and said, 'Sorry, lads. If you want close company tonight, it's drawn lots and a bit of a ride.'

They had reached the city after some fifty days.

It lay beyond vast sweeps of cultivated land, the kind of fields and orchards that had scrappily surrounded Khish, magnified to an immensity. Days among plains of cabbages, among plaited fences of wheat. Nights under the latticework of apples, grapes. The roads were good again, better than at Khish. Towers, and wooden houses of one or two storeys, appeared, like and unlike the other places of the country Livdis had known. Nothing was quite the same, even the dress of the slaves in the fields, the women at the wells, being obliquely dissimilar.

Livdis tried to meet the unending challenge of alteration bravely, but since the incident with the Traveller girl, he had felt awkward.

People came from everywhere for the Magister's blessing.

The outskirts of the city were a sprawling suburb. Behind uneven walls, a timbered mass began that gradually petrified to stone.

On the crest of a stinking street hung with torn washing over the channel of a sewer, roosted a stone church. They rode into the courtyard, while most of the neighbourhood stole out to regard the Magister.

Presently Livdis followed Anjelen into the church. It was cool, but some goats had been penned near the doorway. Only the area by the altar was still sacred; the church served as a hospital and byre for the surrounding district. A lay brother came and kneeled before Anjelen and kissed the unwashed paving at his feet.

At midafternoon, a canopied carriage filled the court. The Magister was driven away in it, with his scribe. The rest of them made do as they were, but there were ten guards from the cathedral, encased in crimson, black and gold, with gold buttons on their helmets, and the stemmed cross printed and embroidered and inlaid upon and into every material.

They clambered the nasty streets, past abattoirs and boneyards, into the better lanes, and beheld the stone heart of the city disembodied by haze, brooding in a glaring sky.

Anjelen went away into marble, with the scribe, the boxes, Mechail, and the – perhaps a curio – dwarf. In a court the four soldiers from Khish were paid off, and left to agoraphobic startlement. Livdis was allocated a house, church property, some hundred feet vertically below the cathedral, where he next enjoyed a false home-coming to unknown servants and Jasha, whom he did not even entirely want.

What was it Anjelen had said to him at the vision's brink? *Exist or die?* It had not meant anything so simple, had not been, surely, only a threat. Anjelen had seen in him something of rarity.

Livdis consoled himself with Jasha, inured himself to the current life, which would be an interval. He did not think of the sleeper, or of girls with blood dripping from their wrists. He reminded himself, he was worth something to the priest.

The market, where Jasha searched about for provisions, lay on the bank of a muscular brown river wider than any encountered on the journey.

The core of the city was stone, many buildings raised on a platform, dominating the surrounding miles of timber and plaster. The core had towers pointed with pinnacles and bulbs of metal rusted green, and the river cut beneath the platform, where there were broad arches crowded by blackened statues. The river then descended through the city, and at its lowest stretch brought fishing boats, and cargo vessels with slanted sails, to the market.

The wooden city was carved and painted, and sometimes caught fire, in summer, causing panic. There were churches everywhere, painted wooden churches and churches of stone, and the mighty marble cathedral upon the central platform. Bells rang at sunset, dawn, midnight. The city nights were noisy with drunkenness, street music, the churn of carts and drays. These sounds were quite unlike the constant noise of the forest, its leaves, the nocturne of creatures to whom night was day.

Frequently, day and night, Jasha had heard or seen funeral processions. A burial ground lay up behind the district where Livdis was housed. Professional mourners waving their arms and shrieking, attended each bier like crows. There would be a priest speaking prayers aloud, lost in the outcry. Before him, at the procession's head, went a man holding up the long-stemmed cross of Father Church. If the funeral was a rich one, the cross would have gold and gems, and the mourners would amount to a flock. Often the cross was wood, the priest in homespun from one of the painted churches, the mourners only two or three women whose screeches were hoarse with effort.

In the market Jasha, attended by the male servant, picked her way between the heaps of vegetables, the human heaps of beggars and the leprous. She quested for fish like a gannet, for the fish came inland along the river and were salt, almost unlike anything Jasha had ever eaten.

A ship lay out in the river, too big to move into the quayside dock. Jasha looked at the ship, its trees of masts, the looped-up sails of dull red. She had, for a moment, a sense of being in two places together, here in the city, back in the warp of the forest. Why was that? As she stood examining, glancingly, the sensation, a woman's voice broke suddenly like light into a wordless song.

Jasha looked about. The song was extraordinary, exquisite, limitless – no one took any note, and the man-servant stood deaf, picking his nails.

Jasha saw, some way off, the figure of a girl, perhaps her own age, seated on a bale of something. Her hooded head was tilted back. Intuitively, from her posture, Jasha told that it was she that sang.

The domesticated courtesan of Livdis turned her reptile face, her slender body, all over in the direction of the

138

voice, moving impetuously and fluidly, as she did when psychically aroused. All that was in her mind was the earth mound in the wood, where she had occasionally sat, with a doll made of cones and reeds, in her earliest and most normal years.

'Lovely fishes,' said a man, brushing into Jasha, not realizing she was in the grip of anything but her usual greed. She might have darted by him – but, as if quenched in his mundane appeal, the unearthly song was done. The hooded, muffled girl seemed to fold out of sight like an impossibly thin surface turning sideways.

'Fishes, fishes,' insisted the fish-seller. Jasha eyed him, bought, handed the slimy-smelling package to her attend-ant. That was all there was to be done now.

'*He'll* be pleased,' he said.

Jasha ignored him, as now she ignored the evanescent phantom girl.

She did not bother about Livdis, who was not always charmed by the fishy meals. He would anyway be in a better humour this evening, as he always was after Anjelen had required his attachment on some jaunt. Mostly the captain's duties seemed to involve waiting, in ante-rooms, refectories, about the cathedral. But Livdis talked of his adventures all night, strenuously assuring himself of his necessity to the Magister. He had never mentioned Mechail, and appeared to know nothing of what had become of him.

At the market's edge, Jasha looked back, to where the singer had seemed to be. This was not like Jasha. She could not have said why she did so, and anyway the bales were empty, the air raucous with unmelodious elements.

Jasha found herself instead with her once or twice con-sidered, three-fold picture of Mechail. There was the man-wolf at the fountain, and the naked man beside the streams that she had washed (all his white length, and the black triangle of hair, on whose cushion his penis rested, some-times hardening briefly in her cleansing hands. Otherwise, he never woke. There was a fearsome scar over his heart). And next there was a Mechail who lay in a dark chamber, where figures entered, and moved him about, or washed him or fed him as she had done. They exercised his limbs, even the club of the left arm. This last view of Mechail was an insight. She never mentioned it, did not ponder it. She wondered only for a second, on the street that led uphill to the house, why she had linked Mechail, the three images of him, ordinary or insightful, to the singing in the market behind the beggars and the wizened fruit.

'Are they making you wait, Magister?'

Anjelen raised his eyes from the copy of the Book indigenous to the cathedral. It was quite beautiful, in its fashion, but the ornamentation was a little crude, and jewels were missing from the covers.

'To live is to wait, Administer. By this means we learn patience.'

'Naturally. I didn't infer – you know, Magister, we're at your disposal. Faithful servants of the order, under God.'

The Administer, a plump and clerkish man, touched his hand to his crucifix of silver, and bowed. His head was shaved for the heat, and when he walked into the city, a boy minced before him to wave a censer of spices. The Administer never asked after the young man who slept like a corpse in a chamber off Anjelen's apartment, the cathedral servants recruited to serve him, or the dwarf in the corner. He had done what the Magister wanted of him, would continue in exact duty. Even his chancy and pointless remark (all transport required time), might have been meant for commiseration, a desire to assist further with sympathy; at worst a yearning to pry.

Anjelen the Angel was centuries beyond such men, and their foibles and their whims. He corrected the Administer perhaps for form's sake, as a priest should his inferior. But the man, a whole universe to himself, was to Anjelen as unimportant as a louse skittering across a distant gallery.

*

'Bloody salt fish – can't you find anything better? I should beat you—' The maid cowered behind the door, wringing her hands as Jasha tended her irate soldier at the wooden table. 'Well, what do you say?'

'I like salt fish.'

'I know you like it. Who pays for it? Am I to be made sick of the filthy stuff to please you, you woods trollop?'

He had been sent back after attending ten hours in the cathedral. Anjelen had not called him to do anything. It was a waste, with no excuse. And now, this.

'Didn't I get the lout to trim your grapevine? To turn the soil out there? Can't you grow something?'

'There's cabbage, there.'

Livdis rose glowering. Anjelen's behaviour had made him feel experimented upon, like a beetle set to run about, and this he had not admitted. He longed to strike Jasha in her ugly face – Anjelen had given him Jasha, too, a type of marriage. And all at once Livdis did not care to strike her after all.

Outside, just then, another of the funerals began to gurn up the street, squawking and wailing, with a whine of pipes. It was after sunset, but then, there had been such processions at midnight. Was this why the house had been allotted to him? Because it was prey to miserable rackets?

Livdis pushed at Jasha's arm and the ladle swung, smoothing fishy particles across her second green dress. (He had paid for the material, the thread and needles.)

The noise of the funeral was very loud, and it was now ridiculous to attempt communication even in violence. Jasha stood with the ladle, and the maid gibbered at the door, and down below the male servant would be snoring on his pallet. Livdis attended on the funeral.

So that when the cacophony lessened, the fresh sound came directly in to him, surprising, disorientating him. He turned his head, involuntarily, as Jasha had in the market. A woman's voice, of a strange richness, vivid with music, was singing on a high wordless winding of notes.

The last howls of the funeral had flapped away. The beautiful singing was left behind, stationary.

'It's a beggar woman from the market,' said Jasha.

Livdis moved across the room and slapped out the shutter. He looked down, and in the darkness that was the street, he saw the woman, with her hands upheld in an odd way that made her into the shape of a fork, the third middle tine being her hooded head. Her lower face caught some light and was almost visible, and as she opened wide her lips to go on with the wonderful song, he saw only blackness in her mouth. She had neither teeth nor tongue.

He started round from the window, the night. He was aware he had seen a frightful thing, not comparable in any sort to any horror of battle or disease. He did not know what. He thrust it from him.

'Will you throw her a penny?' said Jasha.

He thought she looked sly. Absurd.

But the song had stopped. He let himself glance out again, and no one was there.

The ship parted the river at dawn, and everything gave before her. Even the big ship of the previous day, she that had lorded over the water, made haste to haul herself aside.

The new ship was massively upright on the river, fully rigged, her mowing oars bringing her in silent as a shadow behind her charred balcony of a prow, the jaw of a sea-beast, a leviathan, out of whose calcified prongs rose the cross of the Christus and the Church Paternal, blacker than the west had been an hour earlier, and tall as a house.

The flotsam of the quays gave her a name: *God's Ship*. A crew of slaves looked back on the watchers with unseeing eyes. Too great to approach the bank, the Ship of God put down a black boat that rowed in to the wharf.

A space was observed about the enormous ship, and about the boat.

At midmorning, guards from the cathedral cleared the quay. There were reports of passengers.

At midday, the sun impaled on the zenith above the blocks of white sails, each marked with a black crucifix, the Ship manoeuvred herself, the water churned. And when the maelstrom settled, she was rowing herself away behind her leviathan jaw, her house-tall cross, going out again, to where the salt fish were, and what else besides?

Riverine glooms and gleams tilted in the candlelit cabin which had become Anjelen's chamber. He made every place his own, it seemed, the soldier thought, standing before him, uneasily entranced, unbalanced, as by the slight feeling of seasickness the motion of the ship had induced. He and the woman slept under awning on deck. The crew of the ship were swarming and silent, seeing to oars, rigging, the cleaning of the vessel, the preparation of food. Two days had passed, and now it was night again. An hour ago the copper ball of the sun had gone into the river. Now a yellow half-moon hung over the water and the banks. Flat rolling land spread away, the urban wheatfields and vineyards diminished, and the horizon was only earth meeting sky.

Since boarding, until this moment, Livdis had not seen, nor been called to, his master. Even Jasha had not been obliged to see to the sleeper, who occupied a smaller cabin close by. The dwarf, seemingly trained in the city, now attended to Mechail's needs.

'Soon,' said Anjelen, sitting before him (Anjelen, the one changeless thing), 'we sail by a village on the shore.'

'Yes, Magister?'

'A prosperous village, which has a decent road, going on to one or two towns. Or there are horses available. Cities would be accessible to you.'

'What do you want me to do there, your grace?' said Livdis. Then, having spoken, understood.

'Yes,' said Anjelen. 'You've served me very well. You'll find I'm properly grateful.'

'You're putting me off.'

'Paying you off.'

'But I believed—' Livdis caught himself, sounding

petulant as a girl who had been promised wedding and got only bedding. 'I thought your grace engaged me as a bodyguard, in the long term.'

'Why did you think that?' said Anjelen.

It was no use. Livdis' disappointment was nearly painful. He felt cheated. This, coupled with nausea, was maddening. He rummaged after the weirdness of the forest, the words murmured to him there – surely Anjelen had a purpose for him?

'I gave up a fair living at Khish,' said Livdis. He now sounded menacing and small-minded. 'I reckoned your grace had some – how shall I say? – *theme*. An ambition, perhaps. For which you'd want support from reliable men, a captain with some knowledge of how to go on. That's what I reckoned.'

'Did you.'

'And here you say you want me off at the next flea-bitten hole, lose myself. Months from my birthplace.'

'That never worried you formerly, captain.'

'I was led to believe I'd profit, your grace.'

'You shall.'

Anjelen motioned to a table. There was a box on it. Livdis would have liked only to stare at it, and away. But he wanted to see, too, what the Angel thought him worth. So he went to the box, lifted the lid, took out the leather bag, which was very heavy. Loosening the string, Livdis saw silver, and gold. It was a most fetching wage. He should rejoice and take his leave. He waited there, with the bag in his grasp, seeing an empty vista after he got off the ship. He could not visualize what would happen to him, if he left Anjelen. And although such a blankness would never have troubled him before, as the purposeless days at Khish had not, he did not want that wilderness again. He did not want to return to being nothing much.

And he heard himself say, lightly, 'Is your grace testing me? I tell you, when I meet a man of proper calibre, I'd rather continue with him and let the cash lie. You've seen how I've served you. Never asked any questions. And there have been some strange goings-on.'

Anjelen said, in his beautiful voice, 'You have a little drop of vision, captain, which enabled you to perceive more than others. A very little drop. Otherwise your loyalty was, patently, appreciated.'

'No, no, you're out after something, your grace. I can scent it. You've great powers. Keep me on. You won't be sorry.'

'You prefer to follow me than to take your wage and seek elsewhere.'

'I *will* follow you, your grace.' Livdis grinned. The awareness that he had been proved, that he was winning through, made him festive. 'Where are we going? Some religious stronghold? That's what I'd guess, from the rumour at the quay. Well, I'm your man.'

Anjelen rose. He crossed to the cabin door and opened it. The night was lined by the shine of the river, and as the candlelight of the cabin bloomed out, the half-moon answered it from the plain.

'There is the village, captain. Downstream, less than a mile.'

As if it were the exactitude of symbols, Livdis beheld an ant-hill hummock of dwellings, worthless hints of opaque lamps.

Livdis remembered the tongueless woman who had sung under the city house. She had been a herald of the voyage, sent to alert him. The music of her song had no impediment of words.

'God bless the village,' said Livdis. He was proud of his flippancy. 'But I've seen what you can do. Maybe glimpsed what you *are*, Magister. Let other men take your gold, and offer *me* the chance of glory.'

'Oh, it isn't glory I offer you,' said Anjelen. He turned, and half his pale face was there, like the half face of the moon. Then the door had closed. The night and the village were shut off.

Livdis confronted the Magister, with only the length of the doorway between them.

In those seconds, Livdis tried to read the mind or soul

of Anjelen, Angel of God, and did not succeed. For the eyes of the Angel blotted away everything else.

'Since you refuse to leave my service,' said the Angel, 'I can only reward, instead, your stubborn constancy.'

Something happened which outstripped any waking fantasy Livdis might ever have had.

The Magister leaned forward, and set his cool lips upon Livdis' own, and his right hand upon Livdis' heart.

The kiss was brief. The mouth, dry and smooth, barely real. The hand imparted a warmth, leaving him a fraction later – the tingling heat of it remained. Livdis gazed on the Angel, which now drew back, seeming to become the single division of shadow between the candle lights.

What could a man say to this? Livdis struggled with emotions of excitement, disbelief, others he could not have named.

Where the priest had touched him, a fire flamed, and his heart raced and galloped beneath it.

Again, Livdis tried to speak. Now he could not. Truly, could not.

Something else was happening, not like the thrill of the kiss. Its marvel was twisting – what was wrong? From Livdis' mouth came a sludgy noise, a sort of burp – frightening him—

He was *afraid*. The shadow of the Angel was running like black ink, and either side the wings of light engorged, and through it, this insectile, molten shape, there bored an eye of scarlet.

The scarlet bolt was in his breast, the breast of Livdis, burning and gouging at him – he flung both his hands towards the spot where the hand of Anjelen had touched him, and for an instant, appalling, unthinkable heat scorched his palms, before his whole body forgot that flesh was not fire.

The soldier strained his jaws to scream, but out came only a coil of boiling blood over a blackened blistered tongue. Through the netted mail of Khish, buckling and soft as tallow, the blades of three boiled ribs burst forth under the heart. The figure that had been Livdis toppled over, kicking, while scalding fluids seeped and sprang out of it, steaming, and spraying the legs of a wooden table to whiten them.

Shortly, with a slow hissing, the carcass subsided. It had been cauterized of life.

Presently the Magister Anjelen moved out upon the deck, and two or three of the slaves entered the cabin, closing the door.

Under the awning aft, Jasha was seated, mending one of her dresses in the moonlight.

Anjelen glanced at her as he stepped by.

But Jasha kept her eyes upon her work, not looking, not seeing anything. She would sleep alone tonight, as if she had always done so. And in the morning too she would be alone, as if she had always been.

Chapter Nine

Where the river entered the sea, a range of mountains lifted, a rock at a time. Below these mountains, which, as the season turned through autumn into winter, were like lead, a floor of stones stretched towards the water.

The sea clashed against the land. As the winds blew, winged breakers fought with the sinews of the estuary. The tides drove to and fro.

On calm days, separated by the leaden mountains and the beaches of grey stones, the sea was blue and brown and the sky blue and white, with monumental clouds.

At dawn, the east pushed the sun up out of the ocean. Days were short, for the mountains swallowed the sun prematurely.

The coast beyond the estuary, the strand between material immovable height and liquid restless depth, lay in the silence of ceaseless sound.

One came to an area then, where an arm of rock struck out into the ocean across a desert of sand. The sand was black as coal dust. A debris of black shells had formed it; it glittered and contained small shards like razors. The occasional gull that alighted there made blood sacrifice.

Twice a day, the sea drew off from the promontory and the black beach, and twice returned to cover both. About sunrise, at this time of year, and in the aborted twilight, the black beach and the rock lay bare, and it was possible to gain, if any meant to, the building, for whose foundation it seemed God had fashioned the promontory.

The Christerium had the look of a beast lying on the rock with two paws tucked under it (the foregate), and the massive round tower with its domed skull, a raised head. The single eye, a sea-facing window of colossal size, glassless but ornately latticed, was blind by day, yellow by night, and reflected then far beneath in the water that swathed the rock.

The second birth, the rebirth as a man, commenced with pain: in the eyes, in all the body, especially at the left shoulder joint, the upper back. And pain had also a sound, a continuous and omnipresent crashing. It was the sea, but he did not know it.

Sight flooded in his eyes with light like knives.

He had it all, and knew it all. Like the sea, too, the past gushed over him, drowned him, and bore him rushing into the pit. Unbelievable, intrinsic, inescapable memory. He was Mechail Korhlen. He had lived, and died. He was the wolf in the wood, in the splintering ice. The ice-womb had cracked and out he came, howling, screaming louder than the torrent of the sea—

In a slender room dressed with five hanging swords, some shields painted with strange designs, owls, herons of silver and gold, suns, moons upon black and red, there the skinny priest dipped his neck like a drinking gull:

'Magister, we have been forced to bind him.'

'How?'

'As you suggested. With chains.'

The skinny priest looked up. He was of the Brotherhood of the Christerium, one of a colony of black ants.

The Magister stood before him, garbed now in clothing which the Christerium recognized.

'Does he cry out, still?' said Anjelen, with a pitiless gentleness. Behind him a glassed window set with westered panes of purple, orange, blue and cochineal, seemed to be a fire caused by his body.

'Less now, Magister. He looses his voice. For two days and the night, he roared.'

'Offer him water, as I instructed you.'

'It's offered. And the gruel and broth. He butts them away with his head, like an animal.'

'I will see you again at noon tomorrow.'

'Very well, Magister.'

The skinny priest went out. Anjelen moved from the window, and its picture was recreated: a tree of burning fruit about which a serpent twined, with the breasts of a woman and the head of a cat.

Anjelen was clad in white, a tunic embroidered with gilt, white breeches and boots. The lacquer crucifix lay on his breast, its ruby blinking, and on his left arm was a wristlet like a carapace of silver and steel, having in it a dagger. A longer blade, a sword, pointed from the belt of white leather, in a sheath crossed with black and scarlet and set with devices of gold, among which were visible stars, the head of a fox, a wheel.

The colours of the window dyed Anjelen's clothing and skin. He went under the swords and shields, entering another room, wider, with a beamed ceiling. There were chests and standing cupboards. Upon tables lay books, a map held by brass weights, the skull of a lion, the crystal globe. In one corner, a water-clock in the shape of a tower was lowering a gold moon into the evening. Another window, poisoned mauve and green, showed an angel riding upon a winged creature, partly wolf, but horned.

Anjelen darkened in the gloom of the chamber. He moved about it, lightly touching objects, until quite abruptly seating himself in a carved chair. Its familiar likeness had been in the Korhlen Tower, Nilya's possession.

The window dulled.

Anjelen spoke, and in the three lamps upon the tables the wicks caught fire. It was not magic, but science. A balance, like that of the clock, responsive to a quiver of particular and exact sound embodied in six words, shifted and struck tinder. It had taken some hours of his life to perfect the trick. There were many rituals, some of use, some of waste, which had their miniature places by the ultimate passion, upholding it, like the praises which burnished the glory of God.

After his voice gave out, his reabsorption into terrible sanity was a matter only of hours. He had known it instinctively, and so he screamed and shouted, blasphemed and raved, for as long as he was able. While he did this he was demented, sometimes even expelled from consciousness, or no more than partly aware.

But knowledge was relentless. His throat tore and blood came from his mouth. He fainted, and could, reviving, only whisper.

They had chained him to a wall in the cloudy cell he never looked at. The chains held his arms out sideways, not much raised, that he might continue to breathe. There was even a stool to sit on, when he was tired. If they found him senseless, they kindly propped him on it.

He had a great longing now for the water he had refused, and to lie flat and sleep. But when they intruded on him again, he writhed and lunged the length of the chains at them, his eyes starting and bloody spittle on his lips. He chased them off, like reality. But it all came back again, these servants, and his life.

He had prayed to die, and got this. *This.*

Eventually he noticed a blob of matter, like a frog, squatted across from him on a matching stool. The frog mewed. It was Krau's dwarf.

'Go away, you thing,' Mechail whispered to it.

At which the dwarf hopped down and puttered over, bringing a bowl of water. It craned and strove to reach Mechail's mouth, and in the end he took compassion on it, leaned down and drank.

It was an act of despair. Mechail had given up his pursuit of an oblivion which would not have him, either.

But the dwarf was gone. Mechail pondered instead a face circled by twisted silver. 'Look at me,' said the face, which was without features. 'Know me.'

The left shoulder . . . it burned and tore, but it was

mobile. The arm. The fingers of the left hand, in chains, flexed themselves.

This made him cry out again, or try to. But everything save his voice, was much stronger now; unconsciousness would not come to relieve him.

Finally he sat down on the stool, his numbed arms held out idiotically.

There were no windows in the room, but some source of light entered through a panel in the door. Gradually because he let it, this illumination pushed out the corners of the cell. Then, the door was opened.

He expected the dwarf, which had vanished, to re-enter possibly with jailors or slaves who would attempt to wash or massage his body, and he braced himself, now very wearily, to protest.

A man walked into the room. He wore white, yet he was darkness. Eyes, a crucifix – Mechail knew him, as he had known all persons he had seen consistently each day when he lived. The man's face was as customary to him as Mechail's own face in a mirror – more so, for he had not often looked upon himself. But none of this sprang from contact or familiarity. For Mechail had been *made* to know him.

'Are you calm now?' he asked. His voice was like an instrument, playing across sleep.

'No.'

'You would appear to be.'

'Give me time. I'll begin again.'

'Time is what you have,' said the musician.

Mechail flinched. He stood up again, pulling on the chains.

'There's no need then, I think, Mechail Korhlen, to explain your recent history over to you. You remember.'

'What I remember is impossible. Against the law of God.'

'Why should you suppose that? You must permit God to grasp His own law rather better than fallible man, who has perhaps misunderstood.'

'You argue like a priest,' said Mechail.

'Within my order, I am a priest.'

'And a magician.'

'An inaccurate term, employed by those unversed in the alchemic sciences.'

'Unchain me,' said Mechail. He put back his head, and in the gaunt unshaven face, the feline-lupine eyes stared on from out of the ice.

Anjelen went forward. He ripped open Mechail's travel-worn tunic and the foul shirt in one amalgamated and unhesitated wrench.

'Look at yourself,' he said. And Mechail resisted him, the bell of the voice tolling, the power. But the eyes pressed against him like night against the pane of ice. As if by a cruel claw his head was forced again downwards, his vision bent on his own body, his nakedness. There, like a coil of burned rope inset over his heart, the scar.

'That is you,' said the Angel of God. 'Look at it. Accept it, and what you are.'

'Undead.'

'Much more than that.'

'Possessed by some demon – I mocked your bloody God, and for this—'

'Be quiet,' said Anjelen. 'God is not mocked, though you may think you are capable of it.'

'And you are the Devil's,' said Mechail.

Anjelen had drawn away from him. 'I've scarcely begun on you,' he said. 'But the first lesson must, it would seem, be firm.'

Before Mechail's disturbed and swimming vision, the figure of the Magister, the teacher, seemed to draw in upon itself, becoming yet more thin, more elongate, hard as diamond and almost as clear. The black eyes were flat.

Something else began to be in the room.

A mass of filmy stuff, not unlike a ball of fog, yet oddly corporate, a fog smoked out by flesh. Circling together, it formed within itself a fretwork of skeleton, and sinews, that flushed suddenly to opacity and grassed itself over with hair. There was discernible an image, an animal of belly and sides and limbs, the muzzled head. Until through its skull there pierced the human eyes of a wolf, gleaming and wet with life. It solidified to being, and before it was quite completed, still edged with vapour as if from some monstrous cookpot, it advanced, lifting the long head through which a wall, a piece of doorframe slowly melted. Then it had been filled in. Was impenetrable, tactile.

Beyond this creature, the figure of Anjelen, a statue, the soul gone out of it. For demonstrably, the soul was now inside the eyes of the wolf. And from the very fabric of the soul, the wolf had been formed.

With this etheric thing Mechail had hunted in the forest of his madness, with this slumbered, and drunk blood. And it was this that led him, through phantasmagoria and illusion, under the hallucination of the ice – just as, in its other form, it called him forth again.

The wolf snarled, and reaching up effortlessly, seized Mechail's forearm, in the manacle, clamping closed its jaws. The wolf breath was hot, *living*, and the teeth dented into Mechail's skin. In that moment, Mechail dreamed they might tear him open, as the man's hand had ripped the shirt. In a sort of ecstasy he gave himself over to another's will, as once before. And the chains dropped both his arms at once, heavy as millstones, and his body, losing its balance, fell.

The wolf sprang and was on his back, macabrely playful as in the wood, its four paws planted on his spine, the weight of it pinning him prostrate.

Jasha had not entered the Christerium. She was a woman, and no woman might go in at the gates, the Magister had told her on the day of arrival. (This was the sole dialogue she had had with him since he spoke to her in the forest.) Having mounted a dangerous stair from the black beach, Jasha was left on the platform, under the wall by the foregate, in the company of two slaves from the ship. These men, who bore a chest between them, she then followed along the outer wall, which was fluted by huge buttresses, and sliced with raw light and shade from the sinking sun that the mountains were eating. Above the bastion, upper portions of the inner edifice sometimes arose, with here and there a leaded wound of window. On the further side of the Christerium the promontory of rock altered its shape, dropping and broadening out into a second, lower terrace. Here a path of smoothed blocks descended to a smaller building, also walled close, and having one narrow stooped gateway. This outer house was the Doma, the female adjunct to the fastness of the priesthood.

The slave men who bore the chest carried it along the path to the gate, which stood open, and there set the burden down. They turned instantly and went back up the rock.

Jasha stood on the path until a female voice summoned her abruptly from inside the Doma wall. 'Enter. Hurry. You're expected.'

In an after-glowed courtyard, figures were bearing off the chest Anjelen's porters had deposited. Another made tugging motions at Jasha. 'Come quickly now.'

Jasha did as she was bid, in her usual way, without meditating on it.

Presently she had gone with her guide – a spindly hooded robe, a childish voice – along a corridor and up some steps, and across a hall where a few thick candles were being lighted by slave women. At the summit of a sloping passage beyond, a wooden door was sounded by the spindly robe, for which purpose it produced a fist. No one made answer, but silence seemed an affirmative; the guide pushed wide the door and indicated Jasha should advance.

In the low-ceilinged room, a fat woman sat behind a table, above her lamp and books and counting-beads. She too was robed in dusty black, and hooded. But round her forehead passed a scarlet band, which glared more vividly than any other thing in the chamber, far brighter than her eyes.

'You're the woman Jasha, servant of the Magister Anjelen. Shut the door. Do you know where you are?'

155

'The Doma,' said Jasha.

'Yes, that's so. I am the Administress of the Doma. The house exists to serve the Christerium. Men don't enter the precinct, and only male slaves approach it. There are four classes of women in the Doma. The slaves of the house. The Sisterhood, whose duties are spiritual, the lesser echo of the Christerium. Our handmaids, who do such work as the Christerium allots the Doma, gardening and harvesting, the making and mending of clothes, such tasks as these. The fourth class of women are those who come to us unvirgin. They may not participate in service, and are granted shelter only in unusual circumstances. Since you belong to this class, you'll live apart. The sister outside the door will conduct you. In your lodging you need care only for yourself. The worship of God will be accessible to you. Cause no commotion, stay clean and tidy and behave modestly. You will bind up your hair. Commit no trespass, and think pure thoughts. Is there anything you want to ask of me?'

Jasha saw through the woman's mask of fat and eyes into a glaucous spirit that was now righteous and then afraid, and beat its body with a rod.

The fat face, as if it guessed the depth of the scrutiny, gave way and respread itself in haste across its bones.

'Are you unhinged, girl? What do you mean by staring like that? You're the servant of the Magister, or I'd never permit you in the Doma.' Jasha waited, regarding the Administress under her lids. The Administress said, 'You can't gain by your master's rank, here. Here you're nothing. Now go with the sister.'

Beyond the wall that girded the lodging, came and went the blue sea-days of earliest winter. The other side of the stone yard, another wall shut off the Doma, although sometimes its sedentary noises were to be heard, the bell of its chapel, and the murmur of its creatures – but frequently the ocean, infinitely more vital, cancelled them. Above the Doma, and visible on the wall-top, were the remote hulks of the mountains.

There were two other unvirgins, besides Jasha. They were an elderly pair, who emerged from their cells at daybreak like mechanical crickets, to sit in the sun, and retired again when the sun had gone over. When one of the slaves of the Doma brought food, at noon, and some hours after sunset, the two crones would eat it uneasily, with their few brittle teeth. Sometimes they argued together, or attempted a game of counters on a board of yellowed squares. Now and then they went to the chapel, at the permitted times when the chaste women of the Doma vacated it. Jasha they viewed with slight interest. They did not speak to her.

Jasha turned a patch of soil by her cell door where a stone had come up, and inserted there pips and seeds from the vegetables and fruits meagrely included in her food. Taking water from a well just the far side of the yard partition (to which the unvirgins were allowed access), she cleaned her cell and the yard, and swept up with a broom garnered from a slave.

Gulls paraded along the outer wall, paying her more attention than the two crones. There was no shortage of salt fish to eat.

Jasha watched the sea. Like the forest, it moved and sounded continually, and was filled by mostly invisible entities.

On the thirteenth day of her sojourn, she went searching for strands, cloth or cord, to tie up the sproutings of her impromptu garden patch. There were some empty cells further along the wall, with their backs to the sea, and in one of these, having unstuck its warped door, she found the Magister's chest.

She recognized it infallibly, for she had seen it on the journey, and on the ship. The slave men had borne it to the Doma, and the hooded sisters borne it away. Now it lay there, behind only a warped door.

It would have some purpose, being here. To Jasha, so much was obvious. She was not surprised, or curious, except that she had a sense she was meant to come on the chest.

157

As if the Magister had been in the cell, a tiny room costive with dust, cobwebs, salt, Jasha listened, and seemed to perceive an instruction. And as if she had done so, she proceeded to the chest and put her hand against the lid, which was secured by a metal lock. It might be possible to break this, using the table knife or fork left in her own cell.

Jasha began to feel something that was like a buzzing, emanating from inside the chest. There was neither sound or movement; it was a supernatural vibration. In her forest, Jasha had often come across these signals. She left them alone, or not, depending on accompanying sensations; but frequently they portended, anyway, nothing that was apparent to her, leftovers of some earlier force that had departed, leaving merely the psychic imprint of where it had lain.

What was in the chest was sombre, perhaps risky. And yet, it took a grip on her. It was like a noise of tapping in her ear.

Jasha moved away. She had seen that a crimson thread encircled the chest, passing over the lock. Its presence indicated that the lock was now undone, the thread alone a proof that no one had tampered. Such a thread would be helpful, what she had indeed been looking for.

Jasha went from the cell. In the yard one of the crones was carrying water, and looked slantwise at her, as though Jasha was a ghost.

For a week he was a baby, and must learn everything over, how to feed himself, and walk, how to utter prolonged speech even, for the muscles of his throat were damaged.

But he was strong in his weakness, and he had been accustomed to pain and to labouring in spite of it. And the pain lessened as each ability was regained, until only the old curse of the crippled shoulder stayed to be his torturer. And with that, finding how it would *obey* him, the hand grasping and holding, the arm tensing to support and direct, and the fingers making of themselves fences, utensils, a cup – he toiled through the hurt relentlessly. Since he must go on with himself, he would prefer a body that was whole. Each fresh trick the arm accomplished filled him with triumph. And then with a sort of bitterness. He mused upon resurrection sanely, frigidly, and in silence. He probed, without alternative, deeper and more deeply into the well of darkness.

Anjelen, whose name he had somehow learned, maybe only mundanely, overhearing it, Anjelen did not return. (Somewhere, in the limbo of belief, the wolf's paws had gone off Mechail's back. It, and its maker, went away.)

But those moments, never dreamed of, *real*, they too were of the dark well.

Two or three slaves still brought food, oils for the massaging of his body. Krau's dwarf fantastically presided at these scenes, as if it had been made his personal attendant. Why dispute that?

Mechail disputed nothing.

From a high embrasured window by the bone-hard bed, he saw rock, stones, shoreline and water. The quantity and energy of the water persuaded him it was the ocean. The walls of the edifice which contained him, constructed of grey stone, sloped to the sea. When the waves withdrew, there was only rock and a waste like soot.

He woke at sunrise, generally, the enormous gulp of sky flaring, the sea racing out of the jaws of the sun.

Acres of sea where there had been miles of forest. This tower for the other.

That man had brought him to it, the voice which had claimed him.

Mechail asked nothing of the slaves, demanded no interview, or to go out of his room. His habit had once been a dreadful self-sufficiency. This had become stronger, with the rest of him. The discipline of loss.

Often his back and shoulder split in small tears, or round punctures would appear and bleed. Sometimes fragments of bone wormed through. He would discover them on the sheet after sleeping, or sticking from his skin like the quills of a porcupine. Having no mirror, his right hand alone could inform him that the hump upon his back was reduced. Of course – he had healed of death, why not of something so ordinary?

In sleep, and he slept a great amount, every incident of his life seemed meticulously re-enacted, making sure it was learned by heart. He even dreamed of the tree where they had thrust him, and of the hammering of the sword into his heart.

A storm came from the sea and swept over the wall. Squeaking like frightened stoats, the crones immured themselves in their cells. Jasha observed the storm through the cracks of the shuttered cell window. She had swept and cleaned the yard to no avail. And now sea water sluiced under her door. Outside, the seedlings would be destroyed. She climbed on the wooden shelf provided for the mattress, and sat brushing her hair with the brush Livdis had bought her in the city. She had understood all along that Anjelen had murdered Livdis; she had sensed the murder approaching like quiet thunder. (She had unbound her hair for Livdis, so it reached the floor, and he had sought her nakedness through it.)

When the storm ended, the water mostly sank away. Jasha took her broom and swept the puddled debris of the ocean along the yard. Reaching the significant cell, she pushed at its reluctant door, to see what had happened to the chest bound with crimson thread.

The chest still stood on the floor, reflected now in a scoop of sea around its base, the dark box of it, the solitary red line. Then Jasha saw that the rough action of the water, or of some sharp thing contained in it, had sliced the thread in two.

Jasha put both hands on the lid. It was unlocked, and moved upward easily, as if recently oiled. An old dried ugly smell seeped up and filled the cell. The chest was packed with bones, misplaced and broken, lying in a heap the tinge of dead leaves, upon a scatter of rags. A black spider had spun there her complicated web, and now hung starved and mummified in it. The skull lay sideways, as if sleeping.

Carg Vrost's daughter lowered the lid of the chest, stuck back the severed thread, and walked from the cell. She spat at the doorway, as the women of the woods village had done, after laying out a corpse. But it was a ritual gesture, meaning nothing.

One morning, after the rising sun had woven its strip of woollen mosaic in the carpet across the floor, the door was opened, and a man entered. He wore a priest's robe, not in the manner of Beljunion, but black and belted with cord, a face scoured of dirt and hair.

'I'll wait outside while you dress yourself in the clothing there. Then we'll go to breakfast.'

'I breakfast here,' said Mechail. 'And what are you?'

'Today you'll eat in the Common Hall. I am a godbrother of the Christerium.'

'And what am I?'

But the priest only answered, 'Here, you're Brother Mechail.'

'And who told you my name, and how you're to call me by it, like a priest – by which you insult me – and where I'm to breakfast today in those – clothes?'

'The Magister Anjelen.'

Mechail picked up the garment which had been delivered while he slept. It resembled that of the godbrother who stood before him.

Until now, the clothes left for him had been makeshift – breeches, shirts, underlinen like those of a well-to-do peasant. Or a servant in a little town. (There had been a journey through towns, wide country, a city, and over water – he recalled none of it, and yet, he did. Maybe his very flesh knew it, having been travelled with such a distance. And somewhere, there had been a woman's hands on him . . . But that would have been the laying-out, would it not. Before the chapel, and the resurrection.)

'Get out then. Let me put on this slave's sack.'

'The robe of the Brotherhood.'

161

'Slaves of God.'

'You are correct,' said the scour-faced man.

Mechail pulled on the robe. The belt was of black hempen cord. It must be his difference should be hidden here. It must be that *here* was a religious house. Somehow that had not occurred to him before. Where had he thought himself? *The Christerium.*

The godbrother led him soon enough, and wordlessly, through corridors, down stairs of granite, between walls whose bleakness was mossed over with tapestries, or plastered and figured with the patterns and shapes of men. There were saints with haloes of ancient brown gold-leaf, raising hands of blessing and obfuscation, under trees of fruit, palaces that burned. They were unmistakable evidence of the nature of the place, but Mechail paid them no courtesy and barely a glance. He had been a rustic prince, and the things of God angered him then, and more so now.

The Common Hall was an appropriate cavity in the building, barred with rows of long tables and benches. A kitchen adjoined, whose smoke swilled into the sky above a court they had crossed, coming in. It was a blue day, decorated sometimes with gulls.

The breakfast was of the type they had already been bringing him, a porridge with fish, and swarthy bread, a cup of water.

Several sorts of men soon crammed the refectory, some in the black robes of priests, others dressed for labour. There was no consorting. The priestly faction sat at the inner end of the Hall where there was a fireplace lighted. There were sufficient in numbers that Mechail was not amazed to go unstudied. Perhaps as a hunchback he might have gained attention, but the deformity was hardly to be seen now – the robe had made no concession to it.

No conversation; nothing of value on the tables: pottery, wood, tin.

Mechail pushed back his bowl and cup.

'What next?' he said to the godbrother who had brought him in.

The man said quietly, 'The Ceremony of the Bread.'

'More bread? Better than this?'

'The bread of God.'

A bell started sounding.

This is justice. To hate God and his men, and end here.

Anjelen entered Mechail's bruised mind, a warrior more than a priest, or a wolf, leaping—

The artisans at the tables were getting up and passing into the court and away somewhere, and in their turn the priests got up, Mechail's escort with them.

Left at the table, with only the tin and pottery to keep him company, Mechail might follow, or not.

He could feel a new quill working its irritant route upward to evacuate the skin. The air was harsh with winter brine, unlike other air he had known. He must follow.

The crowd of men was moving on under some arches, through a corridor of upper storeys, over a cloister whose stout pillars were bound with wintry vines. In the cloister garden nothing grew but a mat of ice-green grass. There were no trees, no softening thing. In angles of the walls, leering beasts of stone craned out, a bull with a fish caught in its jaws, a serpent crowned with a princely tiara, and there a man's head upon which a bat perched, gnawing at his hair.

Abruptly, Mechail found he was in a paved yard, where the church of this place, a rounded mass, went up like a column. Two windows stabbed it high above, heavy with obscure stained glass. The doorway was chiselled, toothed, embroidered, and beyond, in darkness, the incense smelled to high heaven.

The slow boiling wave of men flowed into the church tower. Mechail followed to the door, and there his guide had after all anticipated him, and waited.

In the church was a gloom rained through by the sequins of the glass. 'Come, this way.' The godbrother led him now into climbing a stair, up into a gallery. A strange human head of stone poked from the wall. Its beard grew into a hand that fingered Mechail's sleeve as he went by. He rounded on it, but gave it up. The gallery was carved all over by plants and flowers of stone.

They halted. There was a press of bodies. But just below, drawing the eye against its wish, was the great, glamouring altar, draped in black velvet fringed with gold and scarlet, and on the altar a huge crucifix, a terrible magnificence of pure gold, blinding with cut sapphire and emerald, and with a white Christus of alabaster with bloodstone wounds at palms and foot, and in the side. On the forehead of the Christus, the crown of thorns had flowered with roses of ruby. The gallery hung level in the air with this crucifix, which seemed to float, coming slowly nearer. The impaling nails were studded with diamond.

Mechail turned dizzily. There were the windows instead, of saffron and garnet and chrysoprase, each showing the battle in Paradise, the Christus in victory upon his charger, the fiery sword, the thunder-plumes, the trampling of the damned, and the Devil in his pit like a pulsing coal. But forward above the altar, a disembodied window shone that was paned with sky, pale singing blue, across which a white cloud bannered.

Between this window and the altar, a stairway came down out of the wall. Nine men stood on it. Like the heavenly army of the Christus in the glassed windows, they were dressed for war. Their mail caught the colour of the sky, the stained fires of the heavenly battle; they were men of metal dipped in a river of jewels. From their helmed heads, where vizors were lowered to mask eyes, colour-ringed white horse-tails fell. The rainbow of white cloaks had no device. Mail-gloved hands rested, each pair, on a sword. The spiral of their bodies ended directly over the crucifix, over the agonized head and peaceful eyes of God-in-man, the wreath of blood-red roses.

Mechail looked at the warrior-priests of the Christerium anchored in space above him. Something crawled in his belly, unnamed, not aversion. There was a tingling of the flesh, and an emotion strong as fury. For the warrior who stood the nearest to the altar of the Christus, half-masked though he might be, was Anjelen.

164

There had begun to be singing, a choir of young men in the dove-blue of the seaward window. A youth swung out a golden censer, a spicery of smoke. There stalked, through the parted crowd below, a man swagged in the splendour of a king. His black robe had been redrawn in silver, across his shoulders a white and scarlet shawl; his torso was covered by a breast-plate of gold, and on his head was a golden diadem armoured, like his hands, with gems.

'The Primentor,' said the guiding brother beside Mechail. But even in the tangle of the forest they heard of these beings.

The Primentor, a king of the Church Paternal, strode to the altar and dropped to one knee, in a blaze of lights, to salute it. The cymbals of his gold sounded, even over the singing, which next ceased. Turning, the Primentor raised his arms, a great staff he carried of gold catching fires like the warriors behind him.

'Exalted and glorified is the name of God, Lord of all and Maker of all, Who cleaves darkness from light. Our mouths are full of the praise of Him, as the sea is full of its waters.'

And after the loud ringing voice of the Primentor, the men in the Christerium tower intoned their answering prayer, every man, a hubbub of resonance in which all words were lost. But all the men in the Christerium moaned on and on, their praises like the sea. Every man, but Mechail Korhlen. And one other?

Anjelen, where are you, in this?

The Primentor stood under the altar, until the crazed howl of voices was sucked back into the stone. And then he cried out: 'Our son, Anjelen, Knight of God.'

And Anjelen, called up as if by a prayer, came off the stairway, down to the altar. And the Primentor turned, and embraced him, as a man in a dream embraces lightning.

And Anjelen spoke. He said, his voice carrying without stress, 'By God's grace.'

God's Knight. And magician. My devil.

Mechail stared down at Anjelen, masked and mailed, white as any winter snow. *Mine?*

The Primentor had stepped aside. He was a beautiful doll, redundant now. It was Anjelen who stood by the altar. His voice filled the atmosphere, as the smoke of the censer had done. Not a word failed. The voice played like a melody.

'It happened that, by the shore, they had no bread to eat. Then bread was brought the Christus in a pannier, a single loaf. How was it to be He might feed a multitude from this single loaf.' The voice sang from Anjelen as if from a statue, his lips seemed not to move. In this way, the wolf had come from him.

A priest bowed before Anjelen, holding up a basket. There was one loaf in it.

Anjelen did not accept the loaf in his hands that held a sword. He said, 'With God, everything is possible.'

And then Mechail saw the loaf in the basket split and become two loaves, and these also split and doubled themselves. Suddenly the basket was exploding with bread. It rioted ludicrously over the altar steps, cascading among the men who crowded below.

'He's a sorcerer,' said Mechail, aloud. No one reproved him.

But behind the vizor, the black eyes of Anjelen seemed to see Mechail.

Men were stooping and picking up the bread, passing the loaves amongst themselves, sniffing and pressing their lips to them. And they were kneeling, line by line. They knelt to Anjelen.

Bread continued to rush from the basket.

Then Anjelen had gone back from the altar. He stood by the lowest stair, and the crucified Christus crowned in roses hid him.

With a biting pain, the quill pricked from Mechail's healing shoulder, making him shiver. He put his hand there and felt the quill through the cloth of his priest's garment. He ripped it free. He said to the guiding, guarding priest, who ignored or no longer noticed him, 'I don't like your God, or these tricks.'

When he had got down into the belly of the church, men were reverencing the bread, pawing and kissing, making love to it.

Mechail must thrust his way through the mob. As he did so, one of the loaves was put into his hands. He took it, and bore it outside. He crossed the paved yard and went into the cloister, the green grass and bare vines.

He examined the bread. It had the appearance and smell of baking, but he could not bring himself to put any in his mouth. Would it taste of the Body? The Host . . .?

He could not recall the way back to his room – but he was at liberty.

From the church tower came the droning of prayer. They had reverenced Anjelen, like a god.

Mechail cast the loaf across the grass. At the impact, it broke into two pieces. It looked like two stones, lying there.

Chapter Ten

Dusk (a sapphire borrowed from a Primentor's diadem), and he had travelled a day through the Christerium, unchallenged, guideless, going where he would, as if there was on him some cryptic, esoteric mark by which all might know him. The complex building was a small town, or city. It had its basements, terraces, pinnacles, its cisterns and roads. For the third of one hour after their Ceremony of the Bread, a close quiet had stayed it, deserted, noiseless but for the sea. But then a slow flush of activity coursed back. There were men repairing walls, the wheezes of a forge, the smell of kitchens, a loud debate in rooms where novices learned.

Everywhere, the priests glided, like movements in a mechanism.

He was tempted to question them about the things he came on and saw: Why are there yards where men wrestle or spar with staves? Is this religious? Or: What lies behind these locked doors? Are there secrets allowed?

Where he did ask (mundane questions), he was answered courteously. Thus he discovered two further refectories, the Halls Novitiate and Ordinate. At the latter he ate about midday, off a plate of pewter. There were paintings of suffering martyrdom on the walls to spoil the food, which was only salt fish and bread, augmented by salads, soft fruits, a thin mixture of wine and honey.

He beheld a long library in the Christerium's south side, where old priests bent over tomes and parchments like figments of a picture of a library. There was a bell tower. One great brazen bell, three lesser bells of iron. There were avenues between walls of stone that ended in stone, and steps up to the roofs. The sea was visible there, the sky, and further aloft, weather vanes, turrets, drainage-channels, and windows which, as the day waned, lit into topaz, violet, the ubiquitous rich burning red of priestly power. In the dusk too, from the heights, he saw the Doma, the women's house, light itself, but did not know – did not care about – its nature.

In the twilight the gargoyles, which lurked in every cranny, peering, growling, amused, distressed, thrummed with sympathetic awareness and potential sentience. They might surely now detach themselves, winged heads flying off over the taller roofs, snakes, that held ringed and severed hands in their jaws, hurrying along the shadow alleys. A mossy stone frog by a well jumped suddenly away. It must have come to life.

Anjelen. Mechail had thought of him constantly as he roved the labyrinth. Anjelen was the Christerium, yet dissociated from it. Knight of God. Wolf, Angel, priest, sorcerer. And *known*. Known as had been no other.

Mechail sat on the well's edge. The sky was a Primentor's amethyst now, and in the well was a jet. The black well where all matters might be consigned?

'Mechail Korhlen,' said a mild voice nearby, 'your servant's here, seeking you.'

Mechail looked up – as he had thought, they all knew him – and beyond the shade of the priest, he saw another, larger, frog. The dwarf.

'That isn't mine.'

But the faceless shade was pacing off, and the dwarf sidled closer.

'Stay where you are,' said Mechail. 'I'll sling you clean across the yard. You understand? *He'll* have knocked you about; Krau. Did they tell you I killed him?' The well of jet was duplicated in the dwarf's eyes. A gargoyle . . . 'What do you want?'

The dwarf trotted closer still. He put out one crabbed hand, as if to pluck something from the air.

Mechail said, 'You serve Anjelen now. The wolf, not the raven. Get away from me.'

The dwarf made his mewing sound.

The sea was audible, returning to the promontory with long sighs. One of the iron bells began to toll, the nightly summons to prayer.

After a minute, the dwarf turned and went from him, vanishing into the dark between two walls.

The night did not seem cold; there was no wind. Stars shone, the unseen corpse of the Christus fastened to heaven by diamond nails.

Mechail leant his head on the wall behind the well. He saw his mother, inside his head, vividly, her frail face and thinning, greying hair. She held an apple and a silver knife. She cut into the apple. It bled. He watched the blood as it flamed down over her wrists. Her hands were like chalices of crystal. A snake in a crown wound her like a tree.

There was an icy thirst in his throat, a yearning for wine. He cursed God, Who had abducted his mother. And the old priest Beljunion ran from the library and thrashed him with a book—

The well had upturned in the sky and made it black. A sea-crawled silence lay deep as the drift of darkness. Not a window glimmered. Was it so late?

Then something moved, down among the lower walls and courtyards, the long flight that had brought him here. A tendril of sea fog . . . it wove from corner to corner, ascending, twitching itself about the dragon-like gargoyle at the stair's foot – and where it entwined, the fog remained, caught like a vine.

Mechail got up. He stood while the snake-tail of fog pleated itself up the stair towards him. It unrolled to his feet, coiled them like a runnel of milk, and flowed on. Mechail kicked the fog aside. It came undone.

He went down the stair, through the circles and eddies of fog, breaking them with his hands.

There was no moon, solely stars in the enormous height,

the building of the night bigger than the Christerium. At the bottom of the stair a priest was standing motionless, one arm lifted and the hand outspread. His eyes were open and mirrored the starlight, his lips were slightly parted, taking a breath to climb the stair. Now, he did not breathe.

Mechail went by, and past the dragon in its curl of fog.

In the areas he walked through, the fog hung in garlands. The mechanism of men, that had moved so assiduously through the day, had been stopped. They slept upon their feet, their frames canted in everyday positions now become, through immobility, uncanny and dismaying, arms at angles, one foot off the ground, a head craned foolishly or mouth stretched in dumb talk. They had been snared in the open as sorcery overtook them. On some of the faces was a look of surprise, stasis had been too swift for fear.

At the door of the Ordinate Hall, they had been going out from their meal. Not a candle stayed alight through the length of the room behind them. Here and there a cup had fallen from stiffening fingers. The men in the doorway were packed together as if they had come to see some sight – which then turned them to rock.

In a passageway a novice ran, his long holy skirt upheld. His body pitched forward, he poised only on the ball of the left foot – but did not topple.

Mechail realized he had remembered the path to the church tower of the Christerium. Or, something led him there, some final invisible guide. He did not resist. A sort of hunger pulled him on.

The church tower stood higher than any height of the Christerium, coming between the earth and the stars. In its ruffle of embroidered stone, the door was shut.

But when Mechail reached the door, it gave at an ordinary pressure. Of course, only a man the spell had missed could enter.

The church seemed in darkness. Then a quiver of

tenebrous light bloomed out, like a lamp beneath a river. A floor of polished tiles ran towards the altar.

Its vertical shape was draped now in the white of snow, and on the white, a thorn crown was worked in black and gold, from which dripped several colossal rubies, smouldering. Above, the crucifix, the head of its Christus lost in shadow. But the diamond nail in the feet glittered.

Under the altar were the white Knights of God, ranked four by four like columns, and as motionless, yet breathing and awake. The swords were sheathed, and the helms set aside. Eight male faces, dark-capped with hair, eight brothers in stillness, and the veiled candles beading in a brotherhood of eyes.

Against the altar stood Anjelen, their focus.

The Angel.

And the hand of the Angel beckoned, and at the gesture, chords struck in the stones, the air, the floor itself seemed to tremble, projecting themselves towards him. Mechail also took a step. But another was first. From somewhere in the recesses of gloom exiled by light, a young man had risen. He moved towards the altar as the tiles and stones had tried to do. A youthful priest or novice, naked but for a linen loincloth, a coronet of ivy on his head.

Mechail watched him enter the web of the candles, and approach Anjelen by passing between the pillared Knights. The boy kneeled to Anjelen. Mechail could not see the boy's face.

Anjelen spoke, in that voice, recalled from infinity, like music, like silence.

'They hung Him on a tree. He was perfect. For the sins of the world He suffered and He died. He said, Do this in my name.'

The boy had put back his head to look at Anjelen. Anjelen leaned to him a little. From a wristlet on his left arm, Anjelen withdrew a knife. He put his left hand behind the boy's head, tenderly, as if with a child, a son. And then, with one stroke, partly invisible, he slit the young man's throat. Blood jetted out, so red it seemed alive; the head lolled over upon the supporting hand. Now Mechail beheld the face of the boy, not yet dead, unafraid, and the eyes not closed, serene.

'Drink,' said the Priest Magister, the Knight of God, 'for here is the wine of the Immolation. Did He not say to them, *This is my blood.*'

The nearest of the Knights moved. There was a chalice of silver. He held it and caught the spurting blood.

Then he served his seven brethren, lifting the cup, which each man accepted. Each man drank from the silver brim, and gave back the cup. When the seven had drunk, the eighth man drank.

And then Anjelen, who all this time had supported the calm-eyed, bleeding head, drew the boy up the length of him, raised his body like the chalice, and drank from the brim of the severed throat.

Darkness smothered the lights like a wing.

Mechail stood in blindness, and felt eight drawn swords of steel hedging him, a circlet of thorns. But Anjelen was there too, free of the dying boy whose blood he had supped. Anjelen was no part of anything, but like the moon which pulls the tides.

'What is it, Mechail Korhlen, crack-shoulder, Land-holder's get, what is it you want?'

Blood. It was blood. The red living blaze of it, the fire—

His *thirst*.

Mechail lunged forward, and the crossed swords warded him off. In the blackness Anjelen moved like a black planet.

'Not for you, this. Not for you, sulking howler in chains, denier of self. Did you die in the forest? Do you live now?'

His thirst – and yet, this blasphemy – even against the God he had reviled and hated. *No*. But the fire, the burning, the white wrist and the cut apple and the silver chalice of the throat— And the wet rose on the thorn—

Mechail thrust at the swords; they flew up and away.

The great door was ajar; beyond, a lesser blackness, reminding him of something, once—

Dreaming or waking. In the paved yard, against the threadbare curtain of the night, Anjelen sat upon a black horse, which walked across the yard, into the cloister, leisurely. Mechail heard the hooves striking the stones, the only sound above the sea.

There was another horse in the lea of the tower. A chestnut mare. Mechail had toiled to bring his muscles to their strength again. Hitching the skirt of his priestly robe clear of boots and breeches, he mounted without awkwardness. He had never indeed mounted a horse with such ease, his whole back agile and of use to him.

Now he must follow the Magister. The drinker of blood.

They had shared blood before, in the forest. The blood of beasts which did not satisfy.

Not for you—

It was his sister, in the alley by the peach trees, feeding him from her wrist, after he slew Krau. Puss – or Chi; did he even know which? And in the death trance, her child's blood had sent him down again to existence. His mother, Nilya, had brought him that albino child, to drink from. Had any of it been real, any of it a dream?

He did not call after Anjelen, only rode behind him, through the Christerium, which, in the pre-dawn nothingness, was simple of access and egress. Here the high wall, the small gate, open, and outside were rocks, and the ocean, and the second wall of mountains, all just barely visible, unnatural, as if created and unfinished. Out to sea the sky was a cavern. The dawn star came up entire on the waves, the diamond from the feet of the Christus.

Anjelen rode along the rock, in the direction of the mountains.

If he is a demon, if I am – the sun must destroy us.

But they had walked under the sun many times, he and Anjelen.

In the outer building (the women's house), there were

a few lamps alight. Had the sorcery not affected that place?

A breeze slaked the rock. The black sand lay below as if the heart of Anjelen's secret evil order had poisoned it.

And Mechail followed Anjelen while the sea began instead to run away.

Tongueless and toothless, the beggar woman sang in Jasha's sleep, a beautiful melody that faded as Jasha raised her lids.

It was sunrise. The wretched cell was scraped with sunlight.

Jasha got up and put on her second green dress, and unbraiding her hair, combed it with the comb Livdis had given her, before braiding it again. Despite the instruction of the fat Administress, Jasha did not bind up her hair in the Doma.

By the door, in the patch of earth ruined by salt water, none of the new pips had put out a sprout.

Along the wall, the cell with the chest of bones hung flat on the lit sky.

Jasha went to the cell and pushed the door, to see.

Things had changed, which did not astonish her. The current in this room was now charged and potent. As for the bones, they lay along the floor in proper arrangement, everything positioned as it should be, even to the head, hands and feet. On the left hand, on the forefinger, a ring of twisted silver had been placed. (In the woods women had sometimes tied bones in the trees.)

Jasha went out again and closed the door.

One of the crones came staggering into the yard with her pitcher.

Jasha said, also to see, 'Shall I help you?'

The crone cried out, 'No – no—' and crossed herself, almost dropping the jar.

The second crone was watching from her door slit; Jasha felt her eyes. The second crone had already informed the other old woman that Jasha was a witch. Some of the priests of the inner orders, who came and went at the Christerium, kept girls, either to use them carnally or in unholy rites. The sacredness of the fane provided a flawless counterpoise and camouflage for corruption. Such ideas were never frankly spoken of, yet the working women, especially, held off and overlooked by the religious community, vigorously believed in them, and spread their spores. The higher the station of a priest, the more certain he had other inclinations, to lechery, to devilry, at best to alchemy.

The crone unvirgin had once been a buxom whore at an inland village. She had heard of the Christerium, to which the villages round about paid tithe, as to their landholder. She had never thought to end at the Doma. But in her age, a bastard son, supposing this would be nice for her, or for him, packed her off here with a gift of money to the sisterhood – he was a robber.

Jasha the crone detested. For Jasha was what she had once been (young), but more successfully.

The crone muttered, addressing herself by name. She had paused, to allow a legitimate amount of time. Now she would totter to the Administress with her tale.

Solid stone, the slopes of the mountains. In spots they had ground down to boulders, and these ground down to the pebbles of the beaches, so to sand. Seaweeds and winter moss patched them, and lichens where the sun came. Gulls nested there in colonies, screaming when the two riders passed below.

The sun beat heatlessly on the stone, the men. It was a white day. A wind blew higher up, tossing the sere false grass in the clefts and strewing out the clouds.

The forward rider went by a straying path, moving behind outcroppings and leaning thunder-heads of rock. Yet, like clockwork creatures, they both maintained their pace, their division from each other.

About two hours after dawn, Mechail glanced back and saw the Christerium beneath on the promontory, forepaws tucked in and head lifted at the sea. When he looked ahead again, Anjelen had disappeared once more. Turning up the path, Mechail beheld a chapel wedged into the cliff. A hermitage, some retreat. There were no windows, and the doorway lacked a door. The black horse had been tethered to a ring in the stone wall. Mechail rode up, dismounted, and tied the mare to the same ring.

The sun fell in a crescent within the door, and gave itself up. The rest of the interior was void.

After the speechless night, Mechail addressed black day.

'Sorcerer, are you here?'

No voice returned the challenge, but there came a flaring hiss and a candle ignited in the darkness' heart. It was a yellow stem with one russet bud. Then something disturbed the light of it, a pulse of black went over and over, was gone, and went over again.

About the candle, some bird or huge insect was flying. Mechail glimpsed it – the wings were soundless, and through their tissue the flame faltered.

Two futile actions of the hand – half reaching for the sword or knife a landholder's heir would customarily carry – and, less appropriately, half marking his heart with the cross.

It was a moth. He saw it now because now it clung upon the wall above the candle, over the stone slab which provided an altar. A black moth with wings outspread and two points like sparks on the pins of its antennae.

Then, the voice came after all from the darkness.

'Do you remember at last?'

And memory was like an ocean, crashing on the beach of his mind, but he could make nothing of it but breakers, foam, a myriad tumble of smashed thoughts.

'The beginning,' said the voice of Anjelen. 'The drinking, and the vice which held you. The mirage of the long hunt, the insect and the moon. The soldiers led away through the wood.'

As if from far off, Mechail felt a falling, the merciless blow. Agony lanced his left shoulder, his spine, and in his hand a claw dug slowly through the bones. But he did not cry out, for in his mouth was the taste of rubies beyond price.

On the wall above the light the moth expanded and altered. It became a man upon an unseen crucifix, the legs and torso stretched, the head thrown back, the arms outflung. And in its breast a single nail of scarlet fire. And then Anjelen stood there, on the altar, a mailed warrior, a sword at his side, and on his breast a cross of black lacquer with an eye of a scarlet jewel. He lowered his arms, the pale hands. On the pale face the depthless opacity at least of three hundred years inside a mask of skin.

'Do you understand what you have seen?'

Mechail said, 'No.'

'But you believe that you have died, and live.'

'Yes. I must.'

'And the mode of your life, what is that?'

'Some demon.'

'A night-thing, a vampire which craves human blood?' asked Anjelen softly. And behind him stirred the great wings of power. 'Forget the superstitions of Korhlen Tower. Think of what was shown you in the church below.'

'I dreamed it,' said Mechail. 'And maybe this, too.'

'Dream and reality. In the world of life, the barrier is slight, between them. What the ignorant term magic is only the science of true things. Come here, Mechail.'

Mechail walked forward, as the young priest had done in his crown of ivy and his nakedness. He had not feared, nor did Mechail.

'What of your father?' said Anjelen, when Mechail stood before him, under the altar.

Mechail lifted his shoulders, the whole and the healed. The pain was gone. He was only thirsty, ached to drink, and even the red candle-flame that burned at Anjelen's feet was like a hint of wine, and the red jewel on his breast.

'The seed of a Vre in a forest Tower, that made you,'

said Anjelen. 'Here's the riddle then. You are also my son.'

Anjelen was no longer on the altar, he had sprung down. The jewel in the crucifix welled over. Liquor played along the gem, from the small wound in Anjelen's throat.

'This is my blood. For I will make you into what you are. You're mine. You will be myself. As, in her way, she was, your mother. Take my blood. And after, you will drink in remembrance of me.'

And as gently as he had cradled the skull of the dying priest, Anjelen drew Mechail's head down until the fire burnt his lips.

There was the faltering image of the wrist of a girl, the scent of peach trees. And then the crimson rose flowered in his brain. Flowered and burst, and its petals fell in drops of flame, fluttering through his body.

As the breast of a woman had given him the white milk, the vein of the man gave him the red rose of life. The rose of blood.

He drank until his body was filled by fire, until he was no longer human, a being of light, until the sun blazed in him. His flesh seemed clear as glass. He felt the soul that was in him. The soul was what he was, and the flesh adjunctive, malleable. There was nothing of himself he might not command, and little of the world.

And then the fire softly died, and the rose folded itself and slept.

Mechail strained wide his eyes. He lay on a rock under the noon sun. The chestnut mare cropped lichen nearby. No chapel. No companion. Only the Christerium below, and scintillant sea that came and went.

Dreaming or waking.

Chapter Eleven

With the scorching sting of seven wasps, the rod smote the fat woman's thigh. The seven thorns with which the rod was equipped drew immediate blood, snagged and tore the flesh. The Administress bit her lips, and straightened her arm, and her psyche, for the second blow.

The door was rapped on.

The Administress knew a human relief, a shadowy emotional disappointment.

'You will wait.' She spoke firmly. Her hands wavered as she dressed herself again in her robe, knotted the girdle, and laid the rod in a wooden box. 'Enter now.'

One of the novice sisters opened the door, came through, and stood with head bowed as if in shame, the posture of humbleness expected of her.

'Lady, one of the old women from the unchaste women's court has come here. She wants to see you and won't go away.'

A strange galvanic tingled through the body of the Administress, about the island of her painful wound.

'Send her in to me.'

The novice went out, to be replaced a minute after by the elder of the two crones. She had been a harlot once; no trace was left. She was like any peasant hag of the villages, only a little better fed, uncouth, dirty, partly senile.

The crone expressed her gratitude at being received. In the peasant way, she referred to the Administress, thirty years the younger, as *Mother*. The Administress found this irritant, along with the cringing, fawning subservience of the old woman. The Administress preferred the slave-like subservience of her sisterhood, that never attempted to placate or win favour, flatteringly knowing such were impossible.

'Very well. You're here. On what matter do you wish to see me?'

'It's the witch,' said the crone. 'The young one in the court. She does bad things.'

'What are you talking about?' said the Administress. She felt a pang of unquiet.

The crone said, 'The witch girl who lives in the court.'

'Do you mean the young woman who's the servant of the Magister Anjelen?'

'I mean the bit of a girl with the long hair and the fine dress.'

'You can have no complaint against her.'

'Yes, yes I have!' shrilled the crone.

'Be careful what you say. This girl is under the protection—'

'Only I saw what she does. First she planted herbs for use in her witchcraft, but in this holy place they never prospered.' The crone cackled. She said, 'At night she abuses herself. Yes, I've seen. She sticks her finger into herself.'

The Administress said sternly, 'How is it you were watching?'

The crone quailed. Then rallied. 'I heard her groan. I thought she was ill, and went to look in.'

The Administress doubted this story. Besides, self-abuse, though a messy, demeaning process, was a lesser crime in the feminine gender, it wasted nothing. The sisters must abstain, but in a common woman, an unvirgin, it might be overlooked, only a light penance given. And again, the green-eyed girl had not seemed much in need of fleshly things. For the growing of herbs . . . this had already been reported. A supplement to diet, most probably, some sign of peasant industry not to be discouraged. And while she rationalized in this way, the Admin-

181

istress, who had abhorred and feared Jasha at once, thought, *Quickly, you old wretch: something more.*

And the crone said, 'Otherwise, a chest was put in an empty cell. There are human bones in it, and the witch goes in and plays with them, dressing them in rings and flowers. *Communing* with them. Godless.'

The Administress was aware blood was soaking out of her skin into her robe, from the cruel stripe she had given herself. Terrible self-doubt, a reasonless dread that now and then came upon her, drove her to the rod, by means of which she beat her demon of panic away. She did not like others to see evidence of her chastisement. That she must resort to hurt was not, to her, a symbol of piety, but rather of weakness.

'You've spoken. Go back now. I'll consider what you've said. If it's true, something must be done.'

'*True* – it's true.'

'To lie to me would be ill-judged.'

'I don't lie. I saw her. She worships bones, and calls the Devil over them.'

'Be silent. I've listened, and will act as I see fit. Go back to your cell.'

The crone pulled a sour face, her eyes full of malevolence and thwarted hunger. She retreated. The Administress crossed herself. She was feeling better. She did not need the rod, now.

For Jasha the sea was the forest (droplets, leaves), and the court the piece of ground before the bothy door. The broom leaned there, a water jar, the earth patch was turned. In the winter afternoon, Jasha hung her second shift to dry on the cell door, tied by its hem. The shift puffed and bellied, as if a fat woman had got into it. Jasha watched this omen, and because of it was not surprised when, preceded by two of the sisterhood, the Doma's Administress trod into the yard.

'What are you doing?' said the Administress to Jasha instantly. Her tone was accusatory. It was dangerous: Jasha had been well-lessoned in such nuances.

'I washed my shift,' said Jasha. 'The breeze will dry it.'

As she answered she was aware of the two crones straining their inadequate ears in the adjacent cells. Some mischief had been started. As though she guessed it in detail, Jasha glanced about, searching if there might be some escape. But the only exit point was shut by the bulk of the Administress, her two sisters, and the pair of pot-faced slaves who brought up the rear.

'So you're cleanly. But you don't bind your hair as you were told to.'

Jasha looked through the Administress' left breast. Jasha was waiting for the next clue to behaviour.

'You're disobedient,' said the Administress. 'Unruly. What do you say to that?'

Jasha looked up into the eyes of the Administress.

After a moment, the woman said, unable to keep it in, 'And if I tell you I know you do unlawful and unholy things, what will you say then?'

'No,' said Jasha.

'*No*?'

'No, I don't do anything like that.'

The Administress frowned. 'You're pretending to be simple, but to have been the servant of a Magister you can't be less than intelligent. Exceptionally so, to have fooled him you were sufficiently godly to stay in his service.' (One of the hags muttered in her cubby.) The Administress raised her voice. 'You, sisters, go into the third cell, there. See what you find.'

The two sisters made for the cell where the chest and the bones were supposed to be.

Jasha did not feel fear, but an electric swarming of animal alarm. She would, if she could, have sprung away, leaving everything behind. It was still a preferable gambit, although she must knock down the fat woman to get by – the slaves would likely fall back to let her through.

The door of the third cell was breached. The sisters stood there, like two witless creatures. Then one said, 'Lady . . .'

The Administress surged forward and gazed in, her heart beating with a disturbed anticipation, nearly pleasant. At the same instant she was horrified.

A chest was in the cell, as expected; that was nothing. On the floor lay the skeleton, each bone in the right place, the bone feet together and bone hands crossed at the sternum. Under the skull was a cushion which Jasha must have stolen from the chapel – though she had never been noticed there – where they were kept to ease the kneeling of the older sisters. The skeleton had been dressed in a green gown – identifiable as Jasha's. The bald ivory head was crowned with a garland of green winter weeds. On one thin digit was a silver ring.

The younger sister emitted a giggle. She was between fright and an enlightened view of sinister hilarity.

The Administress did not seek to reprimand her. Instead the woman turned about, after Jasha. In that way she was in time to see the two slaves reaching ineffectually to prevent Jasha bolting from the courtyard.

'In the name of God' – the Administress heard, with some shock, her voice rising to a screech – '*stop her*! Witchcraft!' She added more soberly, 'Necromancy. Seal this door,' she snapped at the goggling sisters. 'I must send to the Primentor.'

Beyond the court there was a cry and a vivid crash. The fleeing girl had run into obstacles.

The Administress pushed aside the useless slaves, and beheld two more of her sisterhood lying bleating and whitened amid a great broken urn of milk. Others were transfixed as Jasha the whirlwind blew by. She was a dissolving being of flying plaits, about to abscond into a dimension outside the Doma.

'Seize her! A witch! Hell's spawn—' screamed the Administress, alive and demented.

At last a portly, doddering sister coming from a side alley with her tiny prayer book in her paws, reached out and grasped Jasha on an impulse peculiar to observe, like the paroxysm of a drowning cow. Nor, having got a hold, would she relinquish it. Jasha writhed and struck, bit and pummelled (silently, wasting no breath), to no avail. And like slow lees running in a barrel, other sisters now spilled themselves upon the couple. Jasha was imprisoned by flesh and dark robes. The vernacular noises now rose everywhere. 'A witch! Witchcraft!'

'Witchcraft,' repeated the Administress. 'Rites of bones.'

She began mentally to pen her message to the Christerium's Primentor. In all her time here, she had never had cause to communicate with him. As for the Magister, Anjelen, he must learn from the Primentor. It was not her part to tell a Magister anything. (And he was not only a Magister, but a Knight of the Church.) A knot of fear tapped against her heart. She knew, unrealized, a devastating pride, inexpressible, at meddling in the affairs of angels.

Her prison lay somewhere in the Doma. She had been bustled there and did not know, to describe to herself, where it might be. To detect this in any case would have been valid only if she had seen some means of escape, which she did not. (Jasha was practical. Mostly life was superfluous to her process of living.) The door was bolted, and barred. There were no windows or apertures. A candle burned inside a clay lamp, with other candles lying by. She must ignite each tallow vehicle of light from its predecessor, as that one died, and so it went on, an area of time marked out by these fluttering, exhausted and extinguished, reincarnated fires.

Having no other time to contend with, Jasha began to remember her childhood.

She did not remember being born. It was strange. Suddenly she had seemed to flash into existence, as if the man, Carg Vrost, had made her up, perhaps from vegetable matter and rags lying about the hut. Her soul evolved and grew only as her body did so.

She learned Carg Vrost was her father, and the mound of earth, the grave, her mother.

Carg Vrost did not know what to do with her. He gave her away to a village.

Only in the village did Jasha, her growing soul and the debris of which she had been shaped, begin to take on the proper mortal contours. Now she had beings to model herself on, other than the rodents, animals and insects of the forest.

Jasha tried to conform, to be as like a mortal woman as she could. Chameleonly successful, she sensed and never questioned her differences, only hid them. Going back to her father was a sensible move. She had learnt all the mimicry she could, for that period of her life, and she would be safer with Carg Vrost, who was insane. To return also was what a good peasant daughter might do. Jasha would always, when let, do what others expected of her. Even to running away, possibly, in the Doma. But that was too her bestial instinct, blind and unwise.

They wanted to condemn her. To run away had added to their evidence of her villainy.

The bones in the cell had been dressed; she had seen them herself. She had not done it. Or at least, her body had not done it. Jasha would not take responsibility for the deeds of her soul, grown like a plant in the compost of her flesh.

When the prison door was finally opened, two slave women ran directly in and up to Jasha, and seized her. Jasha did not resist. The women were very muscular from their manual labour. A sister stood in the doorway, who turned at once without a word, going off along a corridor outside, and the slaves dragged Jasha after.

Presently she found herself (there were gaps in her observation, confused by the new illumination and extension of architecture), in a hollow place of dressed stones, which had one light only, a lamp held in the claws of an upright beast of iron, lion-headed, with the robed body of a girl. Behind this curiosity was another effigy, balanced above a great book upon a stand.

'Confine her,' said the figure above the book. The voice

was sexless, or of both sexes at once; it was humanity it lacked.

And the slaves moved Jasha out into the space, where the lampshine fell down on her, and with a sudden stooping had bizarrely secured her, by her feet, with two manacles connected to a ring in the floor.

Jasha kept completely still. She looked up into the light. The thing there was a woman, or had been one. It had breasts, shapeless outpourings of them, and the belly of childbearing, but these children were ghosts. There were eyes revealed by two slicks of clammy yellow.

'You are called Jasha,' said the woman above the book. 'A servant of the Magister Anjelen. Yet you have practised witchcraft.'

'No,' said Jasha.

'And you persist in denials. Even the time allowed you for reflection you've misused. Don't you know, God sees into every closed room, every heart? Tell me now, what was your purpose?'

It came to Jasha she might need to invent a purpose for this thing she had not done, describe some plan she had had for the brown bones. For these women were intent upon her as a hunt.

But she delayed too long, could, in those moments, offer nothing, and above the book a pair of hands were clapped together like the apparatus of a trap meeting.

Someone came at Jasha from the edges of vision and awareness. Another woman, from her odour, but whether a slave or out of the orders of the Doma, Jasha could not tell. It became irrelevant. This woman took Jasha by the throat, forcing back her head. Jasha tried to resist now – she encountered some breastplate or apron of metal – her hands rebounded.

But the hands of the unseen woman had a scent of earth, as if she had been peeling vegetables not ten minutes before. They crawled across Jasha's lower face, and prised open her jaw. A fearsome finger entered over Jasha's lower lip. A black fingernail – invisible, invoked, tasting bitter as a medicine – then a fist was all of it in the soft cave of Jasha's mouth. Jasha's instinct was to bite, but she could not. She was held. She fought, and her hands were smitten away. The earthy fingers closed on her, intimate and thorough. An incredible shock, and a sound – felt rather than heard – introduced pain like a burning knife. The hand immediately ejected itself. In the spill of light it was now stained black.

'She has snapped your tooth,' said the woman above the book. 'She'll break others as efficiently.'

Jasha put her tongue's tip down against the shocked pain which had been, moments earlier, a lower canine, whole and strong.

'What,' said the woman, 'was your purpose with the bones?'

'Witchcraft,' Jasha said. Blood ran along her chin.

'Speak then. And I will write.'

Jasha thought swiftly and said, 'My mamma taught me.'

'Continue.'

'It will call a spirit.'

'That was your intent?'

'Yes.'

'Your mother taught you this spell, you say?'

'Yes.'

'For what end did you practise it?'

Jasha said, 'I don't understand you.'

'What was your aim in working this spell?'

Jasha was not ready. At her hesitation, she felt a stirring behind her, the heat of the woman with the hands of earth drawing near again. Jasha said: 'I've done it many times. Calling a spirit.'

'You must say why.'

What, what could she say? Why did the women of the village fiddle with their meagre magics?

'It tells me things.'

'Ah.' The woman above the book seemed satisfied. But she might want more.

Jasha's brain whirled with thoughts. Then an image formed. It was brilliantly clear. Before the woman asked her anything else, Jasha said, 'The spirit shows itself in the shape of a moth. A black one, with red eyes, large as a bird.'

The pain in Jasha's mouth had put out tendrils, up into her eye, into her neck and down into her breast. She felt a gruesome anger at what had been done to her, but without true object, for she might spring upon neither of her tormentors.

'Once, my da tried to kill the spirit,' Jasha said. Her words rambled across each other. A jumble of old tales in the village, a half dream spinning in her head. 'He got the village men, and they ran after it, through the forest. But,' she said quickly, weakly, 'it does no harm. Only tells me how to grow things, and the weather . . .'

'And will it be fine tomorrow?' asked the woman above. 'A dry day?'

Jasha put her own fingers into her mouth and tried the broken canine, snapped off at the level of the gum. It was a dagger's edge.

'The Magister's my master,' said Jasha. 'What does he say?'

'Nothing. You're ours, here. The Magister won't protect you.'

Jasha knew a deep terror.

She wondered if they only meant to frighten her, but their behaviour was extreme and exacting.

'You can go back to your room now,' said the woman with the book. 'You've been sensible, speaking up. It's saved us both much unpleasantness.'

'What penance will be set me?' said Jasha.

'A sister will visit you, to discuss the condition of your soul. Provided you repeat your confession to her, she'll instruct you in the proper prayers.'

Prayers could not be atonement enough for the summoning of spirits. The interrogation too had been brief, almost superficial.

There was a shift of planes behind Jasha. The heat of the woman with the earth fingers went away. The two slaves were there, undoing the shackles, seizing her again as roughly and competently as before.

Jasha realized for the first time that she was faint. She allowed herself to become loose-jointed, mindless.

The slaves bore Jasha out. Jasha's consciousness swam in her body along the windings of the Doma. Escape remained out of the question. There was no hope, therefore nothing to struggle for.

Back in her prison room, she was left on the pallet, and the candle, which had gone on burning in the lamp, darkened.

Jasha lay in the dimness, licking at her wounded tooth. The woman torturor had not given her back the broken piece.

Within the gourd of Jasha's skull something fresh was waking, moving about. She did not know what it was, or examine it, she merely watched it in her trance. It concerned the Magister Anjelen, who had brought her here, the Magister who would not do anything to assist her now. The idea was not hope, was formless, and might be useless. Even so, in the seconds before the lamp guttered out, Jasha sat up and lighted another candle.

Since a Primentor could not enter the Doma, nor an Administress the Christerium, they conversed by letters. There were four in all, hers the first, rather long and convoluted, telling everything in a flowery and self-conscious way, that of a virtuous child striving to please a stern father.

The Primentor-father's reply was short. What had been discovered was grave. The girl must be examined. The Doma should inform the Christerium of results. The third letter contained these results – Jasha's wholehearted confession. What penalty should be applied? Surely the severest? The fourth letter, from the Primentor, endorsed the view of the Administress. Final religious consolation must be allowed the girl, since she had repented. But, once her soul was washed, her living body should be taken from her. She only did wrong with it.

The means of death which the Primentor had originally prescribed were not those put down in the letter. It happened that the Primentor had consulted with one other. This other (the Magister Anjelen), had voiced some cool aggravation that he had nurtured a viper in the bosom of his household. He suggested that to wall up and starve Jasha, the common price for sin paid in the Doma, was a death both too lingering and unfastidious, and too bland. Fire, said the Angel of God, turning his night of eyes upon the Primentor, was the ultimate bath for the deviant soul. It had been the oldest and truest method of the Church in the education of city and village alike. They should not shrink from it here, at the Christerium's gate.

Thus the letter concluded with these words: *You will, with all due observance of the lawful procedures, take the woman to a suitable area beyond the Doma, and there, at the first hour of morning light tomorrow, burn her as a witch.*

That afternoon when he had returned to the Christerium, Mechail began searching for his mentor. But Anjelen was elusive. From the first priest he encountered – the porter at the gate – to the novice met with on a flight of steps, they knew of Anjelen. But his whereabouts they did not know. They spoke of him as of some pervasive phenomenon, as if he might be anywhere, nowhere, detectable, unreachable. And they too, come back from the sorcery of the prior night, apparently knowing nothing of it, were yet a party to it. They had been ensorcelled. They had lent themselves to the power of Anjelen, and were poisoned.

Mechail did not attempt to breach their amnesia. Finding the entry into the Christerium properly manned, the aisles and walks populated by waking persons, he knew only that he had expected nothing else. A groom came and stabled his horse, which had been real enough. He heard the bells toll for meals and churchly observance. He considered the church tower murmurous with worship, where the Knights of God had taken their communion of wine which was blood. And of blood, he thought of that.

But he could not have said, Something is changed. He was adrift.

And eventually, the last one, the novice met on the stair, who pointed, and then, gathering his skirt, led Mechail up to some apartments in the south wall. 'Here are the rooms of the Magister Anjelen.'

The rooms were empty, of course. (Why of course? Because here also he had expected nothing else.) But he gained access merely by opening the door after the novice left him there.

Mechail spent an hour in the rooms of the man who had fed him blood. The outer apartment was very narrow, hung with weapons, the inner was a magician's chamber, with skulls and books and devices set about. Everything was rich, and the windows had wild colours. But a slender bed behind a curtain presented a single bolster, an unpaired blanket.

Traces of Anjelen were there in oblique and careless quantity. As if the rooms had *emanated* from his body, out of his brain.

At length Mechail descended.

He relocated his own lodging. He caged himself within it, and waited. For Anjelen. Or some word of Anjelen.

And he longed for Anjelen, like a lover, could think of nothing else.

But that day passed, and that night passed. In the morning, they brought him food, as before, and at noon, when they did not bring him food, he sought the Common Hall. He went among the brotherhood, unnoted, the mark still on him, giving him access almost everywhere. Giving him nothing, in fact.

Day by day, he was driven about the Christerium. He began to memorize the positions of buildings and sections within it. This dismayed him a little, as if the edifice grew smaller, less significant. He climbed to Anjelen's apartment – empty. He asked direct questions: Where will I find the Magister Anjelen? And now the answers were exact: He is praying in the church. He is in the library, the courts of exercise. . . . But, entering these areas, Anjelen was gone. Mechail seemed to miss him by a hair's breadth.

There was an evening that Mechail went to the stable, to look over the red mare they had given him at Korhlen, or her duplicate, evolved in the dream. And the groom, a lay brother, brought her out on request, *his* property, burnished and supple and actual, for his review.

Mechail by-passed the church, where they were singing an evening devotion – they had let him go in, let him push about there, trying for Anjelen. He went to supper in the Ordinate Hall, under the martyrs. Eating here alone among the brothers, he bit upon a notion. Having pursued, he had gained nothing. How if he took himself off?

He thought of the mountains. Himself riding slowly, Anjelen a measured distance behind.

The morning they were to burn her, Jasha, knowing how near death was, like a dog outside the door, had asked for water and washed herself all over. She unfastened her hair, letting it uncoil like a flood to its full length, which Livdis had so enjoyed. She had guessed the format of death from previous rumours, and had meant to bind up her hair again very tightly, keeping it close to her and out of the flames, for in that way she would protect it and her body longer; a pointless, yet again instinctual, delay. But they came for her too soon, before she was ready, and tied her hands, and her hair stayed unbound.

They brought her wine to drink, no food. (The night before they had given her the last rites, and the wine of the Sacrament of the Christus, and a large dinner of bread and fish.)

In the morning, in candlelit darkness – the very last candle was half burned through – a thin sister squatted before Jasha and told her that after the payment of pain, God would receive her. She need only continue penitent, entreating the pardon of Heaven, she need fear nothing more. Jasha did not argue with this. Her terror of the fire was ordinary, she knew there was no chance of evasion. She relieved herself several times, and drank the wine, and was taken out with tied hands and loose, flowing hair, frowning a little with stress.

After a long walk through the worm-trails of the Doma, Jasha emerged with her escort of two sisters and guard of four slaves, on the rock terrace above the sea. Torches were lighted, everything else was grey, except eastwards, over the water. Here the morning star blazed, and the rim of the sky had worn thin. The tide was going out, and the torch-headed procession wound down after it, passing along the stones above the beach, southerly, away from the Christerium.

The mountains began to form out of the sky. The colour of shells was in the east. Gulls cried. They did not bother what the women did, torchlight and burning girls would be all one, all equally incomprehensible and uninteresting, to them.

South of the Christerium and the Doma, between the sea and the stony slopes, a platform had been put up.

Some twenty or so of the sisterhood were standing there, and the Administress.

As with the gulls, none of it made any sense any more to Jasha. The pale morning faces were clownish, everything which was being done was absurd.

The Administress stepped forward and began to read aloud from a prayer book, over the rustling of the sea.

Jasha caught snatches of meaningless words. God was the redemption and the Christus the Saviour, and there was no death, all was according to the will of the Lord. What could such phrases have to do with Jasha at this moment?

There was a ladder up the flank of the platform, which seemed hastily botched together out of the stones from the beach. Sticks of wood and straw were piled on all sides. Jasha was forcefully assisted up the ladder by the four slaves, who next pushed her down into a sitting position. Jasha was required to lie flat, as if in a bed. When she had done so, the women secured her with ropes. After all, it would make no odds, the fire and her hair.

Perhaps it was a kindness to lay her out like this, that the flames should have all of her the more quickly.

Jasha believed in God, but only as a demon, one more supernatural element capable of interfering. Beyond life, she credited nothing, and had seldom thought of it, for she was young. She would pass through agony to oblivion. This stunned her, but maybe also there had been a drug in the wine, to dull her and keep her tractable.

She turned her head against the resisting hold of ropes and hair. The sun was coming. Jasha wondered how long it would take her to die. It seemed she should die as swiftly as possible, in order to minimize her pain. She put her mind to it.

The Administress concluded her reading and shut the book. She signed herself with the cross.

There was a peculiar stillness among the women on the shore. No breath of doubt or compunction seemed to disturb them, only the composed dread of something unavoidable.

The sky was suddenly rose-red. Enormous rays streamed upward. More terrifying than anything, the everyday sun broke out of the sea, boiling.

A slave woman, probably picked by lot, approached the foot of Jasha's stone couch. She carried a torch, whose flame was no longer visible in the sunlight, and bending, touched this invisible essence to the straw and bundles of wood. There was a smell of charring, and smoke thundered up. The slave withdrew.

Jasha lay behind a wall of smoke. Even the sun was outside, bloody and distorted.

The heat came. Flaming embers fell upon Jasha. She heard herself scream far off, at their shocking little hurt. Was it really to be now?

One moment she was bathed in sweat, then her skin crisped. She felt it dry upon her bones like withered leaves. Then her hair and her dress caught fire. She saw fire clothe her. And all at once she was cold, freezing. Her teeth chattered, she shivered uncontrollably. She could not scream now for the cold, but as the ropes burned through, she leapt upward. There was no thought in her, no word she could utter. She had become fire. *Jasha* was gone.

Like all the other mornings, this one. Mechail, walking to the stable yard of the Christerium, only wondered again if they would refuse him the horse. But she was brought, and Mechail mounted her, careless, coordinated. The porter opened the small gate, and the rider passed through.

The sun was rising below, and moving between the mountains and the sea, he saw all at once something went on at the brink of the black beach.

He had not seen women for a while. Though he had dreamed of one tending him as he slept. These were women in the flesh, females of some sisterhood – the building below the Christerium? They were acting out some scene at the water's edge. He rode nearer.

They faced all one way, out to sea, not hearing him or imagining he could exist. On a block of stones something was burning against the sun.

He knew a male indifference, bred in him, and at the same time, curiosity. For (here), anything might be some clue to or link with Anjelen.

He kept riding forwards, and he was less than twenty paces from the group of women, when the dawn wind fanned in over the water, parting the smoke that clouded from the platform. In that instant, something sprang upright on it.

Mechail saw clearly, against the smoke-hung round of the sun, a shadow-girl, with upflown wings of orange fire— She stood on the platform, as the elemental aspect of the Magister had stood on the altar.

The horse pressed on, seemingly unmoved by flames. Mechail watched, and the smoke blew in and furled away again. Then one of the sisterhood on the beach shrilly screamed.

Out of the raging fire, over the burning layers of wood, came walking a girl brown as bronze with eyes like green glass. Pieces of fire clung to her and spun off. The flaming orange of her wings was gusting up into the sky— They were great washes of hair which had caught alight, dispelling in cinders now, like a swarm of flies. All the hair was burned off. Her skull was brown and bald. Her very brownness was the baking of the fire. She had been *cooked* in it. But not consumed.

She stepped on to the beach. Her eyes were devilish, so green and wide. He pondered if she could see anything through them, or if she would fall dead at any second.

The women of the sisterhood were shrieking and scattering along the beach. A fat woman pitched about in the riot, turning back, running, once dropping to her knees, crawling on sideways like a crab.

The fire flailed, devouring the batches of wood and other tinder propped by the stones.

The horse had stopped, refusing to go farther, tossing its head.

Mechail found that he dismounted. He went towards the cooked girl as if to a prearranged meeting. Heat lashed from the pyre, and a second heat radiated also from the girl. Behind her, beyond the fire, water poured along the beach.

She parted her lips. They were not blistered, but fused to a brazen smoothness. One of her lower teeth was broken. A golden bubble of flame issued from her mouth, popped, burst. The girl poked out her tongue like a lizard, and made a croaking noise. Then she went down on the ground.

Mechail could not handle her scalding body. He hauled off over his head the priest's habit, under which he had kept on the shirt, breeches and boots also gifted him. He threw the habit on to her, swaddled her in it, and took her up, limp and heavy, carrying her awkwardly down the beach to the hem of the water.

When he rolled her among the waves, her flesh hissed like metal and the white steam rushed through the air.

(Along the shore the women ran and wailed, diminishing.)

In the sea, the girl breathed. Her eyes were shut. Mechail lifted her hot head from the breakers. Presently the sea had pulled off from her, still drawing out towards the sun.

There was no explanation for what had occurred. But it was like the blade in the heart under the tree. It was the same thing.

Despite the fact that he had never looked at her before, he knew the girl was the one who had put her hands upon him during his journey. As with Anjelen, it was as if he had known her all his life.

When the steaming and hissing lessened, he touched her surfaces again; she was only very warm. He picked her up and bore her to the horse, and put her over its back. The mare shook her head again, protesting and less docile. Mechail remounted.

Up the beach the Christerium cut its shape from the sky. The distanced women still scuttled towards their building.

The other way were the mountains, blank as a desert. His scheme had been to ride back into them, and he did not intend to alter anything.

Before him, the brown girl, her uncanny slimness and her boy's buttocks, and not a hair left on her. He was careful not to touch her again as he rode up the beach.

Chapter Twelve

Perhaps it was some story Nilya had told him as a child. Some chivalrous fantasy. To rescue the burnt girl and ride away with her. It seemed so perfectly natural. And now, of course, he expected to be pursued – by the women of the sisterhood, by the Christerium. The burning of a witch. Church business.

He did not know where he would be going, and maybe had not reckoned to go far before Anjelen accosted him. Anjelen would have now a double reason to do so.

Mechail arranged the habit over the girl's body, to protect her from the cold day. On to his own body he put another shirt left behind in his cell, and a blanket brought from the bed. They were not sufficient against the winter. But he would reach somewhere soon, and extra clothing might be begged or purloined. Or were the mountains empty? Certainly they did not look real. The notion of dream and illusion persisted.

By the end of the morning, veined dark cliffs were all around. The Christerium was hidden. There was no indication of being followed, and from the overlooking heights, no sight of any collection of humanity. By afternoon, gulls no longer wheeled overhead.

The girl did not stir, although he saw her breathing, and now and then she coughed, a healthy barking.

The sound of the sea was gone.

The sun, the only thing to come after them, moved ahead and jumped abruptly down behind the crags.

Last night he had appropriated bread and a jug of the

watery wine from the Ordinate Hall. Slight provision, now there was the girl.

As the light ripened, he led the horse into a shallow cave, and made a fire there near the entry, against the coming of night. He wondered how the girl would react, if she woke and saw the fire. But she did not move, only breathed and coughed in the cave-back where he had put her.

Mechail sat by the fire, while the sky over the mountains changed to honey and then to ash.

It was as if he had had to sit down with himself at last. He could not avoid it. And so he looked, and saw. He did not feel alive. No, he had not done so since he left off struggling and howling. Only the obsession with Anjelen had intervened, the dizzy memory of the taste of blood, its visions. These seemed to hold Mechail together like scarlet threads. He feared this on examination. Yet, too, he feared to abandon it, for there was no other purpose. There was only otherwise the bronze girl and the iron mountains.

The sky was indigo, and stars glinted. Winds slid down the mountains like shale.

They came as wolves, five of them, out of the flesh of the night.

They made no sound, beyond the pad-pad of wolf feet on the stone. There was no jostling, nothing very wolf-like, beyond appearance. They would be his Knights of God, Anjelen's fraternity or army, the men who had clustered in the church to drink the blood. They had seemed, none of them, to have an individual intelligence, but to draw their life and movement from Anjelen, and this impression stayed. The ten flat gems of eyes danced around the cave-mouth. One wolf led the rest. The other wolves, as if loosely attached to it by hidden strings, walked and sat, shifted paws and heads, when it did.

And then there was a surprise. Krau's dwarf came up the rock, and entering the zone of the firelight, began to turn cartwheels.

Mechail watched this, the wry memory of the Cup Hall in his brain, the stupid laughter, Vre Korhlen and his woman Veksa, and his brother. They were phantoms, yet they lived. Even Krau, maybe . . .

The dwarf concluded his acrobatics, and stood up, looking at Mechail. Something in the gaze of the dwarf had altered. Mechail did not see what it was, only that it was there, like a fish darting in murky water.

When Mechail glanced back, four of the wolves had drawn away. Where the fifth wolf had been, a man was sitting on the rock. After all this, Anjelen.

He was dressed in dull dark red, that the highlights of the fire turned applicably to blood. The garments were priestly, rather than in the warrior mode. By this alone, Mechail sensed that what was before him was not the body of Anjelen, but like the wolf, one of those physical copies or reflections taken out of the soul.

It was the presence therefore, again, of a magician, which bore down upon Mechail. The advent of Anjelen was not as he had hoped. It was removed, vexatious, accomplished by deceit. Unsatisfying.

And – 'What do you want, Mechail Korhlen?' the being of the Magister asked softly. 'Not merely answers, surely? You suspect there are none, and maybe this is wise of you. Besides, you've provided yourself with further questions. Running off when you might have remained. Must I be your nurse-maid? Did I not give you enough in one hour to sustain you for a month, a year? I had prepared the Christerium for you. You were to be its pupil. But you ran away. And with what provisions? A burnt witch. Don't lie down with her, Mechail. You know you must abjure the carnal act in any form.'

Mechail said, 'I never had a woman, when I lived.'

'You are a priest. You'll honour the rule of chastity, if no other. The Christerium, by giving you instruction, will reveal your way to power. You must be patient, Mechail. You must trust me.'

Unsatisfying. A sluggish frustration, growing.

'Why trust you?'

'As your old priest told you in the forest, even unseen, God is with you. Think what you've been shown. How many miracles are necessary?'

Mechail said, 'I don't understand any of what you say.'

'That's your stubbornness. Go back to the Christerium and learn.'

'Are you there, then?'

'Wherever I want.'

'*Are you there?*'

'Yes,' said Anjelen. He smiled, very quietly, like an elderly man who does not care to conceal contempt or mockery any more. 'I sit in the narrow room with the swords and shields. They made that apartment for me perhaps fifty years ago. The girl asleep in your cave,' said Anjelen, 'was given the name Jasha.'

'I've – heard her name.'

'Yes, probably. She washed your body and fed you, when we journeyed. You needn't fear for her health. She was set a test by me, and has got through it. She's strong. But you have other responsibilities. There.'

The clerk's hand gestured into fire-tinged shadow, to where the dwarf crouched, with its head down, like a dog and not a wolf.

'That thing was my brother's toy,' Mechail said slowly; the conversation felt its way along a precipice, the drop was immense.

'He's yours, and is still yours.'

'Mine . . .'

The dwarf, who must be illusory, raised his head. The coils of black hair slithered over him. The ancient face, another rock of the unreal mountain.

Abruptly, as in a slant of lightning, Mechail saw his own face, his own hair, own eyes of a different shade, his features, his physique, defective as it had been in the Tower – all the same, only compressed and crunched together into a new horror – of *emphasis*.

He started back from the sight. It seemed to fling him towards the abyss, compared to which the black well he had idly speculated upon looked no deeper than this shallow cave which sheltered him.

'To be afraid,' said Anjelen, 'is a distraction. Accept fear with the rest.'

'Tell me your plan for me.'

'I've told you, the lesson is to be learned.'

'I'm to go back, to the Christerium? And the girl?'

'Leave the girl. What could she be to you? Let her make her own way.'

'What else?' said Mechail.

'What else would you have?'

Mechail felt heat rise through him.

'You gave me blood,' he said.

And the voice of Anjelen replied: 'Never speak of it. You'll pluck that flower again. Yours now, to give and to receive.'

'What of God?' said Mechail. 'Your Christus, whose name you take in vain?'

In the silence, he must stare at Anjelen, but the fire was sinking, and almost nothing might have been there on the mountainside.

Yet the voice repeated, 'Go back to the Christerium.'

The serpent of the wind slipped along a ridge.

The slope was void.

About three hours before sunrise, he managed to wake the girl. She had looked so extraordinary in the faint firelight he had kept up through the dark, he could not believe she could revive as human. Possibility and metamorphosis had charge of the night. She might make again the noise of a lizard and sprint off on all fours.

But her eyes opened, simply pale green. Her metallic look had quenched itself. She could only have had a lasting brash summer tan.

He told her what they would do, and she comprehended, offered no protest. She got up, and dressed herself in the priest's habit. She started to seem like a tanned boy acolyte with a shaven head. She did not sob, or babble entreaties for details of what had happened. She knew, presumably. She was an excellent practitioner of Anjelen's teaching of non-question and acceptance. Had it been lavished also on her?

Mechail assisted her to mount the horse, and mounted behind her.

He was unmoved by the pressure of her body against him.

She did not even ask where they were going, though she was netted up in Anjelen's design, and might have done.

They rode into the mountains, south-west, away from the sea, and the Christerium.

The mountains belonged to the Devil. He should have foreseen. Huge stone arteries bulged, there were natural stairways and pylons. The gaunt grasses and mosses grew in parts, and fed the horse an unnourishing diet. Sometimes there were streams that fell from height to deep, or stagnant pools, demon prints from the infancy of the rocks. Higher, they saw deposits like salt.

The second day of their ride, there was an abandoned village, huts like crows' nests above. Not even birds nested there now.

Mechail saw nothing alive, beyond the weed-like flora.

They fed themselves sparsely, the girl and he, from the bread. The girl – *Jasha* – who looked like a bald boy, picked some of the grasses and chewed them. She had stopped coughing.

They did not speak to each other.

Did the mountains have an end? For if they were some sort of hallucination, why should they?

They rode by day for as long as they could endure it. The girl was resilient. She had been a peasant, he thought, one of the soldiers who attended the Magister had taken a fancy to her. Her value to Anjelen was obscure. But, no questions. He did not inquire, either, of her.

At night they sought some cave or cranny. He lit a fire. The girl did not seem to mind it. They slept apart.

It was cold. No one existed. The mountains had no end.

On the third evening, having got over a ledge just wide enough to condone their passage one by one, and the horse drawn along by its rein, the leaden iron sameness cracked, and there was downhill a vista of boulders, several miles of it, finishing in another country. The landscape was vague, for light was seeping away from it. A sunset, which they had never properly beheld in the mountains, floated on the earth. Space was vast before them. They backed at it. They settled for the night where the ledge broadened into the terrain of boulders. Starved and unhinged from the cold and upper air, they watched the gulf of open sky and far-off ground rinsed into darkness, and the stars budded in all directions, so many of them.

That night, out of the enormous sky, the stars fell. It was snowing.

The girl was silent beside Mechail, but she clung to him, spread all her slender girl-boy's body against his, gripping him. It was for warmth. She fetched the horse nearer, too, tugging on the rein. Mechail covered her head with the blanket. Snow entered into their starving mouths, tasting of strange fruits.

Before morning he wept. He did not know why. Grief, or pain, whatever it was, seemed as essential to him as breath. The girl was sleeping and did not wake. Mechail averted his face from her, not to mask emotion, but to prevent his tears adding to the freezing moisture that enveloped the blanket.

The dawn was now what the mountains screened. When the sky started to lift and lighten, the snow finished. It had painted a thin white skin across the rock and boulders.

He was so cold he could barely move, but he and Jasha unfolded themselves, and leading the horse, commenced the treacherous downward climb.

He wept again during the descent. He was thinking of Nilya. He could not let go of his thoughts of her, or of the agony they brought him even now. He clung to this agony, as Jasha in the snow had clung to his body for warmth. Maybe the pain fuelled his will to survive, maybe it fed him.

They slid, stumbled, and the bruising barriers of the boulders saved them. The mare fell once, but they got her on her feet, unharmed.

As the sun flashed over the tops of the crags, the snow melted. Waters raced down the slope. There were birds in the sky – far up as the stars, they looked.

Trees leaned out below, bare-armed hags, beautiful.

At midday they rested. There was no food left, a mouthful of the strengthless wine. Mechail gave the dregs to the mare, who sucked them gently off his fingers.

'There's a river,' said Jasha.

Mechail saw the river. It flashed with lights between the trees. It took Mechail six, seven minutes to discern the clutter of bothies, from which a low smoke was circling.

By day, the sun shone into the hut for an hour, from the high window-slit. Jasha would unfasten the shutter to allow the sun to enter. In the same spirit, she kept house, brushing the floor, simmering soup in a cauldron. She even went to make bread with the other women, when this facility was offered. Before they approached the village, he had supposed she would be taken for a boy, a novice from the Christerium of which, probably, they had heard. But this did not happen. Jasha was taken for what she was, a girl wearing a priest's robe. No comment was passed on this, or on Mechail's equally unsuitable winter garb.

A few people had wandered out of their homes and stared, and next a burly man came up, bearded and wrapped in a coat of fleece.

'You want to stay here? You have money?'

'No money,' said Mechail.

'An exchange. The horse,' said the man.

'We need the horse,' Mechail said. He thought, *We have to go on. Further.* He visualized pursuit but it was a phantom.

'The saddle then. We can give you straw for saddle.'

They were making everything very easy.

After the exchange, the man led them to the hut, which was standing vacant, but tidy, the thatch sound and the hearth clean.

'Bring us food, and kindling,' Mechail told the man. The man, seemingly the holder of the village, took this order as a matter of course, sending another fellow running. He himself left the wayfarers in possession, more interested in the saddle than their history.

No one interrogated them. The woman who brought the curds, cheese and vegetables pointed out the well. The boy who brought the logs had nothing to say, or ask.

The first day, they ate, and then slept on the pallet Jasha had fashioned, a mattress stuffed with leaves and dried fern. The horse had been given residence in the lean-to.

Towards evening, Mechail woke, and saw Jasha freshening the fire. A cauldron hung over it, smelling of herbs and onions.

'Supper's ready,' she said.

The first time she had spoken had been about the river. This was the second time.

They supped on the soup she had made.

He watched her. Young women were quite alien to him; he half liked, half doubted her proximity. Her face was shameless in its hairless nudity. Even her eyebrows had been scorched off, though somehow not the lashes – the wetness of her eyes maybe had saved them. When she raised these eyes, he glanced away. He did not want to look into them.

They sat in silence again, after the meal, under the rusty firelight. And outside there was a soundless pressing in the air. He turned towards the window. And Jasha said, 'It's snowing.'

'If the snow settles, we may have to hang about here.' She nodded.

He said, 'I don't know – they could send men after us.' She shrugged.

Mechail looked at her, at her eyes. 'You think not?'

'You're to go to him,' she said.

'How do you know to say that?'

'He fetched you from the forest. Once was enough.'

Well, she was a witch, she knew things. He knew it too. It was self-evident. He had turned his back upon Anjelen. And the sense of Anjelen's presence – was gone.

What had happened? Mechail had turned from the excitement of the blood like a drunkard from his flagon. But at what moment had the dream faded to this depression and despair? Worse, far worse than in the wood, when he had prayed for death. For now, there was no escaping. He must fly, but flight was circular. It brought him back.

He wanted to sleep once more, and more deeply. He wanted to go away into sleep as if into another land. Where no one could find him, where he could lose himself. But that was death he wanted, not sleep. Sleep would have to do.

And in the womb of darkness two nights later, the fire now a crimson smear upon the edge of sight, waking then, he found her body laid against his. He had committed it to memory, her body. It did not seem separate from him. He reached quietly to touch her. His hands came upon the shallow curving flank, the soft cup of a breast. He explored them, wanting mostly her heat, her liveness.

A fox gleam caught her eyes. She too was awake, guiding his hands now by movements of her limbs and pelvis, allowing them to feel of her, head to toe if he wished. She was completely acquiescent. She put her own hands upon him. A flood of sensation had knotted at his groin, her fingers alighted there, bird-like and fluttering. For some minutes he lay in a kind of stupor under this ministration, which seemed to draw all of him upwards, to suspend him as if in water. Then some genetic code of lust thrust him over on her, lifting off her hands, parting her thighs, some urgent victory shouting to be taken. As he possessed her, there was a singing in his ears, the rush of rivers. A handful of images coursed across his mind, women naked in a green pool, a white girl writhing with a red man, the ghosts of sleep-pleasures – but burning through these was the fire-rimmed picture of Jasha, her hair, its absence, her breasts, the column of her throat, her fox's eyes, the line of her lips, and her flesh, the sheath of her that mouthed him. And the fire itself was inside him, blazing up. He forced against her, into her, desperate to reach the end. Desperate, despairing.

Soon she began to help him. The exquisite torture of her hands, her caresses, probings, became unbearable. He reared suddenly away from her. His body came out of hers, still engorged, the weapon of the fire locked for ever upon its rage and pain.

Mechail cried aloud. The noise shook the hut.

Gradually his pain subsided, the unreleased erection lessening like a healing wound. His whole body, muscles, bones, throbbed as though after a beating.

The girl bent over him and offered him water. He drank some. He said, 'Did I hurt you?'

'No.'

'That's good.'

'It'll be different tomorrow,' she said, out of all her sordid little store of wisdom.

Mechail did not answer her, for tomorrow had no place in their dealings. Her tomorrow was not his, his tomorrow, like his yesterday, being a valley of the Shadow.

Book Two

ANILLIA

Chapter One

Every morning early, the old woman Marika would go to milk the goat. She was the only one who could do it, for the goat had ideas of her own, and would kick. The other women in the chapel of the Handmaidens of the Christus were afraid of the goat.

Warm, deceiving and sad, the light of autumn lit the courtyard, and chapel building. But the berries were thick as red drops of blood all over the bushes at the door. It would be a wicked winter. The forest, standing behind and about like an army of bears, its darkness still green, would change rapidly to a place of snows. Marika feared the winter. Her uncomfortable joints turned painful; sometimes she froze in her bed and could not move until another of the Handmaidens came to rub her with heated oil.

They were a tiny order, scarcely recognized by the Church. (The town was miles away.) Rejected surplus daughters, useless to those families that had cast them off here, they carried on their lives in memory of the elect who had tended the Christus, washing Him, anointing Him, bringing Him water on the road to the cross, and grouped weeping about the tomb from which He finally evaporated. *Their* number varied, according to the text. But in the chapel there were only five, the youngest being in her fifties.

As Marika went along under the wooden walk, saying her beads thoughtlessly, she began to feel something, an influence, like an ebbing of temperature, or the stirring of a nameless memory. She stopped, concentrating on this feeling. It was neither pleasing nor dismaying, yet it intruded. Now and then, when she was very tired, Marika might see out of the corners of her eyes things that were not there – usually in the form of cats running. Out in the courtyard, across from the goat shed, Marika had now the impression of just some such non-existent movement. She blinked. She continued, no longer telling her beads, until she came to the bucket, which she took up.

When she opened the shed door, the goat, who generally frisked towards her, jumped away, and lowering her sandy head, displayed her sharp little horns. 'Hoo, sweetie,' said the old Handmaiden coaxingly. 'Come along, let mother milk you.' But the goat kicked up her heels.

And now Marika seemed to see again something moving which was not there – but to see it out of the back of her skull.

She was too stiff to turn quickly, so she levered her whole body about. And dropped the bucket.

The courtyard had a single door, which was bolted inside by night. The stone walls went up ten feet. The fourth side of the court was closed by the chapel, with the sleeping cells attached, and only the chapel door leading into one oblong hall divided by low pillars and screens of pinewood. The outer door of the chapel was also kept locked at night. The window slits were high and thin. Otherwise there were the kitchen and the eating hall, but these had entries only to the courtyard. No one was in the kitchen yet. The Handmaiden whose duty it was, was lazy, and breakfast normally late. But a girl stood by the wall, opposite the goat shed.

Marika's dull eyes had an impression of paleness, the pallor of an image that awaited painting. There was definition, but no proper contrast, although dark hair lay in a tail over one shoulder. She was dressed, the girl, in a linen shift. Marika stared, and embroidery seemed to come out on the shift like a stain. But Marika could not trust her eyes.

She reached to cross herself, did not. She called querulously, 'Who are you? How did you get in? What do you want?' And behind her the goat bleated anxiously.

The girl spoke, her voice musical, but husky, and hesitant.

'I slept . . . here.'

'No business to. It isn't allowed. *Where* did you sleep?'

The girl made a swimming gesture that apparently selected the base of the kitchen wall.

'How did you get in?' repeated Marika.

The girl looked at her. Her pale face was hardening in the air. Marika seemed to see it much more clearly, and she was struck irrationally by the purity in the face, like that of one of the saintly masks on the screens. She had a childish, decided urge to colour the lips of the girl pink, and her eyelids brown for assertion.

'I was wandering in the forest,' said the girl. 'And I came to the door.'

Marika squinted across. Abruptly she noticed that the court door was unbolted. This explained everything. It also filled her up with outrage and fear. They had lain all night at the mercy of brigands, drunk peasant men, wild beasts.

'How can you have been wandering in the forest?' said Marika, righteously. 'Where's your home?' *She has the look of a wealthy house.* Marika remembered her own domicile, unseen, unvisited for forty-nine years. She had been the bastard daughter of a carpenter. She grew up in the kitchen until the wife had her thrown out. Then her father sent her here. She had been afraid and miserable in that timbered house, and now only recalled it in spasms.

'I don't know where I came from,' said the girl. It was a stupid utterance, but she voiced it with gravity and self-assurance. 'I opened my eyes, and I was in the forest. It was night-time. I heard a wolf howl. I found the wall, and the door.'

'Why didn't you wake anyone?'

'I didn't know anyone was here. I lay down in the yard.'

Marika after all did cross herself. Once a woodcutter had been put out in the courtyard by his two brothers.

He had fallen, they said, but more likely one of them had brained him in a fight. He was conscious but did not know his own name, or where he was, or his brothers. This girl did not seem like that. She was not dazed. She understood about wolves and walls and doors.

Unsupervised, the Handmaidens were by now equals. They drew lots for their duties. Marika could only think, wanting to be rid of the responsibility, of passing the girl on to the youngest of the order, the fifty-three-year-old Doya.

'Well, come along, come along,' said Marika, fussily, and beckoned the girl. The girl approached, was next to Marika. And then Marika caught the smell of her. The old woman had never smelled such an odour – it was not unpleasant, not even strong. But it was like no other scent Marika had known in the world. Marika backed away. She thought of the holy perfume of the saints, the special aroma of sanctity – surely this was not some manifestation of it, the girl a vision sent to test the chapel . . .

'Go in there,' whispered Marika, frightened, flapping her petrified hands at the chapel door. 'Go to the altar and kneel and say a prayer. And I'll fetch someone.'

The girl said, 'What am I to pray to?'

'To God – who else!'

'God. Yes, to God.'

Enigmatically, the girl went in at the chapel door, and turning her head, obviously located the altar. Marika watched her until she went out of sight, then rushed to the cell of Doya.

Doya was sitting on a stool, braiding her grey hair, like ropes, and binding it around her head. She could read and write, and had the looks of a male human horse.

'There was a girl in the yard. They left the wall door undone. She's slept there.'

'What girl?' said Doya crossly. She hated her durable body, and hair, found their impositions tiresome.

Marika heard herself begin to whine like a fretful baby, trying to evoke the uncanniness of what she had just seen, heard, smelled.

Doya cut off her recital. 'Some slut thrown out of a village. Carrying too, probably. We haven't enough to feed her likes.' She rolled towards the chapel in the joy of action.

Inside, it was dark, slight shafts of the promissory primrose light slanting down from the windows, spanning but barely altering the gloom. On the screens of ancient polished pine, the saints' masks looked at eternity aimlessly. They were turning a blind eye. While the area of the altar remained sacrosanct, the rest of the chapel had become a large living room for the Handmaidens of the Christus. Here they sat by day, sewing and mending, reading their copy of the Book, which was missing many pages, and scraps of other books amassed from time to time from pedlars, telling their beads, making dolls, gossiping. Sometimes the goat would come in to join them. They did not shoo her out, being afraid of her, and Marika liking her. When the goat defecated on the floor they only cleaned it up, grumbling.

The chapel showed signs of this truer life, the group of wooden chairs about a dead brazier, a dropped spindle, a cake left mostly uneaten on a plate – though mice had been at it.

Doya evidenced annoyance that these things should be revealed to the straying girl. Doya's head cracked about, her nose leading the search.

Paleness in darkness, the girl knelt before the altar. On her shift the embroidery was of fruits and leaves done in green and red. Her eyes were lowered, but if she prayed Marika was not certain.

Doya marched over. The girl raised her head, and looked straight before her, at the altar, where a small ivory Christus writhed on a wood crucifix.

'What name do you go by?' said Doya.

The girl seemed to contemplate a crystal balanced before her invisibly in the air. Presently she said, 'Anillia.'

'Hoh,' said Doya. 'A fine name. From the towns, or some holder's Tower. *Anillia*. How is it you recall your name, and nothing else?'

217

'I don't know,' said Anillia, gazing on the crystal. 'But I do recall other things. My age is fifteen years. My hair and eyes are black. I'm a woman.'

'Of course you're a woman, you slattern. Are you in the family way? Is it some peasant feud you've been muddled up in, and cast out with your enemy's brat in you?' Doya was coarse. She had been the mistress of a Landholder's soldier once, and did not mince words. She was well-versed in woods feuds, and Tower feudings, raids and babies.

'I'm a virgin,' said Anillia. 'I know all those things. About my body, and how I am. That I'll bleed once a month. My womb.'

'Be quiet,' said Doya the coarse one, amazed into modesty.

Marika, peering from the doorway, thought, in jumbled words: *She talks the way the Woman must have talked, in the Garden. Taken fully formed from the flesh of Adam.* And the roots of Marika were brushed by a supernatural quivering. But then the girl got up, and she stood before Doya, pliant and stem-like, yet dried hard now like butterfly wings or lacquer.

'I have nowhere to go. I've come from nowhere. Will you take me in, in a charitable manner?'

'No, no,' said Doya, becoming limp and flustered.

'I'll starve in the forest. The wolves are gathering for the winter. What will become of me?' The girl's beautiful voice held no appeal. It put forward its arguments logically. *See, it's this way.*

'Doya,' chittered Marika from the doorway. To her surprise, Doya was glad to come over to her. 'Doya, we must tell the others.'

'She speaks like a lady,' said Doya. 'Maybe some terrible event's broken her memory and her wits. She's no peasant.'

'Could she be – some saint?'

'You're addled, you old fool,' snapped Doya.

The girl went on waiting by the altar, shaking out her hair now with slow fingers. Then she moved her left leg, poised on the right one. She pointed her left foot, staring down at it. She put her hands over her breasts, fleetingly, laid them on her flat virgin's belly.

The first Woman, fashioned from a rib. Made a female and sprung into Eden, without a past, *knowing*.

Doya and Marika went to the other Handmaidens, who were gathering in the eating hall by the kitchen. There was a quarrel over the absence of milk, and a spat with lazy Urzi, who had left the wall door unbolted and swore upon the angels of God she had not, threatening her sisters with a cook-pan.

Next they debated Anillia. The three who had not seen her were eager to amend this. They went to look at her, and returned, wobbling their heads (on which the uncovered hair was done anyhow in the mode of some aging women comfortable together and lacking the male irritant).

The girl was a lady. She had lost her memory and talked oddly. Her shift was unsuitable for the wood, but richly embroidered. Most of all, she was young, and new.

They had better keep her, care for her, drink at her life like thirsty birds.

The forest. It gave birth to things, was full of legends and fables and strangeness. All the women of the chapel, who had their beginnings one way and another in the forest, were aware of the forest's separate and continuous pursuance of being. Each of them, at the start, had been dewed by the pagan elements of the forest. Marika and Urzi carried ghostly childhood recollections of a young man garlanded with ivy and flowers, tied to a tree, and screaming as he was beaten with birch branches; Doya's mother had had a basket of minute skulls, mouse and squirrel and ermine. She would clean them, and she and Doya would take them out and tie them by moonlight in the bushes.

Anillia, as she sat in the grey wool gown they had found her, her hair in a long plait down to her waist, said, 'It sounds like the sea.'

219

None of the Handmaidens had heard the sea, although they knew of it. Trying to catch out the amnesiac, they asked questions, why the forest sounded as the sea did, what she meant, and so on.

'The leaves,' said Anillia, 'when the wind blows.'

'But what does the sea *look* like?'

'Like water.' Anillia paused. 'No, like green curds. Like a fish's back. Like blue glass that pleats itself over and over.'

'And were you often by the sea?'

'I don't know.'

Sometimes, Anillia would add her statement that she had been *nowhere*. That she came into existence like a tear, squeezed out of the eye of night. 'I was nowhere, then I was here.' Yet she said this less and less. It was as if she accepted their formula for her, to save them all trouble. With their herbalist quackery they had examined her for injury, and made for her poultices and brews. But she seemed quite perfect and whole. She ate and drank, had bodily functions, and was a virgin as she had said.

They taught her to sew, and she was adept. Doya set about teaching her to read. Here, at first, the girl was halting. Then suddenly she outstripped her teacher. It became obvious she had known her letters thoroughly. If this memory could return to her, why not others?

The Handmaidens had phases of prompting Anillia with a monotonous and ceaseless and aggravating persistence. They brought items for Anillia to regard, touch or taste. They took her on their little limited walks about the edges of the chapel. The woodland was turning to roan and yellow against the high hedge of the pines. The vegetable garden and two or three fruit trees were dropping their harvests, and Anillia worked beside the Handmaidens, stronger and more able then they. (How had they managed before she came?) Apples and grapes and cabbages did not startle Anillia. The tracks of crow and pigeon, stoat and fox, were familiar. But she did not know her house, her infancy, her father, her fate. The trials and promptings of the old women she endured with apparent calm.

She seemed to have no impatience or bad temper. There was a melancholy note to her, but that was to be expected.

Her unusual odour had slowly dissipated. Only Urzi had been able to smell it, as Marika had. Urzi had said it was like fruit sugar, but Marika disagreed. Finally Anillia only smelled of youth and girlness. That, among the Handmaidens, was odd enough.

Winter came like a long, sure wave. The days were short, speckled with sun and darkling cloud like the frantic last birds that foraged in the courtyard and about the vegetable strips.

The Handmaidens of the Christus had grown used to Anillia. They hardly every questioned or prompted her any more. Urzi, without telling her, was weaving her a new dress on the loom in the chapel's west corner, behind the screen with the masks of Saint Mechailus and Saint Eda. The gown was oatmeal colour, and had borders of rosy foxes and blue grapes.

'The priest's on the hill.'

Doya broke the tidings as she rushed into the chapel. Everything must be tidied. Always the man took them by surprise, always berated them for their slovenly and impious style.

The Handmaidens fled about, snatching up articles, sprightly with panic. They had hoped they would miss him until spring, the priest; he had not bothered with them two years. It was mere luck Urzi, emptying slops outside the yard, had seen him riding along the forest's edge, on his mule. He came from the town, a lengthy journey he disliked, visiting the outposts of the Church to see what they did wrong.

In the twelve minutes' grace they had, they achieved very little. Besides, he guessed how they went on here, these frowsy, sluttish women.

He rode to the chapel door and there tethered the mule. Doya went out to greet him, her head covered in kerchief and veil, purple-faced from her exertions, and angry at him, striving to be meek and courteous.

'Good day, sister.'

'You're most welcome, godbrother.'

'I'm parched too, sister. I've been riding since first light.'

'Will you come to the eating hall? We can serve you milk or ale.'

'Milk, if you please.'

Old prude.

They gave him milk, and cakes with honey and poppy-seed (to subdue him).

Then, he inspected the chapel. Its yard, its sheds and kitchen. The body of the religious chamber. The altar was dusty, and mice cheeped from the candle store.

'Why is that brazier there?'

'It grows very chilly here, godbrother.'

'The chapel isn't for your comfort, but for prayer and meditation. Can it be you still use this holy place for your female pastimes? Despite my previous admonition?'

Doya frowned.

The godbrother delivered a short sermon upon the fallibility of womankind, her trustlessness and addiction to futile habits. 'In your sisterhood you must be doubly vigilant.' He said they should all have penances, fasts, watches. 'Now, I'll inspect the cells.'

He found many things he did not approve – there had just been space to hide their non-religious books. In the last cell, sorting the patches of bark she had been gathering, he came upon Anillia.

The godbrother shied. 'Who is this woman? She's not of your order.'

'Yes, godbrother. We took her in, and—'

'This is irregular. Who dedicated this girl?'

'She was destitute.' Doya attempted to explain that which she herself did not understand.

'Has the girl got a tongue? Let her speak. You, girl. What are you doing here?'

Anillia's dark eyes gazed on the priest without affright, without respect, neither with any insolence or rage.

'I was lost in the forest, and they sheltered me.'

'Lost? Lost?'

'She doesn't remember, godbrother, her house or station in life.'

The priest said they would go to the eating hall, where he would question the girl. How was she called? Anillia answered quietly with her name. The priest had become sharp-eyed, his natural spiritual cruelty augmented by something more worldly.

In the eating hall, the Handmaidens were swept out. He sat in a chair and directed the girl to a stool. He proceeded to interrogate her as the Handmaidens had done, but with a nasty edge, trying to catch her out by silly, scornful tricks. Anillia did not say to the priest that she had come from nowhere. She clove to the persona the Handmaidens had fabricated for her. She remembered nothing, save a few basic facts concerning herself: her name, her age. It was as if she had been born that moment in the forest.

'Well then,' rasped the priest at length, his spurious cunning used up, trying something fresh, 'since you've been taught skills by the sisters, since you've had a month or two to contemplate your lot, if I were to ask you your *supposed* position, how would you reply?'

'I've no idea, I regret.'

'Your speech and voice, your comportment, suggest a child of high birth.'

'Perhaps,' she said.

'In Khish,' said the godbrother, naming the town as ominously as if it were a celestial province, 'records are kept. The Church, you can be sure, will investigate you. If you've committed some crime and are attempting concealment, you should confess it now.'

Anillia – smiled. This facial gesture ruffled the priest. There was nothing presumptuous or challenging in the smile; indeed, the girl lowered her eyes. And yet the smile was not fifteen years, it knew so much. Possibly not concerning the smiler's origin, but the meaningless tumult of mankind – concerning that, a great deal.

The priest went his way in the afternoon. He wished to be somewhere more comfortable for his dining and sleeping. He left a shower of penances in the chapel, like a sticky deposit. The Handmaidens would try to observe them, not wanting to offend God, until it would come to them, as always, that it was the measly priest they offended, not the young man whose white body, black hair crowned with thorn, hung upon the wooden tree, spilling his blood for their sake. Then they would lapse. In the matter of Anillia, however, they were to stay rather unhappy. They sensed malicious disturbance at work. Though the girl seemed cool as rain, they feared to lose her.

Snow fell thick that winter, and the wolves and the winds howled. Marika hobbled upon two sticks. Urzi made soup and thin pies with a little salt meat in them and dry vegetables saved over, porridge, and bread of ground pine kernels. They drank ale against the ice. The courtyard looked full of white bolsters. The chapel grew too frigid for society. They spent all their days in the eating hall, and prayed there too, having moved the Christus in above the oven. No one had ever caught them out at this. No one ever came in winter.

On the first of the holy feasts, Urzi gave Anillia the dress of grapes and foxes. Anillia thanked her, and accordingly appeared in the dress. Urzi was wounded by a dark disappointment. Seeing the doll in its new clothes, Urzi was aware they were not good enough.

Some days, it was so still in the white desert, they heard the faraway clack of an axe upon a tree, five or six miles off.

The white moon lit the snow by night.

The goat came to camp in the eating hall.

There was often the smell of wolf about the yard door.

After an age of winter, they began to speak to each other of the spring, as if it had happened once in the history of the world, and never would again. They told Anillia about the buds and birds, and the summer of leaves and flowers, as if she did not recall them. But as with all essential external things, Anillia too had her compendium of the seasons. They listened nervously then to what she said, in case some hint might drop which would, at this late hour, reveal her. Yet she mentioned only fisher birds at streams, and wild mint, asphodel, dragonflies, roses, swallows. Then added, 'The sea is blue as though it burns. The gulls lay their eggs like stones in the rock.'

'The sea,' said Doya fiercely, 'you've lived by the sea.'

And they held their breath.

But Anillia said, 'No, I never did. Someone, maybe, told me.'

When the spring returned after all, its green veins glistening along the wood, the Handmaidens beheld it with mixed feelings. All through the first spring weeks, emerging from their hibernation, glad to have lived the winter out, they were watchful. When the courtyard barricade was open, they looked up at the ridge of the forest. In the end, they did not see the robbers until they were at the door.

There were two men, and their outriders and their servant. The garments of the men, both of whom were quite young, were costly, with deep fur trim; they had gold rings on their fingers; they had horses.

The elder young man straddled the yard door, and looked at Doya the way certain young men look at a woman they reckon past her sexual prime and thus of no imaginable interest. And Doya looked at him as do such women confronted by such men.

'Holy lady,' said the young man, 'my name is Tarosar Crel. This is my brother. These, Crel guard, and our servant. Can you give us a roof for the night?'

'No,' said Doya, satisfied.

'Excuse me, holy lady. The guard and servant can make

do in your yard, or outside in the woods. I meant for my brother and myself.'

'We're a religious house of women. The Handmaidens—'

'Of the Christus. Yes. We know of you and your gentle hospitality to forlorn travellers. We will of course make an offering to the chapel. It's been a savage winter. My brother and myself, you see, were sent here to take care of a dispute . . . these peasant overseers can be trusted with nothing. The house of Crel owns land in the forest. My father is at home in the town. Khish. We've brought our own provisions, which we'll gladly share in return for the cookery cleverness of your order. A cut of beef, fresh, some wine . . .'

All the Handmaidens were at the door, like mice, their hungry eyes watering, and their hearts giving warning.

'The godbrother told us of your chapel,' went on Tarosar Crel. 'Charity being a feature of your calling.'

Their hated priest had been busy. They guessed it all while knowing none of it. They limped away from the door and allowed the young men and the servant in, while the guard slouched off and made a cursing bivouac under the apple tree. Powerless, these women, before youth and maleness. And before their own guilt – sweet fruit was always forbidden.

The beef was too tough for most of their teeth any way. The wine was not given generously. And vast inroads were made upon the bread and spices, the goat cheese and ale.

Marika, still hobbling on one stick, had crept across to find Anillia in the chapel. The Christus was back over the altar, and Anillia had begun to put spring flowers before him in a crock. Marika clawed mildly at Anillia's arm.

'There's boys come. Doya said you should hide yourself. Best not be seen.'

Anillia regarded the old woman.

'Why?'

Marika had realized there would be difficulty.

'Chancy,' said Marika. 'Noble young men – they'll rape a girl soon as look at her.'

'Do you think so?'

'Too likely. Doya knows.'

Anillia did not argue. Marika had thought she would, although not of the form of the argument, for Anillia was serene, only smooth ripples went over her surface.

'I should go to my cell, do you mean?'

'Yes, go now. They're in the eating hall, stuffing their bellies with all our bread and cheese, while Urzi roasts the beef.'

Anillia's cell was the sixth, tucked up against the sheds.

Anillia moved out across the slushy courtyard and stepped into her cell, and drew closed the warped and rickety door. Marika pattered unevenly after, and whispered there, 'Put your mattress against the door. Then if they try, they'll think it's stuck.'

Marika waited, to hear if the mattress was being dragged into place; but she did not hear it, and soon she hobbled off to the hall, where the cheating meat was beginning to smell lyingly beautiful.

When the repast had been eaten, or sorrowfully abandoned, the two noble sons of Crel, who had spoken mostly to each other in low tones, laughing, making sly obvious jests about old women, turned their attention once more to Doya.

The younger brother, Gden, belched behind his hand loudly, feigned embarrassment and begged Doya's pardon. Tarosar said, 'Yes, do excuse him, madam. At least, I gather from the godbrother, you were used to men once.' Doya was about to bridle furiously, when Tarosar continued blandly, 'But you've a maiden here, haven't you? It would have been a bad thing to have offended her. Nobly reared, I believe, and something of a mystery.' And Doya saw that over his spoilt-boy's eyes was abruptly a carapace of steel.

'The godbrother,' said Doya, 'interviewed the girl.'

'Yes, so my father was told. She called herself – *Anillia*.'

Doya felt a sinking.

'What is it?' she said.

'Well, since there's nowhere to speak privately . . . I'll assume you administer the chapel, lady. To come to it outright, this girl may – or may *not* – be something to my house. To Crel. It's my mother, you see. She's mourned for years. There was a daughter lost to her. They were on a journey in the forests, and the stupid child wandered off. I remember this, being eleven at the time. Uproar in the women's apartments. Solace unaccepted. She's sickly, my lady mother.' Tarosar's steel eyes gave a slight dismissive flick. 'Hearing the outrageous tale, I was sent to investigate further your foundling. My father likes no page left unturned.'

'But – how old was the lost child? Years must have passed,' boomed Doya indignantly.

'Quite so. It's a curiosity, isn't it, madam?'

Doya could not find her voice.

Tarosar Crel realigned his eyes, and said, 'I'll need to talk to this girl, in her chamber.'

'*No.*' It was Urzi who spoke.

'Obviously, your Administress may be present, if she wishes. Meanwhile – can you read, madam? – I have a letter from Crel himself.'

And there the letter was, with Crel's seal of two swords.

Doya scanned it. It might have been in another language. And yet, through its nonsensicality, she perceived that what the young man said was supported by parental testimony. This came to her as if through magic, for the words she could not see. Near the letter's end she did manage to pick out this sentence: '*We had christened our daughter by her grandmother's name, that being Anillia.*'

How had she lived in the forest, child to woman? Peasants had adopted her – but how kept her so couth, how not abused her? Had she changed to stone for ten or twelve years, to be awakened by the hand of God on the predestined night?

'She doesn't remember anything until that time she came to us,' said Doya stubbornly.

'But she claims a name of my family. We can't take

that lightly. She may be some farmer's daughter up to mischief, or is it witchcraft?'

'*Never.*'

'You can't be sure, lady. Only God and his angels are all-knowing.'

Doya scowled.

'When will you see her?'

'Now.'

'Very well. I'll go in first, to prepare her.'

'If you want,' he said, careless, certain of his rights, authority and wisdom.

It was early in the spring, and frost was on the evening air. The bitter stars seared above the courtyard.

No lamp burned in the girl's cell, but when Doya called, the door was opened. Doya talked hurriedly. 'Those men. They say you have the name of a child their family lost. A Khishan house. They're all in with Father Church. What can I do?'

'There,' said Anillia in the darkness. 'If it must be.'

Her tone was so fatalistic, so cognizant of what would happen, Doya recoiled.

'Do you think it's possible?' Doya said. 'How can you be theirs? They may harm you, if they suspect you're a liar.'

'I'm theirs,' said Anillia.

Doya took this like a blow.

'You *do* remember?'

'No. I've no single thing to remember. I told you. I came from the nothingness. But I'll be their lost child.'

Doya crossed herself. The cell seemed to her dank and cold. She retreated to the door, and outside the horrible sons of Crel stood swaggering. The younger one had brought a lighted lamp.

'Go in,' said Doya.

She no longer wanted to mount guard over the chapel's fosterling. Suddenly she could see only the oddness of it, the pale girl sprouting amongst them, twining about their lives like a slender vine.

The lamp went into the cell, and Doya heard the girl, Anillia, say softly, 'How may I help you, sirs?'

Doya thought, *I must stay. It's dangerous for her with those louts.*

She clumped briskly back across the court to the eating hall, bracing herself for the outcry of her sisters.

While in the cell, the light constructed a slim female figure clad in a woven gown, patterned at neck and cuffs and hem, her combed black hair loosely bound with a blue ribbon. She was very straight, marble in her bearing, yet she dipped her eyes, and folded her narrow hands together.

The two sons of Crel from Khish looked her over.

Suddenly the younger one, Gden, who was drunk, blurted, 'By God, it's her.'

'Shut your mouth,' said Tarosar. 'What do you know? You weren't even born. And she was two years of age. You,' he said to the girl, 'do you say you're a daughter of my father's house?'

'I don't know who I am. I don't remember. Just my name.'

'Say you name.'

'Anillia.'

'Can you read?'

'Yes.'

'What else?'

'I don't know.'

Tarosar said, 'You're to come with us to the town. She's nagged and whined ever since she heard of you. Our mother.'

The girl made no move, said no word.

'*It's her*,' said Gden. 'Mother's face, in the painted enamel, when she was young.'

'Do you want me to strike you? Hold your noise.'

Off under the fragile arches of spring they took her, the two young men, the four outriders, the servant.

Birds were singing.

Doya watched crossly. Urzi skulked in her kitchen,

burning food. The two older women had fallen sick. But it was Marika, seeing the light shadow flit away, who knew she would not live into another spring.

Khish was a walled town, centralized at its garrison, churched in sparse stone, compressed to alleyways, not yet into its summer stink.

Pigs roamed the lower streets, and further up there was a market, through which the Crel party rode. The girl, grey-cloaked and hooded, was mounted before the younger brother. He had not laid a saucy finger on her, taken no liberties. He already believed she was his sister. The journey out of the forest had been uneventful, uncomfortable. They never spoke to her beyond the merest and shoddiest politenesses. After all, she was only an errand they had been sent on. A task set by their father, for the sake of a mother they did not much bother with.

The nicer area of the town was behind the market, up above a church whose colony of stone gargoyles jeered and grimaced in the dying of the light. Wooden house-fronts fenced the street. Above a black door, a pair of balconies painted with scarlet fruits, and an iron lamp hanging between, already lit: this was Crel.

Inside the door, the big hall was hung with carpets and axes, with candles on a stand burning, and a fire on the hearth, where some women had been sorting coloured silks. At the slam of arrival, servants erupted like disturbed mites. Cups of hot ale were brought the brothers, who stood by, stamping their chilled feet. The girl they set on a bench, and left there, something found in the woods – what else was she?

Next a steward came down the stair and up to Tarosar Crel, to advise him his father would have them all into the upper study. Gden made an immediate move forward, like a well-trained horse. Tarosar performed a show of finishing his drink. 'I'm cold. It's been a lengthy ride.' The steward stood quietly, his hands folded.

While this went on, three women appeared on the stairway. One held up a candle in a sconce, which lighted them strangely, in a dramatic manner. The first woman wore her hair in a snood of beaded wool. She had on a costly red robe trimmed with fur, and two rings that flared. She was also in the middle stages of a pregnancy that, for her years and general look, was untimely and unsuitable.

'Oh, Tarosar, Tarosar,' she called out. She had a feeble voice, drawn thin and insufferable by, it would seem, the constant use of whining appeals. Tarosar for his part jerked up his head, at once annoyed, impatient, a response as trained as the former equine movement of his brother.

'Good evening, Lady Mother.'

'Tarosar – is that the child?'

'Go to your room, Mother. Father will see me now.'

'The child—' said the whining voice, and the emaciated figure, unbalanced by its belly, started a course of strengthless staggering steps.

'*No*, Mother.' About the hall, in the doorways, of which there were several, the house servants had gathered, watching. *Damn the woman, making display of herself*. Tarosar now took a vicious stride, as if to reach his mother and wring her neck.

The Lady of Crel halted. 'But—'

'You must wait, Mother, as must we all, on Father's word.'

It was then that she looked past him, over to the shadowy bench where Anillia had been sat. The woman who had lost her child put her hand to her side, slowly. Very clearly, but with no awareness, the gesture said: *Did you come from me?*

Anillia lifted her head. The hood fell back, and the pale face was visible, marked with its dark eyes and set round with smooth dark hair.

Crel's Lady started to sob. She held out her hands towards the girl on the bench.

'Damnation,' said Tarosar. '*The Christus*.'

Anillia had got to her feet. She walked across the hall, and went up the stair until she was in front of the sobbing woman. The woman touched her, her face, hair, shoulders, fearfully, staring.

'Are you?' said the lady.

'Madam,' said Anillia, softly, 'I only remember being in the wood. Perhaps they told you that. The trees, and then the chapel. Nothing before.'

Crel's Lady began to stroke Anillia's forehead, and hair.

'You wandered away,' she said. 'It was snowing. I was carrying your second brother. I was sick. I didn't see, until too late. They searched. You were naughty to go away. I told you: about the wolves, and the white bears, and the wicked god of winter who lives in the forest.'

The man who had come down the stair behind her, parted her women, and put his hand on her arm. Crel's Lady melted into stasis and muteness.

'Go up to your chamber,' the man said. There was no unkindness, and no kindness in this voice. 'You must let me deal with this, madam. You know you're susceptible.'

'Yes, sir.' She stepped aside. As if blinded, she no longer saw the girl. The Lord of Crel looked at one of his wife's attendants. 'A dose of Black Poppy,' he said.

The woman nodded. The lady made a small sad noise, without protest. They drifted off up the stairway.

Crel turned and gazed over Anillia's head.

Now Tarosar moved quickly, with Gden on his heels.

The figure of Anillia was caught up in their advance, borne in the wake of Crel the father, along a gallery, into a room where a fire burned between two dogs of stone. The space was bright with flames.

Tarosar propelled Anillia into the light's very centre.

Crel positioned himself, and gazed only at her.

He had a large face, its features coarsened and spread, the whites of the eyes tarnished, the pupils honed.

Presently Crel turned to his sons. They rendered him an account of what they had got from the girl, and from the women in the chapel. (Gden was halting, Tarosar blustered.)

In the brilliant red and yellow illumination a false cheerfulness lit up the hard flat scene.

When the sons of Crel had spoken, Crel sent them out.

This time, he did not look at the girl, but into the fire, at a hanging on the wall, a cup on the table.

'You have a touch of her, when she was young. The priest says I must humour her fancy, and this priest is important. You'd be about the proper age. Maybe you heard the name from the peasants. If you're lying, better be careful. Be a daughter to the house, and perhaps it will go nicely for you. Expect *little*. Whatever you are, you're not much to me. They said you were a virgin. Is that so?'

'Yes.'

'My wife has her whims. See you make her happy. She may be carrying another boy. You can go out now. There's a girl in the passage will see to you.'

As she walked to the door, he spoke her name very harshly, and rather differently. She glanced back.

'That was her pet name for the child she lost,' the Lord of Crel said. 'Do you answer to it?'

'If you wish.'

'You're a cool one, a cold one,' he said. 'Aren't you frightened?'

'I remember nothing to be afraid of.'

'You'll learn a lot of new things to fear, I've no doubt.'

She said again, 'Yes.'

Outside it was spring, and later summer. Rain, warmth, and finally great heat pressed on the frame of the house at Khish.

Lady Crel felt the cold, and fires were built for her, and the chamber burned. Then suddenly she would be in a panic-stricken fever, and the fire would have water thrown on it and all apertures would be breached. This large room, with its glass windows, each with a small ruby pane, its curtained bed, its ranks of herbals, relics in boxes, its population of tiny statues of saints and icons of the Christus, was generally also full of women. It smelled of scents and tinctures and medicine, and of feminine flesh and hair. The men of the house avoided it, though sometimes they might be heard going past with a clash of maleness, dogs and boots. Sometimes the lady would take exercise, walking slowly about the interlocking corridors of the house. The corridors, windowless, were dark and gloomy and, as the summer fermented, had a yeasty odour.

Otherwise there was a little closet awarded for the girl's private use. Here she slept, if the lady did not want her company. The girl was not often in her closet. At first, day and night, Lady Crel would need her. By night Anillia would sleep on cushions near the bed. By day she would read aloud from some book of vacuous tales. Night or day she would be listening as the pregnant woman unburdened herself over and over of the same dismays and frustrations. She was a being unable to let go of any pain or unhappiness, distrustful of any enjoyment. Soon she began to say to the girl, 'Can you love me, Nilya? No, it can't be possible. If you only knew how I've longed to find you. But I can't expect that you'll cleave to me.' The lady would sometimes garland Anillia with strokings, compliments, gifts, expressions of thanks. The lady did not require Anillia to call her *Mother*. Anillia – Nilya – was to call her *Lady*, just like the servants.

These months might be thought to have unrolled interminably.

The lady's servants, especially her favourites, hated Nilya. She was their rival, and – patently a schemer – might eventually be put over them. For this reason they did not do her any harm, save with their tongues and eyes.

The patience and equanimity of Nilya were marvellous, and endorsed the view that she schemed. Why else was she never taxed by the lady's endless complaining, her procession of maladies, and pettiness? Nilya was an imposter and a clever one, a serpent; best beware.

'She's got no soul,' said the youngest of the lady's servant girls at sunrise, as, with a fellow servant, she prepared the herb drink for their mistress. 'Maybe she's a demon.'

'No, she can touch the holy statues.'

'When the priest comes, he'll suss her out.'

The priest, a godbrother loosely attached to a church in Khish, was an object of some uncertainty in the house. He had visited the lady one day, in place of the other, the elder, sour godbrother, who liked to give penances. The elder priest was loathed and dreaded, mocked in secret. The new priest was not mocked.

When Anillia – Nilya had been in the household two months, the new priest paid a call.

He spoke briefly to the lord householder and the sons of Crel, below. Crel had some vague connection to the Church authority at Khish, but they had been given to understand this priest hailed from elsewhere, presumably the city of Chirkess. He refused their wine, and drank only water. This would have been a rampant insult from any other. The elder godbrother never refused anything; he was a nuisance with his expectations of a good dinner. Then again, you knew where you were with him. It was the information of the elder dinnery godbrother traded with this other one that had been relayed, in the revelatory form, to Crel's wife. Next she clamoured, piping and snivelling. The new priest, standing there in his plain black, belted with hemp at a sword-thin waist, had added meaningly, 'God instructs you, sir, to succour the weak. Your wife is breaking her heart. And if the girl turns out to be yours, how can you refuse her?'

The new priest, though lowly in station, had upon him the full mantle of the Church, that canopy of power, invisible and invincible. Crel sent his sons to the forest.

Having exchanged his latest warmthless courtesies with the Crel men, the male priest ascended to that chamber of women which men so seldom dared.

There was a stir when he was admitted. Not because of his sex alone.

All the women in that womb of a room stared at him. The servants were covert. The lady was suddenly flushed with life, gracious, her pleading changed into the true desire to please. The girl now called Nilya also gazed at this godbrother. Her look, though sustained, was level, neither spying or evading. He did not seem to notice her. He sat down before the lady in a chair that was brought, apparently impervious to the raging and inappropriate fire. He had, of course, no jewellery, but extraordinary eyes.

Their talk was of the spirit, of consolation, the duty of a woman fulfilled here in exemplary sort. The lady relaxed as she heard him. He had such a beautiful voice, his words were like a balm. For those few minutes she became possessed of herself, knowing her worth, not caring for the censure of others.

Then there was a little pause. And the lady said, half playful, 'And do you see, godbrother, who's here?'

He turned, and looked, at the girl they called Nilya.

'This is she?' said the priest

No one had supposed he would be astonished or overtly intersted.

'She's a treasure to me,' said Lady Crel. 'How I try her. She's my own angel,' and back into her tone, unavoidable, there stole the yearning and demand for reciprocity. For the Lady of Crel gave too much and asked too much, that was her curse, which had brought her to what she was.

The priest rested his black jewel eyes a moment more on the lost child. Then, to the lady he said, 'And does she remember any more of what befell her?'

'No, poor lamb. She never speaks of it.'

'God's mercy, perhaps,' said the priest. 'His ways are beyond mortal knowing.'

When he left, he blessed them all. Caught in the broadcast ray of it, Nilya did not avert her glance.

Afterwards the women chattered of the priest – Lady Crel let them do so for a while – but Anillia kept her eyes down on the embroidery the lady had given her ('She does work finer than any of you!'). The eyes of Anillia, which might have resembled those of the mother in her youth, did not resemble at all the brown pebble eyes of the brothers, the corrupt honed eyes of the father. Of all the eyes thereabouts, the eyes of Anillia resembled those of the priest from Chirkess.

Chapter Two

For almost seven years Anillia was the servant-daughter of Crel.

Her position was not worse than that of many girls who had grown up in a household, subservient to father and male siblings, attendant on their mother. And yet, naturally, Anillia was not such a girl. She was the cuckoo's egg given back to the cuckoo.

In the brass coffer of the summer of that first year, Crel's wife gave birth. Her screams tore the house a day and a night. Crel went out upon business and the sons went hunting, Gden raw-eyed from terror.

The women ran industriously everywhere, Nilya with them. And near sunrise, having watched the lady of the house turned to a shrieking, heaving, mindless beast, Nilya, with certain others, beheld her split open like a carcass, and from the scarlet depths a devilish thing, a child, was purged forth.

The baby was a girl. Therefore more or less useless to the house. They had gone to so much trouble, favouring the woman, and she had done this. As she waxed stronger – for despite her several chronic sicknesses, Lady Crel was quite hardy – she put on her guilt and her slavish resentment. She did not nurse the baby, but dandled it when it was fed and clean. A bond, like the peculiar springing cord which had issued from the woman's interior, began to be seen to tie close mother and child, both helpless victims, mewling together in their abject corner.

This, obviously, spelled an end to the other idyll. *This* child was not lost. It had been absorbed, carried about, suffered for, thrust out in agony, witnessed and evident to all. It was a girl, also. The urge to name it *Anillia* must have been poignant. Instead, the father rendered his sorry female offspring the name of a saint, Plina.

As Plina grew, she seemed to push Nilya from the room by the size of her cries and her wants. The servants were gratified, and encouraged it. They noticed aloud that the poor baby wept when Nilya was present.

Nilya began to be relegated to her closet, which contained a narrow bed, a stool, an ewer and basin, a thin window having no glass, only a shutter for when the winter came.

The winter came, and went, and other winters, springs, summers. There had been a day when Crel had spent an hour with his wife, and she said to him, 'That girl – there's something I don't care for in her. Her eyes—' 'The priest finds no fault,' said Crel. The lady wilted, hard-done-by, martyred, comfortable in her accustomed miseries. Yet it was established. The doubt of the mother over the daughter.

Nilya proved efficient at her women's tasks, however, and was obedient, unobtrusive, occasionally even of help, for the schooling they believed the women of the chapel had given her had made of her a better scholar than her father. There was too about her that potential of marriage, for, though no beauty, she had for a man some hint of allure, and Crel's physician had made sure of her virginity. As a recognized child, she might utlimately bring Crel a return.

For the dark priest who had persuaded Crel to take her on, he was long since gone away. The other Khishan godbrother saw to the women's spiritual needs.

Time, which seldom heals anything, nevertheless will confuse ancient pathways with fresh ones.

Plina swelled into a fat and lazy parasite, clinging to her mother, the new axis of the womb chamber, and Nilya floated in the world of the house as if she had always been there, like the tapestries upon its walls, the lights which, with difficulty, entered its corridors.

'She's older than he'll want. But then, a town lady doesn't age so fast. They live softer. She'll have to be examined, her seals must be intact.'

'Do you mean to be impertinent?' said Crel, angry for his house.

'Not at all,' said the agent, amiably. 'I'm a woods man. Blunt. And I speak to you for a noble Tower.'

'Forest lordlings,' said Crel. 'Barbarians.'

But it was foolish to stand on too much dignity, for the very fact he had allowed the man into his hall to discuss such matters said most of what needed to be said.

'Well, sir,' murmured the agent, who had not refused wine, 'he accepts the girl as your daughter, and worth something, whereas another landholder might want to inquire.'

'Anillia is my daughter.'

'For himself, there's been trouble, getting permission to wed a second time. The first wife died in circumstances that the Church frowned on. There was talk. Unfounded, of course. He's eager as a boy, casting around, wanting the perfect woman. It's the prestige he asks, her birth and fitness. He doesn't look for much in the way of a wedding dower – indeed, as I've said, he offers generous tokens for his bride. Horses. Some tithe rights to various of his lands.'

'It's dubious,' said Crel. 'Why does he think I'll part with my daughter, pack her off into the wilderness?'

'Love,' said the agent winningly. 'He loves the notion of her.'

It was apparent the agent had sold the girl as a wonder of high town birth, nobly linked to the upper families of Khish, and to the Church. For Crel, it was a means of doffing something unwanted and making a profit; where another house would baulk, the Tower was ready. The agent would gain his own advantage from each side.

*

Nilya was examined in the traditional way. The crone prodded at her, and the accompanying women peered, and the pronouncement was made: a virgin and healthy. Though nearly twenty-two years of age, she had a girl's body. She should offer sport and bear soundly.

Her scholarly accomplishments were noted too. The godbrother, after a good dinner, interrogated her on her religion, and offered the public opinion that she was pious, he could find no flaw, though privately he set her three penances.

Flawless then.

The lady, her sometime mother, came and spoke to Nilya of her wedding chest, those garments she might take with her. There were even a few pieces of jewellery she might keep, former presents. The second daughter, Plina, scowled and pawed her mother's skirts. The lady had become more firm. Nilya had never loved her, but Plina was her ally, her familiar, they grew as one, fatter and sturdier.

'Have you been told the name of your husband, and his house?'

'No, madam.'

'One would think you'd no inquisitiveness to learn.'

Nilya was composed. She had never altered. Only, her utter patience had frozen slightly, as if it encased itself in frost.

The name of the bridegroom was Kolris, Landholder of the Raven Tower of Korhlen. It was an antique house, proud and mighty. The Lord of Crel had done well by the young woman who, for seven years, they had sheltered like their own.

'We give you to Korhlen as our daughter. I trust you consider yourself to be so. To say otherwise to this lord would be dangerous.'

It seemed Kolris Vre Korhlen would be coming in a day or so, to view his bride. (A savage custom, to want to look, before signing the contract.) Nilya must comport herself as the women had instructed her.

241

They had drawn her from the forest, now they dropped her back into the deep sea of the trees.

Plina pulled a foul face at Nilya, under her mother's loving hand.

The Landholder, Vre Korhlen, arrived with his men, his horses and a pack of dogs. The house of Crel, which had anticipated nothing else, reeled at the coarseness and the foment.

They dined noisily at the table, in the hall. They were clad like what they were, creatures of skirmish and slough. The soldiers who guarded the Vre wore battered mail and gaudy adornments tacked on for their excursion. The Vre's nobles were scarcely better. But the Vre himself wore a collar of gold, some rings that took the eye. They stank, all of them, from the long journey which they did not trouble to wash off. Mud and ordure-splashed, seethed in old sweats, just so they plumped down to the feast, and belched and cracked the bones, and called for more drink as if at home.

They had clothed her in a white linen dress that she herself had embroidered at neck and hem with flowers and fruit. On each wrist she wore a bracelet of coloured enamel. Her hair had been combed out, lying fanned over her shoulders. She had on a pair of pink silk shoes the Lady of Crel gave her in the first two months – her feet had stayed slender. She did not look twenty-two, sixteen or seventeen at the most, a grave, slim maiden. They had said she should keep her eyes lowered. In the forest, women were of necessity modest.

Thus, her eyes were downcast when he came in, hot with wine, a bear from the wood.

In the corner an elderly woman and a young, servants of the house, kept watch. They eyed Korhlen under their lids, disdainful of his uncouthness, suitably intimidated by masculine swagger. A woman was always an inferior. God had organized her lot.

Anillia's bridegroom came right up to her, and breathed

in her face. After a minute he made a sound. He said, 'Aah.' It was satisfaction. Then he said, 'Look up, wench. Look up, I say.'

So she looked up. He was fair-skinned, red lipped, black bearded. But neither those things, nor his features, did she properly see. Anillia saw his total maleness. The incontrovertible stuff of which he was made.

'Nilya,' he said thickly. 'In the forest, you'll be my lady. My wife. You'll give me sons.'

Nilya said, 'Yes, my lord. I will give you a son.'

And he was pleased with her, this white lady who handed him such a promise, straight out.

Even through his drink, he had seen that she recognized him in some manner. She fired him up. He could not wait. Though he would have to, at least until the summer. That was how they went on at things, these town folk.

But he had been fortunate here. After the first wife, that crazy bitch . . . a reward.

'Nilya,' he said again, mouthing her name.

Night, in the town, did not have the movement or pressure of the forest night. Live wood had surrounded the chapel; the dead wood of Khish, boxed groves of houses and hovels, gave off more noises, less ambience of sound. Then, in the month before her journey to her wedding, Anillia woke to the long note of an owl, the rasp of summer frogs, the paper-fingering of leaves and the needles of the pines.

The moon was in the glassless slit of window, yellow, gravid and low. The closet had its light. The room was what it had always been, ungenerous and dull, unchanged. But, at the bed's foot, the priest was standing in his plain black habit.

Anillia never dreamed. Only gradually, as the years passed, had she begun to have thoughts, even. Initially she had acted by mimicry, unspecified instinct, out of the pure vacuum which was herself. A kind of knowledge underlay her responses, but it was as abstract as it was pervasive. She had come to be more human, internally,

243

learning humanness by rote. But still she did not dream, and did not therefore believe that she was dreaming now.

'Anillia,' he said, 'get up.'

She slept, as was reckoned proper, in a thin shift. The shift hid nothing of her body, but she did not attempt either to resist his order or to cover herself against his scrutiny. Scrutinize her he did. There was nothing sexual, even physical, in his regard. His black eyes were impartial. He had looked to be twenty-eight or thirty when he visited Lady Crel's chamber seven years ago, and now he was no older. No *younger.*

Anillia stood in her shift and he in his priest's habit.

He said, 'Do you know me?'

'Yes,' said Anillia.

'Who am I?'

'I don't know who you are,' she said.

'You know so little,' he said. 'You were born out of nothing at the age of fifteen.'

All this while, as they spoke, Anillia heard the leaves of the forest, then the sough of the pine trees in the wind that was like the tides of the sea she had never looked on.

He said, 'The godbrother, and the women in the chapel, gave you the Book to read. Do you remember? The Book says: *The man slumbered, and as he slept, God took from him a rib, out of his body, and from this rib was fashioned a woman. And the man said, This is now bone of my bones, and flesh of my flesh.*'

Anillia, meeting the eyes of the priest, nodded.

'You,' said the priest, 'I made from my body, flesh of my flesh, bone of my bones. I can do such things. Do you credit me?'

'Oh,' she said, 'yes.'

Beyond him, the closet room had opened into an avenue of the forest. It was night there also, folds and layerings of blackness upon the pale black membrane of the sky.

'I formed you to be what you were, Anillia. Fifteen years. Your youth, your skin, every hair. I gave you a heart to beat, and a sealed womb, and a brain behind your seeing eyes and hearing ears and speaking lips, and many skills recorded there, so you could pass for mortal. You're my instrument, Anillia. You must do what I can't, and *will not* do.'

'I know. I've always known,' she said.

'Do you fear it?' he said.

'Not yet.'

At the end of the avenue of trees there was a greater Tree, huge and darkly glowing.

Though it was far off, it was clearly to be seen, and the burning fruit, which hung there, came slowly out on it like the moon from the cloud. Something coiled in the Tree. A huge snake. But it had a woman's breasts and arms, a cat's head about which tumbled unbound hair. Its cat's eyes were grey and cold. It plucked a fruit from the Tree with its woman's hands, and ate it. It plucked a second fruit, and held it out towards Anillia, who was now, without any motion, under the basalt stalk of the Tree. When Anillia did not take the fruit, the serpent woman again bit into it. Blood burst from the apple at her bite. The blood scattered through the air. It did not touch Anillia. One drop had lodged on the black habit of the priest, on his breast, at the centre of a black crucifix he wore.

The crimson eye of the blood stared out.

Anillia, who had felt before merely the transient intimations of human emotion, experienced without warning the weight of despair. She had no name for it. She identified it, namelessly, as she had this magician who had fathered her from his psychic flesh.

'When I've served your purpose, you'll extinguish me.'

'When my purpose is served through you, you'll find rest.'

'Death,' she said.

'That's nothing to you,' he said. 'You are unborn, unliving, soulless.'

'I have a piece of your soul,' she said, 'your life.'

'For a little while.'

They were in the wood, under the Tree, where the cat-woman-snake bit into the bleeding apples of unending life. Though he was before her, he was not there. Not in the magic forest, not in the closet room at Khish. He was miles off, in a cliff of stone beside a plain of water. He had caused everything to happen, her existence and her fostering, her marriage that was to be to this chosen man, stinking of true life, able to make inside her uncanny body a male child, half human and half demon: the son *he* would not fashion from his loins.

On his breast the black crucifix flexed itself. It was an insect, nailed to him by the drop of ruby blood, some other aspect of what he was or might be.

After despair, she learned hate. She had watched it in others, small hatreds. This was vast. She knew that he saw it in her, for to him she was a crystal. He did not mind it. She was his vessel. Do what she would, she must perform his will. Her only other option was to die. And she did not want death. He could fashion her again.

'Tell me your name,' said Anillia. It was the most human request she had ever made. Superstitious and grasping.

From within the ice-black nights of his eyes, he told her he had many names and none. But he spoke to her, and the voice said, 'I am called Anjelen.'

'For an angel,' she said.

'I'm a priest,' he said. 'In my order, this name was given me.'

The Tree was fading, going away.

The moon shone through the network of the pines, through their boughs and through their trunks.

Anjelen, the magician priest, took up Anillia's hand, and her forefinger burned cold. A welt came up on it, and turned to a silver ring, twisted like the tail of the snake in the Tree. She was malleable still; he could do to her anything.

'I've no choice,' she said. 'You're merciless. I can't escape you.'

He let her hand fall, and the ring stayed bright and hard and *real* on her finger.

'Your will is mine,' he said. 'How can it be otherwise?'

246

And then everything, all of it, the forest, the sky, his own body, drew in, poured inwards, into the fragment of the black cross upon his breast. Its blazing crimson star went out.

A moth, large and black, was flickering across the moon in Anillia's window. It flew into the night.

The moon sank slowly, and left the bare room in darkness.

In the last days before her journey to the Raven Tower, they noticed grey strands were starting to grow in Nilya's hair, like winter weeds in a garden.

It was excellent this had not happened earlier. The barbarian lord would not have liked it, such a sign of ageing or debility.

Chapter Three

On her wedding day Nilya wore a gown of saffron, and a maiden's veil of white thread sewn with red and green ribbons, and yellow flowers gathered for her from the garden of Korhlen. Her women, who arranged her apparel, were making the best of things, their faces strained and their eyes inflamed from travel and crying. Crel had given them to Nilya as a part of her dower. The two girls did not want to leave Khish, where they had had to leave too their families and friends, and the town existence they considered to be life. One had pleaded long and noisily with Lady Crel that she should not be sent away. The lady, sighing and adamant, had bemoaned the girl's lot, and severely dispatched her. Obscurely, the Khishan servants also feared Nilya. They did not cause her therefore any trouble, to pay her out for their doom. Nevertheless, they were bitterness personified.

The trek to the stone Tower of Korhlen had taken nearly a month, the journey laden with baggage, and the outriding guard of Crel. Once the lands of Korhlen had engulfed them, some of the Korhlen garrison appeared to escort the bride. She arrived near sunfall, and beheld her future home, the stub of the Tower and its infestation of outbuildings and village. (The Crel men were not impressed by the Korhlen inn.)

That night, Nilya lay in a small chamber, over in the wooden agglomeration of women's quarters – a bridal tradition. She saw and smelled the hints of what Korhlen was, smoke and peach trees, dogs, goats, pigs, open fields and sluggish sewers. On a willow below her window, seen at dawn, two little dolls, male and female, had been hung together, their loins tied close with a string. Later, when Nilya came out to be wed, the dolls were gone.

She was married to Kolris Vre Korhlen in the Tower chapel, by a young, fat, slightly simple priest, who spilled the wine of the sacrament. Korhlen's nobles packed the chapel, with the witnesses from Crel. Nilya's husband was as she had met him before, buoyant and bright-humoured with wine and optimism.

After the ceremony, the day-long junketing began in the Cup Hall. Under the Raven banner of purple, russet and green, Nilya sat with her lord at the high table. Dogs and servants ran about the room. There were slaves with torques of bronze, and scars, and blank faces.

Kolris pressed the food upon his bride, urging her to eat. Beneath the board, once or twice, he rubbed her thigh. For the area and order, he was not coarse, quite decorous, probably. Nilya's girls from Khish had been fumbled several times. It was a wedding, phallic and ready.

In the hot afternoon, he led her out across the court-yard. The big doors were thrown wide, and beyond, the fields ran away in their summer green to the labyrinth of the forest. There was a rough platform, on to which Kolris Vre Korhlen drew his wife. Peasants and villagers of the estate, the field slaves and their overseers, all allowed a holiday for the marriage, stood about to gape at the new lady. When she had been shown, the Vre took his bride back into his Tower, and upstairs to the bedroom.

A slave had come to disrobe him, and been sent away. Nilya's Khishan girls, accustomed to town weddings, had followed to the door, already affronted, only to be shouted off.

They were alone now, husband and wife, lord and lady. Man, woman.

He drank in a swallow the wine from the cup of thick glass braced with gold.

'Do you remember, Nilya,' he said, 'in the town, you vowed to give me a boy?'

'Yes, sir,' she said.

'But the getting,' he said, 'the getting is what I've looked forward to. Believe me, girl?'

Nilya lowered her eyes. Within her seethed something like an ocean. He must not, should not, see. No one, least of all this man-creature, would help her.

He did attempt to unclothe her quietly, but when the garments proved awkward, he ripped at them, then stood back. 'Take this off.'

She went behind the screen, because she had understood that was what a woman of her station did. She put off her dress, her veil, her stockings and shoes, and came out in her embroidered wedding shift.

He advanced again, almost gambolling. The heat of him was portioned from the fiery day that droned in the western window. He burrowed in her neck, and fingered her breasts. Then, lifting his face from her, his eyes narrowed. 'What's that in your hair?'

'What do you mean, my lord?'

'That stripe – and there – and there.'

She realized he meant the grey strands that had grown since the night Anjelen manifested before her.

She shook her head slightly.

He said, frowning, 'Your hair grows old. But the rest of you is young.'

Then he pulled up her shift, and grasped the centre of her body, between her legs.

'Nilya,' he said, several times. He began to unwrap his own flesh from its bridal finery. Then, 'You do it, girl. You touch me.' He directed her hands, where she was to hold him, and how.

His short, rounded weapon was hard, and turkey red, its seed-sacks dilated. She found him ugly, like the stunted bulging Tower itself, ugly and alien. His body forced itself upon her, the strength and texture of it, its amalgamated smells, for he had cursorily bathed for the marriage, its rights to her that could not and must not be resisted.

He pushed her, laughing, to the bed, where the curtain was open. They fell in upon the sheet. She was pinned. He ran his teeth along her nipples. With a weird correspondence of humanity and femininity, she felt a scream rising in her throat. It was as if he tortured her. She had known, she had had *demonstrated* before her, that the end of her function – the birth of the child – was horror, abasement and great pain. But she had not imagined very much to this, the prefacing act. Anjelen had not awarded her any knowledge of it, her experience had not, not even the probing examinations had provided sufficient threat.

Nilya fought, but not with her body. She thrust him off from her even as she sank before him, spreading her thighs for his intrusion. The hurt was awful, as if he meant to burst her. He grinned again and said, 'Bravely, bravely,' and broke her in, gouging a funnel of raw fire inside her. And wedged there, he told her of how she felt to him, how succulent and good. And he forced himself through and through her, and with every grinding blow, he groaned in delight, as if it were her pain that pleased him. All that she watched as she lay beneath, his subject. The seed would presently erupt from him. Her womb, made to receive such seed, would, in the midst of agony, bud. The child of Anjelen, in those moments, should begin to be. *Out of this*.

Nilya fought. Without a sound, without retaliation, without dissent. Her body, too beautiful for any of them to see it, too real to be real, became only a rejection. Created by will, her vestige of that will surged up throughout the entity of her, asserting after all her *self*.

The man, the second instrument of Anjelen's wishes, had reached his climax. He made noises. He arched and laboured upon the apex of his bride's loins.

She had blindly known her purpose. She had revealed it to Vre Korhlen at Khish, when she answered, *Yes, a son*.

But now her body spoke differently. The pages of her skin, her wild hair, her sweat, her temperature, her aching womb, each atom, each cell: *No. No.*

The semen of the man, leaping with its vitality and function, struck upon stone.

He leaned over her, ill-tempered in defeat. She had not been what he looked for. She was cold, inept, a killed rabbit. The streaks of grey in her hair should have warned him. Blood and seed stained the sheet. The old women would have that for the proof. But she—

He glanced into her eyes. They were like heavy polished wood. She had cheated him. He knew she had. He gave her a shake, playful, menacing. 'You'll like it better now,' he said. 'But you must try.'

He offered her the wine, which she drank. He could ply her with that. It would be a long night. By morning, she would be better.

She lay on the pillows and the red sheet, a white body saying No, with shut womb and dumb mouth and wooden eyes.

The Lady of Korhlen had her own chamber, lower in the Tower. It had an eastern window, this room, where the sun rose over the humped clouds of the forest. Here were installed the articles that Nilya's former owners at Crel had given her, and the objects applied by her new owner, the Landholder. Among the latest gifts was a glass mirror. (The Khishan maids marvelled at it morosely.)

The bed had green curtains. Nilya sometimes lay to sleep there during the long summer days. At night she was seldom in this bed. As at Crel, she was summoned to her owner's bedroom, to be employed.

There was a walled orchard under the Tower, passing for a garden. Nilya would go down to the garden, and sit on a stool beneath a tree, embroidering, while the two girl attendants sat apart, idle, making chains of flowers, sometimes shedding tears over vanished Khish.

Every seventh day, and on the holy days, Kolris went to his chapel to receive the sacrament. His wife accompanied him, and the upperlings of the Tower court, the stewards, the captain of the garrison, the surgeon. At intervals it was necessary that Nilya go to the chapel, and confess to the priest. He was nervous of her and, in any case, performed his function oddly. How he had attained such position as he had was a mystery; perhaps his wits had curdled in the forest. Nilya made a confession based upon elements the Lady of Crel had relayed, and matters over which the old women at the chapel had cautioned her. This had always been Nilya's method. Now she kept her itinerary as simple as the Korhlen godbrother's comprehension – pride, slothfulness. It became a set piece between them, and then the gentle penance he imposed. Soon, he was comfortable with Nilya, and babbled about the woods, the great avenues, the arches, everything built to God's glory, a living chapel. There were trees so tall they touched the stars. In Eden, the first garden, there had been such a forest, and there the Tree of Life or Knowledge had stood, guarded by a snake. Nilya listened quietly, until he spoke of this. Then she seemed to herself to see through his sad, blurred eyes – into the other eyes, black, always watching her, through a shadow on the stair, a pane of opaque glass, continually maybe through the optics of those who did not see so far. After this, she distanced herself more thoroughly from the priest at Korhlen.

She did not live. But, she persisted. Each day was like its predecessor, and as she moved across the landscape of it, she beheld on its horizon another day to be, exactly the same. Minor details were variable. That was all. She was like a sundial over which the light of the sun, the dark of the moon, passed and would pass again and again.

Every evening she would dine with her husband in the Raven Cup Hall, under the banners and the smoky beams. When she had been at Korhlen a month, he ceased to go out from the Hall with her. He would tell her to visit his room in an hour, or in two hours. Once she stood up, all the women hastened to vacate the Hall, whereat it became a male den. Uproar thundered from it then, booming over the surrounding places of the hold, and in its alleys there would be slaves racing for more beer or wine, and now and then a noble puking below the steps where the stone ravens stared.

During the summer, often, for a space of two or three days and nights, the Vre would go hunting. At these times Nilya did not take her left-hand seat in the Hall. There was also the occasion when the Vre was absent with many of his men and half the soldiers from his garrison. There had been a flicker of feud with a neighbouring Tower, twenty miles away. The business was soon settled, however, and all the men came home.

It was following this raid that, summoned to her husband's bed, Nilya found him fully clothed, red with wine and anger.

'Well, Nilya,' he said. 'How are you?'

She remained motionless and speechless before him. She did not frequently waste words, or gestures; so he had observed with some abhorrence.

'I mean,' he said, 'is there anything in there yet?' And he pointed at her slender pelvis.

Nilya said, as if he had been merely courteous and diligent, 'No, my lord.'

'*No*? But what did you promise me, then, in your bloody town? A son, you said. A *boy*.'

'I'm not with child,' she said. 'I apologize, sir.'

He felt something, some rock or iron thing. It stood against him like a high wall. He had only sensed it before.

'When I took you,' he shouted, 'I thought I'd got a bargain worth the effort. But you're watered milk. You're cold dough. It needed the girls I had, out in the woods, to remind me what a woman ought to be. I'd say you put a spell on me, if I believed such rubbish. Some woman's spell. You'll do better now. You'll be a wife to me. And you'll fill yourself with my seed. I want an heir, Nilya. If you can't be a woman, at least you can spawn. Work a spell for that.'

In her face he glimpsed a flight of fear. He was pleased. It might wake her up.

But she said, 'I'll do whatever I can, sir. But the rest is with God.'

She did not credit God. He had never fathomed that, since for him God existed, usually ignored, bribed when needful, a force too omnipotent truly to contemplate. To reverence God was to be devoured; let the priests see to it. Yet, God was. Vre Korhlen did not suppose that this woman could think any differently. And by her invoking of God's will, God was put between him and his rights. Vre Korhlen raised his hand to strike her, and God loomed in his way.

'Get in the bed,' said the Landholder. 'Open your legs.'

He took her brutishly, as many times as he was able. She accepted everything, his violence too, but offered nothing, no response.

The wall remained, and near dawn, waking and having her again, seizing her pale face in his hand, he snarled at her, 'What are you doing, you bitch, what is it?'

But Nilya, flung about by his lust, her face crunched and twisted in his hand to that of an elderly woman, did not reply.

She was his curse. He had wanted her, and deserved her, and she would be his ruin.

'A boy,' he said when she went from the sheets. 'See to it.'

She knew he would tire. He would give in. But not the other. To fight this one was nothing. But the other one, to fight him ultimately would not be possible. In time she must yield; her body, which he had formed, would bend itself pliantly. Why then did she struggle?

Nilya did not know. She had become human, she thought, solely through the process of being and keeping alive. It grew in her as the child she refused did not. She was her own child, her own invention, now. Contrary and will-full.

On the stair, the slave lit her way to her chamber. The two Khishans slept in their annexe. A band of opaline blue lay behind the trees, like the sea in the sky.

*

255

Through the winter, the Tower and its village hibernated. The male feasts in the Hall were more vociferous; the Tower soldiers made merry at the inn. Beyond the walls black crows searched the snow, and ermines darted. The wolves passaged in waves among the trees.

Kolris Vre Korhlen had his wife to bed rarely during the winter nights. A couple of times he struck her, never severely.

One white morning, Nilya saw a slave woman in the snow orchard, and two little girls, about two years of age, who were playing and all the while sobbing at the cold. When the slave tried to coax them away towards the women's quarters, the girl children ran off. If caught, they scratched. Both were white as the snow. Nilya had heard some vestiges of gossip, coming in via her Khishan servants. The Landholder's former wife had been addled, and produced two idiot albino daughters before her death.

They were strange figments of the Tower world. Nilya paid them no attention.

In the spring a slave boy was whipped in the courtyard. After the whipping, rumour surfaced in Nilya's room, as one of the Khishans braided her hair.

'Did you know, they kill a man here in spring, lady. They sacrifice him on a black stone to the wood gods.'

The Khishan was arch and disapproving, as if Nilya, by dragging her here, had condemned her virtuous soul in a pagan pit.

Nilya said, 'Who told you? Do you believe it?'

'It's kitchen talk.'

'Then you must eschew it,' said Nilya, in the severer tone of Lady Crel.

The Khishan sniffed. 'Who knows what they get up to in these woods.'

Nilya said, 'I must send you both home to Khish.'

The girl was startled. She lost her colour and bit her lip.

'Have I angered you, lady?'

'I have angered *you*,' said Nilya, giving her cool, silent smile.

She did not want the reluctant Khishans, but must find them a dowry or they would be shamed. Although she did not care about them, Nilya did not want to do them any harm. They cried for days in horror at this new pushing off. Nilya selected the two most valuable fragments of jewellery that Crel had allowed her, and gave one each to her servants. Late in spring, certain Travellers would go through the forest, taking the Korhlen road, heading for Khish. To such a caravan the Khishans might attach themselves.

'But anything may happen – robbers, those rough men on the journey—'

Nilya blinked slowly.

'You must do what you can,' she said.

Her justice was as cruel as it was fair.

They left off crying and turned again to annoyance and rancour, but they were gone before summer.

Nilya made do with a woman of the Tower, one of the slaves, with a slave's characterless part-aged face, who, like Nilya, expected and demanded nothing.

And each year, then, was like its predecessor; as she moved across a landscape of it, she beheld on its horizon another year to be. And yet, these years were not the same. They were, in their similarity, also fraught with change. She felt the man turning from her, she felt herself harden. Her womb was like an apple of obsidian. However, like hardened things, she was strong. There was some power within her. It was not Anjelen's doing, no essence of him. A few times she dreamed of Anjelen – for she dreamed now. But dreams were all they were, nonsense.

There was a feud in her third year at Korhlen, with an Owl Tower. She saw burning far off in the forest, a column of smoke going up to the moon.

And that spring there had been, she knew, a sacrifice at a stone in the woods.

The Cup Hall by night, often, was a bears' arena. They

scrambled across the tables, brawling. The Vre chose from the serving girls and had them in his bed.

He called his wife to her duty once in every month. She came and lay down; he strode to her, rubbing himself to get erect, for he disliked her so much at last, the sight of her did not arouse desire. He would ride her, thinking of other women, and climax as if to be rid of something. A slave would light her down to the lower chamber.

Nilya was now aware that she had wounded. Kolris Vre Korhlen had seemed, and was, such a brute, skin-thick to the exclusion of spirit, it had not occurred to her her adamance abraded him. She had never thought he would nurture fancies. His inadequate and stilted words had not been politeness but facts. She glanced at him in wonder. She had no sympathies with her own plight, could not feel them for any other. She was not human.

The gift was delivered to her in the Korhlen Tower during the summer of her fourth year as the Vre's wife.

Travellers brought it, folk in bangles, rings and bells and rags. Someone had enlisted their portage at Khish. The gift seemed to come from Crel, but did not. Its confinement smashed off, it was seen to be a chair, very fine, of dark wood ornately carved.

On the back of the chair, among the curled leaves and fruits and stems, was cut the Temptation in the Garden, the Tree and the Snake and the Woman, done in tiny, exquisite detail.

They put it in her chamber.

Kolris came to look at the chair.

'You must pen a letter, write and thank them. Your father at Crel, let him know how happy you are, with your husband.' And when she did not answer, he said, 'Damn you, I could have cast you off for your barrenness, if the first one hadn't cheated me.' And she knew he spoke of the first mad wife who had given him the two little albino girls with pink eyes.

She said, with a flint faint pity, 'I regret, my lord, that I displease you.'

But he had slammed away. Leaving her alone with Anjelen's gift.

In the night, when the stars were in the window and sottish roars echoed from the Hall, Nilya sat in the carved chair. The silver ring (which, like the marriage ring of Korhlen, she had never tried to remove), burned her finger, and the arms of the chair sprouted shoots and twigs, and joined across her body.

Held fast, she experienced the renewed growth of the chair, the tree it had come from, rushing up to hit the ceiling, spreading out until a thicket filled the room.

She was in the wood. And caught with her, amid the tree, were martens and squirrels of ebony, and leaden wolves with eyes of painful green, and a white fox that moved its head like a serpent.

Anjelen came out of the starry sky, perhaps where the window had been. He wore and was ivory, and the crucifix was on his breast, the black moth with the ruby nail impaling it, but now, the nail was a rose of blood that shone, dappling the coats of the beasts in the tree.

'Anillia,' he said.

'What is it?' she said.

'I made you for a purpose.'

'Why?' she said. 'Why?'

'Everything that is,' he said, 'must remake itself.'

'Even your demon race,' she said. 'Find a woman then,' she said.

'You've learned enough,' he said. 'Now you can become one of their kind, for a brief while. Go to your husband.'

She had known she could never fight him. She did not try. She relaxed, and the branches of the chair slid from her. The way was a path of steps that led upward through the forest, under the star-crucified sky.

The fox escaped as she did. It sprang like a white fish through a black sea.

Nilya climbed the steps. The trees parted and she found a door. It seemed made of iron, paned with ice, but it was the door of the Vre's bedchamber. Would he not be busy with some kitchen sloven? No, or Anjelen would not have sent her here.

The shadow of the Angel fell upon the door as she hesitated before it. The enormous wings outspread, the body folded like a pin. And the red jewel, the rose of blood, burning at the centre of the breast.

The door became transparent, and through it she beheld Vre Korhlen on his bed, drunken and naked, and alone. The cup of wine had spilled.

As she went into the bedchamber, the forest seeped away, like a wind blowing down the stair.

The normal world of the Tower was there, the hot room of her deflowering and her duty, the bulk of the bed with its curtains looped aside, and the man lying on the sheet.

She stood over him and he opened his eyes.

'Nilya.'

'My lord.'

He sat up, while the empty cup rang on the floor.

'What do you want?' he said.

'I'm here,' she said.

'Nilya,' he said again, 'my Nilya.'

He reached out to her and gripped her as the tree had done, but he was warm, flesh not wood. He put his head on her belly, and murmured over and over.

When he pulled her down to him, she came lightly, she lay with him, and when he rolled upon her, she held him in her arms. She felt nothing, as he worked within her body, but she caressed him, she murmured as he had done, calling him by name. Far, far away, she felt and heard the short ecstasy engage him, throw him headlong, and leave him like a husk.

As he ended, so *it* began. Inside her, there was a glimmer, a pale lightning within her forest. A narrow beam had passed through her. A mote was settling, like a moth upon a hidden room. In darkest night, the glint of life, insectile, preying. Too late now.

Her husband slept, clutching her fast.

Anillia concentrated only on the child which had penetrated her inner darkness. Presently she lost its miniature fire. It was anchored now. It was one with her. As easy as death.

Chapter Four

She walked towards him slowly, and when she was near enough said, without preliminary, 'I'm carrying.' 'Are you now?' he said. He looked her over. She had done her thick dark hair in three plaits and tied a yellow apron over her dress. Her waist looked no wider than on the afternoon he had had her last. 'It's yours,' she said. 'Is it now?' He grinned, letting the axe rest. He had had her virginity, and thought it probable she spoke the truth. In any case, she was the first girl who had proved fertile through him. He had been a trifle anxious about that. 'I suppose you'll want wedding,' he said. She smiled then, and plucked at her apron. To sow and to wed was the custom. He could build an extra room of logs on to his father's hut, and at the month's end, he would take his bride to stand before the Lord Tree; there was no priest for miles. Thereafter she would care for him and bear his children. All about, the wood fumed and rustled in the heat of the summer morning. The depth of the forest was itself like a dark green womb, teeming with life, *alive*. 'Lie down,' he said. They coupled on the wet, warm earth, and silenced the frogs at the pool with their cries.

At various seasons, the Lord Tree was hung with images and bones. (Marra had herself put a mouse skull there.) When she stood before it with Voif, in her crown of flowers, a frightening solemnity overcame her. She swore she was his, trembling, and the village wise women came to splash milk and blood on the trunk, and the villagers laughed and applauded. Marra had always been afraid of the Lord Tree. That was quite proper, yet on this night of her wedding, it seemed to soar miles high, and all its blackened skulls – some of which the men had climbed to position – the smiling sheep, and spined girdles of snakes, catching the torchlight, winked and leered. The foliage was heavy as bunches of fruit, and seemed made of brass where the flames lit them, of the black sky itself where not.

The procession wound back to the village, the only habitation Marra had ever seen. Then, in the new and splintery chamber behind Voif's father's hut, she lighted a brown candle to the Christus on the wall. But He was made from the wood also.

Voif, when he came from the feast, was too drunk to do anything with his wife. As he lay snoring and farting beside her, she realized she did not much like him, but who else was there to take? She had given herself to this one, and enjoyed his lust, and swelled with his seed. She was also glad to have got away from her mother's hut, where five brothers made a slave of her. One man was an improvement. Besides, he was hers.

She lay thinking of their coition, which had caused this. She knew for sure which time it had been. A mote of fire had seemed to pierce her, and her pleasure was so fierce that after, she could hardly move.

Away through the forest, the frogs croaked at the pool.

Marra was familiar with all the noises of the wood. She wondered what her child would be, if he would be special. She said a prayer in her mind, to God. And then, softly aloud, a chant to the other energy, the being of the forest. The duality was usual to her, as to all her fellows. At sunset she threw meal on the fire to make the sun come back in the morning; she had a tiny icon of a saint, bartered for from Travelling People two years ago. The earth had room for all the powers, and so must she.

*

It was when she was four months gone with child that the terrible thing happened.

In the end of the night, after moonset, her bladder, on which the pregnancy pressed, woke her up. Marra was quite accustomed to this by now, and loathing the indoor pot, went quietly out into the fenced yard at the hut's back. Here, on the women's side, concealed by the log pile and the hollow pine, she squatted and voided her urine.

The night was very still, with stars above the village clearing, and the pine-tops round about edged like knives with a half-invisible gleam. Marra kept her eyes wide, however, for it was late in autumn, and wolves might be prowling.

Never in all her days, though she had listened to uncanny tales from the grandmothers, and herself read portents of the supernatural into many events, although indeed she believed implicitly in the occult other-life of the woods, never, never had Marra beheld anything whose jolting weirdness threatened the stability of her existence. Now she did.

Beyond the fence, where the village track ran off into the trees, something was. It had not been there a moment before, when she cast her eyes that way. It had not emerged but evolved. On the black boles of the pines it glowed whiter than the vanished moon.

At first Marra could not get herself up from her squat, so scared was she. Then, when somehow she had straightened her numb legs and come upright, she froze again, could only hold herself there, with a scream stuck in her throat. For the white burning shape had begun to drift towards her. There was nothing animal in its motion. *It floated.*

By this means it advanced nearly to the fence. It took form as it moved, and Marra, through a blear of horror, saw it was in the pattern of a woman with unbound hair, wrapped in a mantle, and although it flamed white, through it were discernible the lines of the trees, the track, the earth.

264

There was no expression on the ghostly mask. It did not seem malevolent, the eyelids were barely raised. It lifted one hand, abstractedly, and the mantle parted. There in the belly lay a second ghostly image, coiling itself slowly, like a cold serpent. This seemed to be a foetus.

Marra managed to let out a low and sickly moan. With her own hand that had no feeling in it, she tried to sketch a mark over herself, and then the cross.

The white woman poised there, watching her perhaps, or not. Then the coiling embryo in her stomach turned a face outward on Marra. It was the face of a baby un-birthed, unmade, yet a face it was, with two molten pits of eyes and a black splitting wound of mouth. Full of comprehending hatred and terror, it gazed on Marra's belly.

The scream escaped from Marra, and her blood seemed to boil. When she looked again, the white demon had gone, though for an instant something like smoke swirled on the air. Then the men ran out.

No one doubted Marra's tale. They huddled her away from the forest, into her hut. The old women would for days and nights toil at protections for her. They would string her with amulets. Ancient stories would be retold. It was well known, woods devils were jealous of human children.

Presently the awful happening sank into the accepted order of the village's history.

Only Marra felt it still lodged within her, like a sliver of ice.

She began to pray regularly to God and to the Christus. She would not go out of the hut at night to make water.

Her dreams were strange. Her pregnancy, moulding her to a progressive mortality, inflicted the dreams, maybe, and made her a participant in them and a witness, both. Nilya examined them on waking. She questioned the answerless creature within her.

In the dream forest, the trees were colossal snakes of polished basalt. Roses grew that the wind struck into fire.

In a winter dream, down an avenue of massive oaks she made her way, and in their snow-locked drums she heard the howling of men imprisoned there for sacrifice, hung to bleed to death, while the trees took on their voices.

The child in her womb was quick. He moved about, not kicking as the women at Crel had recounted the unborn did, more with a sort of beating and flickering, like wings . . .

Every day she grew thinner as her belly enlarged. It took her life. She wondered if she would die in bearing, or soon after.

There were women in the woods in her dreams. She appeared to search among them, passing through their places of huts under the stars. It had begun with a dream of nonsense. a couple glimpsed mating near a pool among the pines. The child in her had moved then too; although he was at that hour only a month quickened. The girl on the ground, mostly concealed in shadow, had cried out in pleasure. The child in the womb seemed to tug. A sudden nausea woke the dreamer.

There was no true time in the dreams. What was her child – *his* child? Were these the child's dreams she experienced?

Then in her fifth month she beheld a pregnant peasant girl in a hut yard. This dream was all confusion. It was all terror. It was not a dream. She knew she had journeyed, almost like the very first journey, but out of her body now. As *he* could do, Anjelen.

Voif's wife was cooking the supper at her hearth, where a loaf baked in hot ashes. This afternoon of winter's finish was already dark, the sky shut, and the snow, which had come three months before, had closed on the village in a white wall. It was not a luxurious time, if any time was that. The fire spat spitefully as wet new flakes fell into it from the smoke-hole.

Voif lay snoring on their bed. He had turned out to be a lazy proposition. The men had been speaking against him, saying he did not do his share. And in his own chamber, of course, he did nothing. She would have to beg him to fetch in some kindling. Was she to carry it, with her eighth-month belly crowding before her? The feeling of illness which had stolen over her about the start of the snow had grown by small degrees, until she was so used to it she mostly forgot her state.

She stirred the soup, and straightening awkwardly, paused in astonishment as a bolt of agony shot through her. There she stood, with the ladle dripping on the earth floor, disbelieving, until the pain tore at her entrails a second time. Then she gave a cry, and let the ladle go.

She called to her husband. She could not breathe or move for pain. Eventually he heard, and grudgingly slouched out to fetch the women, his mother and the crones.

Marra crouched on the floor, panting and crowing at her hurt, staring at the Christus on the wall, entreating his help.

It was so dreadful. Never, surely, had any woman had such pain at a birth. Her loins seemed pushed aside and her flesh rent. Her very bones would be broken.

Marra shrieked and slipped over, and blood and water gushed out of her, as – merciless – the Christus watched. She should have taken something else to offer the Lord Tree. She should have prayed much harder. It was the demon-ghost she had seen who had done this to her.

The hut room was filling up with women giving vague groaning noises, like the lowing of cattle. One loomed behind her, and took Marra's head on to her lap, another spread the girl's legs wide until the joints seemed to crack. 'No,' Marra whined, as if it could be stopped, now.

The little animal in her belly was leaving her fast, and some thirty days before its time. It butted down the avenue of her body, out of the savaged womb that gaped like a mauled rose.

From some limbo where she had fled, Marra heard her own screaming. She had screamed when this thing had entered her.

The night was snowing. The fire turned blue, and bent about, and smoke was in the room with the stench. The loaf had roasted black.

Marra saw her mother's hard wild face.

'It's a boy. You've got your man a son.'

The women congratulated her.

She felt scoured empty, as if a feud had been fought in her, and was done.

They put it down into her arms.

'There. Give him suck. Voif's made you a boy. Suckle him, Marra.' (Voif's mother, preening.)

Marra bared her heavy breast, milk-ripe, and out of the squirming bundle, the head, which had lovelessly shoved at and ripped her, poked forward to take nourishment.

There was something wrong with the baby. Marra stared upon it as it clamped her breast. The milk needled out, a shrill, sweet, different pain.

The little vampire drew and lapped, its eyes screwed tight against the world, not wanting to know what it did. How hideous it was. A devilish thing. No other baby she had seen had been so oddly formed.

She turned her gaze from it, and watched instead the snow coming through the smoke-hole, as the demon milked her.

'*The baby is a changeling.*'

The women at the glass-green pool of early summer raised their heads from their washing on the stones. Who had spoken? It scarcely mattered. One voice for all.

'Have you seen how ugly it is?'

'The poor sow tries to hide it in the shawl.'

'Like an old man it is. And misshapen.'

'The head's too big. Like a booby, but worse.'

268

'She saw a demon.'

'The tree spirits took her child, and gave her back *that*.'

'She didn't make offerings.'

'Hush. The trees are listening.'

They began to sing over their work, ancient songs of the forest.

> *In the wood, the wood, the wood,*
> *Hang the bone and spare the blood*
> *The wild rose blowing*
> *The wind goes sighing*
> *All that lives must die.*

The murmur reached Marra where she sat in the hut room, her ceaseless work untended, the noon meal lying unprepared.

She stared at the five-month child, the changeling, at his eldritch face and burnt-out eyes. His back was humped. Already the skin on him looked withered, an apple left too long. He barely moved. She had named him, desperately, for a saint; the name had come to her, as if from God. But Voif at once corrupted the name, bleeding it of any power to bless or save.

Marra did not weep. She plucked at her apron over and over, busily, as if this were the important task that must be accomplished.

It was not her child. It was not her fault.

Seeing him, this foreigner who had come from her, striding out into the light of dawn, whole and perfect, from their terrible travail, she knew him as a stranger of whom she had caught sight long, long ago, in some other world.

And is this also part of the priest's design for me? How can it matter, since I shall die?

But she did not want to die. She wanted to stay here, with this one, the one who had come forth from her.

At first she thought Anjelen mysteriously spared her. But then she came to believe that she herself had grown strong enough to be free of him, at least in this. Like the bulb casting the flower, she had been meant solely to decay thereafter. She was superfluous. But delivered of the flower, she survived. Only certain aches and exhaustions stayed in her body – these were to be expected after such a taxing birth. The information came with the women of the Tower, the woman who nursed the child. She had learned she had no milk to give. He had left her barren in that way, unnecessary . . .

There had been the moments with the man. These had meant nothing, naturally, and soon he reasoned out the mistake. He shunned her after that more thoroughly even than before. Yet the child was a boy, the heir he had demanded, and which he thought she had promised him. He looked at her with hate, and a bewildered desire that this be otherwise, not knowing himself, and never her.

The child was warm in her arm. She spoke to him. She remembered Crel's Lady, and Plina, and how they grew together. It stonily amused her to consider the phenomenon, and that it might be seen in her, now.

'Mechail,' she said, and the boy watched her, opening wide his eyes, which already darkened and cooled to winter grey. A winter child, she had named him for the saint on the chapel screen. This was not to protect him from Anjelen, called for an angel. It could protect him from nothing at all. She could not guess what he might come to be.

The lord of the Tower had let her have her will about a name. The boy would be his, soon enough.

How long could she live, to be with him here? A year, a month or so, a few more days?

'No, I won't leave you.'

The world was flowing from its summer of emerald fire down into the amber twilight of the fall. Then the dark returned.

How long would she have?

'While you need me,' she said to the sleeping child, 'while I'm able,' and to her amazement, her human tears spilled across the shawl that covered him. He did not wake.

Chapter Five

The slave woman, as she led her charge along the path, had checked, seeing two white things bob up from the bushes. They were the lord's unsound children, a pair of girls about ten years. The uncombed strings of their long white hair snagged on twigs. Their white fox faces, identical as something in a mirror, peered with the same lip-colour eyes.

'Go off,' said the old slave.

One white girl glanced at the other.

'What's she say?'

'Whrr,' said the other. 'Whooo.'

They laughed slyly, in the same voice.

The slave looked down at her master's son.

He was normally a quiet child. His mother ailed. The new surgeon, even with his urban ways, was no help to her. Some days she would not rise from her bed, and today was one of these. And so the slave brought the child down into the garden.

The trees had been stripped of all their fruit. Windfalls lay squashed on the grass with the assaulted leaves. The orchard was golden, but soon it would be bare, and later, white, like the world.

The snow-girls of the lord's first legal begetting came out on the path.

'That's the witch's boy,' said one of them.

The slave pulled on the child's hand, to turn him back. But he was intrigued, and would not obey. He was only three years of age. The slave, who was elderly, did not relish picking him up, for he might kick or strike her, and she must not lay a finger on him, not even to protect herself.

'Come play with us,' said the other girl, who might have been the first.

Now Mechail tugged. Towards them.

'No, Mechi,' said the slave, calling him by the pet, peasant version of his name. She had noticed he responded oddly when she did so. Now he did not seem to hear. 'Want to,' he said. 'No,' she said, 'your lady mother's waiting for you.' 'Isn't.' He was not to be fooled. He was suspicious of his mother's absences, not really understanding her sickness. He had not been allowed to go in to her this morning. He was defiant, like a thwarted lover.

'You must let him do as he likes,' said the first white girl, to the slave.

'Not if you harm him,' said the slave woman.

The sun had come over the wall, the intent, fading sun of autumn. It soothed her shoulders. She did not want to struggle.

Mechail tugged free of her restraint, and ran at the white sisters, who darted giggling away.

The lord's son already had long legs; he would be tall, handsome . . . The slave watched him uneasily, sure she should not allow this, uncertain how to prevent it. But Mechail was weaving through the trees after the sisters. They had taken his hands in their pale paws.

The slave plodded after, keeping a distance, watchful.

They slipped into a kind of cave of trees, where she saw only the white dapple of hair and dirty dresses, and the russet of the little boy's tunic, like fish in a pool.

Shrill laughter came from the cave. Then silence.

The slave sighed. They would be at the oldest trick, she thought. The girls lifting their skirts to show their bald female places, and urging the child, whose manhood yet was only sketched, to reveal himself in turn. The old slave, standing guard, was distracted by the thinnest memory, barely formed, her own first sexual awareness, the motive for which she could not even recall. Nor was it an animal stirring that turned her mental eyes from the scene in the orchard. Rather the sense of the ceaseless length of her drudgery, measured by such small incidents. It seemed to her she had lived a thousand years. Would it never end? She longed for cessation – and was afraid. Though she prayed to the Christus, she accepted very little of the Church's teaching. Only the Christus Himself was possible, for He was the tree god of the woods, the hop and the grape, torn and trampled so the blood might make the ale and wine, the dead winter bough that rose again to life with the spring.

There was a sudden screaming from the orchard cave. The two albinos came scampering out. (One waved her arms.) They whirled away, crying like hurt birds.

The boy walked out of the shadow slowly. He evidenced no physical disturbance. His clothing was neat.

He could not have done anything to alarm the sisters; he was a good child. But they were crazy in any case.

'Mechi,' said the slave, 'you were bad to run off.'

'Can't stop me,' he said.

'Come along now,' she said. She took his hand. It felt very hot, and dry.

He let her lead him; his weight was heavy in the grass and on her palm. He seemed tired, dispirited.

She took him round to the kitchen yards, where there was fresh milk, but he did not want it. The blood had flushed up in his pale face. Was this a fever? He was prone to them, prone to illness, as if to copy the lady.

As they were standing there and she was showing him the goats, in whom usually he took an interest, one of the house slaves came up: the young male Boroi.

'The lady wants him up in her chamber.'

Mechail did not appear to react to this news, only went docilely with the slave woman, indoors and up the stone stairs of the Tower, as if they were going anywhere at all.

The Lady Nilya's room was not well kept, for she was often there and did not like upheaval. (She had not visited her husband's couch for more than two years, they said. To descend to the garden used her up. She seldom ate in the Hall.) She passed most of her hours, day and night, in this furnished prison. Still, there were some fine things besides the stained and threadbare drapes of the bed, the unswept floor and cobwebbed ceiling. A carven chair that had come from a town, a glass mirror that had been a bridal gift. (It was not sensible to look into glass, it sucked your soul away.) *Her* soul looked almost gone on occasion. She lay propped, with the dark and white magpie hair scrawled on the pillows, her hands lying out as if they had not the strength to crawl under the sheet, and her eyes shut. Her sickness filled the room, and yet there was no smell of it, which was curious. She bled too frequently from her woman's cleft. There should have been an odour, of disease and despair.

The child stood by his slave nurse, and would not look at his mother. The slave considered unskilfully: He had done something wrong – but what? And mysteriously the lady knew it – but how? She was a witch. There was something to her that was not anything to do with the frail thing in the bed.

'Leave him with me,' she said now, and the slave, letting fall the boy's hand, her responsibility for the boy's life, turned and left him.

'Mechail.'

Her eyes were open now, very black, clouded. Could she see him? It would seem so. He would not look at her still. He examined a hanging on the wall, a picture of the forest, with birds in the trees, and animals thick on the ground, but it was dulled and worn.

'Mechail, you must come to me, here.'

He advanced sluggishly, stopping to look at things he had seen a hundred times.

Anillia lay as if, in contrast, seeing him for the first.

She was very sick today. She did not know this from the pain, which constantly flared from its accustomed relentless ache into a series of stabs and twistings, nor from the almost constant haemorrhage. It was a day that held the foretaste of oblivion, the longing to give in and so to be no more. She had clung to the cliff face for such a while, ripped at and buffeted, burning with the agony of her fight for survival. And now her grip gradually loosened. She began to perceive the beauty of death.

Only the child had made her cling to the rock, after all. For three years, and more, she had held herself in the state of being, not in order to cheat their creator, but because she had come to love. The child was her love, her only love. She could not, could not abandon him. Others thought him virtuous, stern. But he was cursed. She had realized as much.

The dreams had begun to warn her. Though initially she dismissed them as symbols, or, where she believed she had gone travelling, as misjudged interpretations. The child, which could not walk or speak at first, surely the child was not capable of soaring out so far, free of the body? She had pursued the slight ghost of it through the interminable forest of mirage or actuality. She did not exactly discover the goal of the child, asleep. Indeed, often she only slept, and was left behind. She had questioned him cautiously, evasively. From his manner and his replies she came to think he did not properly remember and definitely did not know what he did. She had asked if he ever dreamed that he could fly. Yes, he had said, like the birds that hovered over the Tower cote, but he was lighter, and there were trees. Once he saw wolves running below on the earth. Once he saw her following him, and went back to play with her, but she vanished and he woke and just the slave woman was there.

He was too young to have to go to the priest. She was glad of that. He was too young to be much with his father the Vre – this too was fortunate.

Intuitively, Mechail seemed to grasp Kolris Vre Korhlen was not his sire, was nothing to him. Mechail feared the man. When he had been taken into the Hall, on feast days, he clenched his small, brooding body hard, to keep from touching the flesh of his father. (The man knew it, blaming her.)

Not a word of explanation had passed between the mother and her child. It would do no service.

She supposed, although even of this she was in doubt, that there must come a time when Anjelen, if he still bore that name, would set foot in the life of Mechail, to claim him. Or did that matter? The ambition to remake himself had seemed passionless with Anjelen.

She had been dozing in a haze of coppery pain, when she beheld her son in her mind under the orchard trees, with the two white twins. A ring of the unnatural shone around them, bright and quivering.

'Those little girls are your sisters,' said Nilya now.

He did not ask her how she knew about this. He was aware of her uncanny insight in regard to him. He had never seemed troubled by it.

But when he spoke he stammered, which happened when he was nervous or dismayed.

'They – have mouse eyes.'

He had reached the bed. Nilya put out her hand and took his shoulder. He flinched. He was hot, and his face was like a paper behind which something was on fire.

'You hurt me – hurt me—' he stuttered, not trying to shift away.

'What did you do,' she said, 'to frighten your sisters?'

'One – one – one,' he said, 'one showed me her chest. She has bumps there. Then she say, Show us your dagger.'

Plainly, he had understood what was meant by this. He studied the floor. Presently he said, 'I told them I'll show something else. I show them a thing I see in the wood.'

'What thing?'

'A thing.'

'Say to me what it was.'

'Mamma—' he blurted. He was not allowed to call her this. The Vre had shouted at him after this third birthday, he was to be a man, he was to call her *Mother*.

'Mechail, you must say.'

'It was me. The me I saw. The me I am there.'

She said, 'You must show your mother, now.'

'Can't.'

He had drawn some oblique ignition from the two girls. They were fey, perhaps energized.

But it was what *he* was that enabled him to do all and anything he did, these magic terrors.

'Who are you,' she said, 'in the wood?'

Suddenly he condensed himself, hunching over, angling his body, distorting his features. All at once she was shown, if not by psychic shape-change, then by childish imitation, another child, hump-backed, buckled, with an ancient face. A dwarf.

Her heart crashed in her breast like breakers from a sea she had never looked at. The pain gouged her with claws. She saw him miles off, her child, she spoke to him in a low, clear voice.

'You shaped yourself into this?'

'Yes, mamma. But it's me.'

'It is not you. Why do you say that it is?'

'I make it me.'

'How?'

'Don't know,' said the child, and became a child, trembling with grey eyes gone to white in a hot, mad, bestial face, like a wolf's face or a cat's. 'Inside me,' said the terrified child, 'it's there, and I see it, the shadow go up the wall—'

Nilya battled with her body, to come back to him along the miles of pain, to comprehend what he said.

'He hates me,' said the child. Something had broken loose. He stamped and screamed and tears and spit whirled off him. 'Mechail *hates me*! Don't want to be him, don't want! Like this! Like this!' And then, and then, she saw him melt and alter like a candle when the flame slips down it. She saw, but only for a second, Marra's changeling.

Nilya felt a rush of blood scalding from her. She swam upwards from her body and hung for an instant over the room, where the shrieking child threw himself about, beating himself against the walls, the posts of the bed.

Her last thought, deadly and precise, went down with her into unconsciousness. *He has done what Anjelen did. Out of himself, he has made another.*

★

She was ill for some weeks, and the child was also ill. They lay in separate chambers, where they were tended by women, differently.

As had happened before, her body, managing to heal itself, regained a temporary vitality. Sickness repaired her. She rose from it as if she might now get well.

The boy too came back from his fever to his former docile, serious ways.

The autumn was turning red, and burning out.

There was a dispute with the Wolf Tower. Kolris Vre Korhlen went raiding with half his garrison and was away most of a month.

The red went to charcoal. The forest turned to iron.

The albino girls sat on their bed, in their apartment of the women's quarters of the Raven Tower. Night approached early now, and the moon had risen, the colour of their eyes frozen in a pinker sky. The bed was islanded with spangled cushions and peculiar toys – stones with faces, bunches of feathers – while their pet civet hung from its rafter. Everything listened. The room held its breath. Sometimes one of the sisters whimpered. Then the other shushed her.

They had closed their shutters at sunset.

Perhaps it would not come, tonight.

The slave women brought them food once or twice a day, and entered maybe to clear up after them, but Korhlen's daughters were unpredictable, and better left alone. Their father did not care to hear anything of them, providing they still lived.

There was no one therefore that they might tell. They had not thought of it. They consoled each other in this, as in everything else, and as best they could.

Outside the shutters was blackness now. The sister who had been christened Charina had lit the three candles, with exaggerated care, as she had once been taught to. All the complex and horrible demons which had got in to people their mad imaginations in the first year, woven of night, must be kept at bay by illumination, the candle, as by the sun of morning.

Perhaps it would not—

A weightless tapping and flickering of sound began, between the darkness and the shutters.

The sisters clutched each other. The second twin (who had already acquired the cat's title: Puss) buried her head in her sister's breasts and hair. While a devil-thing, bizarrely attracted to them and having the shape, it seemed, of a bat or small bird, fluttered on the wooden slats.

Charina did not hide her head or eyes. This had happened for five or six nights, and she was becoming curious. Fearful still, yet she wished she might slip the shutters open a crack, and see. As in an antique tale, might she not persuade the demon to mount upon her finger, and taking a sip or two of her blood, it would in exchange offer her a reward. Could this not be worth attempting?

But Puss burrowed and whined. Charina stayed where she was. It never lasted long, the visitation, so therefore her temptation was also short.

Slaves who passed at all hours of day and night, through all areas of the Tower and its buildings, had seen, some of them, a shadow. They had seen it in the kitchen yards, and in the walk before the chapel, by the Women's Garden. They had seen it in the boughs of naked orchard trees, on a skeletal willow, and a balcony of the female apartments. They marked themselves listlessly, and went on. Some who, from woods parentage, knew how, made amulets, but in a desultory way. For what were they preserving themselves – they had no lives, being only the lord's property.

Two servants in the Tower had glimpsed the shadow. In a cellar, on a stair. They did not ponder what it was. A trick of a candle, a spider's web.

Grey, transparent, with a minuscule glint of brilliant red that was there, then gone, like a sudden dazzle over weary eyes.

The night was so black, it made colours and forms.

Nilya's body, weak from bloodloss even in its spurious and ephemeral strength, gave to her eyes very often such dazzlings and formations. In the dark, waves of flame rocked over her sight.

She stood at her window, and below were the muddy lights of the surrounding Korhlen village, and farther off the walls of the wood, and the moon already high.

She left the child alone now. It was practice for the grave. She had gradually stopped herself loving him. There was no point to that.

Foolishly she had begun instead to pine for her beginning, her brief girlhood in the lorn forest chapel, among the elderly Handmaidens. She wanted to go back. She wanted her fifteen-year old, new-minted flesh, that did not hurt, that bled only on the proper days, that had black hair and was not afraid.

She had learned to fear, and to weep, as she had learned to love. These awful things were linked to one another, fearing and loving and weeping.

Her sham of strength made her frightened too of death. But that would vanish. Ultimately, she would be glad.

Nilya returned to her hearth, where the illusion of warmth and comfort was. And heard behind her, on the shutter she had closed, something tapping and rustling like a lost bird.

She looked at once, fixedly, at the chair. But it was innocent. No branches, bare or clothed in leaves, reared from it. The snake did not hiss, the apple did not bleed.

'Go away,' she said. She clenched her bone hands beneath her throat. It was not Anjelen who was here. He had no need to be.

Then the tapping of thin wings ended. Where the fire shone on the tapestry, there she saw the shadow shape itself swiftly, like a pale stain. It pulsed, nothing else. It might have been a clot of smoke. But the rubies of its eyes were spikes of reality. They glittered.

It could pass through walls, or manifest within them. It had no need to rap at a shutter, asking admittance. It was presumably unsure what it could do, until it had tried.

'I have nothing for you,' she said. 'Whatever you're wanting. You must go back, go in again. Leave the Tower alone and leave the forest alone. You have only to wait.'

The huge moth, transparent still, flew down on to the chairback. It folded its wings. The insectile image was that of the Devil, horned and winged.

Nilya bent to the hearth. She felt the weakness as she did so, it was always by her, ready. Taking up a stick of wood which burned, she went towards the moth. It seemed to pay her no heed. Then, as she thrust the fire into it, into the pin of its body, it disappeared.

She was too drained to ask what had occurred. She let the wood fall back into the hearth and set herself on her bed, where she lay and longed to be a girl again in the chapel in the woods, before she had known anything, when she had known everything.

Snow had come, and the forest was a country of the white moon. The river had not frozen, it was broad and the current swift. The boat was driven smoothly on; she need do nothing, nor the snow girl who sat before her in the bow.

Nilya felt the joyous redemption in herself. Her body was young. Looking down, she saw on her dress a border of foxes and grapes, the weaving of the Handmaiden named Urzi.

In the crystalline shade of the winter afternoon, the white twin – which one she was, Nilya could not tell – looked like a ghost.

Great-antlered trees, cedars, oaks, lined the river. The pines went up beyond, hill on hill, in galaxies of black-rimmed snow.

The boat ran on, and there was a break in the trees, and here the roses grew upon their stalks of ebony, red, as red life in a heart, the only true colour of the glassy day. But the wind blew like the ice mantle of the winter god of whom the lady-woman in the house of Crel had once warned her straying daughter. The wind blew and the roses bent and streamed on the sky, and up from each there lifted like a crimson bird the core of redness, and ribboned away. It dropped to the white snow and stained it, it unravelled in strands and tresses down and down and poured into the river. The river was red.

'Look at the blood,' said the albino.

The boat ran, parting blood and water, and on the shore the roses stood, bled of life, withered papers in the dying wind.

Then, the albino raised her hands, and caught on her finger a moth with wings of fire and darkness.

'Did they burn you?' said the albino girl.

Anjelen said, behind Anillia's ear, inside her skull, 'The first wine will be male. A victim of his anger. Or a killing in the wood.'

If from a woman then, said Anillia, *do we swindle you?*

There was no answer.

The girl laughed. Her hands were empty. Then filled by an apple, red as the roses from the bleeding of the shore.

Anillia stared into the sky, to seek the moth that burned with the fire with which she had pierced it. It had seemed to her a ruby blazed inside its body, the flame she had given in her fear, her death of love. For this *was* love, this loss, these silences.

I am dreaming, dreaming in silence, in a bed of stone, my womb is broken and under me the earth gapes.

I shall wake up in the Tower, in the snow night.

But when I am dead, no waking.

The boy sat by the glassless window, and beyond its painted shutters the snow glided down, so the Tower seemed to fly slowly upward into the night, but never arriving. Otherwise, his situation was mundane. The well known square of room, the hearth in which pine cones charred with a hot glow, and sometimes spat. The old woman was busy at some darning. A few toys lay scattered, a wooden bear, a cluster of round beads for rolling . . . The boy himself perched in the window embrasure, the old woman had helped him there. Now and then she would admonish him not to get down without assistance. He must not fall. The conception of falling was not beyond him. It would involve injury.

The curtains of the small bed were drawn back, and even when he slept, would be so, that his watch-woman might be sure of him.

Abruptly, the door opened. His mother's servant stepped through. Mechail did not need her announcement: 'The Lady Nilya.' But he did not attempt to spring from the window. He waited. The slave had told him that his mother was sick. He had not seen her for two months, perhaps more. He had cried in the night (when the slave thought that he slept) noiselessly, to prevent her hearing him. He half imagined that his mother had chosen the sickness, had gone away with it, leaving him behind. One night, he dreamed she struck him, which she had never done. He had supposed that he was in the forest, someone stunted and misshapen and hated. He did not know who this was, yet it was himself, Mechail, called Mechi. His father came in, to a chamber made of logs. His father was no longer the Vre. He pushed Mechi over. A woman in an apron sobbed, and another one shouted in the door. But it was Nilya who sped across the room with a lighted torch in her hand. She smote him, against the heart. A red nail went through his body. He woke and held his misery to him, stifling its notes in the pillow while the slave slept at the hearth.

Now, Mechail's mother walked into the chamber. She wore white, and with her cold austere face, her black eyes, she had the look not of anything feminine, but of a masculine saint, out of a book his father had once shown him. (The book with the fearful Devil depicted in it, in scarlet, eating the eyes of the damned.)

'Why are the shutters standing wide?' said Nilya, without any emphasis.

'He wanted to see the snow,' said the old woman. She hung there, between apathy and grovelling.

Nilya only said, 'Close them. Then you may absent yourself for an hour.'

The slave went to the window, and putting the stool under the embrasure, and firmly assisting the boy, she got him to the ground. Next she pushed the shutters together and inserted between them a piece of woollen cloth, as always, to keep out the draught. Then she left mother and son alone.

The boy stood on the floor, and looked at the hem of Nilya's dress.

'I've not seen you for a long while,' she said presently.

'Yes.'

'Can you guess why that is?'

The child waited again. At last he said, 'Why?'

'It's because I shall have to go away quite soon.'

Mechail said, not looking up, 'Is he sending you away?'

'Not at all,' she said, for he meant her husband. 'I'm going to die.'

He did not, she thought, understand what she meant, and yet she beheld that he started to cry, mastered the crying, and remained before her, like a small rock, isolated in the middle of a great plain.

She had not, in fact, ceased to love him. No.

She remembered how she had held him, put him to her dry breast for his solace, how he had begun to walk, and to speak to her – but already the blight had come on him, even then.

She went forward and lifted his hand, which unresistingly he gave her. She led him to the hearth, and sat down there on the slave's stool. He looked up, at her eyes, and away again. Time was like the snow. It had no enduring substance, and might thaw to mud in one spring day. She could not dally.

'Tell me what you dream, Mechail.'

He looked at her directly and suddenly then. His eyes were hard with mature pain.

'You hated me.'

He had raved before how he hated himself, or the self he had been made to be. Was that forgotten? Did he know anything at all of what he was, and what he might do? She herself, dimly recognizing his essence, which in some way was also hers (the things of Anjelen), sensed in the child complete knowledge, but hidden from his heart and reason behind a screen of ignorance.

'Why do you say I hated you?'

'You hit me with the fire.'

She collected herself, putting off her panic of longing to draw him close against her and charm the dark with sweetness. The dark was not to be charmed.

'And this was in your dream?'

'Yes.'

'What then?'

'I woke up.'

'But if I struck you, then I could never have known it was you.'

He said, almost guiltily, 'It was in the forest. I was the other one there. His back's all twisted, and they hate him too.'

She was so cold. She wanted to clasp him in her arms, and to fling him from her into the blazing hearth. Both at once.

'Mechail, do you fly in your dreams still, like a bird?'

'I don't do that any more.'

'Surely you do. Like a black bird. And you tap on my shutters to wake me.'

He gave her one sidelong, doubtful glance.

'It wasn't me,' he said.

She said, 'Who was it then, Mechail?'

He lowered his eyes. He took a fold of her dress between his fingers. He said to it, with a dragging deliberation, 'When I grow, what will happen to me?'

'You are the Vre's son, and his heir,' she said, cruel, to see. 'You'll be trained to the duties of the Tower. One day you'll be the lord here.'

He held the fold of cloth patiently. He said, 'No, but, but what else?'

'Your father's son.'

His whole body made an irritated sloughing gesture; it

conveyed Nilya was lying, fobbing him off, in the way of
the adult echelon. He did not have the words to press
her, and she too struggled for words that he could not
evade. She put her hands on his arms. Quietly, she said,
'There's a great moth which flies here. Have you seen it?'

'A shadow,' he said, 'on the wall.' His eyes were down.
He *knew* – and he knew *nothing*.

She thought, *I shall be dead soon. What does it matter?
Anjelen has him.*

'Mechail,' she said.

She drew him to her. He crammed against her body,
as if to get in again, inside her, out of the alien world.

Eventually he said, 'After you go to die, will you come
back?'

'No, Mechail.'

She visualized the vast dumbness and void into which
she would return, the womb of oblivion, out of the alien
world.

It seemed to her he saw it, through her inner eye. His
questions stopped, finding themselves ineffectual, as hers
had done.

A kind of crash, like a dislodgement of snow or rifting in
the ice, surged through the Tower.

Nilya raised her head from her half-sleep. Seated in the
wooden chair, in her mantle, her hair loose, perhaps she
had been attending on something. Was this the advent?

She stood up. Her hearth was clinker and the candles
low and guttering.

She had never heard such a noise before, not in the
stone shell of Korhlen. Had she only dreamed it? But her
dreams, confused and tattered, had swarmed away. The
echo of the noise persisted. It did not seem to have been
physical at all.

In a pair of minutes, she began to detect shouting and
movement in and about the house.

She thought of a raiding, enemies of Korhlen—

She knew it was nothing like that.

Nilya walked a few steps. She felt curiously tall and

287

weightless, chained to and yet detached from her body. There was no pain, no illness. The flesh which had contained and fashioned her freakishness was distant. Her death must be imminent, hovering in the room. But it was not her death which caused shouting through the Tower.

She did not stir herself to learn. It was as if she had already been told, although, by some slip of space or allocation, she had not caught up with the facts. When the fast steps came outside her door, this was a repetition.

The servant entered as bidden. She had served Nilya some years, lifelessly, flawlessly. Now her face had character. 'Madam, oh, madam.'

'What is it?'

'A beast came through a window – it attacked your son as he slept.'

Nilya listened to this.

The woman said, 'The second steward sent me to you.'

Nilya became aware she must go down through the Tower to the room where her son couched, in the wooden bed with the Raven of Korhlen on its curtains. She did not think to ask the nature of the attack, or of the animal, or whether the child lived. She knew it all, had known for months . . . Yet she moved as if she were dazed. That would be suitable.

And then, when she reached the chamber, it was empty. A guard stood at the door in his mail, and tried for her with unsteady eyes, but let her by.

A piece of wool lay on the floor. It was the padding from the shutters. These were ajar. Between the wool and the bed, which showed a slight disturbance, as if the covers had been thrown off in excitement, brilliant red blood had made a tiny pattern, only spoiled at the edge where something, perhaps the boot of a soldier, had scuffed it.

The fire was burning cheerfully. The toys had at some earlier point been put in a cupboard.

Between the parted shutters, the sliver of night was black as frozen glass.

Nilya cast about herself. What would a human woman do at such a moment? Scream or fall to the ground – no, she must seek her husband the Vre, demand to hear what had happened, cry out before an audience—

The gap of glass night in the window exerted a drawing pressure on her. She turned from it, and beyond the open door she glimpsed a huddle of slaves, who instantly swirled about like vapour and were gone.

These creatures knew, as she did. The Tower was full of *knowledge*.

On the stair, another soldier glared at her.

'Take me to the Vre,' she said.

He took her, like a visiting harlot, up the Tower again, to the bedchamber of her husband. And this room also was vacant.

'Where is he?'

'The Vre's with his men. But he sent the captain out after it, and some of the garrison—'

He would not conduct her into male territory.

'My son,' she said.

'Yes, lady.'

She found she had turned again to a window, this one glassed, but still the pane of night. Her mistake – the blackness took firm hold of her, and the white.

The moon seared on the snow, looking too big, as if it dropped towards the earth.

The soldier was sidling out. He would only have sung her some story of a feral animal getting in at a shutter. A slave, cornered, might babble of a demon.

It had no significance if she did not learn the facts accurately after all.

The thing which was her son had come from him, separate and alive, to kill him. Like herself, he had instinctively rebelled. A murder which was a suicide. Had he succeeded? She felt nothing, at the theory of his harm or death. Something pulled at her, magnetizing her through the window into the moonlight, where she saw, on the round and blind white disc, the ghost of the moth, with blood-drop eyes.

Her body stood like marble at the window, and she went forward down the corridor of night, after the flying thing which was Mechail, the soul of his soul, while dully behind and beneath her she heard the baying of the wild hunt, the Vre's captain and his men pursuing a nightmare, a madness, between the flashing swords of the pines.

When her husband, the lord, entered, she was partially aware of it. She did not greet him. He spoke to her roughly, of the unimaginable truth, bolstering it all the time with suppositions: an animal, a felon, the lies of slaves. And when he went from the room again, she stayed by the window, meshed in night.

She was still standing at the window when he re-entered two hours later. Vre Korhlen's wife, the Lady Nilya.

If she had moved at all, a hand, or her eyes, he could not make out. She looked just the same as when he had left her, a figure of the snow night.

'Sit in the chair,' he said brutally and loudly, 'or take yourself to bed. What can you do, just stand rigid as if you were in church?' His voice rose on each sentence, to make her hear. She was his disappointment. She was his youth which had bloomed into middle age, his incoherent hopes never met with, whatever they had been. His craving for a son realized in the unliking boy, *hers*. But this bitch had not sought her child, half-dead in the surgeon's room, under the incompetent and ramshackle bandages. Bitch, this *bitch*. 'Did you even go to look at him?' he roared at her. 'Well, Nilya, you'll answer me.'

'No,' she said. 'I can do nothing.'

Foil to his, her voice was a forest away.

He drank wine in his cold house. And soon left her again, his marble wife, against the wall of night.

And in her body she was sleepily wondering, *How did I talk to him, I am here—*

Here, where Mechail's benighted soul had come, this valley under the brim of the woods.

The moon had gone down, or changed to black. In the starlight, she picked her way between the trees. The ground sloped. She saw the tracks of something dog-like on the snow (a wolf?), and *felt* the snow, as if on bare feet, but only cool. She had no pain. She was light, under the stars, between the sky and the earth. She was forgetting why she had entered the valley. The creature which led her had disappeared. She needed simply to be. It was good to be. Young, and whole, walking on the snow . . .

I've become a girl again.

She touched her long loose hair, and brought a lock of it across her face. No white, no threading of age and terror, or disease.

She was Anillia again, just born, moving through the forest, towards the chapel.

No. She was dreaming.

Then, the tree line broke, and she beheld the chapel lying there, a casket of stone.

The pleasure, the shock of the pleasure, sent her springing back.

Her body received her. She hung in it, as though in an upright coffin balanced at the window frame of Korhlen's Tower. Yet also, she stayed in the valley. She sensed, and nearly saw, herself, miles away, a figurine upon the snow.

It was unnatural. A mother must go to her child.

She forced the coffin body of pain to motion, and drove it out of the Vre's chamber, and through the Tower, to the place where Kolris had informed her their son lay, in a stupor.

She saw the surgeon, frightened and inadequate, masking himself with his town manners.

And she heard herself murmuring, attempting the correct platitudes.

Continuously, distracting her, something uncoiled and uncoiled from her inner self, like yarn unwinding from a spindle. It delighted her, this sensation. She longed to go away with it again, back to Anillia in the wood.

The fool who was the surgeon told her Mechail was a healthy boy.

'Not so. As a baby he was often sick. My fault. And this —' A mother's protective guilt. But her body spoke too keenly. 'Don't let my son suffer.' *Kill him, kill him,*

*you monster, binding him up for a travesty of life when all
he wished was death—*

Cheat Anjelen.

But the surgeon was afraid. He would botch and run
away.

Now he asked if she wished to see her unconscious son.

'I've done him enough hurt.' (She should not have said
this. But the fool would not fathom it.) 'I won't go near
him.'

She drifted out of the chamber. Her coffin Nilya body
had now thinned to mist.

She should have gone in, smothered the child. He had
wanted and chosen death. But she would not shoulder
Mechail's cross.

She reached her room through a shifting insubstan-
tiality, which was what the Tower had become. *Lie on the
bed; they'll think you faint or sleeping.*

She shut her eyes, and instantly rushed out of herself
and through the walls and back along the unwound cord
of power and found herself, Anillia, walking slowly in the
snow, towards the chapel—

Whose door was a shadow door. She approached
through a darkness likewise of shadow. The dawn star
was pinned over the roof.

It was not the chapel of the old women. It was empty
and had been pilfered. The eyes of the saints on the
obsidian screen were all picked out.

She walked through the chapel.

Above the altar, behind the screen, a window, a gape
of paling blackness in a lattice of roses and thorns. A
crucifix was on the altar, with an iron Christus. It seemed
to form out of the dark, and overhead, a lamp. There
should be a watchlight in the bowl, to signify the presence
of God. As she considered this, the light stole up inside
the lamp, yellow as a flower of spring.

Ah, she thought, *because it is a dream.*

She had come to see it was no dream.

She stood in the bleached greyish ascetic's robe the
Handmaidens had first given her, her black hair running

on her neck and shoulders. She saw what she had done. To this, illness and yearning and rage and love had brought her. As Anjelen had done, as Mechail had done. From some astral material of her soul, or of some physical element not fleshly, she had made flesh. She had made Anillia over. A bitter joy infused her.

And then, in the paling night, the moth rose, circling out of the darkness, round and about the burning lamp.

Anillia, as she had seen the albino do, lifted her hand and called the moth.

It flew towards her, avoided her fingers, tangled itself into her hair, as the child had often done in play.

Such love. It boiled in her at the infinitesimal contact, the paper wings against her throat.

Mechail . . .

'Live. Live and deny him.'

Then the soldier stepped over the chapel threshhold. The hunter.

She was transfixed, but the chrysalis of the knowledge, all of it, split open inside her newly sculpted brain. It was a concept horrendous, ethereal, jesting and lawless, a resolution of beings evolved of chaos. If it was more joke than plan, more enterprise than jibe, meant nothing. It might be done.

So she offered her whispering cry to the soldier, the captain of her husband's garrison, twenty-nine years of age, Carg Vrost, strayed broken-handed and partly mad, from terrifying night to chaos night.

'*Help* me.'

He looked very young, the captain, and old. Agony – the broken hand – had pulled his face against its bones.

'If God is here, He'll watch over us. Stay very still, lady.'

As he came towards her, she cringed. It had been too easy – how could it be that she was real? An illusion, he would find her out, and the thing which had flown to her for protection – but he could not destroy that, of course. She forced herself to the stillness the soldier had imposed, and from the whirlpool of emotions within her, let down the long bright tears, becoming for him what she seemed.

He seized her hair in his ruined hand, and screamed aloud. In that moment, as the sword descended, Anillia acknowledged her reality. The blade grazed against her head, a slight, peculiar wound that borrowed all her sudden strength. She fell.

The moth, cut free in a net of hair, went fluttering also to the floor. The soldier tried to trample it. The moth flew up, over the screen, towards the window, where the cold sun was rising.

The soldier, the captain, would believe that sunlight put paid to demons. Perhaps some demons were susceptible to it. Not their kind.

Mechail, the child of Anjelen, knew what he must pretend. She saw, somehow straight through the screen, the beat of wings that went into the fire of the lamp. And then something poured out of the bowl.

It was a reproduction of the tortured altar Christus, a crucified man, arms outflung, impaled at the breast by a single scarlet nail.

Mechail said to her, *I have been made to live. I shall live to be this.*

She shut her eyes, and lay immobile until the freezing sun crept over her and Carg Vrost knelt at her side, feeling at her for signs of survival.

Presently she allowed him to revive her.

'The light,' he said. 'We're safe. It died.'

Above his shoulders she beheld motes sparkling in the air. They might have been the psychic atoms of her son.

Carg Vrost left his wrecked hand lying over on the floor, as if he had already hacked it away. He used his elbows to lean on, and put his right hand into her garment.

'Apple breasts,' he said. The heat of desire soaked through his mail, his skin, into her Anillia body, which was young and whole, ready as fruit to be plucked.

She thought of the dwarf child conceived in the wood.

The motes sparkled as they came down on her.

She put her arms about the soldier. (A forest away, the

294

exhausted vessel on the bed at Korhlen convulsed, trying to refuse.) The new-made virgin girl in the chapel wound Carg Vrost with her limbs, opening herself like a fragrant flowery grave.

Chapter Six

During the last months of her life, the sick woman spent most of her time with her son. This was a contradiction of her former recent avowals and actions. But then, the child had been crippled. The story ran, a dog had savaged him. It seemed sure he would not grow straight. There were whispers in the Tower like a straying of the winter wind that yowled about the stones and shook the timbers. The whispers, like the wind, had their own language.

The child had been very sick. He had almost died. The woman paralleled the child's course, as often in the past. They were like two fragments of some other thing, from which they had been broken off.

Mechail then came limping up from the vat of destruction, formed in his new, wrong shape. With the child's weeping acceptance of pain as some outer element, intrusive to his body, not inherent in it, he bore what he must, and began to sit and to move in the upper world of life, white-faced and fleshless as a winter twig, also twisted like one. Nilya too was there, moving about with him, sitting by him. And she was like a pale leaf. She would not endure where, incredibly, the ruined child could.

The concluding time of her illness made her look young, and when she slept, which was frequently, or sat as if sightless, in some trance, her face smoothed to a pallid oval tile, having only inked-in eyes. Conversely, the child seemed old. Their ages had drawn together, as if she hurried back, he forward, to meet for some final conjunction.

They seldom embraced, or even touched each other. Their own bodies were not worth much to either of them, they did not wish to share the debris with each other, only the soul which had formed inside the skin, that emanation of the heart and mind which is given to hoping it is immortal, but may only be the cipher for something more elusive, which is.

Nilya saw that Mechail had now eradicated from mind and memory all self-knowing. He rose from the river of death purged, solely a small boy, a cripple. What he had done to himself, or willed to do, was wiped away with the deed.

As the voice of the Tower did not tell the truth of it, neither did Mechail, even in dreams.

When the spring returned, the soldier worked at the earth by the hut door, as best he could, one-handed. Scraps of vegetables lingered in the soil, and as he had repaired the hut, he set to nurturing its sustenance.

The girl watched him from the doorway, when the weather warmed and brightened. She was not much use to him.

The wound in her scalp had healed, and the hair grown over. But internally the blow had done something to her. She would nestle against him, trusting and child-like. She would sleep for prolonged lengths of time, and he could not wake her . . . Her breathing was so slight then it seemed carried on by some reflex – will and life were gone. She was *unoccupied*. And sometimes she would shriek, and beat at herself, like a clockwork doll whose mechanism was faulty. She was also pregnant.

After a day and night in the chapel, burning bits of wood on the holy floor for comfort, he had gone to hunt, and found this place. He brought her here. He began next to call her Jasha, after a girl he had once met at a brothel near Khish. It was not to insult the girl from the chapel that he called her this, but only in order to attempt some solidity, some reality.

Carg Vrost had had a vague scheme that, when the

spring came, he would make the trek through the forest, searching out Korhlen's Tower. By then the stump of the hand he had had to amputate would be healed. And if he had to leave the girl big with his child, then he would do so. But spring arrived, and Carg Vrost did not make the effort to go away. He did not know the woods hereabouts, and his forays to and fro, hunting and gathering, gave him no clue. To find Korhlen on foot and alone would be arduous. Then, the girl was pathetic, he pitied her. What she might have been he could never discover. What had he robbed her of, beyond her chastity and her sanity? His arm hurt badly. He boiled roots in an old iron pot left in the hut, and applied poultices. There were days that were black-tinged from fury and desolation. For all these reasons, he did not go away. And for another reason, too. He had been spoiled, as she was, by the thing which had happened to them. As if they had been gouged by fire, or infected with leprosy. They were marked, cut off from the human herd. If he should think of his life as it had been, it was as though he thought of the life of another man. If he imagined himself returned into it, he watched himself with wonder and disbelief, very nearly with fear.

In an overgrown part of the Women's Garden, the Vre's wife sat in her carved chair. She had been carried down in it, and set under the ripening maelstrom of the peach trees. The child was playing methodically nearby, walking a toy bear. He could only use one hand, and his disjointed, occasionally angry and surprised movements reminded her of those of the soldier, Vrost, at his husbandry.

Summer had starred the garden with flowers and birds. Only gentle domestic noises came from the Tower. The Vre was off on one of his hunts.

It was like the forest, here, the forest's softer and more smiling interiors. She had only to lapse, to go there. But she was so weak now, her awareness had begun to be tried by the passage. When inhabiting the flesh of her making, the mad and pregnant girl from the chapel, Nilya now felt feverish and also ill. She preferred at last to control the Anillia-Jasha body as if by strings, hovering over it, jerking its arms and legs. (It was able, in any case to perform most functions from copied memory, mindlessly. Just so it showed affection, or breathed.) Once or twice she had offered it to the soldier, but he did not want sex, or fondness. He too had gone quite mad. As Mechail played strengthlessly with the bear, Nilya manipulated the human and unhuman toys she had garnered in the wood.

The baby in Anillia-Jasha's womb should be born in the coming winter, early. Nilya could not see what it was, or even if it was alive. It might be a monster, worse than the dwarf, far, far worse than Mechail. The baby had been formed from the seed of Carg Vrost, in the matrix of demon-made stuff that was the mad girl. But the baby was also Mechail's, galvanized by the psychic motes of him. An incestuous and impossible amalgam. But Nilya did not care about it. She did not care.

She wanted to sleep now. She wanted to be free of both of them, Anillia, Nilya. She wanted to be free of Mechail, whose rope of love was knotted painfully into the tendons of her spirit. She wanted to go out of all things like an extinguished flame. *Rest*.

The boy glanced up.

One of the male slaves was coming across the turf, over the flowers, the sun preposterously gilding his torque of slavery. Nilya had seen the man before; he served inside the house. His face was petrifying slowly, changing into an organic impaction.

He held out, on his hand, a small object of a kindling crimson shade – absurdly, the slave Boroi was bringing his lady a rose.

Nilya lay in her chair, her portable forest, watching him drawing closer through her old sunken eyes. And the child watched, too, absently.

The garden had become silent. No sound entered. They seemed enclosed in a sunny enamel world.

Boroi kneeled down. He had stopped looking at Nilya. He was perhaps five paces from her, near enough she had now caught the reek of the offal he was holding. Not a rose, but the bloody heart of an animal, freshly slaughtered against the dinner of the lord's return tonight. Blood ran through Boroi's fingers into the flowery ground.

'What are you doing?' Nilya said. Her voice was another woman's. She heard it, the pointless question.

Boroi bowed to her and got up, and went away, taking the rose heart with her. There was blood left in the grass, the white and yellow flowers were red.

He had been making an offering to herself, or to the child; actually to neither. It was for Anjelen, the blood. They sensed Anjelen, they detected him. And if he had come here, as one day he would, they might do nothing, treating him only as a man.

Above her, in the tree, something made a trickling sound, a tiny doll of bone stirring in the breeze.

The priest at Korhlen had begun to suffer from fits. He rolled at the altar, spume coming from his lips, wetting himself. He was to go; a replacing priest would be sent to them. Nilya wondered if this priest would be Anjelen, in his humble robe, his ageless face, his cool hands and winter eyes.

'Mechail,' Nilya called faintly.

Her son approached her, clutching the toy bear. The pathos of his predicament tore at her like a bird of prey.

She took him in her arms, and thought, *Soon I shall be rid of all this.*

Carg Vrost delivered his child on a frozen night, pulling it out of a screaming and scalding body into a country of white glass.

He was not conscious as he did so of the being of a woman, up in the air, herself aloof from the agony of birth, letting the girl's body below thrash and spasm, rupture and bleed.

Presently the body died of its ordeal and was merely spilled there, like a skin. The ghost-thing too evaporated.

Vrost was left alone with the latest creation of uncanny impulse, a female offspring, wailing.

He had unearthed a village that summer, and got from there a goat. Now, having cut the child loose and cleaned it with rough accuracy, he fed the unhappy mouth with milk, leaving the dead dry breasts upon the mattress.

The daughter of his loins apparently looked at Vrost, then. Her eyes were greenish.

She would have to have the same name, he could not bother with inventing a second one.

He felt nothing for the baby but astonishment, even that tempered by inertia.

Later he buried the mad girl, and stuck his sword in her grave as an afterthought, for its cross, and because it had ceased to have any significance either.

The wife of the Vre died before dawn. She had been bedridden for a month or more, and they marvelled, some of them, she did not go sooner.

They kept the tidings from the boy.

The new priest, in the spring, would take him in hand, lesson him in God's will, the trust that must repose in the Christus.

The Vre looked healthy and glad. He had, maybe, already seen someone he fancied.

They took Nilya's body through the cold weather to the stone brick of the Korhlen vault. She was clothed in white, and one necklace that had been Crel's. The silver ring was removed from her finger after death. (A difficult task, it had sunk into the flesh so far it seemed to have grown there.)

It had been easy for her to die. She had sprung from her physical case so often, practice perfected her. She slid out of her sheath and hung above herself, or above something which she had been and which she no longer recognized.

She had hoped and longed for peace. Peace did not occur.

The huge walls of the Tower that had penned her body impinged upon her essence in other ways. She was obstructed by intimations.

301

Live mortals came and went, like hot, thick winds. The stones were like the edges of a knife. Nothing had any familiarity. She was trapped. And then the fabric of the building gave, rent—

That which had been Anillia, and Nilya, walked through the gulf of the forest.

Overhead roared the great bonfires of the stars, and between the pillars of the pines the hollows were full of night as though of blackest blood.

The Tower had not had exactitude. The forest was nothing but.

She knew herself invisible. She knew that she had died.

Alone under the enormous trees, she looked back towards her corpse, the shadow of the vault where she would be laid. She pictured how her flesh would fall like snow and grey leaves, and the bone would stain to darkness.

She did not want the forest. She desired the void.

Had she condemned herself to this, never to cease, never to rest, the penalty of the true ghost?

Recollections of her beginning came to her, or to what there was of her. The Handmaidens' chapel and its door, through which she had passed, not yet sufficiently corporeal that wood or stone could hinder her – although she had undone the fastenings of the door when her framework hardened. She had lain in the yard.

She lay down on the flank of the forest, where the snow was folded, and under it the skeletons of roots. She lay where a stream had fled all autumn. On the pillows of the winter she stretched herself as if for sleep.

How bright the stars, that never ended, the perpetual moon, and the wood that was for ever, the eternity of the earth.

But she was transient.

It was as though she closed her eyes, composing herself for slumber. The void was before her, beautiful, a balm. She let it have her, like the gentle sea.

She slept.

And was no more.

Chapter Seven

When the tree danced from the forest, the women and girls who had been gathered at the clearing's morning edge flung up their aprons, screamed, and darted back among the village huts.

Voif the woodcutter stood watching in the door of his bothy, the axe ready to his hands. Not far off, his father and brother kept a similar stance. All along the track, in the doors of the wooden houses, the village men waited, as the terrible tree careered on. But the women scattered through the village, calling and shrieking, to hide themselves.

The children had been hidden too. Voif hoped that his damned wife had had the sense to secure that thing which had come out of her belly. Six years of life were in the thing, which had a name, but was a curse.

The tree pranced on, shaking its mane of leaves and moss, the scales of bark that plated it rattling.

It was, as ever, a horrid sight, inspiring fears already deep-seated in the bedrock of the mind. That was the intention of it, a part of its purpose. Its origins were almost as old as fear, after all.

In shape, it was a pine, but a pine also blended with the other trees of the autumn wood, the larch, the cedar and the birch, the stunted oak and profligate alder. And it was the underlife of the forest, the ferns and vines, the ivy, funguses, lichens. All these dripped and shivered, clung, hung, glanced to and fro, and out of the leaves and growths, the bare branches stuck like claws, raking at everything and at itself. In the topmost heights of the tree swayed the tied black dead crows and the bones of rats, and knotted there were the wreaths of flowers and ribbons, the rings and beads. The tree was all the forest, and on it were the offerings of the human animals of the forest.

They cut wood in the village. It was how they lived. Logs for building and burning, and sometimes to trade for other things, elsewhere. They harvested the forest, berries, nuts and fruits, mushrooms and truffles, the herbs that might heal, the reeds for bedding and weaving, the leaves for dye and simples, the roots for beer. The beasts of the forest they slaughtered and ate. They rifled the nests and holes for eggs. And when they had a few goats, a sheep or two, they pastured them on the forest's back to bite up its green hair called grass. They took everything they had out of the wood. They even cut adornments from its veins, its limbs, the cone kernels of its children unborn. For so much, something must be returned.

The tree came crashing and thrashing through the earth street.

It was not much more than six feet in height.

Men ran from the doorways, they ran at the tree, surrounding it. The tree stopped in its rush, its branches shaking. Voif, who was lazy, and disliked, was the first to bound forward. He smote the tree sidelong with the axe. There was a booming noise, and the tree screamed.

Another man struck the tree, and another. It boomed again, and the branches snapped and showered, bells and bones rang together. The tree cried out. It had three voices.

Eastward, the sun was shining through a break in the pines, a long needle of light that carved across the street. Caught in its ray, the red autumn leaves in the tree ignited like fires. Liquid fire began to ooze out along the ground. The tree was bleeding.

Voif stepped back, with the other men. The tree swayed, and on three pairs of booted feet, visible now, it lurched away.

Mechi had so far looked on from the hollow pine beside

the family yard. His mother had stored him here at sunrise, with a sharp instruction to remain and a precautionary blow. The same system had been resorted to the previous year; before that he had been stowed with other smaller children in one of the crone's huts. (There Mechi was tortured by these children, but that was not unusual, they inflicted punishment upon him whenever possible.)

Mechi beheld his father Voif smite the terrifying tree which had blundered into the village like a sick and vicious wolf. Mechi did not understand about the tree, he had not done so last year. The event, unexplained to him or, apparently, to anyone else, was an experience of unique tribulation. And yet, now, there was added to his confused alarm the proviso of repetition.

For the dwarf-child, somewhere in the region of six years of age, there was anyway no centre of security or calm. It was hard to disturb a life that had only been a series of traumas. He accepted each jolt and plunge, each abrasion, every nonsensical injustice, equally, if not without a qualm, certainly without analysis. He blamed no one. Felt no specific guilt. He did not think, simply was.

The tree had begun to lumber away from the village street, starting to circle the huts, leftward, letting down its trail of blood behind it. The men went after, shouting intermittently, but moving quite slowly.

As Mechi lost sight of them, a sort of rasping came from below. He looked down into the entry, the great yellow crack in the body of the pine, where dead leaves and various refuse had gathered. There stood also another child, a correct child, with a small neat head masked in damask skin, a normal childish shape. Dark curling hair had given this child the pet name of *Curly*. It had been said that Curly was the bastard son of Voif, got on a girl of the village not shy of her favours, but then again he might have been the by-blow of a young man who was lost one winter, a popular and useful member of the village who had hunted for its cook-pots. Voif had an attachment to the boy, nevertheless, which the flighty mother did not discourage, since it was helpful. Voif was happy to think there was proof he could sire healthfully, for the stigma of the changeling had mired him; he blamed it for everything, his inability to do much work, his lack of cronies, the crabbing of his wife.

Curly, who was four years old and must have been immured in the crone's hut, had got out. He had witnessed the coming and wounding of the tree, which maybe was not desired.

Now he beckoned Mechi.

Mechi sat up in the pine, watching the younger child. No one had ever shown Mechi any kindness, any wish to be near him. Curly was no exception. If he wanted Mechi for something, it would be something bad.

Curly was smiling, making drawing motions.

Mechi sat and stared, and did nothing else.

Soon Curly pulled a face at him, and spat into the tree, as he would have seen his elders do in the dwarf's vicinity. Then he waddled off, the pink and proper child, in the direction the men had taken and the rampaging, bleeding tree.

Having circled the village the tree burst back into the wood. Here, not far from the pool, it was killed, chopped down by the axes of the men. Enormous gouts of blood shot from it, branches flailed, it collapsed to the ground, grunting and crying aloud, and the three pairs of booted feet were towed in, until only a mess of splintering boughs, mosses, dying live foliage, and red gore, lay there in an untidy mound.

The woods men regarded their work. They were never sure that they had done what was required quite fully. This attitude came of a conflict of superstitious respect, bewilderment, awe, impatience. There was no man any more in the village to instruct or coerce them in the rite. Every year the tree must be slain, the three men drawn by lots encased in their shields of toughened leather and wood, beaten black and blue, until the bladders of weasels' blood tied about them split and spilled. It was a blood offering to the earth, a peacemaking with the forest, a symbol both of tree-felling and the sacrifice of human flesh. A hundred years before there would have been a death in earnest, but they had turned progressively reluctant to give up their own.

Voif, who had never had the ill luck to be selected by lot to suffer in the constructed arboreal composite, wiped his lazy axe on the fall grass.

The fellows in the tree were groaning and cursing now but not yet at liberty to get up and attend to their hurts.

'Well,' said Voif's father, 'it's done. May it be done right.'

The men mumbled assent.

They put their axes into the shelter by the pool, from which the women would presently retrieve them, and went, sulky and brooding, not speaking to each other, along the track that led to the beer vat. It would be ready-provisioned against their coming. After ingesting mugfuls of the bitter liquor, they would wax more cheerful. There would be an impromptu tour of the traps, which generally after a tree-killing turned up a medley of little game, as though to reimburse and reassure. By dark they would be ready to eat, and to sleep. Tomorrow it would be done with, only the thick heads to mar their world, and to obscure it, too.

The rest was for the women to do. They would have to come out and clear up the wreck of the tree, allowing its inhabitant scapegoats to get out, beating them freshly with brooms and spoons, chasing them off. (They too if able would later seek the vat, and its dregs.) The women would bury the broken muddle of the tree, speaking their own charms over the wood and blood.

Behind the men, as they slunk to their recompense, something short pottered through the fern. They did not think to look back.

'What do I know about it? It's your brat.'

Marra, with the blood marks of the tree still on her filthy apron, her hair like a black and frowsty nest, filled the doorway of her hut. Misery had made her fat, she slopped inside her dirty clothes, and looked out of her fallen face with shrivelled eyes as dry as raisins.

The other, the pretty plump slut Yula, stood panting and crazy, Her hair was plaited, with a spray of berries in it. She wrung her clean apron in her hands.

'It's you, you witch. You've done something.'

'What could I do?'

'The Christus knows. With that thing in your house.'

Marra uncoiled like a turgid snake. Her juiceless eyes gave a sort of flat flash.

The neighbouring women, who had come out to see, gazed at them with interest, and the crone – from whose smoky, noisesome hut Curly had escaped – sucked her two pairs of teeth, glad someone else was to take the brunt.

'You should have more thought for your bastard,' said Marra. 'But it'll be easy enough, I suppose, to get yourself another.'

'You hate any true child. Any child that's a *child*.'

'You speak too quick, you whore, you trollop!'

'Feared your old man got me with my Curly, while the Devil got up *you*?'

Marra came like a rolling barrel from her hut. Her fist was raised, in the manner of Voif's fist when he hit her.

Yula hurried backwards. She liked her face, though she had only seen it in water and the eyes of men.

'Keep off me, you pig's sow. What have you done to my boy? You tell me that.'

The women were leisurely mustering behind Yula. Although they were not entirely friends with Yula, Marra had long since become an object for jeering and avoidance. Her mother was dead. Her husband was no use. Her son was a monster.

'Tell us what you've done, then,' said one of the village wives. 'Where's Curly?'

Marra turned at bay, her fist lifted high.

'He's nothing to me.'

'Too busy coddling your lovesome babby,' said Yula with venom.

Marra went to strike her, but the other women were close now, and swarmed over her, dragging her off. She bellowed in frustration. And through the door, inside her unswept, unhygienic home, the dwarf-thing was suddenly to be seen, trying to conceal itself behind a basket.

'Look there,' said the crone. 'There it is.'

'*Changeling*,' breathed the women.

Yula said: 'It's a bane on her. Now she wants to hurt me.' She gave off an unexpected, appalling scream. 'Curly! The Devil's taken him!'

And from a slight distance, Marra's mother-in-law murmured, 'She soured my Voif's luck. It's down to her.' Words of a preventative and deflecting nature, employed before, but not in Marra's hearing.

Marra had stopped struggling with her neighbours. Like the men who had had to be the tree, she was battered and bruised. This day was hot with violence always, as if the untotal rite invited compensation. Last year, a stone had struck her. She never saw who cast it. Maybe it had been meant for Mechi, above her in the storage pine.

The women of the village, whom Marra had known from her own childhood, were grouped about her, their faces alight with menace. Behind, in the hut, the evil changeling, her blight, crawled. With no warning, save the premonition and omen of six years of Hell upon earth, something dropped from Marra, leaving her naked.

She sank on her knees and smothered her face in her hands. From this mask, her voice exploded in a series of caterwauls. There was also a shower of words.

'Yes! It's the Devil's! A changeling! It's brought me so low. Kill it! Take it away from me!'

In the traps – was nothing. By one, the footprint of a hare in the soft mud indicated an uncanny rescue.

The men, heavy in their beer-sloshed guts, went to their village to a supper of dark bread and slush of beans.

The sun, which had been a faint crocus in the east, was now an apoplectic porcine red, low amid the western trees. Frost was on the air, the salt breath of winter.

From the roof holes of the bothies, smoke smirched the sky over the clearing. There was a silence on the village, which should have been imperfect – a clatter of plates and bowls, the stroke of a spoon against a pot's side, perhaps the song of a woman, singing the day down, or her fretful offspring into sleep.

Yet the aura of the village this evening was less solid, like a piece of ice – cold, and to be shattered. You could not walk in there without some happening.

The drink, that made them stupid in one way, heightened the extra senses of the woods men, so all together they hesitated, peering into the place like beasts that had never seen the clutters of humankind. They had already had one surprise, they were not sure they wanted another.

'What's up?' someone said. 'Those idle wretches had better get busy.'

But they had *been* busy – this was the reason for the frozen silence.

As the men stamped into the village, the women emerged. They came out of Marra's horrid hut, and from the yard, and from the house of Voif's father. They perched on the street with a blind look they sometimes, if rarely, took on, the outer expression of some intransigent inner mood over which there would be no getting.

The men observed them doubtfully.

Then Voif's mother stepped forward, and Yula was next to her, which was not usual.

'She's lost her boy Curly.'

Yula had been crying, but she too had the blind look, it had covered her panic.

The drunken woodcutters laughed. (They hoped, but guessed it was not only this.) Voif appeared, showing Yula's child Curly wrapped up in his cloak. 'Little scamp followed us. Wanted to be a man with the men.'

Yula started and moved forward, not fast enough, as if she had just woken up. Half of her had stayed blind, in the realm where refinding did not matter.

In any case, Voif's mother caught Yula's arm. 'Speak up, son,' she said to Voif. 'You hold that boy there like

310

your own – we won't talk about that. But what of the other?'

Voif's face went red in the sunset, then sallow. His unshaven jaw clenched.

'What are you on at, Mother?'

'You set Marra to carrying. But after it came out, the baby wasn't natural.'

Voif balanced there on the track for the second time that day, uneasy, belligerent, and now the men stared at him, and the women with their fixed, unseeing glare.

'They say,' said Voif's mother, 'it's a changeling. Demons spirited off the good boy, and left you that – booby.'

She spoke as if the idea had never before been mooted, and the women nodded and shivered as if they too had just recently heard it.

Voif, for his part, seemed astounded.

And the men waited, as they had waited for the tree.

'Listen,' said Voif's mother, 'she's been a poor wife to you, Voif, your Marra. But she was sorely tried. To lose her wholesome infant. She swears that the ghost that frighted her vowed it would be this way. She'd look in the cradle, and find *that*.'

'What ghost?' said Voif. It was more that he needed prompting than anything else. He could not discover Marra in the female crowd.

But the women ignored his question. They were not to be gainsaid. It was one of the crones who spoke up now. *She* croaked: 'Your Marra said to kill it. Take it in the wood and cut its throat. For the trees to drink the blood. That's best.'

At this utterance, the silence reaffirmed itself. It formed thickly as the burgeoning frost.

When it had done so, Marra walked from her hut, and she led the child, the demon changeling, by a rope tied firmly to its middle.

Facing her husband, she glared at him with the same eyes that all the women had, and even he saw that she had found her family again, her fastness among her tribe.

311

'Voif, take it to the Lord Tree. Offer it up there. Sacrifice.'

'No,' said Voif.

He glanced at the dwarf. It had not been physically harmed, it did not bleed (yet), only hung its huge head. Its grotesqueness and its helplessness revolted him. He had often struck it from his path. It was witless, felt nothing . . .

(In his arms, warm, and silly from the drops of beer the men had administered, roistering brave Curly purred in his sleep. Voif's drunkard's eyes moistened with tears. *Here* was his son. Be rid of the other, then.)

The women were like crows on trees above a dying thing.

The men shuffled. One of them belched softly.

'I won't,' said Voif, clutching Yula's son. 'I won't kill it. If it's a demon – that may make them angry.' He paused, to let his downhill speech gather force. 'Like the tree,' he said finally. 'Do with it like that. Every man, if he wants, to strike a blow. You women, you're so pert, you do it as well. Then drive it out. Let the forest have it back. Can care for it, if it means to. If not, God knows, it'll die soon enough. *Mechi*!' Voif bawled.

At his name, the dwarf looked up. But the eyes of the dwarf had no understanding. Burnt stones. The changeling had looked because it had learnt the noise of its name, like a dog.

At first, it was no worse, no stranger, than on former occasions. Harsh, incomprehensible words, the bleak cages of faces from which poked iron eyes. Even the rope was not unknown. His mother had utilized cords before, to tie him in the yard when she did not want him under her feet. Though she had never tied him in the pine, possibly desiring him to stray.

Then, when the adult world rushed on him, there was, despite all the foretastes, a unique and extraordinary terror. Individually he had been subjected to the cruel pinches and slaps of his mother, to the beatings of his father. Mechi endured these. The children had, in addition, attacked him whenever they were able to corner him – the resultant marks were put down to rough 'play', as if he had ever 'played' with anyone. Mechi survived the attacks of play.

The village swooped like a storm of wings and beaks. It was a shadow-substance. It put out the sinking sun. The lashes and punches and smacks came one by one and then in a torrent. Mechi gave a thin squeal that was not even vaguely human, let alone childish. He tumbled beneath the onslaught, went down, knotting his deformed and blunted body tight, attempting to preserve himself through instinct that had no relevance to what he had been made to be.

It was the rope, wound round and round in the flurry and squeezing the air out of him, that eventually laid him prone, apparently lifeless.

By this time the dusk was on the wood, hardening its soul of darkness. In the shade, the men took Mechi the changeling away, and under the Lord Tree they shallowly cut his arms and his feet, giving the blood to its roots. For that, the Lord Tree would protect them, or protect the dwarf-child, whichever seemed best to it.

In utter night, one of them, not Voif – for his back had started to pain him, he lagged, was discarded – flung the changeling into the wild heart of the wood, coming away stumbling, between black streamlets and ebony posts, great bears of pines, the embers of stars, leaving fate to do as it would.

Mechi did not know. He lay partially stifled, torn and tenderized by blows, under the long eaves, and the frost gave him a coat of silver dust, gilded the lids of his eyes, and where his blood still dripped, it set to crimson exquisite petals of stained glass.

They could never have told him the stories, the legends of the wood; had he overheard them, ever?

Along with the tales of sprites and demons, the lurers and mischief-makers, were those of abnormal guides and helpers. Old as the first saplings of the forest, perhaps, the saga of an orphaned or abandoned child, isolate in the centre of the trees, fed by copper-breasted thrushes, covered over against the snows and dews with thistledown, led along tracks of the ermine, and the snail to safety.

The world was cold and black, devoid of catering birds and remarkable animals.

Mechi woke, or revived, and extended a small thin mewing sound to the nothing all about. And out of the huge building of the night, a hoarse voice – unhuman and inhuman, a fox, most probably, or its close kindred – gave unintentional answer.

That was all.

What further lesson did he need, the dwarf of six years, in the callous uninterest of all things.

Long, long after he had closed his eyes again in exhaustion and pain, a sort of ill boredom – uninterest to match uninterest – the pale light rained through his lids, making itself obvious to him as an external agent.

He reopened his eyes and squinted in apathetic dread. What could it be but an enemy?

A woman of white flame was walking through the forest, and she flickered like a candle.

This was curious, even to Mechi. He gazed, too wretched to pay much heed. His eyes fastened on the apparition by themselves. His brain, numbed and out of practice, mulled over her image.

She was a ghost. Something like that. In the flamey pale face, which was smudged through with night, the eyelids were closed as his had been. As she moved – a long-haired ghost-woman in female garb, with breasts – her hands were slightly extended before her. The ghost of a dead dreamer, seemingly she walked in her sleep.

By the spot where Mechi had been flung, the sleepwalker stopped, among the corrugated arteries of the pines.

Her head half-turned upon its misty stalk of neck, her hair was in a plait and it slithered away. She was all white.

She glowed, but lit up nothing. And the dying leaves and needles showed through her hands.

She could not see him, for her lids stayed down, yet, when she averted her head it was as if she beckoned him.

Curly had beckoned Mechi, for trouble. His mother, her face bending towards him, she beckoned and tied him with the rope. The man who lived in their hut, called Voif, he beckoned, and the storm of the village fell.

But there was to the white-fire woman something Mechi knew. It was a weird and groundless recognition. And he felt magnetically led towards her, as she began to go away, the weightless steps of her sleeper's feet completely insubstantial on the black earth.

So somehow, for he was in no fit state, the dwarf-child hoisted himself from his pit, and followed her.

That night, early, the winter had come.

The winter god blew through the pines his argent breath like smoke. The armour of the cold had begun to hammer itself together. He scorched off the leaves and touched the pools to glass. Birds fell dead from boughs.

Through this Mechi limped behind his guiding ghost. Weak and sore and already himself ice-kissed with dying, he kept to her.

As the forest changed to diamond, Mechi bumbled through it, like something out of time, now time had ceased.

Near dawn, a curious susurrous commenced in the wood, a tinsel of life that had survived the night and groped towards the returning sun.

When the darkness watered into grey, the woman of white fire faded until she was no more than a shimmer on the eyes.

At the edge of the narrow stream, maybe randomly, she vanished, dissolved away.

Mechi stood there, where the crystallized bushes went into the opaque mirror of the ice. Presently he sat down, and rested his big ancient head on his little bent and twisted knees.

He experienced a limitless sadness maybe new to him,

315

it had such depth and height. It was the season's death he felt beside his own.

Then the sun came up and some roses of light caressed the stream, which, after about the half of an hour, cracked. Greenish beryls of liquid trickled out like tears.

The Traveller girl approached the stream with her jar not long after. She wore a brown scarf patterned with black and scarlet beads, and there were ten cat skulls in her necklace. Mechi did not see these intriguing items. He had lapsed into a stupor. The woman however, as she leant to smash the enduring ice on the stream, noted Mechi. She took him, according to her own creed, for something ripe with potential, the marked of God. She woke him soon by pressing some warm milk to his mouth, and quietly, kindly rubbing his temples. These activities astonished Mechi. But he accepted them as he had accepted the spite and wickedness of others.

Chapter Eight

Soon after he had laid out the body of his master, the slave was sent to work in his Landholder's inn. The work, as expected, was filthier and more taxing than previous labours, when he had waited on the heir, Mechail. Conversely, he was not much overseen or as liable for a whipping as he had been. At the inn everything was slovenly, and the overseer always drunk. Korhlen was altogether a ramshackle place, beyond the tough stones of its Tower. Servants and villagers availed themselves of the inn, as would pigs of a sty, or the Tower garrison burst through the door. Sometimes Travelling People, pedlars, or, less often, bands of soldiers or traders, would put up there perforce. Boroi had been at the inn a few hours when, in through the door and the westering light walked a down-at-heel stranger. His pony he had left carelessly tethered, and from his condition he did not seem to anticipate anything of the inn save what it would have and be. He sat down at a table, under the low black beams, in the gloom. Boroi was sent to serve him. There was a transaction of cold and greasy meat, bread and ale, and coins for the Landholder's coffers.

When he had eaten, the stranger, a trader in small goods, lay on his bench, a straw pillow under his head, and snored. If the villagers came along at evening, he had said, he would reveal his wares. When the overseer leaned by in his leather apron and the ale mug that long ago had grown into his hand, garrulously telling of the heir's death – slain by enemies – and of the sombre tone of the Tower and its village, the trader had seemed not much bothered. Any talk the overseer might have liked to add, concerning the dead heir's crooked back, the bastard son's ambition, the two prior wives, one mad and one reputedly a witch who haunted the forest (and the current live one, a hussy), failed in the bud. The afternoon went to gold-leaf sunset and the inked-in dark crept slowly up like water from the wood, and the snorer snored on his bench. Then a group from the village entered. One of them called out they came to drink respect to the heir, as an excuse. A cup clattered, and the trader roused, rubbed his eyes, yawned and stretched himself, and swung his legs to the floor.

His goods were of an average sort, but from a town, perhaps to be prized. He did a little business, and bought a jug of drink.

The black ink of night had filled the inn. Boroi and a girl went about to light the candles and the pair of torches at the door.

Outside, dogs howled over the fields, fell silent. Talk turned to omens, to the ominous evening. (In the Tower chapel they would hold a death watch.) The overseer came, put his feet up, joining in the dedicated drinking. The slaves, unsupervised, assumed the attitudes of vacated automatons. Only the girl, who had flung the sprinkle of meal on the fire for the sun, went out to hang something in a bush. Boroi knew, without seeing. It would be a male figure made of a rag, with a thorn through its breast.

'The second one, his mother was an odd woman, no mistaking. She looked a girl till the day of her death, but winter grey. The boy took sick whenever she did. She brought him to it. A winged demon feasted on his infant blood. It was that warped him, body and mind. No fit heir. You can bet, someone saw to *this*. Esnias—' the village man spat on the rushes. 'The Esnias Tower would never dare take on Raven that way.'

'Shut your mouth,' said the overseer, vaguely.

The villager said quickly, as if to atone, 'Maybe something came from the forest to claim Hump-Back, and killed him.'

'There's a hundred things can happen in the wood.'

The overseer banged on the table for service. His personal jug had run dry.

Boroi went to the table with the new jugs in his arms. With his hands that had, this day, washed and clad Mechail's carcass, he put down the liquor for the villagers, the overseer, the trader. They formed a crowding black circle, the light at their edges; they leaned into the black as if towards a lamp.

The trader was drunk now, like the overseer. He looked up at Boroi, with fleering jollity that did not notice the slave at all.

'I'll tell you a story of the forest,' said the trader. He pointed Boroi, not noticing him still, towards the hearth. 'Heat up that broth. I'm hungry.' As Boroi crossed to address the food, he heard the trader begin his tale.

'It's not make-believe. It's something I saw with my own eyes. I was there, see? I was a bit of it. Fourteen or fifteen years back. I'd come from Khish. I was courting a village girl, further north than here, out of my way. Coming on winter. I was travelling with ten others, wanting to get to some decent inn or huttage before the snow started. You know that fear. Like being driven by a pack of white hounds.'

The villages grunted. They knew. The vast snowscape, the danger of straying too deep in the forest, white death moving softer than a smile.

Boroi stirred the kettle of soup above the hearth.

'We were nowhere. The guide lost us. Then he says, Oh, there's a village over this way. Not much, a dump, but it'll do us to get us out of trouble.'

There had been a heavy frost for several nights. They had found a hare and a ground squirrel caught in it, frozen.

Dark came, and frost again. It was very cold, and they had found no shelter. They made a camp among the trees, a big fire, agreeing to take a turn each watching, for wolves, for snow, for any enmity.

The trader was woken suddenly and sharply. '*Listen*,' the watcher said.

There was something terrible in being wakened so violently, out of turn, one moment far down in sleep, then brought up into an icy blackness, tree tops, spiked stars searing, and with the fearsome injunction to *listen* which might presage anything.

The trader lay, his eyes full of the senseless conflagration of the stars, and out of the endless sighing and plinking of the frost-forest came the cry.

'Christus,' said the watcher.

'It's a fox,' said the trade, the townsman who had learnt just enough to put him wrong, hoping. 'Sounds like a woman being murdered.'

'I can tell a fox. No fox.'

The cry resumed. It went on and on, and stopped. And continued.

The other eight men were sitting up about the fire. They exchanged broken lines, concerning the Devil. The crying drew closer.

Every man was on his feet, a knife or a haunch of burning wood in his hand, when from the trees a creature rushed.

The trader in the Korhlen inn drank from his cup. He glanced to be sure the unnoticed slave was stirring his soup.

'So,' said the trader in the black circle, 'it was a woman. Just only that. A village wench, in middle life. Ugly and ill-clad. Not dressed for the weather either. But fat, from somewhere that could keep its own. We thought her cracked, and so she was, so she was. But seeing us, she dropped on her knees and started in to pray. She didn't pray to God. No. You'll know what I mean. She was praying to the Lord of the Wood.'

The villagers shifted, lifting their faces and elbows from the black to catch the light again, drinking.

Presently the mad woman came to the camp fire, and

320

at the heat of it she seemed amazed. They saw her fingers were blackening; she had been bitten by the frost-beast.

They offered her hot beer, and she had a sip.

Then she would only point away into the forest, making at them beckoning and entreating gestures, not touching them.

'What, what is it?' they said.

She clawed frantically in the air.

'Come,' she said.

'Come where?'

'Come, come, come!'

'It could be some trick. Robbers.'

'Let it rest till morning,' said someone.

The woman wept, and opening wide her mouth began again her scream-cry. And she clawed now towards the stars, as if to draw them down instead.

Not every man would go. Four of them accompanied the mad woman, of these one being the trader from Khish.

'I was sorry for her,' he said to the Korhlen inn. 'Those other three, they thought there might be something in it, money, or gear.' He looked at Boroi the slave and shouted 'Bring that broth!'

As Boroi brought the steaming bowl, the trader told of a long walk through the glacial frost, and of first dim light, and then a village over beyond a frozen pool.

'Now, I said to myself, it was the way the light was, made it look like it did, that village.'

For the village was grey, and slick. It gleamed and shone dully as the pool had done. The straw roofs were made of raw metal shavings. The walls, the fences, the midden – were thick, and without colour. Above the roofs too, hung something strange. It was a smoke cloud, and it did not alter its shape or position, and it had the stirred appearance of soiled cream.

They went nearer, the woman hastening in hops and flaps, a demented bird.

The village was not, as it had seemed, made of ice. Rather it was coated so densely with ice that every piece of it had been sealed up like grit in a grey jewel. You could make out portions of the huts, their window-slits and doors, the rain barrels, the woodpiles, but they were deep down, *inside*, like fish in a winter stream. There was some washing frozen, standing stiff in the air and twice its size. The earth underfoot was an ice floe, and one by one the men fell over, and hauled their bodies up, too cautious to blaspheme in such a spot.

Somewhere in the centre of the village, the woman stopped and looked at them. She was too cold to shiver, although her teeth chattered now and then. She said clearly, 'It was the punishment. We cast it out, and its own kind worked on us.'

The men crossed themselves.

The woman began to ramble. She spoke of a child, and of a demon, or a ghost. Then she cried out and beat her hands on her stomach, and the ice-village echoed, and the men stared round in terror. One went sliding away, back to the camp in the forest. Two stayed, and the trader. The dawn would soon commence. They would be safe, then.

The woman spoke coherently after a moment.

'What I say next,' said the trader, 'is what she said. Believe or not. You know the wood.' The Korhlen villagers nodded. Boroi sat on the floor by the hearth, awaiting further orders. At the door through into the passage, the girl slave squatted, perhaps listening.

The woman said that here was her village, and at midday, when the sun was directly overhead, it began to grow very cold. They made up their fires, they called the young ones in from the street, they shut their doors against the winter and each other.

But it was so cold, so cold. They huddled to the flames of the hearths, and these flames gave off no heat. They put on beer to mull, and drank it, but the boiled beer was like a quaff of snow. It burnt their throats with *cold*.

'Cold,' said the woman, 'cold, cold.'

They were afraid. They could not get warm. They stuffed rags into the cracks of shutters and door-holes. They hoisted whole logs into the hearths, and torrents of fire shot up, and here and there the roofs caught, but the fires went out, dying of cold.

'He'd gone and left me,' she said. 'He was over in her house. Playing with the brat with curly hair. Trying in his coward's way to be hardy for the child. *His*, maybe.'

She herself had gone out of doors. She stood there on the street in the biting of the cold, knowing it was retribution, and they could not escape. From all the huts came moanings and prayers. But from Yula's hut the child squeaked, for her man threw it in the air and caught it. The man laughed, a big unreal laugh. Only Yula huddled at the hearth, over her boiling freezing kettle, making offerings to woods demons, cutting her fingers and letting the blood drip.

The mad woman was by Yula's hut. She put her eye to a break in the timber of the door. Yula had stuffed the aperture with her best apron, but the woman could see through the stuff, which only tinted the room yellow.

She was conscious that very little mattered any more, the mad woman, as she did this. And yet she was also mortally afraid, for she felt coming towards her a great soundless pouring thing, like an enormous wind. It bent back the boughs of the trees, it drove the atmosphere before it. Where it passed it dug furrows in the earth, and still it made no sound. She longed to run away, but to fly was pointless. She glued her eye to Yula's door instead. For then, in the instant of horror, she would experience Yula's fate as well as her own.

The man threw the child into the air.

The child squeaked. His face was pinched, and the palest yellow item in the tinted-yellow room. Voif laughed. Yula cut a new finger, and her yellow-red blood sizzled on the cool flames.

And then the mighty wind of nothing issued from the forest.

The mad woman's body had tried to leap forward, to run away from the punishment, and she clung to the timbers, and she felt this: a huge numbness, like a blow, on her left side, and the hearing thudded dead like a plug slammed into her left ear, and her left eye whitened over. But she had her right eye to the break in the timber. At that second the apron too turned white – but instantly crisped and withered and curled off into the hut. She saw perfectly with her one eye. She saw this: Yula was raising her arms and opening her mouth to shriek, and she went grey, even her hair and skirt. And Voif too was grey, and suddenly a bad tooth that he had near the front of his mouth fell out on the floor and stuck there. But the child called Curly, he was up in the air. At the second of the coming of the wind of punishment and nothing, he had been suspended. There he stayed, a grey ice-child with wide-open mouth and white marble eyes and grey granite curls—

And it had been this which made the woman run away despite knowing she must not and could not. And the horror of it drove her, so she did run, staggering and crowing for breath and half blind, and the ice seemed to snap in chunks and splinters in her half-warm blood. And she came out of the village, and ran into the forest, and where the gush of punishment had ended, she crashed to the ground.

She did not come to herself for a long time. It was sunset and the sky and trees were red and black and red. She could see shadows with her left eye, her left side trembled under the skin and flesh, with a crepitation like shaken icicles. She looked back at the village.

It was fashioned not of ice but of blood. The sinking sun dyed it. The colour of heat and life.

But then the sun sank and the village was frost and glass and death.

The mad woman rose and ran on. Later she let out her cry.

A soft bloom of sunrise was on the village at the end of her recital. The trader and the other remaining men glanced at the bulbous ice-huts. They had no desire to investigate, any of them, to verify her story or try to disprove it.

But the woman was insistent still. She beckoned them,

and they were compelled in some way to attend, to follow to a dwelling at the edge of the village, Yula's house presumably. And by some means – her desperation, her connection to the supernatural – the mad woman caused them to look in at the hole in the door. They saw it was as she had said.

'I looked the last,' said the trader, 'not hanging back, see, simply waiting my turn. The sun came up as I bent to squint through the door. I felt its warmth on my left side, as she'd felt the strike of the ice.'

In the room of the hovel was the tableau the mad woman had described. Three figures of stone, trapped by ice, and also by time. For, between the frozen arms of the gouge-mouthed man and the swag-belly of the roof, a child of marble hung as if from a string.

'Nothing held him there, but he *was* there. A boy about three or four, curly-haired, with the white eyes of a blind dog.'

They were dead, seemingly. What else could they be?

The trader thought to move away, stunned though he was. But as he removed himself from the timbers, a spark of light spun by his cheek, like a flying thing. It was the reflection of the sun, touched off from the metal of a buckle, knife or button. It went in where his eye had been, through the break in the door.

There came a loud sharp click.

It was inside the hut.

'Look!' shouted one of the men, 'the sun's melting the houses.'

The trader did not look at this. He pressed back to the door, and frowned in at the hole. And saw what he had supposed he would, not realizing he supposed it.

The ball of frozen child up in the air was shuddering. The light had caught it, a needle of white-gold, at the heart. The light had bored into the ice, which melted in a round dark wound. As the trader watched, the shuddering and melting stopped. The marble child dropped straight down. It hit the floor. It shattered. Like a goblet. And from the smashed bits of it, the scattered hands and limbs and head, the cracked torso, the sugar of curls, the purple blood expanded, smoking in the cold.

The trader drank up his broth from the bowl. When he was done, he met the faces again, the Korhlen villagers he had entertained with his tale. They wore the shifting masks of persons who have been found out in their deeper fears, but they nodded at him.

'Believe or not, as you want,' he said. He saw they believed. 'I still dream of it. We went away fast, never looked at the other huts, with the melted ice running down them like waterfalls. The woman we took on to the next village, left her there. She never spoke again or made any noise. Her sight wasn't good, and she'd lost fingers.'

The overseer turned and called through the silence. 'More drink here!'

Boroi got up.

In the blue first of morning the screams rang across the spring vault of the world. The Tower was their fount, although the cries travelled. When they ended, there began a special dread.

Boroi, who had been sent to empty slops and turds, had gone up towards the Korhlen house on hearing the screams and yells for help issuing from the throat of Krau, the Vre's bastard. It was not to offer assistance that he had gone. Indeed, he would have been too late.

But standing by the garden way of the courtyard, in the dawn star's ghostly glow, he beheld Mechail Korhlen, the dead heir, risen and walking. And Mechail, Boroi's erstwhile master, went by him like the god from the wood, and in the avenue under the trees his white sister came to feed him blood, before he sprang over the wall and was gone.

Before the burial of Krau, slaves were sent into the Korhlen vault, to freshen it with herbs. The stink was hard, was impossible to dissipate, but it did not distress Boroi, the carrier of slops, when he entered. He had no business in the tomb, but went unchallenged, so many of his kind had been in and out. It was afternoon, the inn overseer slept . . . Krau slept too in the chapel, in place of the other who was gone.

The inn had rats, of course, and Boroi might have trapped one. That might have done. But the instinct which urged him, unthinking and uninvolved, dictated something else.

She was easy to find. She lay there on her stone shelf, unmistakable under her cobwebs. Her skeleton had darkened with the years, and the strands of hair paled and fallen away. But the Crel necklace trickled about her neck vertebrae, piteous as water. There was, too, something in her dead posture. Boroi, who did not think of it or inwardly respond, perceived. Her pose was of one sleeping. All about were others, lords of Korhlen and their women. Near enough was the bone heap of the earlier wife. So dead that looked, so *departed*, even a non-sensitive could be sure of it. Kolris Vre Korhlen's first bride was at rest.

But the Lady Nilya, she was another matter.

Perhaps Boroi would have come anyway, when the tomb was opened for the purpose of burying Mechail. Or another might have seen to it, and might have done so now if Boroi had not.

The pungency of the herbs strewn on the floor was acid against the pall of decaying ivory, the ashes of flesh.

Boroi, using a kitchen knife from the inn, cut shallowly across his upper arm, high enough to go unnoted, clear of the worst dirt of his toil. He let the blood drop on to the bones of Nilya. The bones absorbed the blood swiftly, as if dry and thirsty. Only a single splash, misdirected on the stone, stayed liquid, like a ruby.

Boroi drew back, bound his arm and lowered his sleeve. He licked the knife for his own blood. Then stuck the blade away out of sight and left the tomb immediately.

When he was gone, a spider on a silver thread, starving, scenting the blood, began depending herself into the brown cradle of Nilya, to spin.

*

Some while after, when Boroi had been taken from the inn to hunt Mechail undead through the forest, a fantastic and terrifying event occurred, to do with the Magister Anjelen. The summer forest froze to winter, and from a frozen pool black wolf-demons burst, routing the hunt. Soldiers and slaves alike flew in all directions, and most vanished, for the forest regularly drowned things and people, in the way of the ocean.

Boroi too was lost, that is, from the lists of the Vre's power.

Torqued in his slave bronze, Boroi loped through the wood, meeting no one, unpursued, wild as any of the other animals, as thoughtless. It was summer, the land stocked like a larder, and sheltering as a tent.

Chapter Nine

Beauty was not essential to the trade of harlotry. The multitude of women and boys who served the city were for the most part not special in appearance, save that as their employment took its toll, they shrivelled, or assumed the fat, bruised look of dying fruit. The girl therefore who began to be seen about the fringes of the market, the quays, and in the slender streets that led towards the Cathedral Burial Ground, was sometimes remarked on. She wore her hair in three plaits, two of which began exactly just behind her temples and ran down to her shoulder blades; the third and central plait, which was the thickest of the three, fell to below her knees. In colour her hair was like black ebony, and it shone. Her skin was white and smooth, and her eyes dark and polished like a saint's in a mask. She was neither gross nor skinny. She had the body of a well-bred virgin from the countryside, fourteen or fifteen years of age.

Added to her physical allurements was the enigmatic way she came and went. She was often not to be seen at any hour of day or night. Then again, dawn, afternoon, dusk and midnight thereafter, she would be spotted, perhaps followed. There were those who had propositioned her; she approached no one. She was always willing, it seemed. But then again, who did anyone know who had gone with her, to say what she was like, or what she charged?

Oddest of all, report had it that, for her business, she went into a narrow house on the Lord's Hill, which was

Church property. There had already been lodgers in this house earlier in the summer, when a soldier roomed there with his servant girl, or she might have been the servant girl of one of the priests – what *they* did was never questioned. A Ship of God had come up the river, and the soldier and the girl had gone off with their master, a Magister. The house was then thought to have been shut up. But the prostitute began to enter it.

The Administer smoothed his bald head, caressed its silken texture, and sniffed at his pomander of spices. He found the information the merchant had brought him rather trying. The summer was ending but it was very hot today, and not so long ago he had had to deal with an unnerving man, a master of his order, here in this very room. The Administer had said the wrong things, being afraid of such mistakes. He was still anxious, whenever a messenger arrived or Church legate from another city . . .

The Christerium at the coast, housing as it did, Knights of God, was a power mostly unseen but ever present in the city. Its riches were said to fund civil and religious bodies alike, and doubtless did so, although even here the Administer remained unapprised. About the city and its conurbations, the Christerium owned, reportedly, one hundred properties, of which several were streets of houses, some of these being kept to serve travelling officials, military agents, spies, or other beings in the pay of Father Church.

Not long since, the Administer's dangerous and troubling guest had put his guard captain into a house on the Lord's Hill. Now apparently a whore was in residence there.

A bell tingled outside.

'Enter,' shouted the Administer, and left off the soothing stroking of his own skull.

One of the ordinary priests entered, and bowed, an apprentice godbrother destined for some cranky town or larger village – the necessary surplus of the schools of a cathedral.

'I have an unpleasant task for you.'

The apprentice priest did not change expression. It was to be anticipated, this. Not only were the small fry trained here, but continually plucked from their tutors and prayers for errands. The Administer outlined the problem of the holy house and the whore.

'I must ask you to watch the house. It can't be trusted to the secularity. Such a man might be tempted, or paid off. The Church, as you will have been told, attends to its own affairs. When you have your facts in order, return to me. Our military arm can then see to it, in whatever strength is needful. Meanwhile, your studies must be kept up as best they may. You are excused, for the duration of this labour, any penances or observances you have incurred.'

At first the apprentice godbrother was not displeased. He was by nature indolent, and since his family had given him to the priesthood at his twelfth year, he had found the offices of his vocation a ceaseless penance in themselves.

Where he could he skived, and where he could he faked, and where he absolutely could *not* do either, he performed his deeds exactly, so that many had been fooled and thought him assiduous, dedicated. For he was also greedy in proportion to the indolence, and wanted the little power the Church could give him. Even when he had fallen in the carnal way, he took great care, and it seemed they believed him chaste beyond corruption, now. Indeed, what he had been asked to do tickled him. He hoped he might see a thing or two, although he was too wise to attempt any act himself. However, after a day and portions of a night of watching and waiting on the narrow house, the apprentice became gloomy and dissatisfied. For nothing happened. No one came in or out. Not even the ugliest or most virtuous of women went near the place.

He had decided against asking questions in the street, for he understood the Administer's information had been well-grounded in news from the area. Besides, it was beneath the dignity of the Church to go about asking such

331

questions. Instead he took up his vigil in a house opposite, where an elderly servant of the Church saw to his needs. Once, the apprentice went out and walked the neighbourhood, and looked the narrow house over from a closer vantage.

A tall tree presided over the back of the house, where there seemed to be a tiny garden or yard. In the heat of the afternoon, the leaves of the tree resembled beaten dark greenish bronze, and if a breeze disturbed them they hissed and whispered together like a nest of snakes.

On the second day the apprentice rose late, having given the servant to think otherwise. The usual morning was spent, dozing at the partly open shutter. The afternoon likewise. In the evening, with the coming in of lentil stew and wine, he gave evidence of enormous alertness.

'Have you seen anything, fellow?' asked the apprentice of the servant, to be sure.

'My eyes aren't sound, godbrother. I can't see farther than my arm's length.'

'Be careful what you put in the stews then,' jested the apprentice.

The servant was apparently also hard of hearing, since he did not laugh.

Soon after sunset, a burning red one that turned the city into Hell, there started to be light in a window of the narrow house.

The apprentice godbrother gaped at it. He realised he must, due to his unvigilance, have missed the advent of the harlot. Quickly he fabricated a tale of having glimpsed her arrival at sunfall, indistinct in the fiery shadows.

The light was pale and wasted, perhaps from a single and inferior candle. Then it sank, and presently he saw it reappear, less brightly, at a second lower window-slit. It vanished again, and next, the door of the house was opened.

By now the avenue was dark, but for a pair of torches set at the head and tail of the street, by the munificence of the Church Paternal. The lighting-up of the doorway was like an eye into revelation.

For a moment the watcher had the keen impression that it was the girl and not the doorway which was lit. She was so white, her face and garment, that she seemed of all things in some virginal sacred glow. But then the candle must have been put out. She dimmed, and was only a female figure in a doorway in a commonplace pastel summer gown.

The door shut, and the woman began to walk away along the street. She walked slowly but in a measured form.

The apprentice scurried down the stair, nearly bowling over the servant who was passing through the corridor below. ('Out of my road, you old pest.')

On the street, the apprentice was glad to find the girl had not not yet disappeared. The slowness of her stroll had taken her only as far as the torches at the street's end. He fell in modestly behind her, not hastening too much lest she became aware of pursuit.

She struck him as a fine piece of goods. Slim and succulent, with big black plaits of hair, like corded silk ropes, down her back. He had not seen her face properly, and looked forward to doing so.

The harlot chose to go in the direction of the quays, along towards the wide river, a not salubrious precinct at night. Since he was clothed as a priest, the apprentice primed himself with the view that very seldom did any try their hand against the Church. He must trust in God. The apprentice, who trusted no one, and certainly not God, the cruel and terrible overlord who could only be flattered and bribed like any master, stalked his prey along the lanes between the craning buildings, stepping over sewers, dodging broad lamplight, waiting for a vision of a face.

Where there were taverns, and clumps of men, he thought any second she would get custom. But though whole gouts of drunks and ruffians turned to regard her, none grabbed, and very few called. She herself did not seem to see them. (He crept by.).

What was she after? Sailors possibly off the boats, or

traders from the market. What was a smell of fish and bitumen if they had ready money?

But the harlot wandered on – it seemed to him now it was more wandering than walking, as if searching idly through a garden or a wood – and gradually she swerved from the river for the upper city, the marmoreal island with its undercuts of water, the Cathedral, the houses of stone.

Under an arch, beneath the statue of Saint Eda the Smith, the harlot got a buyer, and in the light of a torch there, as she came out of the dark with her victim, the apprentice godbrother saw her face at last. It was all he could have wished and not what he had suspected. She was a young girl, not more than fifteen years, and as yet untainted. Apple-heart skin, exquisite mouth, but eyes very cool and strange. Though he thought her comely, the apprentice had an idea she might actually be unhinged in her wits. For she looked like a sister from a cathedral doma. She looked as if she had never gone with a man, only lain down before the Christus, with a white rose in her hand, the womb of purity, sexless.

This man was a wealthy nobody, some shopkeeper's son on the prowl. He obviously reckoned himself fortunate, and attempted to steer the girl towards a handy inn.

She spoke then, and the apprentice, from his skulkhole, heard her. 'No, I've a house. Come there. It will be nicer for you.'

'A house, eh? Well, you're a surprise. But I've never cared to have it up against some rotting wall. No games, mind. I've got my dagger in my belt.'

'That's good,' she said. Her voice was musical and soft, yet crystal clear.

The layabout took a double meaning, and chuckled. He twined her arm, and next her waist, her breast. He was eager, and the apprentice, aroused himself now and looking forward to their antics, which he might at least overhear, moved behind them, regretting the long trek back.

Once or twice on the journey, the layabout complained of this. 'Where are you taking me? I said, no games.'

'My house is over there.'

'The Lord's Hill? That's a joke, you sprite.'

But of course it was not, and the idiot duly marvelled at it. He had already drawn his dagger – the one in his belt – to be on the safe side, but the girl led him to the house door, and opened it, and they went in.

It was by now midnight. A bell rang from the marble dome of the Cathedral to mark the hour.

The apprentice godbrother gave an abrupt, irreligious oath. He had heard another noise. He knew what it must be at once. A thump of drums, the wail of pipes and tinkle of discs struck with the nails, a drone rising and falling and a sudden shriek. There was light advancing too, a dozen flaring brands, and under these the roiling, howling thing with a wooden box in its middle: a funeral procession to the Burial Ground above the hill. These burials, having gained a plot in sanctified earth, the Cathedral graveyard, honoured no one. The rites went on at whatever time a priest could be found to perform them – noon, dawn, or the black spaces of moonset morning.

The apprentice slunk into the doorway of the harlot's house. He had hoped to get to a lower window, and that the deed would be essayed on this side of the dwelling. Now he would hear nothing, over the mourning racket. And besides light might discover him—

Something made the apprentice, at that fraught instant, push against the door. It was a primitive and unreasoned wish that he might get in. But the door gave. It gave way, and opened itself for him. Before him lay the entry, and a wooden stair. Old stale rushes spiked the floor, unswept after the previous tenants. There was a balm of faraway fish dinners, and a peppery note of the hair and skin of the mingled genders.

Everything darted through the apprentice godbrother's brain. The noise from the encroaching funeral would conceal any slight noise he himself might make entering the house. If the woman and her client were busy, he would take a look at them, and slip away again before the man left her. Should something reveal the priestly presence, he must claim his status. The well-off loafer would no doubt fly in fear, and might even offer acceptable bribes, as fornication on holy property was a serious affair. From upstairs, the apprentice heard a man's loud and lascivious amusement. Then the funeral procession, piping and squawking, came level with the house.

The apprentice ran tiptoe up the steps, and at the angle of the stair saw directly above, on the sinister side, into a slice of candlelit room. It held the bed. His luck was gleaming.

The girl lay there, flat as an icon. The man had flung off his cloak and boots, and undid his breeches now, taking out the ready second weapon. He stood against the door but to one side, as if purposely to assist the watcher. The man played with himself. He said to the harlot, 'Take off your dress. Go on. I'll pay you well, if you're worth it.'

The girl got up, and without a word lifted the garment straight off over her head. She wore no shift; only her hair covered her now, and that at the back.

The watcher swallowed a lump of wetness in his mouth, and wondered if he might allow the straying of his own hand to his own member, now up hard as a rock against his belly. (The funeral had gone past.)

She was young and unflawed, milk-white, with pearly breasts that had flower buds for their nipples. But jet-black, the beast of the Devil, her furry woman's part, an animal waiting with its wicked mouth to take and devour.

'Yes, yes,' the man from the upper city mumbled, 'that's what I like. I'll pay you well.' He pushed her over on the bed again, and got on top of her, kneeling there and licking at her breasts. And then he guided his penis to her face, telling her to suck at it. In a curious serpentine way she did as he asked, as if tasting some alien food. Her eyes were wide and blank as mirrors in darkness. The watcher found the look of them put him off, and he wondered if the active man felt this also. But soon enough the penis was retracted from her exploring lips. The harlot drew up her white legs, spreading them in a practised manner at variance with all else about her. Her customer dived into her, and began to buck and dance, holding up his body on his palms and elbows, and staring at her breasts. (The apprentice imitated the bucking movement manually, faster and faster. They were in a race now, and he must win in order to be off the first.)

But the man was young and virile, and he enjoyed what he did. He kept stopping himself, holding back, growling and gasping. And finally he said in a blurred voice, 'Move with me, make out you love me—' and the girl clasped him with her arms and writhed beneath him, her plaits roiling over the bed and her legs the colour of cream – and the apprentice godbrother burst in a turbulence of hot semen, shuddering on the stair and biting his mouth closed to prevent any sound. The customer could no longer control himself either. He came with a wavering yell that shook the beams.

'Lovely, you're lovely,' said the customer. 'I'll – I'll give you gold. A gold coin, and we'll do it again—'

The apprentice, having wiped his hands neatly on his nose-cloth, was preparing to step down the stair and leave, for he had had all he needed.

But what the harlot said just then stayed him stock-still.

'No gold. Give me a little blood.'

'*What*?' said the man on the bed.

And outside, *What*? thought the apprentice.

'Just a very little,' said the girl mildly, like a child. 'Your own knife can make the cut. In that bowl there. A few drops.'

'You're mad,' said the customer, drawing himself off from her. 'What do you want – *blood* – for?'

'Your strength,' said the girl.

'You're crazy. You're not a whore. For the Christus, what are you?'

The girl said, lying under him, soft and pure and undaunted by the frightened anger in his face, his big

337

body shivering, 'I don't know. I remember a chapel, and women. But I was a virgin, then.'

'You crazy slut!' The man pulled right away, and stood over by the door. 'Are you a witch?'

The girl said nothing now.

The apprentice godbrother on the stair, riveted, rehearsed in his mind a prayer for protection, knowing the tricks of his own trade. Witch? She must be a demon, no less. Something of the Devil's. They must take her, examine, exorcize, burn her. But he alone was not fit to do it. He would need the full power of the Church to deal with this.

'Give me a little of your blood.'

The repetition was terrifying.

'Here – have this coin – it's yours—'

'I don't want your gold. Your blood. Then you can have me again.'

'Have you? Christus spare me.' Her customer crossed himself now. The vampire, it seemed, was impervious to this layman's gesture. She reclined there, and turned her head and looked on him with her black and unearthly eyes.

'You must,' she said. 'Do it at once.'

And then something happened that filled the apprentice with such fear that he understood himself truly in the presence of a creature of the Devil. The woman did not stand up – she became for a second a pale thick oily strand of tallow, faceless and bodiless, which coiled and arose, and reshaped itself. And there *she* was again, before the big layabout from the upper city, and her refashioned eyes were like those of an angel of Hell, and behind her stirred great invisible wings. *'Do it.'*

And whining and shaking like a sick slave, the man crawled upright from the slice of doorway, out of sight of the watcher. Unseen, the knife must have effected its craft.

With no warning but a sort of scuffle and crash, the man came leaping from the room, clutching his belongings, barefoot, and brushing by the shrinking apprentice on the stair. And probably thinking this was the Devil Himself, the man screamed and hurled himself down from the house, falling and getting up, and running along the street. Something had splashed the watcher's cheek. It was a fleck of blood.

In abject dismay, the apprentice tottered down the stair after the first escapee. He did not want to be alone here with a vampire. He had seen her glide across the door, and fancied he heard her drink the blood from the hidden bowl. That was enough.

Out in the street, he too bolted – not for the house opposite but away up the city towards the Cathedral. It seemed to him as he went it was his dearest home, and that he would confess there his sin of masturbation, grievous though the penalty would be. He had been besmirched by evil. He was at risk.

The seven guardsmen of the Cathedral in their black, crimson and gold, a fence of black crosses on their garments, their mail dazzling, galloped up the street. They had been fearfully admired and nervously avoided, stared at, pointed out and commented upon all the way. Obviously they had work to do. The captain carried his sword drawn, symbol of physical violence. The three black priests, who rode behind at a slightly less precipitate speed, were ominous as crows. One nursed before him a lacquered box, chained shut with silver. It would contain a copy of the Book.

Reaching a narrow house on the Lord's Hill, the onslaught clashed to a halt.

The soldiers strode to the door and hammered there with fists.

There was no response. The door stayed fast closed, the windows above, shuttered.

Presently a quantity of observers beheld the door unlocked – it was Church property, there were available keys. The soldiers went in first, making a noise like a fight as they flung through the rooms, up the stair, beating at things or turning them over. The shutters clapped open.

339

It was then possible to see guardsmen milling through the small upper rooms. Flaunts of red and sable, and steel.

Then the captain was in the doorway.

'Lordly Fathers,' he said to the priests, 'she isn't here. Not a trace.'

So the priests went in, and five soldiers stood on the street to guard the horses, but one slammed in again with the captain, porting the box with the Book.

It became clear next, from the scent of incense and a low moaning noise, that chants were being sung, and a bell rung, and vapours burned in each space of the house. It was an exorcism.

Finally all the shutters were banged to. The priests and soldiers issued out and closed the door, which was then boarded up, and signed by a red seal showing the dome of the Cathedral.

No word was exchanged with any of the crowd, in the street, at overlooking windows. The Church attended to its own.

The priests and guardsmen rode off. The captain had sheathed his sword, but that meant not much.

That evening, sunset was not red but angrily overcast, with leaden clouds that promised boiling summer rain. Veins beat in the grey forehead of the sky.

Some said they had seen the whore, a girl clothed in a white or pale dress, arrive at a mixture of hours of day, night. She had been accompanied more than once. A few claimed to have seen men rushing from the house after, as if overwhelmed by cognizance of wrongdoing. Others slunk off in the usual mode.

There was a selection of watchers tonight. They had sensed she would come, like the deer to the pool where the hunters wait. Naturally, she would find the door locked against her, and a seal of Father Church sternly upon it. If she ran, she might get away. It depended. The eyes of God were everywhere.

The harlot had company. She was the preying cat, not the harmless deer. She was the snake winding the tree

340

and the First Woman offering her apple breasts and soon the fatal Apple itself, downfall of men.

He was some labourer, covered in stone dust.

They reached the door, and in the damson dark plainly he did not see anything untoward, and she, putting her hand on the door, did something— A board cracked, a second. The door swung wide.

Once the pair had gone into the house, the watchers, not having the temerity of a godbrother, could only wait to see.

How many men she had let possess her she would not have known to say. Since her body came and went much as did her appearances in the city, her awareness was random. She had been attracted to the house, and to certain other areas. Questions did not suit her, she pondered nothing. She had sketches of memory – a chapel of virginity, and also carnal obedience to a man, or men, faceless spectres who had taught her what to do. She had no emotions. She moved so quickly, in and out of the plain of corporeal existence, they had not yet had time to catch up.

Twice, her consorts of the streets had asked for her name. A twist, more lapse than recovery, unfolded her recollection. The name she gave was *Anya*.

The stonemason was uninterested in names. They went up to the room of the bed, and lay down on its blanket, and copulated. He wanted nothing unordinary, and was very swift.

Then he offered payment. It was cheap; she had not stipulated a fee.

Obviously, as the apprentice godbrother could have warned him, *Anya* wanted a particular reward.

'Give me a little blood.'

The stonemason raised himself. 'Blood? What for?'

'Your strength.'

'It's true, I'm strong. You think so, eh?'

Some were afraid at her request, others aroused again.

The stonemason only accepted the charge, judging it light. He would have enough money now for a drink.

Going to the wooden bowl that stood under the window he gave himself a nick and let fall a slight stream of red. 'Fair luck to you,' he said. 'It'll do you good, that will.' And left her.

Anya drank the blood. It meant nothing to her, was not nourishing or enticing, did not fill her with hopes, needs, ecstasies, or the grasp of anything. She was drawn to do it, as to the house, as to manifest. There was a kind of defiance, however, so she tossed her head, and her plaits whipped away and thudded down, the heavy hair thick enough to smite her.

Outside, unseen, unknown, the stonemason had been apprehended in the street by three silent Cathedral guardsmen. Terrified, he was led off for inquiry.

What Anya did upstairs was nothing. Maybe she would have faded out of being as she had faded into it. Or she might have been about to extinguish those candles she lit by night, through a dreamy out-reaching, the image of a flame upon an altar lamp. But suddenly there were loud and threatening steps within the house – two of the soldiers of the Church coming impatiently, with a torch, for the harlot.

They walked into the room with the bed. There she was, candlelit with the incriminating bowl of scarlet halfway from her lips; she had been drinking very slowly, possibly forgetful she had wanted to.

'You're to come with us.'

Anya glanced at them.

Then she came to the doorway, so calmly they allowed it, and let her by. They had seen, these soldiers, those who went resigned. They let her go on first down the shallow stair. She passed a turn, and they heard the bowl drop. They bounded after. And she was gone. Gone. Solely that.

One searched the house all over again, and the other pushed out from the door. 'Is she here?'

Two brethren guards emerged from their concealment, shaking their heads, startled.

In the glare of the torch, at the threshold of the door, was a single slender footprint marked in wet blood.

At this they frowned, crossing themselves.

Another funeral was starting up the street, raucously. The soldiers stood in stupid wonderment, looking at the blood footprint, and each other, and the man who came out subsequently and said the whore was nowhere in the house. And unhearing they listened to the cries of death, and one beautiful voice singing thrillingly in the mourning song.

'A witch,' said the soldier who had searched. It was proven.

The funeral had captured her like a web. Conceivably her curiosity – *life* had made her curious, she returned to it so irresistibly – her curiosity made her pause. Or else an element of funerals, buryings. Or her dematerialization under such circumstances confused her. She had fled, without fear, on impulse.

The corpse in the coffin of painted and carven wood was that of a woman. Anya could see it. A young woman, dead in childbearing – Anya told this too, not considering it or musing on it.

The funeral was of medium worth, as the city would have it valued. The priest walked before with a long-stemmed cross of silver. A boy swung incense from a censer. The gaudy coffin had flowers, berries, leaves, and two angels, upright, grieving in long curled hair. Five musicians in black dashed cymbals, tapped drums, and a pair of pipes gave their lawless cry. The hired women sang. They were the last of the procession, behind the torchbearers and the mourners, who were all indistinguishably bundled into darkness of cloth and heart.

Anya re-became at the back of the women singers, and found that she raised her own voice in the funeral chant – of which she had no knowledge, following its melodic scale easily, not bothering with words.

As she did this, making her purpose as it were out of the materials to hand, a nebulous wash of remembrance broke through her consciousness. She was all at once notified that, while she walked here, she was somewhere else. And she sensed the direction of her other self illogically, infallibly. This did not perturb her. Meanwhile, she thought – actually thought, in the way a human thing thinks, as opposed to her former recent sensations, which were not thoughts of any type – she thought that she had done this before, sung in a street, a market, under a narrow house. She had abruptly come to be, and given voice like a bird waking with the sun. The singing was a paean. It was triumph, of an obscure sort. The music that came from her was marvellous, comparable to that of a trained woman singer at some high court. Yet it was an irrelevant skill. A skill maybe not even hers, but inherited. It was additionally a skill impossible. On those occasions of her singing she had not always had a tongue, a throat, a mouth to resonate her song. Nor did she have them now, for this manifestation was most economical.

The singers who brought up the rear of the procession, professional mourners prepared to carol or shriek, whichever was paid for, initially did not take in the third voice augmenting their own. They were, after the general custom of their work, slightly daft from incense they had inhaled, a perquisite of the job. The drug assisted in their acting, and also inclined them to minimal hallucinations. About these they were always in two minds, both disbelieving and superstitious.

Therefore, when one of the women realized that another walked behind and sang, she glanced over her shoulder, and in the flouncing orange torchlight saw a cloaked figure that, at any other moment, would have reduced her to paralysis. But this woman only shaped on her breast the cross of the Christus, and seeing her fellow actor also on the point of turning, touched her arm, and shook her head. The second woman obeyed the negative, did not turn, and crossed herself over in the same way. They went on, singing and steadfast, with just the glitter of madness somewhere under the surface of their eyes. Even the one who had not turned knew what her sister had meant to impart. Death walked after them, having come in person to attend the funeral.

The Cathedral graveyard lay in a dip at the hill's top, and was walled in granite. By night, the four gates were guarded under Church authority, for many of the tombs in the place were richly ornamented. Above the gate where the funeral entered was a vast granite cross with an iron sword crucified upon it, crowned by the white skull of a wolf. The marker was ancient, and denoted the strength of the law which operated on all Church property about the city. It hinted too at an affiliation with the Knights of God. Perhaps one or two persons in the city had, in living memory, looked knowingly on any such warrior priest. They were mysterious, and by inference fearful, like the angels and heartless fanatic saints from whom they took their names. The wolf was a symbol of theirs, however. And the Burial Ground was nightly guarded, as was well publicized, by half-wolves bred on the fiercest dogs.

Once through the gate, the route was readily to be seen, for it had been lit by flaming brands. From the highways so created, the savage wolf-dogs kept away; they had been trained to that. But the rest of the graveyard lay in darkness, like a black dead wood of stone, with here and there the wolf-soul roaming in it, a hint of flat yellow eyes, a ticking of feet, or, on nights of a large moon, howling from the moribund avenues.

The funeral procession wound along its predestined course, to its selected grave, ready-dug and gaping. (Two grave-diggers stood by, to fill up the grave after they were gone.) A woman began to weep among the mourners, and the professionals left off their song to utter sharp yelps of pain and loss.

Death had ceased walking behind them. Oddly, despite the evidence, Death had decided not to attend the burial. It was holy ground; perhaps Death respected that.

Death, in fact, had wandered off into the dark land all around. Its aspect of a forest had drawn her, or the stones.

The voice of the priest, speaking over the coloured coffin, sank down behind rows of black things with enormous crucifixes and giant winged beings upon their roofs.

She – Death – moved past an urn of rock in which a fire had burned.

The voice of the burial itself had died.

Anya-Anillia, what there was of her, stood on a high table of earth, under the thunder sky of night which had no rain, no rain even of stars, for these were hidden in cloud and the breath of the city, its smokes and sighs.

She looked down, over the straight paths, and the edifices cut from night. (The funeral glowed half a mile off, like damp embers.)

There was a soft ticking as if fallen leaves blew along the slope at her back, and as she turned her head, she glimpsed a cross higher than her body, with an animal crouched on it, leaning down under its humped, distorted wings, its eyes burning cold. An angel with the head of a wolf, regarding her motionless, winged with its own thin hackles, forefeet gripping the crossbars. But before Anillia, a pit opened into deep night. It was one of the truths of the Cathedral graveyard.

Even the very poor might buy burial here, for a pittance. If they were awarded no token to sign the spot, they did not expect such bounty. The last consolation having been spoken, they saw the soil begin to drop upon the fragile box. They did not see how, at dusk, the soil was scraped off again, and the lid of the coffin, when thought necessary, levered up. On the bodies of the very poor, the wolf-dogs fed. They knew no better, and did not mind. Later, if needed, any remains were tidied away.

Below, in the pit, a white, white body gleamed, the corpse of a young man whose black hair streamed along the ground, having been dressed and combed by someone who had loved him, unwittingly for *this*.

Anillia, or that which was Anillia, gazed on the wolf-feast, the myriad dots of bright eyes, the wolf-angel on the cross. At her back, two more of the kind had stopped to wait.

Any who trespassed on the unlit ground knew what to anticipate. A handful of robbers had perished. But Anillia was occupied with her succession of memories.

The face of the cadaver had been gnawed off, and his hands and feet. And yet, because of him, Anillia reviewed a man lying by a river, and one washed his white body, and dried it with her hair. He was not dead, he slept. His face she recognized, having never before seen it in maturity. She soothed his skin, and spears of love tore through her, too awful to be expressed. There was a scar over his heart. This was her son. She put him to her breast, and now, miraculously, gave the child suck: he drank from her.

One of the dog-wolves, impatient as the guardsmen at the house, leapt up on the back of the cloaked woman. She did not fall. It was the animal which slithered and lost purchase, rolling off on to the earth, macabre and ridiculous. There was not enough of her there to get a hold on. At the same instant, she was too strong.

She had no flesh herself, or very little. She had appeared to be Death, and did so now to the wolf, which abruptly cowered and whined, going away with its belly down, and another, catching its fright, or perceiving her in a new way, copied it. Even the wolf that was an angel up on the cross threw itself off into the darkness, and ran between the tombs into the pit, to eat real death with its kindred.

The illusory cloak fluttered from Anillia. She was a tawny skeleton, with perfect eyes, black as night, night hair in three long plaits, and on the cage of ribs, two breasts like pale flowers grown upward from an invisible heart.

The last wolf-dog, the weakling and runt of the pack, came to her and rubbed itself on her bones. Rising on its hind limbs, it propped itself against her steely nothing of unbody, and licked her breasts, the flowers of milk, eagerly, gently.

In the pit, the others, as if embarrassed, demonstrated

their proper function, ripping the meat in chunks from the carcass.

The wolf-dog slipped down on to the ground. There was no upright thing any more to hold him. He sniffed at the soil, where she had been, or seemed to be.

Over the graveyard, the well-off funeral was done. The grave-diggers, the grave fully secured, were dousing the torches and hurrying for the safety of the gate.

Chapter Ten

They had left the brown bones in the cell lying on the floor, dressed in green and garlanded with weeds. The door was closed with a chain. The room would need exorcism, and the bones some merciless disposal, at the guidance of the Primentor – this guidance had not yet been offered on the day Jasha was to be burned as a witch. The bones were presumably the property of the Magister, Anjelen. Why the girl had charge of them was questionable.

A dreadful miracle took place on the beach, at the witch-burning. Flame-haired, unconsumed, the demoness rose from the pyre. The women of the Doma scattered in maddened terror.

A second miracle took place.

The Primentor summoned the Administress, and met her under the Christerium wall in a tent of black cloth. The winter wind was blowing from the sea, they drank mulled wine. He treated her with respect, so all her inadequacies burgeoned in her like a crop of locusts, beginning to slake themselves on her dignity, her self-worth. She promised herself the rod a hundred times, because the Father praised her, and put in her his trust. But she bore the session with outward calm. She did not confess her faults.

These things, these appalling occult things, were indeed the works of the Devil. And yet, what had risen from the pyre was an apparition, sent decidedly by the Evil One – not, however, the girl herself, who had perished in the fire. So the Devil tried their faith. She must resign herself. Their very piety provoked Him.

Presently the Primentor, the King of that potent and shadowed world on the brink of the waters, conducted her to the burning platform, and there he pointed out to her a remnant or two of bone, black as only burning could make it. The Administress did not doubt, did not go forward to be sure. She had not the learning, being herself unscientific, to tell this was not the bone of a woman, but of some animal recently butchered.

The hysteria was all over. The Administress returned to her Doma, called her flock of dark hens, told them of the new miracle, and sent them to pray, for herein they must be doubly vigilant; they had angered more than normally the Enemy of God.

After this, the Administress beat herself until striped in blood. Until the pain blotted away the sight of Jasha lifting like an angel of fire, bubbles of flame on her lips, and her eyes greener than the sea.

The other bones, the brown couth bones in a green dress, were left behind the door of the cell in the court of unchaste women. There had been no instructions concerning them. Might they not be harmless, loosed from Jasha's sorcery? And might they not, too, have to be rendered up to the Magister Anjelen?

Anillia had not slept inside a vault, coffin or chest, but inside the fretwork casket of her own skeleton. It was a sleep approaching eighteen years in duration. It was a deep sleep, that birthed dreams. From some of these she emerged visibly, a ghost. And later, from her dreams she stepped out in a robe of fleshliness which, if it would not have stood all the tests of the body, was still capable of physical possession, and the drinking-down of blood. The bodies projected from her dreams, too, were able to light candles, and to open doors that had been boarded up, by flexings of a hand – more exactly, of a will.

Anillia had been built by will. She had *become* will.

It was will that drove her back, over the river to the

sea, where her bone bed had been taken. And here it lay down, the will of Anillia, and called out something from another, who also came forth in dreams, to pass through doors, to assemble and to clothe – by will. Jasha served her mother, brain-blind, soul-canny.

After Jasha had been torn from her story, Anillia began to dream herself into being.

This was no longer manifestation of spirit, phantom, proto-flesh. This was the flesh of the first making, what she herself had made for herself that second time, the girl in the second, ruined, chapel, Jasha's mother. But the fibres were tougher, with the fresh pliancy of the exercised muscle.

It commenced, if any had seen, with a clouding over, mist or pollen on the bed of bones. The skeleton whitened and knit together in slow, still conjoinings. Then the misty cloud turned intransparent. It made a country of undulations, the dry pool of a navel like a shell, the hidden liquid pools of eyes. Hair grew out like trickling water. It was black hair, as ever, as the eyes had stayed black. Yet on the head there was hair enough to make three plaits. In other words, the hair of Jasha, through the lens of Anillia, in the way the city had been shown it. Otherwise the body was flowerlike and young, a vanity, a pride, a redemption of all hurts, of sex, of childbearing, of disease, and of death.

When everything was ready, like the queen into the mansion, the land-locked soul of Anillia came up from the other otherness where it had lingered in its sleep. It filled the body, as the body had filled the green dress. It opened its eyes, and saw, while the live brain shone outward, and the heart beat, and the lungs inhaled their first breath, let it go, and took, as a right, another.

The garland of weeds, dying in any case, she threw away – *they* had been Jasha's fancy. The silver ring, which had been grown before everything else, a faithful copy of that ring which her master had grown from her the last, that she kept. As for the necklace of Crel, it had been discarded at Korhlen, irrelevant.

351

So got to her feet, the sleeper, not stiff or bemused after her prolonged drowse.

Anillia remembered everything. But there was more. Not only her own life, her lives. For Anillia knew what Jasha knew, had seen, in sleep, what Jasha saw. Anillia, as firmly as she recalled the offering of Boroi's blood, recalled equally the journey over the hills and plains, between rivers, in the ship, to the end of the land. Her bones had been rattling alongside in the chest where Anjelen had had them thrown – she knew this too – got like trophies from the forest vault on his visit there, her skull due to rest with the other skulls perhaps, the impedimenta of his magician's chamber. But all that while she had seen through Jasha's eyes, seen in sleep. And now, woken completely, she remembered. Anillia remembered everything. As if it had been yesterday.

What had detained her in the world was only love. What brought her back was love. Love's name was Mechail.

He was not a corpse gnawed on by wolves. She knew how he would appear. She had seen his face, his nakedness as a man, as she had seen him when a child, free to her now, through Jasha's medium, as then.

She knew things too that Jasha did not know. Or that Jasha knew without knowing.

Anillia knew the hour when Mechail had died, and that he came back from death.

It was easy to be whole, and to live.

But between them, the black and white tree of Anjelen, its branches of swords, its wolf-skull heart.

Anillia remembered red blood.

Woman was the vessel, the apple, passion as sin. Anjelen was man the sterile sword, the erect phallus that killed. *Anillia remembered Anjelen.*

There was also hate. Hate's name was Anjelen.

Anillia had had her sleep. She was not tired any more.

She turned to the cell door and rapped on it, and outside the silver chain, previously blessed and bane of witches, snapped in two parts and clinked upon the ground.

*

In the high wall that loomed upward into blackness and became the sky, there was a small gate. On the sea a line showed, scarcely light. Below, the Doma in silence, and the long shore, and westward the herded mountains. A few stars. Only the sound of the ocean.

The figure that had come up easily out of the Doma scratched under the colossal wall on the Christerium's lesser gate.

The porter slept. In his sleep he heard the scratching. He had been warned to expect no one. He did not wake.

But the scratching clawed inside his brain. He opened two slits and let himself look forth. The candles were burned out, and everything seemed only night. The scratching.

'What is it? Who's there?'

'I'm on the Magister's errand,' said a soft voice from eyeless black.

'What Magister?'

'Anjelen.'

The porter collected himself. The voice was not masculine, not even a boy's. It was a woman's voice. No sister would approach. Some servant, mistaking her orders?

'You go off, you hussy. One of the men must see to it.'

'No. I'm here for the Magister Anjelen. Do you dare keep me out?'

'No female can enter—'

'I will put it into your hands,' said the voice of the woman.

The porter was sleepy. His head was thick. He took the key and unlocked and unbolted the gate. In the hierarchy of the Christerium and of the Church, he was nothing, an opener of doors. Sometimes he had had women, confessing only sections of the sin. Years ago there had been a village girl who had come over the mountains with her family, to barter at the Doma. She had bartered too under the rock, with him. It was not quite unknown to him, then, to allow a woman's form to shadow the gate.

A shadow was all she was. He strove to make her from the dark.

'What is it?'

'Put your hands together, and hold them out,' she said, playfully. This aroused him. He heard himself laugh, and he did as she said, and next moment she had leant forward as if to kiss his fingers. By the time he felt the knife and knew it, it had cut deeply into each of his wrists. The blood spilled up before he understood, and filled his palms. And as if from a cup, she was drinking.

The knife was from the Doma kitchen. She took as she found. As he unseamed his lips to cry for help, she rested her smooth fingers there. Such vitality was in her touch he could not get out a whimper. He sank on his knees and she undressed him, pulling his habit off over his head and flopping arms as efficiently as she had pulled off her illusory whore's garments in the river city. He had fainted before she finished. She shut, locked and bolted the gate, hung up the key, and in the priest's robe, went into the Christerium. If it was absolute no woman had ever penetrated there before, she must have snagged and warped some of its weave of power, its male dominion. But there was no signal to that effect, only soon the buzz of voices from the church above the sea, the first office of dawn.

High in the high south wall of the Christerium, dark thought in a stone mind, the one whose name had been taken in vain sat motionless in his carved chair. Physically present in that room of his, that matchless chamber of candy-coloured glass and glass like venom, among the tables of skulls and crystals and wands, and instruments of precision, the most precise instrument of all, Anjelen, was intent upon other distances than those below his windows.

He was at meditation. This, for any who might have entered and seen him. (The door was never locked. Who had gone in unasked, save only Mechail?)

The beads of prayer were under Anjelen's long fingers.

The crucifix stood before his face with the bleeding of the Christus. The cross on the breast of Anjelen barely rose and fell to any breathing.

He was away. Like a drop of nothing in the air, he watched to see how they went on, the two who had eluded him.

That was what Anjelen was doing.

The white sun climbed, and the grey beast brooded above the sea.

The noises of the Christerium, its chants and domestica, arose in the usual way.

There was no oddity of notes from the Doma. The elderly unchaste women had been moved from their court, and were not about to notice, with rheumy vision, any breakage of chains.

The sea came back along the beach of blackness and tongued the stones of God.

Late in the morning, a novice going along one of the upper walks found an artisan, who was of a party repairing structures against the north inner walls. The artisan was lying beneath a gargoyle representing a lion maned with vipers. He had been attempting to drink the water which ran from the lion's mossy mouth, but had gone down. The man bled from a tear in his wrist, presumably occasioned in accident by one of his labourer's tools. He was delirious, and spoke of the Devil, so the young priest did not listen closely, being afraid.

In the early afternoon a brother of the Christerium beheld one of his fellows lying, apparently in a swoon, near to the Ordinate Hall. The man's wrists were slashed. He was in a chancy way, and only babbled of a woman. As a potential suicide he was treated with suspicion.

No one, as it happened, had gone near the lesser western gate.

Some imagined, as the evening drew on, the mountains swallowing the white sun, that a ghost had brushed by them in this corner or that. One came to sensual awareness after being passed by a hooded youth in a habit too large: he sought a penance.

As the light began to go, the sky mapped itself with yellow. The sea blackened. The black gulls wheeled.

In the cloister by the church tower, under the shadows, a red-belted priest left off his devotion to his beads, seeing a hooded man approach.

The priest knew at once that what was in front of him was not a figment of the Christerium, that it was alien, and lethal. Then he saw the pale face of a girl come out like the moon from a cloud.

'Hush,' she said. And before he could disobey, she pointed at the great tower, the beast-neck-and-head of the church. 'Take me in there.'

'Woman,' he said, 'get yourself hence.'

'I was always here,' she said. 'I am Anjelen's.'

Bewilderment and fright came over the priest. What she had said bore with it so many connotations.

Above the dusk-deep court, shaded now like a wood, the square of sky shone. The priest glanced at it for aid. But there was none. The woman had taken his hand, how cool she was. 'You must do what I say,' she said.

It seemed to be his awe of the name of the Magister that forced him to respond, but secretly he knew that it was she herself who had bound him.

The bell started to toll in the tower. This was the hour just before the evening prayers.

He led her over the threshold, and the church was ready lighted, flowing with balsams, and the vast window of the Triumph over Hell gone to wine and obsidian, obscured in its meaning.

She followed, and by following moved him to lead her. He found he went towards the altar, draped tonight in purple, with fringes of bullion, and sewn with enormous pearls that were the tears of God. The Christus leaned on his cross, miles above, wounded by diamond, crowned with rubies of rose and blood. The window without glass held twilight.

356

'Get me the Host,' said the woman to the priest. 'Your holy bread.'

'You're mad—'

'And you must do as you're told.'

She was behind him, and as she spoke, suddenly he felt the pain of two blunt awls strike him in the arm. He turned on her with a gasp, and saw her there, a green-clad thing with its head dipped like that of a snake. She had bitten him viciously enough to break the skin and part the vein. His own blood ran down his hand, and she, she licked her lips.

He was horrified, recognizing himself in a confrontation with the Devil. No, he would not go for the Host.

She began to speak again. He could not help but hear.

'The body,' she said, 'the body of your God made flesh. White and sweet. *Fetch* it.'

His hands were on the concealed door before he fathomed what he did. It was like sex, the forbidden act. His head swam, and he gave her his wrist again, too, before she drifted away.

To an open tower high on the wall, the gulls were attracted, blown in across the pools of heaven. All day they scavenged, sinking in the ocean for its fish, mining the cliff faces for insects and lichens. They had become, over the generations, brutal and cannibalistic, slaying and eating each other, or gobbling the eggs of unguarded nests. Sometimes scraps came their way from the refuse of the religious buildings, and once or twice in fifty years, sentimentally, priests had fed them, calling them God's poor creatures, these fiends from the upper air with beaks of death.

The sky was a curious tawny silver, and from this height the water looked much the same, only darker and scarred with froth. The blackness of the gulls swarmed over the black silhouette of the turret, and its open sides, circling and arrowing down.

The figure of a woman was there, holding up her hands. She extended white wafers, and the black gulls snatched

357

them from her fingers, screaming, circling away and in again, and sometimes she threw her bounty, and they caught it on the wing, the black wing, and the white flesh of the Christus was in their gullets, but for a handful of crumbs that flighted away on the wind.

A night cloud was rising from the sea. Like the tide and the gulls, it had come in on the platform of rock, the island of the Christerium. But the turret poked above it still, to where the light remained.

The food was all gone. The gulls continued to circle, lifting off in stages, to be certain not to miss anything.

There was one gull which was larger than the rest. It did not go up, but dropped lower. It was falling farther off, the vault of heaven—

A rushing of wings, like the roar of a gale. The sky went dark, flashed out again, and something alighted in the eastern opening of the turret.

It came from the Book, from the dimension of the past, the myth, the dream.

A slim black sword that was like the body of a robed man, two huge wings, raven-black or blue, that fanned up to frame body and face. The face white, and the white hands, standing on the blackness, and in the palm of either hand, a blazing rose. The Angel.

The girl in the turret looked at the male angel, who was God, honour, chastity, discipline. She was woman, chaos, disorder, rebellion.

They looked at each other with identical eyes, the woman, the angel.

She said: 'Do you remember me? You made me for a purpose. Do you like what you made?'

'You're here,' the Angel said. He was wingless, and only poised inside the turret with her, a black-habited priest with a thin red cord at his waist, a ruby in a crucifix on his breast. His eyes were still the twins of hers.

'Mechail,' she said.

'*Not* here,' he said.

'My son,' she said.

He said, 'Mine.'

'And I am your daughter.'

'Fashioned from the rib of my mind,' he said.

'There are several of us.'

'I have all your names,' he said.

She said, 'My son, Mechi the Dwarf that my son made by will on a human woman in the forest. Jasha, that I made in another body of my will, from the seed of a human man.'

'You can do things, Anillia,' he said, 'that I have never troubled with. The lighting of lamps, and opening of doors. *Magic*.' He spoke contemptuously, a man's voice now. 'You, and he, have done a great deal I should not have troubled to do.'

'And will do more.'

'No, Anillia,' he said. 'You should rest now. I brought you from Korhlen to allow you rest.'

Anillia said, 'I've drunk the blood of your Christerium, your chaste priesthood, some of whom shivered and let go their semen with their blood when I drank it.'

'That's nothing to me,' he said. 'They're dross.'

'Mechail,' she said, 'drank the blood of a woman—'

'But the first blood Mechail drank was that of a male. His own.'

Anillia turned her head. Against the dark night which now had all of Heaven, she seemed to burn like a white flame, but he was the darkness.

'Go to sleep,' he said. 'Go to sleep, Anillia.'

'Whatever it is you want,' she said, 'I'll take it from you. You shan't have it. Then, I'll sleep.'

The dark light of Anjelen went suddenly out.

Anillia seared white upon black before she too disappeared.

After their vanishment, no night had ever seemed so full of unseen things.

Book Three

JUN

Chapter One

From the first seed, which fell like a burning moment of time into the hot soil of the beginning, the forest was. Long before it became shadow and substance, and covered over the land, it was a condition of the land. In the earliest days, when men made their way between the slender stalks of it, its bones no wider than sticks, they spoke of it as the great wood. It breathed with winds, wove like a spider a tangle of undergrowth, gave birth out of its loam, was a hive of hidden life.

And when the forest had grown tall, dense and constant, so that trees might fall and not be numbered, the soul of the forest was strong enough that what passed through it or took refuge in it made offering.

At first the offerings had been random. What died there left its decay, its skeleton, its cooling blood. Trees grew from the spines of foxes. Out of the dead cups of human skulls the pines went up.

It began to be that these gifts of building were anticipated.

As though the trees had whispered of a need.

There were those who lived from start to finish in the great wood, never saw another place and disbelieved what they heard. Was not the world one whole forest, perhaps split here and there by waters, and yet the trees grew in the waters too, and only mountains lifted, and the mountains were clothed in the forest.

The forest was mother and father, womb and grave,

living and extinction. They worshipped the forest, for, being all things, the forest was also God.

In the spring evening, the Chosen, Jun, sat on the ground outside the Woodman's hut, playing with the hare. The hare was nearly white, a spirit-like albino of the forest which came in the afternoon or at dusk to drink the milk put out for it. Sensing, it seemed, that the boy was also special, the hare allowed him to pet it, and would jump over twigs that he held out, or toy with a grass rope. Sometimes the Woodman would ask the hare questions, and the hare would demonstrate its replies by particular movements, or the shape of droppings left on the edge of the clearing. Now and then a spotted snake would also cross the clearing, and the Woodman took note of its track. Latterly, the Woodman too would ask Jun to do certain things, such as selecting from a scatter of objects in the hut, or answering a riddle. By now Jun was empowered: as he had approached the god day by day, he had waxed more magical. To touch Jun brought a blessing, but very few came to the Woodman's clearing, which lay below the Tree. The Woodman was the intermediary between the supernatural and the people. The earth there was galvanized, wondrous and danger-filled.

Very soon, several hundred would come to the clearing, but that was different.

From the clearing, in winter, and in spring when the lesser trees were only starred with green, it was possible to behold the Tree, the Lord. It towered up, smooth and purely black. It looked eternal, and so it was. The first tree of the forest, it had spawned every other, of every kind. For the Tree was not of one kind only; even the child could see this for himself. From the huge trunk, the limbs lent out like a crown of snakes, and the leaves, though some were like needles, were fleshy and silken, while others were heavy flags with long veins and ribs in them. The Lord never lost foliage, even when the snow came. This the boy had seen for himself as well, for he had lived here in the Woodman's hut all winter, under the Tree.

The Choosing was in the late summer, after the garnering and harvest. Male children of nine or eight years were brought to the Woodman, from the hutments round about. Even from the Landholder's estate in the valley they were brought, unknown to the master. He was a convert to the religion of the Christus, the tree-god in other form. Misunderstanding the truth of sacrifice, the Landholder would not countenance what went on in the wood, turned a blind eye to it. His forefathers had come to witness, and at certain eras, when required, had themselves taken the Woodman's part – even once given a son. This was no longer conceivable.

The nearness of the Lord Tree to the estate, once the reason for the construction there of a landholder's house, was now awkward, and strange.

Perhaps prudence had caused the snake and the hare to make no choice of boys from the valley.

Of those picked out, a careful scrutiny and interrogation was performed, both by the elder men of the hutments and by the Woodman, their priest. The child must be virgin, must not even have set hand to himself. He must be perfect.

Jun was nine years. He had been worked hard, but never beaten with a rod. Sexual desire of any sort had not yet found him. He had no scars, no irregularity or deformity. He was a quiet boy, with an oval face and thin well-made body sheathed in white skin.

He wanted the honour and the bliss of the Chosen as much as any of the others, but he did not aim at it, did not brag or show off, or make anything of his beauty. There were three other sons in his household; he could be spared. The grace of his choice would see the family favoured. Only the woman wept a little. They usually did.

He did not mind going to live with the priest Woodman in the clearing. It was a wonder. It was the road to Heaven.

For half a year then he was between the god and the

world, drawn ever nearer to immortality. He was treated gently, fed the very best, given nothing to do that was not pleasant, instructed in secret rhymes and spells whereby to prove himself at the instant when God took hold of him. Nor, obviously, did he fear that moment. He had been taught it was a commencement, not an end. He would be enhanced, changed, lifted up where the pine-tops balanced sun, moon and stars. They were a brotherhood, all those that went before him. He would become the forest, he would become the god. Even the hutments knew that. No, Jun did not fear.

The hare ran across the glade and bowed once to a reed which grew there.

The Woodman stepped from the hut and asked Jun if the hare had bowed.

'Yes,' said Jun, and the Woodman, who had been kinder than Jun's father, smiled at him.

Jun had been in awe of the Woodman. He was perhaps more respectful now, for through the months Jun had watched his priest carry out sorceries both harmonious and unusual. He could call beasts and birds, and seemed to know their speech. He had caused a hemlock tree to burn with a still blue flame that left it entire. In lesser ways, the Woodman entertained the child, making items disappear and reappear, or altering them to a semblance or actuality of life – an axe that chopped their wood, a bowl of beans which made patterns . . . The awe had been enriched by love and trust. A son among a crowd, Jun had never properly known how to love before. In this cocoon between two worlds, there was a margin to find out. The Woodman, now his father on earth, who would give him into the hand of Forever—

'And which animal do you think,' the Woodman said now, 'will you want to be the first?'

Jun knew that once he had become a part of God and the forest, he would be free to experience and to do all things.

'A hare,' said Jun. 'I'll be a hare, and run here to show you.'

'Do that,' said the Woodman gravely. 'One who went before you, long ago, he came to me as a raven, and told me a word of the other life – but not much. He wasn't allowed to tell too much to me, I being mortal still.'

Jun was jealous of the raven.

'I'll tell you,' he said, *'more.'*

'No, you'll think as the god does. Don't mind it. I'm glad for you, the joy and strength, the happiness you go to. Of them all, my best.'

The shadows lengthened, as they lingered there. The mighty umbra of the Tree came down and put its blackness upon them. They were silent in the midnight pool of the Tree. Neither had reason to disbelieve. It was only that the priest knew that the child might suffer, somewhat, before his transformation. Yet it was the price. He himself would have paid it, to be what the boy would be. He was sad to see Jun go. He would look for a black hare with beautiful eyes.

'Tonight,' he said, Jun's protector, 'we begin the last teaching. In seven more days, your day will be here.'

'Truly?' The boy was eager. He forgot the priest, reaching forward with sudden spiritual desire, for godhead, sanctity, *power*.

His death began at first light, when the Woodman roused him with a warm hand on his brow. There was a cup of holy stuff to drink, a wine manufactured from crimson and brown buds of the wood, the flowers of its floor. Jun did not know what the drink was, did not query. After he had taken it, the enormous half-sickening excitement in him quieted, and a marvellous new emotion, nameless, enveloped him.

The Woodman washed Jun in a tub in the hut. Blossoms were crushed in the water, which had been heated. Jun's body was rubbed with aromatics of the pines. He was clad in a goatskin, which had been dressed and was soft on his flesh. Jun felt joy, not knowing quite what joy was.

Outside, there was a mist brushed on the clearing. The sky had a high greenish light.

Two young women came across the glade, and between them, without speaking, set a garland on the boy's dark head. There were wild roses in it, he could smell their scent, and cones from the pines, ferns, asphodel.

The two women went away speechless, and the Woodman came, and led Jun over the clearing by hand. (Only once, Jun looked back, hoping to see the hare. But never mind, he should play with the hare as a brother soon enough.)

Outside the clearing, there were people packed between the trees, and as still as the trees, standing up straight like the trees. Jun had never seen this before, since no children but one attended, and no woman who had not born a child. Jun glanced about, for his mother and the man who had sired him, but he could not be sure. The mist veiled everything, and his eyes did not focus normally, and anyway, he did not care.

The Woodman led Jun lightly, steadily, up the slope. Towards the Lord of All.

Not once had Jun gone to the Tree. It was forbidden. Only the priest might go close, might *touch*. Sometimes he made simple offerings on behalf of his people – carved bone, fruits of the harvest, never, never blood.

They reached the tree.

It was like the whole world.

It was the meaning of the forest, and of being.

A pillar, dividing sky from ground.

The child looked up the length of it, fearless in joy, and saw eternity in the tower of its blackness, in the serpent boughs that flew from it, the wings of leaves and needles. Its colour was perhaps green, but then again it had no necessity of hue, or even texture. It rang and boomed with an immensity of silence and in its immobility was volition. An axis.

These matters the child understood without words. He gazed and was dazzled, felt the god already stretching out.

'Jun,' said the Woodman, tenderly, 'Jun, you must

stand here, and let them put a hand or finger on you. Will you do that? For their sake?'

Jun nodded.

He waited in the whirling stasis of the god, and dimly was aware of the fingers and hands on his breast, forehead, arms. A procession passed him. Probably he had known some of them. He was already transfigured. No one expected anything else.

After a while, the procession dwindled, and then it had gone back into a circle, surrounding the Lord, and leaving the Woodman and the boy alone there.

The priest held the hand of Jun.

'My best, do you trust me?'

Jun nodded again. He smiled.

'Drink this,' said the priest. There was a tiny polished acorn which he put to Jun's mouth. Jun swallowed something that surprised him; it was bitter. He blinked, and the priest said swiftly, 'Now you may go and embrace the god. When you do that, you'll be gone from me, and from us all. There may be pain, but that will soon be over. Do you see?'

Jun smiled again. The priest turned him, and there was the pillar of God. It burned like the flame in the hemlock, but black as a winter river. Jun went slowly to the Tree, and lay against it, and put his arms about it. Then he felt its heart, he felt its *life*. It was as if he grasped the centre of all things, the pivot, the fountainhead. He loved the Tree. He gave himself to the Tree.

Far away, someone had torn the goatskin. A sharp thin stinging blow came on his shoulders, and was repeated. It was repeated many times.

Jun felt but did not feel the smart of the briars striking him. He was absorbed by the Tree.

Even when there was another pain, twining his head, curious and startling – he half made to think of it, could not – for neither did this concern him. Only the Tree. Salt fire ran into his eyes, and tears welled out between the lids, so he closed them.

Fire was coursing down his arms, his feet burned wet.

Jun rubbed his cheek against the Tree, and pins of pain stabbed his temples. But then the Tree had gripped him. The Tree pulled him upward, incredibly, by his arms, up and up into itself, into the hub of the world—

Miles above the earth, the child hung, and tipped back his head. He did not bother to look. He was suspended in ecstasy, of which the pains of his body were becoming part.

Above them, the spectators at the sacrifice, whipped and crowned with his second wreath of thorns, the perfect boy swung from the cords of the pulley that bound his wrists. The veins there were already severed, as were those at his ankles. Blood trickled scarlet down the whiteness of the briar-blemished body, down the inebriate and sacred pallor of the face, and splashed the diverse structures of the leaves. His full weight was on the ropes. From the pressure of that, the innocent phallus had engorged. The sight was cruelly exquisite, not obscene or even shameful. It had nothing to do with human lust. Already he gasped, stifling on the ropes. The blood went out in bursts, rocking to his struggling heart. If he knew anything any more was not obvious. The god hovered in the black canopy of the Tree like an eagle descending.

Gradually the worshippers fell to their knees, or full-length on their faces.

The agony in the Tree excluded them. They could only offer it. They were envious of Jun, they loved Jun.

The Woodman stood dreaming, proud of the accomplishment, the glory to which he had sent the best of all the fair and good.

An hour after the sun was up, a gold round in the sky, the wild hunt came over the hill and into the grove where the centre of the forest and the world of the forest had root.

Groups of the congregation were still present; some had paused to catch a trickle of blood from the leaves, which was allowed them, a terrible and divine undertaking. The Woodman was under the Tree, keeping vigil, his old eyes shut. He was an elderly man, this might have been his last officiation. So much was now certain.

The riders of the wild hunt were a storm of green and reddish brown, like levels of the wood itself. In the midst was a purple raven flapping on a square cloth. Immediately they were known, and the people separated from the Tree, flung off from its aura. No longer devout but screaming in fright, they tore down the slope into the pines, where some stumbled, or were chopped to the ground by the clubs of the pursuers.

The Landholder reared in his stirrups, roaring. He was calling them vile and profane things, in the name of the Christus. The grove of the Lord Tree seemed blasted, singed. And the Tree itself had gone to immeasurable distance, leaving merely its emblem, but the Landholder, under his Raven banner, mistook the emblem for the Tree and railed against it. There was a white-faced riding Christus-priest too, frothing at the lips, shrieking of Hell, damnation, pits and traps.

Then the noise broke into pieces. They flew off and went to nothing. The elderly Woodman was staring up from beneath the Tree, staring up blind at the Landholder. One of the rough soldiers of the Landholder had driven a sword into the old man, directly through the heart. The Woodman died moment by moment on the blade, shaking his head, sighing.

The Landholder glared about from his horse. The whole grove seemed to have turned red with bleeding and cloaks and rage. So he shouted again.

'You see? I've put a stop to it – your bloody barbarism. I warned you! I told you. No more. Did you listen? You listen now. I'll bring you to the true God by my sword. I'll save you from Hell by steel and the rod. I'll have you, I'll have you, you filthy, godless excrement.'

Mailed men were dismounting. They stood attentive. As this happened, the Woodman was pushed off the sword and curled to the ground. The soldiers kicked at him, and laughed, and the Landholder bellowed: 'Shut your row.

Do you see that child up there? Hung like a bit of butcher's meat – God's cross—'

And the priest shrieked awful curses, till his throat cracked.

Then the Landholder pointed out who should be striped with the rod, and he sent the soldiers through the women, hacking off great raping swaths of their hair.

'It's over,' said the Landholder. 'You'll give no more of your boys to that abomination.' He looked round, and there were his men, with axes ready. 'Cut down their Tree,' he said. 'Cut it down, make it into kindling. Fire it.'

There were no more cries. Now the silence was complete. It was the ending of the world. Pointless to resist.

But a sound came, impossibly, of the first axe upon the Tree.

The Landholder turned his horse abruptly and cantered along the slope. His priest sat there a minute longer, gnawing his mouth, then he too made off.

The soldiers, the dregs of twenty places, paid by the Raven Lord, loyal to the Christus, leered and hurled their axes at the Tree, while the red and white child depended above them.

The forest people free to do so escaped. They ran away. Those who could not averted their faces. They escaped as best they could.

The sun was going up the sky. The thudding of the axes went on like hurt in a wound. The trunk of the Tree was like iron. It would take hours to fell it. The soldiers blasphemed the Tree. They took intervals to drink, and to possess three of four of the comelier women left behind.

Conversion to the Christus had scoured the topsoil of the forest from the soldiers of the Raven garrison. In a stone house in the valley, they took the body and blood of the god, and forgot those similar rituals their progenitors had acted. The new god was more stern in some sort, yet also He could be fooled. You had only to confess, and to pay – in a fast, or a coin – and He forgave you. With the old god, so a part of them vaguely remembered, forgiveness was not anything to do with it. Wrong was wrong. There was no blame, the god did not sob at your sins. But if there was a punishment, you could not buy it off. It was like life itself. Like birth, like breath. Inevitable.

The giant, black and freakish Tree began to give way in the afternoon.

The grove was puddled by tawny lights, and the differing foliages of the tree shimmered with them.

The men had long ago stopped glancing up at the hung child. He was dead. They would have to get out of the path of him, when the tree came down. Then give the brat a proper burial – the Landholder had vowed it – up here, in pagan ground.

The men did not look forward to that. They had done a great deal of killing. Few of them had killed little boys, and never in the foul, disgusting manner of the sacrifice. (They had violated the women particularly viciously, for their wickedness in attending here. The men who had been beaten lay on the turf motionless. It served them right.)

Suddenly, as the sun started to dip into the western sea of the wood, shooting through every intervening bough in showers of chrysolite, the Tree twisted from the axes and turned around upon its riven base like a gargantuan wheel. It seemed to take the measure of the grove, deciding if to go towards the south or the west, the sun's death.

The soldiers leapt away, shouting.

The architecture of the Tree, like a beam of the sky, stroked slowly sidelong with a deceptive smoothness. It met the heads of the pines, a young oak, and smashed them into splinters. From the forest below, against the dying blaze of a sun now entirely visible, birds went up in breakers, calling and trilling. Every tree left standing seemed to give out its creatures like a cry. The undergrowth rushed, and a cold wind passed over.

The length of the Tree, the long beam of Heaven, struck the earth.

The ground shuddered. It *moved*. From a hundred

hidden valves and vaults, a murmur rose, and faded in the air like smoke.

Then came nothingness. It was like the stopping of a heart. The whole landscape seemed hollow.

One of the soldiers stamped his feet noisily. 'That's done. Where did the corpse go? We'll have to have it out.'

The boy had gone with the Tree and the pulley and the ropes away into the sunset, downhill. The spume of leaves and birds was sinking there. It had happened none of the captives lay where the Tree had fallen.

The lines of ebbing sunlight shone across the smashed grove. They lit the levelled stump, and one at a time, the soldiers turned to see it.

The hybrid Tree had had huge rings, the centuries of its liveness inscribed within it. They were uncountable, so many. Each ring bled. It was ichor, it was blood, in the dying light it was red.

The Landholder's men stared at this phenomenon, the bleeding of the Lord Tree. They found out, glimpse by glimpse, that the ruined grove had been splashed and dotted by blood. That they themselves were dappled. That their axes and their hands were crimson.

The blood bubbled up from the stump. It poured over and spilled into the ground. The countless rings of the Tree were no longer to be seen, the blood had obliterated them to a lake of ruby, gleaming back the sunset.

As the framework of a thousand victims had blended with the Tree, grown into it and become the Tree, so their blood, feeding it, had filled the Tree. It was vegetable, but also flesh. Tree, but also man. But also god.

A vessel deep inside the severed trunk erupted.

A fountain of blood sprang into the sky, high as (once), the great Tree, a pillar of fire by day— But the last sun shrank into wood and the sky was an opal, and the fire of the pillar of blood sprayed across Heaven and came down again, drenching the grove beneath.

The soldiers ran screaming, and the horses, tearing from their tethers, raced out with them, neighing and voiding themselves in fear.

The country about was another land. As if a wall of glass contained the grove.

Men and beasts vanished as a second wall of darkness ascended from the earth.

It rained in the night. There was a cloudburst. The forest flooded with sounds of water. Things washed away.

After the rain, the sky was clear, and the stars cracked with cold, shrill light.

When the Christus-priest should come, quavering with his cross and faith, in the morning, nothing would speak of anything in the ancient grove but the debris and black stump of a fallen tree.

The punished peasants would have made off; that was to be expected. The corpse of the Woodman, and the child, too, they would be gone. Plainly the peasants had taken these bodies.

The Landholder would hunt the people of his woods for months. He would get slaves. He felt some onus on him yet, to make straight the way of his God. It would require two years of putrid luck, rotten harvests, disease and small terrors to cause another thought to enter him, like a thorn under the skin.

The child had not been dead, at the moment of the Tree's severance. Dying, adrift . . . As the life began to wash from the Tree, Jun lay at the brink. He was the Tree's possession, had been given to the Tree, had given of himself. When the Tree fell, Jun was smashed also, every bone of his body snapped, dislocated, and the skull fractured. Jun did not die then. Most of Jun died, and left him there. And the spirit of the Tree, its thunderous, endless power, which was the forest, and the world as forest, entered in.

To Godhead all is possible. Where the psychic dimensions overlap, a million angels might dance upon a pin: the teaching of the Church of the Christus.

As the steel rain sluiced the grove, the body of Jun mended itself carefully, piece by piece.

When the eyes of Jun opened, in the starry night, something looked out of them that was not boy and was not tree, having slight memory, having no specific aim or longing.

When the body of Jun arose, and walked away between the walls of the wood, there was only one last impulse, like the faint taste of wine left in an empty cup.

It was the impulse, therefore, which went down into the clearing.

The soldiers had also, on a brief sortie, knocked flat the Woodman's hut, meaning to return and burn it. Anything of worth they had looted, but there was not much. A charm or two the forest people had already taken to comfort them, as they had absorbed the cadaver of their priest. The rest of his dwelling sprawled under the injured trees: shorn logs and turf roof, a table in four parts, the tumbled stools and broken vessels.

The pale hare, which had come for its milk and not found it – only outcry above in the grove – came back in the starlight, as if searching. It glowed in its pallor, turning its head, its long forefeet raised, steepled ears listening. When the other hare appeared, the albino retreated nervously. The second hare was stronger. It was dark like the darkness, and propelled itself in a hesitant silky lope. The coat of it was rough as leaves or needles. It rustled as it moved, like the forest overhead. Its eyes were the eyes of a human child.

The white hare darted away.

The black hare went haltingly about the wreckage of the hut.

No one was there, no hint to allay the sunset of a memory.

The black hare lifted to its hind limbs, in the posture the albino had adopted, copying. Then it *shifted*. Like a cloud over a moon. The child stood up from the cloud. Jun who was not, now, Jun.

And the child who was not Jun, that went away into the night.

Chapter Two

The hostel kept for travellers by the religious women was a dismal affair, cheerless and cold. Godbrother Orro was sorry for it. The snows, which had vanished from the forest, lingered in the stone walls, the fireplace with its trickle of flame and few grudging, thin and unencouraging logs left by. The Church instructed that they should be hard upon themselves, but not, surely, on the poor benighted travellers who must seek this haven? For himself, Orro was used to the comforts of the brotherhouse at Timuce. The family Esnias, that owned the land in the forest, had built the brother house and the chapel there on the forest's edge. The ground was full of Esnias graves. A pious and belligerent household. And busy. In return for its support, the priests must be prepared to obey the Esnias Tower, besides the Church, let alone God. Vre Esnias had decided that the Hermitages and Domas of his woods should come under scrutiny. He selected Orro for the work. Such tasks normally devolved from Khish, but Orro had not argued. Vre Esnias was suing for pardon from the Church Fathers at Khish, for a feud murder of an overly violent and publicized nature. Everyone must help. But uncomplaining Orro, in his fiftieth year, had found the spring journey difficult. He took this out on no one. Where he discovered laxness he mildly upbraided, and where repairs were needed, he only prepared a report for his Vre. Perhaps the harsh Handmaidens here might be persuaded to more altruism by the gift of some slight luxuries.

A vicious scratch on the door announced that the Administress had arrived.

Orro bade her enter, and in she came, an ugly warty woman full of resentment and dislike. Though eschewing a mirror, she had cherished the image of her face in her mind. Hatred of God was what had driven her to worship Him. She was a Tower daughter and had refused a marriage; the man doubtless had looked askance at her.

Orro spoke gently.

'I've been writing here. Certain items should be sent you, for the upkeep of your charity.'

'Vre Esnias is godly,' she snapped. (Esnias was not her Tower.)

'Please sit,' offered Orro.

She took the unfriendly chair – he had been making do with the rheumatism-inducing stool. She folded her ugly hands and flashed a bitter, unconscious glare at them. She said, 'There's another matter. We want your help sorely. I wondered if you'd see for yourself, but of course, you are so *burdened*—' She bit her sarcasm off. Who more than she could be burdened, but who bothered with *her*? 'In your painstaking efforts for Lord Esnias—'

'Something's amiss?' said Orro. He was used to this. There always was something. 'Can you tell me what it is, sister?'

'I hesitate.' He waited. Presently, her hands opened a little like fly-eating flowers. 'Godbrother, our two novice sisters— You must believe me, I don't put any faith in demons. God is too strong. However, the weak and fallible—' She broke off again.

After several long pauses, and a pair of promptings, she informed him the two novices had come under demonic influence. They themselves had conjured it, but it grew palpable, they gave it life and vitality. The older women were afraid.

'What form does this influence take?' he asked. He had heard this tale before, indeed since his beginnings at Khish. As for the woods, the pagan ways were still prevalent, and the isolated villages rife with stories of ghosts, unusual creatures, changelings and sprites. Already, not far from this sisterhood, he had been regaled by fantasies of a werewolf in the vicinity. Obviously, with the winter, there would have been wolves about. But the villagers insisted that a beast had prowled the forest there for generations, part wolf, part man. They left it offerings in a glade, and the offerings were always taken. Orro's innocent comment on the gratitude of polecats and rats was not heeded. He blessed the village, but their charms against wolf-men were not removed. On an oak tree by the glade of offering, wolf skulls hung in rows, decorated with tarnished ribbons, mummified blossom.

'They say,' said the ugly woman, 'an angel appears to them, in the wood. At first they hid their foolishness, only giggled and wept over it. Next our sister Resa accused them of spying on some peasant youth who went bathing in a pool nearby. This they denied, and then came out with their notion.'

'An angel,' said Orro. 'How strange it is. We credit that the pure and holy often saw such things, but always in the past. What is immediate makes us suspicious. And yet we suppose, don't we, sister, that through the Christus the chance of miracles remains.'

'Yes, godbrother,' she said. He perceived that she did not suppose this.

'Then again,' he amended, 'caution is essential. Truth will prove itself despite our doubts. Did you wish me to talk to your novices?'

She said that she did. Really she did not know what she wished, except that someone be chastised for something.

He anticipated the two girls might be pretty, or else ugly and unwanted like the Administress – envy or frustration a contributory cause, something like that. But they were very ordinary young peasant girls, healthy, shoved into the order to please God, not because they could not have attracted husbands. Then again, it was the peasants who leaned fervently towards the supernatural. It turned out (they spoke freely), that this image of an angel was mostly a redepiction of the myths of childhood. The angel was the god of the wood, a being they reverenced and made sacrifice to, and who, represented by a virgin youth, had, a century ago, been sacrificed in turn, the forest over, to keep the bond of blood between the trees and the people.

'It was dusk,' said the younger girl, who was brown-haired, an uncommon fairness that perhaps her village had not liked, 'and I'd been sent to fetch water. I was frightened. It's not good to be in the forest after dark. And I knew that I mustn't say the rhyme my mamma taught me, only trust in the Christus, so I prayed. Then, when I looked in the water, I saw something white and gleaming. I looked, and there was a naked man. He hadn't a stitch on him.' There was neither prurient interest nor disdain in her voice. 'But his hair was long and black as the wood in the dark, and he had black wings. So I kneeled down, as he was an angel. I shut my eyes and asked what I should do. But when I looked again he was gone.'

The brown girl confided in her fellow novice. Next evening they contrived both to be out. And for some evenings after, since he did not at once show himself again.

'Why did you think that he would? If it was an angel, surely once would be enough?'

The girls were puzzled. Orro beheld they reasoned to the peasant format; the forest was itself based on repetition.

And sure enough, the god of the forest returned, and each girl saw him. The second girl said she did not see any wings, only a sort of shadow that went up at his back. But he shone like the moon.

Thereafter they were granted their vision six or seven times, usually at dusk, or sunset. But once the darker girl, going out in the early morning, saw a whiteness passing through the pines beyond the chapel. That had been the angel, too.

A light-hearted, self-congratulatory hysteria grew up between the girls over the vision. When it broke the surface of their chapel, and Sister Resa put in her word, they were shocked and enraged. They had seen plenty of peasant youths, clothed and unclothed, enough to know them from an angel.

'And no other of the sisters has been privileged, as you have, to witness this?'

No one else, they said, was sent to and fro in the wood as they were.

He could believe that. They were young and hale, the rest of the women getting on.

'Tell me,' said Orro, to whom talking had been easy, 'why do you think, yourselves, a divine sight was vouch-safed you?'

They could not find the words. But from their faces he read an absolute: they were fresh and full of credulity and faith. If the Christus had hung before them on his Tree, with wounds of roses, they would not have questioned, only bowed down. The Administress would have demanded an explanation.

'Lord, I beseech you, deliver me from evil and from the sinful waste of my own unwisdom—'

Orro prayed, properly, on his knees, hurting and discounting it, in the chapel of the sisterhood. The plaster of the walls was chapped, like the skin of their hands. One should ignore the flesh, but surely, surely, if the flesh were ill-treated, it became clamorous. An iota of kindliness stayed the flesh in quietness. It would be good, if allowed. For he detected that the most devout and godly, of either gender, had been the well and happy. Lust might be put aside, but the headache, the chilblain – ah, they were the very Devil. God did not always require martyrdom. Sometimes He wanted, simply, love.

Orro examined his love of God at the altar in the forest. He thought, *I shall go out. Let us see. Will their demon manifest before a man?*

He did believe in demons – of the mind and of the earth, both. Anything was possible, the world being like damp clay, able yet to take an impress of all powerful things.

When he was done praying, he stood up, and rubbed his hurting knees. He had healing hands, even for himself, and soon walked to the door and looked out.

The sun was setting. The sky was like a lake of glimmering clouds, warm and cool, settling softly, unfearful of the night. Birds played, and the trees shook themselves. But the pines were already black at their hems.

As he crossed over the yard, he glimpsed the lighting of the candles, and heard the sisterhood arriving at the chapel for its devotions. The two novices would be with them. They had directed Orro, guilelessly, as if to oversee an assignation with an approved lover – but it was not actually like that.

Orro, leaving the buildings of the sisterhood, felt for a moment a predictable misgiving. He had felt it before, on the spirit-searches and werewolf investigations of the previous months. He hoped Vre Esnias enjoyed colourful reading . . .

The forest, where it took up its weave beyond the chapel and the wall, was now quite black. There were the ghosts of shapes, like mirages, not reassuring. The nights were cold, warning the waking leaves and buds of another winter of judgement to come. Yes, the forest was repetition.

He reached the pond, at the correct moment, as the dusk started to swell, a vast blue bulb. The pond was clear, fed by a streamlet which sprang down into it. Save for the ruffle of this entry, the water was a blue mirror.

Orro waited against the trees. He was not frightened, but apprehensive – yes. For all the mundane or imagined nature of prior events, he sensed this moment was not of that order; something had happened, did happen.

There was a glow at the corner of one eye. At first he took it for a trace of final light cast aslant. Then he realized, and moving his neck slowly, he turned and saw. An avenue opened between the trees. At the end of it, perhaps thirty paces away, a figure stood against the black curtain of the inner wood.

It was not like the ghost-shapes which the first twilight had formed. This shone, like ivory, and as solidly.

Orro looked, steadfast, blinking now and then, for his eyes had begun to water, from tension, or some other thing.

He determined gradually the body of a young man, unclothed. The hair of the head was long and black and burned out into the darkness of the trees. The hair at the loins was black. The eyes and brows were an impression of blackness. The face was shaven. The figure was totally couth. It could not be assumed to be anything average, explainable.

As Orro watched, the man moved, and was coming forward along the path, towards the pond.

Orro had an urge to be gone. It half surprised him, how forceful a hold the situation had got upon him.

There were no wings. That was an illusion, probably to do with the black mane of hair on the darkness . . . With a start, the priest saw that the wrists and ankles of the young man were circled by wounds, which still bled.

The god of the wood. There could be no doubt. The god of pagan belief, in his role as sacrifice. Each year they had slain him, and then, at harvest, he was born again, chosen, blessed, adored, given back to the trees and the earth in thanks, after the winter drew away— But these practices were no longer common. The Vre at Esnias had muttered about a neighbour, the Raven house of the Korhlens, saying spring sacrifice went on there, for all their parade of a new chapel, a priest, and offerings to the church at Khish. But again, Esnias did not care for the powerful Korhlens. One did not always do well to leap at such bait. Besides, the pagan rites were so often represented in small ways, or wedded to the rituals of the Christus. Who did they see upon the cross of wood, the peasants of the forest, but their old god again, the perfect scapegoat, flawless and dying in consent, to set them free of sin and sadness. Orro suspected that at Korhlen the act, if done at all, was managed symbolically. It was not always practical or compassionate—

The young man, white and black, passed Orro.

From his body, which was indeed unblemished and beautiful, and that of a man about nineteen years, an odour came like the growing of the leaves, bruised grass. Pine cones were caught in his hair, tidily, a garland.

He was by the water, and on the water he reflected.

Orro felt a tightness in his chest, he was cold, and there were tears in his eyes. It was like a vision. He could not confuse it with anything sacred. It was profane, yet so completely pure neither could he resist it.

He found himself thinking that the being must evaporate. But that did not occur. The god of the wood went about the pond, and into the threaded loom of the trees on the far side. The light was going out, and only the night and the wood caused a vanishment.

It would be sensible therefore to say, This is some questionable joke that the local people are perpetrating against us. But Orro did not say this, inwardly, or aloud, on his return to the Doma.

The ugly woman came in and sat before him with her hands held tight one to the other. She was eager as a hound. He dashed her questioning at once: 'Your two novices are quite innocent of any blame. Some slight penance may be set them for wilfulness, but they're very young. There's no wrong been done. I'm sure you'll be glad to learn my verdict, sister.' She was not and said she was, prim in disappointment. He could guess she might write to the Vre at Esnias, complaining that Orro was a sentimental slacker, moved by youth when duty should be paramount. He doubted Esnias would pay much heed. 'As for this thing they have seen, yes, I attest to something, but I don't classify it as demoniac. It asks investigation, however, and some restriction here. Please send neither your sisters nor novices to get water in the early morning, at sunfall or after dark.'

She said she would abide by his ruling. Now curiosity had hold of her. She knew she must be meek and circumspect, but she tried vigorously hard to elicit from him the features and type of what he had beheld. Orro did not satisfy her. He left her wanting, and she was used to that. She accepted frustration as a familiar, poor wretch. He did not relax until she had gone.

'None of you should be afraid. God has us all in His hand.'

They looked at him dubiously. It was ridiculous to say such words, and yet there were no other means whereby to address them. They understood the idea of religious parlance. It consoled them even as they mistrusted its assurances.

'Bring your ordinary weapons,' said Orro. 'I believe you won't have to protect yourselves, except in the most routine sort.'

One said, after a long hiatus, 'But it's always been done, godbrother. And then it leaves us alone.'

'Since my great-grandda's time,' said another.

'Before that,' said a third.

Orro had already gleaned from their speeches and asides that the wolf-man, and their offerings, had been indigenous in this area of the wood, and in other areas surrounding, for a hundred years. It was very likely. Pagan acts had been universal then, and the Christian ethic a force rushing in a narrow river through the trees.

'Because something has gone on for a long while,' said Orro, 'does not make it right. If you've been in error, let's correct the mistake.'

They grumbled, but he was there before them, the tangible aspect of the Christus. Had the wolf been there, speaking to them, it would have gone another way. What if the wolf did speak, then? No. It was doubtful the wolf would be able to do that.

Orro had put facts together in a fine mosaic. One heard stories of the woods. Children left to perish in the forest by parents who could not feed them, adopted by a family of wild creatures, growing without the human estate, into strange versions of the fox, the wolf.

The rumours of the wolf-man, the sight of the naked boy, though they did not marry, yet they were a pair. It had come to Orro, through a mysterious and instinctive process which once or twice had assisted him in the past, that the god of the wood was in some form a symbol of the soul of that which ravened and raved about the villages of his previous visiting, the fleshly werewolf god, to whom the offerings were made.

The villagers were uneasy at Orro's reappearance, and his request. Before, his tampering had irked them. Now he wanted them to go out with him, to seek, to hunt the wolf. He insisted that it was not supernatural, save in the most finite manner. They could not argue. Orro represented the Christus, and the Esnias Tower.

They moved under the oak with the decorating wolf skulls. It was midday, the pine forest bright and dark green, slanted with sunlight, a warm and hopeful day. Alders at the stream were clung with beads of emerald, and the immature birches that had insinuated themselves bore feathers paler than apple skin.

The grove opened, the glade with the severed trunk, and the (new) offerings lying there, already scavenged by birds. A cloud of finches went up at their approach with scraps in their beaks.

The men stood about, with their primitive spears and knives, and Orro with his crucifix and his priest's habit, glancing this way and that. Did the wolf truly dine here, at the trunk of the tree? He went forward and examined the spot more thoroughly than he had done before. There were long scratches on the side of the offering table, he had taken them for marking and weathering of the bark . . . Across the glade from the trunk, something dully red showed up in the fern. Orro went to see, and found a rabbit's pelt, torn wide like a purse, and the money of the flesh devoured. These remains were left for him like a signal. With what would he have to deal? Orro did not allow his former nervousness to sweep through him. He had no choice. It was not a matter of feelings, but of conviction.

Orro beckoned one of the men. He was a hunter of the village, supposedly capable of tracking a beast to its lair

– they had boasted of the wild pig he had got them. Now, he was shy, reluctant.

Not a word was exchanged. He knew what the godbrother wanted, and pushed on through the bushes beyond the glade. He had not brought his two dogs.

Orro, not perfectly confident of the man, had already begun to search for symptoms in the fern and creeper. Suddenly a kind of track came visible to him, patent as if it had been carved against the trees and through the undergrowth. Of course, it was not quite animal.

The pines darkened and closed in, a night in day. Green twilight flickered with points of sun.

When the hunter started to prevaricate, Orro knew that they were now approximate to the wolf-place.

Orro was not afraid of wolves. It was spring, game plentiful. Winter was their murderous time, or when a madness came upon them, as with men.

Orro waved the hunter back. 'Stand there. I'll go on alone.'

'But godbrother, the signs are muddled here—'

'No. They're so clear even I can see them. You and the rest must remain. Be wary. You're not to run away. But I excuse you this.'

Muttering again, they fell back. They were like figures cut from wood, mossy, with the points of sun catching their eyes. They did not move.

Orro went between the trees. They shut behind him and the wooden figures were gone. The ground ascended to a ridge, where a stone outcropping pushed clear of the earth. It was thick with an ivy mantle undisturbed for years, save at one juncture. The entry into the rock was black. A coolness and stillness hung down, enclosing it. Somewhere a bird trilled, as if beyond a wall.

The priest climbed up towards the cave, and saw a bone lying in the tree roots. It was not human, a hare's from the look of it. There was a wolf stink about the cave, not very strong. There was no other smell, but that of the forest, its buds and liquors. Orro had been awaiting the stench of a man.

'God be with me, put over me His mighty shield. I am not alone. Even in the midst of foes, You are with me, Lord, if only I believe.'

The words of the prayer whispered, soft as the touches of the pines upon each other, and Orro stepped up, and looked in at the cave-mouth.

There were no wolves, had been none for several decades. Old relics of their occupancy, the continued practice of their kind, had kept their odour and their aura faintly attached.

The thing which slept on the floor of the cave was a twisted pattern of dark and pallor, snake-like, fearful.

Orro's comprehension hammered in his chest, with the shaken protest of an ageing heart.

As if the noise of it went out into the drum of the cave, the creature there stirred.

From the shambles of blackness, paleness, the snake neck turned. A mask was raised.

Through a black mass of hair and beard, like some showering out of the trees, the tangles of the fern and briar, the white face of a man rose on the air, as if disembodied, floating like a moon, and the black eyes met Orro's, directly now. They were not the eyes of a wolf, or a wolf-man. An adamant intelligence informed them. It was this, and not the terror of the wolf, or the half-wolf, which caused Godbrother Orro to withdraw himself. He moved about ten feet down from the rock opening, and there, in a trance, he heard himself speaking softly, calmly, to sooth and charm: 'Come out, come out, now. I won't hurt you, and you mustn't harm me. God is with you, brother. Come out.' He had been so primed with what he must say, how he must not startle or incite, that now the words flowed from him. The will of Orro had made him still, had made him stop and attend the emergence of this thing from the wolf cave. But Orro himself was helpless. Inwardly he prayed to God for understanding, and his heart beat at him.

Then, perhaps in answer to his voice, or simply because

it was the hour when it must be, what he had called came out of the cave.

At first, he came out as a wolf. On all fours. Orro had heard of this, and that the legs and arms in such a case were deformed, grown into unnatural shapes to accommodate walking and running as a beast. But next, the wolf stood up. It stood as a man. There was no deformity.

What Orro saw, though, was peculiar enough. As the ivy mantled the rock, the long hair mantled the man-thing; it was a cloak, and through the fabric of it Orro saw the naked slender whiteness of the body, the bones of the face. In the cloak of hair was the young god of the wood, the being he had watched at the Doma pond. Orro had known this would be so.

His prayer had been blind. It was sometimes inadvisable to theorize, to question, or to understand too much. Faith, not understanding, was frequently the key.

The young god of the wood poised on the slope, looking down at him.

Orro said to him, 'Will you speak to me? By the grace of God, are you capable of it?'

For several moments the face of the wolf came back, and then the hair of the face seemed to fall away, and Orro glimpsed the shaven face of the other twilight. This might have been a passage of shadows, for a little wind blew through the pines, all the motes of sun shifted, and returned.

'I speak,' said the wolf, or the god, or the young man of nineteen years on the slope. 'What shall I say?'

Orro was stone, like the rock. He could not have moved, or shouted.

'Do you want me to tell how I hunt? How I catch the black hares and break their spines, and feast on the red meat? Or the ermine in the snow? On the streams where I drink, and the water like the jewels from the pedlars that the women wear in the villages? Or the mailed men I see who ride about here? Or the men who cut down the trees, and the trees where they hang the dolls and skulls?

Or the ones like you are, who worship a tree crossed over with a single bough?'

'Dear merciful God,' said Orro. 'How long have you lived this way?'

The young man smiled. Orro could tell that he smiled because of the eyes, for the beard – which had come back with the wind's fall – obscured the mouth.

'Years to ten numberings of ten,' he said.

It was the way the peasants sometimes counted. Ten of ten – one hundred. One hundred years. The boy was crazed. He was twenty at the most. Besides, he could not have lived in this manner for more than two years. For he could speak, articulate, his voice came from him fluidly.

It was not a smile, more scornful than a smile.

For generations, the wolf-haunting, the offerings.

Faith – not theory. It was not wise, yet, to understand.

'You,' said the wood god, 'are like my other. He was a priest. You remind me.'

Orro shivered. And the wind blew again.

He said, 'We must take you from here. Do you remember your village?'

'Gone,' said the young man.

Villages of the forest died, as people died. In two years . . . possibly . . .

'Will you come down?' said the priest, courteously.

'Why?'

'I'd like to take you somewhere that you can be cared for.'

'I care for myself.' The wolf said (how had he thought the wolf could not speak?), 'I live on blood.'

'Come,' said Orro persuasively. The Devil was here, that he knew. The Devil, and the elder things. Now, in this instance, the elder things had not joined innocently with the Christus, they were apart, wicked and insuperable. Only through the Christus could this fallen creature be salvaged.

Orro found that the boy had begun to walk down the slope, lightly. His face was utterly expressionless. There was no ferocity.

I will take him to the men. Dear God, they mustn't run. There will come a moment, perhaps when he sees their village, or when I try to take him inside a hut – he'll panic and want to escape. The power of evil too will attempt to wrest him away. I shall need the men to help me.

The boy followed the priest along the uneven ground. Orro did not make physical contact with him, fearing that this might stimulate him to flight to violence. Orro walked a pace or so in front. The boy walking after him was like a burning flame at his right shoulder.

Through a gap in the pines, Orro saw the village men standing where he had left them. They beheld him at the same instant.

Orro moved into the open avenue, and let the boy come up with him. As Orro stopped, so did the boy.

He isn't a boy. What I saw by the water – his soul, some emanation of him – old as parts of the wood. Can it be? A hundred years?

It must be left to God.

Firmly Orro made a peaceful gesture to the wooden men below. To the creature from the cave he said, 'Now will you come down with me, go with us to the village?'

'They won't allow it.'

'Yes, if I ask it of them.'

'Why do you want me to go with you?'

'For your sake,' said Orro. He said it urgently, not meaning to. The boy laughed, but it was a wolf's growl. Something left over, he *had* lived with wolves, he had learned of wolves— 'Your name,' said Orro, 'do you remember?'

'Yes.'

'Will you tell it me, and let me use it?'

The men had not run off. They were watching the priest talking to the wolf-man.

'Jun,' said the boy.

Orro thanked him gently, and went on towards the men.

They stayed put, they only stared. They continued to stare over Orro's burning shoulder as Orro spoke to them.

391

'The Christus instructed us to shelter the homeless, to care for them. This is no demon, but a man. Do you see? Here in the daylight, but bereft of everything. Now, you'll help me.'

Why did the beast from the cave have no smell but the smell of the wood? No scent of animal or man? No sweat, no foul breath from blood and marrow? Healthy and often in water, did that account for the absence? Even the flesh of women freshly bathed gave off aroma.

'He speaks,' said the hunter from the village.

They had seen it. It frightened them more than anything else. Were they right to be frightened, more clever than the priest?

The men were sidling, they were circling round, making the priest and the boy the centre of a ring – cornered.

'No,' said Orro. 'Don't—'

Just then the boy, unseen behind him, let out a snarling, slavering roar. Spit from his mouth struck the side of Orro's face. It repelled him; it was hot and fresh.

There was a whirlpool. Orro was knocked away from it. He staggered and turned and saw the boy on the ground, frothing and kicking, long jagged claws lashing out on hands and feet and the white teeth bared to bite. Wolf in a snare. The hunter had magicked the scene into life. He raised his spear to strike. Their placations and offerings were forgotten. They would no doubt decorate the skull—

Orro threw himself between the hunter and the boy, and flinging up one arm, cast off the spear. It was a passion like the ecstasies of joy and grief in childhood. Orro did not reason with it; he knelt over the horrid, foaming, Devil-possessed monster on the ground. The soul – the soul, beautiful and reasonable, shone from the black amber of the eyes.

Orro laid one hand, healing, on the matted hair, the low wide forehead, the second healing hand upon the plunging heart.

And the Devil went out of Jun.

His body uncoiled and melted flat among the ferns. He

turned his head into the curving cupping hand of the priest, and was asleep.

They remained at the village for only two days. The atmosphere of nervousness and wrong-being was highly charged. Gods, demons, should keep their place, like men.

The boy, however, all this while, was docile. He sat or lay quietly on the mattress in Orro's hut, eating the stews and gruels Orro brought him, as if he was accustomed to cooked meats from which the blood had been leached. He was not sick, and did not need any nursing. Exercise he must have missed, but he was patient about that.

Orro told him, 'Tomorrow at sun-up, I'll take you to the chapel, the house where I and my brothers live.'

The boy looked at him. Orro had trimmed his hair and, using fat and a razor, had shaved him. A whole face emerged. To Orro's hands the boy responded with repose. There was no danger, it seemed. To Orro he seldom spoke, and then in fragments merely. The wolf was leaving him, though during the first night he had crouched by the hut door, staring up into the tree tops and the moon. The ancient youth of the wood was leaving him too. Perplexed, Orro beheld a man usurping the creature which had been surely more fascinating, yet terrible. It was the man who must be led forth, to God. For the extraordinary soul, what priest could doubt, having gained some inkling of the purposes of Heaven, that it had showed itself in such dark glory as a promise of sanctity. Within the frame of animal corruption, as in the past, there flamed a chance of something marvellous, greatness, saintliness, a warrior of God.

Jun loped beside Godbrother Orro's mule. Without escort they traversed the green paths of the forest. Spring was pungent. Now Orro was not troubled by any fear the beast would come to divide Jun from him. At dawn, midday, evening, Orro would kneel to pray. The young man would kneel by him, copying what Orro did.

'You learn swiftly,' said Orro, filled with rare rich happiness.

'I've prayed before,' said Jun.

Of course, the way back to the truth was always simple, if no resistance were made.

At Timuce, spring rain netted the stones of the brother-house, and beyond, the scrawl of village wavered in smoke and water.

The Administer sat in his chair with the cushion of red velvet, and Orro stood before him on his tired and aching legs, not bothering with them.

'The Vre should be entertained by these notes of your journey. You've been most thorough, and written with some wit. But this, about the boy—'

Orro watched his Administer acquiescently. The rule of obedience was ingrained. One must not disagree, for in the end dissent was futile, and God moved all things as he would. Nothing was ever lost. Even the fall of the sparrow—

'I see, godbrother, you have some audacious notion of wrestling for his soul.'

'That's true, Administer. If I'm impertinent, I will step aside. But someone should do it.'

'My friend Orro, your modesty – no, you're to be commended. By all means. I give him into your charge. I'm much impressed by what you've already wrought. My only doubt – it seems the boy must be, perhaps, a little simple in the mind. His years as a beast in the woods tell against him. Oh, not in his demeanour, which, as I've seen myself in the past ten days, is exemplary – astonishing, under such circumstances – but this idea of longevity, to which you seem also to subscribe.'

'Administer, maybe Jun is speaking in other terms than mortal time.'

'Yes?'

'Of spiritual time. The years of darkness – how can he measure them? If he's in some way unhinged, that too is at the root of a strange holiness.'

The Administer regarded Orro. The Administer was

very fond of the older man, his favourite among the brothers at Timuce. Orro's humble erudition and sweet, nearly naive, piety, delighted him. With another man, the Administer would have looked warily and long at this unison, the wolf-boy and the priest. But Orro did not have the sins of the flesh. Or, if he had ever had them, they had become for him irrelevant as the hairs shaved from his face.

The boy, in himself, was remarkable.

Clothed now in the habit of the novice, going daily to tuition in the Scriptures, and to the devotions of the priests, he behaved for all the world like the son of some well-born family at Khish (better than the barbaric boys of the forest Towers). It was scarcely credible that *this* had snarled and ravaged about in the trees, tearing rabbits with his nails.

'You believe, Orro, that God himself has selected this youth?'

'I daren't think I know so much of God, Administer. And yet, haven't we a score of saints who came from bizarre and awful beginnings, out of the sinks of the worst crime and depravity? As if the Devil himself had cauterized them in earthly fires. I think I do believe that Jun, who evidently was a pagan from the oldest heart of the forest, has been brought to the Christus, and that I, probably through chance, was made the instrument of it. I'm glad not to relinquish him.'

The bell of the Timuce chapel tolled. The Administer got up from his chair, and together he and Orro went to the glass window edged with blue crystal.

Looking out, they saw the courtyard in the rain, and through the rain, the brothers were passing to the chapel for midday prayers. Behind came the novices. Last of all, Jun walked in his dark habit. The hair was cut to the nape of his neck, shining like a raven's feather in the wet. He seemed to have walked across the court to the chapel a thousand times.

The other novices were frightened of Jun. He gave them no reason, and no attention. Orro had seen Jun in the chapel, before the ebony crucifix on which hung the Christus, crowned with the thorns of agony, his hands and feet pierced by the nails of death. Jun *knew* the Christus. Somewhere in the black of the emblematic hundred years of the wolf-forest, Jun had become the possession of God.

'Forgive me, Administer. I must go down, or I'll be late.'

'Yes, go then, godbrother. For your report to the Lord Vre Esnias – it shall be sent today.'

The Administer at Timuce watched Orro's hastening figure appear in turn below on the court. His rheumatism was bad now, and he limped when hurrying. This would have been the last long journey he would make. For the report, the Administer would himself command alterations, without vexing Orro. Orro, anyway, as compliant as he was, would never object. He argued only in debate, but then so masterfully one was pleased to find him harmonious elsewhere.

It was only over the wolf-boy that the Administer was to exercise caution. The rumours of a werewolf were to be left in to titilate the Vre; he was to learn too that a peasant lad named Jun, who had shown a vocation, had been accepted as a novice at the brotherhouse. The lurid, intriguing and fervid passages concerning the 'angel' at the Doma pond, and the speaking animal from the cave, these were to be excised. The Administer, who accepted that God moved all things, thought that men were also capable of a great deal of locomotion. The Vre at Esnias, a drunken rioter, on his knees before the priest one minute and out killing enemies in the woods the next, was not a fit vessel for the pouring in of such a tale. God knew what the Vre would do with it. God knew what upheaval such speculation and such dreams might set alight.

Orro himself would benefit from the omission, for the story suppressed would leave the brotherhouse serene. Orro's orphan might then grow as best he could, to a nonentity or to a prodigy. As God willed.

*

396

In the evenings, after prayers and supper, the novice, Jun, would go up with Orro to his cell in the brotherhouse. The cell was a room of some capacity, and full of books. It had a brazier too, in which hot charcoal sprinkled with herbs sent up a restful smell. Here, at a table, Orro taught Jun his letters. The boy's progress was like much else about him, his character, and apparent modes of thought. He could, by the fifteenth day of scholarship, read. Thus he read, forging on, seemingly privy to the ideas held inside the words. Then would come a sudden block to mental activity. The least taxing phrases became incomprehensible. When this mood fastened on Jun, he did not turn again into a wolf. Yet he became a *shadow*. Orro could see before him then a wooden man, like and unlike those the villagers had represented, below the wolf rock. Orro abided these breaks, these goings away. To reclaim, he must be a practical gardener. That his plant grew so fast at other times was a wonder.

Tonight, Jun read fluently for one hour. The text concerned the Commencement, the world unformed and forming, the paradise on earth, the Man and Woman, the Serpent and the Tree. Already Jun had been tutored in these portions of the Book. To Jun, maybe, the Garden of Eden was the forest; how else might he picture it? (In the same way the children of the wealthy in some city might visualize Eden as the walled garden of some well-to-do house, with paths and arbours, and the trees in pots.)

Sometimes, when Jun had read, Orro would talk with him, concerning the subject. It had appeared at first to Orro that Jun came to theosophy with a brain uncluttered by the trivia of life. And yet, Jun's brain was full, if not of the trivia then of the minutiae. Jun did not reveal that he had inhabited with men, save once, in childhood (when there had been the other, pagan, priest, of whom Orro reminded the boy, or so the boy had seemed to imply; he did not really refer to this era, merely it was occasionally to be glimpsed in a thicket of other things). But, living so long apart from humankind, yet Jun had seen them, watched them, knew their capers, and had kept within him their speech. Then again, he did not entirely have, beyond a phrase here and there, the idiom of the peasants, did not properly speak to any pattern. This alone would make it simple to form his expression, his syntax, in the mould of the brotherhouse, which was to the good. It was the language of debate and prayer. Clarify outward communication, and inner meditation could only improve.

As for the knowledge of minutiae, it was, too, benign. If Jun had for ever and only come from wolfishness, what would the concepts of Man, Woman, God mean to him beyond flesh, *blood*, the elements, fate – those very forms which a priest must cleanse away.

The room was rosy from the brazier, and the books of old leather, some polished and one or two with glittering crusts of gilt, made it soothing to Orro. On the wall the wooden cross and the Christus were less stark, less tortured.

Jun's eyes (from a lifetime of acquaintance with dark eyes, the most general of colours, Orro saw in Jun's eyes a blackness that was different), Jun's eyes rested on the cross.

Orro had never inquired of Jun if he wanted anything other than to be a priest. The priesthood was to be Jun's salvation and release; you did not ask whether or not a starving man would choose to eat and drink.

'Will you tell me how you picture the Garden,' said Godbrother Orro.

'The world,' said Jun, 'before it was spoiled.'

'And there were many sorts of trees, were there not?

Jun smiled, just a little, without mockery. The child in him, still dimly there, answered a memory of the Wood-man under the grove. But now, a man a hundred years of age, Jun did not respond in words.

Orro tried a second question, to see if the adult intellect could make its leap. It seemed to him the spring for this was inherent in Jun. 'You've been taught by the brothers about the life of the Christus. If I were to ask you how it is that the story of the Garden could become the story of the Christus, what would you say?'

'The Garden,' said Jun, 'is the Tree. Men are imperfect. One must be chosen who's perfect. He is God. The sin is the sin of loss, the separation from God. God becomes man to bring men back to Him. The Christus dies on the Tree. His blood rains on the ground from the wounds in His hands and feet. The blood's to be drunk. The power of God which can't die enters with the blood into man, and the separation is over.'

Two emotions, perhaps three, went through Orro. Each was sharp, almost stunning.

Initially it seemed to him that never before had he heard the truth of death and resurrection, the pity of the human Fall, its redemption, so adequately, so profoundly stated. But, at the same second a shock came over the priest. For he grasped that this was not the orthodoxy of the Christus which was being presented before him, but the ancient pagan religion of the wood. Orro had always acknowledged the inevitable association of the pagan rite of recurring sacrifice to the mystery of the death and rising of the Christus. Never before had he seen it conjured in this appalling image – for Jun, the Christus *was* the god of the wood. A fragment of the elder hierarchy, one of millions, a branch of a colossal Tree. The Christus was wondrous, but nothing new, or special, inviolate and unique. The Christus, for Jun, had always been, always worshipped, a festival of sacrifice and a gift of blood. For *this* reason, Jun came to the Church as though he had always known it. And it was wrong, was horrible, fiendish – for the seed was the wood, and the apogee, the sunrise, were the Christus – not, *not* the other way about.

'Jun—' said Orro—

And Jun gazed at him, the never-before-seen colour of black in his eyes, the face pale and lucid, nearly empty.

'The Tree,' said Jun.

The charcoals in the brazier settled, and the light fanned up the planes of the room, as light and shade fanned through the forest. The wood, walled outside, had got in.

The third emotion which had begun to well up in Orro took hold of him firmly. It was terror, nothing like fear, vaster than he was, seeming to push his soul up halfway from his body.

Vines grew over the plaster, webbed the ceiling, clusters of leaves hung down. The books were buried in the leaves, a spotted snake went rustling through— Behind the plaster stood the pines in upright rows. In the midst, in the air, the crucifix spread out its arms. It became a tree, tall, opening a multitude of boughs, like an oak, a pine, a tower. The white god hung from the tree and the scarlet jewellery of his blood rained on the ground.

'No,' said Orro, hearing himself from far off, 'the Devil is here.' He began to pray. His voice was so faint and dry. A stupendous silent roar was issuing from the wood.

The face of the god on the tree was not only Jun's, but a million faces, among which he could not find the forgiving beauty of the face of the Christus, the truth and the way.

When Orro regained consciousness, his room was vacant but for himself.

The reading book had been laid neatly aside, with its marker in it. Nothing was overturned. The brazier cracked rosily. No vines, or serpents. The wood had retreated.

Orro got up and went to his crucifix, and kneeled down. He could not look at the crucifix. He shut his eyes.

'Lord, *what am I to do?*'

Chapter Three

It was at midsummer that, arrangements completed, a novice of the brotherhouse at Timuce set out on a journey southward. Letters had been exchanged. The approval of the Esnias Tower had been sought and freely given. The novice, a scholar of unusual aptitude and expectations, was to join the novitiate of the Church at Khish.

On the morning of the departure, the Administer at Timuce received the novice, Jun, in his chamber above the chapel courtyard.

The Administer sat in the sunlight, and watched the sun bloom in its turn on the young man.

Jun was quite marvellous. He would do them great credit, and if he rose high, no doubt he would remember their kindnesses to him. In the few months of his residence at the brotherhouse, the Administer had found himself increasingly impressed, compelled. Observing Jun, and interviewing him from time to time, as was necessary, the Administer had come to believe – if not all Orro's flight of fancy, then very much of it. Strangely, as the novice progressed through victory on victory of learning, dedication, intellectual brilliance, it was Orro who had stepped aside. The Administer never asked why. This would be like Orro, to labour earnestly for such a pearl, and then humbly to leave it to the best ministrations of others.

'And today you start your journey,' said the Administer to Jun, who stood before him burning white and black in the sun's rays. 'A long ride, I regret. But you're prepared. At Khish, you'll be amply rewarded.' The Administer extolled the priestly library at Khish, the religious building and its ornaments, the clarity of its teachers, and its connections to the city of Chirkess, and to all the vaster arms of the Church Paternal.

Jun, at the appropriate instant, thanked the Administer.

'I shall be happy to learn of your successes. Perhaps,' said the Administer, 'you'll write to Godbrother Orro.'

Jun bowed his head, raised it. With such sparing, graceful mannerisms, the young man – who had been a wild beast – conveyed his intentions. His script was refined, also. There would be no problems in reading his letters.

The Administer prayed with Jun, blessed him, and sent him forth.

It was a shame Orro's health was so poor. The mission which had given up this astonishing treasure had otherwise not done the elder brother good.

When the star had gone away, the Administer went down in person to visit Orro in his cell. The godbrother had a summer fever, and had been excused all but the midday devotions, over which he fretted; they had only been able to keep him in his bed by the warning that his morning and evening cough disturbed the others at prayer.

'How are you doing?' said the Administer. In Orro's reddened eyes, he thought he saw the grief of Jun's going. 'He will do very well at Khish.'

'Yes,' said Orro, 'very well.'

For a while his hot dry coughing racked the room. Presently, he said, 'I should like to make confession to you.'

The Administer was surprised.

'There's surely no need – you'll have confessed at the normal times—'

'I have, but I left out, always, one item. I must confess it to you, because you won't believe me, Administer. Another confessor might have done. Besides, it's now too late. I alone will carry the sin of its secrecy.'

'My dear Orro,' said the Administer, 'you know quite well that you'll be well and hearty in a week or so.'

'Probably. But let me do this.'

'If you insist,' said the Administer. 'I can see it's troubling you.' He went to the bed and made over Orro the sign of the cross of the Christus. 'In the name of God, our Lord and Father, and of the Redeemer who upon Himself takes all our transgressions . . .'

'It is my fault,' said Orro, 'my grievous fault. I was afraid of being thought a liar, or a fool. Or else afraid of being taken seriously. Jun,' said Orro, 'is a demon.'

'Orro.'

'No, not the Devil. I think not the Devil. But out of that torrential army of Hell, an angel, a prince come on the earth.'

'Orro, your malady—'

'Excuse me, Administer. Not my malady. I'm powerless. I can't do anything. I was blinded. He blinds us all. What is so terrible, he reverences the Christus – he *worships* God, as I imagine the Devil also does, irresistibly, in some hidden room of his palace under the ground. How can the Devil not worship God? He, of all things, *knows* God. It's love makes the Devil fight with God.'

'Orro, lie back. Look at you. Now you must have a herbal. This is too bad.'

'I've spoken,' said Orro. 'It's over.'

He stared through the walls of his room into the forest, and saw Jun riding away on his mule, with the servant from Timuce who was afraid of him, and was fascinated by him. How green the wood, how high the trees. The figures of Jun and the servant were small and finely fashioned, like toys.

'It's over,' said Orro again, and went to sleep.

The journey to Khish was a long one, as the Administer had regretted. Coming from miles of greenness and darkness, out of the tunnel of the forest which was all he had ever seen, the young man emerged on the plains before the town of Khish, where the grain grew and the sky was a low roof: an alien landscape.

Under the roof of sky the town walls appeared.

403

The streets were narrow, and the houses hung together, and in the ravines below, pigs and sheep grazed on grasses rooted in mud and garbage. The town of Khish, whose sigil was a key, stank ripely, and the servant from the forest held his nose, but the young novice seemed not to mind the stench.

They rode to the church, which was of stone. A round window, set with glass like petals, fractured the sun.

At the church in Khish, the community of novices was thirty strong, and held within itself a well-educated, secretly arrogant, sometimes dissatisfied elite. These were the second or third sons of wealthy houses, given to the Church Paternal because they were superfluous to the genetic necessity of a family, and might turn out useful in the ranks of God. A few had believed themselves possessed of genuine vocation, a longing to serve the Christus. All had suppressed their anger at the rigours of religious discipline. It was either the refining process needful to bring them in to God, or the penalty of junior status which, with the coming of a better position – that of the priest – might be alleviated, avoided. Some of the novices had entered the Church from lowlier backgrounds, accepted as fodder; there would always be a job for slavish servants, the travelling priests, the messengers, those sent to the forest to counsel drunken Landholders, or into the villages to minister to the hopeless souls there. These lesser novices kept themselves apart from the aristocrats, in subtle and careful ways, for they were lessoned and worked and prayed communally. Occasionally, small, unobtrusive tests were set the inferior novices, tiny ordeals the priesthood overlooked. For although in the eyes of God all were equal, in the opinion of men this had remained a fallacy.

When Jun arrived at the Khishan novitiate house, word of him had gone in before. Jun was supposed to be a peasant, a clod. Some impertinent adroitness in learning and theosophy had brought the acceptance at Khish, and maybe some conniving also by a too-partial provincial Administer.

Jun was first seen at the evening meal. He had been travelling for almost a month, through the summer forest, to Khish. He appeared as quietly among them as any of their number long-established. He did not even attract undue comment by an effect of being travel-worn. He had no barest look of the peasantry, or even the rough and ready Tower nobility in the woods (a by-blow of which several had said he must be). He was slender, with long immaculate hands. His face, lightly tanned, had the carven symmetry and none of the lapses of an ascetic man two score years older. The eyes sought out no one, but here and there, where they seemed to pause in thought upon some object, they were already the eyes of the priest, the initiate – of one who *knew*.

They saw him generally once more at the late evening offices, and reckoned to again during the offices at dawn. Between these times, Jun evolved in the novitiate dormitory.

This dormitory ran along the whole south and half the eastern arms of the cloister. A narrow corridor gave upon some forty partitioned cells, each with its narrow strip of window, its wooden pallet, chest and stool. Invariably, one candle in a pewter holder rested on every chest, along with such books as had been provided for study. Less frequently personal belongings, inappropriate and sparse, lay by the books, while in a dozen of the cells might be found a whole stand of candles, or a crucifix and beads of greater richness that the iron and enamel on the wall. Such interesting cells were located in the southern arm of the dormitory. Here it was the priestly aristocrats of Khish were given, without any word or acknowledgement, their quarters.

Twenty-three young men studied, prayed, slept, dreamed, applied penance, fretted, made vows to God and to self, in the southern dormitory.

As Jun entered, by the east door from the cloister, the other portion of this area, he must perceive at once that

405

all the lights were extinguished here, but, at the turn of the corridor into the southern arm, candlelight flared brightly at plaster: all the candles *there*, it seemed, were still burning.

If he was aware of being watched, and Jun *was* watched, he gave no evidence. He entered his prescribed partition, laid down the bundle he had brought with him from Timuce, and without fumbling lit the single candle on the pewter holder.

Opening the bundle next, he removed two books, and placed them on the chest. It seemed he was not prepared to sleep as yet. Instead, he raised the topmost book's worn cover, and drew the stool up against the chest. Leaning his head upon one hand, Jun read over the life of the Christus, from the Scriptures the Administer had presented him.

After perhaps ten minutes, in which Jun moved only to turn one thick ochre page to reveal a drawing, crudely but determinedly done in red, white and brown, certain figures that had just now traversed the unlit east dormitory, blocked the doorless doorway into the cell.

Still, Jun did not look up. He might be unaware of them, but that was unlikely. They had come softly, but with a smoke about them of night beasts.

The man who stood directly in the doorway, just inside Jun's cell, was twenty-one years of age. He was handsome, and his body had been built by exercise with horses and with swords. He had known women too, in his father's house, and out of it. His father's eldest son had seemed set to die. Most of his life the novice Wedsek had known this. Then, in Wedsek's sixteenth year, the elder brother rallied, changed by some wonder into a glowing bull. Wedsek lost his position. A whim of his aunt's – the mother was dead – had Wedsek delivered to the Church to thank God for his brother's salvation. A fearsome rage had overcome Wedsek. He had absented himself, roved drunk and howling through the alleys of the town, made a drunk's plan for riding off to Chirkess, going for a soldier, a hired sword, anything better than *this*. In the middle of his outcry, one night he became sick, maybe from the drink, or from other abuses of the flesh. And as he writhed in a screaming delirium, a vision fell on Wedsek like a cool white rain. He did not afterwards properly remember it, and this enabled him to embroider for himself upon the theme whatever he desired. He gave himself up to his father's (his aunt's) will, and went to God at the church. He stayed for himself however, as a soldier. That had been an element of his vision – in mail, he had hewn with a bright blade for the Christus. Heaven's choice, he had said no, until Heaven put him wise.

The warrior, Wedsek, stood now in the mouth of the cell of Jun, the bumpkin and upstart.

Wedsek ruled supreme among the novices. He was admired for his physical looks and prowess, covertly for the fierce and sinful life he had thrown away for God. He had been the talk of them all, and his pronouncements, in that little, airless, closed world, devoid of women, and offering only adventures of the spirit, were a sort of law.

Instinctively, Wedsek sensed the danger of Jun, the threat of him.

'Who's this?' said Wedsek.

Jun, even now, did not respond.

'The fellow from the woods,' said a novice at Wedsek's back. 'The one they think can make into a priest.'

'Ah. *Jun* is the name. I remember, it's so outlandish, a *woods* name. What you'd call your dog.'

'But you haven't a dog,' said the novice playfully.

'Perhaps Jun will be my dog. It's true. I miss the curs from the yard. Can Jun bark? Can he beg?'

'He *can't* hear,' said a second novice behind Wedsek in the dark of the east dormitory.

Wedsek entered the cell, and planted his hands flat on the chest top. He lowered his head, and with the eyes a girl had once compared to brown mahogany, he glared smiling at the bowed head of Jun.

Jun looked up. The candle lifted its slim flame between them, lighting for each the face of the other.

Wedsek saw close to what he had witnessed in the

refectory at the novices' table. It startled him a touch, maybe he had expected some change.

'I am Wedsek,' said Wedsek, 'formerly of House Crel. But that's all past. Now I belong to God. What do you say?'

Jun spoke. 'Each of us belongs to God, from the moment of his conception.'

Wedsek straightened up. He went on staring down into the composite face of Jun. There was everything in it, and nothing out of true there. There was no way in, for even the black eyes were impervious. This was a man of thirty who had passed for a youth of eighteen, being strangely without any marks of age.

Wedsek discovered he must fall back on a stupid sparring tone.

'Great things are mentioned of you, Jun. They think you'll beam and glitter.' Wedsek imagined to himself the listening row of black cells, the low-born novices, straining their ears. 'Do you say God summoned you to the priesthood?'

Jun nodded, slowly.

'That's presumptuous,' said Wedsek. It was his own credo; he would never have stipulated the fact at large.

Jun did not reply. He went on sitting at the chest, with one hand which, like the face, was not that of a peasant, on the book, and he did not move, did not blink or swallow or glance aside.

Wedsek caught himself sweating in the hot night.

'Let's hear you,' said Wedsek, dissatisfied, 'say a prayer.'

Jun rose, without hurry. He was as tall as Wedsek, and though far more slender, seemed purely hard, steel to brass. Jun's black eyes were yet fixed on Wedsek, and Wedsek felt a sudden weakness, a kind of fluttering as if something were trapped in his throat. *He* now wished to look away, but could not, by God.

Jun began to speak again, in his sombre and musical voice, already priest-trained to a standard rare even in the cities.

'O most mighty and compassionate God, Who like a gentle father regards the works of men, and hates no thing which He has made, revoke death from the sinner, let him only repent and resort him to Your service. Mercifully forgive us our trespasses. Spare us, for whom the Redeemer died, though we are vile, the mud and the dust upon the earth. Meekly we acknowledge our crimes, weeping for them. Send us then Your help that we may endure, and live through You, until the Final Judgement.'

There was silence. Thick as black snow it filled the air of the eastern dormitory.

Wedsek drew a breath.

'I commend your cleverness,' he said. 'You must have had good tutors at your wooden chapel in the forest.'

'Wedsek,' someone said anxiously behind him.

The accomplices, driven by feelings of unease, were withdrawing up the corridor.

The baiting of the newcomer was at odds with everything, even with the night. He was not food for them after all. They had started to believe that here at last was one unlike the rest. They would have no choice but to leave him alone. Tomorrow they might think differently, or not.

But Wedsek stood before Jun, unable to find a crevice, a crack, a flaw. And Wedsek blazed inwardly with an old nameless wrath he had reckoned was finished with him.

'Don't tire your eyes,' he said to Jun, 'you have to be in the church at dawn. No slacking here, we're diligent. I'll watch for you. I've taken an interest.'

Then Wedsek bolted, with leisurely swaggering steps.

Jun's candle filtered through his shadow along the corridor, until he reached the turn.

The novice Wedsek fermented the red emotions of anger and unappeasement inside his strapping and disciplined body. His flesh he could control, even the night-hungers of sexual appetite, but his brain and heart were prone to elude him. He took exercise, as was allowed him, in the cloister garden, wrestling with the fruit trees, hoeing, and repairing the paths. If he sometimes also snatched space to hurl stones at a mark, to weave and feint with a stick, fighter's moves, he confessed the truancy. Later, when a priest, he might regain his rights to ride, to train with sword and staff – it would depend where he was sent; he had longed for a city, the vast cathedrals like a lord's court. They had an inner guard, priests allowed the practices of a warrior, or so he had heard. They rode hunting too.

His mind did not exercise so skilfully. The esoteric labyrinth of religion did not lure him. He toiled at it as best he could. The plain thesis of God was enough, and the rest a trimming . . . Though he admired it vaguely, it was superfluous to him.

Two months of brown and arid town summer went by, the square and market, the houses, hovels, transmuted to a desert. The summer stinks increased, but there were the golden sunsets to alleviate them, and the blue-green dusks in tiaras of stars. Wedsek got some peace at sunset, going up to the walk below the church roof when able. He would tell his beads (rose quartz, jasper, the gift of his aunt), he would think of the blows he would one day smite for the Christus. Sometimes he recollected his debauch in the town: then he smiled. *That* Wedsek was another person.

Yet, when he thought of Jun, Wedsek was restless; he sensed the old Wedsek lying in wait for him. It was a test of faith. God had called him. He must resist the spearhead of rage he felt at Jun. An upstart, yes, a wretch who should be taught the lessons of Wedsek as well as the schooling of the church books—

Wedsek wasted time on his fury at Jun. It would not go. Each time he beheld Jun, the monster uncoiled its length within him. And when Jun was not visible, the red emotions bubbled in their vat.

Jun made no mistakes. He was exact. If any penances were set him, Wedsek surmised that Jun fulfilled them strictly, but in total privacy. No public punishment was ever the lot of Jun.

The other novices, even the resident godbrothers and the brother tutors, the Khishan Administer himself, probably, seemed to note Jun. And Jun did beam and glitter. When he read from the Book in the refectory at a meal, the quiet might be spooned up with the soup. The beautiful voice commanded. It brought the words out of their sleep and gave them freedom to order the reactions of men. Jun carried out all duties, the lowly, the holy.

Jun was valued. Respected, revered.

Very little was said of him. When he entered a room, the nave of the church itself, eyes went to him, and away, as if with the essential thought: *He is here*.

For himself, Jun was courteous and remote. He had no elected companions. One morning, as the novices paced the cloister with their books of study, a servant came running on some task from the kitchen. He knocked the volume from the hands of Jun. Jun stood quite still, and the servant plunged to his knees, scrabbling for the book, to hand it up to him. And it was a ludicrous scene, for there were three others also kneeling before Jun, novices, trying to fish up the book for him. One of these was a fellow of Wedsek's, a cousin from a noble house.

Wedsek took him aside later. 'What were you thinking of, you dolt? Some slave from the woods.'

'Jun isn't a slave.'

'What is he then, that everyone bows down and crawls before him?'

'I don't know, Wedsek. I heard the brother librarian talking to his assistant. He said Jun was the clay from which the saints are formed.'

Wedsek laughed. 'God's heart. May the cretinous fool be forgiven.'

'I didn't hear your jibe, Wedsek.'

'You dare warn *me*?'

'Here, we are all one.'

'Jun is not.'

Wedsek's cousin hung his head. 'No.'

Beyond him, in the corner of the cloister up against the Confessional wall, the marble cross on its basalt plinth, nine feet in height, the outstretched Christus impaled by gold and crowned with golden thorns, looked away into the opposite corner, where the book had dropped and the novices and servant had scrabbled.

That evening, the duty came to Jun (a deed the Christus himself had once performed for his disciples) of washing the hands and the feet of his fellow novices, in the refectory before supper.

This act was never ridiculed by the aristocratic novices; their hauteur forbade their even speaking of it. They carried it out when it fell to them, frowning and careful. It was too apparent a trial to be flunked.

In the refectory, the candles were not yet lit. The day came down from the high windows, itself the colour of used wax. The shadows were long and syrupy, pooling from everything that did not move. The priests and the novices who took their places crossed this chiaroscuro in combing bars. Seated, they too cast heavy shadows, and if they should lift their hands, the light filled in the blood of them like garnet.

The Administer, the serving priesthood of the church, assumed their seats.

Through the door came Jun, preceded by the youngest (common) novice, a boy of thirteen, who held the bowl of water, the cloth and the towel.

The light of dying day painted the face of Jun to golden ivory.

He walked to the first of the novices, knelt, accepted the cloth, dipped it into the bowl and then wrung out the water on the waiting feet, murmuring as he did so the proper phrases of service, the prayer notes to God. The first novice stared at him, as if afraid. When Jun brought the towel to his feet and wiped them dry, the novice shook, his shaking visible. Jun clasped his feet within the towel. The shaking ended. The novice sighed, and Jun let him go.

To everyone the servor went, and anointed him with the water, and clasped him in the drying towel.

Each man looked unsure, amazed, *altered*. The law of

silence was on them. Only the one who read, or the Administer, might be heard in the refectory. It seemed they yearned to speak. Of what?

Jun came to the cousin of Wedsek, who sat by him on the bench. Wedsek watched from the corner of his eye. He braced his body, as if for the shock of pain.

Jun kneeled before Wedsek.

'As it was done, and in the sight of God . . .'

Wedsek did not understand these sentences he had listened to so often.

The water was tepid, pleasant. That was nothing. Then the towel came, dampened by the other feet, high-born and low, not to be winced at. It was not the towel – the clasp of the hands of Jun ran through the towel. Was it a heat, a laving of vibration that moved the fluid of his blood about? Like the fireside after snow, like wine.

Wedsek stiffened his frame, muscles, bones. He resisted.

And Jun drew away and, his ministry accomplished, was gone. Wedsek did not see into what or where. A dissembling of shadow.

Wedsek could not sleep in the scalding cauldron of the night. He might get up, go and draw water from the well in the garden, douse himself.

He rose from the hard bed and put on his habit, in the dark. He felt curiously ashamed.

At the doorway of his cell, Wedsek stopped, knowing why. He was not going to the well. Along the cloister lay the Confessional, where every night one of the godbrothers took his duty, sleeping on a pallet, ready to be waked by any who, in the dead hours, would creep to be heard.

What was it Wedsek would say? *I have a jealous hatred of him.* Was it that? *He has usurped what I wanted.* But what had Jun usurped – was it not there for all the men in this priestly bondage? No. For it was the mark of one chosen. It was the knighthood bestowed by Heaven – Wedsek writhed at the confusion and inadequacy of his words, and at the confrontation with his disappointment.

413

He would have to go to the elderly godbrother in the Confessional, he would have to blurt out that he wished to rob Jun of life. That he wished Jun had never lived.

As Wedsek emerged from the south dormitory door into the cloister, he saw Jun come out of the eastern door.

Perhaps Jun sought the well, as Wedsek had thought he himself meant to. Or the latrines. Oddly, Wedsek had never seen Jun visit them, in all these months, when every fellow novice had been encountered there at some hour of day or night. Well, did a saint *void* himself? Unthinkable.

Wedsek grinned, and as if he had detected the noise of Wedsek's lips in motion, Jun looked back at him.

Only three dim lights burned in the cloister, two beneath statues of Saint Eda and a nameless angel, and one above the plinth of the Christus on his marble cross.

Jun received a faint brushwork of this light; he seemed a figure of the darkness, something of basalt like the plinth, shining.

Well, Wedsek thought, *well*—

But Jun had turned away again. He was walking along the cloister, towards the statue of the Christus. Did Jun seek the Confessional?

Wedsek began to walk after Jun. An abrupt bravado was on him. If Jun had some sin that kept him sleepless, what was he but a man, an ordinary miserable thing of skin and hair and sludge, like the rest.

Wedsek had quickened his pace. Both men moved soundlessly. At the refectory turn, where the steps led down into the garden, Wedsek realized he could catch Jun up. Wedsek reached out and delivered a weightless blow to Jun's shoulder.

'God's serenity be with you, Jun. Where are you going?'

Jun had halted but did not turn, now.

Wedsek felt a pressure inside him that might be incipient triumph.

'Some miscreancy to confess?' said Wedsek. 'The poor old godbrother needs his sleep. Tell *me* first. Let's see if it's worth waking him.'

Jun did not turn.

414

Wedsek put his hand back on Jun's shoulder. It did not have the width of brawn, but it was shaped and flat, knit with lean muscle. Wedsek came around and gazed into Jun's face, which now had half the light from above the plinth washed along it. And Jun's, too, was a statue's face. The eyes seemed all burnished blackness, without white. There was a surge in Wedsek. He knew undeniably the instant had come, the contest between them. He, or the other.

'No, I won't let you go in and disturb the poor doddery priest. You must make your confession here, to me. I'll absolve you.' Wedsek pressed on the shoulder. 'Kneel down, Jun.' The shoulder did not give. It was like welded bronze.

Jun spoke to Wedsek.

'You misinterpret. It's the Christus that I go to. The beautiful image with the golden thorns, and the nails of gold through His hands and feet.'

Wedsek lifted his eyes, looked aside involuntarily towards the place, and Jun somehow had gone by him, was pacing up the cloister into the light.

Wedsek strode after him.

'You *wait*, you peasant, on my leave to go.'

Jun turned this time. Before Wedsek could predict, Jun's hand had flashed up and struck Wedsek across the cheek. It stung like icy water. Wedsek started back as if afraid. He was not. He was not anything. This went on too fast—

'Look at the statue,' said Jun.

Wedsek could not take his eyes from Jun's eyes. He seemed to see right through them, through two black gems, to where the Christus hung. The lamp above picked out the white features, the agonized crown. A shadowy moth was flying about the lamp, attracted to it. And suddenly the moth flew into the lamp. There was a spurt of pale flame. The Christus seemed to contort, rolling up His stare towards the sky. From under the thorn crown three scarlet threads unwound. They slipped down the

415

marble forehead, the lids, across the eyeballs, out, like tears. They ran together on the lips, staining them red.

'In the name of God – God be with me—' Wedsek picked out his own muttering. He no longer saw through Jun, for Jun had left him again, without leave. Jun was standing under the statue, black under the whiteness.

Worms of blood were running from the wrists and feet of the statue under the golden nails.

'*In the name of God—*'

It was a miracle. He witnessed a miracle. Make it stop. He could not bear it—

Wedsek trembled from head to foot. His bowels were liquid. He tried, over and over, against the vocal expressions of prayer, to apply inner reason: *What is it? What is it?*

But it was that the Christus bled from His wounds. And Jun was there, looking up.

No. Jun was on the plinth. He had put up his arms and spread them out along the crucified arms of the Christus. Jun lay against the statue, three feet from the ground.

Wedsek did not know how Jun had ascended. It hardly mattered.

The instant had come. It was not the instant. It was all time, none.

Wedsek opened his eyes, and the statue was clean white under the dull sheen of the lamp.

Jun stood before Wedsek. Jun's wrists were red with blood, his palms full of blood like flowers. His lips were red and wet.

Wedsek kneeled down.

He did not know what to do. In terrible horror he floundered. And then he *did* know. It was so easy. A tide of thankfulness broke inside him. It was not battle. He was not unchosen. Jun was God's, and Jun chose Wedsek. Wedsek the warrior of God stretched himself out and kissed the feet of his redeemer.

Chapter Four

Late in spring, the grey church at Khish was dressed with
asphodel, and lilies. An altar cloth of white and green,
sewn with brilliants of glass but fringed with silver,
replaced the darker cloth upon the high altar. The higher
streets of Khish, too, dressed themselves with blossoms.
A Factor had come from the city of Chirkess, to ordain
the fledgling priests. The Factor, looking down his long
nose, was entertained by the noble families of Khish. The
beads he told were of sapphire, jade and pearl.

At the church, the Factor was inquisitive. He pried. If
what he found was in order, an indifferent complacency
bloomed from him. Where there was any fault, he smiled,
and made a note on a parchment tablet.

But concerning the twenty-eight novices due to be
remade by him, he was sanguine.

'An abundant and healthy harvest, Administer.'

The Factor observed, through a magnifying lens of
crystal, from the gallery above the nave, the novices passing to their devotions. It was the Factor who undertook
their final interrogation, who set them their final and most
rigorous fasts, instructed them in the death of their male
bodies, the birth from chrysalis of their spiritual being.

'There is one. The others attend him. In another situation this would be a bad thing, but I believe that here
we see a special gift. This is the novice of whom you wrote
to the Primentor at Chirkess?'

'Just so, Father Factor. That is Jun.'

'I'm impressed by him, Administer. I did not expect to

be, despite, excuse me, your letter. Jun. He won't, I suppose, take ordination under such a name – of the peasantry, pagan most likely. It would never be correct.'

'The name of Saint Junion was recommended to Jun, as bearing some relation to his own.'

'Yes, yes.'

'But Jun declined use of this name.'

'Indeed? Do I detect after all a hint of disobedience?'

The Administer said, 'His rejection was made without any show of wilfulness. But the name Jun has chosen for himself as a priest may not please you, Father Factor.'

The Factor raised his long thin brows like quarter-moons of wire. 'I'm agog.' The Administer offered Jun's choice, and beheld the Factor's pallor tint itself. 'That's a lofty selection. I'm unsure I can approve it.'

'Jun told me very simply that he coveted the name of an angel in order to uphold constantly before himself an unattainable goal. He must strive towards it, could not turn from it, the name, like the flesh, being undetachable during life from the soul.'

'He theorizes like one already in the Fraterium at Chirkess. Does he aim to get there?' The Factor put his crystal to his eye, and looked at a blister upon the chamber wall. 'Of course, this isn't an archangel. Nevertheless . . . to fix on an angel so closely in service on the Unsurpassable Sacrifice . . . I will have to question your Jun.'

The angels stood by the right hand of the Christus, who was seated amongst His disciples. Before them ran the table with its metal cups. The young men wore clothing like that of the priesthood, sombre and seemly; the Christus was clad in white, His head rimmed by the sunburst that swirled up into an arch of white roses overhead. Under the left hand of the Christus lay a crimson rose whose stem had emitted awful black and curving thorns. The first serving angel was fair, blue-robed, with wings of fleece. He carried on a silver salver the bread that was to be the Body. The second serving angel provided a note of fire to complement the rose. Black-haired and sable winged, he was attired in red. And in his hand was the chalice for which the Christus already reached: the chalice of the wine of Love, at the Last Supper on earth. The wine which was the rose-red ichor of the Christus: *Drink, this is my Blood.*

The mural had been vital thirty years before, but damp in the wall of the chapel had somewhat affected it. Despite that, the details were clear enough. And the name of the Angel of the Blood of the Redeemer, who in a mystic story repaired after to the foot of the cross, catching the precious drops in his vessel that they might not sink and be lost in the ground, this name, though commonly obscure, was documented in the lists of the hosts of Heaven.

'And do you not think, Jun, that you aspire beyond your station?'

'Father, I aspire to be a priest. That's far beyond my station. I aspire to do the will of God. That is beyond the station, and the knack, of most men, even the best.'

'You argue very ably. This sophistry was taught you here?'

'Pardon me, Father. I only speak the truth as I judge the truth to be.'

The Father Factor leaned back in the chair which had been set for him. He regarded Jun with his narrow, too-clever eyes.

Jun was not ordinary clay. He had presence and enormous power, even so young. His voice could break and make the hearts of humanity. Already the novices, and half the priests here, were under his sway. He was a radiance that it would be idiotic to ignore.

'If I were to say to you, Jun, that this name is not to be yours, that you must put on with ordainment some other, how would you reply to me?'

'This is the name of what I am to be. Name me by some other name, I will abide by your command.'

'You're saying then, that you'll obey outwardly, and inwardly rebel.'

'No. Now I go by the name *Jun*. That is not who I am. Yet I answer to the name *Jun*, without rebellion.'

'If Jun isn't your name,' snapped the Factor, wary, and bristling, 'what is your proper name?'

'Man,' said Jun. His eyes rested on the Factor, and the Factor grew still, measuring, weighing this paradox like the quality of peerless music. 'I am Man, the universal name we answer to, the race made by God in the image of the Most High.'

Inwardly the Factor preened himself, for peerless things delighted him always. He had never grasped that, save with God, this also was a sin and a snare.

'You must allow us time, Jun, to consider your request.'

Jun bowed to the Factor.

It was already decided. The Factor would permit this novice to have his way. Jun should garb himself in the name of the Angel of the Blood, which name was Anjelen.

After the fasts, the inquisition of faith, the day.

They rose four hours before the sun, two hours after they had lain down.

There was moonlight in the cloister and on the garden, powdering the apple trees and the vines on the wall. Each man bore a lighted taper. They entered the church.

The novices separated, like islands, and one by one knelt down. Kneeling, each man extinguished his taper, like an act of will. Then they were alone there together, in the cold spring night and the shining darkness of the moon.

Only on the altar, like a mountain, the lamp burned before the crucifix.

The Watching must last three hours.

It was the passage, in darkness, out of the dark.

In the final hour, before the sunrise, the golden wind would blow into the hall of stone, the dawn of rebirth. Candles, singing.

Before that, the meeting with self, utter and inescapable.

Only the star on the altar to be a guide.

How many men had kneeled here in this dark and cold, and in this form. Longing maybe for visions, or simply for the stamina to endure the Watch. How many minds had wandered from the vigil, slipped back into the past (the warmth or bitterness of childhood, the years of growth, before the going away into this), or forward, in greed, material dreams in the margin left for a meeting with the spirit.

Some fainted at the Watching. No one tended them. Some sobbed, or prayed aloud. Some abandoned the taxing posture, taking up again the painful kneeling stance only when it could not be avoided. Once, or twice, not more, a candidate had fled the church, some inner demon having found him.

This Watch was unlike any other.

Separated in their islands of self, the waiting men had union. It was the power of the novice Jun, feeding them and upholding them. They felt it like a sea of soft lightning. It supported them, it refurbished.

And above them all, the lamp burned on the altar. And beyond the stones of the church, the morning trod slowly nearer to the east.

And in the mind of Jun, soon to be Anjelen, what was *there*?

The mind that had been a boy's mind once in the heart of the wood, and that had emptied, and that had filled again with the wild abbreviated eternity of the Tree. The mind which had lived as a wolf, and a god-thing, to which a decade was one hundred mortal years. The mind that came up from the shadow, and stayed a shadow.

The mind of Jun was like a globe of glass. A million things were engraved on it. Lights and midnights played over and within it. It turned, and gave out, like silent chimes, all that it knew, had learned, had lived, and, too, it kept in, withheld, stored, and wasted nothing. Like a globe of glass, its clarity. And yet, like a forest also, dense and convoluted and *full*.

Not the mind of a man, or of anything supernatural in the spiritual sense.

Its intellect it employed as a beast of the field might use instinct.

Not human. No, it would regain humanness only gradually, and maybe solely through imitation.

Jun knelt straight as a post. He did not change his position. His breathing was barely visible. His eyes were open on the altar lamp.

He did not go back over memory, or forward into future.

He existed moment by moment. Each moment was new.

He was not accessible, scarcely alterable. He did not even know, Jun who was to be Anjelen, *what* he was, his purpose, his desire. He grew now as the Tree grows, blind and certain, upward into the sky.

In the hour before the dawn, the golden wind blew. The church doors opened, and they swept through the hall of stone, the boys singing in their white, and the priests with their candles. The Administer came in a robe of white, and the Factor in robes of red and white patterned with yellow brightness, and the utensils of yellow brightness were set on the altar, now like a green hill of flowers.

'Father, I present to you these, whom I believe, in the sight of God, to be worthy of the office of priest.'

'If there is any impediment, let it be spoken directly.'

And on the Factor's admonition, a minute was counted out by a sandglass, after which a bell was rung.

'Now, even as the Son of God ordained particular men, who through His will became the saints, so are we given to make for Him a priesthood.'

The service proceeded, and the heat of the candles drew up the scent of the lilies, and the incense clouded down.

Outside, inch by inch, the blackness lightened and the stars went out. The moon was left, like mist, on the edge of a wall.

The Factor, the Shepherd and the Maker, stepped

among the kneeling men, and laid his hands on their bowed heads.

'As it was done, receive now the spark of the fire that is God. Whose sins you shall forgive, they are forgiven them, who speaks to God though you, he shall be heeded.'

The dawn, despite everything, was overcast. No flame was in the east.

The Host was elevated, and the Wine of the Christus.

Silken grey light began to come in at the windows of the church. The light flickered like the candles. In the world, it rained.

The Bread of the Body was given to the priests who had kneeled as novices. The chalice was brought to them. They drank the Blood.

The rain reflected on the face of the Christus hanging on the crucifix above the altar.

Anjelen sipped from the chalice, the Wine of the Redeemer, and the cup continued to the mouth of Wedsek, like a kiss.

And the rain tears slid from the eyes of the Christus, reflecting the weeping of the sky.

'To Chirkess, these four or five; yes, I shall recommend it.'

Four, the sons of rich families, had been bought their places by charitable awards. The fifth priest, Jun (Anjelen), had won the prize for himself.

The Factor smiled upon the Administer.

'Impressive chances lie before them. You've done well here.'

Anjelen stood in the chapel, under the mural of the Supper.

Wedsek and three others, the new-minted priests, stood where the chapel opened to the church.

They waited on Anjelen.

At length, Anjelen turned and looked at them.

'Chirkess,' said Wedsek. 'It's sure.'

Anjelen said nothing, did nothing. He made no movement, was expressionless.

From his body, or so it seemed to them, the power of the fire of God flowed out.

They were rewarded.

Chapter Five

To those who had never seen a city, Chirkess gave a drab fulfilment to their assumptions. It was a sprawling town that had not checked itself. It spread along the shore of a narrow river, and up the hills to the east. A current wall was being built to contain it, since it had outstripped the other. Chirkess had an Overlord, and was capable of making war. The towered building of her temporal power stood near the water, and the garrison was there, the wharves, and a few ships. The Cathedral of Chirkess, completed twenty years before, rose on a hill, surrounded by its own stout walls, and having its own military presence to defend it. It was the Cathedral that had the greater pretence to being a city. Ensconced within the battlements were the necessaries of life, granary, stables, candle-makers, forges, breweries and butchers' yards. There was a garden of beauty and harvest, an armoury that frustrated the lord below, a library that disconcerted him, since he could not read. Learning was yet the magic of the priest-hood. And it was picky and canny whom it taught. There were ten clerical priests allocated to the court of the Over-lord, aside from his confessor. He could not do without them.

For the priesthood of this place, save where they went about as tutors, advisors and spies, Chirkess was only the Cathedral.

The snow had been especially harsh that winter. The river froze completely. By-passing the lord's house, the citizens went up to the gates of the Cathedral and cried for help. They were chastised by hard words concerning their transgressions. Men kneeled praying and lamenting in the cold, dead snow. Then the Cathedral sent them bread, by the cartload.

The first wife of the Overlord had died two years before of a colic. He had had to attend to a year of penances, strictly watched by his confessor and religious counsellors, before the Church Fathers of his city awarded him permission to take another wife.

Now, the snow, the spring, the summer were gone, the lord's wife was with child, and early autumn blazed along the hills and fired the beautiful garden of the Cathedral.

In through the west gate of the Cathedral precinct rode a hunting party. They wore dull red and black, immediately recognizable, although they might have been lords from the city, as the priesthood.

They passed the forges on the slope of the yard, and went up to the kitchens. Servants came out to collect carcasses, two deer from the plains; they had been grazing on the wheat, which the hunt had trampled in its career. The farmers would have to thank the Church for its kindness.

Above, over the grouping of walls and buildings, the Cathedral's great north tower arose, fluttering the banner of the black knot-cross on blank white, masonry capped with blue tile, and rimmed by gold, and with the vast eye of indigo, ruby and green beryl looking west and down into the city towards the river. The picture in the window was of the death of the Devil as a dragon, and the Christus ascendant. It was the colours which mattered. On clear nights, this was the jewellery moon of Chirkess.

Just visible too, across the roofs of the Cathedral behind a complex of small courtyards, a lower, squatter tower, round as a wheel, showed its grey shoulder to the garden.

This tower was older than the Cathedral. It had been an outlying garrison of the town a pair of centuries before.

As he rode up from the kitchen, Godbrother Wedsek, thinner, harder, pleased with his hunting and his prospects, oddly tense and bemusedly out of step with his life,

426

glanced at this second, south tower. Almost he winked at it: an assignation.

Few servants entered the south tower. The trees that grew up against it from the garden walks below had partly rooted in the lower walls. Black moss and creeper licked out from the blocks of it. A series of window slits high up sometimes emitted faint light.

The lower room of the south tower, gained by a small warped door, put up the armoury of the Cathedral, weapons antique and edgeless, modern and harsh, hanging together. An inner stair led on to a further door, always kept locked.

There were gargoyles along the heights of the tower, having strange faces, their eyes masked by the visors of helms.

Sunset began in the river valley, and gradually the western gargoyle faces reddened.

Wedsek, having stabled his horse, had walked down into the garden. He should go to pray now, in the chapel. He was not ready to pray.

He stood beneath the south tower, looking for Anjelen.

Wedsek's first sight of Anjelen, every day, was sharp and accentuated, as if there had been long absences. Through their three years at Chirkess, this had never lessened. In fact it increased. Wedsek's feelings appeared to him a curious mixture of awe and envy, the subjugation of the self to another, the outcry of self to be acknowledged.

Anjelen had not failed Wedsek. Neither had Anjelen fulfilled Wedsek. There was a sort of tarrying. It seemed Anjelen could wait a hundred years. Wedsek understood that he himself could not.

The door moved surreptitiously in the ivy, and elderly Magister Egar emerged. Next came the three pupils who had today been with him in the under-rooms above the armoury. Wedsek beheld his fellows Behri and Kopis, and Anjelen alone in their midst and burning with a black motionless flame.

Egar paused on the step inside the trees. He waved

427

Behri and Kopis on, and leaned upon the shoulder of
Anjelen. The Magister spoke to Anjelen, eagerly, intimately. The other two came down, and found Wedsek.
Their eyes were cloudy. Behri said to Wedsek, 'The peace
of God. It's possible to make light in a lamp.'

'Yes?' said Wedsek.

'He showed us. Certain words—'

'Be quiet,' said Kopis. 'Those are secrets of the alchemist's chamber.'

'Rubbish. The trick of doing them's the secret. Neither
you nor I, yet. Anjelen, however—'

'Then, when Anjelen gives you leave, you may talk of
it.'

Wedsek said, 'Anjelen will tell me.'

'Yes,' said Kopis grudgingly. 'The *other* brotherhood.'

'And you,' said Wedsek, 'don't speak of *that*.'

They stood in triangle in the peace of God, lips formed
to create blows. The pupils of the alchemist were in their
habits, a red cord at the waist. Anjelen too was dressed
in this fashion, and the aged Magister, whose lizardine
crucifix of emerald and gold ignited on his breast at the
sinking sun. Wedsek in his priestly hunting garb, short
habit, breeches, boots, had put his right hand across his
body. The hunting knife on his hip evidenced what was
supposedly not discussed. There was the inner order at
Chirkess, as on other heights of the Church, brothers who
carried weapons, might exercise and hunt.

Egar and Anjelen were coming nearer.

Wedsek caught the quick soft gabble of the elder priest.

'The ignorant call such a man a magician. The bones
of the word are apt enough. They imply learning, the
follower of truth. But alchemy is science. It can be said
to be as simple as the adding up of beads on a string.
This *you* master.'

The Magister was a trifle deaf? His murmurs were audible and perhaps should not be. Already his eyes had a
film on them. He hurried to pass on his knowledge.

But Anjelen. Wedsek had seen or guessed so much of

428

what Anjelen could do, those prodigious things like dreams only half remembered.

'To give hope to the faithful among men, for this you learn to offer evidence of supernatural acts. In such a form, you must learn. Otherwise, the deed is unholy.'

'Do you say, your grace,' broke in Kopis, 'that we should mimic the miracles of the *Christus*?'

The Magister turned to look at him. He gave a sudden snake-like smile. 'If God grants you the talent so to do, my son, why not? If God does not grant the talent, well then.'

Kopis reddened like the gargoyle heads aloft in the setting sun.

Egar said to Anjelen, clearly, 'What you learned this afternoon required of me one year of my life. Go in God's peace.' He blessed them carelessly and ambled off towards the body of the Cathedral, with a wandering, somnambulist gait.

From the north tower of the window, the bell for prayer voiced its summons.

Wedsek repressed, as ever, his irritation. He must go in and wash himself and put on his priest's habit and rush to kneel in the Cathedral with the rest.

Anjelen looked at him. Kopis and Behri had started off. They had gone into the courts beyond the garden.

'Don't you mean to pray?' said Wedsek abruptly.

'Life, for the priest, is a prayer,' said Anjelen.

'But the rituals must be observed.'

The darkness was coming to cover Anjelen, the bright-burning black flame of him.

Wedsek relaxed his body. 'I'm in no state to pray. Filthy from the chase. My mind elsewhere. I'll play truant, and confess tomorrow. And you?'

But Anjelen was now moving towards the courtyards, the Cathedral. Wedsek got suddenly in his path.

Anjelen halted.

'I find it difficult,' said Wedsek, 'to be a slave of God. I'm God's warrior.'

'The two are one,' said Anjelen.

'Tell me what to do.'

'You know yourself what you're expected to do.'

Something rose through Wedsek, three years of waiting, like a tide.

'I was the son of the noble house of Crel, at Khish. They presented the Church with me.'

'Did they.'

'I had dreams of something. Of the might and glory of God – *you, you* were like the sign of it. That time – the blood on the lips of the statue—' Wedsek stopped. He pointed up to the south tower. 'Tonight. Is *that* only a ritual? Where does it go to, Anjelen? You know, I've served you. You aim at something. I *know* it. I'll follow you – to Hell.'

'Believe,' said Anjelen. He was a shadow, like the trees. 'What you worship is old as the world. Is the world. Believe in me.'

'I do,' Wedsek whispered.

'The rituals are not the passion,' said the shadow. 'But the passion has created the rituals. The rituals are games. As a child does, learn by them.'

A cold wind sped through the garden, smelling of the river and the dusty, dirty sprawl of Chirkess.

The evening star had risen.

Anjelen was going on towards the Cathedral, and Wedsek ran to his cell, to dress himself as a priest, to obeise himself before God. Subdued, convinced. Unsatisfied.

No servants at all entered the upper chamber of the south tower. It was large in scope, approximating the space of a lordly hall, in shape a seemingly exact round, like the wall without. There were, between that outer wall and the inner, both of stone, certain apartments and offices that complemented the round chamber. Four arched doors connected to them, east, south, west and north. Four crimson curtains on rods of gold obscured the doors. On the eastern curtain was a sun in gold and on the western curtain a crescent moon in gold. In gold upon the south and north curtains were a heron and an owl respectively. At the centre of the great circular floor, which was laid with a heavy paving of pale stone, lay a brazen disc, inset by a cross of black marble, its arms of equal length. From the disc a sort of web or tracery of gold ran out to all points over the floor, a pattern mathematical yet obscure, disturbing if regarded for too long. Twenty pillars of stone rose around the room, close to the circling wall. They were featureless to their tops; here they became stone trees, carved with branches and foliage. Three or four fruits of gold and silver hung in each, representations of the pomegranate, the pear, the quince and the peach. The roof of the chamber was painted blue, and marked by golden stars in the form of constellations, perhaps, yet these too were uncomfortable to the eye if gazed at more than a few moments. The centre of the roof held a colossal depending lamp of brass on a chain of gilded iron. It displayed the beasts of the Apocalypse, an eagle, a lion with a serpent's tail, a bull with the lower part of a fish, an angel, all leaning out on wings of silver, with the lamps hanging from them in necklaces, ten bronze cups of oil to each figure and all alight.

Beyond the pillars, between them and the inner wall, a strip of chequered floor ran around. Above this, in the alcoves of the wall, lit by forty lamps of black iron, were forty carved stone faces, some of animals and monsters, some of men in torment and joy. As the lights shimmered on them, their expressions slightly altered or intensified, an audience compelled to watch for ever.

At midnight, the summons to prayer collected the priests of the Fraterium of Chirkess into the Cathedral. They went to their places and knelt down. Then, in at the door, there came a battalion of mailed men, armed, helmed and vizored. Over the armour the tunic was white. No man in the Cathedral turned to look. Not the officiating priest, the Administer, the two Magisters, none of the higher or lower orders.

The Knights of God, of whom, at Chirkess, there were then sixteen, stood throughout the last ceremony of the evening. When it was done they went out again, and their brothers remained, motionless, to let them go.

The warriors passed along under the wall in the silence, entered the garden, approached the south tower. All the doors stood open. They ascended through the armoury into the apartments of the alchemists, and came up into the round chamber of the great lamp, via the south door of the heron, from which the curtain was drawn back.

The sixteen men assumed their stance around the wide central disc, the brazen plaque with the cross. The positions had been marked out, every one, with a little cross of jet set down there on the edge of the disc. Each man, arriving, kneeled as he had not done in the church, touched his fingers to the small cross, and then to his lips. After that, he rose, and withdrew the helm from his head. In the auburn light, the faces recognized one another, without salute. They were not, here, as they had been.

The curtain on the south door dropped, and that to the north looped aside without visible agency. Through the owl door came a figure like that of a woman (no women were permitted here) cloaked in black. The figure advanced a few paces and began to sing to the glory of God, in a magnificent female and unreal voice. Raising her head and her hands, they might behold she was a skeleton, with palms of bone and skull of ivory. She sang of the fragility of man, lest they forget. An hour of time to live and to be. Only in God was life everlasting to be found.

When her song was done, her head and hands were lowered and put away, and she glided backwards from the chamber, out of the owl door, and the curtain sank.

At the centre of the central disc, where the greater cross had been inscribed, a mechanism operated. An inner panel parted from itself four ways, and out of the dark below came up a golden thing, like a vast coin. A black cup stood there, from which incense smoked, raw and sweet.

One of the Knights lifted his eyes, looking upwards; Wedsek.

Presently, from somewhere within the lamp of brass, a

sword hurled itself down towards the cup, stopping suddenly three feet above it, quivering and ringing, on a metal thread. The blade of the sword appeared to burn.

The curtain on the west door of the room raised itself, and a figure in white entered. It had a white hood, a vizor of silver, and in its hands a sword of steel. Though another doll, it spoke with a male voice.

'Say now, brethren, why is it that you gather here?'

Tonight Wedsek, who had not turned to glance at the west door, must speak the words of the vow. This fell to every man in turn, for two or three gatherings at a stretch.

Across from Wedsek, Anjelen.

Wedsek spoke loudly, with all his ability, to Anjelen, whose eyes seemed not to see anything that was in the chamber.

'We are here for our faith, to pledge service to our Lord, the Christus, by means of prayer and duty, and, with these, by force of arms and the sword. We alone, Knights of God, have committed ourselves to this, without blemish or stain of earthly wants, vainglory, or the jealousy of the world.'

Angelen had spoken on the last occasions. The calendar of these rites was irregular, fixed by planetary conjunctions. It had been two months before.

And when Anjelen spoke, the stones had seemed to shift and shine, the sword to brace itself. A high honed singing note had whistled round the chamber. The lamps fluttered, reddened, sprang up more vividly. It was as if the roof would give way and a hand of light hover there, or a molten dove fly down. But these things had not happened. Wedsek did not suppose he was capable of creating them, if Anjelen had not done so. Nevertheless, his nostrils stung by the powerful incense, his nerves drawn like strings over the instrument of his heart, Wedsek tingled to unconceived possibilities, and stumbling on his words, had to collect himself. Then, as the Knights responded in unison, he experienced a deflation of his soul.

Wedsek chafed against himself. These mysteries were

romantic and proficient, but the marvels came from the alchemist's art practised below. Ignorance and paganism were the enemies of the Knights, and no battle was demanded save the spiritual fight asked of any priest. While the brushing wing of God must be taken on trust.

The responses were over, and the white-robed doll went backwards through the west door.

The eastern curtain of the sun lifted away, and a second white-clad priest-doll entered. Its face was masked in gold, and on a golden tray it bore the Chalice, which was of smoky green glass. The doll moved towards the disc and the circle of Knights, along a gold line in the patterned floor. Wedsek, over the sputter of the lamps, his own breathing, heard a vague sound of wheels.

When the doll reached him, it halted. It had not been given a voice. It was Wedsek who turned and took up the green Chalice, within which the liquid looked black as gall.

'And He gave them the wine,' announced Wedsek, 'saying, Drink, this is my blood. Hereafter do this always in my name. For He was the Sacrifice, dying for our sins, that we may be redeemed through Him.'

Wesdek moved about the disc, inside the rim of it, giving the Chalice one by one to each man.

And when he came to Anjelen, Anjelen only accepted the vessel, drank from it, and let it pass.

Last of the sixteen, Wedsek too sipped from the Chalice. He then replaced it on the tray of the automaton, that instantly backed across the floor and vanished inside the eastern curtain.

Children's games, by which to learn . . .

The Knights knelt in prayer.

'*Show me the path, Lord.*' Wedsek, in his brain: unsatisfied.

So in the henna smoke of autumn, Wedsek the unsatisfied went to his prayers, fasted at his penances, scourged himself, walked proudly as a Knight in mail once more to the room of symbols and crimsons, and rode in the chase on the plains below Chirkess. What he missed, and did not know, or must not know, was what his body hankered for – the fruit of the body, male life, the vaunting and lusting, the making of himself over in children, the responsibilities of which he would have been most capable – the management of a household, the ways of the world. But instead he had the bread of cold white love, the wine of sacred fire. From these exquisite ghosts he had tried to fashion for himself an alternative to that from which he had been sundered. These phantom foods must become, for Wedsek, savoury and devourable as the feasts of the flesh. But they had not, they were of another order.

Wedsek took the Christus as his Overlord, but the Christus would not come down from His cross.

Anjelen stood now between Heaven and earth. Anjelen was the only hope.

Out on the plain, the far side of the narrow river, the willows and the birch groves were full of the embers of leaves. The country passed down into red valleys of oak and poplar. Fir trees gripped boulders in their claws. This was woodland, but not forest. They hunted there, beyond the levelled grain where nothing fed now but the crows.

There were no great silences in these woods. The ending of the year would strip them bare, relining them in the white coat of the ermine.

They had hunted a wild pig. It had led them a dance. Firstly they were glad to get off such a distance from their fane. Then the sun went westerly and the day was running too.

Anjelen never rode at the forefront of any hunt. Its excitements did not touch him, apparently. Like the firs, he stood out black on the colours of the woodland, black hair and habit, and the black horse.

The six other men had gone rushing on. Wedsek said, 'No trace of it for an hour.'

Anjelen said nothing. He was looking about him slowly, deliberately, not for game, it would seem. At the foot of the trees, the scarlet leaves lay in dry pools.

Wedsek glanced here and there. Up on the naked bough of a tawny ash, he saw, clear as surprise, something hanging from a bit of thread.

'Look – what is *that*?'

Anjelen did not look, he had already seen.

'The skull of a fox.'

The gaunt and broken thing reminded Wedsek – of what? A gargoyle from the church at Khish, or from the chamber of the Knights of Chirkess.

'An offering,' said Wedsek. He drew his knife and was about to slash the thread, to cut down this pagan atrocity.

'No,' said Anjelen.

'No? This godless frippery—'

'Not godless. What we do in church, they do here, under the trees.'

Anjelen had stopped the black horse.

Wedsek leaned about to see him.

'There's only one God,' said Wedsek. His voice sounded strained and anxious, unnerving him. 'This is worship of false gods. The Devil.'

'There is only God,' said Anjelen. The black eyes were there. Wedsek gave way to them. He felt a surge of alarm. He was glad. 'Don't you realize, Wedsek? Since there is only God, whatever is worshipped, must be God? They come to the ash and hang a skull on it, and spill blood at its foot like the red leaves lying there. The Tree must have blood, but it makes return. What dies for the Tree, who dies for it, becomes the Tree. Man and Tree. Both are one. Both Sacrifice and Lord, victim and master, together. And what else is the Christus?'

'I—' said Wedsek.

Anjelen had dismounted. He walked to the ash tree, and the skull began to move in the wind. Before Anjelen had reached it, the skull had become a wolf's head made of silver that swayed back and forth. It was a bell, it rang out. It was like the bells of the Cathedral, the little bells of the ceremonies.

Some sort of overcast had spoiled the sky. A vast cloud had come down on the tops of the wood. Everything grew veiled. A circle of darkness with a lid of shadow held them in.

Wedsek saw Anjelen under the ash tree, which towered now, into the grape-purple overcast, and was lost there, with the silver drop of its wolf bell ringing dimly.

Something fluttered. A huge moth, playing round the light of Anjelen, for only Anjelen gave light. He wore mail, as in the chamber of the Knights. His arms were outflung, so he seemed pinned by nails of black fire upon a cross—

Anjelen said, inside the brain of Wedsek, 'I will make you into what you are. Become mine.'

Wedsek moved towards Anjelen. As in certain dreams, he experienced nothing of the world, did not sense his footfalls on the grass or hear the leaves crushed under them.

Anjelen was the statue of the Christus, mailed. The moth flew away from it, but the burning nails pierced on, and from them ran the rubies of the blood. Not murky wine in a chalice, true ichor, so very red.

He did not hesitate, Wedsek, he set his lips to the wounds in hands and feet, in the side where the lance had torn the heart. Huge inner seas belaboured him, he hung like a lost leaf on the tree, until the gale shook him free into nothingness.

'And you will do this, in remembrance of me.'

They had found the wild pig. They cantered through the forest after it. The trees were much thicker here, fir and pine and spruce, hemlock and cedar mingled with the leavened autumn oaks. Branches cut at their faces like swords. They ducked and wove in the saddle and the horses ran on.

The boar was like a brown barrel rolled before them, hurtling through the undergrowth, breaking a way.

Wedsek heard the other men shouting. He held up his left arm to defend his eyes.

He was not quite sure how he came to be where he was. He had paused with Anjelen, to discuss some token of theology – odd in itself, for Anjelen, knowing his preference, did not turn to Wedsek for such debates.

It was dark in the woods, dusk in day, though the sun itself must be near to going down, for frequently there came, ahead of them, a smouldering flare of red, as the wild pig raced towards the sunset.

Wedsek too shouted aloud, to try to start fervour or even agitation in himself.

And then, suddenly, in the manner of such a headlong advance, a glade burst out, flinging itself across and around them. It was enchained with red sunlights, thick with mast and fallen leaves, and there stood the barrel of the pig at bay.

The Chirkessian priests, who hunted like nobles not peasants, cast their spears. The boar, quilled with death, reared and plunged down. Two men were off, and digging in their knives. They poised, action over, abruptly quite still, black on the flamey lights, and the forest settled round them.

The boar had not made any sound, as it died.

Wedsek swung off his horse, and went to look. The other two drew aside, and behind him, Wedsek heard the soft trampling of the horses, reined in on leaves.

The pig was strange. It was not made of flesh, but rather it was like a nut from the trees, an acorn or walnut, a closed cone. Where the spears had penetrated they had cracked its shell. The long fissures ran over its smooth carapace. Its snout was carved, its carved eyes shut. From the parted jaws stuck brown clean walnut teeth and a grained tongue like peeled bark. It was a vegetable of the wood, a pod, a seed.

The vegetable boar turned his stomach, but Wedsek was not afraid. He remembered he had tasted Anjelen's blood.

Wedsek woke, roasting under the single cover, which he thrust off impatiently.

He had been dreaming. He lay, trying to decipher what was dream, and what a memory of the afternoon's hunt.

438

'In the name of God—'

He threw himself upright. He stood. And the night's coolness sluiced down to tone the heat of his body.

There had been no curious, no lawless or blasphemous or wonderful thing. They had hunted in the woodland over the river, and come back with a pig—

There had been a skull tied in a tree and he had chopped it down.

No, Anjelen had prevented that.

God is God. Whatever is worshipped *is* God.

Anjelen flew up to the statue of the Christus, and kissed it, and wounds sprang out on Anjelen, and from these wounds Wedsek had drunk the Blood which was the Life.

Trembling and shivering, Wedsek dropped to his knees. He prayed, gripping the edge of his pallet, and beyond the partition (which at Chirkess, was of thin plaster), he heard the snores of Godbrother Kopis.

He is the Devil. Anjelen—

But how could the Devil copy the sacred stigmata of the Christus?

Anjelen, the Angel of the Blood.

A thrilling terror sang through Wedsek. He seized the scourge with its knots, and beat his shoulders. He was possessed by great strength, both to inflict and to bear.

The Factor sat in his room high in the castle-Cathedral of Chirkess, and watched Magister Egar search about him for a chair.

There were one or two of these items, fine pieces of dark wood, with cushions of damask. The room towered with books, elaborate artifacts of religion in costly materials – ebony, marble – a painted panel of the Agony pointed up with gold-leaf, and a sapphire in the aureole of the Christus.

Magister Egar could no longer pick out these things, as he could not, without difficulty, detect the alchemical splendours of his own cell. Chairs might be confused with cabinets.

'Allow me to assist you, Magister. This room, I'm afraid, becomes overcrowded.'

The Factor guided Egar. Egar allowed this without rancour. He accepted his plight, as God had averred all men must, meekly, without a single cry or kick.

'Some wine? My stairs are steep. The days are cold now.'

'Thank you no.'

'Then how may I help your grace?'

Egar looked, or more precisely blindly stared, at his knobbed hands, deformed by rheumatism, agile only in pain.

'One of our number. A godbrother. We've spoken of this young man before.'

'Indeed, your grace.'

'Anjelen.'

'Ah yes . . . Anjelen.' The Factor added, 'I ordained him. He was Jun, then. Are you pleased with his progress in your science, your grace?'

'He has genius,' said the Magister. 'It seemed God had given to me the son I might never have. And for this audacity of mine, I'm punished.'

The Factor did not tense himself any more than he had already. The reflex was, in him, the coiling of the snake before it strikes. Anjelen, the Factor had always known, was a creature of lightning. He might be dangerous to fools, and half-blind old men.

'Can you explain yourself, your grace? I'm startled. Why are you punished in Anjelen? I hear nothing of him but excellence.'

'He's a Knight of God.'

'Of course. As were you yourself, formerly, until the prescribed age, Magister Egar.'

'And as you are yet, Factor.'

'I have, according to the tenets, nine further years in which to offer my service to God in such a form.'

'And Anjelen, favoured by you, was elected to the Knighthood.'

'Yes, Egar. While you selected him for tuition in your

arts. Father Church, as we know, must encourage the flowers of his vine, not stifle them.'

Egar said, 'When last did you attend a gathering?'

'Of the Chirkess Knighthood? Well, Magister, not for some years. My task has been frequently to be abroad, on the work of God. Elsewhere I have attended, of course.'

'The ceremonies of the Knights here have passed by rote to Anjelen again. Now, he changes them.'

The Factor lifted his thin cruel brows.

'How is this known to your grace? You're no longer of the brotherhood of the Knights.'

'Alchemy plays its part in the ritual. I must oversee the procedure.'

Oversee? This blind man?

'Don't you, your grace, delegate younger brethren?'

'But they must report to me any oddity.'

'Reveal the oddity then, your grace. I'm most concerned.'

Egar looked up, peering at the Factor through the mists of his dying eyes. Egar spoke too loudly, out of deafness, and fear.

'The Chalice returned to me with dregs not of wine — but as I think, of blood.' The Factor was as motionless as a viper under a rock. 'My eyes deteriorate daily, and my hearing is muffled,' said Egar. 'But I can smell and taste. The stink of blood gone cold was evident to me.'

'This accusation—' said the Factor.

'I accuse no one. I ask you, Father, in your role of Knight, to attend the next gathering in the south tower. They must admit you. Under the secrecy of the order, they may reveal what occurs. If not, you may demand it.'

When Magister Egar was gone, the Factor of Chirkess opened his calendar in its plates of ivory, and gazing through his crystal lens, deduced the proper night. Dullness had actually absented him from the rituals, though he kept up their privileges. The blaze of his living eyes the blind one had not seen.

Seventeen Knights had come in mail to the ritual in the

441

tower, but behind the pillars with their dripping fruits, forty lit stone faces fleeted and blinked. There a man bitten by a cat, and there a sheep toothed like a wolf, a wolf with the horns of a ram, a child with three eyes . . . Perhaps not all the Knights of Chirkess had noted one extra was among them. But then they had grown dazed. Three conjunctions of stars and lunar orb had brought them in swift succession to the round room, which now changed itself. They had waxed and waned too, away from the room by day and night, doubting, questioning, yet held like flies in ice.

The crimson curtain of the heron door had sunk, the lamp of the apocalypse hung like a smoking planet.

There was a quiet, like winter on the land outside.

The curtain of the owl door raised. The lights in the lamp turned brown.

And in the brown light, Death rode out through the door.

Death on his pale horse of bones, in his mantle and hood, and crowned with a diadem of golden owls.

Death sang, in a boy's alabaster voice, of mortality. A raven of black bone perched on his left hand.

When Death was gone, the floor parted. And out of it there arose the kingdoms of the earth.

A plateau of waters and mountains, forest, and deserts of snow and dust. And golden cities shone there. It was the view from the height, the Temptation. And incense wafted from the censers of golden cities and the deserts of cinnamon.

Next the sword fell. But it was a hundred swords, which dashed like rain. Their blows smote the Knights of God beneath, insubstantial, potent.

And the seventeenth Knight, he endured also the swords of Heaven. *He has learned better alchemy. These are a mage's tricks.*

The swords were done, and through the door of the moon came the figure of the sword doll.

'Say now, brethren, why is it that you gather here?'

The Factor glanced, under his lids. It must be Anjelen to speak the first responses.

Anjelen, in his extraordinary voice, which thirty years of training would not have made, which only God could have articulated and tuned to construct this music, said: 'We are here for our faith.'

The Factor, once a seasoned campaigner of these rituals, at Chirkess and in more mediocre circumstances, and more illustrious, was used to the fluffing or forgetting of the lines, the stammers and inadequacies.

When Anjelen said nothing else, he was offended, deeply and horribly, thinking for a moment that Anjelen had fumbled, and failed.

Then, he saw, from the bearing of Anjelen, that nothing had been mishandled. It was Anjelen's formula to say no more. These words were all there were, now, to be.

And ordered up by them, out of the customary rhythm but obedient, the doll of the sword withdrew into its wall.

The Factor flicked his gaze now along the attending Knights. They stood as they must according to writ, as if in the eye of battle, straight and speechless. Their eyes were glazed from the incense, as they willed themselves into a trance. He could remember that, the forcing wish for some rare thing, which had never come.

But now the curtain was rising up over the door of the sun.

The Factor let his eyes travel once more, and watching the door, saw then come out of it not the doll that bore the cup of the wine – no, nothing like that.

From the door of the sun slowly walked a figure, human, male, unmasked, naked white but for a linen loincloth, and on its head a garland if ivy and briar from the winter woods. Not a boy, but a young man. Black hair and eyes like black agate. And the whiteness not solely colour, but power.

The Factor, who was also God's warrior, directed his sight like a dagger through the circle of Knights. Anjelen was there, shorn and mailed. Yet, too, Anjelen came slowly over the golden tracery in the floor, mostly naked, a stream of hair like a mane across his shoulders.

Much better alchemy.

He found the evaluating words in his brain, and shook, the Factor in his ardour.

But the Chalice – where was that?

The hands of the figure, the second Anjelen, were empty. He was the sacrifice, equipped only for eternity.

Anjelen spoke again. The voice came as before from the mailed body in the circle, while the other approached across the paving.

'And he gave them the wine, saying, Drink, for this is my blood. Hereafter do this always in my name.'

The lids of the eyes of Anjelen the Knight were nearly lowered, and beneath was only blackness. There was no white to the eyeballs. Two slots like night in water.

The Factor trembled, and held himself alert for any flaw. But the perfection of the almost-naked man had moved into the circle. He had lifted up his palms, which were full of scarlet from the wounds of the nails. He went to each of the Knights in turn (missing only one, his double), and gave them to drink from the chalice of his hands.

And the Factor waited, shaking, but in control of himself, his intellect poised to receive or to rescind.

Each Knight drank the wine. The chalice was before the Factor. Like the rest, the Factor did nothing but lean forward to drink. As he did so, he scented the body of the creature, the holy odour of arboreal things, not mortal, not flesh. The blood lay like a jewel, and as his lips hung on the moisture of it, strange fire began. Abstemious, he did no more than touch to the fire his tongue. Not meaty or salt, not *blood*. Not blood or wine, but the spirit of God transmuted through the intermediary vessel. A red rose flowered behind the eyes. The petals unfolding and unfolding like waves or wings.

The ceremony was over. The creature that was of God, or was God, had gone away like the mechanisms. The Knights stood in their circle.

The Factor, having opened his eyes, beheld the rose of blood unfolding away into the face of Anjelen, and the eyes that had no whites were altered now, passing for human.

'What have you witnessed?' said Anjelen.

The Factor replied, 'You are more than I supposed.'

So, in some concealed sort of reverie, he had long planned that he would confront his Lord. Rational always, this man, for the Factor adored the logic and the intellectual soul of his religion. It was this he worshipped in the person of God, and took for God. The Christus of the Factor had, of necessity, been a prince, having for speech oratory and wit, having a weapon as a mind, beauty for a voice, an unblemished frame in which Godhead had poured itself – these were essentials of the God-in-man. God could not be shown forth in any other caste. Nor should God, returned to men, be greeted by rude outcry, exclamation, gross silliness. In calm reverence the Factor knelt to the lightning flash.

'I have given you the Blood of the Life,' said Anjelen. 'And in recompense, I ask the same.'

Each of the others, these spellbound warriors, they had offered back the gift, in this chamber, in some chapel, cell, some ruined tower, somewhere.

'Take what you will from me,' said the Factor, 'Lord.'

There was after all no one else in the chamber. It seemed not any longer a place of stone, but the vault of a tree, veined and ribbed, with beasts that looked with eyes of topaz and obsidian out of its galleries. Above were branches of stars in a neutral sky, not day or night.

Anjelen was with him, inside the tree. Anjelen struck the man's throat lightly and from it a fountain sprang. Painless, sure.

The Factor sat reasoning in his brain, savouring the ecstasy of the rite, praying deliberately and serenely to God. Thanking God for the salvation of mankind, for the promise fulfilled. And all around, the shadows watched as Anjelen drew the Factor upward, weightless like a child of two years, until the brim of the Factor's severed throat came to his lips. Anjelen drank the blood. And it was dark in the chamber, like the wood, black as the forest, under the trees.

The Magister, Egar, could only half recall, at the start of it, how he had prayed lovingly, earnestly to God, to melt away the frost from his eyes. But the methods of God were pitiless in their purity. The blindness came on, as the deafness did, gentle as breath in sleep. He must endure. Egar, by his own mathematics, measured his decline. A few months more, and they would have to lead him by the hand. A year, and only the highest notes of the singing, the twitter of the birds, the rasp of a file in the forge, would reach him. He was being walled up alive. Yet, still he trusted God. The teacher was stern, He beat and upbraided you, to bring you to the ultimate knowledge. As a tutor, Egar had modelled himself upon God. The side of his tongue was slicing as the whip, but he expended punishment only on those worthy of it, the bright pupil who had grown lazy or inept, the fanatic who was careless.

In Anjelen, when Anjelen had come to be, Egar had not perceived any kind of son. This cliché was wrung from him in the vicinity of the Factor, like a cry of hurt striving for speech. Anjelen was like the last light, before the night fell down. In him, Egar achieved a résurgence of faith, his trust shored up. For God had sent Anjelen to take up the torch of understanding. Egar showered the gold of his science upon Anjelen. *I don't matter. Truth matters. Here the vehicle is. I need not be afraid, for there is justice.*

Egar crouched now, out of custom, over his bench, with a book open before him and the utensils scattered about. He could see them dimly, even the letters written on the page, though not their meaning any more. He liked to touch these things, the lembics and pestles, the silken half-skull of a man which was the reminder of mortality, but also an object of miracle in its exact structure, one other proof of the genius of the Creator – as was the foetus of the dog inside its tube of crystal, the rock with the imprint of an animal old as the earth. He liked to touch, and now he must see by touch. He ran his fingers over contours, but he recollected the smell of blood in the cup.

The Factor had not spoken to him of the ceremony. As usual, the Factor stalked about the precincts, occupied by Church business. He had taken to wearing a high collar against the cold, a recent affectation among the Knights of God, as if to rival the red waist cord of the alchemists' school. Egar had not been able to discern the collar, but he had heard it remarked on.

Anjelen had charge of the mysteries of the alchemical ritual of the Knights' gathering. He alone would in future order them, conducting them from the chamber above, which Egar would have thought was not feasible. The Factor and the Administer had both condoned this new regime, Egar being disabled and doddery. Dismissed from his role, he would have no excuse to ascertain if the Chalice was again returned bloodied – or empty.

Thus, he knew it all. That evil had taken root, spread its leaves, grew up and pushed against the roof. The Cathedral was filling, day by day, with its spicy, pleasing perfume. Every pillar and brick was bound with tendrils. There was no defence.

No knock, loud for his deafness, drummed on the door. No step or rustle of a male robe could be audible to Egar. Nor had any shutter of light and dark teased at the remnant of his vision.

Yet he was aware at once, as in the corridors, in the dining hall, the cloister, alone or among others, that Anjelen was here and that the Devil, therefore, had come into his room with him.

Egar stayed still, one hand on the skull of man, the other over the emerald crucifix on his breast.

'You honour me,' said Egar. 'For what inconceivable reason do you need to visit me here?'

'You,' said Anjelen, 'are my tutor, Magister.'

The voice penetrated unhindered, as no other sound ever would again.

'No longer a tutor to any. Egar's found wanting. He has no work.'

Anjelen began to be visible, and for a second Egar wondered, in a corrupt hope, if he might see him fully and clearly, as he had heard him, the form, like the voice, of the Devil, burning through. But Anjelen was a shadow, only darkness, a pillar of smoke.

'I taught you the great science,' said Egar. 'But you didn't need my little lessons.'

'Yes,' said Anjelen, 'to give a name to what I do.'

Egar said, dismayed to be inflamed by this dialogue in Hell, 'Of course. If men can say, There is an alchemist, there is a magician, they miss the other name. But you were, for such a mighty one, curiously bungling over the blood.'

The shadow shifted, it drew nearer. It did not answer. Egar thought in sudden despair that after all, the cup had not been Anjelen's negligence. It was only that it did not concern Anjelen. He might do as he wished, suborn, destroy, hypnotize, anything, as he wanted. And even if he did not, where he hid himself and took trouble, as in the learning of alchemy, it was merely for convenience, a notion maybe, an alternative process of moving forward. Never, even in his meditations on God, had Egar glimpsed a supremacy like this. But then, he had never been this close, to God.

Then Anjelen pressed one hand on the forehead of the Magister.

The contact was momentary, cold and quick, and gone.

As it departed, it took all the rest. The room vanished. There was a greyness, but without colour, without even the vaguest blur of configuration, no depth, no brightness, no shade. In Egar's ears, two doors had swung shut.

He was within, closed inside the walls of his own head. Under his hand, the skull felt farther than a star. He could not believe in it. He let it go.

No fire of terror broke in Egar. He stayed. He searched for God, knowing that this ordeal was as random as anything Anjelen was prone to award, that he, Egar, had no special claim on the mercy of Heaven. Closed within the tower of blindness and unhearing, the sin of the seeing and listening Cathedral could not infect him. A blessing?

No terror, and yet, after an hour, a frightening childlike thing, which said, *How long? How long?*

'Deliver me,' said Egar, feeling the vibration of his voice.

Soon someone would come, after the prayers, or dinner, and see what had happened to him. He would say nothing of Anjelen, even supposing he could will himself to be intelligible with only the vibrations of his throat to guide him. And soon too this corpse body would dismiss him. That must now be certain.

Or would he live on, healthy for a decade or more, kindly led, impatiently spared, like a man with a boulder clasped on his head, his ears and his eyes changed to stone, sniffing about in the nothingness for the odour of the Wicked One? Egar gripped his hands together, held himself in the trap, and waited, waited, waited.

Chapter Six

Winter was Chirkess.

The alleys, hovels, houses, were made of snow, with black abrasions of mud before the doors. The smoke composed a cloud that seldom lifted. The river prepared to freeze.

On its terraces the Cathedral seemed bewitched. Was it possible to enter the gates? The gatherers of sticks and dung who wandered the streets glanced up without response at the mansion of God. It had not yet got to the stage of pleading for bread.

Unlike the city, the Cathedral garden had kept its cadences, paths freed of snow, laid in white squares, tented with white trees.

To Wedsek, it seemed he had walked in this way, a pace behind Anjelen, for miles, for weeks.

Anjelen appeared to tell his beads. Appeared? Doubtless he did so. About the garden elsewhere, the black figures perambulated. The pink winter sun shone on them, and slicked upon rounds of enamels, eyes.

They had reached the statue of a saint burdened by snow. Anjelen paused. He looked about him, and all the black figures in the garden stirred like reeds brushed by a current in water. So it was when he advanced through the building. None dropped to his knees, obeised himself; the Administer received Anjelen's bow. Yet, they were Anjelen's. His priesthood, his warriors, his disciples.

I have drunk his blood. He has had mine.

A shameful glory, like a blush, until the skeleton of Wedsek seemed to catch alight.

He might do anything.

Wedsek would follow Anjelen, to Hell or out of Hell. Whatever Anjelen was – Son of God, Son of Night. It had never come clear which.

Anjelen stood by the statue, and Wedsek murmured, 'Well, then.'

Anjelen's eyes moved over him.

'I mean,' said Wedsek, 'tell me, what would you have?'

Anjelen said, 'I have it.'

'What is your mission?' said Wedsek.

Anjelen told his beads. They slipped like a dark snake through his long fingers.

'What,' said Wedsek, 'is there for me to do?'

In various ciphers, this phrase had been now and then placed before Anjelen. Replies sometimes were elicited, but they had had no substance.

'It stands still,' said Wedsek. 'Like the winter. Is it just that? What are you waiting for, my lord?' And he said again, with iron passion, 'My *lord*.'

Anjelen did not speak.

'I ask only what you have in mind – the future – a month away, a year. But what is it?'

Magister Hyrus came through the garden on his route to the Cathedral offices. (Egar had become decrepit and was no longer seen.) The Magister did not acknowledge Anjelen, and yet the very garments on his body seemed to make deference. It was the will of Anjelen that nothing be overt.

Wedsek balanced on the edge of the unnameable, and questioned it. The return must come, the whirlwind, the silent voice: Where, then, were you when I laid the foundations of time, gathered up the seas and lit the singing stars of the morning all together.

But Anjelen now gave nothing.

The snake of beads coiled through his hands, and behind him a slender tree, powdered white, made the same ebbing motion at a coil of wind.

'The lord in the city's churlish,' said Wedsek. 'Some bother over alms. Anjelen,' said Wedsek.

The Christus had drawn men to Him, from their work, their boats, their families, out of living into Life. *Do this, for me.* They wandered like young wolves over the land.

Even a reprimand might serve, to solace this inquiry.

'Anjelen, we're *brothers in blood—*'

A finger fell on Wedsek's wrist. He started at it. The bush at his elbow, clothed with snow and motivated too by the wind, it was this which had caught hold of him. And the white tree moved again. But Anjelen did nothing at all.

There was a moment of perceptiveness for Wedsek. He beheld, by means of some magic glass of basic human sense, the inner room of Anjelen's consciousness. Wedsek could not have said what he saw there. He recoiled at it. It was instinct which told him how and where to see, and instinct which blotted out every iota of the view. The tree grew, it ascended. It needed no more. It *was.* And the magnificent and blazing brain lay around it like a dragon to guard, to burnish, helpful and, finally, superfluous.

The white tree quivered and the bush tapped Wedsek's arm. Anjelen was still, not even the beads sifting over his hand.

Wedsek knew himself orphaned, and did not know why or from what. Nothing had happened.

Twelve white Knights rode through the city, after the bread carts. The provisions were sent unasked, on a freezing noon under sky like lead and swagged with new snow. The Overlord had been heard, in a peevish fit, to say it was his employment to supply viands; the Cathedral had its own work. The Cathedral, then, preempted him.

There was a different tone to this. It was militant. And the Knights in their mail, beings rumoured of and partly mythical, looking as if they had leapt down fully armed from the Cathedral's cornices and columns and the warlike window; they stoppered every protest. The Cathedral guard, with the red buttons on their helms, might have

452

attended the carts, and indeed did so, sitting by on their horses in the slush and ice as the godbrothers and novices dealt out loaves. The Knights rode up and down, princely and obdurate.

Along by the river, the Overlord glared from a window, and saw it going on in the square below the Cathedral. He reportedly inquired who and what were the Knights. On being informed, he denied that this brotherhood, these priest-warriors, were ever seen; it was an act of faith with them to remain invisible, and to conceal their ceremonies.

But black and steel and white, the Knights were there, and behind the vizors were the half-faces of remote and devout men encountered elsewhere in the capacity of religion, or of the priestly hunters who rode through the city too fast to gain recognition. The hunting had been blatant enough. The Overlord chafed, but his wife was giving birth in another room. She might die. Priests were always necessary.

The captain of the troop was Wedsek; he had been given this position five days before. Soon Anjelen was to be created a Magister. The winter went on and on, and the unloading of loaves was like the winter. But constantly Wedsek felt a vital spring within himself, at his own image in the mail, the way in which his men took his orders – inconsequential, of no importance, yet redolent of war for all that. Say, the city had been besieged, and they had come off the ramparts to feed it . . . *God give me battles*.

Wedsek rode back and forth along the carts. The people of the city had stared, and fresh ones arrived all the time and gawped in their turn. Wedsek absorbed their curiosity and slight fear; the faces meant nothing, their gender or sort. Until, in the tail of sight, Wedsek beheld Anjelen, on the snowy street, at an alley's corner, gazing with the rest.

Of course, it was not Anjelen. This Wedsek knew even as he glimpsed the apparition. Something in Wedsek knew a great deal, and tried continually to tell him the facts, but Wedsek, as most men grow to be, was fast at avoidance. He looked, and saw a young man, perhaps sixteen or seventeen years – Anjelen himself, though he must be past his twenty – first year, looked not much older (save in the eyes, the eyes). It was the eyes, oddly, of the boy on the street which were Anjelen. Not the core of them, not the expression or intensity, the (misleading) profundity of mind and thought. But the shape and line of the brows, perhaps the extreme blackness of the irises – that might only be a trick of the darkling day.

Wedsek did not consider. He saw the boy, who was Anjelen humanized and adjacent. Wedsek reacted.

'You,' he said. The boy froze like the river, and Wedsek rode over to him. 'Have you had your share of bread?'

The boy looked nearly frightened, yet he kept his dignity. He was some labourer, by his dress: a leather apron over rough and partly threadbare clothes.

'My mamma will have got it, sir. My dad's gone. She's collect for us.'

Wedsek disliked the boy's babyish use of *mamma*, frequent enough among the lower pockets of town and city, and in the back woods.

'Why then are you standing gaping?' said Wedsek.

'I never saw Knights before. Knights of God. My grandda said, was a lie. You never see them.'

'But now you have,' said Wedsek. He laughed suddenly, pleased and disgusted at the conversation. The likeness of Anjelen came and went like a ghost. When he could catch it, Wedsek was quick to disarm and unnerve it, and shocked as he did so – and then the mirage faded off like steam, and he thought, *What am I doing here with this?*

The boy lowered his eyes. When he did that, the resemblance to Anjelen was piercing. But it was an Anjelen fourteen years of age, before the massy power had set on him like stone.

Wedsek thought: *His family may starve. This one fellow to support them all, probably.*

'What work do you do, boy?'

'On the wall,' said the boy, proud of his trade, which

would be that of apprentice still to some mason or block-layer.

'Don't they feed you?'

'Soup,' said the boy. 'Glad to get it.'

'And your house?' Wedsek did not know why he asked.

'Over by the wharf inn. I'm Larl.' Alert now, hoping for attention. It would do no harm to be neighbourly with a Knight of God.

'Get along,' said Wedsek. 'Don't neglect your work, or your mother. Remember God.'

The boy's face sank inward. He was not Anjelen.

Wedsek, sitting the horse, face of steel vizor, steely lips and jaw, watched him go off.

For some while, Knights of God were seen about the city of Chirkess. They rode by on fine horses, as the hunting priests had done. Their arms were carried with authority.

The show had been made, the largess distributed. The Overlord had ceased his whining. His child, a boy, was delivered safely, and in his letters here and there he made no mention, that his priestly secretaries noted, of any annoyance or untoward matter.

Then, once or twice, God's Knights were seen after sunset, on the broader streets, the flash of mail under a torch, the snow-white tunic with its cross-cut of black. Faces masked by metal.

The Cathedral must have ordered it. It made the robbers and low-life uneasy, and if the whores slipped away like mice, you would find them in their usual underground haunts, the taverns and hovel alleys.

Let God's Knights patrol Chirkess if they liked. The winter was hard. On and on. Soon, there might be more bread.

Nights no longer made for sleep. For the priest, in any case, there never was much slumbering: the midnight praying, the prayers in the black early hours of morning, interruptions to nature that became habitual. Between midnight then and the first devotion of morning, the

455

Knights of God rode about Chirkess. Not all; not all were inclined to it. The insubstantial order that had sent them out, attendant on the bread carts, had evaporated. Yet no further order came to draw them in again. They were like pale eagles, not easily mewed.

There had been a gathering of the Knights. Anjelen did not preside over it, but was merely a player. The rite was bizarre in its meekness. Not one of them spoke of this, as they had never discussed the Rite of Blood, like a dream or vision, which occurred before.

Now three Knights were in the square below the Cathedral, riding lightly with a soft noise on the snow, and the faint jingle of harness and of three swords in sheaths of silver and hide, like the thin white wind that blew weightlessly along the ground. From the river came a weird hollow sound of emptiness, as if from a huge and unrung waiting bell.

Towards the mouth of this the Knights rode. They had drunk the Wine of the Sacrifice (bitter vinegar), and real wine they had brought with them from the refectory, for, along with their exercise and horses and hunts, red meat and strong liquor were permitted them.

'The Factor,' said one of the mailed men, low, under the windows of Chirkess, 'didn't vouchsafe his company, tonight.'

So, one of them had alluded to it after all.

'He has a chill,' said Wedsek. He had not heard any report of that; in some obscure way he was protecting the night from extraneous things.

'He'll return, our Factor, when Anjelen—'

Unstayed, the man did not finish. They halted beneath an archway, heavy with its cap of snow. Everywhere the city lay smothered. In parts a dull glow from some fire of rag-pickers under a wall, or the individual tinted smokes curled up from holes and chimneys, and from two taverns with an orange window apiece. In the house of the Overlord were tall lights, and a sentry walked along the roof, his own armament chinking. The wharves and the one ship moored there, ice-locked, with a greenish lamp at her prow. But mostly the scribbles of white darkness and the nullity of fools who slept.

'The wine tonight,' said Wedsek, 'it failed us.'

They sat the horses.

The man who had spoken before, Riazi, said, 'But it was the best the kitchen had.'

Wedsek said, 'The *wine*.'

In the slough of snow city and night, they had made a circle of three. Their faces under the vizored helms were alien, each to each. It was in the manner of the south tower, after the curtain of the heron door fell down.

'What's your meaning?' said the third Knight. He was a man from a nowhere place, a town beyond Chirkess. He had been bought all his stations, would be a Factor in a brace of years, was a Knight almost by default. Yet, he too, he too under the vizor and the dark, made up the circle.

'It's given to us,' said Wedsek, hearing himself, half amazed, and not able to stop, 'to act the rite to its utmost. We're beyond ordinary law. We're God's. And he instructed us.'

'Anjelen,' said Riazi, again.

'Do this in my name.'

'And after, in rememberance.'

An excitement, cold and hard, an icicle slanting upward from their circle of power, a white and glistening sword of urgent and willing *want*.

'He gives us his jurisdiction. It's the way of it.'

Wedsek felt the trembling in his body. It surprised him a little. He had not yet caught up with himself.

'Our blood,' said Riazi, 'is it capable of translation into the wine – without Anjelen?'

'Not our blood. To him, we give. To the king and lord. Without withholding. But for ourselves, as he does, we'll take.'

Their eyes glittered. The real meaningless wine of the kitchen had gone up into their skulls like sorcery. They trembled also, Wedsek saw. They were with him. Anjelen had united them, his disciples. The train of events opened here, the fabric of everyday life torn on a wild light. Go through, be proven in this war. For the enemy within had shown himself now. He was prudence, human edict, the codes of a priesthood outgrown, for a king might rearrange his kingdom how he chose. Perhaps Anjelen had waited on them, as they on him. *Do this in my name.*

Do this—

'I know one who's intended for us,' said Wedsek. A deep insensate thrill went through him, at the rightness of it, and because they were of a mind with him, these men. Not one, but a triple being, and he its head.

They rode into the bell of the shore, where there were the wharves and the ship. The garrison loomed downriver.

They came into a space between the houses, with one end open to the sheet of the river ice. A stooping inn, closed, unlit. A torch-pole smouldered in front of it, and a house leaned there, one room and some cranny above under a tumbling roof. Smoke from the chimney. Outside, a water butt, and a workman's mallet left by it, too battered and worthless for anyone to steal.

Wedsek halted, and the other men, Riazi and the bought Knight, did the same. They had not exchanged further words.

Wedsek dismounted, and walked to the door of the hovel by the inn. Round about, nothing moved, nothing looked out, not even a rat from the winter refuse. But he was masked, what could any see? He knocked lightly on the door, a familiar note, not threatening. And a woman's voice called quietly, 'Is that you?' 'No,' said Wedsek. (Then she gasped.) 'Send out Larl.'

There was a nothing. Next a flurry. She said, 'Why? What do you—' and he said, 'Don't come to the door. Send Larl. Hasten.'

From the back of the room Larl said, 'What is it, mamma?'

Wedsek called quietly, 'Larl, come out.'

'It's the old fellow,' muttered Larl, meaning perhaps some overseer off the wall.

The boy drew the bolt and put his head round the door, and beheld the Knight of God, one of three, on his sill.

'You must come with us,' said Wedsek.

'I haven't done anything,' said Larl, frightened now and not dignified. 'I haven't – who's said I did? Didn't. I never.'

'Dress yourself, and come out,' said Wedsek, 'or we'll take you as you are, in your shirt.'

'I'm not guilty of it.'

'On God's business. Do you resist?'

'No,' said Larl. He came out, and he was already dressed in everything but the leather apron, a coarse blanket round his shoulders. He had been sleeping by the fire, for he was warm, and there was soot on his cheek. He looked not at all like Anjelen, and then, very like him.

The mother was flapping inside the door, trying to get out too and see. Wedsek said, 'Go in, woman. Do as you're told.'

Larl walked before Wedsek to his horse. The door had shut. Alone with the Knights on the snow, Larl withered. He began to cry. Probably he had blasphemed God at his wall-building, or else committed some theft or lechery. He reckoned he was to be punished, not honoured. Wedsek touched Larl on the shoulder. 'Calm yourself. You're chosen. Special to God. Get on the horse.'

When Wedsek had got Larl lumpenly on the beast's back, he led the horse away between the houses. The new wall (Larl's wall), was far from finished yet; there were a hundred ways out, through the alleys and along the river bank, over the fields and into the groves of apple trees and the deathly vineyards.

The excitement was as cold as the night. It beat in the breast like a hammer.

They avoided areas of fire or activity. They passed one live and mobile thing, some wretch scurrying between the house-backs, who glanced, and went away the faster. There was no moon, only deep shadows and the patched whiteness of ice and snow and stars.

*

A ruined and deserted mill, a pool like a tear wept out of the river, and of varying thicknesses of ice, presumably having been broken for water on the previous day. Tall, blackened reeds standing like sticks of decayed sugar, like bars.

They gave the boy from the city some of the kitchen wine, and it cheered him up.

The Knights smiled and nodded, also drinking from the flagon. Wedsek laughed with Larl. But Wedsek felt no laughter. His whole body was primed and shining, sparks darted along his veins as he gestured, walked, breathed, sometimes startling him, but only with pleasure, like the first drunkenness he had ever known.

Riazi brought a wreath of ivy from the mill. He put it on Larl's head, and there before them, still laughing and cheered, they began to see the sacrifice, clad in a workman's clothes and blanket. The clothes did not matter. Only the final clothing, the skin, must be stripped to bring forth the naked blood.

Wedsek said to Larl, 'What we do now is sacred. Never speak of it. On pain of the severest penalty. Do you understand?'

Larl nodded. The garland had sobered him, cold from the snow.

'Swear,' said Riazi. 'On God's name.'

The boy swore. His eyes were like a child's. He was not Anjelen.

Yet, Anjelen was there. Wedsek felt the face of Anjelen covering his own like the vizor.

They made the circle, not speaking the secret words. In the mind of each the phrases flowed by, and, ready, they turned to the garlanded youth at the circle's centre.

Wedsek took hold of the boy, and with the sharp knife, cut open his hand, between the palm and the wrist. Larl uttered an animal cry. Wedsek held him. 'You must keep faith. You swore.' Larl gave in, submitting to Wedsek as Wedsek had submitted.

And Wedsek took Larl to Riazi, and lifted up the ruby hand that was jet in the starlight.

'Drink, for this is his blood.'

Riazi bent his head, and sucked blood out of the hand. Then Wedsek propelled Larl to the third Knight, the outdweller, who also lowered his helmed head, and swallowed the blood.

Wedsek pulled the boy around. The night was burning with a fierce pale flame. Wedsek strained Larl up his body, over the mail. He saw that Larl had fainted, from cold, shock, or strong drink. Wedsek grinned, but it was not a grin. He sank his teeth into the little wound, and bit the blood up from it, gulping, thirsty, and it was the Wine. He had made it so. The Wine of God.

When he could make himself stop, Wedsek found he was loaded with weakness, and putting down the boy on the ground, he shook violently. He wiped his mouth and cleaned his hands in the snow, and the cold ached through him, into the pit of his skull, his feet and loins.

They used the snow too to stop the bleeding. Bound up the hand with the boy's own rags.

They were like naughty urchins now, earnest to end the prank, cover up and be off.

The third Knight – Wedsek had forgotten his name – wanted to leave Larl by the mill.

'He'll live. He'll find his own road back.'

But they hauled him as far as the new wall, threw him flat, and spilled liquor on him there. He was reviving, whimpering.

'Recall your oath, or it's death,' said the third Knight.

Larl nodded.

They left him in the shelter of a hut and rode through Chirkess, wanting to get away from each other also. Near the Cathedral, Wedsek spoke. 'We too were bonded. Don't talk of this. Don't *regret* this.'

'You had his blood like a wolf,' said Riazi.

Wedsek stared him down, and the eyes of Riazi shrank back into the vizor-slits. They would have to see each other again at the morning devotion.

'Blood is life,' said Wedsek. 'Only Anjelen can judge me.'

He thought: *Anjelen will know. No need to tell him. And God too. There's nothing to confess.*

Winter waited in Chirkess, lay there like a white beast, on its belly, brooding.

Men moved about like ants on a marble slab.

The snow turned gradually beige, and muddy, and nothing rebuilt it.

There was a bare blue sky, and the snow soaked into the earth, and there were white flowers, paler than the eyelids of the dead.

As the snow melted and the sky returned, on that day, almost spring, five old women going down for the fish beyond the garrison wharf found a body among the jumbled stones of the new wall.

The snow had kept it. It's eyes were open. Male brown hair straggled like weed where the asphodel was trying to come back. The boy was some fifteen years of age, clad as a rag-picker, in rags. There was a delicate gouge on his throat, and he had been let blood. Killed in some brawl, poor thing. The women clucked over him. There were fights and murders in any city. There had been two or three like this during the winter, all young men.

They left the body alone, only diverting to it a garrison soldier who came to ask their business with the fishermen.

It was the bought Knight who had begun the second phase. This man – nameless to Wedsek, who could never recall his name, had never heard him addressed by it only by the title of *Knight*, or *Godbrother*, while the man seemed to assume always Wedsek had memorized his name, and Wedsek did not correct him – he it was who, after the first time, had sought Wedsek in the cloister, both of them habited in the black of their order of humble brothers. 'When is it to be again?' 'When what?' said Wedsek, scared as a child, for once the fit had worn off, like all drunkenness, it left him compromised by self-doubt and reproaches. 'After the next gathering, do you want to do it then?' 'What happened with the boy—' started Wedsek.

The other broke in, 'It was you said *Blood is life*. And Anjelen has judged, hasn't he? When he keeps the rite it's a rite of blood, and otherwise milk and water, old men's mumblings. Do you see the Factor there?'

Wedsek said, 'What we did that night—'

'Was *good*. Was in the order of things,' said the bought Knight. He was hoarse with his purpose. He, plainly, had not believed any wrong done or danger enticed. He felt no shamed embarrassment at the memory of the labourer left against the wall. It was the bought Knight indeed who had declared Larl might be abandoned at the mill.

Wedsek resisted. But nights after, he rode by and saw the quiet uncomplaining smoke going up from the chimney of the house by the wharf inn. The mallet did not lean there, but neither was there any sign of distress. Everything was well. Larl had recovered, had not made an outcry. Perhaps he even boasted of the event in his heart, that he was chosen. Or else he had been terrified, as a man is who confronts a demon on the work of its master, the Devil. Which? That was the question for all of it.

But Wedsek's conscience grew slovenly. He calmed and thought of what had been done, not with the elation of the hour or the unease of the aftermath, but objectively.

The bought Knight did not nag on at him, pawing and whining. He treated Wedsek respectfully and distantly. Whereas Riazi avoided Wedsek, and Wedsek wondered for some weeks what had been confessed, there. For Riazi might have come to look on their act of blood as a crime, mistaking—

Mistaking, for it had not been a crime, a foul deed. It was an expression of worship, just as they kneeled, as they toiled, as they read from the Book, fasted and chastised themselves. Like that, but more.

When the gathering of the Knights came again, after some time, the proper conjunction delaying itself, it was the milk-and-water ritual the bought Knight mentioned.

The dolls were wheeled out, and the Chalice with the sooty drink.

Anjelen, far away as a dark star. Anjelen was away from them all now. Alone. At prayer, at table, in the cloister, mailed in the upper chamber of the south tower.

And Wedsek did not approach Anjelen.

When the dry gathering was over, he nodded curtly at the nameless bought Knight.

They rode into the city. And by a tavern they found a drunken man of about twenty, who thought they were the Overlord's soldiers arresting him, when they dragged him from the barrel where he rested in his sot's daze.

They went to the ruined mill again, but to a different part of it, where trees came thickly down towards the water. They did not need to give the man wine, he had had enough. For themselves they had taken no drink but the one sacred sip in the tower.

'Not the palm of the hand,' said the bought nameless Knight.

'Where else?'

'Where it was done with you, and with me. With the holy Factor, too.'

'The neck? It might kill him.'

'We lived. We have only the little scar. The mark of the fellowship Anjelen made. The blood from the throat – richer. Close to the heart.'

This did not move Wedsek. His desire was of some other sort, but evidently the nameless Knight of God was thirsty; a heat came off him like the smell of fire.

Anjelen had employed magic, when he took the blood. The power of what he was.

The idiot of a drunk leaned on a tree, swaying and murmuring to himself, not truly aware of them any more.

Wedsek had dismounted. He drew his knife, and crossed to the man. Wedsek felt, strangely, a savage sorrow. He longed to console the drunkard. He did not bother to say that this was sacred, or secret. The boy whom he had briefly believed resembled Anjelen had somehow demanded that, and if he could, Wedsek would have been faithful also to him, selecting him again for this, and maybe – how curious – paying him when it was over. But then again, he had not wanted the boy to be involved a second time, had not really wanted the boy at all.

'Get on, do it, do it,' said the nameless Knight.

'You take my orders,' said Wedsek. 'You *wait*.'

Silence then. Only black icy crackling, soundless awful night, and the river washing by below, and the trees growing under the whiteness.

Wedsek had cut the side of the man's neck, a shallow quick cut from which the blood spurted. The man did not cry out, but he shouldered himself up against Wedsek, shuddering, making stupid worried moans. 'Hush. Hold steady.' Wedsek soothed him like a nervous horse. He beckoned the other Knight over impatiently. Again, they had not vocalized the ritual words. Had not even thought them through. But they had spoken them in the tower. The nameless Knight approached in a hurry, grabbed and sucked for the blood. It had already run down across Wedsek's hands. It was not hot, only warm. It repulsed him. He did not think he would take it. This was not the Rite of the Blood—

'You, you,' said the other Knight. 'It's good.'

Wedsek's gorge rose, and as he did so he lowered his head and put his lips into the blood. They were like vegetables, flowers, fleshy curving borders to his need. The blood filled his mouth. It was the Wine. Just as before. Perfect. And he knew then it could not be wrong, or rather that it could not be a mistake. This was meant.

When he had had enough, he dropped the man on the snow. Disgusted, uninvolved, he watched the nameless Knight kneel down to drink again, gobbling.

Wedsek leaned, and pulled him away.

'Leave it.'

The Knight sat back, accepting Wedsek's command.

The blood pushed from the neck vein, not easing. Despite some care, Wedsek had cut too deep.

He reached into his belt for the tinder. He struck flame.

'What are you doing – someone might see—' the nameless Knight, he was frightened now.

Wedsek stared into the face of his victim. The man was not unconscious, but horror had deprived him of everything else. Wedsek ran the yellow flame, which had given sudden white and red colours to all their faces, into the spout of the wound. The drunken man shut his eyes. He seemed to fall asleep. The wound turned black. It rusted down, and the blood stopped.

They ported him on Wedsek's horse back to the edge of the city. It was another freezing night, the snow packed down like rock. Probably he would not live, but they had not tried to take his life.

Two gatherings in the south tower fell close together in the space of a month.

Wedsek could not shake off his companion, the nameless Knight. This one's craving was obviously cannibalistic. He had performed extemporarily, and taken to the deed. It surprised him, but then he accepted it. He was a man who liked to please himself, hold nothing back, or off. He had none of the normal human appetites for sex or wealth, food or power. Wedsek distrusted and hated him, but they were, as he himself had said, bonded. Riazi meanwhile had revealed nothing.

They hunted. They found. In each case, the man died. The third victim was another drunk, convenient. He bled violently, and by the moment Wedsek kneeled to cauterize the wound it was too late. This appalled him, but alarm had no room for itself in his goings on as now they were. The fourth victim was a boy – thirteen, fourteen. He pleaded with them, never consenting. He spoilt it all. His blood stank and burned and only the cannibal enjoyed it. Wedsek came from him all doubt again.

None of the victims were discovered, so far as Wedsek heard or knew. Save one at winter's end. There was a raw rumour in the city's lower sinks. Priests were called on to exorcize a graveyard from which spectres erupted to rape the soul and suck the blood.

Hearing *that*, Wedsek felt a whirling panic to explain. Should he confess at last? He did not confess to any of it.

Nor did Riazi. Let alone the cannibal Knight without a name.

Then the conjunction fell again for a gathering and Anjelen was to have charge of the ritual, out of turn, but this might be blamed on a casting of lots.

In a sweating anticipation, Wedsek sought the nameless Knight, as never had either really sought the other, only coming on each other after the gatherings and setting off without a word.

'This will change things,' said Wedsek.

'For tonight.' The other Knight had no look of anything except maybe glee, a man glancing forwards to his supper.

Wedsek yearned to strike him.

'No more will I go out and do what we did.'

The Knight smiled. *Smiled*. 'Where's the harm? Some louts. The city doesn't miss them.'

'We won't speak of it,' said Wedsek. 'But I'm done with it. You can do as you want.'

The bought Knight frowned. He relied on Wedsek's partnership, the physical edge it had given them to be two not one, and the comfortable kinship, where neither could let down the other.

'How abruptly,' he said, 'your liver blanches. Do you want to cause me trouble?'

'It's forgotten,' said Wedsek. His skin stiffened with allergy. *I could kill him. But what then?* The bought one was numbered, not a miscellaneous lout of no merit. 'It seems to me we misinterpret. I need the guidance of Anjelen.'

'And do I?'

'You'll do as you want. I've said so.'

'Another order.'

Wedsek left him. He was in turmoil. He longed to go to Anjelen and kneel at his feet, pleading. He wished to stand there and declare the act of blood to Anjelen, boldly.

Anjelen came across the cloister in the shadow of evening.

Wedsek stood speechless, and attempted to read

467

Anjelen's face, but of course learned nothing. Then Anjelen spoke to him.

'The gathering tonight isn't for you. Absent yourself, Wedsek. If necessary feign illness.'

'Why?' Wedsek blurted. He saw eyes. There was nothing else. 'Why? What have you heard of me? I didn't—' and Wedsek recalled the first boy, the one who had seemed to have an appearance of Anjelen. *I haven't done anything – who's said I did?*.

Anjelen was already moving off. The decision was made, engraved in stone. *Absent yourself.*

Would it be admissible to disobey? What would happen – God knew, and only God.

The ground, where the green spring grass was coming up black in the dark, seemed gurning and roiling, trying to pull Wedsek down into Hell.

The other one – had he received such a warning? Had Anjelen gone to him, gone up to him, too, and demanded this?

A sweat poured from Wedsek, and his bowels pressed and quaked. In a kind of mindlessness, he stumbled out of one court of madness, to a second.

That night a man went to a tavern down beyond the wharves. This was not unusual, for though it was long past midnight, the tavern kept open until sunrise, and then would dilate itself again for business if any knocked urgently enough. It lay at the confluence of five alleys, and there was mud several feet deep, a swamp at the door, from the melted snow and the fecund, thawed spring river. The man, who arrived about two hours after the midnight bell from the Cathedral of Chirkess, wore dark clothing of fine cloth and cut, but nothing about it to render much information. He might have been a clerk or officer of accounts from the better end of the city. But he was tall and well-built for a penman. They thought they could see why he was slumming: he would want a woman, with which species the inn was reasonably stocked.

The girl nicknamed 'Flowers', the best one, the favourite, went up to the man about two-thirds of an hour after his entry. He had been drinking heavily and quickly, as if he hungered for something else. A fair sign.

'Good evening, sir.'

The man glanced at her. He had eyes like shiny brown wood, but the whites were reddening. He was in need. It was most obvious.

'Can I bring you more ale? He never serves the good liquor to strangers. I'll tap the nice barrel for you.' Such a ploy, agreed long ago with the innkeeper, often worked wonders.

'This will do.'

The man spoke indifferently. It was not the street voice of Chirkess.

'Well,' said Flowers, 'but I can sit down with you? It'll save me my feet.'

'Sit,' said the stranger, 'if you want.'

After a long hiatus, Flowers said softly, 'Are you sad? Your eyes are tired. I'm not prying—'

'But you'd help. In what way? On your back?'

Flowers perceived she had one wise in the etiquette of tavern girls, and so she had, for Wedsek Crel had known plenty of that tribe before his family and his delusions sent him to God.

After a while, he shared his cup with her, and noticed she was ready to drink the less good liquor. She was pretty, the most attractive of that sort he had seen. And he thought about it, how he had come out dressed in his hunting garments devoid of any significant mark, like a man unordained, owing no one anything, and now sat slurping ale with a whore.

Next she offered food. Poor fare: soup, bread – the inn was not splendid. Wedsek said, 'I'm fasting. It's a penance.'

'But your priest didn't mention the drink, eh?' she said. She giggled, and they were in a conspiracy together against the legions of God. 'Those godbrothers, they get fat for all their fasts and sore trials. They don't know how it is to be a proper man.'

'No?' he said.

'Or a woman, either.'

'They want you to give up your sinful actions,' he said.

'Oh,' she said, 'and starve. That's very well.'

'Like the women who followed the Christus,' said Wedsek. 'They came to him in scarlet, but he robed them again in white.'

'White like cold snow,' said Flowers.

Wedsek the priest looked carefully, thoroughly, at the girl. A few years ago, he would not have dared to do so. His manhood would have engorged even to sit so near, to smell her, her youth and spice. But now, the rigours and the disciplines had trained him. He was drunk, a little, and full of anguishes and angers, but he did not want her. He was almost sure that, even if he had made a foray on her willing body, his own would not have answered – in the flesh perhaps, but not in actual lasciviousness. He would have been able to possess her, but just as nimbly to resist.

She had light fawn hair, a wild bush of it, and eyes like black berries. Her breasts were to be seen through the dress. Even the small cross she wore of carved cedar drew the eye to them. He looked at her breasts, at the buds of the nipples. He imagined putting his hands over them, and a twinge, no more than an itch, crept through his groin, and was gone.

He had taken control of himself. Wedsek ruled Wedsek. He was in every sense a full man, and had formed himself to this calibre. And Anjelen thrust him off.

'The way you live,' said Wedsek to the girl called Flowers. 'How can it go on? Some disease, a childbirth, poverty inevitably when you lose your prettiness.'

'Am I pretty, then?'

'Have you no family? Couldn't you find other work?' He was recollecting, nostalgically, the girls of Khish, what befell them, and the old ones, unwanted, beggars at the age of twenty-five shedding their hair and teeth from ailments and malnutrition.

'But I like this work.'

He visualized, quite suddenly, changing her. He saw himself sent off from the brotherhood of the Knights, roaming like the wolf of God, bringing the lost lamb back into the fold, in his jaws. It was a joke, and he recognized it as such, and yet it got a hold on him. The ale was to blame. The only drink he had been granted.

'Do you say your prayers?' he said to her.

She smiled. 'Sometimes. Can you teach me how to pray so God will hear me?'

'Yes,' he said simply. He believed he could. He recalled the vision in his fever at Khish, and that God had selected him, and later Anjelen had done the same. It was essential to retain these facts. All was not over for Wedsek. Life had purpose and symmetry.

'You can teach me then,' she said. 'To pray. But we'll have to go up to a room; he won't stand for it here. I must seem to go with you. He'll beat me blue otherwise.'

Symmetry, purpose . . .

The room was no more than a cubby, but it had a door, though no window.

Wedsek was exactly aware that the girl supposed him to be playing some perverse game. That he wanted to humiliate her or pretend to pious magnanimity. She did not for an instant suspect that he was a priest, who might hear her confession, pardon her, advise her on the correct atonement, and put her forth like a new-born child, free into the world.

But she would starve, as she said, if she did not practise her trade, and the innkeeper below would beat her. No man would wed her now. Her other options were drudgeries as bad, though not profane.

'Have you never,' he said to her, 'seen me about the city?'

She looked sly a moment, wondering clearly if she had happened on a rich merchant, one of the Overlord's friends.

'I don't reckon that I have, sir. I'm sure I'd remember.'

'The Cathedral,' said Wedsek.

She appeared genuinely astounded. She did not think

him to be lying. Before she could say he was a guardsman or servant of the church, Wedsek shook his head.

'A priest,' he said. 'I'm on God's errand. He sent me here.'

'Oh,' she said, 'is that how you'd like us to do it?'

She was brazen, but under that, afraid.

Afraid because omnipotent truth had found her out, he the hunter, the wolf of God— He detected his own bewilderment, a snagging of the symmetry, but before he could pick at it, she said: 'No priest would come here. Do they even let them out at night? But, if you like . . . godbrother.'

'I am a Knight of God,' said Wedsek.

All at once, her slight fear became an antipathetic fright.

He saw through it, as if to a book of written words, dicipherable, having only one meaning.

She had heard some awful thing, in connection to the Knights of God. In a fashion the upper city had not, or did not care to, she had been privy to some incoherent garbled tale, of riders by night, and takings off, and blood – and blood.

Wedsek stood looking at the girl. Her skin was rosy from the hot, cramped room, the two fat candles burning, rosy with blood. The blood of women – it was unthinkable, unspeakable, and forbidden, that the lawless and unclean gore of women be associated with the flawless male blood of the Sacrifice.

'You don't want me,' said the girl.

'I'd like you to pray,' he said.

'No. I don't want to. You don't want me for what you ought to. He'll make a row downstairs. I have to go down to him—'

'You must not. Kneel here, and pray.'

'I have to go and see him.'

'You have to kneel with me here, and ask God for His forgiveness.'

'You can't make me.'

She sprang towards the door, but she had secured it,

472

snaring him, coming in. And as she fluttered at the bolt, Wedsek took her by the arms.

How extraordinary she smelled, of female skin and moistures, of long hair, and living sweet meat, and terror.

He had her. He pulled her against him. His arms were around her body. She was so heated she boiled against him like a cook pot. She struggled, and stopped, went limp.

'I'll do whatever you like,' she said, 'I won't tell. But be quick. He'll want me down—' She was lying desperately and not uncleverly. It might have fooled another man, but Wedsek did not want her for this, some corrupted and accursed coupling. He held her still in her boneless state, her hair over his lips.

'What prayers do you remember?'

She stammered, 'Forgive, forgive me, Lord, that I am fallen, fallen—'

He had his hand on her neck, did not know he had put it there, to feel the rush of her voice under his fingers.

'Don't don't,' she said.

He pressed her head back into his shoulder, and leaning over towards the vibration of her voice, a power gushed up in him, something he had forgotten, did not know, and that he altered, for the symmetry threaded into another mode. He had her flesh there by his mouth, and her hair, and then he tore through them, with the fangs of a wolf, to get at the red blood he had seen under her skin.

She attempted one scream. But her own life-fluid choked her before she could release it – the noise was like a sexual one, and fetched nobody, even if they heard it.

When she died, Wedsek never saw. He no longer saw her at all. He ripped at her, with teeth and hands, crushed her open like the white and pink carcass of a flower. As he did this, he drank from her. It was not the Wine. It was the *truth*.

What finished him was what normally would have done so. Orgasm unlocked the valves, his penis ejected its

473

spasms of agonized joy. Then, he came to himself, in the customary manner.

He found he was sinking down on remains, *remnants*, that were not now like anything human, brown leaves of dress and petals of skin, soiled in a sump of blood and semen, and he did not understand what he had done. It was as if a demon had claimed him in sleep and thrown him here. Wedsek slipped forward heavily into the mess of death and self-betrayal, fainting. What else was there left to do.

Near morning the man came up from downstairs to get back his best girl, the favourite, Flowers.

Unable to enter the room, he summoned assistance.

The door was broken down.

And there on view to all the occupants of the inn, lay unconscious Wedsek, and his deed, and the result of it.

Chapter Seven

Of the nature of the deed there were to be three versions. It was to be an act having the flesh of reality, but three souls, only one of which was spiritual.

After the rearrangement of the scene at the inn (the removal of bodies), during which the soldiers of the Overlord had presided, the priesthood came. There were seven black priests, including a legate sent by the Administer. Ten of the Cathedral guard sat their horses by the door.

Those at the inn – most of its present population – who had witnessed the upper room, were questioned. Having rendered their picture of the event, they were next told of what the event had actually been composed. This was not as they had thought. Yes, evidently an extreme butchery had taken place. A woman had been murdered. In the carnage lay a man from the Cathedral of Chirkess, already in the pandemonium identified. But perhaps not a priest; why had this conclusion been drawn? Nor could it be said that the man, lying senseless on a bed of ribboned skin and blood, was the author of the death. Why, also, should such a thing be deduced? Would the murderer not have fled at once? It was a fact there was no window to the room, but there were beings which could pass through walls. That was not to say, either, that the visitation of a demon should be presumed. However, the room was to be exorcized, just like the city graveyard.

Through the enactment of exorcism, a type of conclusion was laid down on the proceedings. All prior ideas

and theories were unsettled, and gradually began to dis-
lodge themselves.

After the exorcism, the room was boarded up, and
sealed with the sigil of the Cathedral at Chirkess, a long-
stemmed knot-cross guarded by a heron and an owl.

The body of a woman, shovelled in a box and covered
over – not much else could be done with it – was not
examined. The marks of what might have come to her
were to be identified from description, apparently. Her
employer at the inn must deal with the corpse. She was
a whore, for all his avowal of her other tasks. Prayers
would be said for her.

The unconscious body of the man, carted off by soldiers
of the Overlord, was prized back from them.

It was made plain that this dish was not for any earthly
table.

The man, whatever his rank in the Cathedral, was the
Cathedral's own. No secular law could touch him. Be
sure, the harshly righteous arm of Father Church would
spare nothing. God's justice outstripped for ever the petty
retribution of men. That, then, the popular soul of Wedsek's Deed.

For the Cathedral itself, the soul was this: breakage of
vows, disgrace, a brawl, untidy, unclarified. Woman, the
temptress, the apple of sex, the serpent of breasts and
hair who twined the Tree, she had worked her mischief.
If there was blood, it was immaterial. The act of horror
was unchastity, by which the door had opened upon the
galaxy of Hell. Demons rushed out. Demons lacerated
and rent. And there lay the priest, ruined.

Within the inner mechanism of the Cathedral at Chirkess, the soul became the ethic, the unseen cluster of
filaments, that knit up a stone chamber, lit by candles,
having high slitted windows showing only darkness,
almost square save for that outer windowed wall, which
curved with the shape of the south tower.

Externally the gargoyles in their helms and visors had
outstared the sinking sun. Inside the room, the men in
their black habits sat their wooden benches, with gargoyle

faces from a nightmare; for these were the faces of a foreign land whose language Wedsek did not know, whose customs he had not been lessoned in, and who hated him – worse, who cared nothing for him at all.

He was dead, but he stood there at the floor's centre, upright and aware, though not exactly of how he had arrived, who had conducted him. Even, for a moment, he had glanced about for the Administer – the Factor – could find neither. And for Anjelen. But how should Anjelen be in this gathering, this crowd of black crows masked in faces?

For himself, Wedsek did realize what he had done. He did not suppose himself possessed, or insane. He had fallen. From a huge height of self. It was so peculiar and unbelievable, so vividly obviously inescapable, that he was able to regard it all blankly. As if he had sheared off his right hand.

And he was dead.

He had accepted that too. Although he dreaded, childishly and irrationally, the instant when it would be spoken.

Magister Hyrus sat in a carved chair, across the floor. He did not look at Wedsek, but precisely through him, through his forehead.

'Among our brotherhood, there has been one. A man named Wedsek, absorbed into the benignity of God, living in the Fraterium at Chirkess, as our brother, in the holy and blessed ranks of the foremost servitors of the Lord.'

Wedsek stopped looking into the face of Magister Hyrus. Wedsek looked at the floor, where his own godbrother's habit, put on him an hour ago, met the booted feet of the mail he had had put on him a few minutes before the habit. This vaguely puzzled him, and his mind slipped off into some thicket of conjecture, before he drove it back to listen to the toneless voice of Hyrus.

'But the Devil will throw down any man. We must be always vigilant. There will come to us those that are wolves and vipers, clad like the gentle deer. From our hearts we must pluck out the poisoned root.'

477

The candlelight reflected in the floor, which had been laid with faded coloured tiles that did not matter.

'He is priest no longer,' said Hyrus. 'Strip him of that.'

And two men came at Wedsek from somewhere. He was unprepared for them, and though resistance was irrelevant, almost he did not object, but it was ineffectual anyway, the slight motions he made, the two or three half-expressed words.

They slashed the habit he wore, with little knives, trimly, and pulled it off him. He stood in the mail, then, yet disarmed, swordless, without the helm.

'Into the world he must go, but for him the world can be nothing. The world is God's. Fashioned by the Creator, like the Garden, for man. God is in all things. And for this one, who has been called Wedsek among us, there is no longer any God.'

Hyrus rose. Wedsek looked at him, not meaning to, into the bright flash of a sword. The sword was Wedsek's blade of Knighthood. Hyrus pointed it at him with the candles running gold along its steel.

'From this hour, there is no way for you to God. His eyes have closed to you, He does not see. His ears are stopped against your cries. Even the Christus, the Redeemer of men, cannot intercede. Though He grieves for you, though you are an agony sharper than the nails, the lance, the tearing of the thorns, yet He must let you depart into the desert of all-night.'

Wedsek flinched. The light of the sword flew off at him like drops of venom.

'Go out, and roam the wild places like the beast. Avoid the houses of God. Enter no church, kneel at no altar; it can avail you nothing. Wander the earth, until death, and then travel down into the dark, where the worm and the maggot shall have all of you. For, at the last, there is no trumpet and no song that can raise up you, the accursed of God. You are excommunicate. Your soul is dead.'

Curiously, the sentence, spoken, like the acceptance of what he had done, did not pain, cripple, drive mad. It was more a colossal blow, which stuns.

Two – perhaps the two who had cut away his priest's robe – had Wedsek's arms. Their grasp was inexorable. Not rough, but like some mighty engine, which pushed him from the room of stone, through an aperture of stone, some foyer or passage, and in, in at a door of the round chamber of the south tower, but wrongly, for there was no door save only the four curtained entries, and this some crack in the wall that could not be. And then the hidden door was shut, had ceased once more to exist. All that existed was the chamber of the gathering.

The Knights of God were already there, without him. He had come late, yet they had attended on it. They had been shown too where he would enter, for they faced him in the form of a horseshoe, he in its open end.

Wedsek did not count the Knights. Anjelen must be here, among them. But he would never learn. For they were cloaked in white, every man, and every man leaning on a drawn sword, and over every helmed head a white hood that fell below the lips. No face, only the holes of the eyes, edged in silver, through which they stared at him. Or, maybe, they did not stare, having no care for him, the dead man.

Above, the massive lamp, brass and gilt and bronze, angel, lion, bull and eagle. The lights flamed on it. And in their niches behind the pillars of fruits, the stone faces leered and snarled and howled, and the floor had tessellations, and at the centre its brass disc was crossed by black marble.

The clockwork in the floor operated abruptly, and Wedsek was jolted; almost he shouted. Up came the golden thing from the floor, and on it, a broken sword. If it was not Wedsek's sword of Knighthood, it was the symbol of it.

A voice, Hyrus' voice, repeated out of the air:

'Go out now. There is no other way for you. Roam the wild places like the beast. Travel down into the dark. Your soul is dead.'

The horseshoe of Knights parted. Perhaps they were

not men, but alchemical dolls, for they moved so exactly, smoothly.

Another door that did not exist had cracked open the further wall. It was between the crimson and gold curtains of the owl and the moon.

Wedsek did not move.

Conceivably, he did not move for more than the quarter of an hour. Time ceased. Nothing more was said to him. No gesture was made. The Knights of God stood in two white lines, white faceless faces of snow, silent.

There was nothing. No one to hear any cry. Not Hyrus, not Anjelen. Never, never God.

Wedsek finally began to walk across the chamber, skirting the broken sword, to the crack of door, into, and out of it.

Beyond, a faint glimmer of a lamp, a narrow twisted foul stair, like the course from a privy. Down this he went, for it was the only route.

At the bottom, a last door of wood, which gave at the mildest, most inadvertent contact.

Outside, astonishingly and inappositely, was only night, and the city. Was this Chirkess? It did not make much difference. It was a town of the earth that was God's as the ground was God's, the river and the trees, and all mankind. And he, Wedsek, a shadow that would wander there, unseen and immaterial. Dust.

The great pale ship, full-rigged as if with cloud, and every cloud striped with its black brand of the cross, clove down through the land. Where there was still ice, and here and there the wide river was rafted by it, the crew swarmed over, and made its way, with mallets, and with fires. By night, the cool spring moon shone through the sails. The dawn was stirred by oars, the mauve light in the water was broken. Birds rose, like prophets, announcing.

On either side of the river, islands of land, plains, valleys, hills, horizons of rock and mist, pushed at the sky. On the black, wet fields, the slaves and peasants stayed their work, to look. The overseers saluted the ship.

Women crossed themselves, and some kneeled down. Some brought their children to see. The ship was like a vision, lucky or fearful. It could be used as a date: that was the evening the Ship of God went sailing by.

There were villages, towns, cities. By night their rose-red windows, by day their markets and their quays, where all the craft teemed back, to let the great ship pass.

On the deck of the ship, the Factor stood, and the other, the one he had brought with him. The Factor pointed, but seldom spoke. He understood that he acted out the Devil's role, if with a difference, showing to his Lord all the cities and the kingdoms, demonstrating by such mighty, little things as the clasped children, the running fisher-boats, and the power that the ship represented, the omniscience of the Church. *All this can be yours*, said the women as they crossed themselves, and the sailors staring on the quays.

The ship herself had come from nowhere, on to the river at Chirkess, summoned like a vast whale from the deep of the sea.

It would be possible to reach the sea. It would be possible to hem along the land for weeks, showing, demonstrating, the people bowing low, and the earth itself, spreading and waiting under Heaven's sway.

But the man, the Man, what did he think? Were the kingdoms of the world of any use to him, this second time? He watched stilly. The Factor sensed the smallness of almighty power held up to view in the polish of those eyes.

'The Saviour was, and still may be, betrayed by one of the elect. On the perfect branch, one rotten purblind stem.'

The Factor was with Anjelen, standing in the well-furnished cabin.

'Nevertheless. I will go my own way, Factor.'

'Of course. How should I doubt it? I have shown you this, that you might see. But I'm yours to order as you wish.'

Anjelen had been made a Magister, at an age far junior to what was general, or recommended. In Anjelen's case, the general and the recommended were of no importance.

But the vileness of the dead priest, Wedsek, had besmirched them all, the beauty and sacred strength of the Rite of Blood. Anjelen had recoiled from it, not in any obvious or cited manner. It was visible through this declaration. Despite his station in the Church, he would take on himself a mission that fell to those godbrothers of the lowliest sort, that of the mobile priest, who toiled where he was sent, on the very road, ministering, admonishing, trackless and sometimes untraced.

'I can't gainsay your decision. However you must, thus will you accomplish your vocation. But I, and the Administer, as your officers, will see to it, my lord, that your path is swept and prepared for you. There'll be letters sent to the churches and religious communities. By any means you choose, you will be able to enter in, command, and receive every assistance. At the very least, there will be no chance that you yourself can be disobeyed. I don't imply by this,' the Factor added, 'that you would be incapable of such authority.' He smiled, displaying his logic and his jest to the Infinite. 'But there need be no stupid disruptions. No muddling of your purpose.'

'Yes,' said Anjelen. 'Then you'll see to it.'

The Factor looked briefly at a ripple of disappointment running the length of him. To the gift, such a casual return, as if Anjelen did not care, did not see it's cost and value . . . But this was foolish. One could not judge him. One must look for nothing but to serve.

The Factor knelt, and Anjelen blessed him.

From the hand of Anjelen came a scorching cool energy like a drink of the eternal.

It would all be seen to. Couched in clever and tactical language, not offering too much that might be misread, cause scandal or doubt. Yet, through the inner method of a priesthood built upon assumptions of the Return, the Absolute, particular signals might be given. Not as a Baptist had given them, splashing noisily in the waters of wonder, but as the sophisticate and cunning modern man of letters might. Each missive a labour like that which facetted a jewel, heralding the promise, stating nothing. And Anjelen might pass through the land like an angel. Where he sought shelter, preference, military aid, such should be his. There was a daunting suspicion, already posited, that news of the third soul of Wedsek's crime had reached into the most potent bastions of the Church. That the Knights of God, who had been proud at Chirkess, were to be disbanded, pushed back into the cellars of ritual. Even, God forbid, if that could happen, Anjelen should work unscathed.

The purpose, the exact structure of this second attempt upon mankind's salvation, mooted in Anjelen, who could divine it?

One need not bother. Faith, not witless but pure of sight, was the token of the Factor's service. The brilliant mind did not question God. It knew it need not.

'All my life is yours. Until you come into your kingdom,' said the Factor, pledging himself.

Anjelen was only white and black, only eyes, only fires, only the dreams of men warped like wrecked stars from their parameters.

The Factor did not guess, kneeling there in his stupendous arrogance of humbleness, that Anjelen's kingdom, which was not as the Factor, anyway, thought it, would not occur for something in the region of a pair of centuries. That Anjelen, who could still be leisurely, would not do anything of much plan until this man was long, and by-the-way, dead and buried, lying in his grave for the last trumpet of Heaven. The Factor was spared that, both the foreknowledge and the awakening. He had not been the first to confuse the tree – the cross – with that which hung on it.

Chapter Eight

Once, among the Travelling People there had been a traditional necklace, worn by their girls until the day of marriage. It was a show of wealth on one side, a measure on another, but also flirtatious, since for any but a prospective father-in-law or bridegroom to make proper count on it was an offence liable to feuding. The necklace was made up of quartets of beads, each representing a season of the year, a white bead of enamel or alabaster for the winter, a green beryl or stained quartz for spring, for the summer a piece of brass, or nut of gold if it could be got, and for the autumn's freckled fall, jasper, garnet, amber, bloodstone or painted clay. Four beads comprised a year. By the age of six, there were usually enough to go about the neck, unless the necklace were very rich and the gems very tiny. By the age of eleven or twelve, most often the maiden was wed and the chain ended. The rare woman who achieved fifteen and still could add to her virgin necklace, did not. She was too old for marriage, and who would waste beads on her?

But the years themselves continued constructing their necklets of seasons, the winter white, the green spring and golden summer, the shattering leaf-fall of red and brown.

Like a broken mosaic, like curtains and clouds, waves, moods, they passed over the land, which, in its length of age, might perceive them more swiftly and flittingly. How fast they came and went, the lights and shades of time.

Snow descends, melts away, beryls stitch through and

bloom into a golden rage that fruits and chars and drops and is done, and then the snow descends, and again, and again.

The trees, those that shed and those that appear change-less in their black-green spikes and furs, they stand fixed within the whirlpool, the coming and going, the flushing up and withering, clothing and unclothing, the colours. The trees grow. They drain the nurture from the soil, and put down their claws into the arteries of the earth, levering up unnoticed as they do it, rocks, the foundations of houses, the flanks of mountainsides.

Sheep like grey boulders strewed the hills, under a white plain of sky. The baked grass cheeped in momentary winds.

These were days of the summer's golden rage.

Something else, too, raged on the hills. There had been talk of it, south and west, towards the town. Men went searching for a great wild cat, for it was not the white-bead time of the wolf. Snow killings, of that sort, were not uncommon.

On the hill structured like an axe head, grazing, the grey sheep clotted together under a thorn tree. Sometimes they rubbed their bodies on the trunk.

The shepherd was beneath the hill, sleeping by the stream where he had eaten his raisins and cheese.

The stillness was improbable. Something must pen-etrate its globe.

The sleeper felt nothing. He snored, with his cheek on the breast of the earth.

But the sheep, one by one, raised their flat-nosed heads.

They scented the predator, death, before hearing and sight discovered him. The stench of the meat-eater, always fearful, except in man, whom they trusted, and who cut their throats at times of festival and famine.

This was not man-scent. But nor was it like anything, not the cat or polecat, or the fox, the wolf, the dog.

The sheep began to move, restless. Thought stupid,

instinctively they knew the trusted shepherd was also use-less to them.

A wind, or something, slid through the high grass beyond the thorn, and the sheep ran.

They ran bunched together, a horde of dirty innocent rumps and small black feet.

The scent came after them, running them down. It had a sound now, heavy and yet vigorous, blundering but sure.

Where rocks came up from the hill, the sheep separated. They bleated shrilly, veering away in groups of three or four or five, and then one ran alone, and there came sudden confusion, a matted animal darkness that reared up and smashed down, and under it the sheep was slapped into the hill-side. It lay pinned, and the dark smothered it up, and its baby-like bleating ceased. The blood oozed through the grass, and the dry hard ground refused it. Over the lip of the hill it trickled, from the mound of greyish and darkish life that died and fed together.

Blood did not rouse the shepherd; it had not made any sound, as the other thing had done, although the crickets in the bushes by the stream had dulled his ears to that.

Then the day began to ebb. The sun spread into an elongate and awful image, of a molten pupil-less eye. The shepherd drew himself out of the country of sleep and was back in the land.

Glancing up, he beheld his flock away to the east of the hill above him. They did not graze, but had posted themselves into the ground, staring westward from the sides of their heads. He knew the beacons of their fear, at least.

He took his staff, a young man not yet eighteen, and shook the shaggy black fleece of his hair out of his eyes.

When he came up, cautious, over the brow of the axe hill, he saw nothing at once, but then the sun itself tweaked a yellow ray into the heap of wool and blood. A carcass, partially devoured, that had been a live thing when he had seen it before. So quickly, death achieved his spell. The shepherd had never applied the formula of that to himself.

He looked hurriedly everywhere, recalling the tale of the giant wild cat. He was not afraid, only furious at his loss. Then the grass lurched upwards, and the shepherd gave a grunt, hefting his stick, ready.

Some devil of a Traveller, some homeless robber, dangerous, the leg bone of the sheep in his hand, but outmatched, worn and cragged and shaggy and unkempt, with patches and streamers of white in a blackish mane and beard – too old for the wandering, stealing life.

The shepherd did not issue his challenge in words, but he strode forward, hunching the staff, growling.

The old man was against the sun, but a twist of his head let the spread light into the beard, to reveal gobbets of blood and fat. He had been eating the repast as it lay, warm and raw.

Bestial, unlawful, preying on the flocks of others—

There were teeth too, some broken but all bared in the mouth.

And then the itinerant robber, the ageing man, was no longer anything of the sort.

The eyes in their gaunt hollows flared a coppery red. The red infused the whites, and they vanished: two furnace ovals slotted with black. The mouth had become a cave, fenced by the jagged fangs between which the red meat remained. The hair, the rags, were pelt. And the leg bone of the sheep, clamped close to him to gnaw, was not for a weapon, for now it was slung away. It was a wolf the shepherd saw, a summer wolf on its hind legs and tall as a tall man.

The shepherd plunged his stick across the body of the man-wolf. He felt no astonishment as the maimed gnarled paws in their thin gloves of grey old man's fur reached out and took the stick, and snapped it. And then the wolf weight leaned on the shepherd, the heat and roaring and the stinking breath and the pale scarlet eyes. One blow of a paw snapped the stick of his throat a second before the teeth shut fast in it.

★

In the village, where the stream went down in a fall of green water, and some trees grew, the women at the pool with their jars saw the man first, as he came along the track. They lifted their arms to shield their eyes from the sinking sun. Even on the blaze of sunset, they saw he was not like other men. Turning to each other, they exclaimed.

'She's in luck.'

'It's what her mamma prayed for.'

The man came into the village, and stopped by the women, looking at them. He was about twenty-four years, a young priest, his plain dark habit belted at a thin ascetic's waist with hemp. He rode a black mule that had on it no baggage at all, not even a gourd to store water. His eyes were marvellous, like a saint's in a picture. This village clove to the Christus, and even had a small stone box under a fir tree, where it had worshipped when the local godbrother was still alive. But he died at length, and unfortunately the religious fathers in the town had not been able as yet to replace him. The village did its best, and married under the fir tree by the stone church, before the village's holder. But it was not the same. As for ancient ways, a girl might sleep with an acorn under her pillow, or tie a ribbon or a flower into the fir to mark betrothal, pregnancy. They did not otherwise do more than scorn such things as superstition. When the elderly women threw meal on to a fire at sunfall, they said *Christus bless us*.

So, it was good for Gisla that the priest had come by, the day before her wedding. The groom would not mind, but she would be glad, and the mother in her grave, doubtless.

The village holder's wife, who was at the well, went directly to the priest, and asked for his benediction. He gave it with a breathtaking elegance against the sinking sun. No peasant, this, but one on some journey from a town. 'You're right welcome, godbrother. Will you stay tomorrow and do a service of marriage?'

That night the young priest sat in the holder's hut, where the holder made stout conversation with him, intimidated, but anxious for stories of the town, from which it would seem the journeying man had come. The holder's wife waited on them. She was sorry that the priest ate so little of her cooking, but also pleased with such firm unworldliness. He had said the evening grace for them, and would speak the morning grace for the entire village, sixty-five souls, at sun-up. His voice was so musical. He drank only water.

There were four other villages across the hills; he might go there too, but maybe not. Maybe only here. Then they could remember and boast of him. He did not seem to expect payment of any kind, no barter or tip. The low summer fire played on his face like melody. He had the beauty of all still things of vast, contained and secret power.

And that night, on the hills, the man-wolf lay low in secret grass, his belly full of meat and blood, watching the stars, and the curved anvil of the moon on which was hammered out the night.

Sometimes he recalled sufficiently he was a man to make a fire, but manlike tonight, he knew it would be unwise. Earlier, there had been a band of men on the hills, on the axe-shaped hill, with burning brands. They were looking for their shepherd, and they found him.

Far off, more than a mile away, in the quiet, he heard the uproar from that village, and dots of lights between the hovels there, but distant, removed. The sheep had been driven down. Warnings would circulate in the area.

A couple of times, after he had killed like this, a goat-herd, a pair of woodcutters, the resultant wary searchers had come on him a day or two later, and he had been in the mode of a man, and having alerted him to the danger of a marauding slaughtering animal at large, they subsequently took him in, and he dwelled with them in their settlements. In the second village he even stayed a year, working in the forge, teaching them to fight – they thought him some strayed soldier. He had been trying perhaps to evade what was in him, but the phantom of his purpose was close at hand, two villages off. And when the eldritch dawning lamp moved on, he too went away, after it, as always.

He had had several interrupted man-lives. They were never properly real to him. Only what he followed, and which never beckoned, never looked back. Yet surely, his pursuit, the loyalty of it, and the obsession, these were known, and accepted. What he did, too, in the guise of a beast, wolf by winter, cat by summer, the white and red seasons, the gold and green. He had killed a Traveller girl once, with just such a necklace on her, unusual now, possibly not hers either, or accurate, for she was less than twelve years and the necklace, when he idly counted it after, in the blood, was fourteen seasons. He did not rape her. He did not experience any sexual thing. He had never gone with a woman, though here and there they offered. The one terrible time, that had purged him like the rupturing of a boil. That was how he saw it. Not crime, not fall, not anything but a sickness, from which he came forth.

Often, he was uncertain what he truly was – never who, since he had mostly forgotten – but whether man or beast.

Yet, one way or the other, he was a god's. No longer the Father, but the being who had proceeded from the Father. From the Creator, or from the Evil One. To this god, he belonged. And therefore, he was safe, the wolf-man, the man wolf. More than condoned, his acts were predestined and exact in the sight of the Lord.

As he shifted on the hillside, his joints ached. Sometimes in the heat, as in the cold, they hurt him. But he did not fret. When he was a man he limped, but discounted it, just as he discounted the name he gave those who asked, *Wedsek*.

He never entered a religious building. He did not want to. In the wilds, that was not so abnormal. In the woodland of the south, now and then he had been attracted to some bush or tree or grove where the skulls of animals were hung, bells and coins, pieces of hair, and wooden effigies of tiny men.

Only five occasions had he followed so close he had seen the god walking near before him. Twice this had happened in darkness. He always yearned for it. He yearned for the god to look back. To come to him. But how should the god see Wedsek? It was enough that he knew.

It had begun under the wall of Chirkess, the unfinished new wall, wrapping the city slower and slower, running down.

Now the memory was smeared and inchoate, bits of things, such as when he lay in the reeds beside the choked-up pond, in an agony beyond agony, agony of the soul, which died from a death wound inflicted only hours before. Strange recollections of a dawn coming up, a deadly and accusing glow, and panes of brilliance in the pockets of water. There was a visualization of an exchange of clothes made – violent – some theft conducted upon him. Of other garments purloined in turn. Of a bank near a tavern down from the wall, above the river. Staying here some while, and they flung him scraps like a cur. Of the sense that all men knew him, but no one did. Paranoia of fear replaced by horror of personal dissolution. Invisible, mistaken for other things, wandering, days and nights, reeds and water, stone and wood and thatch, and trees. Silences without number that were loud with frogs and birds, the calls of men, or women with a catch of fish, and then the road that washed out of the city, straight down under the wall like yards of blotted rope. And the figure on a mule, the priest like a prayer coming on. And scrambling to the roadside, among the debris, and seeing it was the god, on the mule, with palms of sunlight and shadow cast before its feet.

And thus, Wedsek followed. There was nowhere else to go. Like the door, the stair . . . like life itself. No method but progression, after some goal, actual or ephemeral or false.

And then, this composite of time, the jumble of the beads, white and gold, green and red. Day and dark, cold and warmth, pain and momentary alleviation of pain, and food. And the wolf. Where the wolf began, how should

Wedsek tell? In Chirkess, probably, those months at the very start. Or earlier, with the boy. Or in the round chamber. Or under the tree, in the drink of Everlasting Wine, from the vessel of Anjelen.

Anjelen.

Anjelen.

Everything and all things – were Anjelen's.

Anjelen was the world. To follow him was to follow the cycle of the world. to follow the circle of death to birth, through existence, to death again.

I am the truth. And the Life.

Not lost.

For thirty-one years it had gone on. The wolf-man on the hill, sated by his murders and their blood, staring at the stars, he could not calculate and did not want to. It had blurred together and grown tough, like the layers of a plant. Thirty-one years he had followed Anjelen. Now an Anjelen riding a mule. Now walking. Now in a town, a village, some city outskirt. Anjelen entering a church. Anjelen changeless. A few years older. Only a few years. That was all the time it had taken. Four years or five. Or thirty-one.

Wedsek lay back deep in the summer grass.

A half dream moved on him, like the moon upon the ground, so for a moment he was elsewhere, young and laughing, in an inn, in his father's house. But then sleep came, and Wedsek was a wolf. He chased the sheep on the hill, and took them in his jaws. But overhead were the black sky and the white stars, like the eyes of Anjelen his Maker, who loved him.

That morning, he blessed the village and said for it the grace. At midday there was the wedding. The bride, Gisla, came from her parents' hut, in a coloured apron, and with flowers in her hair. She was laughing and happy. The groom was bashful and aggressive by turns, but he bowed to the priest and looked in awe at him. The priest was only maybe a handful of years the bridegroom's senior,

492

but educated, born obviously in a town, travelled and learned, and besides in league with God.

They went to the stone building that had been the church. The floor was scrubbed, and before the oblong unglassed window, a spray of the green wheat was in a jug, and long-lashed daisies. The statue of the Christus on his cross rose on a stone table beneath, a wooden rough-chiselled object. There were a few utensils of pottery. A wooden goblet, smooth from the handling of observance, stood for the wine.

The priest spoke, simply and mildly, all the correct words of the ceremony, much better than the holder's gabble.

The bride blushed and paled before him, drinking up his presence, the omen of it, on her day of days. The shuffling bridegroom mumbled when he must.

The Host was elevated, into the light of the window.

Everyone partook of the Body and Blood of the Redeemer.

After the wedding, they went over to another table set up in the street, piled with cakes and loaves and syrups, beer and ale, and a sheep which, roasting since sunrise and lancing the air with human hungers, was rushed at with carving knives.

'You'll stay and sup, godbrother? Brighten our feast?'

The holder's wife was still anxious he should eat of her cooking.

Their first cups were lifting when three men prowled on to the track above, along the hill.

'Look, who's there, wanting to feed off our table?'

The women called out, mocking these late and uninvited arrivals, but the men on the hill did not respond, and their faces, as they came nearer, were grim.

Getting to his feet, the holder called two of his own men. It was the worst manners, to spoil a marriage.

The bride and groom were busy eyeing each other. Birds sang in the trees and the gold sun was over the highest roof.

The priest sat calmly, looking on, as the holder marched

up the track and met the visitors there. A dialogue ensued between them. One of the fellows from the other village pointed away across the hills. Every man glanced in that direction. Then the holder brought all of them to the table.

'Give these a drink, wife. Listen here. It's not the hour for it, but they've come out of kindness. To warn us.'

One of the newcomers said, 'There's a beast, perhaps a sick wolf, killed sheep up to pasture.' 'And the shepherd with them,' added a second man. 'A terrible killing. Man and animal part eaten, and the blood all ways.' 'I've seen the work of wolves,' said the third, the oldest. 'Never like this, not even a pack starved crazy.'

'Our goats are down today,' said the holder. 'We've this to tend to.' He indicated the table and the bridal couple. 'Happy for us.'

'Who did you lose? Your young man?' asked the holder's wife.

'That's so. Poor wretch. He tried to fight it off, broke his stick somehow, on a rock, maybe. Then it was at him. The throat,' said the neighbouring villager. All at the table sighed, but the priest, where he sat by the whey-white bride. (Omen less sweet.) He did not seem provoked or uneasy, not even consoling. Of course, it was the way of things, such deaths, on the hills, in the woods.

They would have to get the men from all the villages, search for the animal and put it down. It might have the children. If it found the pickings choice, it would stay. They could not know, although their priest, he knew, that this devilish carnivore would soon be gone, as soon as the priest was gone, in fact. The beast, following, would prey elsewhere.

Over the wedding meal then, preparations were made. The wan Gisla was cheered up, and affectionately cursed by her husband when she begged him not to go on the hunting. 'What? You're not changing me into a ninny. I'm a man.'

The priest sat still as darkness through it all, not eating, having only sipped from his cup or perhaps not even that, his hands folded on the table. Once, he too looked at the hills, flint, madder under the tawny base of the sky.

'Not tonight. First light tomorrow. It'll rest itself then, or go to drink along the stream. We can catch it then.'

'*He* won't want to be stirring early.'

But the bridegroom declared that he would, wedding night or no.

The stars wheeled. In altered time, he seemed to have learned how to watch them, so he saw their motion, and the long silver snail-trails they left behind, which slowly dried to blackness.

He did not want to devour again. He had had an abrupt hankering for brown bread and broth, and curds, and picked apples, and ale. It was a man-space come on him. Maybe tomorrow he could go down to one of the villages, play the forager, the orphan soldier. Anjelen was in the lowest village, to the north. During the day there had been a festival there, and Anjelen had sat out in the street with them, and later he retired into the largest hut.

Perhaps Anjelen would consent to stay and be their priest for a pair of seasons, the red and white. This had happened before. Then Wedsek certainly could revert to humanness. He might make a place for himself in a close community, and one day, as they hauled logs or tilled some field, Anjelen might pass by on his mule. Anjelen might raise his hand in blessing, a special moment between them, half a jest. Or one day Anjelen might summon him. *Do thus and so, for me.*

A black hare darted over the hill-side. At first Wedsek was not sure of it, but then it went by again. Fearless, it paused, upright, its horned ears erect, with the stars embroidered about them. Then it was gone.

Wedsek lay down. He dreamed a few seconds: the hare was Anjelen and had come to call him to some meeting of angels on the plain below.

Something woke Wedsek. He sat up at once, attained his knees. He could not recall if recently he had kept a knife or not. But he had. Uncleaned and rusty, it came loose and he got up with it.

It had killed the occasional wolf, in the winters, when they had come on him alone and would not leave him be. One time he had climbed a tree when a pack of seven or eight encircled him. He lay along the boughs three days, eating the snow and a piece of a kill of his own – perhaps its smell had attracted them. Finally they had given up and gone away.

But this was a summer wolf. He saw its shape now on the rim of the hill. It was whole and sound, not crippled nor favouring any part. Its eyes flashed. It trotted to within three yards of him, and halted.

Then, he saw the stars begin to point out through its flank. It went to a sort of smoke, and flowed off, and Anjelen stood up out of it, but he was the wolf still, black on the sky.

Wedsek was too amazed to feel joy. But he dropped back to his knees.

Anjelen spoke to Wedsek, and Wedsek learned he had forgotten the meaning of Anjelen's voice.

'How you stick to me. Here and there I shook you off, but you returned. Constancy such as this, Wedsek – or do you not recollect your given name? – asks some reward. What do you want from me?'

'Whatever – whatever you say.' And Wedsek's voice, out of practice, gravelly and strangled, made him ashamed. It was good enough for the rabble of the villages, but not for Anjelen. 'You tell me, Lord. Is it time?'

'Time for what, Wedsek?'

'For me – to serve you? The hour. The day.'

Anjelen said, 'Do you know where I'm going?'

'No, lord.'

'To my beginning,' said Anjelen. 'A long journey, doubling back on itself. Acres of earth and time. Too many years, Wedsek, for you. Though for myself, little enough. I have my own road. And on it, always, I hear this intruding step which is yours. How frequently in some village street have I seen the outcry over the wolf

or the cat or the wild man who's killed the flock and the
shepherd. It irks me, Wedsek. You, always in my way.
You've forgotten Chirkess. Your gross buffoonery, your
acts of mindless inaccuracy. What's God to you? You can
grasp nothing. What am I to do with you?'

Wedsek wept. Berated, he did not properly understand.
Human speech had been reduced for him to the simplest
phrases. Concepts, sentences, this tirade, had now no real
relevance.

'Don't let me go,' he said. 'Don't leave me, lord.'

'What is it you want?'

'You,' said Wedsek, in a broken, embarrassed humili-
ated croak, 'the truth, the path. You. To follow you.'

'You want the Blood,' said Anjelen. 'Blood which is life
as you came to believe it to be. You and all of you. In the
roots of the world, they knew; but now there is a race of
blind worms. Blood. That's what you ask me for.'

And Wedsek, who had fantasized bread and ale, tingled
at the mystery of the devouring, of the vase of the throat,
and the Wine.

'Come then,' said Anjelen. 'Follow me. I'll give you
what you crave. I'll give you all and more, till the cup
runs over.'

Gisla had gone to her husband a virgin. The union had
been hearty and determined. He was no ninny. He hurt
her and was glad, for her loud cry proved him a man.

When he slept, she lay and solaced herself with the hut,
now hers, the cook-pots and spinning wheel, her apron,
the priest-wedding.

Tomorrow, she thought, *tomorrow I shall—*

And heard a noise out in the street.

Just before sun-up, the men planned to be off hunting
the marauding cat, those whose heads were not too thick
– she was gratified to note how many cups her husband
had swilled. Could this be some early riser? Or had the
holder put men to patrol the village?

The footfalls were odd. Shuffling, limping and loping.
Was it the beast, which the women had whispered might

be more than natural, out there, moving down towards her house?

The shutter of the small window hung wide on the summer night.

Gisla slipped from her bridal bed, wincing at the bride's pain, and went to the window. She was half afraid and half fascinated. She had always been the first to crowd to the ghost stories at the fire – and always the one that shrieked in her sleep afterwards.

A skinny waif of moon shone on the street.

Something roved along the track, unsteady and uneven, as if deformed. It was of great size – and then she saw it was a man, a kind of man, but in some way so ghastly that she would have cried out again. But next she saw another thing. A blackness unrolled before the uncanny man. It was like a black light on a black taper, and as it came, the ground under it turned also black, a stain spreading both in front of it and behind.

Gisla found she could not cry aloud, could not make any sound. She tried the name of her husband, but it would not come out. Like the sheep on the hill, she also knew intuitively that her helpmeet was useless to her.

The dark in the street had stopped, and just beyond it, the other, the man-beast.

Gisla held her breath. Every pore of her body was aware that she was seen. And she thought of the shut door, and the bar down across it. She was safe, for she had not the strength to shift that bar alone. She must walk away from the window, shake her husband, or crawl in beside him under the sheet.

The thing that was a man was crossing over the moonlight towards her. His eyes were filled by Gisla. She seemed to see herself staring back from two sightless panes. The darkness on the track had spread everywhere. It made pools and puddles; she wondered hopelessly if it were only water. The black light that had rolled before the beast-man seemed gone. She stared about for it. She must leave the window. The man was stalking, stumbling near. *Get away, get away*. As in the nightmare after the story, it was not conceivable her feet could move, her arms or body. She tried to draw back, and in that instant, the man-beast-thing was at the window. He smiled on her and reached out his hand, so gently she scarcely saw it, and then he had her, by the face. His grip was clasped around her forehead, cheekbones, his fingers in her hair, and he pulled her forward, forward, until her head was out of the window, her neck braced on the sill with the breath pressed out of it. She kicked, and coughed, and the husband in the bed muttered she must be quiet, he had to be up early, and Gisla coughed up her breath and the man leaned to her and tore the flesh of her cheek out with his teeth.

The stool by the window was kicked over.

'Gisla, shut your noise, you bitch . . .'

Gisla had shut her noise. But there was another noise now.

The bridegroom surged up on his elbow and swore at his reeling head.

'What are you at in the window, eh? Come here. Get me some water, for God's sake.'

There was Gisla, in her wedding shift, her head vanished into night, and in from the night came a feeding sound, and something smeared in down the wall, glittering.

As the drunken groom tore from the hut, Wedsek, still holding up his first prize with one fist, caught the second, and banged its brains out on the door-post. Then Wedsek drank and fed from two dishes.

To the racket this had made, he was oblivious. Under the aegis of his protector and god, he might do anything. Anjelen had given him this, and to do this. And Anjelen had been there at his side.

But then the darkness of Anjelen furled away, like a black leaf blown along the earth, and fetched up in the doorway of the largest hut, the holder's house, and there it was Anjelen again, the priest, who seemed to have come out to greet it . . .

Wedsek saw the village running at him from twelve

directions, all the huts and hovels there were in it. Men came with axes and knives, and women ran out behind them, children muddled in their skirts, while dogs leapt through the air. The sound was a madness. Like a festival.

The man-wolf let go both the dish-vessels of his kill, and stood at bay a moment, as he gathered himself to fly.

But a voice began to speak to Wedsek in his head, whose marvellousness he had again, incredibly, overlooked.

'Stay, Wedsek. This I give you.'

Wedsek glanced up. A dog was coming down, launched for his neck, glaring and slavering. And as it hung there, a knife slewed through it, nearly taking the skull from the body. The dog fell on Wedsek and the hot blood splashed his lips, tinctured with honey, for the knife had come uncleaned from the wedding breakfast, from the slicing up of cakes.

After the dog, a man's full weight struck Wedsek. The man screamed between wrath and terror. His throat gaped like a ruby.

'Drink,' said Anjelen from the high tower in Wedsek's brain, 'take your fill.'

Wedsek too had fallen. The earth was black and slippery and red. Somehow the red was visible in the moonlight, the only colour.

Blood jetted over Wedsek's face.

He tried to push it off, the heap of bodies, the fountain of blood.

A woman had collapsed on his chest. She made sounds. She too tasted of the wrong elements, herbs and bread.

The knives had turned in their hands, or flown after them from the hearths, or else the veins of their necks burst spontaneously like glass at great pressure, and out the crimson fire-like juices sprayed. And they crashed and sank on Wedsek.

The taste of all the blood was wrong. It was only blood. It was not holy. Not Wine.

'Drink,' said the voice.

The scalding salty vileness poured in Wedsek's mouth, he could not avoid it. He tried to gulp his way free and, as he did so, spew it forth again. Burning hot, the blood gushed down his nose, and laved his eyes.

'Drink,' said Anjelen.

Wedsek struggled and floundered. All their weight was on him, the weight of mankind, the sins of the world.

The holder's wife sped last from her hut. She clutched at the priest where he stood, impassive as a stone in her doorway. 'Brother – in the name of God help us—'

She looked at the heaving mass, like erupting mud.

She rushed forward with her ladle, and as she met the wall of flesh, felt the vein in her neck give way so terribly she barely believed it. Her ladle skidded across the track. She lay on a spasming dead child, disorientated, dying.

Buried in skin and meat and bone, drowning in blood, Wedsek heard the voice say from the mountain-top of consciousness, 'Drink.'

And the cup ran over.

He had been dreaming of blood and heaped bodies, in some form the Day of Judgement. Black shadow coiled along the ground, and all that place was changed to blackness, a black season, a black bead upon a chain. He supposed, waking himself, sipping from the cup of milk left by his bed, that he was an old man and his kind had such dreams. The ending of the world was, for him, close at hand in a personal way. Yet, he had nothing to fear. Though he had been disappointed, mentally and intellectually, he had been enabled to contend with and subdue the vice of impatience. In his seventies now, the snatched peace of a painful physical age deterred him from much complaint.

Only he regretted, he could not help it, that he had never seen during his years as a man, the advent, the coming of the Second Kingdom on earth.

The boy rapped at his door.

'I'm ready. Come in and clothe me.'

The boy, clumsy and nervous, entered, and the Factor yearned for certain other men who had waited on him with skill and charm. But he had outlived them all, for their duties and advancements took them elsewhere, and now he had fetched up in this city, in the Cathedral apartments, with this lending.

'Today, I shall go upriver.'

'Yes, Father Factor.'

'To see how the building progresses.'

'Yes, Father Factor.'

There it was. Not a glim of interest or enthusiasm. Did this pudding of a novice understand anything of what went on? Ah, to adore excellence and end in the care of a moron: God's lessons. But anyway, Anjelen had spoiled the Factor for the value of any man.

My life has gone in his service. He knows it. The marks are everywhere. And in my last letter, which surely will find him at some hour in Chirkess, I reported upon this latest thing. My gift at the feet of God.

He must not be proud. That was a misdemeanour. But to cherish the work would be allowed.

The Factor was rich, and into his project his riches had flowed like blood (blood – that dream – no, the Devil soured the sleep of the just; don't think of the Devil, for old men thought of him too often).

Robed and gowned, and with his gold crucifix and beads of jade, sapphire and pearl, the Factor was carried out in his chair, to the room above the marble hall, where he breakfasted with the Cathedral's Administer.

'You're visiting the new church, Father Factor?'

'Not a church, my lord. Much more than a church. The palace of God upon the ground. Heaven in the everyday.'

The Administer frowned. The tiresome dotard came nearer to blasphemy with every phrase he uttered. But there, his presents to the Cathedral here had been lavish. And it was said he had himself been one of the Knights of God, before the order fell to disrepute – a dangerous old gentleman.

The voyage upriver, in the huge white-winged ship, took some days. There were sand bars to be avoided. Flat miles of unkept land wavered in the heat on either side the ship. The rowers strained.

The Factor took the notion, as he sometimes did now, that all this was one continuous dream, which included waking and sleeping. Might he not at any moment see Anjelen himself coming across the deck in the sunshine, as on that other journey? The Factor had tempted Anjelen with earthly power, and Anjelen had rejected it. How beautiful that seemed now. How perfect. But who had built for the Christus a temple of gold and crystal and white stone, in the days of his years?

Where the river entered the sea, a range of mountains soared aloft. The breakers of the estuary flailed about each other peevishly. It was a calm summer day.

They came to an area where an arm of rock struck out into the ocean across a waste of white sand.

Twice a day, the sea drew off from this promontory, and it was possible to gain access to the building whose foundations now showed above the rock, balusted with scaffolding, and strange detritus, like the leavings of giant molluscs.

They had to wait for the tides.

When the elderly man was carried up the steep, lethal ascent in his chair, the workmen on the walls above wondered at it, but he was a priest: only the extravagant best would do for him.

The enormous seaward window was already sketched in.

The Factor sat some while, gazing at it.

He doubted he would see it finished, any of this, as he would not see the completion of the other, non-corporeal, edifice.

The overseer stood before the Factor, giving good account. The Factor listened, wandered, listened again.

'And there, down the cliff, a Doma for women, to house the sisters of the order.'

The Factor was not interested in that. Women had never interested him. It was sensible that they should be allowed to kiss the hem of the garment of the Christus, perform their little adjunctive duties. They had their part, as did the animals, and women had souls too, for the

503

Christus had said so, but not souls as men had them. That was not reasonable.

'The Christerium,' he said aloud. '*His* house, when he's ready.'

The overseer waited out this rambling politely. He was not positive whether or not to remark to this ancient father what had happened with the sand, if it was worthwhile even, for probably the elderly priest would not take it in. The legate and the factor minor from the city had both assessed the phenomenon as springing from the dead shells of crabs and other sea creatures turfed up by preliminary excavation. This did not entirely explain it. Some of the labourers, the artisans even, had been perturbed. A divine service was held under the promontory at low tide, to ease their minds. For the white sand was going to black, a curious soft bruise that spread away from the cliff towards the sea, like a shadow poured out there.

They had heard the buildings were for a special purpose, not Cathedral or Fraterium, something more. Those ideas of a palace of God on earth, common to all churches, had here some extra resonance. Why then the blackening of the sand?

The old Factor was shivering now in the bright day, and the anxiety-ridden attendant asking if they should heat some wine for him. But the Factor only said, '*His* house,' again, and stared up at the tower of the seaward nave and the etched window and the sky. And the overseer decided he would not bother with the story of the sand, which after all might indicate nothing of any significance.

Chapter Nine

The journey had meandered: acres of earth and time. It had been the journey of growth, of the coming to estate, and to such purpose as he could recognize, Anjelen. Wedsek's intrusions were not of such great moment. He sloughed them when it seemed to him they had become so. His judgements were just, and blind. To kill brought Anjelen no delight. Even power did not delight Angelen. But the vitality of what he was, maybe that sparkled within him, the passion of pure strength that must know itself in every move it makes.

The years that elapsed before he reached his objective – the return, the point of starting – were their own device. He delayed, and as he did so, matters sorted themselves, coming also to their own fruition.

Other elements, too, fitted themselves home in their places during this period. The churches Anjelen might enter as a godbrother, as a nonentity, and as a Magister, and more – as a prince – ranged far and wide. The Factor had seen to his work well, along with others who had impressed themselves into Anjelen's service. Anjelen might be anything in the name of God now. That he had not gone up into the highest spheres, to the purse of an Administer, the throne of a Primentor, displayed only that he felt no need to, that his requirements did not encompass that. Between him and the outer world of littleness there were the white and magenta screens of higher Church Authority. It was convenient. But for himself, he did as he liked.

The forest, as he finally came back into it, was altered. The cores of that fervid terrain were denser, deeper and darker; like sinking wells. But elsewhere the brand of man was on everything. Roads thrust through, clearings made bald. Not a taming of the wild, but a witless living with it, a going about under the shadow of black and mighty things too large to be seen. They did not know what they did, nor would they be forgiven.

He rode into Raven lands, where the best road was, and went towards the Landholder's house. It was the Raven tribe that had set themselves to root out the old worship, more than twenty-six decades ago, when Anjelen had been Jun, the Chosen, nine years of age, under the Tree.

There were no outriders, no servants from Khish. Anjelen rode a mule, the mount of a godbrother, with two or three suitable pieces of baggage, and a gourd to store water, for it was a dry spring and many streams had run to their gravel.

The house of the Korhlens was unimpressive, seen from above. The stonework of the defensive central Tower, the barns and outbuildings. The women's apartments, segregated, were of wood, bright with darts of paint. Orchards wound round it all, and fields went to the door. They had not yet thought to make an inn, although traffic might swell on the road in these parts, and push them to do it.

The priest met with the Vre before he had quite got down to the house.

The Landholder and ten of his men came pelting along the incline from the wood, with carcasses of deer snarled among the horses.

'What's up?' said Vre Korhlen, riding headlong at the priest. He eyed the priest as a dog might eye a beetle, deciding whether or not to squash this inane interloper.

The priest reined in his animal, sat and waited. Most men in his circumstance would show some emotion on their faces, annoyance, nervousness, a desire to placate or chastise. The priest showed Korhlen nothing.

The Vre's tunic was diagonally coloured purple, rust and green, and from a collar of gilded bronze hung the raven of his house in heavy silver. He was well dressed for his hunting, and the wristlets and boots of leather were chased with gold. His left leg stuck out from the side of the horse uncouthly. It was braced with three rings and two stems of iron. No ornament that, but a malformation coped with as best he could. It had not, apparently, stopped him in much.

'What's up?' said Korhlen again, beside the priest.

'I am on the business of the Church,' said the priest. 'Will you afford me shelter at your Tower?'

'If I must, I must, I suppose. We have our religious, Godbrother Vezion.'

The priest said he had heard so.

'And heard he's weak, too soft on us, no doubt. That's why you honour us with a visit?'

Out here in the forest, tough, feuding (Korhlen feuded now; the priest would have heard that too), they had small need of the Church. It pursued them as best it might. But even the Vre's wife was hale. She had borne him a healthy son five months before, and was good for several others. The Vre was not desperate for any holy favours.

A mill was being built, up from the house and the Tower. On the half-sown fields, in the broad light outside the wood, the peasants of Korhlen toiled; and clearly immediate, there came the rap of a rod on a man's back.

Over the valley, above them now, the undulations of the pines, the immovable vista of darkness.

They rode into the yard. A stone flight led up to the door of the Hall, which stood wide. The Vre dismounted with a clash of his leg-iron, and a sort of roar to match it. 'Come in, priest, and take a cup.' Vre Korhlen gestured to a man, some steward. 'Fetch Vezion! He'll tell you what we're up to, our heinous badness, all that. You can set what penances you think we want, godbrother. We'll do our best with them, but we're busy, at Korhlen.'

The Vre's contempt was jovial. Plainly, he thought the

Church nothing to be afraid of. It had its uses. In fact he was quite pious at the proper moments – talk at Khish had led the priest to believe so.

Nevertheless, the Vre did cast at the priest an occasional searching glance. This one was not like the other ones, the grumblers and mouthers, the stragglers of God who wandered about the forest. Nor was he to be jollied with drink. He would accept only water. Well, let him have it then, and be damned to him.

Godbrother Vezion, when he got there, was unhappy. His rumpled face tried to straighten itself out, he tried to sing the praises of the household, the perfect wife and mother, the abstemious nobles, the brave soldiers, the wise and patient Vre . . . while close by ravened the wretched, drunken, godless Esnias Tower, constant source of fighting, their boundaries running down the Raven's in so many spots—

'I've been given the apartment by the west barn,' said the visiting priest. It was not a shining area, a former storeroom, damp in winter, broiled in summer, always tumbledown. 'Perhaps you would spend an hour with me before the Tower dines.'

'Yes, yes, or course.'

When Anjelen was gone to the awful apartment, the Korhlen priest plucked his lord's attention. 'I think – we should be wary, sir.'

'Why? Don't puddle your drawers. I'll save you from him.'

'I think – he is more than he says or seems. I've heard, my lord, of a travelling priest, like this one, ascetic, with compelling eyes—'

'Were they? Looked half mad to me.'

'He's rumoured to be a Magister of the Cathedral at Chirkess.'

'Then what's he doing here?'

'God knows,' said Godbrother Vezion with simple faith.

When he went to the west barn apartment, Godbrother Vezion had reached the stage of tremor. He had some cause to be distressed. He was alert for the visitor to be cognizant of this and ready with traps. What could Vezion say? *Here I'm at the mercy of my master.* Your master can only be God – that was the correct reply to his mewling.

The dark priest from Khish, or Chirkess, had given as his name Godbrother Jun – an unlikely title. Jun was no name of any recognizable sort, the kind of phonetic the lowliest peasant might fashion in the depth of the wood.

But Godbrother Jun, anyway, was sitting waiting. He had somehow contrived for there to be a table. On it were spread only three things, but these surprising. To the left of Jun a vitreous globe, polished, to the right a dagger with a bronze hilt. These were the accessories of a mage, the Magister, and recollections of what Jun might really be – a false name? – drew near. Before Jun, opened, was the most alarming evidence of all. It was a book, quite small, but beautifully coloured and illuminated, of the Scriptures, or part of them. One of Jun's pale hands lay on it. Vezion noticed for the first time that, along with plain wood beads, the other priest had a cross of bare black lacquer on his breast.

'Here I am, brother,' said Vezion, with tremulous heartiness, the latter learnt off from the Lord Vre, the former all his own.

'Here you are. Do seat yourself. The stools are not of the best, but we must make shift as we can.'

Vezion sat. He looked at the Book dubiously. His copy was poor, with passages omitted or inaccurate.

'Is that fair thing from Khish?' he ventured.

'From somewhere.' There was to be no doubt; Vezion faced an interrogator. It therefore startled him afresh when Jun went on: 'With the recent birth of the Vre's son in mind, I've been reading this section. *Blessed be God, that He gave to me a son in my old age.*' Jun looked at Godbrother Vezion.

Who smiled timorously and addended, 'Although of course our Abraham here, the Lord Vre, is hardly old—'

'But,' said Anjelen, 'we may take for his age the length

of the family line. The Ravens have held this land for some centuries.'

'Just so,' said Vezion, wondering what would come next.

What came next was that the immaculate black-haired head was lowered again, and the exquisitely trained voice – a city, a city – read on: '*And it came to be, God prompted Abraham, saying, Go you into godless country and there make a sacrifice to me of your son.*'

Vezion waited, alight with fears, expecting now theosophical debate. What did Jun want of him? The usual argument that God had required immolation of His precious gift in thought, not deed, in order to be sure of the fidelity of His servant?

'*Sacrifice,*' Jun repeated, coolly, and lifting his head, looked at Vezion again in that manner from which it was not possible to turn, and which it was such a horrible discomfort to behold.

While the *word* gave the key to it all. And Vezion quailed. Was it better to be honest at once? Obviously. Events had been discovered.

'Please understand,' said Godbrother Vezion in a shaking bleat, 'that it's very difficult for me, alone here in the forest, to deal with such – aberrations. The Vre's a godly man, I insist that he is. But these old rites loom large. One day I may bring him—'

'What are you saying to me?' asked Jun.

Vezion, up to his throat in the mire, stumbled and went down. He stared at Jun, through obscuring mud.

'Why, that – that what the Vre has done – that the sacrifice—'

'Can you be telling me,' said Jun, most gently, 'that Vre Korhlen plans to offer the blood of his first-born to appease God?'

Vezion said, 'I'd assumed from your inference, Brother Jun, that the sacrifice at Korhlen' – emboldened of necessity, Vezion's tone was firmer – 'was to have the attention of the Church Fathers.'

Jun said, 'Of course.' He said it without any threat at all, and so appalled Vezion.

'Indeed, how could it be otherwise,' said Vezion. 'There's secrecy, but some account always gets out. They've done it since they first took the land. An offering to the god of the wood, a token in payment. The worship of the Christus stopped it. Then, some bad luck sent them running again to the ancient gambits. Not, as you'll be aware, human blood-letting – no, no. An animal, a sheep or pig, sometimes a horse. Every spring.'

Godbrother Vezion broke off because he got no response.

Godbrother Jun sat like a pale and dark stone, and regarded him, and at last Vezion could only lie there in the mud, suffocated and will-less, for what would follow.

'The eye of the Church,' said Jun, 'sees everything. It is the earthly minister of God.'

'Is he to be punished?' said Vezion. In his eyes was a vision of Vre Korhlen stripped of his possessions, land, wife, child, worst of all burnt alive as a pagan disbeliever, a practitioner of obscene rituals. In Vezion's heart was fright for himself. His own stripping, and maybe worse. He meant, *Am I to be punished?*

Jun answered him. 'You yourself are held quite blameless. I stress this, since I see you suppose you've condoned a crime. Vre Korhlen has acted ignorantly, but through his ignorance has yet approached a virtue. I am going to place in your keeping now, Vezion, a hidden truth. You must cherish and guard it.'

'Yes—' faltered Vezion.

'What,' said Jun, 'but the ultimate sacrifice, was the Christus? Through his death he accomplished two things: the payment for earthly sin, and the assurance of eternal life.'

Vezion went on staring. His face was quite smooth now, childish, fascinated. Choked in mud, he had reached the moment of soporific ecstasy. The vitreous globe glimmered, the dagger pointed at him.

'You must understand,' said Jun, 'that blood sacrifice

511

is neither alien to nor outlawed by the Church. You will find the Book threaded with it. To the unlessoned, naturally, the practice is never revealed, for it must not be profaned by the unlearned and vulgar. For the man here, he performs in unruly and impious rashness a very profound and sacred mystery. He needs only to be tutored, and shown how, by God's grace, he may acquit himself of the action better.'

'But,' said Vezion, 'it's a pagan thing—' He was so becalmed, he did not know what he said, or he would, definitely, never have quibbled.

Jun answered patiently and rationally, '*Go you into godless country*. This was the word of God Himself. This deed must be done on pagan ground. Try to comprehend, Vezion, for as with all complete truths, the matter is both dauntingly complex and utterly plain. All is God. It is therefore impossible, when at worship, to worship anything but God. The rituals of the wood are also God's rituals. Their form is unlike, yet also entirely apposite. The tree, the flesh, the blood. The thorns and the roses. Put away the little, infantile things, Vezion, and accept the great Truth. The secret of the rose of the Blood.'

'Yes . . .' Vezion whispered now. 'The Wine, and the Tree—'

'What's been done is very well,' said Jun, 'but it lacks. It falls behind.'

Vezion felt as if he slept. Yet his brain was clear as the magician's globe, his hands were firm with excitement, gripping as if they clenched the dagger.

'The Vre has feuded for a month, and taken, I believe, certain prisoners.'

'Yes,' said Vezion. 'Thirteen Esnias soldiers. Only five can fetch ransom.'

'Long ago,' said Jun, 'slaves died by the score. But then, it came to be one man, a Chosen. And then a Chosen boy. Boy or man. The youngest of them. Tell your master the Vre. Before he dines.'

Vezion got up unsteadily. He said, 'There are other families in the woods, who sacrifice men.'

'I know it, Vezion. You reveal nothing astounding. But they're special here. The ground is special, here.'

Dinner in the Cup Hall had been strange and strained. Vre Korhlen had seen, in the orb of torchlight, the new priest down at his out-of-the-way and ill-served table. Vre Korhlen had seen his raven-haired wife too, in her saffron dress trimmed with green and scarlet, the child brought in for show, and given a lick of wine on a knife handle. He had seen his twisted leg, as ever, stuck out to trip unwary servers, the slaves, the rowdy Tower court. And when the women went and the drinking began in earnest, the first fisticuffs started, the first beer and bones rolled, and the dogs went dashing, and five men were kicking and pummelling among the trenchers. A bears' cave by firelight it was, constant as life. But he got up and left it, and went out into the scented spring night, down among the peach trees to where the chapel was.

There, in the stone vault as cold as winter still, he stood rubbing his wrists in anger, glaring at the new priest who had dared come here and know the secret and give it up to him in a fresh and fearsome way. Agitated, he did not simmer his words. He flung them raw.

'What bloody trick is this? What do you want, you crawling black-skirt?'

And the new priest, Jun, he said to Vezion, 'Stay here and pray to God,' And to Vre Korhlen he said, 'We'll go up the hill now, to the place.'

'What place is that?'

'The place of the sacrifice.'

'It's a pitfall. God rot him, that numbskull, what's he told you? You take on his lies? I won't be caught. Up there, at night? The stone – God knows, its bloody roots go down as far as Hell.'

'No more protests,' said Jun. 'You'll be silent now.'

Vre Korhlen opened his mouth wide to describe how no man gave orders to him, but a peculiar and vast murmur, not physical, neither imagined, quivered through the chapel. It was like the breath of God. And Vre

Korhlen stepped off from it, caught despite his avowal, because he believed in things unwordly.

Jun was at the door. He went out of it, not looking back, and took the track up towards the mill, as if he knew the path well. He did not pause to invite or command the Vre again. But the Vre walked after him. And Vezion, as instructed, knelt down on the paving to pray.

Birches grew about the grove. They had come up like white maidens in the mornings and the afternoons, the dusks and midnights, to coronet the ground. Inside, the grass was rank, strewn with mushrooms, cones, thick as horse-tails, with a ferny compost odour and a sweet fragrance in the dark. And there, at the centre, as at the centre of all things, was the Tree. It leaned now. It had lost bark, branches and foliage, every bough, every inch of height and vestige of wood. *But nothing else.* A black stone stood crooked in the ancient glade. Chopped down, eviscerated and petrified. And it was the Tree.

Above was a hole of night sky, limpid and bluish, with salt-grain stars.

Jun moved about the stone. He stood the far side of it, and bowed his head.

'Well,' said the Vre, angry and afraid, the bravado of food and drink leaving him as if in the gusts of the night breeze, remembering eventually maybe the strength of the Church Paternal. Confused. For what did this one want, this renegade, who had apparently wed the cross of the Christus to the old dark shore of the wood? 'Well. What is it, damn you?'

'Be still,' said Jun.

His voice came like silver through the night. Now, here, rather than exacerbate, it soothed. Like a bell, softly it rang between the silent spaces.

Then, out of the black stone which the Tree had become, the Tree began again to grow.

It rose up, dim and ghost-like, hardly black, like a column of smoke that was also water. It put out limbs, and these put forth branches. Leaves like phantasmal metals, and needles that were smoky crystal. And in the belly of the Tree there were to be seen, like the skeletons of things in black amber, the spines and ribcages and skulls of men. Thousands of them there were, all folded, each behind the other, and away, to interminable distances where they grew slender as twists of ivory. All the young men who had died and become the Tree. The Sacrifice, over and over.

Jun raised his arm. He struck the Tree. From its side a stream of blood erupted, the colour of blood even in the dark, and elsewhere eyelets gave and arcs of whitest water poured out. The Tree was the source of everything, of tears and the rivers, of the blood of death and birth.

There were eyes in the skulls inside the Tree. They looked on calmly, glowing.

High above, a man's white body hung between earth and Heaven. Stars were the three blazing nails which pinned him there, his arms outflung. His head was crowned with the bitter thorns, in which the blood had gathered like roses.

'Here,' said the voice of silver, 'is the kind Father who feeds you. In return, feed him. It is God. God is only One. It never finished, and must go on. To the end of the world, it is with you.'

If Vre Korhlen made a noise now, it was not audible. If he thought of wife or child, land or goods, the priest or himself, was in doubt.

The Tree gleamed and flickered and was and was not. All the forest was there, the miles without number, the teeming of life within it, its centuries past, and to be.

'Father, forgive me,' said Vre Korhlen. He knelt down. *'Yet, if I walk through the Valley of Night, be with me, Lord, O be with me, Lord.'*

The man was dragged screaming. He had fought bravely in the battle with Korhlen's men, and reckoned to be got home to Esnias before the summer. When they fed him and washed him, he felt lucky. But then they took him out and soon he guessed, for he had heard of such rites,

515

and that perhaps Korhlen subscribed to them. It was no easement to him that he had been better prepared than hordes of former captives meant for the Tree, and other captives due in future for the black stone.

They tied him to a rock.

It had not yet come to include a rite of manhood, the proving of the Landholder's heirs as their people's shepherd and priest. It was the Vre who took the knife. Nor did he cut the throat or neck veins, as he had thought fit to do with the animals butchered there.

He drove the knife in and upward, to sever the stomach and carve the heart. The ghastly scream, gouts, fountains of gore. As it should be.

The forest gave, and must have back, in some measure. It had always been so.

And as the summer swelled, the fields fattened yolk-yellow, the streams ran clear, the beasts proliferatively dropped their young, and his own wife hung heavy as a grape on the vine with his second child, the Vre beheld that what he had done was good. If he recalled its connection to the Christus – who could say?

Three years later that second son was to die, of a childish ailment not unknown in the forest. At the next spring sacrifice, Vre Korhlen took his first-born, then almost four years of age, with him to the stone. He let the boy witness the sacrifice, and going to him after, anointed his forehead with the hot red blood. The small child, Kolris Korhlen, did not flinch or cry. He had already learned, at the hand of his bluff iron-legged sire, better than to do that.

Chapter Ten

At thirteen, when Catra became a woman, they had
decided that her wits were not quite sound, but that did
not matter so much as the other thing, over which they
had worried. Ten was a normal age for puberty, and there
were fears her lagging brain had slowed her body. But
then she woke crying and the nurse ran down to the
mother with the red-splotched bed linen. They were
pleased with Catra, and made a fuss of her. Now she was
a worthy maiden. Now she might marry. So Catra was
pleased also and smiled. She was a winsome child, after
her own manner. If not too much was asked of her, she
could pass as adequately as another girl, being only more
docile, more tractable, which was to the credit. Otherwise,
she was something of a beauty.

Her hair was unusually fair, like bleached cloth, fine
and soft, and her eyes very pale blue. Where these pearly
looks came from no one deduced. Perhaps fortunately for
her mother, no man of this description was among the
Hill Tower kindred, or servants, and none had ever been
noted in those parts. Catra's father was the fourth brother
to the Landholder, low in the crowded ranks of aristocrats, and his wife had already equipped him with two
sons, black-haired and brown-eyed like all the rest.

It happened they had been waiting on Catra's coming
to bud. An alliance with another Tower was thought suitable, following a slight disagreement. No daughters were
legally available, but Catra, and another girl of twelve –
fully a woman, but of even less vital birth, thought too

removed from the Hill Tower's Vre to be an acceptable offering.

The union was to be with the Raven Tower of Korhlen. Her nursemaid told Catra all this, as Catra sat plaiting flowers for a chaplet, under the jagged stones of the wall. Below lay the forest, as it lay everywhere, a ruffled blackish carpet from which peaks of emerald, ash, grey and slaty blue expressed their heads. Catra was afraid of the forest, and in her infancy had had terrible dreams she could never explain concerning it.

'And he's a wonderful man, the Vre, a Landholder like lord uncle. And young. Not twenty-five, they say. His first and most precious bride you'll be. Won't you like that?'

Catra said she would. Already she had been given a gown embroidered with lilies, a necklace and bangles, earrings of blue enamel.

'And you shan't mind going away from your mamma, shall you?' queried the nurse.

Catra shook her flaxen head, a little doubtfully, but 'mamma' did not represent very much, if rather more than 'father', both of them stern and judgemental, spoilers and punishers. 'As for me, I'm too old to go. But you'll have the girl with you, flimsy bit though she is—' The nurse left off, seeing Catra had jumped, and that her dilute eyes filled with tears. In her hands the flowers were crushed. 'Won't you come with me, Nursey?'

'No child,' said the nurse, gratified to have caused pain, for who else valued her?

An hour later she was less gratified, for Catra had wept herself into a sodden state, and there was the lady, Catra's mother – for the nurse, too, a punisher and spoiler.

'What did you mean by telling her?'

'I thought no harm, lady. I'm not to go. It's better she grows accustomed. Once she's a husband, she'll forget me—'

'Yes, so she will, and sooner than that. From this day on, you won't see my daughter.'

After the nurse, snivelling reflexively in turn, had

departed, Catra's mother paced her small stone chamber, which, situated above the stable court, was summer-doused with smells unwanted. Catra's mother did not herself feel comfortable or used to her daughter. Thank God this offspring had not been a boy; she would never have heard the last of it. To this hour, she remembered Catra's getting. A sudden frightful gurning and moving in her womb, so that she knew it had received a child. That night had been full of phantoms. She had heard mutters from the servants, of a ghostly figure seen at the edge of the forest, a robed man . . . And there were dolls hanging in the trees that the Vre had had taken down, for he did not like pagan ways on his Hill.

By suppertime, Catra was appeased. Her poor, limited mind generally could not keep anything for very long, even grief, though her instantaneous reactions were often febrile.

Calmed with sweets, she fell asleep, drifts of unbound, light-washed hair on the pillow. For what was needed, she would do.

Catra went to Korhlen, to the second stone Tower like, and not like, her childhood home. She was thirteen, child-ish, but not flamboyantly missing any element of herself. She took some boxes and chests amongst which were apparel, combs, beads, and a cithra she had almost learned to play, whereon she would pluck innocent tunes, and sing softly to herself.

Her bridegroom came out at her in the yard. He was black-haired, with a warm colouring, quite young, and surely young enough. But he frightened her and she squealed, and that seemed to amuse him.

There was only the 'bit' of a girl to sustain Catra now. The girl was one year older than Catra, and mentally old enough to be her mother. For that reason she had been picked. The girl served Catra in all particulars, was her advisor: she had even instructed Catra in the duties of the wedding night, and been met with a sheer disbelief that did not augur well. Catra had seen, to be sure, goats and pigs at such activities. But a man with a woman? It was not kindness that had protected Catra from these sights, only decorum and, mostly, naivety. Perhaps Catra *had* seen them, and misunderstood.

'He'll hurt you,' said her maid. 'You can cry out, but not too much. Let him do everything he wants. You must on *no account* deny him anything. It's the law of God.'

Catra went to her bridal in terror. She kept glancing at the red-lipped groom, whose eyes shone and who to her seemed aged as her father and her uncles. Alone in their bedroom he was due to turn into a monster.

Sensing her fear, knowing himself fear-inspiring, and thus not noticing her oddity, Kolris Vre Korhlen attempted to reassure. He reckoned the Hill Tower had lied, the girl was not much more than eleven, but he had had a girl younger than that, and was not put out. It showed the Hill Vre's desire to ally with him. And she would be all the better for children, the heirs he must achieve. For Kolris had had no children, for all his romps, though he had consented to acknowledge a pair of boys as his own, down in the Korhlen village, for the look of it. Could it be God would hold off from allowing Kolris the rights of fatherhood? He dared not even think of this. Blame his women all he would, fifty years before, the lack of an heir would have been enough to oust him, and at this date he would have to fight day and night to retain leadership. Catra had been examined and was a virgin. He would see to it she was true to him. He would sow her until God gave back an affirmative.

After the wedding, the feast. Catra was improved, she enjoyed the food, especially the pastry people, and the pastry ring Kolris cut and gave her to eat – it had sugar on it. Oh, after all what could be going to happen save they would ascend to bed in the Tower and sleep there? Though it was a disturbing thought, this great man wallowing by her, yet certainly she could endure it. She would not say no, and flout God's law.

When they had been lighted to Kolris' chamber, left there, and the servants had gone, Catra's maid with them, the Landholder sat down on the bed, and pulled Catra to him. He was rough in his handling of her, but that did not particularly upset her; all her uncles, when they dandled the pretty simpleton, handled her the same.

'Do you know what comes now?'

Catra lowered her eyes. She said she did not.

He said, 'Come, someone told you. Your mother.'

No, her mother had not told.

Kolris, in his twenties, strong and already erect from her proximity, said, 'Then I must show you, mustn't I? You don't want to stay a maiden. You want to be my wife.'

Then he began to undo her dress, which the clever maid had already made an easy task for him. He was therefore able to do it quite gently, not to make her start, for she was so youthful and tender. There would be enough bruising.

At first Catra was meek, then she was scandalized. The cloth slipped off her breasts before she was moved to squeak (an uncle had once done this; there were reprimands all round).

'No, no,' said Kolris, young enough to be mild, all his life before him. Anxious enough also to want to plough the furrow straight.

But Catra struggled, and then he grasped her firmly, and not bothering to kiss her mouth, rubbed his face against the small and lovely breasts, rocking her on his knee. He had had a great many girls, all willing to go with a Vre, but they had taught him a few of the things they liked.

Catra wriggled, but then, she relaxed. Body-pleasure, which she could never have associated with the flat instructions of the 'bit' of a maid, began to move inside her, her veins and loins. She snuggled herself into Kolris, her husband, and allowed him to find out what any man might, who had dared lay all his hand on her, that she was at high temperature, a woods girl after all, glad and hot and willing.

When Kolris rolled her down and tried her, having to

force to get in, she, with yelps of pain and amazement, thrust up to meet him. She opened herself wide and kicked his back with her bare pink feet, scratching his ribs and buttocks with her fingernails. She reached orgasm in a few moments, and only then did she cry out as it had been permitted her to do. Kolris crashed upon her, gasping.

Later, if not by much, when he wanted her again, she was more than ready. Later again, when the candles had burned to stubs, and the roars from the Cup Hall were dull with ale and exhaustion, she put out a leaf of hand upon his private parts, and tickled him into a blaze. She had learned swiftly. He even wondered what she had been at, this sprite. If he had not had such positive proof of her sealment, the new red blotches on the bed, Kolris might have doubted her. But no, she was true, and if she was a minx it was for him, only for him.

As for Catra, she fell asleep at last, curled like a blissful sea-thing in a cocoon of warm bedclothes. She had neither remorse nor shame. Her simplicity provided her with the talent of acceptance. There had been sugar on all the night.

Hung in a balance of bright spring sunlight, the Christerium had leaned on its forepaws above the sea, its head raised, its one seaward eye staring. So he saw it for the first time. (Anjelen, for whom it had been made.) But what he thought of it, what he felt for it – useless to apply such notions to him. He felt nothing but a sort of oblivious rightness, as at a detail in its proper place. And he thought? Some abstract thing to do with architecture, contours, the play of shade and sun. The diamond brain made its assessment. The tree that was the man discounted all, aware only of the benign weather change, the correct season, something like that.

But for the Christerium—

You will know him by certain signs.

He himself was the sign. From coded and mystic precursors they would discover him, from some clue of description physical and spiritual. The Factor had performed his labour well.

The porter at the gate did not question Anjelen. The porter's face went sallow. He took one look and let in the dark priest, who was on foot, carrying nothing.

All the gates, and the doors, opened.

The higher brotherhood came out to meet him. Some of them kneeled. In the church of the Christerium the bells began to ring, but the mass of priests did not crowd the walks and terraces, the upper towers and windows, to see. It was forbidden. They understood how they must greet him. Under a consecrated terror of joy they took him in, as it must be, like the awaited guest he was.

High in the south wall of the Christerium, an apartment had been made for Anjelen. As yet it had few furnishings. He would perhaps send for the objects that had accrued on his travels, from the storage in which he had left them . . . for alchemy had become his device, his foliage, like books and learning, like the priesthood itself. He bade them take the silk from the bed. The coloured windows were facts: the horned wolf ridden by the angel – the Manifestation, the snake with breasts and cat's cunning face, who roped the Tree of Fruit. How aptly the ignorant read him, while the wise fell at the wayside.

He summoned the high priest, the Primentor, who arrived with some pomp. In the first chamber, alone together, the Primentor knelt to Anjelen.

'Get up, my lord,' said Anjelen.

'You are *my* lord,' said the Primentor, whose robes flamed with jewels.

'But it should not seem so. I don't ask it. This isn't the time.'

This admonition would one day be passed on to a successor. The Primentor did not guess. Like the Factor, he was to be spared foreknowledge of lethargy, the test of faith that must endure not trial but, worse, a long, long wait. Anjelen was dressed for the Primentor as a Knight of God, for the order, which had been censored in the

523

outer world, was succoured, and flourished, here. From such Knights, disciples would be drawn. It was expected.

A dove-blue choir chanted in the galleries below, like the sound of the sea that, in its way, was the noise the forest made, the hush and swell of waters, leaves.

His title, at the Christerium, was Magister. Not much was seen of him. He was not discussed. He came and went as he chose, through the days, the months, the years, the decades. Sometimes he was absent, although present. At others he was reckoned to be there, but was away in the body. He led particular ceremonies of the Knighthood. The Christerium was, at his advent, close to three hundred strong, aside from its servants and slaves. (The adjunct women of the Doma did not count in any sense.) The numbers grew. The sanctum had an ambience of its own, although in general parlance it was supposed a seat of high learning, a remote kernel of piety and devotion, in another way, something which knit the fabric of the earth. Anjelen had imbued the Christerium. He was in every stone, every pane of glass. The gargoyles were aspects of his darkness and his piercing fire. The pictures of the windows and the walls reflected his soul, his intellect, his mythical nature, his actuality, and his demonic unsubstance that would never make sense. All unawares. It was as if his blood – the sacred and profane and dreadful blood which he used to feed those he took to himself – that blood ran through all the secret arteries of the building, and down into the very sand, that now was entirely black to the edge of the craving, pouring sea. There was a drop of blood also in the crucifix over his heart. Heart's blood, perhaps. A tear of blood let fall, crystallized, and turned into a flower that in turn turned to a ruby. He must have created, or garnered, the gem himself. It had not been left for him, they would not have presumed.

Thus Anjelen, at the hub of the edifice that had been formed to enclose him, to magnify and make straight his way. The palace on earth.

It was his study. His chamber of science. There he worked on what he willed, which had nothing to do with the religious or miraculous reveries of the Christerium priesthood. It was the business of a tree. That was what he toiled at, in the exquisite rooms of tinted lights and hanging swords inside the shell of stone. On the spore-spreading mindless brainless bloody and insensate propagation of the wood.

And it was there, and in this way, that he formed the blonde girl Catra out of the mere genes, the semen, and the ovum, of a male and female.

That she must wed into Korhlen was his purpose. Korhlen, the area of the Tree. For that he made her, without great effort. Free of his body, in various guises, wolf, hare, man even, he moved about the forest's edges. He observed the boy child, once carried in to the Raven Cup Hall, grow, as it might have seemed in a few days, to the youth of manhood. Kolris. Who was beaten by his father of the twisted leg, into a shape. These psychological semantics did not concern Anjelen. He noticed only that the Landholder of the Korhlen Tower must pick a bride away from his own kindred, and that he would be likely to make an alliance here with this Tower, or here, with this. That light hair was unusual and might entice. Anjelen constructed Catra to fulfil such essentials. He constructed her in the womb by introducing into her composition at the moment of conception (the man and woman thrashing on the mattress), the etheric splinter of himself. He melded with her, and through his will and his invisible physical presence, she was conceived. She was conceived also female, and after his design.

Catra had two fathers. Not the semen of Anjelen, kept close as treasure, but the psycho-fleshly matter of him. It was that which fused with sperm and ovum, and which made her. He fashioned her like a pattern, next concentrating and perfecting a little at a time. He did it unfeelingly, seeing her from a great way off, through alchemic and biological knowledge, and via a godlike callousness that experimented, almost frivolously. He expected only success. And from that high view, he did not jib when coincidental fate itself removed her possible rivals to

Kolris' marrying hand. Sickness came, and carried them off, or other suitors. He, if needful, would have seen to it, one way or another. Luring by omens of the forest, through dreams, into disgrace, killing through hallucination, whatever was necessary. He might accomplish so much, this magician-priest, looking in his glass of quartz, manipulating, just as he had structured the embryo of Catra.

Catra came to term and was born. Anjelen saw this. He was in the room, somehow, unnoticed, a germ of flame upon a wall, in the corner of an eye, a mirror . . .

Catra was his, but he had been careless. It was all done so blithely. He had not made her, after all, quite right. The first experiment in genesis was a failure.

The Tree, spreading seed, reproducing its life, did so blindly.

One failure did not spell so very dire a dismay. Yet also Anjelen was becoming human, he had a mortal brain, transcended though it had been.

Add then to the inconsequence, the barb of intellectual irritation. Longevity had begun to impress upon him a man's occasional mental symptoms. Partial pleasures, almost angers. The hint of wormwood.

Catra was simple. His play with her had addled her wits. Yet, that might not interfere. Korhlen took her, wedded, bedded. Her use was to bear a single fruit. It was now feasible.

And in a near impatience, the Tree waited in its grove of marble and shadow and painted saints. For a burgeoning of the Korhlens out of the vessel of Catra: Anjelen's son.

'Don't cry now. You're my good girl, my clever little wife.' Kolris Vre Korhlen embraced his shivering woman, and her flaxy hair skeined over him, smelling of wood herbs and night. 'I'm pleased with you. It's a shame you must go over to the women's rooms once you're in the third month. But I'll visit you.'

She clung. Kolris fondled her breast, put down his head

to suck at the candy star of the nipple. Could she make him a boy, this fragile lily? Why not? Who would have thought her so lusty a lover, so hot. She would bear well for him. He had hung her with necklets and put a comb of gold into her tresses, but the comb made her hair look more grey than fair.

'You'll like to give me a boy,' he said.

'No,' she said, and struggled, and he took it for teasing and pushed her back, but she was frightened, as if doing this again might make another baby in her, astride the first.

She had heard the tales, the birthing in agony, the woman shrieking and split. Did not the whole belly come apart, and the surgeon have to sew the mother together again?

Catra did not confide in Kolris. The accurate explanations of the Hill Tower maid had only caused more fear. The child did indeed come out of the belly, through the passage whereby it had entered. It emerged between the legs. There was blood.

Catra fought off her husband. She did not want to be penetrated. She wanted to forget that thing in there. Her belly was growing round and hard, and in the mornings she retched and vomitted, and one of her teeth had begun to ache, and the maid had said she would lose it because of the baby, which ate her strength, the man must pull out the tooth with pincers. And maybe the baby would be pulled from her and she would tear in two.

Kolris hit his wife, to quiet her. He would not force, not wanting her to miscarry, but he was sorry his hour of relief and exaltation had been spoiled. The girl was backward; he had been stupid to ignore it. He must have her watched, in case she harmed herself and the child.

The Christerium was in darkness, but only that which holds a wood, for here and there the minutest lights were burning: the candles of some, late reading, the bakery ovens, the lamps at the latrines, and under the niches of prescribed statues, in the corners of walks where the gargoyles stared, and over the supreme altar of the church.

The church tower stood higher than any height of the Christerium. In its ruffle of embroidered stone, the door appeared shut, but was not secured. Any might open it, enter. None would do so, now.

Within, the church did not long stay in darkness. An undersea radiance bloomed out. It did not quite touch the landward windows that showed the battle of Good with Evil, the fallen Devil in his pit of garnet and chrysoprase. But the altar opened like a flower about the core of the lamp, the white and scarlet stamen of the Christus on his cross. The altar drape was red. It was embroidered in gold and picked out with large drops of fire opal. Before the altar, on the polished floor, there lay a vast crown of thorns, woven for the head of a giant. It was fixed there, in the island of light, sparkling faintly where it had been splashed with some fluid.

Under the altar stood twelve white Knights of God, in mail, tunics, cloaks, helmed and plumed, with swords at their sides. Twelve male faces, capped with metal, alike in the stillness as twelve pillars. Eyes beaded from veiled, smoking wax.

Directly by the altar, Anjelen, a Knight, the angel, god-in-man.

Soon after sunfall, Catra's labour pains started. She had been ill and restless all afternoon, and her women had looked for it.

The midwife came to the women's quarters.

Catra shrieked.

'If the lady screams now, what will she do when it really comes on her?' joked the midwife, a burly woman who had borne thrice with considerable ease, and assisted at every difficulty with a contemptuous matter-of-factness. Trouble was for others. Perhaps they had deserved it.

Catra shrieked.

'She's very slight, very small,' whispered the maid from the Hill Tower.

'Slight she may be, but that's a great one she's got in her bag. Now, push, lady. You can't leave all the toil to he and me.'

Catra shrieked till her voice broke. Her eyes were insane with horror. She bit and struck the women who tried to help her, and only the bullying midwife got the better of her.

'We are here for our faith.'

The novice had come from the side door to the north of the nave, seeming to emerge from nowhere. He had thrown off the robe, and was naked but for a loincloth of linen. On his head was a garland of autumn flowers. He entered the aureole of the candles, approaching gently, half-timorously, like a ghost. His face sightlessly adored Anjelen.

'They hung Him on a tree. He was perfect. For the errors of the earth He suffered. He said, Do this in my name hereafter. And He gave them the Wine.'

The midwife slapped Catra's back. The girl lay on her side. She had been in labour for ten hours, and it was almost dawn. 'Heave, girl. Get him out.'

Catra whimpered. She had let her maid come and hold her hands. Catra had no more strength left to her to fight any more, her maid, the child, or the pain.

Blood, water, wine soaked across the sheets and into the straw laid under them.

Catra tried to scream. She had no voice.

The maid stood up.

'Call the surgeon. He must help.'

The midwife, red from her exertions and in her butcher's apron, laughed in the girl's face.

'He'll only want to cut her up. Best to leave it to me.'

The boy put back his head to gaze at Anjelen. From the silver wristlet on his left arm Anjelen drew the knife. He put his left hand behind the boy's head. With one glancing stroke he sliced open the throat. Blood jetted—

—It gushed out black and crimson, and in the centre of the blood the leaping thing rose white as a fish under the muck.

'A boy!' called the midwife. She seized the child as though in hatred, severed from it the link of birth, shook and swung the baby, scraping out the three holes of its face with her finger. The child voided its lips and nostrils, and wailed in the tone of a nightmare mouse, so thin and reedy, so *unhuman* was its noise.

The midwife glared at Catra, lying almost but not quite sunken as a sack, her eyes like colourless pools in hollows of dust from the moon.

'She's big still.' The midwife pressed on Catra's belly.

Catra managed to scream. Her cry was exactly like the child's.

'There's another to come out, God have mercy.'

'And this one is no boy,' added the maid with venom, holding the thing over the basin of water, a little white fish-rat with invert loins.

The Knights of God drank from the chalice one by one. They were moved, but decorous.

At last, the last of all, Anjelen raised the novice boy to his lips, kissing his forehead in a kiss of peace. The boy could not die, unless Anjelen willed it. The boy only need to believe, to give of himself, and so he did.

Anjelen drank from the brim of the well of blood, as the Tree had done so many countless times from the blood of men.

Catra was unconscious when the second girl was squeezed from her body. This girl was like the first, perhaps more flaccid, tinier, an even poorer specimen.

They supposed Catra could not survive. But she did.

Her husband was kind to her, the Landholder's lady in the Raven Tower. He said she was not to fret. She would give him a son next time.

Catra knew she would never let Kolris, for all the

delight of it, into her body again, for she had learned what resulted from such unions. Anyway, she could not think that her rent flesh would ever be fit again to receive him. He had ruined her.

She lay in pain all day in her bed in the women's house. When at length they coaxed her out into the garden he had had made for her from the orchard, she sat passively. She did, so far, what she was told, even to nursing the two white, boneless, rat-like daughters. But her milk was thin, and a nurse was got for them. The nurse did not like them either. They had strange eyes, too pale. Presently their eyes changed to a pink colour, quite pretty, like rose glass in a window. A white down appeared on the heads of the creatures. They were albinos. They would be odd, like their dam.

Even then, Kolris was kind. Catra had proved he was capable of generation. Unluckily, she herself was faulty. He had begun to ponder if an annulment of the marriage was procurable, and his words of sons were offered only to cheer the ailing wretch.

A letter to the Church Fathers at Khish, however, had gone unanswered five or six months. Which, even allowing for the onset of winter, was a long while. Winter, after all, was now over and the roads clear. He would not dare write again so soon. Wait and see. She was unhealthy and might die. Why make her miserable? There was still time.

Kolris Vre Korhlen did not know that his disappointment had been, in an oblique and unlike way, shared. That something, like the form of a black eagle perched upon a crag, looked down and watched his world through a globe of glassy stuff. That something walked his woods, went over his fields, and left the print of a wolf.

This unguessed participant was close in every way but the physical.

The slaves of Korhlen murmured, and threaded the trees with effigies, and now and then cut the throat of something at the forest's brink. The sacrifice to the stone in spring was looked for in a parched desire. And Catra sensed a sound of footfalls drawing near. She began to have the bad dreams she had endured in infancy and childhood. (There had been a child, then, gone astray, as sometimes happened, in the forest, the daughter of a good family. Word spread, and the nurse had blamed Catra's dreams on that, having herself recounted the gossip in her vicinity.) Surely, however, the infantile legend bore no relation to Catra's adult terrors? A tree of ebony grasped her, turned her round and round, plucked at her. Her hair was tangled in the boughs. The tree had hands like those of some monstrous man, jet-black and gleaming, articulate, hard, and inescapable.

Time moved, as the sea moved on the sand under the building by the ocean. It crossed the forest, stripping and returning leafage. The pines remained, and the granite trees of the Towers, though villages that might last two hundred years might also slip into the ground, vanishing in a week. For the forest jumped, as did the wolf, upon the back of anything fallen, and there devoured it.

Not much time. Enough to heal the silken lining of the thin pale girl, so she could walk through the orchards, and up the stairs of the Tower, and along the wooden galleries of the women's house. Enough to unfold the budded daughters into little white vegetables that skipped and meandered, holding to her skirts, for rarely would she grant them her hands.

These two things had hurt her. They were to blame, as Kolris was, who had put them inside her. She did not regard them as hers. They were two tumours that had been wrenched out of her, and external now, still kept a grip.

Having walked through the orchard garden, where the twin females had, at the persuasion of a serving-girl, tried to pat a ball, mother and children were going back to the women's quarters. Catra, the Vre's lady, lived there now, as was quite proper, although several had thought he would discard the custom, he was once so keen to get at her.

Charina and Chirda made heavy weather of the ascent

among the wooden buildings. Their legs were small for the climb. In keeping with their freakishness, they had begun to speak very clearly, if in malformed and often senseless phrases. 'Mamma,' said Chirda, repeatedly attempting her mother's cold and bony hand. 'Want Mamma.'

'Your mamma's there,' said the serving-girl, coming up behind them. She was embarrassed by Catra's unnaturalness; it offended her on some deep and unreasoning level. 'Lady, won't you take your daughter's hand?'

'No,' said Catra, and brushed both her children off.

The little girls had quaint matching dresses of pale blue, with sewn eyelets to show blue and green checkered petticoats and strawberry stockings. But the clothes were infrequently changed and dirty.

In the long rooms, of which there were four, befitting the legal wife, Charina, and Chirda (the younger by seven minutes), recovered themselves and began to play more earnestly than in the garden, apparently consoled by the icon of their mother.

Charina took the cithra and commenced plucking the strings, her fingers unable as yet to make more than a vague scratching. Chirda draped herself in a long scarf of her mother's, and strutted about. They were like two dolls from the trees, almost without contours, so white, their hair fine as smoke.

Catra lay down on her bed and pulled over the hanging.

She lay staring up at the carved ceiling, where apples were painted a flaming dulled red. But there were leaves too, indigo and brown and green. Catra did not like the leaves. She started a dream, evaded it, sank back and was caught again.

The dim scratchings and patterings of her daughters had become an emission of the forest. Unseen animals patrolling, the scrape of needles against each other. What was in the woods?

Another child had been lured away, abducted by a tree spirit or demon. But Catra had avoided this. She lived on and was older now, a woman now. But no, she was only the age of Charina and of Chirda. She was tiny, and how high the trees towered up, and there was a tree blacker than the others, and like all the others together twisted into one shape—

Catra ran, but the tree reached out and grasped her. It pinched and worried at her, and Catra opened her eyes and found the punier twin, Chirda (though she did not like them, she alone could tell one from the other), had hold of her wrist. 'Mamma, Mamma—'

Catra absently stroked her daughter's head. Chirda had rescued her from the dream of the tree. Charina looked on with pink pebble eyes.

The curtain at the door was pushed aside and in came the servant with food.

The little girls ran to the repast, more curious about it than hungry. They had been weaned haphazardly, and still went to their mother, or the nurse, attempting to suck the breast.

'Now, lady, you must eat. Eat this bread and the whey with honey. See the fruit.'

Catra's maid from the Hill was nowhere near. She had entered into a romance with one of the soldiers in the Vre's garrison. Catra did not miss her, engrossed with depression. She missed her husband far more, although now she was afraid of him again. Catra ate some of the barley bread dipped into milk and honey. Chirda copied her mother. Charina had lost interest and gone to play with a toy of rags one of the women had made her.

Catra looked round the room, and round again, wanting something to happen. It was true the light changed places, going about and over objects, altering them, while the dark also reversed its shapes and positions. Catra watched the motion of the afternoon sunlight. She had not the capacity to envisage an eternity of boredom, and so did not totally despair. She had no suspicion that Kolris might try to cast her off. Left to herself long enough, probably she would have reverted to her basic needs, would have seduced the boy in him, and so won round the man, at least until pregnancy once more hunted her down.

But the light changed in a new way. A strange shadow stood up in the corner.

Catra was at once afraid, and did not look exactly at it. Something of this kind had occurred before. She could not have said under what circumstances, maybe only in the thickets of her dreams.

(Detecting their mother's fear, the two children also reacted, each in her own way. Charina slipped off into the adjoining room, casually, as if eluding one who might, if properly convinced, forget her presence. This gambit was not directed at her mother; there was no cause for it to be so. And yet simultaneously, Charina did not seem to be aware of any motive for deception or flight. A moment later she was playing again in the sunny shadows under a window, plaiting the doll's tow hair. Chirda, however, recoiled, without looking, exactly as her mother had done. Chirda did not remove herself. She bit her nails with her head tucked in, looking nowhere and making no sound.)

The darkness in the corner was like a man, tall and etiolate. There was the suggestion of a face, a pallor, that might only have been a coin of light intruding through the shadow. A reddish beam was concentrated high up, as if on some jewel below the throat, but again an orphaned ray from the sun might have accounted for it.

Catra dropped her bread on to the plate. The red burnished apples in their dish were burning up like round fires.

A tension of terror had fastened on the room. It seemed lifted to another dimension, beyond all help.

Catra put her hands together childishly. She muttered a prayer, and the nearer child, without the formula of words, once more mimicked her.

'Lord, Who is above us, enthroned over the world, we praise Your name and entreat that Your power encompass us and all the earth as it does Your kingdom of Heaven.'

One of the apples dislodged from the bowl. It rolled and lay against Catra's plate.

Suddenly the clutch upon the room slackened. A wave of light throbbed, expanded, ebbed away.

Catra reached out and took the apple. She could not have told why. Perhaps it was the withdrawing of fear at her prayer, as the priests assured you fear would do. Or perhaps some item to hold that was warm from the sun, round like the breast, sweet for the mouth to suck in comfort—

Catra bit into the apple. She recalled biting the hand of a servant in her labour. The flesh had parted and Catra had tasted blood. She tasted blood now. The apple tasted of it. The apple bled. The blood trickled over her fingers from the wound in the apple, and out of the wound came something, bitten open at its centre, still weaving and wriggling – a scaled worm, a serpent. It raised its head, writhing, and it spoke aloud: 'Give us today our food and drink, and forgive our sins that we may forgive those others that sin against us.'

In Catra's mouth, the piece of snake she had bitten out also wriggled. It went into her throat before she could stop it.

Catra screamed and jumped to her feet. The plates crashed, the fruit and milk were spilled.

Chirda screamed too, more thinly, and jumped up. And in the other room, Charina jumped up, stuffing her lips with the rag doll to keep sound in and the world out.

The maid from the Hill Tower, who had brought herself back to Catra's service, hearing the outcry, hurried to the apartments. She imagined Catra or her children were in a pet, and coming in saw nothing at odds with that – save the face of her mistress, which was congested and scarlet, a volume of colour never before achieved.

In Catra's hand was an apple, with a bite taken from it, the crisp greenish flesh gaping like a wound.

Although she did not let go, Catra had forgotten the apple. She was jerking, half springing, her body in a wild dance. The noise she made was no longer to be confused with a tantrum. Then her face went dark and her eyes bulged in their sockets. She curled over and sprawled along the floor, and kicked the broken plates with her pink feet. Froth exploded from her mouth and fragments of apple. Chirda shrieked and Charina stood in the distance with her doll over her face but not her eyes.

Catra's maid fought with Catra, trying to expel the fruit from her throat. But the spasms were already involuntary. There was no longer sight in Catra's eyes.

In the blazing of the awful sun, which now entered all the windows on that side of the house, no mistake could be made.

The servant got up. She sobbed, and called for assistance. Who would come? This Vre would be glad to be rid of his sickly wife.

It was such a terrible thing. And the girl thought how her soldier would comfort her, when he learned of the dreadful accident she had witnessed.

Chapter Eleven

Under her checkered shawl, in the bouncing carriage,
Anillia was sleeping. Outside was whiteness, stemmed and
variegated with powder green and black. Someone sang
to her sometimes, or told her stories in simple words . . .
'And then the wicked god sent his white bear to lean upon
the humble cot, and its walls caved in. That was their
reward, for having tempted his anger. The snow bear ate
them up . . .' The man rode on a horse beyond the
window with his servants; and the man-boy, who was
indifferently cruel, he had been left behind in the town
house. It was therefore safe and comfortable here, with
only the mother, and the hot coals in their box, and
the travelling rhythm, and sleep. Arrival had no form or
allurement for Anillia. She was two years old.

The woman though, the mother, Lady Crel, was looking forward to their journey's end. She was anyway not
so comfortable as her daughter, nor so warm, and certainly
not so redundant from care. Her duties as a wife she found
distasteful but she bore with them, having no choice. Her
spirit had survived despite bondage. Although she had
produced two children, and carried another in her womb,
she had her good looks still, was voluptuous, her condition
evidenced only in the globular four-month stomach
hidden in her velvet skirts. Her skin was lucent, her hair
abundant, coiled and looped through tortoiseshell about
her neat and bird-like head. She pretended often to be ill
to stay her husband's appetite. She had never inclined to
men either in a bed or out of it. Her natural desire might

have been for women, if she had been permitted to discover as much. The first son, who had won for her praise and presents, she had loathed to touch him intimately. The second child, this daughter, Lady Crel loved.

Nor did she fear the forest. There was a legend in the Crel family of a noble of their lineage who had become a madman of the woods. But there was also a legend of a priest of the Crels who had gone astray, found with a whore in a tavern. Lady Crel preferred priests who were abstinent. She had always managed to fall well of them, by her respect, her chasteness.

It was her husband's business that had brought him to the forest. A tract of Crel woodland, a foolish steward. Lady Crel had not paid much attention. The husband had brought her with him, thinking the trek would revive her health – she had generally enjoyed travelling – but she was careful to pretend on with her vapours, keeping him away as successfully on the road, at the inns and in his woodhouse, as at home. The business with the steward sorted (there had been whippings), they returned to Khish through the forest. But then the winter snow came early. Crel was determined they should get back to the town. For herself, his wife had mixed thoughts. If they were caught tonight and could proceed no further, she might not mind it. They were due to stay at one of the larger Domas of the forest, a sisterhood with whom she had had dealings in her youth, for her own family had connections with a forest Tower, and she had received schooling with these sisters. The very old ones she had known in girlhood, and the younger were contemporaries who must revere her. She almost envied them, save she could never have brought herself to like the austerity of their life.

As evening wrapped the woods and the road grew worse and new snow began to descend, Lady Crel imagined their detainment there, at the Doma, among the women, and desired it less. She did not fancy carrying to term and giving birth out here in the wilderness. If only *he* had not saddled her with another baby.

The child slept. Lady Crel looked at her, wanting to

wake her, to have the full consciousness of her daughter's eyes fastened on her face. But Anillia was two years of age and must be allowed to sleep. Indeed, her talent for peaceful sleeping was a useful one.

Lady Crel could not deny that she was half excited, approaching this female place of her girlhood.

It was the dinner hour when they reached the chapel of the Handmaidens of Saint Hrolowice, pitch-black but for the snow glare, the men wet through, pounding into the courtyard with their habitual bombast of impatience, demands and cursing.

Presently Lord and Lady Crel were in a stony chamber, their belongings on the floor, and behind them, to her chagrin, the wooden box of bed thought correct for their married state.

'Well, madam, make yourself as comfortable as you can. I must go and see to my fellows, shoved in the stable.'

'Yes, sir,' she replied. and drew to the fire, holding her side as if it ached.

'They'll bring you supper, no doubt,' he said. He ignored her hand. He pointed to Anillia, who was sleepily awake now, seated on a cushion at the fireside and playing with her wooden doll. 'The child must nap in the cot there.'

'Thank you, my lord.'

'And you and I on the same couch.'

She bowed her head to him. There was a red light in his eyes that was not the firelight but the angry lust she abhorred.

'Tarosar,' she said, 'may I go to speak with Sister Virina? You remember she taught me to read and sew?'

'Remember? No. But I suppose you'll please yourself if you visit her, madam. Eat first. You must take care of your belly.' (He meant of his next son.)

'She's very skilled in herbal medicine. Maybe she can suggest some restorative.'

'And you'll take none of her recipes. Don't you recall you nearly lost the boy, spooning simples into yourself?'

Lady Crel bowed again obediently. 'As you say, Taro-sar.' He had had the boy named after him, and the boy seemed fair set to become a replica, if rather lacking in his father's brutal good sense.

'I won't be abed till midnight. I shall hope to see you here before me.'

As he slammed the door, the child, used to his noise, looked up. Her eyes were dark as her hair, both burnished, her face a small perfection of paleness.

Lady Crel held out her hand.

'Should you like to visit Sister Virina with mother? Mother was in the care of Sister Virina when she was only ten years older than you.' The child considered, mentally striving to go this impossible distance of age which, in any case, she was not destined physically to accomplish. 'Can Dolly come?' 'Of course.' Consenting, Anillia rose, and went to her mother. Lady Crel felt for a sour cold moment the sweetness of her child's freedom. The boy would never ask, he merely *did*. Only his father had jurisdiction over him. And she also, Lady Crel, must *ask*.

Suppose the thing within her now was another boy? She did not like to dwell on that, this absolute closeness of a male. She had prayed for a second daughter. Then the hardship and the agony she had to look forward to at its end would be worthwhile.

She knew the way down from the guest apartments, the circling stone stair, and the bare corridor with its rushes strewn for winter insulation. After twists and turns, the narrow door. Lady Crel knocked.

The door was opened to its widest. Inside was a scene that made her, despite herself, utter a brief cry of pleasure.

She had written to them a month ago, that she hoped her husband would break the journey at Saint Hrolowice Chapel. They might have gathered in this room and been waiting since the day that letter came. They were all there, all the old ones she recollected so vividly, those she had feared and loved, and the younger ones she had half admired, half scorned. And in her chair was Sister Virina, thin as a winter branch, ancient as a white snake, and beautiful, clad in her gauze of skin and sculpted bones, with the great greyed black eyes burning through. Ten women, all in all, to welcome the lady in her crimson velvet.

'And here's the child,' said Sister Virina, when Anillia was led to her. 'Will she be sent to us, to school her?'

'Lord Crel may not allow it.'

Between the two women, the tense unspoken censure, durance in chains. Without these men, *we*—

There had been such teachings, too, with the sewing and reading. The Scriptures themselves pointed them up, for only the male saints were flawless men, and only the Christus, who was not a man, but God.

They said no more of the child's tuition. Anillia sat at the old woman's feet, with her doll, and two of the younger women in turn played with Anillia. A chair was brought for Lady Crel. They asked her how she fared, and the stricter sisters asked after her religious observance, but Lady Crel was pious, and they were glad at her.

Supper was served for Lady Crel and the Administress, Sister Virina, in that familiar room, and one by one the other women melted away to their duties. The little girl might have been taken too, but Lady Crel would not hear of it. Anillia therefore played on with the near-mindless absorption of her two years, making now for the doll a necklace of ribbons, as one of the sisters had taught her.

'Then you're easy in your life, have pleased your husband, are not at odds with your Maker.' Sister Virina paused and supped her wine. Age had given her back certain comforts. 'What then, girl, is troubling you?'

Lady Crel lowered her eyes.

'I don't want this child that's in me. It's a burden.'

'That is a sin. You must cast out the notion. Where would we be on God's earth if no woman ever wanted to bear?'

'I've borne him a son. He should be satisfied.'

'Your daughter you don't mention.'

'He cares nothing for her. She'll cost him a dowry, or may be plain. To me she's very dear.'

'So I've seen.'

'But the boy . . . He's already a man. Like his sire.'

'You must do your duty by your husband, whatever you feel for him. God has given you to him. You have only to obey.'

'I do. Look where it's taken me!' And with a spare, sharp violence Lady Crel tapped her belly.

The old sister raised her brows. Very little could shock her. And though she spoke of marital obedience, there was between them still the unvoiced other creed of womankind.

'The problem has no solution, my girl. To rid yourself of what's in you would be a crime against your husband and against God. Besides very dangerous, now. I trust you had no such idea in your head.'

'No sister. I have the hope that this is another girl.'

'God allots the gender of babies.'

'I've prayed to Him.'

'And perhaps He hears.'

'But sister – sister—' Lady Crel faltered. Her mind was back in the past, and yet she did not quite assay the memory, for the ways of the chapel might have altered.

There was silence, then a sigh from Anillia, who had once more fallen softly down into sleep.

'You must open your heart to me,' said Sister Virina. 'How else do I advise you?'

'Perhaps I'm at fault, sister. But I recall that when I was fourteen years old, in the month that I left you here, I made an offering to God, in a manner before unknown to me. My father wished to give me to a particular man. I won't name him, but I was afraid. I made the offering, asking to be spared that marriage.' Lady Crel stopped. She looked long at her hands, on which three rich rings fluttered the candlelight. 'I can't falsely say to you that I love Lord Crel. But he isn't a fiend. That other one – I might have died at his treatment. And when I ran to you and told you, you sent me with two other sisters to make an offering to the Christus. And I was spared. The creature was killed at his hunting. I'll never forget.'

'What offering then was this?' inquired Sister Virina. Her eyes were blacker than before, unblinking. The room was still. 'Come, now. I must be at late prayers very soon. Speak out.'

'It was years ago . . . We went into the wood. I remember nothing else exactly—'

'See that you continue to forget,' rasped Sister Virina. Lady Crel looked up.

'Pardon me for mentioning the subject, sister.'

'See that you forget, and forget once more, if it happens that again you go into the wood.'

Lady Crel loosed the grip her hands had obtained on each other. Through her brain went the faded bright images of fourteen, the summer of the wood, the towering shadow of the pines beyond, some deep place where a spring bled out like silver from the ground. Sunset had come, and then the night. They had taken off their garments and washed, shy and startled at each other, in the water. Naked, crowned with leaves, they went among the trees. No, she did not remember all the words, the gestures of reverence, the garlands they had hung up, or the turgid wine with its smell of a recent pig-killing, poured along the ferns and grasses. The name used was the true name, that of the Christus. They exhorted Him as a young man standing overhead in the boughs. After, she had been frightened, but not so much as at her wedding prospects. At home in Khish, when they told her her betrothed was dead, she had gone to the church to pray, she said, for his soul. She had thanked God with passion, that he had answered her invocation in the forest.

For what she wanted now, it was a jumbled thing. It was freedom, it was a condition she could not even picture to herself – Crel's death, some miraculous liberty – but in the prefiguring of a second female child, that was how she gave it shape. *Let me only be freed somewhat from men.*

At fourteen she had sent an offering also to the Hrolow-ice chapel. If her boon was granted now, she could send them something much worthier. She could say it was in token of a safe delivery.

Virina clicked her tongue against her fang-like teeth, all of which, though blackened, she had kept.

'You must slip out. If you're able. Go down to the back court, to the door. You must be no later than the second hour of morning. Someone will be there.'

They worship often in the wood, even in the snow, she thought, and was curiously calmed to think so.

'He may wake,' she said. 'Is there something I might give him—'

'Certainly not,' rapped Virina. 'Am I to have you practise against your husband? If he wakes, you must desist. Accept it for God's will.' *Caution.* They must not be blamed.

Of course, she had wanted to drug him against his molestation of her in the bed. But there, if he were to work against her that act he so greatly liked and she so completely hated, coupled to the travelling and the chapel beer – what means were more sure to make him sleep?

Only, the child might wake up and cry for her.

The child must go with her. Into the wood.

That had its rightness. Let the god in the wood take heed of Anillia too, protect and bless her. One day she also would be a woman, and then there would be no help for her but God.

Crel entered the guest apartment a little before midnight. His wife, contrary to his anticipations, lay in the bed in her shift, her hair spread on the pillow.

After he had divested himself of boots and clothing, and drunk the mug of ale warming at the hearth, he came to the bed.

'And how is your health tonight, madam? I must tell you, I'm anxious for your consent. Before long you'll be too hefty for the purpose.'

'I'm quite well, sir,' said Lady Crel

'That's good,' he said, and got in beside her.

With a taut body and some acute discomfort, she endured her husband's attention. She made herself give unresistingly, even when the thrusting of his member seemed to unseat her inner parts and she became partly frightened she would be damaged. She had never evinced wanting love, so he gave her none. The ale had slowed him, he took a time, and when he was done an awful relief made her weep.

'There,' he said sullenly. 'I'll leave you be.' He slewed over and slept instantly.

Lady Crel bit her fingers to end her tears.

Soon she was able to slink from the bed, shedding his wetness as she did so. She put on another shift and two cloaks from the journey. It was no method whereby to venture out into the frozen wood, but she had no option, she could not, as she now was, manage her dress without assistance.

How cold the chapel Doma seemed when she stepped from the red-fired room. Her child, shawled closely, she held in her arms and only stirring like a kitten accustomed to her, unquestioning.

The passages were blued with frost. At the courtyard door a flame burned in a clay dish. No one was there, despite Virina's promise.

'Damnation,' whispered Lady Crel, and cast about her in annoyance, but before she could do any other thing two slight forms came from the passage's farther end.

They were two of the youngest sisters, glimpsed at arrival. She had never known them. Both made her a small obeisance. They wore the chapel's grey robe, their hair bound and hidden in black linen.

'Well?' she said.

'Lady, hush. Only follow and say nothing.'

The other had undone the door. They crept out into the snow like thieves, and glided one by one across the black court. In their pens the wintered pigs grunted at their straw and mush. From the larger yard, over the fence, came the rufflings of horses, sleepless, and snores of Crel's men bedded in the byres and stable. There was a full moon; it stayed yet on the cones of the pines.

The women went through shadows.

At the outer gate there was a hesitation. Then the gate

moved, seemingly of itself. Outside, an older sister, one Crel's Lady had known in her adolescence, beckoned them through, and on.

They went towards the forest, over the wide white space of snow. They stepped defiantly now, although the surface was treacherous, and the moon shone on them for any to see. But the chapel was mute at their backs and all the men slept. The first wave of trees accepted them.

Lady Crel was very chilled. She was uneasy now, for herself, and for her child. This was not wise. What had she been thinking of?

An abrupt colour flitted in the trees, bewildering her. Was there a torch ahead? They came between two hemlocks of enormous size, and she recollected them as if from a dream. Beyond lay the open place with the watercourse – through a palisade of slender young trees she saw the glade. It was not the glade of summer. The stream had vanished under the snow, and in a dark-running hollow near to the surrounding pines a fire blazed like a spotted lion in a tapestry. There were other sisters there, warming themselves. Not Virina, not at this hour, but two more at least that were known.

Without any deference to her rank, and now she was glad of it, they came forward and embraced her, like the girl she had been, then.

She was drawn to the spotted fire. One of the older women lifted the sleeping Anillia from her mother's arms. 'I'll see to her. We'll sit here by the fire and keep ourselves cosy.'

It was dreamlike still, not only the memory, but the changes. An owl went over the clearing with a stark and evil cry, and all the women lifted their heads, seeing only the white sail of a wing, a veil from the moon.

Lady Crel was shivering. From the hot ashes at the fire's edge one of the young women drew up a vessel. She wound it in a cloth and they passed it between them. It was indecorous beer, the man's drink. How invigorating it tasted, and all at once the dull pressure and gnawing of the cold went off. In her boots the woman felt her feet come back, and her fingers in their fine gloves. Her entire body stopped its quaking – had that begun in the open air, or when Crel left her?

It seemed unbelievable that they might go naked under the trees; until this moment she had dismissed such a theory as absurd.

But then she learned that the winter nakedness was of a different sort.

The Sisters of Hrolowice were unbinding their kerchiefs, letting down their hair. One of the younger women Lady Crel had known from girlhood came to her with a wonderful garland. It was of ivy mingled with white ribbons – just such as they had given her child to toy with.

The sister gently put back the two hoods of the cloaks and set the garland in the hair of Lady Crel.

'Do you remember?'

'Yes. No, I—'

'We must walk in the pines, there. It's there we do it. I'll touch your arm when you're to speak. Say what you want aloud. We must know, to raise the power of prayer before God.'

'Will you—' she wavered, said more quietly, 'Do we offer blood, as was done last time?'

'A little blood, from the chickens your husband dined on, mixed in wine. Blood's sacred to God. Look how He colours the berries.'

They began to move towards the blackest stand of pines in all the forest.

The mother glanced back. The older sister sat by the fire, cloaked and scarfed, with Anillia quiescent on her lap. The vessel of beer lay again to roast in the ashes. It was a strangely domestic peasant sight. No beast would confront the fire. Yet, something quivered under her heart. 'Will my child be safe?'

'Come, Lady. We'll only be a tree or two away.'

Crowned with ivy, something in Lady Crel thirsted for the black immersion of the pines. At this moment she was free. No man to lord, no child to hold. Even her womb was light.

*

As if it were a state that must be passed from one human thing to another, the sister slept, the child awoke.

The woman was drowsy from beer, of which she had consumed a drop too much. The child had slumbered a great while, and the unbalance of cold and heat revived her.

Nearby, she caught a murmur. It was soothing, resembling the sounds she had heard in the chapel earlier. Like her mother, Anillia did not fear the forest. She widened her eyes, and, lying on the broad grey lap, looked off at it through the lick of flames.

Where the wood seemed darkest, a shadow of paleness came and went. The child could not decipher this. Soon she turned away, and found where the moon speared into the trees, parting them.

There, in the lighting of the moon's fire, a black hare sat upright, gazing back at her.

Anillia watched. Animals intrigued her.

The hare kept so still it might have been made of basalt. Then it darted out across the clearing. It ran as if towards the women's fire, and the child shifted and held out one hand. But the hare veered off, and was gone again.

It was after the hare had run away that Anillia began to pick up the other sound, which was very faint and clear, and which she knew from entertainments in her father's house. The dainty singing of tiny bells.

Again the child shifted, sitting up, feeling herself to be like the hare, alert and attentive. The sister eased her arm about Anillia. 'Softly,' the woman muttered, but she was asleep, and in her country, Anillia slept too.

The notes of the bells sprinkled the air like figments of the cold. Now they were near, and now farther off. The child looked round and round for them, and the sleeper became accustomed in sleep to her fidgeting.

Anillia's mother was perhaps thirty paces away, inside the wall of the wood. In another fashion, Anillia's mother was a world's length out of sight, lost.

The child looked over her shoulder, and there, not six feet from her, was a fascinating figure, all black, but sparkled over with gleams and glitters. It was a man, like the men in the travelling entertainers' plays who leapt and performed tricks. And it rang and chimed from all the little bells that hung on it, and were tinselly shaken as it moved.

The child reached out her hand again, to finger and ring the bells.

The figure slid back, out of her way.

Anillia laughed. She had slept enough and wanted diversion. She liked this game, and got down from the grey lap to continue it.

The sleeping woman (in sleep), felt after the warmth and weight of the child. And something lay down on her lap, shapeless and motionless, but of the proper weight, and warm. And the woman's arm rested around it protectively, while the child took three more quick steps to catch the retreating bells.

The women circled, their arms about each other's waists, breathing the burning air from each other's mouths. The pivot of their motion, half dance, half run, was a young pine, only a few feet in height. A briar had twined it and grown up with it, perhaps slowing its advance. The snow had been cast from it, and in the needles were knots of ribbons rusty and torn from weather, and some skulls of mice and birds, a chain of bones all sewn together by a crimson thread. It was not to this tree they had brought her formerly. Maybe its youth had significance, or the other had died. How did they explain its ornaments when the priests came to examine them at Hrolowice? Did they undress the tree – or blame superstition on the village half a mile off?

Lady Crel was exhilarated by the running dancing motion. When they stopped she would fall. But the circling ended and she did not. The other women held and supported her. She was dizzy, near to laughing. They sank to their knees, in the comfortable, glowing snow. It would be easy now to ask for anything.

550

One of the women, one she had never known before, began to sing in a high thin voice:

> *His crown is made of leaves,*
> *His sword is made of wood,*
> *He hangs upon the tree,*
> *To save us with His blood.*

And one sprang forward and spilled the blood of the chickens mixed with wine from a clay jug at the base of the tree. The liquid went into the ground at once, as if drunk down.

Lady Crel felt the touch on her arm.

She had forgotten what it was she must plead for. It did not seem to be of any importance any more.

'My daughter,' she said, and broke out wildly laughing. The women stroked her. Lady Crel thought, *It already gives, and will give nothing else. It only asks. It wants, and will have.* And then, *I am a noblewoman of Khish.* She drew away from the sisters and said, 'Give me a girl child. I ask for the blessing of the Christus on my condition,' and crossed herself over in the snow under the tree.

Like the vast cathedral that it was, the forest unfolded a gigantic nave, between its pillars of ebony and ice. The floor was ribbed with glass. The windows stood in their webs of branches, paned with stars. The child had burned her hand once on the moon-white snow, but her tears dried. She did not know the cold as yet, pottering on her booted feet, swathed in her furs and shawls, after the jet-black player of the bells.

And as he went, other things had been drawn to follow him, and this also enchanted the child. A mouse in its white winter hair, a white ermine with gemstone eyes, a tree rat with a plume of tail that skittered and pounced from bough to bough, dislodging soft snow that showered like sugar. These items were like pieces of a story her mother had told her. They were accustomed marvels for which the child had merely been waiting.

But the nave of the cathedral of forest night spread on and on. The child to stumble over roots. She tripped, twice falling, dazed a little more than hurt, but the mouse and the ermine ran away. The squirrel had ceased to scamper above her. She had been allowed no nearer to the magical bells.

And the wind started to ride up the forest, in his armour, with the spikes on his cloak and helm and on the hooves of his horse, just as her mother had said. Such spikes struck at Anillia. Pains woke in her body. Her hands and face ached, and her feet in their boots had given up their feeling, which scared her, for now she seemed to walk on her ankles.

Ahead, the man in gleaming blackness, black-clad in bone-tight flesh, black flesh of jet, black hair of coal, with black, jet-coal face and hands and throat, with eyes lacking any white, teeth black as iron, glittering all over as though strung with stars, ringing with the tiny bells that hung on him. The child waned. She stood in the nave of the cathedral, and her priest halted, and glanced at her, and beckoned her, and the bells sang from his wrist. A hundred tiny skulls they were, of mice and ermines, rats and squirrels.

The child cried. She took a step and stopped again, afraid at her dead feet.

The blackness of the figure of the man had seeped into the snow, a pond of shadow lay all round him.

She did not know, Anillia, two years of age, that she was now in truth all of a world away from her mother.

'Mamma,' she said, and put her shawl into her mouth.

But from the blackness at the rim of the blackness, something was pushing, shouldering up out of the ground. One thing, then another, and another.

Anillia took the wool from her mouth. She let out a banal, inconsequent, useless scream. It had no strength. She did not pin upon it any prayer. She knew, as only a child could, that the nightmare had her, and was unavoidable.

Black wolves pulled themselves out of the ground, and the snow skimmed off their backs . . . like sugar.

They rose up and grouped on the floor of the cathedral, and looked at Anillia with eyes like stars.

She knew wolves. They were in the stories, too.

She knew what wolves did, and that she had no chance.

With a deadness and a dragging tiredness, Lady Crel, who had remembered herself, came from the sacred place, and saw the fire burning and the woman asleep with a bundle on her lap. Lady Crel looked at the shapes of these beings, and did not want them, or anything. Not the child she loved, not the life she disliked, her station, her rings, her sodden cloaks, her shivering body, the dreaded mound of the pregnancy, nothing. Only, perhaps, sleep.

Then walking briskly to the fire, she cursed her silliness in risking *his* anger for a pagan ritual, and was revolted by that old woman, Virina, probably senile, a witch and her mysteries. Yes, Lady Crel longed for her bed, packed as it was, and for the house at Khish, though not hers, and for morning, which was no one's. And she looked down at the dozing sister by the fire, who looked back smiling and patted what lay on her lap pridefully.

'My daughter,' repeated Lady Crel. Her voice was low and controlled. 'Where's my daughter?'

'Why, here.' In the woman's lap lay a dead and bloody hare. She peered down and saw it, shrieked.

The other women ran forward. They formed a clot of hair and skin and cloth and breath beside the fire.

Lady Crel poised in their midst, straight as steel.

She stared into the forest. Ignorant of everything as she always would be, for those instants she knew it all.

Before her she saw also what would come after. The man's fury, his blows, her fever, sickness and shame, his lies to cover her lapse, lies believed in the passage of time. Time itself.

The forest had devoured Lady Crel's girl child. She was gone.

One single image, in that prophetic second, Lady Crel

did not receive. That of a young dark priest and his counsel, of the strange rumour and the girl who would walk back out of the wood, Crel's daughter, no longer wanted, or recognized, no longer the symbol of anything, returned to her: Anillia.

Chapter Twelve

And it came to pass that Anjelen, who had been Jun, made Hell on earth for some through the mechanics of his will. But only in the way of creation, with only, here or there, a wink of malice. He was not a man, yet the emotions of men had grown in him a little, moss upon the tree.

When Catra was born, Catra that he had fashioned in the womb, he saw his work and it was not good. He waited on her growing, to see if even so she might fulfil his purpose. But it had happened that, even before her birth, he had foreseen a second means, and moved among those other lives, tearing them in bits, to make potentially another bride for the Korhlen house.

All offerings in the wood he was aware of, as of the rain which fell there, the snows, and the summer sun. He felt the blood poured at the foot of every pine and oak, every bush and shrub. It fed his soul, or what passed for a soul in Anjelen. So, he knew, in some unthinking, unconsidered annexe of his consciousness, when the Sisters of Hrolowice went out to worship. Then, too, there was the reminder of Wedsek Crel, for the woman had been taken into that house of Crel. She bore the name, and an invisible glint of malignity had prompted Anjelen to work on and against her, for Wedsek's sake, towards that end he envisaged.

To the brain of Anjelen, those crystals and razor edges, what was more simple than to prepare a slot, dug in the soil of history, wherein at a later time, if appropriate, might be dropped the unspoiled seed. For if Catra failed

him, he would make a second Catra. He would make her
out of himself, and from no other thing. The etheric rib,
the flesh made of the flesh. And he would call her *Anillia*
and send her back out of the slot in history and the ground
which he had emptied for her occupancy when he removed
the daughter of Lady Crel.

And Catra failed Anjelen; by her tenth or her eleventh
year he knew it, and began to move elsewhere again on
the waters of lives. He created the second Anillia, and
brought her in to Crel as a woman, by means uncanny and
psychological, by advice given plainly as a sober priest, by
subtle descants on the confused song of the human heart.
And then, while she was at Crel, growing in the mould
he had formed for her, he let Catra proceed into the
Raven Tower of the Korhlens. And there, when she failed
fundamentally, producing her two albinos, her unclean
female fruit, Anjelen shifted events in a similar unper-
ceived manner as before, killed and cleared, and brought
Anillia from the Crel cupboard to become the perfect
vessel for the Korhlen blood. And at last Anillia conceived, and bore, for Anjelen, Anjelen's son, Mechail.

But Mechail in his turn attempted to ruin himself.
Sensing what was in him, what power, what root, he made
to rip it out, and crippled himself, body and mind.

Anjelen watched now his son growing crookedly aslant.
Anjelen watched Anillia, her determined and astonishing
strength, the blowing and decay of the rose, and the claws
of her life sunk firmly in the rock. He knew soon enough
she would not die, for death was not able to stay her. She
was as strong in her way as Anjelen. Maybe that surprised
him (surprise, the emotion of the man, of Jun, if Jun had
been all he was). He stole her bones easily from Korhlen
and took them with him, to him (discarding like pips the
necklace of Crel) about the time he garnered back
Mechail, a wild harvest, from the wolf-wood. She had
earned that.

The dwarf, Anjelen took also, Mechail's own random
creation – product of Mechail's own power, and his bitterness. And the woods girl, the lizardine Jasha, with her

low wide brow and green eyes and brown river of hair. For Jasha was Anillia's Catra, as the dwarf was Mechail's. And maybe Jasha was Mechail's also – Mechail, Anillia, they had made more obliquely, less astutely, yet rather better than Anjelen the mage and master craftsman.

This gathering, then, he had about him for a moment, at the Christerium, which men, in their order, had created for Anjelen as a god. The Christerium, which had no trees, which lay by the ocean, the restless liquid land that offered no spot for a wood to grow.

But the Christerium was itself a sort of forest, with the great Tree being the seaward tower, the branched open-work of the window, the trunk of its stone almost all-endurable. The Tree itself had gone to stone.

Anjelen sat high in the south wall of the forest of the Christerium, in the jewellery rooms decorated by the makes of his mortal part. Like a tree he was stationary, rooted in body. Now at last he too felt a fixing of himself into the ground of that place.

From the petrification of the Christerium he sent out the tendrils of visions and hallucinations and things formed of spiritual flesh that were not flesh. Within, he walked, and gazed outward, and therein he practised the rite which brought him the feeding blood of holy sacrifice potent with its willingness, the Last Supper of Love.

For his priests, they were the undergrowth of the wood, the lesser trees, which both concealed and led the way to him. For his Knights of God, they were the grove, the briar hedge which ringed him round. Should it be needful, they would die for him. As his priesthood, mostly, should be capable of doing.

His disciples, the Knights, the apprentices of his magicianry, attended him at certain times. He let them run in the shape of wolves, or think themselves so to run, and others so to think, also. He loaned his genius to them, as now and then he nurtured them in turn on the human-inhuman ichor of his veins.

And with his blood, he had fed Mechail.

Of all that Anjelen had wrought, or which had been

wrought indirectly through him, Mechail was that being he had sought to create. As might have been guessed (that is, a man might have guessed it), Mechail was the very least of them, the saplings strewn about. Anillia, with her survival of carnal death, and Jasha that Anjelen had tested, sprung from the witch fire; the hunched and crumpled dwarf Mechi, who was also Mechail fathered of himself, risen from the deadly cold, a survivor of that most rigorous of trials, existence itself. Mechail, who had been the flawless flowering, it was Mechail who foundered. The others came to the door of the Palace-on-Earth as tyrants, wolf-like, serpentine, vengeful and questing, *tenacious*. But Mechail would not cling, would not grasp even the extended hand.

He had run away, with the girl Jasha. Struggled over the treeless mountains, and down into a valley by a stream. He had wept, he had cursed God, unable to die, unwilling to live.

It was Anillia who had stood on the high tower and challenged Anjelen, and the dwarf who had scuttled with teeming courage over the boulders of the days with Krau, and Jasha who did not ask but took and held with talons of the psyche.

A painted stroke of violent light seared out and entered, without breaking it, the globe of quartz.

Anjelen, who had lived more than three hundred years, lifted his head, by which any would have told him to be thirty-five, a modicum more, or less, and retraced the passage of colour to its fount, the fruit on the Tree of Knowledge in the window of the outer room.

This, the first physical movement he had made for seven days, did not discommode him. The altered body which he wore was not like that, not human enough yet even for that. In the inner room the water-clock in the shape of a tower lowered its golden moon slowly down the day. The days were long still. Time was stretching itself out more and more. For ever lay in front of the Tree, dappled by metamorphosis only.

Anjelen lowered his head again and looked on his work, Anillia and Mechail, Mechi, Jasha. (Far off, he did not consider the albino daughters of Catra, rambling about in their bright madnesses. They were very nearly all human. He had let them be. Each blossomed as it would.) The clock made a sound. Another hour had passed, time so swift, and so slow. Was it winter or summer in the changeless wood?

Early in the morning of the dark tomorrow, the man named Mechail opened his eyes from sleep and saw a strangeness in the world. It was everywhere. In the shelter of the hut, which during the night had cracked and crumbled, and now let in a view of snows and trees. In the lack of sounds and smells, even so soon familiar, from the village by the stream. In some indefinable thing which hovered there. And in the girl too. Mostly in her. As though all of it seemed focused through her. For she sat by the hearth with a piece of stone in her mouth, chewing on it, as if she ate.

'In God's name,' he said. 'What are you doing?'

She removed the stone. She looked as he recalled, and he thought of how he had tried to have her, had done so, but incompletely, writhing with her before the fire. The fire was low and smoky now in the vapid light, and burned behind her. It showed a halo round her head, coppery and supernatural, until he realized this was her hair, growing back after the other fire on the beach, the witch-burning that he had got her from. Her hair came quickly. Already there were two or three inches of it. He had not noticed yesterday. Had it grown in one night?

Other events had gone on, evidently.

She said, 'I do it now and then, to file the broken part.'

And he understood she meant she filed her broken tooth with a stone.

He did not know how this tooth had been snapped in the first place, for all her teeth otherwise were healthy. He had not asked, she had told him nothing.

He got up and pushed away the blanket – surely there had been others, the lending of the village? Now there was only the one he had brought with him from Anjelen's

Christerium. Mechail stood on the floor of the hut, through which pushed the roots of trees that had not pushed there last night. He thought of his other wakenings, in the body of a wolf, next under ice, next in the cell of the Christerium. Of his humped shoulder, which was now whole and straight. Of his dead brother Krau. Of killing Krau. Of Anjelen. Of blood.

But Mechail's mind raced back again at once to the curious, leaning, tottering hut, and to Jaṣha, that he had tried to have, unable to expel his lust.

In the nothing light her green eyes were pale, like acorns. There was something frightful about her. She was all part of a weirdness that went on and on and which had no answers.

'Jasha,' he said.

She watched him attentively, uncaringly. He remembered her hands on him on the journey to the coast, in a dream, washing him. Her hands last night. Her whore's reassurance. She cared no jot for him, as why should she. In this place, worse than an enemy, she was a being without a reference.

Outside, the village had gone away. There was no solitary trace of it. Trees clustered near, black-green pines, ledged with whiteness from the snow, and over there the gleam of the cold, cold water in its bed of ice.

Anjelen could construct illusions. Anjelen had warned him, by inference if not by words. And *she* had said: *You're to go to him. He fetched you once. That was enough.* Or had she said exactly that? In some way she must be the agent of Anjelen, too. All things were. Even Mechail, after all, for Anjelen had fed Mechail with his blood, promised him power, given him life. A spiritual father. *Magister.*

'Jasha,' said Mechail, 'everything here was his sorcery. Did you know?'

She shrugged. She had done that before.

Beyond the first ascent, the mountains had been all one to her; she took very little notice of them, or of how they were negotiated. She had things of her own to think of.

Even so, it was borne in on her fairly soon, the circling motion, the absence of new landmarks. She had nothing to say on this. It was not her affair, even though she was caught up in it. And Mechail did not ask her opinion. But the descent, the water, the forest, these she beheld with a sort of interest. Thereafter the village, with its huts, helpful, reticent women, the holder who made off with Mechail's saddle. She saw through them, not literally, but in other ways. And despite the fact that, of course, she went along with them, with everything, it did not surprise her, the morning after Mechail had lain with her (or attempted to do so), to wake and find that everything, or very nearly, was gone. Only the trees and the shallow stream remained, with the mountains scowling black and white on the snow sky. The bothy was ruinous, and single. There was no village, and there were no people. She went to look into their supper cauldron, out of curiosity, and there was soup enough for a pair of meals, and bread standing by the hearth, where a few logs still smoked. Not surprised, then, Jasha, but she pondered how he would react, her companion, who in the face of a score of contrary clues, had taken their circular rambling for a journey, and the wood for a village of men. He would now question (she surmised), what they had been fed on, how they had been -- he had been -- fooled so completely. He would ask questions of her impossible to answer, the more so in her more perfect understanding, for how could you explain an object you had seen to a blind man? Had Mechail never heard tales of places, persons, extant but vanishing in a night? Or of the complex illogic of mutated time? Yes, heard but not credited. He would swear and shy beneath this witchcraft, unable to accept. He could accept nothing, for he had accepted it all, swallowed it whole, and it had stuck in his throat, unable to digest itself and become a part of what he was.

Jasha was not like this. She was porous.

In the village the pain of her broken tooth had altered. It occured to her the tooth was pushing up under the snapped crown. She found a slate and began to file, a little now and then, in the same way she worked on her nails. That she had come back out of fire was a fact.

There was nothing else to say of Jasha, at this hour, upon this or any day. Her action with the slate symbolized her as she currently was. There was not even now the instinct for subterfuge.

Mechail stood in the ruinous bothy, and said, 'I shan't go back to his God-house. He plays games with me, even here. God knows, maybe this is a hollow tree.' He stared on the inadequate walls.

Jasha sat composed before the hearth, where the logs still burned and there was a pair of meals in the cauldron. (There was also a lean-to on the hut, where the horse remained, saddle-less, eating from a mound of hay.)

Outside, the snow was not so deep as yet. She had heard no cries of wolves or winds, nothing threatening. All wildlife had vanished with the phantom village. How far off to east was the Christerium? Since Mechail had gone mostly in a circle, she did not think it could be far at all.

Jasha did not tell Mechail she had had a dream.

If she had looked at him speculatively, it was probably an accident. She pitied him, respected his maleness, his therefore potential danger to her, that was all. The beauty of his body did not enthral her any more than the fine aspect of a tree.

'He sits there in that upper room of his. I can see him. Perhaps he lets me see.' Mechail paced about the hut. It trembled slightly, and next door the horse blew and stepped. 'I'm in the net. He hauls me in. But Jasha, I won't go.' And then, as if someone had responded, queried, 'Where else? Nowhere else. Sedentary. He let me get so far and here is where I'll stay the winter out. In spring—' He did not bother with spring. It was alien to him. Useless, the world. Jasha perceived in Mechail all that she was not. She did not condemn him or despise him for his differences either from herself or other men. To live was to live.

562

He did not ask her what she would do, presumably expecting her decisions depended on his. From the innate courtesy of caution, Jasha felt obliged to placate him.

'I won't hamper you,' said Jasha. 'I'll tend the house. How best can I help you?'

'But you can't. Not even in the sexual way.' He was white, he would soon hate her for showing up to him his own lack. 'However, I can't tell you to get gone. Where can you go?'

She sat meekly. They were trapped, she and he, by the season. And Mechail was under a doom, a shadow, or under some dark, *dark* blessing. Whatever it was, as he had said, he had rooted to that spot.

She thought of her father Carg Vrost. He had rooted in the forest. When he died, it was as if the time had come for it. She had known, days before, she would be leaving that place, and had been preparing. His death fit exactly the lines of her destiny. But she would not need to bury Mechail decently.

She heated the stew, and served him with it, and ate a little.

They lay down for sleep in the early night, separately, which would be good in the future time for her to creep away. She wondered if she would dream again, and slipped into sleep quickly, looking for the meeting.

The woman sat as before, on the mound of her grave. She wore Jasha's second green dress, and her hair in three thick plaits, as Jasha had done. The woman's eyes were black as wet stones.

Tonight Jasha went nearer, and felt the summer soil under her feet. A short way off was the hut, not the bothy she had shared with Mechail, but the wooden box of her birth. Until the dreams, Jasha's mother had only been the grave mound.

'Yes, you know me,' said Jasha's mother. 'My name is Anillia.'

Jasha watched her mother, excited by the dream contact as she had never been by anything else. Alluringly new, it had too a completion formerly always missed.

'Are you in the wood?' said Jasha.

'Which wood is that, Jasha? Or, are all the woods of the world one, and all Anjelen's?'

Jasha thought of the very few times she had heard Anjelen speak, and that her mother sounded like Anjelen. Intuitively Jasha believed she might fathom the relationship, Anjelen to Anillia, as Anillia to herself. Jasha looked at Anillia's silver ring, and wanting to vocalize her name, said it in the forest way, once, '*Nilya.*'

Then, the dream shifted, and her mother Nilya-Anillia was riding a horse, astride as a man rode, and clad in a mantle from the priests' place against the cold.

The mountains were all about her, motionless, noiseless, and slowly but too fast day and night fled over them. The landscape also flowed swiftly. There were none of the tremendous geographical difficulties in view that Jasha recalled from her journey with Mechail. The mountains through which Anillia rode were changed, or had reverted to their original condition.

'Where are you going?' said Jasha.

Anillia did not answer: it was apparent, she rode towards the wood beyond the mountains, towards the hut where Jasha slept.

Jasha opened her eyes. The hut was silent. Mechail lay sleeping with his head on his arm like a child.

Jasha got up quietly, and went by him, to stand in the hut's doorway.

It was black as any night, normal, save for the peculiar half-seen gleam on the edges of vision – the mountain-tops in their snow. Then there came a whisper along the icy ground, like the tingle of blood along a vein. Out of the substance of the dark, a woman came, leading by its reins a horse just now ridden in the dream.

A pale sunset had burned on the walls of the chamber, less red by far than the scarlet band that encircled the brow of the Administress of the Doma of the Christerium. Less red by far than the blood she must beat out from her body. Inferior, weak woman's blood. It was the only manner in which, now, she could offer it, for her female courses had ended years ago.

The woman, fat with the blubber of frustrations, thickened by depression, by a world ruled with the words: *You shall not*, contemplated the rod, her terrible old ally, with fear. For tonight she must make fifteen inroads upon herself, she had pledged it, and she was half-terrified. She must not cry out, must not groan. And afterwards, bandaged, she must walk firmly to the Doma chapel. On a chest stood a stoop of rough wine. She would need it, when she was done.

Slowly, she unwound her poor gross body from its wrappings. How she had once longed to be fair – vanity, sin— In the fading of the light, her own scent came to her, stifled, and acid. She readied the rod. She must strike there, on the healed flesh, her belly and her calves – for her thighs were a mass of purpled wounds.

The Devil – he was everywhere. She did not dare to fail. The weight of them all, these women's souls clustered in this hive, depended on her.

She struck, and gasped in agony.

Why, why did this become more demanding, harder, this act of her faith, each time that she gave herself to perform it? Of course, she had learned pain, what there was to dread. But more than that, surely. The Evil One was muttering, dissuading her.

She struck again, and her throat uttered a sharp, shrill cry. She could not control it. She paused, to discipline herself. Should she drink a mouthful of the wine? No, this pain must be borne to the full.

Her hand shook.

She stared at it, shaking, with the thorned rod protruding from it. She thought suddenly of a dragon, a snake. Then she remembered an image from a book once impiously shown her, in her youth, before she had taken her vows. It had been a picture of Eve and the Serpent, but unlike any image of them she had ever seen before. For the snake was a scaled man, and bare-breasted Eve, in a shower of golden hair, had hold of the Serpent's member.

She held it like a flowering stem, and just so the fat woman held now the rod of her correction, like a ghastly flower, like the barbed penis of a snake—

'You know nothing at all of the method of a man with a woman, yet you know enough to damn yourself,' said someone, a girl, musical and disembodied, in a corner of the locked and empty room.

The Administress laboured her body about. Last bars of sun lay on the wall, and in them poised the demon girl, the witch they had burned, and who rose up from the fire. All her hair was down her back, and it was black now, and her eyes were black, and her face was not the same . . .

'Go you behind me,' hissed the Administress. 'Go left of me, to your lord, the Devil.'

'Stupid bitch,' said the Jasha-girl of another face, the music of her voice playing with the coarse language of men, idly, smilingly. 'What's the Devil to me? Or do you mean *your* devil, your Magister in his high place – *Anjelen*.'

The Primentor had warned of the Devil. That their holy actions outraged him. The virtuous could only expect further obstacles, more suffering.

The Administress turned again, lightly as a girl, and struck herself unflinchingly across the stomach.

She felt the blood flow, wetness and heat. No pain. In astonishment, she gazed down, and saw the wound with the marks of the barb in it.

Behind her, the Devil now was silent.

Renewed, the Administress struck herself, repeatedly. She felt the power of God assisting her. The blood leapt from her body and in her hand the rod murmured with a life of its own. The blows landed and she felt their impact – like the slap of a velvet ribbon, no more.

'God be praised!' she cried out, unable to help herself. 'He is with me! I shall fear nothing!'

The joy of the miracle filled the room as all light left it.

Then there was only the sound of the phallus of correction beating on against the thick white flesh that turned

now in dark stripes and arcs, towards the colour of the
night.

'Come here,' said Jasha's mother, 'let me look at you.' As
a mother would have done. Still unsure if this were a
reality, Jasha could yet tell, as she had before suspected,
that Nilya was not a woman from the woods villages. She
was a lady. Her hands, her fingers, felt perfectly real, and
smooth from a lady's lack of use, when she traced over
Jasha's face, stroked the thickly growing hair. Her breath
was real and fresh, and touched Jasha's forehead, cheek.
Nilya's eyes were lit and alive. Jasha was pleased. She was
awake. She gave herself to the scrutiny and the caresses
as does a young cat to its mother's attention and grooming.
When Nilya had had her fill, she merely ceased. Her
hands were removed and, lady-like, laid themselves gra-
ciously back on the reins of her horse.

'Our first meeting,' said Anillia. 'Do you think,' she
said, 'that he's watching us?'

'Maybe,' said Jasha.

'I believe Anjelen means to do nothing. Or perhaps
something so opaque it amounts to nothing. I've begun
to feel that too, suddenly. A quiescence. An immobility
in him that is itself a sort of motion. He made me for a
purpose, and I made you, Jasha, for a purpose. But now
I think we have no purpose but to be, and to continue to
be.'

Jasha smiled. Her instinct – like that of any fox or wolf,
lizard, cat, flower, tree, stone – had always known as
much.

For some while neither woman spoke. The night spoke,
as it had never left off doing, in its unique and hushed
voices.

Then, from its makeshift stable, Mechail's horse whick-
ered, and the beast of the dream, the reality of Anillia's
horse, tried a soft answer.

Anillia nodded. She was gentle and potent, a storm held
in exquisite glass.

'Is he asleep, Mechail?'

Jasha did not question. 'Yes, lady.'

All at once Anillia's hands again let go the reins; they darted up to her breast, her lips. 'I can't wait to see him – and I can't bring myself to see him. And yet,' she said, 'I saw him, through Anjelen's mind, like the globe he used to spy on you. Anjelen's mind formed my brain, and I read his mind, there in the roof of his palace, like a book. Can you read me, Jasha, since I made you?'

Jasha shook her head. She felt a low note of jealousy, primal as the ground, go through her. Anillia, her ghost-mother come back to life, had passed her, moving to the door of the bothy. She stood there now, looking in, with Jasha left behind in the snow.

It was not often that the sisters of the Doma came to disturb the evening meditations of their Administress, after the supper and before the first late office. But one of these women, emerging from a duty in the chapel, had had a feeling of great uneasiness. This centred on the court of unchaste women. The witch had dwelt there, the witch who, burnt to cinders, had sent up a demon to plague the Doma. Was the demon in the courtyard? Something was there, whispering and murmuring. The woman felt rather than heard some illicit monologue of the darkness. She treasured them, these links to the surreal, and having brooded in her cell, presently she sought the Mother of her order.

The sunset was long over and the winter night had closed on the rock, the shore, the mountains. Soon the bell would sound the summons to prayers, tiny in the silence. The woman hurried up the corridor, full of an eager distress. Everything was blurred in a kind of black light, caused by the single candle burning in its alcove before a small stone saint. A hint of the lighted dark fell out on the door, which, as the sister approached it, groaned.

She caught her breath. She waited. She knocked vehemently on the door.

From inside came a curious noise, like that of a large animal rustling and coiling through leaves.

'Lady!' cried out the sister. 'Is everything well with you?'

Then the voice came. It was recognizable as that of the Administress, but only to one who had heard it frequently.

'Help me,' it said, 'for – the love of God . . . for His mercy. Help me.'

'What is it?' said the sister, stupidly, pressed at the door, afraid.

'Get me help,' said the voice, with an unsuitable random trace of anger in it now.

The woman meant to back away, and to run at once for assistance. Instead she lifted the latch and pushed open the door.

The blur of light and darkness mixed, slanted into the room. It divulged there a host of images that seemed without form though curiously cohered – whiteness and black, and a reddish substance that lay in the troughs, and shone. Abruptly there was the scarlet band that bound the face of the Administress, and two wide eyes that glared out beneath, and then some other features, a nose, part of a mouth . . . And with the movement of a snake striking, a firm white hand flared up clutching the stem of a rod – but the hand had no strength left, it fell away cheated.

'Cut off my hand if you must,' said the Administress in her curious voice, altered by loss of blood and weakness, and by the mutilation of the lower lip and chin. 'Make it stop. No more. Help me. You must pray – for my soul.'

And there was a shift of perception, as might come in finding a hidden pattern in a game of some sort played with tiles.

The sister saw, brightly and clearly, that the Administress of the Doma lay on the floor of the room. She was naked, but not any longer with a female nakedness, for her body was a swamp of fleshy slush. In her hand, the rod of correction, which she had used until blood-loss and faintness took all strength from her arm. They were on the floor now, the hand unscathed, quivering slightly, as if only resting. And in it the rod pulsed, its barbs catching each a white point from the candle. And from its upper end a fluid trickled, or appeared to, that was not bloody, milky rather, and already drying.

Hysteria of the same order and attached to the same root as that attendant on the witch-burning spilled the sisters and other women of the Doma round and about, like grey mice running in a maze by night. A distance off, the windowed towers of the Christerium looked on and did not see. Above and below the sky, mountains and ocean made no response. A bitter cold had pierced the lower world of the shore with hooks of platinum and steel.

It had become evident to the Doma sisters there was a demon in their midst.

To enter the Primentor's apartments was a progress, like that of the soul through halls of unknowing, confusion and wisdom, ascending to the Throne of God. Sufficient twists and winds of the passages were involved that all awareness of direction might be lost. Like a labyrinth that rose finally upwards, through a stone ante-room hung with tapestries of red and ethereal blue, and through a second ante-room clad with panels painted in the trials and eventual spiritual aggrandizement of the saints. A screen of figured ivory hid the door into the presence. It too was hung with masks of saints, with eyes of nacre and jet. Long seats padded by crimson velvet were set below the screen for those who must wait, and at the centre an ebony stand in the form of a bull, on which the Book lay open between the horns, for any to peruse, today, at a page which began: *God is in Heaven, and we in the world, therefore let your words be few.*

The priest, who had lived and served since late childhood in the Christerium, had, as it turned out, only passed this way once before. Whatever passage had then been highlighted in the Book, certainly he had dutifully read it, but his awe and trembling had kept from him its message. His mission that day had been slight, merely to summon the Primentor to a preordained office of the Church. But the priest had felt it keenly. Now, fifty years of age, with a mission more onerous, he was both duller and more fearful, for, even through the vestments of faith, he had learned something of this 'world' wherein he was.

After a pause of half an hour, the door behind the screen was heard to be opening. Out and around came the Factor Major, who had gone in before him. Grimly upright, he beckoned the lowlier priest with a thin, uncharitable hand. 'You may enter.'

The priest hastened into the sanctum of his earthly lord.

Over a sea of velvet carpet laid in one long spill of red, and hammered into the floor at each corner with a huge nail surmounted by a golden crucifix, over *that*, and between two high-windowed walls tapering with perspective but clothed with silk of Heavenly blue embroidered by briaries of silver, *there*, was the great chair of white marble, with its cherry-red footstool, and above an arch of gilded wood from which hung fruits of gold, rising to an angelic host painted on the ceiling. In the chair, the Primentor, in his black crossed by white and scarlet. He wore only the jewellery of one vast cross set with two emeralds of remarkable size and lustre, his kingly hand ringed just twice.

The priest went forward along the burning carpet, and kneeled some fifteen feet from the footstool, bowing.

When he raised his head again, he looked at the emeralds in the cross. In any event, to look at the Primentor's face was as barren as to have to read the Book on his previous visit. Study this face as you might, it never came clearly to the view. For the Primentor had been made featureless by his regalia. He was his station. He was every Primentor, and the faceless function of God.

The Factor Major, standing to one side now, spoke again. 'You may tell the magnanimous High Father what you have told me.'

The priest faltered a moment. Then he said, 'My lord,

there's been a disturbance in the women's house, something fearsome . . .'

The Primentor's non-face awarded nothing.

The priest said, 'There was an outcry in the Doma. A
servant approached our gate – a *woman* – then some of
the sisters. We learned that the Administress was
stricken.' The priest was at a loss how to relate again what
he had already gifted the Factor Major.

The Factor bent to the Primentor's ear.

The Primentor said, 'The woman abused herself, mis-
interpreting the ideal of contrition. Or perhaps was
attacked by some animal.'

'Those – may be the facts, my lord. But the women are
shouting about a demon. They say the slaves have carried
rumours that a demon also infested the Christerium, defil-
ing the sacred Bread, approaching the brothers in order
– to delude them.'

'There has been the tale of a vampire, currently,' said
the Factor Major. 'Such stories blow about the villages.
One cannot always be protected from these con-
taminations.'

'My lord,' said the messenger, 'the women insist some
emanation or unholy spirit – perhaps a girl recently chastised there – haunts the by-ways.'

The Factor Major waited for the Primentor to inter-
vene. There could be no laxity in his failure to do so. The
Factor Major resumed, 'The women must put all such
notions from them. They must fast, and pray. The High
Father will send them guidance, in the correct way, by a
letter.'

Seeds of doubt scattered from the air like dry rain.

The priests of the Christerium were restless. They discussed, nearly blatantly, sudden deaths, vampires, Brother Mordin, who had died in the porter's lodge . . .
Worse than the women, these men, for the women might
be controlled.

When the priest had been shooed out, the Primentor
said, 'The Administress, when recovered, shall be
questioned.'

'She may not survive.'

'Can that be so?'

The Factor Major did not comment by his looks on the naivety of the Primentor's reply, since it could not be naive.

'She was desperately hurt.'

'This seems an infection,' said the Primentor, 'in the very form of the reported demons of the Christerium.'

'A fancy of unclean minds, my lord.'

'Yet there were deaths here. And marks upon the corpses.'

The Factor Major drew his brows together, as though to close a curtain against something feared.

The Primentor did not expect anything from his Factor Major beyond obedience, and a certain subservient simplification of events. The Factor Major was his translator, for the environ of the Primentor was rarified, not of this or any earthly world. And his words were not few, merely of another language. Chosen to succeed the previous High Father of the Christerium, he had been swaddled, since the age of seven, in a cloud of what was to be. In time, he must choose his own successor, among the promising boys of the river city. Or perhaps, by then, the Kingdom would have come to pass upon the earth, and it would not be necessary. It was true that the Primentor was faceless. It was his soul which had no face. He had been created as a cipher, not a king but a slave. His master was close at hand, and asked nothing and gave nothing. Yet to his master, to Anjelen, in any perplexity, he must have cerebral resort.

To Anjelen, therefore, like the slave he was, the Primentor had gone, a visitation which could not be accomplished without a progress. Off the godly throne, and through the complexes of the Christerium, with a train of attendants, to the alchemical rooms of Anjelen. And to the Christerium in its knowing unknowing, there was no argument that he, the lordly Father, went suing to a Magister.

Inside the rooms, Anjelen had sat, amid shards of

bright-coloured winter light smiting up and through objects of stained glass.

The Primentor, in his own language, which employed the phrases and phonetics of men, yet through its usage and symbols was quite alien to them, attempted to acquaint Anjelen, the expression of God's renewal, with this latest problem of the Devil, the vampire-demon. And Anjelen had sat in a rainbow, as if colours pierced through him, like the Nails, and he did not answer. Previously, when witchcraft had been detected in the Doma, his participation was exact, and blasting. But on this second visit he had sat like the dead, yet alive. If he heard what was said to him, it lacked evidence. At length the emblem of the king-slave had had no recourse but to say, 'Your wish and your will shall be done.' And to depart. There was in the Primentor then the most slurred and transparent tinge of trouble. Not much, for in a world where God had revealed Himself, undeniably, to exist, slavery was the only option for one enlightened, and took away all rebellion, all individual thought – and thus every insecurity and misgiving.

'You will,' said the Primentor to his Factor Major, 'suppress the wild imaginings of our order. As you say, unclean fancies. Do everything in your power to instill calm. For the Doma, one of the lowlier sisters must have charge of them for now.'

The Factor Major acknowledged his task and went out at once to commence on it. In the chain of incipients he too was a slave, and the inner glim of the Christerium, where he had resided only ten years, was but half-understood, its whiff of Godhead. So, he was more free to feel impinge on him the essence of unease. As he left it, he noted that the great chamber was altered. A storm had begun to brew over the sea, and the high clear casements with their topaz, turquoise and ruby decorations, had changed to lead. A shadow descended.

Book Four

EUJASIA

Chapter One

As they approached, the ruined mass was not quite as they had heard or told it, but that did not alter an inflexible tradition. The yellow sky of a dying summer's afternoon, the brown shadows that mobbed the broken walls and the blond cuts of light between, the bars of young trees that sprang now out of the avenues in shawls of brassy green, these things disguised but did not deceive. The Travelling People searched out and came across other signals. How the dark reflection of mountains crept quickly to this spot. How the shrill screeches of ferocious birds tore the air, as they wheeled above their nests in the huge cliff of a tower. It had been sacred once, this wreck, and was now profane.

The Travellers set up their camp in the first courtyard, where the collapsed gate gave swift access to outer regions. The premature mountain-shadowed oncoming of evening had already filled this yard. There was still supposed to be some esoteric, nescient life in the ruin, but that went on at its eastern end, where the edifice had been better kept up. Others of the Traveller tribe who had passed this way going along the coast, by the city there, to avoid the plains, had recommended a well down the rock, but warned that only the women might go to it; anything else incurred bad luck.

They lit their evening fires, and erected their totems, the skulls of horses and dogs on painted poles, and turned their wagon-sides, thick with black crosses, towards the main area of the ruin. Their flock of cream-coloured goats nibbled at the grasses and tilted paving began to appear.

In their shaggy breeches and high boots, plaited beards, orange jackets, the men swaggered before a knot of leering stone faces that bulged in an outcrop from one wall. All the men then urinated here, under these gargoyles, to demonstrate their determined territory for a few days and nights. Then one scattered a little sugar, a placatory offering.

Fifteen women went together out of the gate and down the rock, carrying their pitchers for the water. The site of the well was a smaller lower building which had dropped headlong in the decay of total abandonment. Much of the structure had been wood and plaster. This had crumbled, warped, worn and torn awry in heats and gales. The stonework too had generally come down, and littered the shore with the larger pebbles. Beyond, the sea was drawing out, bronze and pearl under the hollow of sky.

The women shook their scarves and hair and wigs of crow-curls. As the men had urinated, so each woman spat as she went over the threshold.

The mountains had already taken the sun. The sheltered courts soaked up the shade. The women scattered wild flowers by the well and drew their water, singing thin and cruel as the gulls that circled overhead.

None of the Traveller men would kill these gulls, which might house lost souls. The villages the other side of the mountain pass, where the forest lay, they had their own stories of the ruin.

The women hurried back into the camp and offered meal to the vanished sun, that he might escape the mountains and return in the morning.

Darkness came, and the Traveller hearths were red.

'Come ye the fire, godd'er,' the leader of the band suggested, standing over the young boy who had sat down under the wall. They had come across him on the lower pass. He was walking on the black bare rock in the afterdawn, under the crawled lichens and cliffs clotted by the builderly excrement of the gulls. He could not be more than fifteen, but to their people that was old enough for a man. Besides, he wore the habit of a priest, very much mended. His hair reached his shoulders, flat and drab with dirt, save where there were long streaks in it of old man's white. A journeying godbrother he must be, or novice out on penance. Since he had inadvertently attached himself to the Travellers, they liked to keep him close, for they trusted none but their own, and preferred to behold at all times what he did. Only for the sheddings of nature did they give him privacy. They had not asked a blessing of him, for evidently he was not worth much to men, or to his Father in Heaven.

'If you wish,' said the boy priest now.

He got up and went threadbare with the Traveller leader in his splendour of orange and gold-kinked beard. The women sat together on the west side of the fire, their flame-dotted eyes going up to him and away. The men paid no heed, or seemed not to.

'Ye drink, eat.'

A piece of bread and goat's cheese was given to the godbrother boy, which he took and mouthed a little before setting it aside. Tomorrow, the leader said, they might catch fish in the sea and the women cook a stew with it. The godbrother drank from the cup they handed round.

The night was soundless but for the insistence of the sea, the crack and shuffle of the fires, that tossed iridescence over the disjointed ramparts.

The boy glanced up, and it seemed he saw, high in the standing stone of the south-easterly wall (above the gapes and crevices and holes like caves), two petals of light like stars, coloured mauve and emerald, cochineal and sapphire. He did not, the boy, point, exclaim. No person otherwise of the camp looked at the south wall.

And when a different sound, perhaps music, drifted out from somewhere like a cobweb, the Travelling women sang, and rose and danced, even the old women with half-covered faces, flouncing their skirts and stamping down the paving.

In the head of the ruined tower was a vague shining, like the firelight, but paler and colder, not comfortable.

Some gulls lifted like unseated grains of the night sky, then dropped back into the shell.

'Of all the fish in this water, no fish ye catch that is black.' The Traveller who spoke drank from the circling cup and let it go on. 'Black fishes feed them on the wood in the sea.'

The young godbrother sat under their eye, listening, not looking now at the lit tower head, the two stars that were windows.

The Travellers told over, in the way one who is much alone may come to talk to himself, that a petrified forest lay under the ocean. It was black as the sand here, black as the water by night. The trees were ancient as the land, and once had grown and thrived from the mountains to the edge of the east, until the sea was born and covered them up. Then they altered to basalt, and fish swam between their branches of stone.

In the body of the wrecked building the living trees stirred softly at the breath of a wind.

The chant had ended in the tower. The Traveller women sat down again on the west side of the fire.

Later when the men and women slept in their wagons, the godbrother got up again under the eye of four or five Travellers who were the watchmen.

'Make water?' one said. 'Go wary here. Bushes for ye far enough.'

Above, the two windows were out and might have been sucked away into the wall.

The boy priest came back from his bush, lay on his striped hair, and observed through open eyes that seemed lidless as a snake's, the night urges of the camp, its indistinct flutterings to and fro, and away.

In the morning, a man was missing from the camp. He was not one of the watchmen, but a young husband from the wagons. His wife ran to the leader, fell and grasped his knees. The missing Traveller had gone out in the night, mumbling that he had been called to by his friend.

But the friend denied this, and all made signs of aversion, or fingered the skull poles.

The leader selected six or seven of his men. They would penetrate the building a short distance. Others should search outside.

The godbrother boy joined himself to the inner search. They did not thank him, or send him off. Two of the men kept a constant watch on him, even as they pushed through an archway and entered the inner courts.

By day, the ruin remained mysterious, and indeed showed its physical dangers more boldly. There were everywhere strange subsidences, as if the earth itself had quaked and the foundations given way. Elsewhere steps went up to floors that had gone down in rubble. The sockets of windows gaped. Whole walls had parted company with each other. And between everything the grass and the green trees with their autumn roan beginning on them.

The men kept to the open ways. Entries to the inner storeys of the edifice they spurned. They would not even look at them. Sometimes they called out the name of the missing man.

Emerging through a brake of immature oaks fey and slender and innocent of their age to come, they confronted a broken wall that exposed a heart of red plaster, blackened perhaps by fire, and with something painted on it. It was a man with a saint's haloed face. The Travellers squirrelled off from it, violently leaping the sundered stones.

The south side especially they avoided. They appeared to know the ruin well by hearsay. It had been mapped for them in tales.

The sun was not very high, less than an hour had gone in hunting, when they gave up their man for dead. This was an oddity among their kind. They were normally incestuously fond and protective of their own, and perhaps the ragged godbrother had been told of that, for he expressed puzzlement. Going up to the leader, he said, 'Won't you look for him inside?'

'No. Unsafe.'

The godbrother did not further protest, the leader tried no more elaborate excuse. The men turned back towards the western outer court. The two Travellers who had watched the godbrother marched menacingly at him.

'Come, ye.'

'I'll look about a little longer,' said the godbrother. 'What do I fear? God is with me, and with all men.' There was something sly and amused in his face when he said this, and under the low wide brow, from which the thick filthy badger hair erupted, his eyes, that these people had called blue, might be unlucky.

The men drew back. 'Let be,' said one.

Westward a sharp keening cry arose. Not a gull – it was the woman who had lost her husband, judging almost to the second the search's abandonment, and that she must now count him dead.

'She'll need comforting,' said the boy, the godbrother.

He turned and walked off, slanting back towards the painting on the old smashed wall. They did not go after him.

There should have been, by day, several offices, but this priesthood no longer properly recognized daylight. Like a colony of beasts in the dark, it had gone underground, and was usually active only after sunset. Sometime during the night it constructed a single play of worship before God. Occasionally there was another rite, ceremonious and powerful, for which they rang the bell, the great-throated brazen being in the tower, if only as best they could.

Beyond their daylight hibernation, the meagre priesthood of the ruined fane left ample spoor – they were hidden but not in hiding. It was to be found by any who chanced and glanced on the south and eastern areas.

The godbrother travelled across the masonry, through the half-arches, up or down tottering stairs. He saw a large hall full of benches and chairs hacked into kindling to feed its fire-place, where a few ashes stayed faintly warm. He almost entered, beyond a garden of ivy and weeds waist-high, an endless domain so choked with the grinding down of velum, the erosion of parchments and books, that he shied from it and slammed home the unhinged door. But there had been candles set on the floor in dishes, pooled with cold wax that mice had nibbled. Overhead, through tunnels of omission, might be glimpsed corroded weather-vanes from which no wink of silver caught the sun. Cracked and splintered glass flashed stains of red and blue. But on a terrace there lay a crust of bread, fresh yesterday. In the weedy garden was a crucifix not yet consumed by grass.

The godbrother came on gargoyles often, and always suddenly. They did not make him start, though they seemed to pounce out from alcoves and overhangs, and here and there they lay underfoot, fallen, disfigured, but still grinning in malicious pain and joy.

High up, by a well which stank from glaucous mud at its bottom, the godbrother looked over, and the sea was visible in a gap beyond, blue-black, on the black beach.

Time had dealt quickly with this place. As if the stones, cemented by false dreams and faith, abetted their own destruction. As though it had been built merely of faults.

The wind blew through and the tough young trees bowed mockingly before it, and the motionless stones came ceaselessly undone, minute by minute.

A little rattling at the boy's back might have been only one such stone, coming away. But he turned, the godbrother, to see. The light came at him from one side and the dark from the other. It became obvious that he was not, after all, a boy, but a young man. His eyes were not 'blue' but the green of acid fruits. He gazed with them at what he saw, which had materialized not far away. It was like, at first, a swart toad, standing up monstrously on its hind limbs, so it was too tall for what it must be.

The godbrother's gaze had grown into a cool soulless stare. It held an interest, once more a slyness, but sheathed in pale green like the sea that maybe could think and feel, aspire and want, but invisibly.

'Yes?' said the godbrother, in his low soft voice that brought to mind a woman's.

The toad was a dwarf, but the dwarf was tall – something bizarre and contrasting, that defied vision. The cramped body appeared stretched, like a bend of iron uncurling – yet stuck. This flowered into a pair of lean hands, with long strong fingers, and into a big unwieldy magnificent head, shaggy with black hair. The eyes were black and elder, as they had always been. Both creatures stared at each other. Metamorphosis became obvious, lingering, and cunning, and a composition like bodies made from branches, driftwood, shells, feathers, the moon – then altered into skin and bone, hair and eyes.

'Show you,' said the dwarf. His voice, now he could speak, had learned presumably some use for speech, had stayed mewing, a pawing plaintive sound. He had not learned also to smile or threaten.

'Show what? I've seen,' said the godbrother. 'The Doma's gone to shale. Does the sea dare to come nearer? Will it dare to sweep in over the Christerium itself? Or will the Christerium only fall down in a heap, and the gulls go homeless, poor crying things?'

'Show,' said the dwarf. 'Follow me.'

How novel for this animal, this dwarf, to bring out such a command. Even in the role of servant, he could now deliver an instruction, himself be in charge of an event.

The godbrother with the woman's voice, white-streaked hair, green eyes, nodded, tilted his head anomalously, maybe in acquiescence. And at that, the dwarf turned and made off, trotting as he had done before, dog-like, and the godbrother moved after him.

Almost instantly, the route went into shadow. That was where the dwarf led, the godbrother was obliged to follow if he meant to.

They climbed down behind and under the walls, into a vault of stairways that did not rock but that stank of wet, and where poisonous mosses grew. And then came a gargoyle on the wall, and next another, both with garlands of ivy. Then there was a twisting corridor, and in the corridor, whose walls were painted by warrior angels, swords and wings, a lamp hung, burning sick light, from the beam of the ceiling.

The dwarf motioned, holding up his articulate hand for stillness. He padded ahead to where the corridor angled, investigated, beckoned. The godbrother followed once more. They turned into a chamber which gave on a staircase. This sloped into darkness, although another ill lamp burned at its foot. A curtain of mildew decorated the wall, and all the shadows were there. The dwarf went to the curtain, became a shadow, beckoned again. Together guide and guided withdrew without distaste, above such nonsense, into the curtain's folds.

'Half-blind,' said the dwarf, and then: 'Listen, here comes.'

A pathetic tread was audible from the far side of the room where a doorless space gave on, perhaps, infinity. From its vagueness slid a man in a black robe, tied at the waist with hemp, a priest with rusty eyes, gliding forward as if on runners which themselves knew the way. In his shrivelled hands there was a silver dish, a chalice, blazing. He held it out, carrying it or drawn by it. He went like a pendulum across the room, seeing nothing, and coming to the stair slipped mindlessly on to it and up into sheer blackness.

The dwarf and the young godbrother stepped from the curtain.

'Where does he go then, Mechi?'

The dwarf said, 'To Anjelen.'

'With the solace of wine.'

'I show you the wine cask.'

And now their dubious path was lit at intervals. They entered, in this quarter-light, a space. Here the dwarf darted forward, picked up a candle, roused it with a tinder and displayed – the wine cask.

The Traveller man lay on a mattress, a loudly tinted bundle from which his face had been thrown up, as if rejected out of hair and clothes, as white as flour. From his left wrist the leather armlet had been cut, and a bandage of black stuff wound tightly on.

'Drained but not yet dry,' said the godbrother. He licked his lips as if in parody. 'How salt, salt as the sea, salt as a fish, the blood of men.'

The dwarf stood off. He idled the candle, making the room weave and shake.

The godbrother ambled through the spurting light and leaned under a wall that made pretend it was about to fall direct. He gripped the shoulder of the senseless man. 'Wake yourself. Wake up.' And when the Traveller did not stir, the godbrother bent down and bit the lobe of the man's ear, and out of a depth of nothingness he woke screaming of knives and the dark. 'Be quiet. Get up. You'll be better soon. I'll help you.'

Day entered the mountains, was leached out, faded. Besides, the sky grew overcast. Abnormal colours floated in the sea. The hot wind exhaled greenish rags of cloud that mirrored over the floors of the Christerium and caused the lids and lips of the gargoyles to twitch.

The Travellers had remained in the outer courtyard. On the poles of skulls they had hung flowers, and marked the black crosses with liquor. Within the wagons, on the ground, ran a circle of fires, which the women tended carefully, and where nothing was cooked. The wife who had been deprived lay in her cart, with at her side a small rudimentary doll of cloth and twigs, hastily formed to represent her husband. To the doll she whispered on and on, speaking of their time together, ventures mundane and intimate, secrets of their loins and hearts. She addressed the doll by his name.

The storm sky infused like the sea, in which the flint blood of the petrified forest looked to have been released.

The Travellers ate their raw sparse meal. Coming together inside the ring of fires, they started to perform feats of the sort with which they would waylay the caravans of others, or draw the money of the crowd in a town market. Their acrobatic tricks, like their magic, were to them, as was not always understood outside their tribe, an aspect of religion. By such means they joked with their gods, with God, wheedling, jesting, demonstrating both foolishness and skill, wantonness and self-control. Here, in the ruin, they used an athletic sorcery to protect, to shield, and to drive off elementals of the dark and of the stones. At midnight, a propitious hour, they would be away, and did not desire pursuit.

So they danced between the buffets of staves, turned cartwheels and strode on their hands. So too an oval of willow was brought forth and set alight, and through this final fire the older children, the boys of nine and ten, came diving, somersaulting down in showers of sparks to cries of fear and triumph.

When the very last child had tumbled for the very last time, they held the hoop up and waved it at the sky that was now black and starless. And another child came hurtling through the willow and landed there inside the fires.

The final child was a dwarf man. He had sprung off a walk some ten feet above, over the wagon-tops and through the willow hoop, and come down like rain on the ground.

No one moved. Those that had shouted closed their mouths. They were in two minds. For he also was of a people that they revered, the japes of God, and must be treated with fairly. But too he had burst from the very sinews of the ruin. Tall he was, the dwarf, almost the height of a man, but crouching, with a savage head like a wolf's.

Then, in the entrance of her wagon, appeared the woman whose husband had been lost, clutching together her hands.

And at her, like one of the gargoyles, the dwarf winked. As if they might all, if they wanted, be in with him on *this* joke.

But probably she did not see what the dwarf did. She was riveted by the hoop of willow.

Framed by its limping running flame, standing in the

night air, was a ghost. Nothing else could be sure about it save its vast gush of hair, in which it seemed to have clothed itself, brownish red as virgin malt in the firelight, yet woven with hanks of white.

A handful of seconds the apparition was suspended over them. Then the empty hoop dropped with a hiss. And from the blackness beyond – where nothing was, not even now the bright tears of windows, and where no sounds emitted but sea and wind – a man came staggering.

They let him get to them, the Travellers, this one who had been lost. They gave neither assistance – nor greeting. But when he was near enough, they brought him in through the fires. He stood there then in their midst, but not wholly present. He did not crane about to find his wagon or his wife. She did not come down to him, she did not call.

The leader said, flatly, 'Search him for any marks.'

And they laid the lost man gently down. He did not struggle. And they, they did not need to do more than unknot the black binding from his wrist.

The lost man rested there, on his back, and murmured something only his tribe could recognize, but this they did, and drew around him. He shut his eyes. The leader came to close the inner circle of bodies. He knelt by the man and got out rapidly some strings of words that were just identifiable as a forgiveness of sins. Silence again, and the fires spitting like cats. The leader of the Travellers leaned forward and wrenched at the man with his right arm, holding firm with his left hand. There was a *crack*. The leader rose up and walked away. On the paving where the goats had fed, the lost man had turned his neck right over. His dead features were pressed into the grass.

The woman in the wagon entrance did not keen. She had done that earlier. She went back inside, to snap the neck of her doll.

And like a human wheel, all the eyes in the faces with their coverings of gauze and beard and fleshy tissue rotated towards the dwarf. Might it be they had come on a question to ask him?

Chapter Two

Together in their claustrophobic webby world, dim-
sighted as moles, four aged priests were at a twilight
baking.

There had been slaves and servants once, to fulfil such
chores. The kitchen had been intact, the ovens less
obstinate . . . They had forgotten. Their bread was
unleavened, but that might be piety. The stores of flour
were often full of maggots; they put the substance through
a sieve, lamenting. When last was there fresh flour, cheese
or milk? Meat was a dream, but it was holy to abstain—
Fish sometimes were spewed out on the beach and might
be gathered up. Now and then offerings of food were left,
amorphously threatening, in the westernmost parts of the
Palace on Earth. The offerings were almost idolatrous,
and there had been none for a great while. The priesthood
knew itself beyond the mortal country. One foot in
Heaven and one in the grave.

They bickered over the burning bread and the oven
smouldered, but the stormy darkening sky would hide the
smoke, if any had cared.

Only the gulls, who shared the ruin with them, screamed and came to see.

Once, when younger, they had killed gulls with stones
and devoured the flesh, fishy, and which they had made
out was fish, losing observance of fasts and frugality.

Day had become night with them. Centuries of dereliction might have gone over, changing everything, melting
it into an eternal dusk. Amnesia of the mind, inertia of

the soul. A Fall. Yet all this, these acres and spans of time and falling were only years. Among the number chittering at the bread oven, or creeping about the stairs and halls, might some have been vigorous and upright with black hoods of hair, a decade before? It was a spell, this that had come to them, as it was a kind of curse that worked upon the building. Apple with worm. Canker in the wood.

Across from the kitchen and the dining hall, a slip-stream of pacing went on about the tumbledown cloister, some further phantoms of priests with their beads. In a garden the priestly spiders froze on their looms and sipped the dew. A mile high, or in the sky, a star or a window lit, and another.

The paving before the tower of the church had all come up, depressed like molars out of black gums. That had a look of tombs lifting, Judgement Day.

The base of the tower had become ivy, and the stone bastion rose out of it like a tree. Storms had hammered the two apocalyptic windows; neither the Christus nor the Devil had kept purchase.

A priest crept hurriedly out into the tomb-yard, entered the tower of the church at a gap where the ivy was not. Behind him night came, but in the tower there was night already. The glassless seaward window hung in black space. Beneath, just visible, was the tracery of a stair, and the huge slab of the altar. The altar was not dressed. The horror of the altar was its nakedness. Gone, the crucifix, gold, alabaster, diamond. All the treasures had been taken away. The priest (old like the others), contemplated the desolation, and far above he heard the gulls muttering in their nests. They had spotted the floor, the carvings, the gallery, the altar itself. But it was carts that had swallowed up the riches of the Christerium, one autumn afternoon. The happening was nightmarishly vague, he could hardly recall how or why, only a mighty glittering and its removal, the toiling of horses, and men in the livery of Cathedral guard, and one soldier with a sword, barring the way like an angel.

Standing so, with nothing in his hands for the altar, the old priest became aware of another immobile beside him, a brother in a religious habit.

'The bread's burnt,' said the priest to this other.

'Yes?'

'Isn't it always. Uneatable. But we are not made for luxury.' They stood as a pair, but unmatched. In the dark the old one had not seen the other was young. The old one added, in the same voice that spoke of bread, 'There won't be any ritual tonight. We fail him. God pardon us.'

'The man ran away, did he?' said the second priest, the young one. 'I'd have thought him too weak and afraid to manage it. Who was meant to guard him?'

'Brother Ragis, but he was nowhere near. So long since there was strong wine for us. But the Magister had his. The first cup, as always. Will he be angry now?'

'Have you seen him angry?' said the other one.

The old priest, dislocated by an unusual turn of inquiry, knew suddenly that the priest beside him was not of the brotherhood. The voice was untainted, firm; it disturbed him, it was young.

'Who is it, there?' said the old priest.

'Brother Eujasius,' said the voice. Then it laughed.

The old priest crossed himself. The laugh – its quality – had made him do that. But even as the second stroke of the cross went over his breast, he mislaid the potence of it. For they had begun obliquely to realize, growing up as they grew fossilized and senile, that their webbed world contained the Devil. It was the Devil in the Christus, some awful power conjured, that had cast them down into the Fall whose symbols were all about them.

'Brother Eujas—'

'Eujasius.'

'The name of an angel,' said the old priest wonderingly, like a child. 'Such a high name to be granted you. Where have you come from?'

'Out of the air,' said the voice.

The old priest stepped back. He moved to where he knew some candles stood on the floor in clay dishes, and

lighted one, and all the time the other stayed there, in the
dark. The candleflame curled up, and the old priest beheld
the young priest. Who was not like the Angel Eujasius,
shown always with yellow hair, holding the salver of the
Bread of the Body – *I told him of the bread being burnt* –
from the same coarse unleavened dough they made do for
the Host. It was a blasphemous quip, maybe, this naming
for the Angel of the Bread of the Body of the Redeemer—

The young one went on standing on the floor, smiling
a little. The old priest was reminded of a snake, of something female and debasing.

'Well, brother,' said Eujasius. But then he only looked
all about at the church tower, as if he feasted on its shame.

'You're from the city,' said the old priest. 'You came
along the river to the sea, or walked the plains, begging.
Or from a village. A town.'

'Or over the mountains,' said Eujasius, still drinking
up the ruin, stretching himself and basking in it. 'Stories
are related.' he said, in his low, girl's voice, 'about this
shambles. That there was a Knighthood here, insulting to
God, and which called up demons. Wicked acts. Rites of
blood. And there were suicides, murders, vampires. So
then the arm of the Church Paternal reached out and
snuffed the evil lamp, disbanded the order, burned papers
and tapestries, smashed windows, looted and made off
with the goods. And now all that go about here are ghosts
and ghouls.'

The old priest watched as if enticed. He had seen something else, blocking out the torture of this recital. The
turning neck was young and smooth, the pallid eyes were
clear.

So that when the youth finished his gloating perusal and
returned his gaze to the old godbrother's face, the priest
said, 'You must be hungry and footsore. We have charity.
We'll share with you what we have.'

'Will you?' said Eujasius. His eyes gave off a vivid flash,
some trick of the candle. 'What about your master, the
Magister?'

'He is above such things. We serve God as best we can.'

'And who is God,' said the boy, 'to *you*?'

The old priest attempted to cross himself again, but could not discipline the tremor in his arm.

'Hush,' he said.

And the boy smiled widely and put one finger over his serpent's mouth.

It was breakfast or dinner in the Common Hall. (The Hall of the Novitiate had caved in beneath the snow winters before, the Hall of the Ordinate was flooded by the sea, and barnacles clambered about its figured walls.) The trickle of priests ebbed in through the courtyard door, sullen and loitering. There were so many limits upon where they might go, and here too there was no choice. A single table of planks had been spared, and left up against the fire-place. The night was cool, and a chair burned on the hearth unwillingly, tended by one of the brotherhood, who fed in carved legs, and wretched knots of rubbish he and his fellows had found about the building and not wanted.

The table, rather than lit, was shadowed by seven candles. The priests affixed themselves, and picked like angry old birds at the burnt cakes of bread, a mush of weeds, the brackish water in tin cups.

They had never been encouraged to conversation at the board, and now maintained a silence that was itself fraught and fevered, these voiceless skinny rats and carrion crows upon the unnourishing carcass of vocation and of life itself.

Then, unsuitably, one spoke. 'Pass me the cellar of salt.'

'It's empty.'

'That's a lie. I gathered salt myself yesterday.'

'No you didn't. You're neglectful, brother.'

'Brother Ragis is neglectful.'

The scavenging heads went up, and through the jolting fusc of the candles, discovered Ragis gnawing at his bread. He looked back in turn, frightened and fierce. 'I took the drink. I took him the wine.'

'But the *man*,' grated out the chiding brother, 'what of the man?'

'He must have run off. Who was there to watch but me? And the lord's servant came to me. Take him the wine, he said.'

The brotherhood crepitated to itself, clawing with parchment hands at the table and plates, crumbs and robes.

'The dwarf,' said another one, 'like an imp of Hell.'

Ragis said. 'It must be as the Magister wills it. The Magister sent for me.'

'You cut the vein,' said the chider. 'You cut too deep or more than once, or didn't bind him tight enough. He crawled away and died.'

From the table's farthest end, aeons off from the fire and a mile from the last candle, someone said, 'Brothers, in the name of the Most High, we mustn't squabble before strangers.'

So the heads moved again, and one of the hands, pushing forward a candle, produced a voice that demanded, 'Who's that? Is it you, Yaivin? Why are you sitting in the dark?'

At that moment the night wind swept by the door above the sea, out of all the dark there was and in which the island of the badly lighted table was adrift. The wind was like a laugh. It flaunted the candleflames to blue strands, and let them recover like drowning things. The dark was so easy to achieve, why not sit in it?

'Speak up, Yaivin. Who has he got with him there? Can you see, Brother Ragis?'

The elderly priest Yaivin, who had concealed himself, perhaps unthinkingly, reached forward and brought the pushed candle nearer. It lit then, for the dim red rat eyes of the priests, his own familial physiognomy, and that of the other. And the other sat by, a face above two slim hands which rested on a bit of blackened bread. The shadow kept him otherwise, making odd variances with his hair, sculpting deep hollows at the cheeks, under the lower lip, and all around the eyes that were pale and animal and watching.

'A travelling godbrother,' said Yaivin. 'He tells me he is known as Eujasius. This I dispute with him. But, well.'

The priests looked at Eujasius.

'A boy,' said Ragis, and he put down his bread. 'Is he? Is he young?'

The one called Eujasius said, 'I'm thirty years. Or more.'

'No, no,' said Yaivin, 'that can't be.'

'I seem younger,' said Eujasius. 'Isn't that true also of your master?'

'Our master? What does he say?'

'Our master is God.'

'No, he speaks of the Christus.'

'Once,' said Eujasius, 'you had a Christus on your altar. He was white as the ice and nailed through by diamonds. There were roses of corundum on his head. But the Church Fathers from the city confiscated him, didn't they? What was Anjelen doing that afternoon?'

At the name, Anjelen's, the old priests moved, were twisted about without leaving their seats, to shapelessness, and re-formed like the candles in the wind. It was some inner piece of them, not their bodies, which had writhed.

'Anjelen is Anjelen,' said Eujasius. He raised the burnt bread and broke it. *'Did He not say, This is my Body?'*

Anjelen's priests looked on, and they beheld the scene in which they participated, and were aware of something devilish in the youth who was its pivot, something feminine and reptilian. But there he sat in the centre of the ruin, and the image was on him irresistibly of the Christus at his Final Supper upon earth. The mirror had so distorted for them that anything symmetrical would not have shown in it. But Eujasius showed, he bedazzled them.

They were intent upon their own designs, this flotsam of the Church of God, and he intent, of course, upon his, also, yet not maybe to the exclusion of theirs. A union was forming, victim with assailant.

And on the door which no longer shut, leading in from

the outer court, there came a blow, harsh and fine, more than sufficient for the silence. It was not a courtesy, not a knocking for admittance. An announcement, rather.

The priests turned gratingly on their silted-up bones.

Through the door came the dwarf, the servant of their master, scuttling like a black crab.

They feared it. It was the Devil's imp. It served God.

Tall, for a dwarf. At first, a millenium ago, it had not had the ability of speech, but the Magister had given it utterance, that it might convey his wishes now and then.

That afternoon when the guard of the Cathedral had ridden into the Christerium, when the letter from the city Administer had been read, when the city Factor had walked with his acolytes the rooms, the halls, the church itself, and given forth words of excorcism and awesome promises, and when the priests had thrown themselves down at the feet of these invaders, when one hundred and ninety-two men in habits of black had whipped themselves before the legate from the city, then, running up to the rooms in the south wall, what had anyone met there but vacancy? Anjelen was not to be come on. And later, in the incoherency of their revenance, when they discovered him again, it was by the emergence of the dwarf. *The Magister requests that you bring him—*

Myopically they glimpsed the disintegration of that hour of their humiliation, that afternoon, the biting slash of the honed sword. Then they wandered in the forest of stone and webs, until they were old, blinded, forgetful, glutted with the ultimate sin of Dormancy.

Yet, there burned inside the fog a scarlet secret jewel, their rite. The passion.

The dwarf was in the refectory, standing to one side, and after him came a figure that was just the dream a dwarf might fabricate. Tall, straight, slender, and of a metallic darkness in its black habit, its priestly garment that had withstood the centuries of ten years of desuetude, as he himself withstood all time, ageless, like the full-grown tree.

'Magister!'

They got up rushing like boys, their joints cranking.

'Sit,' he said.

One word. The beauty of the voice made of it a thousand cadences. They reheard, over and over, and sat down.

And Anjelen moved towards them, up to the brink of the candlelight, gazing out across it. And the candlelight stretched up to have for itself him.

The forehead was wide and low and the black hair sprang from it. The eyes and brows were black. The mouth seemed the only feature in his face. His face had no meaning but for the mouth. It was well-shaped, having nothing to it that suggested venality or greed. Yet, it was gluttonous. That was all it was, and all the face was. The gluttony of a drunkard ninety years of age and always at his cups. That young firm mouth, the level teeth. Thirst incarnate.

But the lips parted, and the beautiful voice came from there, music from a swamp.

'On the other hand, you are to stand up before me,' it said. 'Stand then, Mechail Korhlen.'

A kind of motion, a ripple, went along the table. The candles limped and rose. The old priests had no will to be amazed, or even to seek about.

'I said to you, you will stand, Mechail.'

No anger, nothing human in the music of the swamp of the thirsty mouth. But in the black eyes a slight alteration, as if they might for an instant dominate the face.

Yaivin tore himself, a severance of psychic skin, from the hypnotic of the lips and voice, and looked sideways. *Is that his name? Mechail?*

'Get up – his grace commands you—'

Yaivin began to see what was really there, and this was no one. The boy had disappeared, run on lizard feet unnoticed somewhere, into the hall, or past them all and out of the door.

'Magister, he's gone.'

There was a stifled chorus of outrage from the table, old men ranting in creaks and whispers.

Anjelen said, 'There will be a return. After so great an absence, the visit could hardly be so brief.'

'His name,' said Yaivin, 'your grace, he called himself Eujasius.'

Anjelen's eyes went over Yaivin. Yaivin stared, trying to see, to miss no inch of face or second of response.

Anjelen walked back towards the door and the courtyard. His movements were a little stilted, stiff, as if he did not, often, this antique sot, wander about on solid ground. *'The raven shall live there,'* said Anjelen, *'it shall be a maze. Thorns will come up in the palace, and the walls shall be the stones of emptiness.'* He put his hand upon the dwarf's shoulder. The dwarf looked up at him like a dog of iron. 'Whatever God asks of you is good to do, even if it be to grieve. He will come and tell you' – he meant now the dwarf – 'when to ready yourselves. Ring the bell loudly.'

Ragis wobbled to his feet.

'But he *ran away*, that one. And now – this one too.'

Anjelen said, 'Prepare the house, and the guest arrives. Crows come from the desert with bread in their beaks, and from the rock bursts the stream of wine.'

Ragis opened his mouth again, and now the dwarf lifted up a hand of admonition. Anjelen went through the door, night into night. Then the dwarf made a mewing sound, and skipped, and turned a cartwheel out over the threshold.

The men had surrounded him as they had their dead, so there could be no sudden flight. They talked to him with the manners of their own Traveller etiquette, and did not ask his name, which he would have given carelessly, the version that the forest left him. They asked what had brought him to them.

'I go with you,' he said. 'I earn my keep. As you see.' For the dwarf, this was a lengthy vocalization. Once he had begun to utilize speech, he had learned unhesitantly, as with other things. But even so, having got by such a while without them, he was still slack with words. They were tools for everyday or servile matters, not yet the vehicles of concepts, not pretty, or emotive.

The leader of the Travellers asked, 'Where from ye come? Out the church?'

'I shelter here, me,' said the dwarf. 'Bad place. I see your light, and come to you.'

They accepted this, for it was reasonable. But the honesty with which it was delivered did not convince. Then again, though, the dwarf might be God-touched. To a simpleton simplicity was not ridiculous. They would have to test him, as they tested most things, biting gold, striking a dog, once, scorning a bride's chastity in a careful song.

'Eat then,' said the leader, and parted the enclosure of his men to allow the dwarf freedom.

The dwarf ate the cheese and berries a woman brought him, like a small rodent, holding them in his lean man's paws. He did not seem hungry. He had always carried with him a memory of a Traveller girl in his childhood, she who had soothed warm milk to his lips as he lay frozen on the shore of death. But it was only one more memory with the rest. The viciousness before, and after, the jibes, the sticks and stones that helped break and bend the bones of his psyche.

The Travellers watched the dwarf as if he had come to take the place of the godbrother they had watched before. The godbrother was now reckoned lost, like the man who had died to them and whose body was stacked neatly in a cart for burial in other ground.

No further questions were asked. The dwarf rose and went all at once away to the edge of the fires, to a dark spot by a wagon wheel. 'I sleep now,' he said to the man who stood over him.

Then, they watched the dwarf sleep.

He was as still as their dead. He did not make a sound, did not turn. He slept in a ball, like a cat.

'See how he slumbers,' said the leader to his wife's brother.

'I see it.'

'Go, kick him, light. Say to him ye stumbled on him.'

The man crossed over to the dwarf, and batted with his boot at the lower leg.

Mechi did not react. Oblivious, he lay clotted in his ball of sleep.

The Traveller looked over at his leader. The leader nodded. The man bent, and shook the dwarf by his shoulder. All the camp watched, now.

The dwarf did not wake, did not grunt or protest.

Quickly, the Traveller man seized the dwarf by both shoulders and pulled at him, and Mechi unrolled like a carpet. He was also like a man then, properly grown, but in miniature.

'Leave him,' said the leader.

They dragged the dwarf out from among the fires and put him against the wall. Here they made a circle round him of salt, and dropped a cross of twigs on to his chest.

They went on about their preparations for departure, which were prolonged by safeguards.

Mechi had gone back to his master, when called. Which is to say, he had put his other self under the wagon wheel in a pose of sleep, and withdrawn his awareness from it. He had been testing the Travellers too. If they slaughtered him, or what stood for him, in their camp, then he would know to avoid them. Although he would have liked to journey in their company, as in the woods of childhood, before Krau and the Korhlens.

Mechi was changing, but it did not bother him. He lived day by day, as he had always had to, as every lesson in the world advised, had he but known it.

For his years at the Christerium, serving Anjelen, and let be by Anjelen (who was less a man than a pillar of wood, and even when he moved about remained so, save in the area of the one obsessive need), in those years the dwarf had been tutored by inference, and taken in schooling through his eyes. The Magister taught Mechi nothing, yet Mechi was privy to much, actually to great wonders which he merely gazed at. For Anjelen dabbled in alchemy, as if not knowing what he did. These actions would come to be like the abrupt bursting-out of a green leaf on a bare branch, which shrivelled and vanished in half a night. Anjelen's purpose in such sorceries was inexplicable. They were a reflex, perhaps, the hands and mind starting into movement between vast seasons of nullity. But Mechi saw, and knew himself, in an unnamed way, in the chamber of a magician. Magic rubbed off like pollen. And if Anjelen turned on him his black eyes that, gradually, were becoming as superficial as the eyes of a human man, Mechi met the eyes and stared, like a dog at the moon; but the moon was dead.

One dusk in Anjelen's inner room, where the wolf window had mostly cracked to bits whirled away into space, Anjelen was absent, and Mechi had paused to look into the globe of quartz. Three daggers were laid about it, pointing south, west, and north of east. They had been positioned there weeks before, and dust was powdered on them. The globe itself shone, and looking at it, Mechi saw his own reflection. It amused him, for through the medium of the curved crystal, by shifting here and there, he could alter his shape. And in this manner, Mechi refashioned himself in the glass nearly in the shape of a man. Subsequently he would find the chamber empty often, and he would play with the quartz globe. He did not know why he was pleased with the game, or even truly that pleased he was – what standards of pleasure had there been?

But there was a sort of compendium of knowledge in Mechi, as in the others of his kind: Jasha, Anillia.

One sunset Mechi saw his shadow on the wall of the ruin, and it was different. He stopped, interested, untheoretically conscious of what had come about. He felt no tearing bitterness at previous possibilities denied him through ignorance. He felt no spur of desire for what he might now make and take and have.

He played with the shadow. He found it would gesture and walk without him. He rendered into this matrix, *substance*, as they, the others, had done, Anjelen, Anillia, Mechail.

The dwarf created himself almost in his own image. The ectoplasmic projection they had achieved through sorcery, will, madness, dream, Mechi came to as an artist, a pragmatist.

About three years after (three decades of a century of ruination, the spell of the Fall, to the Christerium), Mechi's images bounded and scudded about the walks and courts, and he, his reality, had grown four inches, and his back was mostly straight, and now and then a splinter worked out of it, and he recalled, with no appetite for association, the splinters piercing from Mechail's shoulder, like quills from a porcupine.

Sometimes Mechi, and sometimes Mechi's making, would go to summon the priesthood to its rite of love. The makings, when their use had been served, he let melt back into nothing, but no one saw. They were like water marks drying on the stone. He had got speech by then, which fact spoke too for itself. The business of the priestly rite did not trouble Mechi. The world had never made sense.

It seemed to him though that occasionally he had been made to go about, like a puppet, before he himself began the work of his own volition – but neither did that perturb him. He was a slave. Yet the game itself was appealing, as had been the performance of the tricks the first Travellers had taught to him. The game inaugurated for him himself. (He was also learning *not* to be a slave.)

He sent himself to the Travellers in the courtyard because their people had once been tolerant of him, useful – if he was yet able to think in this style. But to run away was an idea so alien he gave it no title.

Crouched outside Anjelen's chamber, where Anjelen had sat since Godbrother Ragis had come there with the silver chalice of blood, Mechi had approached the Travellers through his other self. If they were afraid and killed it, so what? He could make another, and know to let them be.

But when he had withdrawn from his sleeping surrogate, they only ringed it with salt. And Mechi, as he, in body, attended on the Magister, experienced a weird new excitement, *glee*, an embryo which might at last harden to malice and joy beyond the capacity of any ordinary hating, laughing man.

Eujasius sat on a hill of stones, once a wall of the Doma, overlooking the night sea. The tide was drawing in in scarves of blue foam. The moon was rising.

Earlier Eujasius had gone out along the sand like soot, and explored the limits of the water, encouraging them to come back. There a fish smote up, and Eujasius got hold of it. Till its struggles were finished, he held tight, and then kissed the cold scales up and down.

The fish was all the sea in one flexive drop. On the hill of rubble, Eujasius ate it raw and slow, licking off the silvery blood. He ate everything but the transparent intricate tail and fins, and the tragic head with its black eyes. The perfect skeleton he examined, as if to find the source, what had made it live and spasm, what had gone out of it and left it indifferent to his rending.

Then Eujasius stared along the beach, where the moonglazed sea was mounting up invisible steps of possession.

The sea. How deep did the staircase drop into the floors of it? What palaces were there, what halls and towers and churches made of bizarre shells, and of the materials which only the ocean could design? And was the forest of basalt there, beyond the skirt of the beach of black sin?

Some other thoughts went through the head of Eujasius, who had bathed in the chill salt sea, and washed there with sand and water his caked, striped hair.

Eujasius thought of a blond man who fought beneath him, ripping at his arms until Eujasius broke them. And into the mouth of this enemy Eujasius thrust the hilt of a sword until it had gone through everything into the brain. The cross-piece of the hilt had gouged Krau's cheeks into a lunatic stricture. He had an idiot's grin now, with shattered teeth. The iron pointed out from it like a tongue.

But also, Eujasius thought of the carved chair that had become a thicket, and spread up about the walls and ceiling, and of a white fox which looked out of it, but soon another would come, and then Eujasius must go up to the man in the chamber hung with russet, green and purple, she must part her legs for him and conceive his son. And Kolris Vre Korhlen lay on her asleep, clutching her fast.

And she or he saw the globe of crystal, the brain of Anjelen, and in the crystal the secrets and the learning, facets so bright, like the stars strung over the sea, and as readable.

But also she thought of the path down on to the beach at dawn, and the hot torches against the warmthless sky. The Administress stepped forward and began to read aloud from a prayer book. And there was a ladder up the flank of the platform, and they hurried her, and they tied her, on her back, for the fire—

A light bloomed now on the rock under the Christerium. It swung adeptly down, coming towards the beach without haste or deception.

Not the priests, they would have tottered. This would be Mechi again, sent to search Eujasius out, and Mechi of course would sense where Eujasius was, just as he had done before.

Eujasius rose gracefully, and turning back, approached the lamp.

Beam-lit, the dwarf stood over him. Eujasius cast the skeleton of the fish away.

'Turn a cartwheel,' said Eujasius.

But the dwarf only pointed along the rock. His black eyes were all the dead moon was not. And he looked tall enough now to be the same height as Anjelen, the Magister. Taller.

Chapter Three

After her mother had been inside the hut one quarter of an hour, Jasha had gone to see the horse, taken its rein and led it under the lean-to. She considered Mechail's mare might take against the newcomer, but the two animals moved together for warmth, peacefully, and bowed their heads to the hay on the ground. A limitless soft snow began to fall. From the hut no sound emerged. Jasha waited, and silence pressed in her ears. At last she had crossed the snow and re-entered the hut, quiet as a cat, as if to interrupt them, catch them out.

But nothing had properly altered. Mechail slept where earlier he had elected to, rolled in the blanket on the earth, with a cushion of dried grass extracted from the mattress under his head. He lay on his back, now, his arms across his breast as if thrown there in protection. His breathing was just audible.

Anillia was by the fire, standing up. She was cloaked in black, and dressed beneath in a white gown that looked to be banded and embroidered, garments of her own mandate, maybe, off no loom but her will.

Jasha observed them. The sleeping man and the standing women.

The fire cracked and the soft snow sighed.

'He'll wake presently,' said Anillia. 'When he's ready. He knows that I'm here.'

'Shall I go out again and wait, lady?' said Jasha.

She was not humble, and her eyes gleamed, unblinking.

'In the snow? Why?' Anillia turned and glanced into the cauldron.

'Can you conjure more food?' said Jasha. 'If you're a witch, lady.'

'You,' said Anillia, 'were the witch. They wanted to burn you for it.'

Jasha said, 'What did you do with my green dress that I gave you?'

'Gave my poor unclad bones. Your dress . . . I forget.'

'A soldier bought me that. And this.'

Anillia said, 'Come and stir the soup.' Jasha approached her. Anillia's face was like Anjelen's, and there was about her too a ruby darkness, a luminous shadow. 'Dresses. I recall my maids twittered of such things.'

Jasha looked into the cauldron. It was burning dry. And from the ashes the loaf was gone. Perhaps the woman had hidden it?

Jasha said, 'He'll have to go hunting, or trapping. There's nothing here.'

'Do you think he will? Is it probable you'd starve? The witch-fire didn't scorch you up, and the sword only stopped his heart for a few days. For myself, I died and rotted, and came back, and here I am.'

'It's not good to go hungry.'

'Little peasant girl,' said Anillia, 'put away what you were.' And Anillia gazed at her, the same gaze there had been outside. Jasha did not rummage after answers. She did not care how and why Anillia was her mother. But that Anillia was Mechail's, his possession, this Jasha had guessed at once.

Jasha drew aside. Having moved the pot from the fire in a prim housewifely way, she sat down by the hearth.

Then, as predicted, the man woke.

He opened his eyes on Anillia, a figure flowing up out of the dark, sketched in vertical lines by dull firelight, a stem surmounted by a drifting mask of face. Perhaps in turn he could make out her eyes, their blackness. Would he suppose this icon, which revealed no gender, did not lean to him or speak, to be that of Anjelen?

'Who's there?' Mechail said. And then, 'Where's my knife? I'll need it today, won't I?' Then he sat up, and flung his right hand round on his left shoulder, the deformed shoulder that had healed itself. He said, 'Ah, no. I remember now. All that's over. What do you want?'

'You know me,' said Anillia. 'Who I am.'

Mechail did not look. He had fixed his eyes on the wall, where the tree-sides pushed through. In tiny gaps there the sprinkling snow was visible, attracting the light from the hearth.

'If I know you, am I dreaming then?'

'Was it only in dreams you saw me?'

'Yes. And when I was dead, you brought me a drink, wine . . . no, it was blood, the blood of the child – the albino girl.'

'That was my dream, I must have sent it you. But I'm here, and you've woken up.'

'I don't believe that. Every day,' he said, looking at the snow in the torn wall, 'I thought of you. I see you now as you were then, gaunt and dying. Your black hair became thin and brittle and there were great strands of white in it. The women used to talk about your hair. I remember when they said you died, and I never believed them. The priest beat me. I cursed God. But you were dead. It didn't matter if I believed or not.'

Jasha sat watching by the cook-pot. Excluded, she eyed them, and felt the fine needles of her own hair sewing out of her scalp an inch or so an hour.

'I was called Nilya. The Vre in the Tower made you call me *mother* when you clung to the childish way. My true name's the Crel name Anjelen foisted on me, and which I've made mine, as I've made mine this body whose seed he gave me.'

Mechail regarded the snow falling.

Anillia went forward, two steps, and knelt down at his side. At once, she *became*, for the fire spread across her face, described her throat, her breasts, the three rich thick plaits of oil-black hair. The scent of her, which was young and fragrant, and not quite human, must have been exact

609

in his nostrils. She put her hand on his face, and persuaded it.

'Here I am,' she said. 'The flesh and the life. What do
you want?'

'Nothing,' he said. 'What's the use?'

His grey eyes were white from the snow, and Jasha saw
them clearly as they fixed on the woman's face.

In Jasha something writhed and chirped, so faintly she
took no heed. She stretched out her hands to the fire, and
they were full of clean redness. She heard Anillia say,
'You want only rest. I remember how that was, that wanting. To die and so sleep for ever.'

'Yes,' he said. 'But *he*—'

'Anjelen is nothing,' she said. 'We outran him, you
and I.'

'He's there before us,' he said. 'I can see him in the
future. He claimed me as his son.'

'You are my son,' she said. '*Mine.*'

Jasha heard the smooth susurrous, cloth brushing cloth,
and the snake-like slipping of long plaits of hair.

She formed strands of firelight between her fingers with
the red glow of blood in them. She tilted her head. Her
scalp itched from growth. Did the soil itch like this as the
grass pushed through?

When she looked over her shoulder, Anillia sat by the
wall on the pillow, and Mechail lay against her, his head
under her neck, so each face was set near the other, and
angled alike, saints' faces on a screen of cloak and hair
and dark.

They would not move for some while, or speak,
probably.

Jasha said in a sharp-winged little voice: 'Will you have
some of the broth?' And tapped the empty cauldron.

They did not reply.

Jasha looked back into the fire. It would last until morning, for it must.

Through the winter night, the girl Jasha closed on herself
tightly. As she slept, with her head laid on her knees, her

fluent spine bowed and her hands loose, her hair coiled over her and met the ground. The fire gave to it a bronze burnish, such as often it had had in the city, where it was so regularly washed and brushed and combed and caressed. Jasha dreamed briefly that she walked through the city, going to fetch water for her father's hut, at a well near the market. And she came on Anillia and Mechail lying together side by side, covered with leaves. It was summer, however, and their skins had the green glimmer of the foliage that grew from the houses and hovels. Even their lips were green, like moss. Jasha bent to tap them at the temple, the arm. They gave off a drum-like note. As she walked away on her errand, Jasha saw that the fingernails of the hand with which she had struck them had turned to wood.

She roused when there was a wintry first light through all the holes and crevices in the bothy. Sitting up, she peered cautiously at the place where Mechail had lain against their mother, the lady, and there they still were, as if they had not moved. But their eyes were shut as if by mutual consent. They slept a state of unison, but it was remote and pure, there was nothing natural in it. One sleeper in two bodies. They breathed as one and without detection.

Jasha broke a stick out of the wall and dipped it in the fire which, through the will of someone, had persisted without physical help. The stick caught, and Jasha got up and went out of the hut, holding her torch, into the dimness under the trees.

Birches shone like signposts to the stream, where the phantom village had been. There were pines. They seemed to have grown like her hair, swiftly, abundantly, so established and dense and massed with snow.

The stream was frozen, and Jasha got down by it and broke the surface with a slate. Underneath, imprisoned in meandering rafts of ice, big grey fish were lying. It might be they were an illusion, or something magically created. But she had found fish before in this way in the streams of the forest. Jasha took the ice and the ice-fish in the

611

skirt of her habit, and walked back to the hut. Her feet were still bound in strips of homespun stuff Mechail had given her. This would not be enough to save her from the snow, and yet it sufficed. The fish for hunger, the bindings for the cold, were provisions against her own oddity. Only by these methods did she lie to herself, and then not thoroughly. It had been wise in the past to avoid the probings of others.

On her path to the hut, she searched for edible grasses or weeds that might exist inside the bowels of trees. A handful of such savouries she amassed. And going into the room, she threw the ice, fish, weeds into her cauldron, and began to heat them on the fire.

Later she gathered sticks and branches to dry out by the hearth. There was no broom to sweep the floor. The sleepers did not wake. She took snow to the horses for drink.

Jasha plaited her hair. She recalled the long winters with her father, Carg Vrost, and her summer evenings with the irritable soldier Evra Livdis. She watched the fire and saw pictures in it and told herself stories from them, as the women did in the villages. When the fish soup was ready, she took it from the fire and after an interval ate some out of the cauldron, scalding her hand and lips. She did not like the fresh-water taste of these fish. She had liked the salty fish of the sea-river in the city.

She turned herself about and stared at the woman and the man, who slept. She thought of flinging pebbles at them, or tossing the bubbling soup on them. The vibration of sorcery had begun to come from them; it was not a sound, but it was the only noise they made.

'Will you wake up?' said Jasha. 'Supper's here. I've made you soup, lady. The fire's bright. Come and warm yourself.'

Sometimes she had put wild flowers on the grave-mound that was her mother in the forest. She went out and picked a twig with the snow on it, and put it between the fingers of Anillia's left hand. A silver ring had been on one of her hands, but it was not there now. It had dissolved, like the snow on the twig of frozen flowers.

The fire was black, the room crimson. A sunset covered the wood and through the open door, which stood wide, were fire-coals of mountains, and the rose-red snow. And in this heat of colour, the cold burned.

The sleepers had woken and they were gone. Nothing remained of them but the cushion of grass thrust into a corner.

It seemed to Jasha the woman had put her cool, ringless fingers on Jasha's forehead, as at their meeting.

Jasha went out quickly, and there were no horses in the lean-to. She picked about and found, halfway along a slope, a broad mantle of pink snow pitted by hooves. Then she returned to the hut. Again she provisioned herself with some of the now unhot fish soup. She imagined the cauldron might disappear when she left it. She was glad her hair had grown to warm her.

On her bound feet, she deserted the hut and walked up after the hoof-marks until she lost them among the thicker trees. The crimson was soaking by then into purple twilight. The shades were exotic and extreme, as if to keep her alert. She sought until the light was almost done with her, and then she found the trail again. She sprang along it like a hare.

Despite its effect, the woodland was not yet very old. As the dusk melted out the trees one into another, Jasha sensed slender shoots padding themselves with snow and darkness. Then, after the hues of roses, apples, grapes, the black total of night filled up everything. And as this happened, Jasha heard the syllables of her own name, eerie and bodiless, spinning back to her along the aisles of the wood. It was the woman who called. As if, since Jasha had pursued, she was now bound to go with them. Jasha accepted this. She moved unerringly towards the solitary summons.

They went through the trees, the makeshift invented road pillowing up, giving way, declining, now awkward and now plain. Sometimes, as though to be certain, her own name blew back to her once more. Jasha did not call in response. She had known the blackness of the forest since infancy, and its snows, and the lure of supernatural songs. She was only unsure of how far off they were, the two riders. How long she must travel, to reach them. She did not suspect herself of constancy, or envy, or need, or trust.

They were at the summit of a hill, and in the night without a moon, a vast forest seemed to or did surround them, sinking away, spread in folds towards nothingness, and black mostly, with the glass sheen on it of the snow. On the hill-top one tree, a thin spire, grew towards the sky. The snow had patched it lightly. There were stars upon its boughs, like birds.

The horses they had left below, setting them at liberty to do what they could for themselves. The horses had not seemed real, less so than the forest and the night.

'Why have we come here?'

The black-haired woman said quietly, 'To find the sleep you long for, and that he wished on me. The only rest there is.'

'Anjelen.'

'I know his mind,' she said. 'I know him.'

'Then you're his creature.' Mechail's voice was bored and dull. 'Another hallucination sent to torment me.'

'From the mental rib of Anjelen,' she said, 'I was made. And from my body I made you. And from my mind, at one remove, came Jasha. But also you made Jasha with me – my daughter, and yours. And from your soul, Mechail, the other one. Your dwarf who has your name. But we're all the creatures of Anjelen, or the creatures of what he is. Even he is the creature of that. And the man, that priest formed by others, that inquisitor and magician acting by human rote, losing sight of himself . . . How much more there will be to lose. I vowed against the man he is, to take away what the man wanted. I shall do so. But that other he is, that other's unavoidable. Its plan is our own. What you long for is what it would have from you, though not what Anjelen, the man, desired. His son upon earth, to walk in his ways. His chastity, his father's ambition – those you and I will ruin. But already, he allows it. What Anjelen truly is hasn't any care for earthly wants. It seeded, and has made its life again, in the image of the maker.'

'Where?' he said.

She smiled, and in the dark any watcher might see her smile like a ripple on night water, might see her smile – but not really her face. She touched her breast, she touched his cheek, then she pointed like a sword towards the single tree of stars.

'There is what we are,' she said. 'The root of our life. The one coffin that will hold us safe.'

The winter snow was on the wood, but then in the east an auburn disc rose like a copper mirror, a moon not of winter, spring, or autumn fall, but the summer moon of blood. The world welcomed the moon. It put off winter like a dew and the snows smoked away. In the life of one minute, the ground was black with the night-black of summer grass, and the flowers wounded it to get out. They rushed on the slopes, around the sinews of the trees, drifts like snow, night born and moon born, white and ash, sable and silver and brass. And the liquid pools were throats that gave out the hymn of frogs. A nightingale sang in an oak of ten thousand leaves. The trees were ancient and ripe with their foliage. The red moon shone on the forest like the sun by night.

The woods girl hid herself in her bush of snow that had become flowers. She breathed their perfume as she crushed them with her body. The bush sweated in the furnace of summer. She thought of a summer wood, and the ice age that had come on it, once, the shattered sugar of frozen roses. But that was then. This was now.

Above, on the hill, the man and the woman had stood before the narrow mast of the young Tree, and said their words, which she had listened to. The Tree had grown from their words. It was a column now, a pine perhaps, yet clouded at its top, the moon fired it there as if it burned.

And there were brilliants among the trees everywhere, swarming like fireflies, but they swam up the hill, and as they drew closer they lifted higher and grew larger, and she smelled, the girl in the bush of flowers, torches.

The man on the hill stared down at them.

'What is it?' he said. 'These lights.'

The woman said, 'Don't be afraid. It's a memory. The forest has them, as we do. Remember when you were a child and I took your hand? Like that, Mechail.'

'It's death,' he said, but his voice was longing and trembling as if with love.

'Not death. You know, we can't die, not I, not you. Haven't we tried?'

'Then—' he said. And he looked at her, and all of him was only in that look, nowhere else, and he was nothing else. '*Anillia*.'

'Rest,' she said. 'Truth.'

'In the wood,' he said. 'God's in the wood.'

He reached and took her hand, and so they stood, linked by a small connection of flesh, as the torches burned onwards along and up the hill on every side.

They passed her, Jasha, as she waited. There were men and women like wild beasts, children like fawns and kits and the cubs of foxes. The faces were blameless and intent. They were clothed in pelts of things that stank, and in their own foliage of hair. They were a primeval people. They were like the snake before it sheds its skin. She scented their archaism, yet they were *young* as the tree had been that now seemed equally old and unending and unbegun.

Going by, she felt their insubstantial substance, a wind of atoms.

The burning moon lit the hill like the morning of another world.

The crowd was all about them now, the two on the

hill-top. Jasha saw that their hands parted. Anillia said, 'My best, my love. Will you trust me?'

'Yes,' he said. 'Do I remember this – if he remembers—'

'There will be pain,' she said, 'but soon over.'

'It was all pain,' he said. 'Till now.'

Jasha saw them between the figures of the people, or through their bodies – somehow. She never lost sight of them, Mechail, Anillia. But they also changed.

Anillia's hair was loose, played over her. And she was clad in the skin of a doe, and her arms were whorled like those of women in the crowd, with the dark and red juice of berries. There were daisies in a garland on her head. She stood inside the crowd, as if she was one with them, but she shone through them.

Mechail had been drawn against the Tree's trunk. The men had roped him there, his arms uplifted, his ankles bound. One rope ran about his breast like a briar from the wood. He was naked. Jasha knew his body, though it was without any crippling mark. Like ivory now in the gilding moon, the black hair wound at the head and on the loins with shoots of ivy. His face tilted to the shoulder, as when he slept against Anillia in the hut. It was the aspect of the Christus, the arms outflung, the bound legs, the sinking head. It was the god of the wood who died and was reborn for ever and for ever.

And the Tree was a pine that was an oak; the tines of birches fanned out of it, the alders, and near its crown the sweeps of a willow, and near the roots boughs like the apple. It was all trees in one, and vines broke from its bark and entangled it; it was overgrown, and at its peak it had become a pillar of smoky fire.

The crowd murmured antique words that divulged no meaning.

The men were beating Mechail, with bunches of thorns. It made only the slightest noise, that under the chant was scarcely audible. The thorns started on the naked body, curious stitcheries. They formed and met and ran, and others came.

The ropes of briar had been weighted, and dragged on,

and the man on the Tree was lifted up off his feet. He was a hanging man, no longer an image of the Christus, yet the shape of the crucifix. He was the shape of the Tree itself, upflung towards heaven.

There were no stars, the moon had devoured them.

The slender seams of blood clothed the body over. They dropped at last on the earth under the Tree.

The Tree was hung with the man, and with a shower of other tokens which seemed to come visible only as his blood anointed its base. The Tree was as full of bones as there were flowers on the vines. The brain-cases of goats and wolves with creeper growing through their eyes, the skulls of horses polished dark, the colour of walnuts. And where the skulls were not, there were the teeth, the jointed tails and ribs of things, flagged with ribbons, and with the black bubbles of wild grapes poured from them, and honeycomb dripping like molten gold. The Tree was all trees of the forest, it held all sacrifice, life and death and life, each offering past and to come. It was time bent to a ring, turning like a wheel. And the man hung in it. His face was agonized and sleeping, dying awake. Miles above the earth he hung, and bound to the earth. His full weight was on the briary of ropes, and from the pressure of that, and from the stinging blows of the thorns, the adult phallus of his manhood had engorged. It was not innocent. It was the lust of the body under the provoking kiss of death.

One of the men was at Mechail's feet. He cut the veins of the ankles with a sharp stone.

Mechail's eyes had opened. He looked down on the man, scornfully, tenderly, half-amused. It was the face of a prince given valued service by an unknown slave.

The crowd had moved back. They had knelt down. The agony in the Tree excluded them. And as if the moon burned them up, as it had the stars of the sky, they began to go out in drifts.

Only one woman was on the hill-top under the Tree. The woman in the doeskin, who raised her arms and put back her head so her hair brushed along the ground.

To the watcher, the semantics of these things were useless. Reason was only in the power which roared like sound inside a huge bell.

The woman went to the Tree, and bending there, she kissed the bloody feet, and the blood was on her lips like paint, giving an extra feature to her face that had been only two eyes. The sharp stone was on the ground, as the skulls stayed in the tree. She took the stone in her hand, and then she set her feet into the sides of the trunk, and walked up it, like a stair, until she reached the man. She balanced before him, as though the Tree supported her and she had nothing to do with it, did not have to struggle or catch at the boughs.

'Who am I?' she said, looking into the face of a man that, dying, came alive, as once she had done. 'Do you know?'

'Anillia,' he said.

'I was Nilya, when I gave birth to you. She travailed, she held you to her dry breasts. She couldn't give you suck. She couldn't feed you. Nilya gave you nothing but life.' Stretching up, she drew the honed knife of stone steadily across each of his wrists. Fire ran in two streams, along the ivory flesh of both of them, and the skin of the animal discarded itself from her body. Above the left breast, she cut a new flower of blood. 'Now I can feed you. Drink from me.' And she drew his head against her, his mouth against the rose of the wound. As he took this draught, she held him, wrapping his torso with her arms. The stems of their bodies wove, as the vines with the tree, the skulls and bones with the grapes and blossoms and honey. He lifted his head and looked at her wonderingly. She was not his mother. Her body was not Nilya's. She was the earth, and he became the Tree which rooted in her. She had taken him in. Inside her was the core of the world, its soul, and this he touched. The branch of his loins had grown into her. Her arms were fastened about him. As they stirred together, it was the rapacious thrust of animation, the seeking swelling ferment of years amplified to swiftness, passivity now volatile.

The watcher in her bush of distance looked on at something that was a reflection in a mirror. She beheld an act that was to her, to Jasha, a commonplace, the unimportant, foolish, wanton blundering and plundering she knew, that to others was crime and dirtiness, craving, shame and imperfect satisfaction. But in the mirror of the moon, this she witnessed was not what she knew and had learned. Not copulation, not rutting, not even the making of love.

They were three, and they were one. The man, the woman, the tree of life. As the two bodies of flesh rhythmically and quickly beat together, like two white wings against the dark, the Tree encircled them, moved after and with them. They grew together, they grew into the Tree. And the Tree began to make a cry, low in the earth, miles down, where its roots padded like the paws of a giant cat, cracking the soil so the grass itself ran and the flowers there parted. The earth rumbled, and the limbs of the Tree thrashed in a slow weaving motion, and blood and wine and honey spilled through the boughs, and there were eyes in the skulls that glowed and looked eagerly about. A wind came, and tore along the sky. It seemed to blow the moon up into the forest of the Tree, another skull, another honeycomb.

And far away, in the heart of the wood, the listening watcher heard the two white creatures on the Tree crying aloud. They were arched from each other and from their joining, the two wings of a white moth now spread wide to fly. On their faces no features were left, they had become chaos. The sky burst above the moon. White lightning erupted from it and drenched the Tree in a fountain of liquid silver that, like the black wine and the red, the honey gold, sank into the roots of the tree, the caverns of the world.

Out of a strange prudence, Jasha hid her eyes. She curled over the bush and rubbed her face on the soil, to avoid and to receive everything.

No, Jasha. You must see. Look up.

The thing which communicated with her came from

the ground, too. It did not employ speech, or her name. Yet she was called by name, she was exhorted.

She could not ignore it, disobey. She sat up, and looked again, and as she did so, warm driven rain began to slant across the hill, easing her perception by its interference.

The Tree had already begun to be different. Much of its bulk had evaporated. The jewellery of flowers and skulls was not to be seen. It was a slender oak mated with a pine . . . Two white boughs curved upward from the trunk. They were male and female, and their wet black hair flowed in the rain as if beneath the sea. Their faces had come back, not those of Anillia and Mechail, necessarily, but also male and female, and folded together, a kissing of lips, breast upon breast, the limbs mingled. Stillness now as ultimate as the motion before. The moon had moved westward, more yellow than red.

It was the rain of summer's end. It ceased, and the leaves of the tree turned brown and rose, the needles yellowed like the moon, paled as the moon did. All began to drop from the Tree. And the flesh of what clung there, changing from ivory to grey, crisping like the leaves, like sallow petals, fluttered off, feathers, butterflies. The leaves and the flesh fell. The last ghost of a horse's skull depending as if forgotten far above, shook free and tumbled, fading before it met the ground. Only the bones were left of the man and the woman and of the winter Tree.

The Tree was young and slender. It resembled a pine with many broken boughs. Among these breakages, along the lower trunk, it had a formation like that of a skeleton grown into or out of the bark.

Jasha glanced at the sky and saw the winnowing snow. The moon, like a cold opal, had gone down under the horizon. Time had replaced itself and was. The snow and the winter refurnished the shallow wood.

Jasha walked over the snow, thick as several carpets now under her cloth-bound feet.

When she got to the Tree, it was already muffled fast, transmuting into a white mast without shape or meaning.

She circled the Tree, and her footsteps sealed her presence in the snow, and then were covered up, as if she were not there.

All the Tree said to her, the timbre of its power, was *Here*. *Here*, the Tree said, if in command or assertion of self was not to be known. *Here*.

In the beginning. Blood made the Tree, flesh built the Tree. The Tree had entered flesh, had been flesh. Flesh became again the forest. *Here*.

Jasha struck the trunk with her open hand. It made no sound. Some snow crumbled, and then fresh snow brimmed the place over. Jasha examined her hand, fearful and curious. There was no metamorphosis. Her skin tingled a little, but that was from the cold.

Just then sorcery let her go. And staring around herself, she knew where she was. In the wilderness, in snow and night. She looked at the Tree again, the snow mast that only said *Here*, and that might only be a young pine.

It was mute, like the darkness and the whiteness all about. Jasha had nowhere in the world to go, but she turned and stepped away from the Tree as best she could. As she did so, it seemed to her she had gone like this a million times, out into death-like emptiness and silence, through the wood.

Where the village had affixed itself, against the side of a long low rocky terrace, the winter had piled up white washing, and from the white snouted hut roofs poked with their smoke-holes forcing black into a low stone sky. Every dawn after a snow-fall, the villages dug out their door sills and made paths like tunnels down which they sometimes hurried. But there was not much to do abroad in winter. Only to fetch the logs or fill a bucket with icicles from the lintel. They hibernated like the pole-cat and the toad. But Gedno, who was a hunter, he was out at first light and dusk, to oversee his traps. He was the wolf; and he clambered up the snowbanks cursing and growling to himself, stupidly proud that he did not huddle indoors.

Above, the rock had snapped up through the afternoon

snow, and the trees along its crest showed their contours, though they were white. There had been a moment of sunshine that day which might have induced the things of the wood to emerge. In an hour it would be night.

Gedno got up among the trees, and went between them whistling his promise to the beasts in his traps, the starved ermines and bitter foxes. But when he came among them they were vacant, standing ajar under branches and snow with the morsels of food in them hard as obsidian. Disgusted, he blasphemed God. He almost did not bother with the last of the traps, which he had secreted down by the stream. But then, not yearning to return into his prison, Gedno forged on through the pines and slid and scrambled to the water's edge, which was now a snarl of ice.

There had been something in the trap. A brownish matted rag that was once a rat. There was a woman lying in the snow by the trap, holding the rat to her face, sucking its blood, that ran down her chin and from her wrists and scarred the whiteness so it smouldered. Gedno stopped and stared at her. Where she had come from, God knew, and God had no care. Her hair was a fearful bush. She wore a dark sack that had wound round her, giving her the form of a serpent with breasts. What urged itself on him was that she had no proper protection from the cold, her hands bare and her bare feet sticking out from the snow, yet she was alive, glubbing the blood out of the rat that was like a shred now. And he felt hatred for her, taking from his trap. She meant nothing, only that hatred. But hatred was novel after the winter's tedium.

'You bitch,' he said, and he went and got hold of her, pulling at her. Her head swung. Her eyes were a peculiar shade of blue or grey, half shut and perhaps sightless. She did not pay any attention to him, though at the briskness of his grip she had dropped his supper. He peered at it. The meat was intact. He grabbed it into the pouch at his belt, and hauled her up. 'Where are you from?' It was rare to see an unknown face, let alone a female face.

'Traveller folk, are you? Slung you out for your sluttish-ness maybe. I'll teach you to tamper with Gedno's traps.'

Her bare feet had gone under the surface of the snow. He looked at her hands. They should have been frost-bitten, but possibly she had not come far.

'Where are your men?' he said. He checked the rock and the trees spreading over it. The sky was muffled, anyone might be lurking. 'Some trick, eh?'

The woman did not speak. She had not wiped the blood off her chin, and it set black in the cold.

Gedno's senses were keen, he inventoried the country again. No one, surely, was there.

He must accept her. That was what the priests taught, when you saw one. Venerate God and treat all men with love, and reckon yourself a piece of dung.

'Bitch,' said Gedno. He began to propel her through the gathering twilight, in which she seemed moment by moment odder and more hateful. While in his pouch the drained rat was light as something invented.

When they came down the street, no one was about, and the frozen tunnellings were already rigid. Tonight the world would freeze altogether, a Hell of ice. She was lucky, this trull, he had found her.

He thrust open the hut door, and got her in.

Like the others, Gedno's hut was a room of wood, with one window covered by a shutter. It was lit by the fire, and by a wick in fat that grizzled and smelled in an old clay lamp on a shelf. So, it was a room dyed like blood after the darkness and white outside, and in it were a wife and two brats and a goat, who glared in alarm and distrust, all their eyes the same, red and round, slotted with blind reluctance.

The girl was not blind, no, for she glided her head about, looking back at them. She seemed drowsy. She did not seem to know them for a man and woman, children, even the goat she studied an instant, as if she had never seen such a thing.

'What?' said Gedno's wife.

'Be quiet,' he said.

'But what's she?'

'On the hill in the snow,' he said. 'Now sew up your lip. Put this in the stew.' And he tossed the rat to her.

She caught it, well used to such amendments to their diet, thankful to get it, not aware what was wrong with it. She put it on the wooden table and fetched a knife from the shelf by the lamp.

The children, crawling on the floor, gazed at their father, uncomprehending as always his acts. They did not like the snow-girl. They went into a corner, where they kept their toys, a stone, a patch of fur, and there they eyed her now and then, warily. The goat picked a route to her straw in the opposite corner.

The man thrust his prize up to the fire.

'Now you can skive all winter,' he said. 'She'll help with your tasks. In the spring I can trade her, sell her. She's strong.' He got a bladder of ale from behind the door.

The wife began to skin the rat.

'There's no blood,' she whined.

Gedno ignored her. He drank from the ale-bladder, and bore it over to the girl. 'Would you fancy a taste? Good ale. She gets none.'

The girl looked at him, her eyes had focused now.

'Give it to me,' said the girl.

Gedno jumped. By some obscure logic he had believed she could not speak.

'Saucy sow,' he said. He hit her without weight across the cheek.

Her head went sideways at the blow, recoiled. He thought of a snake, as before. But then she lowered her eyes. Her hair was bunched with blizzards of bits, twigs and slimes, the refuse of the forest.

His wife watched.

'Get on with your work,' he said.

He pushed the ale-bladder at the girl's mouth, which was smooth and whole above the trail of blood, unlike the mouths of harsh winter.

'Who are you then?' he said.

'Jasha.'

'Jassi,' he said. 'Who are your kin?'

'In the snow,' she said. Her eyes were like the frozen stream. 'I forgot, there.'

'Then you're my slave. Maybe you'll remember someone who wants you. Who'll pay me for you, eh?'

She shook her head. Her terrible hair was long, though some of it seemed to have been torn out in her travels.

'No one. My da,' she said, 'he died.'

'Ah. Well. Gedno's your daddy now.'

That spring, Gedno killed his wife. It happened on the village street.

The winter had been long and unkind, but so it always was. Spurts of community violence were often the result of such closeting together, barricaded by snow, breathing the air out of each other's mouths. Yet there had been no village murder for thirteen years, which for some was a lifetime. (Murders there had been farther afield, for that was occasionally their business.)

Gedno had gained a slave during the winter. One day when there was a thaw that brought the snow crashing from the roofs and made the street into a stream, this slave was observed paddling to the well. She was unusual. Her hair was brown and separated into three wide plaits that hung to her knees, her eyes were devilish, fish-like. And her complexion baffled them also, since she was tanned, there at the hub of winter.

Gedno had stridden out of his house to see them stare.

Finally he shouted, 'Tell them who you are, girl.'

And the girl said, 'Gedno's slave.'

Then, over their ale, he described to the men his find. One or two muttered that he must share, his good chance should benefit the village. Gedno disagreed with his fists, and it was decided that she was his, and the profit he might get from her his too.

The village subsisted in the normal manner, sowing and reaping, hunting, and bartering with other hutments along the valley below the wood. But the village also had for a trade robbery of any worthwhile sort.

In the summer there were persons who travelled the wood up and down between far off, unknown cities, or there were strays, and sometimes there might be mounted a raid on an alien village beyond the valley. They took whatever they could, were not particular. Silver coins, for which seldom was there much use, nicer wine barrels, corn in sacks, a horse, a knife. Failing all else they would accept the clothes off backs, and sometimes they had had women, now long amalgamated into the female drudge-hierarchy of the huts.

But it transpired Gedno's wife did not like the slave he had found. She resented the slave. It was not, of course in her contract to resent anything, and when the green tendrils began to worm out of the slush and unwary birds sat in the trees by the well for handy stoning, she came out on the street in her apron, crying and squalling. Gedno had been to the slaughtering of a pig. He was splashed with blood and full of ale. He walked from the butchering hut and positioned himself, watching her. But she only raised her voice. 'You plug her!' cried Gedno's wife.

'Well? She's the slave, isn't she?'

'In front of your sons, in the bed—'

'Swallow your row. Or do I make you?'

Then she howled.

Gedno lumbered over the street and landed a blow on her ear. He noticed that at the impact her eyes comically crossed, and this made him giggle. Some of the other men had come out to see. They all saw Gedno's wife thump into the mud and lie there. After a minute he kicked her, to remind her to get up. But she would not, and when he lifted her head by the hair, her eyes slipped over as if she were interested in the ground. She made a snoring noise and matter came out of her nose. That was all she would do, and soon enough Gedno was aware his aggravation with her was wasted.

The other men were uneasy at first. One even remonstrated, but Gedno said, 'She was a nag.' They could hardly deny it, they had seen.

After this, the slave, Jassi, tended Gedno and his two boys, and the goat.

His sons were partly afraid of Jassi, and they blamed her for the loss of their mother. They called her *Snake*. They devised silly, nasty pitfalls for her, putting grit in the curds, letting the fire go out, spilling the water she fetched. The elder boy crept up to her as she stirred Gedno's soup. 'Want you go.' And when Jassi did not answer – she never spoke to them – 'Make you die.' When this was said, Jassi turned her evil eyes on him. He shrank and shrivelled in her gaze. Later, he wrenched at her viciously, and coming around, she struck him with the big spoon she had been working in the soup. 'Tell da,' he said. 'He beat you.' But Jassi said nothing, and neither did the child. Gedno was liable to lash out at them all. The slave had not been misled into thinking she was the only victim. Besides, she warmed the man's bed – the mound of grasses against the wall where the goat was not allowed. Gedno had got up on her and grunted throughout the winter, initially shoving her to the bed from her allotted place by the hearth. (Those times the wife had lain beside them, pushed against the wall of the house. As well she was gone. It gave him more room.)

As the summer came,, the village went about its habits. The fields were ploughed and the women scattered the seed. The goats went to graze. The men, most of them, took up their thieving. Whole days and nights they were gone. (The slave lay on the bed of grass and the children said banes at her until they slept – these did not take, she was hale and tough.) When the men came back they feasted on the best the village had, and drank. Gedno would come into his house. He would drop on Jassi like a collapsing sodden hog: often he could not finish.

The slave's brown skin faded to cream, contrastingly as the summer heightened and the village's arms and faces burned.

A man said to Gedno, 'You should watch her. Something's bad there.'

'Want her?' said Gedno. 'You must want.'

He did not sell her, barter her, slough her.

By the time the summer waned and the dark night of winter threatened them again, some of them spoke of her as Gedno's wife. it was a politeness. They had nothing to do with her. Nor she with them.

During the second winter, she dreamed of the Tree.

It was neither as she had beheld it in reality, or in the vision, the memory or prophecy of what it symbolized. In the dream it was taller and stronger, it had more boughs, and perhaps it had already an immature architecture of several trees, the pine, the oak, the cedar. It was cased in snow, and between the branches long strands of luminous ice portrayed the true formation of the Tree, or dissembled.

Nothing moved. No wind blew. A zircon sun smelted the sky, and did not rise or sink.

Around the Tree, twining it, was a dragon, scale-made of the ice, its crystals, scintillant, and motionless like the rest. The long head lay along an upper limb. It was remarkably distinct, could be mistaken for nothing else. The Serpent. In its eyes, a faint sourceless glimmer. It held the Tree, guarding it or bracing it, or containing it – what it was to become.

Jasha woke from this dream, and thought the soldier, Evra Livdis, was lying on her, but it was this other one, this Gedno. She submitted, guiding his hands when he fumbled. The dream was like music. (A woman had sung, in a market, under a window.) As the man rammed her body, Jasha floated on the plank of the dream. The two children no longer watched and abhorred. They had given up. Just as Jasha had always known, acceptance was everything, it meant survival. When Gedno slumped, before his weight had even left her, she returned into dreamless oblivion. Her days were busy. She required her sleep.

*

For ten years, Jasha existed in Gedno's robber village. It was enough like an earlier existence, the years in the village to which Carg Vrost had dispatched her. She came to such a life now with foreknowledge, yet even that did not make it difficult to bear, for Jasha. What else could there be?

That she had lived through her lost wandering in the snow wood, until the moment of discovering the trap with the dead rodent in it, still warm and lush with blood, when she had bitten and drunk, not thinking, those events had never been examined, and the ten years of slavery were not. To the passage of time she was mostly immune, going only from day to day. She was not demeaned, nor demoralized. Her morality was not like that.

Nor was she disconcerted by the signatures of time. She noted the ageing of everything, the crankiness of the huts, the height and girth of trees, how animals gave birth and thinned and died, how the sons of Gedno imperceptibly reformed into cloddish men of about sixteen. For all her treatment, under which the other women bowed and limped and were gnawed away, grey-headed, creased like autumn leaves, Jasha grew no less. She did not change. As for ageing in herself, who expects that? Old age, even when anticipated, surprises, seems unrelated, stuck on or in, like pins. Jasha did not age.

The village overlooked it too. They had always reckoned her peculiar, and to stay peculiar was in a way her conformity. There was some white in her hair, where Gedno had sometimes bashed her across the temples – they accepted that as a substitute.

The younger son evinced signals of preparing to rape Jasha, and for this, thoughtlessly, she readied herself. The elder threw his shoes at her, but taking care to miss.

Gedno was large and beer-soaked, and left his hunter's work to his heirs, although they all went raiding and robbing. Some nights she was alone.

She would lie on her back and watch the firelight on the tilted hut roof.

All she had nostalgia for was the sea. The sea had been

the forest, yet so unlike. She wondered where it was, for none of them spoke of it, though once, twice, she had heard a rumour of the building, the Christerium, awkward hissings of corruption and the punishment of those who preyed on ordinary men, fat priests, sorcery going under the auspice of knightly ritual. But the phraseology they employed, even in rumour, was obstructive. They knew virtually nothing, and invented illogically. And Jasha inclined not to have any attention for it, although sometimes she found she had listened closely, as if she meant to bear the tale away for the man Mechail, or her mother, the woman Nilya. But they were dead. They were not hers.

The sea lived. She visualized it. There was a window in a dream from which she saw it come and go, and the dawn meadowed on the water and the black blooms of night.

The morning the priest came into the village, most of the men were heavily asleep. They had been jaunting in the wood and met a wagon taking provisions somewhere; all these arrived at the village. Then there had been a massive junketing. Even some of the women got drunk. Of all things that might follow, an itinerant priest, bearing his beads, and a few pages of the Book, footsore and hopeful of hospitality, was the last thing they had looked for.

Jasha was at the well. The priest came down the track that in summer was baked out plainly as a city road. He nodded to Jasha a big brindled head. 'Give me some water, girl.' So Jasha took him the pot with the water, and he drank straight from it, from its cracked rim, where all their lips had been. Then he glanced Jasha over. And something struck her. In the second year, she had been given the dead wife's clothes, which did not fit yet abstractedly grew to her shape. Under the grass bed lay the priestly habit in which she had journeyed. How if she had been wearing that? 'Where's your husband?' said the priest to Jasha, irked at the sparseness of his welcome. 'Where are the women?'

'Asleep,' she said. And then, 'Do you come from the Christerium?'

Perhaps it was only that the decade of interval, offering nothing, had left her concentration in the past, where the Christerium still reared, important and indelible. Whatever the immediate reason, the priest flinched away and marked himself over in a pushing manner, with the cross of the Christus.

'What can you know of that? Hold your tongue, girl.' Jasha said no more. The priest glared at her and said, 'Don't you know better than to jabber of vice? That place – full of wicked men who worked against the Lord God, using Father Church as their shield – dealt with, shovelled in the ground, and may the Devil have them.' Then, 'Take me to your house.'

'Not mine,' said Jasha, with some fastidiousness. 'I'm Gedno's slave.'

'Slave? What business has this peasant with slaves? What goes on here? Asleep at noon – the Evil One's been busy.'

And then again, as they walked towards Gedno's hut, he said, 'Demons and vampires nest in the ruins. Unsafe when the wholesome sun is down.' And he hit her in the back. 'What can he be thinking of, your master, letting you hear of it?'

Jasha indicated the hut door, which in summer stood wide, emitting Gedno's guttural drunkard's snores, and those of the younger son – the elder was courting a girl and abed elsewhere in a haystack.

'Is it a pigsty?' shouted the priest. He fetched the table leg a brawny kick. 'Up! Sloth's a sin. Yes, a sin. Woe betide the fool who sleeps, for how shall the trumpet wake him on the Final Day?'

Gedno and his younger son opened their eyes. They had thick heads, and Gedno a thick gut, but their ears performed very well.

'What's this?' said Gedno. 'Who dares to come in and kick my table?'

He and his son sat up, each on his wall, and eyed the priest cautiously, unlovingly.

'I am God's,' said the priest. 'If he prompts me to kick, I kick.'

'Maybe,' said Gedno, 'the Devil will prompt me to kick back.'

The priest's face flamed as Gedno's did in drink.

'On your feet, you swine. Up! Up! Do you see me, who I am? I stand for my Lord, the Christus. Sinners all. I shall have labours here.'

He was intrepid, belligerent, and these qualities they unwittingly respected. They got to their feet and presently came to breathe their beer-stinking kisses on his crucifix.

As he had said, he had labours there. He dug out the erring flock from their stupor and brought them to the trees by the well. Here he preached Damnation to them and they, loathing and writhing, sick and drunk, must stay to heed, for such was the might of what he was sprung from, the Church Paternal, of which this roving bully in filthy darned robe, filth ingrained in his neck and fingers, warts on his cheeks, yet remained a representative. He bore upon him, and he knew it well, the seal of Heaven. What might he not give – all the horror of Hell, the limbo of spiritual exile, misery everlasting. And if they did not entirely believe in him, or in his waxen god (so like the dolls the women put in the trees at holy days and harvest), they could not bring themselves to risk it.

She heard them mutter how they would like to spit him, throw him down a hole. She watched as they kneeled and reverberated their confessions. And when she, with the other women, was sent flying for ale and breads, dishes of butter, a cold roast starling, apples, Gedno caught her arm. 'Hide the loot, do you hear?' She did not ask where. 'In the cupboard,' he groaned, 'back of the bed—' And in the hut she stowed the pair of lumpy bundles, which the priest had not seen, or wanted to see. For it must be true, also, he would have a code whereby to deal with villages of this sort.

After he had eaten and drunk, the priest visited each

hut. Here he saw nothing ethically amiss, but he ranted, in his dirt, about floors unswept, the pots unscoured.

'Here's a slave,' he said, daggering his thumb at Jasha, 'keeps better house.'

He returned to Gedno's mansion at evening.

And there Gedno sat faultlessly with his two sons at the fire, where the supper kettle bubbled. And Jasha was tying up the two latest goats that she had brought in from pasture.

'What are you doing, owning a woman?'

'She's my wife,' said Gedno.

The priest lifted his brows. 'She said she was your slave.'

'Oh, once, godbrother. But then I saw fit to wed her.'

'Under some tree. Do you want the service now?'

Gedno scowled.

Jasha turned from the goats. 'No,' she said.

Gedno rolled about with an oath. It took the elder son to laugh. The priest mashed his brows down. 'Are you a pagan, girl? Or what are you?'

Jasha, called Jassi, stood in Gedno's hut, in her dead-woman's apron, her three long brown plaits, her green eyes that measured the floor.

'I won't marry him,' she said. 'He's nothing to me. Tell him to let me go.'

'How did he come by you?'

'I found the bitch,' cried Gedno. 'I took her in from the snow. She'd have died if not.'

The priest, who had made them dance to God's tune, would not force the music for worldly matters. Man had governance over woman.

'You owe this man your life, and gratitude,' he said to Jasha. 'What are you, a shrew?'

The elder son said with a flourish, spitting in the fire, 'She's a fey from the wood. You should burn her, godbrother.'

'And you swill out your mouth with brine and vinegar,' said the priest. 'You must learn to keep quiet where you know nothing.' Then he beckoned Jasha. She crossed the room skirting Gedno, who fumed like the fire. 'What do you say to it?' he said.

'I say,' said Jasha, 'I'll turn into a white hare at moonrise and get up into the forest.'

The priest struck her in the face.

'You've no religion. I can't save you.' He stared at her weird eyes, but they looked away over his shoulder. 'Like Eve, you're for the land below. He's earned you.'

And he went out and left them. They heard his coarse voice speaking aloud a prayer and he passed his beads through his grimy hands, not looking back, shaking the dust off his heart upon them all.

There passed a piece of time then, in the hut, without much movement, noiseless. Outside sounds came from the other huts, the dusk filmed the sky and the valley. Where the priest had gone (boldly, unwisely, despite his earlier tirade, as if night were only another kind of day), the spirits of darkness gathered.

After the silence, the elder son spoke first.

'What will you do, eh, Da? What good is she, the sow? She's barren too. Beat the hide off her. I would if she were mine.'

'She isn't yours,' said Gedno. His voice was deep down in his belly with the soured ale. 'Get out, the two of you. Take yourselves off.'

They got up, and as the elder one went by Jasha, he tweaked her plaits and grinned.

'Shut my door,' said Gedno, 'you rotten bloody bitch.'

Jasha, his slave Jassi, shut the door.

Jasha turned by herself, and then Jasha, and more than Jasha, stood looking at him, but he did not see, and maybe as yet she did not completely know it, either.

'What do I do to you,' said Gedno, 'to teach you manners? A white hare, is it? You'll be a skinned hare when I've done with you.'

He started to hoist himself, and stopped.

His slave was coming forward from the door, out of the shadow, and the fire shone on her lizard's face, attentive and serene, and her tongue flickered between her parted lips; she held her right hand towards him. In the unnatural light, it might have been made of smooth-planed wood. A wooden hand that could not move its fingers, yet was alive with purpose.

Gedno reached and seized the hand, to check it, and he cried out wildly. For the hand was icy or scalding, it scorched him.

'Look in the cook-pot,' said Jasha. Her voice was only cool and mild. Her eyes were black in thin rings of silver. Her tongue darted. 'Look in there, Gedno.'

Gedno tried to struggle, to get up and grasp her, but instead he lowered himself and hung over the kettle so the steam of the vegetables seared his cheeks.

'What do you see?' asked Jasha.

'Bitch,' said Gedno. And then foolishly, 'Let go.'

Through the steam he saw in the soup a black snake that swam. As it squirmed through its bath, its scales glinted and pulsed. He was afraid. His eyes had boiled dry and he longed to close them.

'Gedno,' said Jasha, 'put your head into the pot.'

Outside, it was the younger son who had idled near his father's house. His sexual intriguement with Jasha had been enhanced by notions of violence done her. Perhaps he wanted to hear her scream. Instead he suddenly made out a crazy muffled howling and rattling, the crashing of something metallic. It seemed his father was thrashing the slave with the food kettle, moaning and choking as he did so. While she, oddly, did not even squeak. Then the man's vocality ceased, there were a few thumps, a nothingness.

The younger son grimaced at the darkness. He tried to make it join him in complicity. He wished his brother was there, had not slunk off to his slut again.

In a short while the younger son swaggered to the door. 'Da? What are you at?' And, having no answer, 'I'll come in now. Will you let me? Yes?'

When he came in through the door, the hut was very dark, for mostly the fire had gone out. Something had fallen or spilled and put it out – there was an odour of boiling, wrong and unpleasant, and of charred wet cloth.

636

Gedno's younger son went forward, and tripped over his father's legs, which were sticking out in the mode they had when he collapsed drunk on the bed. They were not so unusual, these drunken legs, but his father's torso in the fire was what the son contacted next, and his father's shoulders that ended at the rim of the soup kettle, where flooded squashed vegetables, peeled ribbons of skin, drowned hair.

The boy screamed as he had thought Jassi would. And the scream, raising his head, let him see someone standing across the fire-place. This someone was not Jassi. It was a man, surely. Tall and dangerous.

One of the goats bleated a gentle inquiry.

'There, now,' said Jassi kindly, to the goat.

'You,' said Gedno's younger son. 'What have you been doing?'

He pulled himself up from his father's corpse and went over the burnt tunic and splashed wet flesh and the sticks and soup to take Jassi by the throat.

Jassi slewed away. Her hard left hand blazed into his jaw, and as he staggered, she stabbed him in the heart, exactly, with the skinning knife from the shelf. They were male blows, set with the precision of one who had been trained to fight, he almost realized as he died.

'What now?' said Jasha's cool Anillia voice. She watched through the dark a moment Gedno and his younger son lying on the fire which they had, between them, totally suppressed. It was with a quirky lightness that she discarded them, and all of this, this hutment, this life, the ten years. Need she have endured even one of them? Could she not, long since, have released herself? But it was as if the seed she had taken with her from their Tree had asked her latency, the opaque soil wherein to germinate. She was with child of them. They had not possessed her. It was she who had possessed them.

She remained on her feet in the dark by the corpses, not noticing especially, looking in at what she now was.

She was the fox that had received the dual soul of a man and a woman. She had always understood how to run upon four feet, now also she might walk on two. She might bite and bark, she might speak and sing.

It was magic and a mystery. It was the ultimate passage of a psychic atom, the ribs of her makers, and she had fastened herself about it and closed it over with her body and her mind.

If she glimpsed now she had ever been incomplete, spare, it was for the reason she might be filled.

They had gone back into the wood. But the library of their brains, their mortal dreams, were hers. She was what they had been, but more.

Mechail, Anillia. And beyond them, the other, the Angel, the root and the destroyer, she beheld him, too.

Jasha stretched herself, waking from her ten-year sleep.

Going to the bed, she took out the tattered priest's habit Mechail had given her. She put off her other borrowings, and inserted herself into the pelt of God. This amused her, and phrases of Mechail's sarcasm, Anillia's contempt, skimmed her awareness.

She knew where she would go. She knew what she wanted. She was lawless as they had not been, no, not even Anjelen. Sing and speak and *bite*.

As soon as she was ready she opened the hut door and stepped out.

The elder brother and a brace of his cronies were on the street, and in the other doorways lights glowed. A tableau of normalcy and so of threat.

'Who's there?' said the elder brother.

They stared, the four or five robber men, and saw a priest as unlike the visitor of the morning as was imaginable.

Despite towering, immutable evidence to the contrary, they began to recognize Jassi, the slave Gedno had been beating – for they had heard a scream.

'What are you at now? Get in, you, and see to supper.'

'Supper's seen to,' said Jasha. She smiled.

She started to walk right by them. They gawped and did nothing. 'Get hold of her,' snapped the elder son, unknowingly sole lord of the hut and the two goats.

'But – it's a priest – I can't go laying my hands on a—'

'It's the *slave*, Christus send you to fry.'

One of them grabbed Jasha.

She turned her head and spat directly at his eyes. The man floundered back cursing, 'Poisoned me – blinded me—'

It took Gedno's elder, now only, son to rush at Jasha, grip her arms. In the chequered light of the neighbouring doorways, at which here and there a man or two had appeared, Jasha was shown to her attacker. Her gaze was grey like steel. It was black, ink on adamant. And it was green like the sea, of which he had been told by his mother at the dawn of his days, before the mould of slobbishness and witless cruelty had clamped him in its vice.

'A white hare,' said Jasha. 'Look there. It's away.'

And he looked and saw, and afterwards two of the others also claimed they did, a white slight springing thing sewing up the street and off over the slope towards the rock and the forest.

He must have released what he held. They said Jassi vanished. Vanished from their sight into the air and the darkness. And that by then was possible, for she had now all the lessons, the making and dispersal of flesh streamered out by will from the soul, the deception of enemies, the grandeur and inconsequence of the magician melded with the fox.

Chapter Four

Three of them went with him. It was as if he had them on a leash. But they stared. The one who called himself Eujasius, the Angel of the Bread of the Body of the Redeemer, he must feel that rheumy concentration, just as he heard their desiccated bones crackle on every step, at every turning. They had met him in an alley of the Christerium, where the dwarf conducted him. Then the dwarf retreated somewhere. Eujasius and the three priests paced on, one leading but always looking back, the others behind.

The chamber where they arrived burrowed in a jumbled block of leaning cells, close under the tower of the church.

'You see that? You will wash yourself.'

There was tub with hot water. (Where from? Their wells were sewers, their cistern a swamp. Could it be they took water from the women's well of the Doma?)

Eujasius, who had bathed in the cold sea, offered no discouraging remark. He said, 'Go out, then.'

'You must wash, you must be clean.'

'Why?' asked Eujasius, innocently.

The priests exchanged their gazes. The one called Ragis said, fussily, 'To be included in our ceremony. For the honour of God.'

They withdrew, and left Eujasius to the bath.

He shut the door to the cell, and hung the habit up over it. Eujasius dipped into the bath, comparing its curdled warmth to the freeze and play of the ocean. They had left him another robe to put on. It was white, or once it had been.

When the bath was over, and Eujasius dressed in this garment, he opened the door again. The unlit corridor ran, unoccupied, to the court outside, only the candle they had left in the cell dripping and flicking at it. Across the corridor's end, over the arch of more transparent black that was night sky, night walls, something went. It was low, a skinny humped back, an eared head hanging. Eujasius caught the whiff of its smell of redness, darkness, and the milky wink of its eyes.

Then, disembodied, the one called Ragis quavered: 'Are you there? Are you ready?'

Eujasius came along the corridor with the candle, and met Ragis in the yard. Shadows crouched, breathing. Over stonework and mounds of ivy, shaggy like the beast which had gone by, the seaward tower flew towards Heaven. By night, the broken top was lost in stars. A bell rang unevenly, with a dolorous, halting clank.

'What's that?' said Eujasius.

'The summons.'

'To what?'

'To the feet of God.'

'Wolves,' said Eujasius, 'pad about your ruin.'

'Oh yes,' said Ragis. 'Yes.'

'Mangey wolves, with invalids' eyes. Is that all that's left to you?'

Ragis averted himself, his whole body. He flapped Eujasius on. The other two were no longer in attendance. All the shadows swayed.

They negotiated the yard, a shattered area, squeezed through a compressed tunnel wolf-haired with creeper, smelling of wolf. They came out on the paved court where the slabs had lifted out like graves. There was light. A torch exploded its fire over the fantastic ivy doorway, ripped at the slivers of tinted glass above, the untidy nests of birds. Some gulls had been displaced by the bell. They yawed about the tower, and they too caught the torch flame under their wings, and were bits of fire, demons . . .

There were wolves in the church, all over the Christerium. Under the faltering of the bell, the screek of the gulls, their shufflings, their panting, ebbed and flowed. A phantom slanted up a roof, among the twisted weathervanes, another flashed between two windows its pupils, the razor leanness of its back. In the tower they crustily inhaled. They were old, stinking, loping on taut chalky legs, cracked claws fumbling. But he let them run, as always. It was their reward, their proof. That Ragis had not been granted the privilege might be the sign of his master's displeasure, or an oversight. There would be oversights, now.

'Walk along by the wall. There's a little door left ajar. Go on, and stay yourself there. You must remain, you understand?' Ragis was blossoming strangely on excitement. He no longer distrusted Eujasius, or doubted Eujasius must be part of what was to come.

'Very well.'

'There'll be lights. You'll see. And the Magister will be with us. You must keep still. Whatever you witness or hear. Until he calls you.'

Eujasius said, 'How many have you brought here, to your God-hovel, for Anjelen?'

'Oh, very many,' said Ragis. He was not thinking or reasoning. He craned forward, at the same moment pushing Eujasius away with one hand towards the wall.

Eujasius moved off along the tower, and found the door amid the litter piled against its base. Inside was pitch-darkness, but he smelled the Christerium church, what it was, what it had been. Laid finely on the musty excrement of gulls, the rot of timber, damp stones, weather, were the hues of incense bright as dust from the stars. Eujasius waited, and nocturnal vision was bestowed on him, on his feline female eyes, rendering up for him his own boy-girl body in its sheath of lacking white, the male body the priests had given him, that even Anjelen had given him with the name *Mechail*. Eujasius had cut his hair with a

642

knife in the mountains, before the Travellers met him. Now, in the dark, Eujasius began to let his hair grow. He guided it under the neck of the robe, suggested it hid there, as it went on, trickling down his back, the male back the priests had given. Striped Anillia hair. *Anillia,* Anjelen might have said, sensing this latest nuance.

Did Anjelen perceive? What did he learn? Nothing. *I read him,* thought Eujasius, Angel of Bread, *what he is.* It was a void. Mindless. Only the craving shone in it, like the ruby in the lacquer cross. And that drew near, floating down through the layers of the building.

The candles lit in the church. The magician's alchemy brushed them into being with the beauty of a glamour. But Eujasius, who *knew,* knew this was only the glamour of practice, almost an aberration. Anjelen was what had revealed itself in the dining hall. *That.*

Nevertheless, the church tower had changed, now it had been entered into the light.

The floor had lustre under its dullness, water under scum. The adornments of the gulls were a mosaic, like secret forms that might be solved. The great altar was draped, and the faded material, like a flower, shone white from within. But there was no gold or gems on it, whose riches were gone, like the great crucifix, and magic did not fake them. Instead there stood now on the altar-top a silver cup in a garland of ivy.

Then the brethren came, the Knights of God.

There were thirty of them. They were clad in mail, helmed, with vizors lowered. The cobwebs of cloaks trailed behind them, and torn, yellowed plumes. They walked with the firm sure tread of ghosts, forgetting they were dead. The mail was blistered, it was rusty, in spots it had dropped away. And it hung on them, too large for their shrunken frames. Yet they fired like fevers, As they creaked forward, to make a circle under the altar, the helms gave to their faces a fearsomely unsuitable and horrific arrogance. They were the cadavers at the feast, crying *Behold our splendour* while the worms gnawed in their bellies.

Outside the light, their creation, Eujasius, regarded them. Others there had been, bemused, terrified, but Eujasius watched, thinking of Anjelen and his black-haired warriors, their swords rainbowed from the windows, the loaves of bread prancing from the basket. A gull shrieked in derision high above.

And Anjelen was on the stair above the altar, descending, as once before, in the rainbow time.

He was not dressed as a Knight. He had on his body, which did not physically alter, the same black habit he had worn in the refectory.

Eujasius nodded. The memory of Mechail provided the thought, *He doesn't bother with it any longer. The ritual, its trappings, bore him. He only wants his drink. But they cherish all he puts aside, the old wolves. What can he give them? What will he spare them from his high table?*

Anjelen spoke.

'We are here for our faith.'

They lifted their heads, every one of them, and one third of each face was tarnished metal, and the rest the triumph of age, motivated by avidity. They hungered. Their old lips and parchment-covered jaws begged. They were dogs of famine.

Anjelen had reached the altar. 'The wine,' he said.

There was no music in his voice. It was the voice of a man. He did not exert himself.

And the withered flower-heads of his greed hung around the centre of his indifference.

And around that, the ruin.

Anjelen's own brain supplied for the brain of Eujasius, like a book, the illusions and wizardry of all times past. There had been forests woven with serpents, budded with beasts. Roses grew from the broken vase of blood. There the melody was, the wings, the power, and the glory. But there was only this, now. And Anjelen turned his head, looking at the gloom beyond the candlelight, where Eujasius stood waiting.

With no particular elegance, in fact quickly, peremptorily, Anjelen beckoned.

And like all the others of the past, as if afraid, mesmerized, staring only into the eyes of Anjelen that were the eyes of a man, Eujasius moved towards the circle under the altar.

The circle parted, to let him go through.

Anjelen intoned swiftly, 'They hung Him on a tree. In the sight of the world. Do this, He said.'

Eujasius had reached Anjelen. He saw that Anjelen was pulling from a wristlet in his sleeve a sharp pale knife.

Eujasius put back his head and looked up into the face to Anjelen. He looked with Anillia's look, and Mechail's. And even that, Anjelen could not discern as he bent forward to force and to have. He had taken this one for Mechail even, and now forgot all that, like all the forgetting. For he was in the summer drought of thirst.

'Drink,' said Eujasius, 'for here is the wine.'

His hand darted out and ripped the knife from Anjelen's fingers.

He leapt away, blithely, and jumped up on the altar, where he struck aside the cup with his foot. It swirled along the cloth in a blur of lights, and poured to the floor with a kitchen sound of pots and pans. Eujasius snatched up the ivy garland. He swung it upon his head.

The priestly Knights groped after him with their eyes and hands, not moving otherwise. And Anjelen was still, all but his mouth, where the lips contorted, lengthened, strove, without opening.

'I'm the wine,' said Eujasius. He laughed out loud.

With the knife of the sacrifice he tore down the robe they had given him, all the way from neck to thigh, and shrugged it off. And there he was, not in the body they had given him before the robe, but in the body of a woman. Jasha's body. Slim and apple-breasted, the hips slenderly rounded, the groin a bird-brown silk, weaponless and clandestine. Her hair rushed free, the wave of it, down to her ankles, carnival striped. Her eyes were the green grapes that made the white wine, having no savour of blood.

'Eujasius,' she said, 'or Eujasia.'

645

She stepped about the altar, parading herself.

The old Knights began to caw and wail. They smothered up their vizored eyes. They turned, they went to their crunching knees. They prayed.

'Woman's blood,' said Jasha. '*Forbidden.*'

Mounted on the altar, she glanced sidelong at the fallen angel, to see what he would do.

He was a graven image. Even his mouth had ceased to work.

'I told you,' she said. 'Whatever you want, I'll take it from you. You shan't have it. I mock your bloody god,' she said.

Anjelen moved away from the altar. He went to one of the old Knights. It was Ragis, moaning and beating at his breast. Anjelen got hold of him, raised him like a bundle of branches. Ragis glared into the mask of his lord, and like a wolf Ragis howled, between terror and exaltation. Anjelen, no longer having the knife, sank his fingers into the priest's throat, where the mail had given way, and tore it out, crudely, to its strings and cords, as if clawing through to find the source of water. The blood vomited up in a scarlet veil that flared across the pool of the light, and tossed on the faded wall a shower of colour.

Anjelen was drinking. In the stone clearing, by night, a wolf on its hind limbs and clad in black, sucking out the life of an ancient child.

And when he let go of Ragis – no longer Ragis, a few remnants of iron, cloth and skin – there came another, pawing at him. Another of the priest Knights had crawled to Anjelen, pleading.

Now Anjelen made a noise. It was the wolf's growl. And hauling up this other one, he bit into the throat, spitting and tearing, while the blood sprayed, glittering through the light, gilding, moistening, making flowers.

The rest of them began to limp towards him, holding up their old men's hands. They wanted. He gave. What other terminus for their service . . . where else could they go to, whom else could they seek? Heaven and Hell were here. They stretched their throats like herons for his talons and his fangs.

Everywhere there was blood. The marvellous red of it was like the panoply of former days. On the altar the drape had a crimson device. How white the drapery looked now beneath this red.

When he was done with them, he threw them aside, the bodies. Their fragile bones sometimes broke at the meeting with the tiles, and so everything was contorted.

There was the smell of salt over the incense. The sea was high and a wind blew against the Christerium. The waves rushed like the blood, and all sounds were lost in the ocean as one year the tower itself might be, drawn under for ever.

Jasha was sitting on the altar. A jewel of blood starred her left breast, some others were on her arms and feet. The ritual was finished, and the order with it. Thirty carcasses were on the floor. The gulls did not cry. Anjelen lay at the limit of the light, with the last of his priesthood crushed under him. And then Anjelen separated from the flaccid lolling thing, he too lolled back and the dark embraced him.

Jasha slipped off the altar. Naked but for her gown of hair, she walked between these drained wine-skins, picking daintily over the floor, until she came to Anjelen where he lay on his back.

He was bloody. More than this. He was bloated, swollen. His very skin looked red, as if it must crack on redness, although it was white in the dark, and his half-shut eyes bulged, sightlessly. His mouth, under the mess of his debauch, was couth and firm. It was not thirsty any more.

Jasha lowered herself to the ground. She laid aside the silver knife, which she had kept, and put out her hands, well-versed, and neat in what she did. Sliding away the habit of the priest, she found the core of the body which, after all, might only have been made of wood. But what was there was flesh, Jun's flesh. In the black male hair the snake of Eden was hard, and lifted up to its own

647

instinctive eyeless life by the tumult of the engorging blood. To Jasha, this was no different to the penis of any man. Jasha knew quite well what to do with it. She bowed over him, the Angel of Death, and put her woods girl's mouth around him.

Anjelen did, could do, nothing. The Tree had grown into his brain. The crystal was closed by leaves. And his belly was full of the Wine of the Sacrifice. His purpose was ended. Anillia-Mechail-Jasha had sprung from him, three in one. No matter humanity's false notions of him, he had become himself his grave.

But Jasha's mouth went on about its business, the satin goad of her tongue. She licked and lipped at the final mortal part, and it answered.

A shudder spasmed through the bloated felled thing beneath her, and into her throat washed out the other drink of life, its salt, the sea of beginnings.

A wave broke against the glassless window. It was a compounded invisibleness that crashed over and sang on the tower. The gulls rose like a second spume. Here was the future, the drinking of the land by the sea, of the world by God.

Jasha kneeled above the angel.

'And that too I took,' she said. '*Your chastity.*'

But his eyes were only slits of white, no black in them. As Anillia and Mechail had gifted her through the Tree in the snow, so from this she had swallowed up the fountainhead.

He and she were wetted by the sea wave. It had cleaned the blood on the walls, and moved the knife a short distance from her hand. Jasha reclaimed it. Without a word or cry, flinging up her arm, she plunged the blade into the gut of Anjelen, forced and drew back. His body gaped, a velvet chasm of blood, and there the rib bones were, like the spine of a large fish. Jasha saw, in the little candlelight the wave had not drowned, that every rib was encircled, ridged and ringed. She put in her hands, concisely, and snapped out one of them, fashioned like carved white jet, a wonder. She extracted from him the rib, she held the rib. Then with both hands she hammered it home into his heart.

There was the faint ticking of waters on the walls. Later the skipping of mice and swoop of gulls. Nothing else. Huge silences built from the floor.

On Anjelen's body the gulls did not squander their efforts. He was obdurate, and cold. In the darkness, and the other occult dark which was his own, he had the shape of a narrow tomb, and out of this the ringed rib protruded like a sword. He did not bleed. His blood had stayed in him, seeming to lapidify. Death, for what he was, must be solely passage. He must transmute, as any god in any story. In the night, before all candles were extinguished, it seemed that Anjelen was changing into stone. But who was left to see?

And in the autumn dawn where the green ocean met the wetly flaming sun, Jasha walked along the beach under the rock.

She was like a sea-thing, maned with weed. Her feet were not cut by the sharp defences of the sand. She watched the water, remembering the fire which had closed over her head, cooked her, eaten her hair, let her go. The fire had been hot to freezing. How icy was the sea.

Behind her, the ruin had become the rock. The tower was an eccentric fretted cliff. The blackness of the sand was only the soot of shelled creatures which had died there.

Jasha thought of a myth of the coast which might come to be. A village by the water's edge, constructed of wrecked ships: the fisherman returning with his tale; how squinting over from his boat, he saw into the ocean, and a woman was there under the sea, a woman in a smoke of hair, walking in a forest with leaves of marble and coal. One day she must rise from the depths, with the winged wave at her back. Angel of Storms.

Jasha entered the water. It was as cold as it had been when she had bathed there. To the eye it was a surging floor, but the way led down. Jasha followed the way. The cold shocked at her groin, her waist, her breasts, her hair spread out on the tide. Was the forest so green? The cold of the water grew slowly warm.

The Tree had made men. They made themselves over into magicians, or went to ground, became the Tree again. But she was a rogue sapling. The mutant plant.

She lowered her head and was gone under the surface and the sunlight, into the water greener than the wood, warmer than the fire.

Book Five

MECHAILUS

Chapter One

Because she had been flung from a great height, Veksa, the miller's daughter, had remained through her accruing years an object of marvel. She was a cipher both for the improbable favour of fortune, and the smiting of fate. Her resolute and double-jointed cunning had fastened on this. Without knowing exactly what she did, she had dramatized herself, to make herself more into the proper image. Her wheaten hair went stark white, yet kept its abundance. Her body, which would have run to fat in the comfort of her Vre's Tower at Korhlen, restrained on the leaner diet of the village, had an unsightly magnificence, tempting still to some, repugnant to others. Though almost fifty years of age, she had kept her teeth; her eyesight and hearing were keen. Her skill with herbs was respected and occasionally feared. Women who had insulted her at first, learned to keep to their own counsel (how she doctored their stomachs they were never sure, maybe their own nervousness saw to it – only when they had begged her forgiveness, when she had pardoned them, did the sickness and cramps dispel). For her own father, he did not much care about Veksa's crash. She had managed to bring away with her from Korhlen all her own and certain extra valuables, which amply repaid anything the dad might reckon he donated at her marriage. They had heard the Vre died four months after Veksa was cast off. That was God's judgement on him, they said in the village, loudly, so Veksa might catch the words. Now, she kept house for her father, but then the old man had a pair of servant girls, she need lift no more than a finger or two, and give her orders in the voice of one accustomed to obedience.

Once a year, in the spring, Veksa would go mad for three or four days and nights. These insanities surrounded the anniversary of her son's death. He had been a wonderful man, her boy Krau, blond, brawny and handsome. The Vre's elder son, a weakling and cripple, naturally envious, had plotted to harm Krau, until Krau had had to kill the monster to preserve himself. Thereafter Kolris Vre Korhlen had had Krau murdered almost under the eye of his mother, before tossing her out into the forest. Yes, God's judgement indeed was on the Vre. And she, as she had said, was glad to be done with that Tower of villainy and blood. But her boy, her lovely Krau, she had only to think of him for enormous tears, fat from grazing in fields of hurt, to sluice down her face, which too was fat, and red and lax, from the beer she liked to drink. The yearly climax of her drama the village attended on with relish. They would listen to Veksa screaming and weeping in the miller's house. They would see her go out into the wood, there – as they knew – to brand evil on the souls of the men of Korhlen. Women who had beheld Veksa at her antics in the oak grove, where sometimes even now a bride might hang a string of coins or berries, saw her rocking a ghost baby in her arms, saw her pierce small lumps of tallow, having two legs, two arms and a penis, with pins whose heads were Korhlen amber.

As for the Korhlen Tower itself, she knew nothing of it, save what the now-and-then traveller might tell or invent. There had been fighting among the Raven kindred, for Kolris had left no heir, stipulated none. The enemy neighbour Esnias had paid some visits, too, and the Owl Tower. But these foragers were apparently beaten off.

Sometimes, when she had fed her dad his evening herbal, in which she mixed a little of this and that, to stay him in a sociable docile mood, Veksa would go into her tiny chamber and put on herself her jewels. There was the necklace of beaten gold her father had given her, stamped with the Korhlen Raven, there were bangles and earrings, the rings and combs and pins, the girdle of golden links, whose tying cords had had to be lengthened. In these she appeared for herself in her copper mirror. And she would say, twisting up her thick hair, sunny in her metal glass, 'Not so bad, my girl. He would have had luck to have kept you, rot him.' Even her red face in the copper looked only peachy. She had had men since Korhlen, better between sheets than he. She would raise her beer cup, drink, remember the one thing she had truly been robbed of. And the slick fat tears would ooze from her eyes. It was the mother felt the anguish. Her lad, her Krau— And then, perhaps, she would recall Mechail, malignly, speculatively. Was Mechail in Hell? As her hatred of him had gone on, perhaps he too continued, tortured and burning in the Pit. But if Mechail had gone to the Devil, then possibly Krau also had descended, as must she. And Veksa would kiss her amulets, and offer a few redemptory prayers on holy days even to the Christus. She must live long in order to expiate her faults, for she was not certain she could give them over quite yet.

The forest was black and bannered with tawny lace the colour of the copper mirror: Autumn. As the sun came up, Veksa was dreaming that Krau stood in her room. He was in his crimson tunic, and the sunrise combed his hair, and he was grinning merrily, but only half his face was on.

Veksa woke in fright. She recognized an invitation from the dead. Though he was her son, she did not wish to go with him, not to that—

She prepared herself for life, dressing herself and putting round her neck the golden necklace, which none of the villagers would ever dare to snatch from her. She plaited her hair up on her head and put the amber pins into the plait.

At her breakfast she called for beer.

'You like your cup,' said her father, who liked his.

'There, Da. I'm drinking your health.'

Outside, in the fenced yard, she sent the thinner serving girl on an errand, and took the arm of the other, who was sometimes, in various acts, her accomplice. 'Go over to Nine Toes' house. Get a dove from his cot.' 'How if he says no, mistress?' 'Tell him, I say *yes*,' said Veksa. A quarter of an hour later, the girl was back with a cindery dove in a wicker casket. Veksa hid this in her apron, showing she had something but not what.

The grove of oaks lay half a mile beyond the village, out in the tawny-flushing wood, where the darkness of the pines surged like a wall. The sun was there. It was a bright morning, even under the trees.

Veksa entered the grove, and going near the oak tree where the offerings were hung, she spoke words, ancient phrases almost nonsensical, that her aunt had taught her. Veksa did not know all their meaning, but she knew their intention. Then, she opened the cage and drew out the dove in her big hands. Used to human touch, the dove was quiet, and Veksa said to it, 'All's well,' as she walked straight at the tree, intending to smash the bird's neck directly on the trunk, before slicing with her sewing knife to let out the blood.

Six paces from the oak she heard the warning of the wood, the fanfare of lifting finches, scraping leaves, that evidenced some onslaught.

Veksa paused, clasping the dove. It was too late to hasten away, she would do best to stay, dumb and immobile. What came?

Through the cloister of oaks, against the black tapestry of pine trees, eight men rode through the forest in front of her. Their mounts were nourished and burnished, motes of sun broke on stirrups, the decorations of reins, and here and there on a jewel, for they were smart enough, the riders, in the forest way. A few black-brown dogs loped with the horses. Veksa felt the strangest thing, as if she had been whirled back in time. It was like the day Kolris had ridden into the village with his men and dogs, out hunting, seeing her suddenly, and the unrealized look

658

on his face that said to her: *Take hold, your chance is here.*
But she had been bereft of her chance. And the rider at
the head of his men, he was not Kolris, for he was young
and slender, clad in black and red like the wood. Then
he wheeled his horse abruptly, swung round at her. She
caught a scarlet arrow from a gem on his breast, and saw
the embroidery worked at his shoulder, rust, green and
purple, the Raven. An enormous bitch dog followed his
horse, and as he drew rein, the dog leaned in on him,
against his boot. And then Veksa saw his face in the clear
sunlight.

Her mouth sagged and her hands undid themselves on
the dove, which, instinctual at last, fluttered up and was
gone among the beams of the wood.

The young man with the Korhlen badge grinned at
Veksa, just as Krau had done. But his face was entire.
That did not help. It would have been more suitable if he
too had been the death's head.

Veksa said some more of her words, a forest spell.

'That won't bring you any assistance,' he said, 'old
lady.'

She felt the bite of that, even in her extremity. Who,
till now, had called her old?

'You're undead,' she screeched. 'Get away!'

'Listen to her,' said the man to his companions.

They were young nobles of the Tower. They laughed
and spat and the dogs grunted. 'My lord's wife,' said the
man, 'is it you?'

'No, no,' she said, 'no.'

'You foul fat witch,' he said, 'shall we ride you down?
For a deer you'd hardly be swift, you'd give us very little
sport.'

Veksa toppled to her knees. She knelt there with the
gold necklace on her throat, and the amber pins in her
white hair. She was sobbing, but this time not for her son
Krau.

'Mechail,' she said, 'I was never an unfriend to you.'

'You lying trollop,' he said. He did not grin any more.
His face was chill and priestly, as she remembered. He

was all her memory, lean and strong and tall, black-haired like rage. An animal face, cat and wolf. The eyes were black now; they must have altered in the grave. She recalled their craziness, the flame that came and went, never going out. And the hunched shoulder, she remembered that, but it was mended, remoulded in Hell, and now he was flawless. 'I don't thank you, lady,' he said, 'for your nice wishes. Where's your son?'

Veksa groaned and covered her face. Under her breast a forge of fire had her heart on its anvil.

'Mechail Korhlen,' she said.

He had dismounted. He stood over her.

'I am Mechailus,' he said. 'I sit at dinner in the Raven Tower, and I sleep in the bed of Kolris. I have what I was bred to have. What Krau would have liked, but Krau's not got it, has he? They threw his bones out for me in the wood, so anything might take its pick that might find a use for them. The crows carried them off.'

Veksa did not cry any longer. She struggled to breathe and to listen.

Mechail said, 'Only think, if you'd been a mother to me. Only think, if you'd been sweet and loving. Now Mechail would escort you back to his Tower, make of you a lady, perhaps succumb to your wiles, if you had any charms left, but you don't, old lady. And anyway, you were never kind.'

Veksa felt some squeezing obstruction give in her body. Streams of loosened pain ran down her arms, and up into her throat. She knew, like the warning of the wood, the forecast of death. She had no spirit left. She bared her face and looked at him. He was not Mechail. He was what Mechail had never been. And his eyes were black like some other's she had seen . . . So funny. So terrible.

'Veksa,' said Mechailus. His voice was melodious, winning. 'Come here to me, my darling.'

She stared, and the bitch dog came forward and leant now on his thigh gazing up at him, and he stroked her fierce head, to and fro.

He had given the dog her name.

Veksa's skull, under the weight of age and amber, sank down on her breast.

She heard them ride off, and the dogs running gladly.

She could not make her body get up to go to the village, and so she fell down on her side in the grove. She lay there feeling the life tick out of her like drips of water. She was stiff as a board. She could not move her hands or feet. She thought of rocking Krau in her arms. Had that been, or was it to come? She hoped it was to come.

Chapter Two

In the spring, the cathedral of the forest, green as an apple, candled with lights. Emerald on the pines. The grass, the moss, the fern. Where men had shorn the trees to make their tiny bivouacs of fields and huts, churches, villages, and Towers, how would it go in the end? Which would have which? For the forest ate the earth. Or would men eat it?

The question posed itself as he slept, but he woke, and the question was not.

The servant, Boroi, was thumping at the door. When he entered he carried the usual things, the water and razor, the wine and bread,

Mechailus said, 'You're my clock, now. Give that here.'

The servant, who had come back out of the wood early in the spring before, no longer wore the torque of slavery. His brown face was a blank, but to Mechailus everything was discernible.

'Come on, then, shave me.'

As Boroi's razor smoothed his jaw, Mechailus sat in the Vre's chair of oak banded with brass. The western window was still dusk and Boroi performed his work by the shine of a candle, that in turn lit the masculine treasures of the room. The rings in their box, the cups of greenish glass. Light ribbed the purple raven on the bed-curtains. When Boroi wiped his face, Mechailus took back the wine and sipped it.

As he dressed himself, Mechailus watched his reflection in the glass mirror.

I know who I am. No need to tell me.

The servant watched him too.

'What?'

'My lord's knife.'

'Yes, here it is. Ready for its day.'

Mechailus was also ready. He wore crimson, tunic, breeches, even the boots a treacled red. On his chest the crucifix centred its four black tines, and in them the crimson ruby, at one with him.

He broke the bread in his hands and gave a piece to Boroi. 'You finish the wine.'

Outside, the dawn was down in the yard with his men, waiting. The slaves of the house were also there, and inside the wall of the Women's Garden, the girls were already about in the orchard, gathering blooms for garlands, their voices wild and vernal, flowers come alive.

Mechailus looked around him. There were thirty men of the garrison and their captain, the nobles of the Tower, all mounted up. On foot, the plump priest, toying with his ash-wood beads.

They brought Mechailus his horse, the sable gelding.

Mechailus went up into the saddle with the agility of the acrobat he had been, and still sometimes would be, to make them laugh or make them scare. Mounted, he seemed to fill his body with his spirit. He was alive as other men were not. Then he rapped the gelding lightly, and it started off, through the wide yard gates and on to the bad old road, dry from a week of rainlessness.

The soldiers, some of the slaves and servants of the house, fell in behind Mechailus their lord. Behind these came the Tower court, the uncouth nobles in tan and purple. The priest walked along, telling his beads.

The fields sprawled under the sky, the forest rose over them, the rim of the bowl. There were no slaves on the fields today.

The feud with Esnias was over. The Korhlen clan had recently scorched out their valour and their quarrel. But they had raided the Owl Tower ten days before.

They turned on to the mill track. The mill was idle, its sails set.

Above the mill the track thinned and disguised itself among blue flowers, and then came in under the trees. Ahead, was visible the clearing, and the grove of birches, filigreed with slim green.

There in the core of the birch grove was the black stone. Mechailus sat his horse, regarding it. *Father and mother. God and self.*

Mechailus nodded to the stone, ignoring at first the man tied there.

The priest chanted, his beads clicked. If you heeded, you heard nothing Christian. They were the words of the wood. The priest knew them off by heart as he knew the Intercession, the forgiveness of sins. He believed that God was in the stone, as God was in the forest. Mechailus, who liked his tame priest, and went once a year to Khish and made liking to the priesthood there in the church, turned his wolf eyes inward at his own smiling. He knew where God was. He spun from the horse, which stood like a rock when he bade it do so.

The victim, trussed to the stone, had been assured of freedom and got drunk. Now he slumped, conscious of nothing, except dreaming maybe of his return to his Tower. (The black stone leaned, holding him close. *Mother and father.*) He was young, naked, only a blue bruise on his cheek to reveal how he had been made sure of.

Mechailus waited, as the soldiers, his pigs of nobles, the slaves with faces creaseless as new paper, formed up around the grove, which, with two years, had expanded itself to receive them.

The naked man was clean, bathed, shaven.

Mechailus approached him. He lifted the black lacquer cross on its silver chain, and pressed its ruby lightly to the alien's lips. 'Your transgressions are forgiven you. Forget tomorrow. We thank you for your gift to this earth.' The knife was in his right hand. 'There is no Hell,' said Mechailus Vre Korhlen. He drove the knife into the man's body, braced for the resistance of flesh and muscle, and removed himself from the jetting blaze of blood, the hue of his garments. The man did not wake, only his brows twitched, relaxed, his head slipped sideways. He was dead. The mystery of the carcass, its mechanical astonishment laid wide, the steam of the blood that had showered the stone and the eternal ground, at these the assembly gazed in stillness, permitting them their honour. Then the shout was raised.

'Give me the cup.'

They brought it to the Vre, the captain and the priest, the nobleman whose daughter, likely, Korhlen would marry, come summer. The cup was of gold, with garnets, made in Khish for festivals.

Mechailus filled the cup from the life blood. He drank from the brim, gold and red. Then the slave came and poured in the blessed red wine. Mixed, the chalice went to the priest, to the captain, to the noble. And then the slave bore it to them all, the circle of the acolytes, and they drank of the Blood of the Life, of the Wine of the Sacrament.

Mechailus said to his priest, 'It was rich, this year. The crops will be sturdy.'

'Yes,' said the priest. 'This one was sound, God love him.'

One of the soldiers came and drew the knife out of the corpse. He cleaned it on a cloth, and gave it back to the Vre.

'Are we absolved, godbrother?' said Mechailus.

The priest said, 'I absolve you, and all here.'

The sun was growing into the clearing in a silver branch. The black stone sparkled.

Mechailus called to his gelding, which stepped across to him and stayed waiting until he mounted.

They had known from the start, the Travellers, that the Dwarf was possessed, bewitched, something to be avoided, but – since they had not managed to avoid him – one to be treated with, bargains not war. For in with

665

them he was. They had left him sleeping like the dead in
their salt ring; riding through the night amid their land-
slip wagons, they found him again, trotting after them.
This time he was in the actual flesh, and though they did
not comprehend that, they gaged it. His knack in pursuit
spoke volumes concerning his vitality, physical and otherwise. He had selected them as companions. They complied. Theirs was a stoic and experienced race.

He gave no trouble on the journey. In fact, he was a
shining addition at the markets and roadsides where they
made camp. He juggled goblets and daggers, became a
human cartwheel, and presently acquired the craft of
guessing what men had in their belts or up their sleeves.
How he did this, without a mate to tip him off, they could
not be certain. But then, perhaps he was a real magician,
a shape-changer toiling back into his proper form. For he
was never a day the same, so they noted. He shot up like
a forward child, he lengthened and expanded. Inside a
month his body fitted his head. And then everything
realigned itself, like a sheet that was straightened. In the
second month, when they moved away from the river
through the late-harvesting grain-lands, the tall dwarf was
a tall vigorous man, well-proportioned and at the peak of
his youth.

They would be able to tell of all this in tales in years
to be, he would pass in among their legends and become
one with them. But for now he was their liability. They
were careful of him, to be fair and to be aloof. They gave
him his share of their takings, the food and drink. Though
he made no hint of anything towards their women, they
drove them off from him. For it was a fact, the women
were intrigued by Mechi, who had sprung down to them
from the ruin by the sea.

He himself, offering no thought and few words, seemed
only interested in the earth, the country through which
they travelled. The city they had skirted he had stared at,
turning in the saddle of the pony they lent him, looking
at the uphill towers, the heavy steel coil of the river with
its ships. And in the villages and ramshackle towns he

666

would go off roving, a man now, nothing to be picked on, and come back just before sunrise, always amused at something, perhaps only the same thing; the ways of the world.

They did not try to slough Mechi. Occasionally they believed he would leave them. When he did not, they were philosophical. Of all the frightfulness, the worst had been that, though he had grown to man-shape and height before their eyes, they had not been able, at any moment or hour, to lay hold of it – for this was the subtle development of the plant in the sun. Yet it grew so fast that in a week they might glance back and measure it against its former self, and startle. They had to offer it, over and over, fresh clothes. If he had stretched like a bowstring in their view, they would have feared him more and shunned him less. This had been as if he tried to fool them with the unconscionable.

Winter began to finger the journey. One early morning two of the young Traveller men, savage with drink from a dubious tavern of the stubbled plain, stole up on Mechi in the lemon twilight. The younger rowdy had convinced himself that his betrothed cast her sight on the man-dwarf, to which attraction the man-dwarf had wheedled her through some hedgerow sorcery.

They meant, so they reckoned, to pin the wretch, cut his throat, haul the body away for the winter foxes, and then bother with what type it was, dwarf or man.

As they were leaning in, Mechi opened his eyes, black and lucid, youthful as something unimaginably ancient.

'And who is here?' said Mechi, who had begun to speak too in another way, placing words differently, so now and then they caught the voice of the trained alchemical priest he must have been.

'Clamp him!' snarled the would-be cutthroat.

The other grabbed and Mechi struck him a blow in the neck that sent him flying. Then Mechi looked at the knife and said, 'Stick it in. I'll die. Bury me. The others will see you and say, *Tut, ye shouldn't have done that*.' The cutthroat tensed for the killing swipe, and Mechi said, 'In a day or so I'll come up from the earth. I'll follow you. I'll bash your knife in through your mouth, through the soft of it, into your brain.' And then he punched hard in the boy's gut and pushed him off to bring up his noisy drink in a bush of frost.

But that was the winter day on which Mechi left the Travellers to their travelling.

He went with nearly nothing: the latest shirt and jacket and breeches, a scatter of coins he had earned, a withered apple plucked from a tree at the wayside. The pony, he left; and they soon found it was fractious with other riders.

Mechi walked over the plains, which were blasted now like the outlands of the punishing afterlife, under a white dizzied sky. It was cold, and Mechi had only cloth wrappings on his feet, which wore and came off. He had become bearded among the Travellers, where before a beard had never grown on him. He knew nothing in his formed brain of the Tree which was all the trees, which sent out and reclaimed its life. He knew nothing of where they had gone, Mechail, Anillia, Jasha, Anjelen. But again, again, in the deepest chamber of thought, he did know, knew it all. Mechail had wrought Mechi through the semen and the ovum of the man and woman in the wood, through the psychic thrust of anger, pain and puzzlement. Now Mechail had ceased to be Mechail. At long last, Mechi might flow up to fill the empty shadow. All Mechail had denied in himself, that was Mechi. But now Mechail denied nothing. It was a saint's name, and Mechi put it on in its fullness, pleased by it, for he had every capacity for pleasure Mechail had put away. Mechi-Mechailus welcomed his uniqueness as the prisoner runs from his cell. He greeted the world like a ripe fruit. He was ready. For he had had to wait in chains.

When the dark began to rise from the plain, a coral hill in the sky was the sun going down, and Mechailus looked over his shoulder, and the Traveller girl was following him still. She was walking as he did, but her boots were stalwart, and she was strong. He had first heeded her at noon, when he sat a while on a stream bank observing the lethargic fish under the reeds. She was about two miles behind him.

She came close, as if they had been lovers, as close as that.

Then she stood there, looking at him. Mechailus in turn looked down from his young man's height, and watched as she took out her knife and made with it a narrow slot of blood in her left wrist, among the bracelets of weasel-bone and painted husks.

'For me?' said Mechailus.

He raised her wrist and gently sucked out the blood from the wound. It was a pleasure, like everything else, a *great* pleasure, like eating or drinking, striding, riding, sleeping, sneezing, making water, having a fantasy of sex. No lesser pleasure of the flesh, and no more.

When he finished he said, to her dreamy eyes, which heard on their own: 'You scratched yourself on a bramble, did you? Tear your skirt and bind it up tightly. Don't tell your kin, you know what they'll do. Put away your knife now.'

And when she had complied with these orders, he drew out from under his shirt the cross he had stolen from Anjelen, or that the Mechail in Mechi the dwarf had caused him to steal. He held it for the girl to see.

'What do you make of that?'

'A black moth,' said the girl, 'with its belly full of blood.'

'You're clever,' said Mechailus. 'What shall we do now?'

Then she put both her arms round his neck, the bracelets and bandage, the warm skin, the tindery inrush of long hair.

They lay in the bushes on the black leaves. He had her several times. She was the first woman he had had, ever.

In the morning he kissed her and sent her away, and she cried a little, but off she went. It was most ordinary. And the plain was the same scoured desolation, and the sky even whiter.

Mechailus overwintered on the plains, in two villages,

and at a deserted inn. He behaved like a man and was treated like one, with suspicion and fellowship. Nothing of moment occurred, though to him everything was of moment, equally, from the village girl he was supposed to have got with child, and had not, to the beryl buds that shone around the inn's edges, the spring.

He knew everything there was to do, but he had never done any of it, and brought novelty and enjoyment to the mundane matters and the gross. When he got to Khish, he worshipped God and the Christus in the church, bought boots, a barber's razor, a knife, a sword that – never having done so – he understood exactly how to ply. He hired soldiers for his bodyguard, and won a black gelding in a wine shop where someone had said five cups and a lighted torch could not be juggled.

The six men he took with him into the forest were enchanted by Mechailus, the novelty and enjoyment. They sensed in him an aspect of themselves that living had trampled over, they copied him, and it poked up its head. They believed his story, too, or taught themselves to believe it – that he was the heir to a Tower, an exiled wanderer, cheated by a stepbrother while the stepmother poisoned the lord.

Armed with this, they reached Korhlen.

The Tower had gone on with its functions, for the slaves had been made to see to that. But otherwise it had changed hands eight, nine times, as this or that one butchered and bundled himself to the crest of the heap. There had been no priest would stay there in five years, few tithes paid, and the church at Khish, having sent messages of disapproval, had heard out Mechailus in a small stone room and seemed not adverse to his tale, either.

But those were the tales. The truth would seem more curious. It would need tales to mask it over.

It had happened, the game of exchanges had come round to Gaj, the steward's son. He had grown corpulent, balded. But of the several who had known Mechail the crack-shouldered heir, he was the only one left of those who had stood by at the hour of Mechail's murder in the wood.

If ever it had been, the evening Cup Hall of the Korhlens was now a cave of beasts. Females, but for the slave women, had been excluded altogether. The men gathered to their fire, the long tables and the high table crossing them, the dogs slinking about among spillages. There were brawls and bouts of insane drunkenness, girls raped across benches; the walls smeared and the raftered Raven banner itself had been torn, draggled, as if they had had to make sure it showed how they slipped.

And that night there were even some Esnias at Gaj's board, for where the tithes had not gone to the Church they had wended to the neighbours, who would be in before too long if nothing else was done.

Mechailus rode out of the forest with his six soldiers when the sky was violet and the dew was down. The poor road was there for them, with the muddle of village below, the inn, the Tower and its buildings, where the lights were blaring. The slave-tended mill revolved its sails. As they came closer, five dogs, gone wild from the Korhlen hunting packs, bounded over the track, baying, thin as strings.

'Omens, sir,' said one of the soldiers. 'So flee your foes.'

Mechailus laughed. 'They won't get so far.'

In the village, half abandoned, unkempt, the few lamps blinked and spies looked out. The inn gate was off and a goat sat in the gloom with Devil eyes.

At the Tower, the courtyard doors were secured but unguarded.

'Who can climb?' said Mechailus.

'What, up there, sir?'

'It was climbed once. The heir climbed it, to escape.'

And standing up on the gelding, which let him do anything, Mechailus gripped the beam, rose like fluid, and was gone over the top.

The soldiers exclaimed. Leaving two with the horses, four followed their lord's example, not so wieldy, but

671

thorough enough to take them too up and down into the
yard.

No one was out, all were in. Between the stone ravens,
that had been hacked and spoiled, up the stair, the entry
was open. Mechailus, ahead of his men, walked into the
Hall.

For a while not one of them noticed. They were intent
on the habitual loudness, liquor, the programme of the
bear-cave.

Thus Mechailus hung over them like a sword, and in
his brain maybe were the recollections of the one whose
place he took, and those also of what he had been, many
powerful impressions of powerlessness. If that was the
case, he did not mind them. Most of all, he had the look
of Anjelen, but an Anjelen alive, with the humour still
there under his lips, although he was a wolf, a priest, a
drinker of blood and night.

Then, someone did see. It was Gaj.

He choked and dropped his cup of wine, and clumsily
jumped up. Through the torch-blear and the candles, he
saw precisely who had come in. And as if there had been
nothing in between, no years, no happenings, Gaj beheld
Mechail Korhlen, who had risen from the dead, come
back again for a taste more of revenge.

Between them, Gaj dampening his drawers, and
Mechailus, an exquisite simplicity of arrival, the Cup Hall
was jogged into awareness in wedges and dots. There were
plenty now who could identify Mechail. How not when
he looked faithfully as he had done more than a decade
ago, save for his straight shoulders, the curve to his
mouth, the eyes the nearest might see were much blacker
than black. Such items enhanced the reproduction, did
not devalue it.

And most of the Hall knew the ghost story of Mechail.
Dark nights it had even unnerved some of them. Even
where they would not believe it, the weight of it had
charge of them.

Mechailus went up the Hall then, between the silent

tables, by the hearth where the house dogs cringed, fawned, wagged their tails, flattened themselves.

He went to the high table where once Mechail's father had sat, with Krau, and the blonde woman Veksa. And the four Khishan soldiers, who knew their job, stayed two at the door, and put two along after him, with hands on swords, courteously looking everywhere.

Mechailus came to Gaj.

'I,' said Gaj.

'You?' asked Mechailus, and struck him between the eyes with his fist. Gaj leapt over backwards. He was dead; that was that.

And Mechailus sprang up on the table among the trenchers, cups, while the men there slewed away, trying for knives, snorting like hogs surprised.

'Here I am,' said Mechailus. 'One of you, name me.'

Silence.

A man fiddled with steel at Mechailus' back. Acrobat, trained fighter, the new prince of the Tower whipped round in a sort of jig. The bright Khishan sword cleavered through a neck and blood hit the rafter, splattered the banner as if it deserved it. The head skidded away like a child's ball. It was easy to kill men. One found it so.

Mechailus balanced on the table, bright red sword, friendly darkness.

'Come on, name me. Shall I offer a reward?'

The slaves were there, male and female, poised stilly, an absolute of acceptance. *They* knew, *they* named, but all without action or words.

Then a man shouted.

'Mechail!'

'Yes,' said the one on the table. 'Mechail, son of Kolris Vre Korhlen. If you know me, take me. *Get on your knees.*'

His voice had an authority that must have come from tutoring in the church schools southerly. Oh yes. *On your knees*, it said, and on their knees they generally went, and where they did not, the four soldiers glanced, and it was thought better of, kneeling.

'You've made wreckage of my father's Hall, his hold,

everything,' said Mechailus, enjoying, not harsh. 'For the Esnias here, they may leave. Take my greeting to the Esnias Tower. We'll return your visit.'

The Esnias men got up and hurried out, cheered to be alive.

'Now,' said Mechailus Vre Korhlen, 'where's dinner?'

It was during this dinner, so structured and momentous, that one thing happened that Mechailus received in another way. While the soldiers fenced him, taking precautions, and the Hall of men strove to emit duty, trapped as they were in a fable, an old thin dog, limping, came in at the door, and crept along between the tables and the servers, the ones who flung things at it, glad of release, the other dogs who snarled. The dog was not wild, it had not hunted in the wood. Its muzzle was grey and it came to the high table, shivering, its dull eyes sure. The dog knew Mechailus, as the others knew Mechail. Oddly now it approached from the table's left, the bitch's side. It had made a bizarre partnership in the buildings of the Tower, and so survived. It knew Mechi, who had starved in the kennel with it. It knew Mechi even now.

Mechailus leant over the table and lifted the dog and brought her up on the table's top. His current nobles, who had not yet fallen under his magic (as they would; in six months he would be able to spell them to his will, even to the assailment of Esnias), reacted with disgust. Then shuttered it prudently.

But Mechail put the meat in his mouth, and so offered it to the bitch dog.

'Here's my lady,' said Mechailus, when she had eaten to his lips and he let go.

He smoothed her gently as she ate.

Later, as he lay in the chamber of the Vre, with two soldiers unneeded at his door, the bitch dog lay among the furs, spine to spine with him, for he had sent the woman away after their dalliance that the dog might slumber easily.

*

'Mechi,' said the fawn-haired girl, 'will you still call me to you, when you're wedded?'

'Of course,' said the young man in the bed. 'Provided you and she are amicable with each other.'

'But you'll make me go now. Will you make her go?'

'And provided you ask no questions about each other.'

When the girl had gone, the dog approached from the hearth. She had grown strong and young, her eyes were clear. She outstripped the other dogs of Korhlen. She could kill any of them she wanted. Mechailus stroked her jaws, her forehead. 'Now rest. Tonight you must be with me for Korhlen's Feast of the Sacrifice.' The bitch dog mounted the bed and lay with her dark head upon her malt-brown paws. She had watched as he drank the blood of the fawn-haired girl. In the room was the scent of it, with the burning cones on the hearth, the spangle of spring.

'Veksa,' said Mechailus to the dog, really to joke, and slept.

A scene engraved in ruby, the Korhlen Cup Hall. The torches red, the flush-red walls, the rafters like cinnabar.

Once, in the winter, their Vre had come to the centre of the Hall and juggled scarlet apples for them, but the apples melted – they were made of blood. Once he juggled with a globe of quartz that burst, and out ran the green sea.

Now he sat at the high table, and led the feast. His pigs and bears were crowned with flowers and ivy. The women returned in all their trinkets and half the roses of the earth. They would get very drunk tonight, and they would come to him, up to the high table, and offer their wrists with tiny and concise cuts, and he would sip from them. The Hall was not as it had ever been, yet noisier maybe than ever before, and looking at it from a distance, where the light shone out, who could not tell by its redness, something.

And beyond the gardens, in the women's apartments,

the glow and sound were muted, like a far red star, that sometimes growled or sang.

'The dog never comes now,' said Chirda. 'Do you remember the dog we fed?'

'She was blind nearly. Once I looked for her,' said Charina. 'I think *he* has her.'

'*He.*'

In the spring darkness without the moon, they sat together on their bed, two small elderly children, with long white fragile hair, and blossom breasts lying on their skeletal bodies like lilies on rope.

'I'm cold,' said Chirda. 'Cold, cold.' She snivelled, forgot to, plucked up a rag from the bed, petted it.

They had met the dog on the grass by the willow tree. They had been afraid, and Chi had waved her arms, but the dog came to them on its belly, seeming to take them for its sisters. They found she was a bitch dog. She trailed them to their cavern of room, and sniffed the moulting civet, and put her head on their knees. Sometimes, even then, a slave would bring them scraps of food. They nibbled them, not having any appetite, and once Puss (Chirda), had snapped at the slave girl with her teeth and drawn a fleck of blood, and had that. They gave most of their paltry meals to the dog, and at night they lay beside her, and Puss hugged her and had dreams, sighing *Mamma*.

Then *he* came, and the dog left them. He never came to them, though sometimes at first, sensing him, they had gone on to their balcony and looked for him.

'Is he on the walk?'

'Will he be kind to us?'

They confused him with Krau, and their moistureless old bodies, prematurely aged to those of skinny hags, palpitated with green shades of lust, but this fell from them like petals.

'Do you remember,' said Puss, 'when Mamma would take us into the wood?'

They sat and stared into the crystal of false memory: *Mamma* had never taken them anywhere. But, in the quartz of illusion, she altered. She grew succulent and dear.

'Shall we go in the wood,' said Puss wistfully, a little crone girl.

Chi got up. 'We shall need a torch, to see.'

They went down from the galleried apartment, past the willow, and along the garden walk. There were lights in plenty now, since the massacre of the Esnias, the burgeoning of the Raven. The garrison guard were on the walls, but drunken. Korhlen was sorcerous. Odd things were said of its Vre. Who would outface jeopardy and try for it, even on the feast night of the sacrifice?

Near the doors, in the yard, a lit torch lay on the paving. Someone might have put it out for their convenience. Chi took it up. Seeing them, one of the soldiers mocked and bowed. 'Off on an outing, ladies? Go careful now.'

They went out through the open square of the doors and strayed along the track, and the soldiers watched them go, attaching no significance, not concerned as to who or what they might be, for they were also merely women.

Anjelen made them, via semen and ovum of man and woman, and the psychic thrust of will. Choked Catra's daughters.

It was a bleak night for spring. By the path the flowers hid their heads, the grass was sleeved with frost.

'Cold,' said Puss. 'It was never cold when we were with Mamma.'

But even in the false memory, Mamma was not with them. They were alone in the forest, up beyond the house, the mill, the grove, into the night.

'In the wood,' said Chi, 'who is this coming?'

'Who is it?' said Puss anxiously.

'He has a black horse. On his shield is a rose. His cloak is bones. Mind the thorns.'

Puss minded them, though none were there.

The forest was enormous, as was the night, and they were one. The towers of the trees resolved in sky and there the stars were dashed, unfinished and not near

677

enough. The frigid grasses splintered, and through the aisles creatures fluttered on winged feet.

'I'm cold,' said Puss.

'The wood's cold,' said Chi. 'Nasty, uncharitable.' She looked about and wondered where they had thrown the remains of Krau, a deed done in some parallel life. On her wrist was a straight pink scar; it had stayed with her, like her sister. Raising the torch, of which she had sole command, she saw the cold black needles of a pine, like claws to rake her eyes, and put the fire into them.

'Look!' cried Puss. All her attention was garnered.

The pine tree was blossoming with gold, so bright, so beautiful. A gust went up its tower into the roof of night. Perhaps the stars would burn better for it.

'Will Mamma come?' asked Puss.

Chi shook her head. She thought of Catra with the worm in her throat, dying on the floor. She pushed her torch into a thicket, and golden vines curled up and away. The dark was glinting with fireflies now. Sparks arced and dazzled.

Puss clapped her hands.

The wood was on fire.

The two albino crone girls stood at its heart, on the pyre, watching. The tinsel vapour of Chi's garment caught alight. As Chi moved to see it, she smiled at last, a very little, and fed her own dress into the circling feeding flowers. 'Pretty,' said Puss. Her white hair was saffron, Chi's hair was silver-red. Such loveliness. The wood began to race with flight and terror. The pine trunks burst like bonfires and the sky howled. 'It's warm,' said Puss. 'It's warm.'